IN TURBULENT WATERS

TIMOTHY ETCHIE

IN TURBULENT WATERS

Copyright © 2022 Timothy Etchie.

All rights reserved. No part of this book may be used or reproduced by any means, graphic, electronic, or mechanical, including photocopying, recording, taping or by any information storage retrieval system without the written permission of the author except in the case of brief quotations embodied in critical articles and reviews.

This is a work of fiction. All of the characters, names, incidents, organizations, and dialogue in this novel are either the products of the author's imagination or are used fictitiously.

iUniverse books may be ordered through booksellers or by contacting:

iUniverse
1663 Liberty Drive
Bloomington, IN 47403
www.iuniverse.com
844-349-9409

Because of the dynamic nature of the Internet, any web addresses or links contained in this book may have changed since publication and may no longer be valid. The views expressed in this work are solely those of the author and do not necessarily reflect the views of the publisher, and the publisher hereby disclaims any responsibility for them.

Any people depicted in stock imagery provided by Getty Images are models, and such images are being used for illustrative purposes only. Certain stock imagery © Getty Images.

ISBN: 978-1-6632-4086-6 (sc)
ISBN: 978-1-6632-4088-0 (hc)
ISBN: 978-1-6632-4087-3 (e)

Library of Congress Control Number: 2022910671

Print information available on the last page.

iUniverse rev. date: 06/24/2022

To the memory of my brother,
Joseph Egharegbemi Atsemudiara Etchie,
and
for the man of all times, Egharegbemi Atsemudiara Etchie,
my late father, who never once doubted but believed
wholeheartedly in the vision God has given me.

ACKNOWLEDGMENTS

The writing and publication of this book would not have been possible without the marvelous contributions of many wonderful people.

It all began with the love of my family and the support of my friends.

First, my sincere thanks and gratitude to my mother, Rebecca Ejiyere, for her prayers, and my wife, Angie, for her love, support, and guidance, most especially for always looking out for me. Babe, thank you for everything.

My heartfelt gratitude goes to my beautiful kids—Temisan, Ari, and Timeyin—who I hope one day will write their own books. Temisan has started hers already. I love you guys more than words can ever say.

Many thanks and special gratitude goes to my brothers—Solomon, Jonathan, and Festus—but most especially Jonathan "Ayabic" Etchie, not just for reading sections of the manuscript and making meaningful suggestions, but even more for the general interest he took in it.

Special gratitude also to the late historian and former chairman of Itsekiri Leaders of Thought (ILoT), Pa J.O.S. Ayomike. Papa Ayomike helped this book in several meaningful ways. He gave me confidence and good counsel.

It was Pa Ayomike that introduced me to Professor Tony Afejuku, who was then head of the Department of English and Literature at the University of Benin.

Professor Tony Afejuku received me warmly into his office and into his home, and in spite of his academic responsibilities, he found time to wade through the voluminous manuscript and greatly influence the final outcome of the manuscript. He was convinced that I had a worthwhile project. I warmly thank him for his incisive guidance and encouragement.

I would like to thank my childhood friends—Henry Demisi, Jonathan Edileh, Patrick Okpomu, George Panama, Vincent Madamedon, Arthur Bofede and Kolawole Benjamin. I appreciate their precious friendship, constant wit, wisdom, and support.

I would also like to thank my classmates and the friends I made at Ambrose Alli University Ekpoma: Godday Igbinoba, Afekhai Elempe, Nefishetu Abu (as she then was), Lucky Izevbizua, Ivie Egbe (as she then was), Wole Akinsanya, Oje Imoroa and Frederick Mabiaku.

I also appreciate the fabulous production, editorial, and design team of iUniverse, who saw this book across the finish line.

Thanks to Chief Eugene Ikomi, my mentor, a man who has made an incredible impact in my life; I cannot imagine anyone to whom I owe more gratitude.

My thanks also to the good people of Warri, who continue to indulge my imagination.

Lastly and most importantly, my biggest thank-you is reserved for God Almighty, whose grace saw me through the production of this book.

When you walk this school,
My friends let your feet be fleet;
When you cross a dark street,
My friends do not be a fool.
Ignore the howls of Owlsmen,
What they foretell is death,
Designed to entrap good men
And take away their breath.
—A popular poem at AZU

CHAPTER ONE

WARRI, MAY 2004

It had been gradually getting overcast, and the sky was black and lowering with the weight of the storm beneath its pouches. If not for the gallant splendor of the departing moon that sent up fingers of faint but burning white fire, it would have seemed as if the world were about to end the very next minute. The rays of the departing moon gleamed white through the black veil of the coming storm and shone bravely upon the earth. In the distance, the wind began to moan. A stream of dull clouds coming up against it flashed down thunder, and quivering lightning followed it.

Large drops of rain soon began to fall. As the storm clouds came sailing fervently downward, others immediately refilled the void they left behind, spreading over all the sky. Then came the low, angry rumbling of distant thunder. Lightning quivered, slicing the earth with its light, and then darkness covered everywhere as NEPA—the national electricity powerhouse—cut the public electricity supply.

At that late hour, with the curfew now relaxed, a young man walked the cold, rainy highway called Warri–Sapele Road. The buses, taxis, and *okadas* (commercial motorbikes) were all parked for the day, so he had to walk home in the rain. It was an opportunity to stretch his legs.

He was completely unconcerned by the rain but very watchful of his surroundings. He walked down the broad freeway with his hands in his pockets. He was decked out in a pair of faded blue jeans, a black T-shirt, and a heavy blue leather jacket. His two hands were in the pouch pockets of his jacket. Inside the right pocket, his fingers were wrapped around the handle of an automatic. The small handgun was a powerful weapon, his companion for the past year. As a leader of the Egbesu Boys of

Africa, EBA, the young man, Isaac Wuru, claimed it a right to carry a gun. He wasn't carrying the gun for fun. He was carrying it to protect himself against the WV, the Warri Vanguard, a roving pack of militant Itsekiri youths who roamed the streets of Warri, searching for people like him.

There had been some killings recently. The thought of those killings caused Wuru to tighten his grip around the butt of the pistol. Only two weeks prior, his best friend had been shot and killed not very far from this place where he was now walking. The WV had killed him. Sixteen 7.62mm slugs were pumped into him.

Walking quickly, quietly, his mind flooded with memories of his friend. Wuru reasoned and tried to grasp how they could've killed Conboye so cheaply. Conboye was a top-notch member of the Egbesu Boys of Africa. He was a good fighter of the Ijaw Nation, armed twenty-four hours a day and "fortified to the bone" with the protective Egbesu juju. He was not supposed to be killed that easily.

Conboye was one of the "gallants" who could be relied on. He had a mind for the cause. An eyewitness's account claimed that a black "V-trunk" Mercedes-Benz had accosted him in broad daylight. Two young men had emerged from the rear seat and, without saying a word, shot him with SMGs, reentered their car, and drove away. Just like that. It was a terrible way to die.

He was about a hundred meters away from the gasoline station when he spotted the car. It was a Mercedes jeep parked at the curb in front of the two-pump Oando filling station. It was a gleaming black car, droplets of rain hanging on its body like fish scales and rain thundering softly on its roof. It carried dull yellowish parking lights.

Wuru slackened his pace, and as he buttoned his jacket, the headlights of the vehicle came on and the engine started. Instinctively, his fingers tightened around the butt of the handgun in his pocket. He saw first a chauffeur's head through the rain-soaked windshield, and then the shape of another man sitting in the rear seat. *Are these the same people that killed Conboye?* he wondered.

He was walking past the car when the rear door sprung open and the man called out to him in an uncommonly loud voice, "Hey—you!"

Wuru looked neither concerned nor baffled. His face was inhumanly still. Quietly he brought the automatic out of his pocket.

"A few words, Wuru!" the man shouted over the rising windstorm.

The bastards even know my name! Wuru turned quickly around, pulled the gun out from his side, and leveled it at the man.

"May we have a few words?" the man said, swaying on his feet as if blown by the strengthening wind and pretending as if he didn't see the gun.

"A few words about what?" Wuru shouted angrily, his finger on the trigger. The man raised his hands quickly.

"I want to talk to you. Can we talk inside my car?"

"No, we can't talk inside your car."

"Okay. I'll walk with you."

"You can't walk with me. I don't know you."

"I'm an Izon. I'm your brother."

Wuru assessed him. He was tall, lean, and well tailored. *He must be a learned man.* "An Izon?" Wuru scoffed. "Let's hear you speak it."

"I'm Vincent Ubangha; I'm a schoolteacher," the man said fluently in Izon.

A barely perceptible streak of lightning climbed across the darkness. There was some silence.

What is the boy thinking of? the schoolteacher wondered. *Is he thinking of his friend wasted by the restive youths of the Itsekiris?*

Wuru might have been carved from marble; the immobility of the face, the stretched gun-wielding hand, and the utter concentration were really frightening.

"Must be very important to come this late to talk to me," Wuru said softly in Izon.

After a brief interval he asked, "What do you want from me?"

"I have an assignment for you," Vincent Ubangha said in faultless Izon.

"An assignment?" Wuru mused.

"Yes. An assignment," the schoolteacher said.

Just then, an electric light reached them. It came from the gasoline station. NEPA had restored power to the entire area.

Wuru lowered his gun. He smiled and then shook his head. For the first time, the lecturer could see the boy's face clearly. He was a born killer, no doubt. It was written clearly in his dark eyes, and they shone with an inner fire.

"Walk with me then. I'm going home," he said, and he turned around and started walking away.

"To Bayelsa?"

Wuru stared through the thinly falling rain and the partial darkness of the night.

"Have you been there before?"

The lecturer cleared his throat, coughed, and spat before he answered.

"I've been there twice."

The roar of the jeep's engine was audible to both of them.

The lecturer fell in step with him. Then the young man surprised him; he did what the lecturer had never dreamed he would do. In the rain-soaked darkness, he swung around, touched him gently, and frisked him hurriedly.

Vincent Ubangha made no protest. Before he could understand what was happening, the search was over.

"You don't trust me?" Ubangha said quietly.

The young man had turned away. "I don't trust anybody." There was an angry note in his voice. "Why didn't you come to the hotel to look for me? Coming out here to stake me out is risky. I could've killed you."

"I want to keep this thing very private and really personal. The hotel's a very dangerous place at this time. I heard they're harassing the customers."

It was true. These were difficult times. A Nigerian naval base had been attacked from the waterways a few weeks ago, and an attempt had been made to cart away great stores of weapons. Some of the boys who mounted the attack were killed. And recently, too, some oil workers, including two Americans and security personnel at one of Chevron's swamp locations along the Benin River, were killed by unknown youths in the area. The Creek River Hotel was one of the first suspected places. Actually, the hotel was put on the red list, and the naval and other security officials up to this very moment were still harassing most of its clients. They said they were investigating the killings of the oil workers, but everybody knew the killers were still in the creeks.

The two men didn't say anything for some time. They were both wet and soaked to the skin by now, and their shoes made squishing sounds as they walked.

"The job I have for you is top secret—"

"All my jobs are top secret," the young man cut in.

"I know, but this is the toppest of them all. And the trickiest, I'd say."

"Really?" Wuru raised his eyebrows.

"Yes, really." There was no mistaking the agitated conviction in the lecturer's voice.

They had been walking for the past ten minutes and had now left the gasoline station far behind.

"The subject's name is Tosan Mayuku."

Wuru turned the name over in his mind. "Is he the one called Picasso?"

"Yes," Ubangha said and his hand shot out, catching hold of Wuru's elbow. "I want this young man killed immediately."

They were now standing under a streetlamp. Vincent Ubangha and Wuru were of the same height, so the young man looked at the lecturer squarely. The fluorescent lights from the streetlamp shone directly on his face.

Vincent Ubangha was a middle-aged man of remarkably handsome features. He had dark obsidian eyes—eyes that were very direct, funny, and cruel at the same time. His mouth and chin were bristled with the stubble of coarse, hard beard—designer stubble of some sort. His complexion, Wuru could see, was dark. What added most to the macabre expression of his face was a ghastly, cunning smile—a smile that was meaningless and stupid.

His attire consisted of a large wide-brimmed hat (popularly called "resource control"), which he held in his hand; a dark brown suit; a pair of beautiful leather moccasins; and an elegant Malacca cane. Even while rain-soaked, he presented a picture of a perfect and elegant representation of a black man schooled in England.

One thing Wuru was sure of was that this was not a quiet, harmless man. This man was a nasty, mean character with evil intent.

"Why do you think I'll be the man for the job?"

The man said nothing for a while.

"I've heard stories concerning him and you."

"Stories like what?"

"They say he burned down your father's house. And he's the one who killed your best friend, Conboye."

"How do you know all these things?"

"I'm a local man. I hear stories."

"You can't believe all you hear."

"You know it's true. You've a score to settle with him."

Wuru didn't reply. He knew Tosan's name was linked to the WV. The story had not been confirmed. Tosan's name was a very popular name in the Warri Crisis. Most atrocities committed by the WV were linked to him. Just like all atrocities committed by the EBA were linked to him, Wuru.

After that bloody battle the previous month, nobody had seen Tosan. Speculation was that he had relocated to Yorubaland—Lagos or Ibadan. But speculation was still running rings around his name as the inspiration of the struggle.

"I'm not the man you're looking for," Wuru said.

"I'm afraid there's no other man that can do the job."

"How do you mean?"

"Everybody seems scared of him. And from what I heard, he's not afraid of anybody. The only man he'll choose not to cross is you."

Wuru smiled. "How much are you paying for this job?"

About fifteen seconds passed in silence.

The lecturer gave no sign of having heard. He was looking at his jeep, which the driver had just parked a few yards away.

He turned back to the young man. "What did you say?"

"I said, 'How much are you paying for this job?'"

"Two million naira."

There was deep silence, no words, no movement—only the slight roaring of the wind and showering noise of the rain.

"Fair enough," Wuru said, his harsh voice almost a whisper. "I'll do it not because I like you. It's because he's an Itsekiri, and there's the story that he's the one that burned down my father's house."

Ubangha looked at Wuru. "I don't care." He turned around and signaled to his driver, who swung the powerful vehicle around and slammed it to a stop beside him.

He stepped into the car and stretched his long legs, arranging himself comfortably into the leather seat. The light on the roof of the vehicle dramatically highlighted the angles and planes of his handsome, dark face. All his self-possession was there, and with it came an unmistakable smugness. He closed the door and touched a button inside the car, and the window slid down with an electric whine. Wuru felt the cold kiss of the air-conditioning pouring onto his face like a bucket of cold water.

Ubangha leaned out of the window. "Meet me at Kudos Bar, say, at five o'clock tomorrow evening. We'll discuss the details."

The vehicle glided smoothly away from the scene.

Wuru stood for a moment, staring at the vanishing taillights. He watched the vehicle blend into the darkness. It was uncanny, like a ghost car or a trick by a magician. But there was no magic wand or any puff of smoke.

CHAPTER TWO

EFFURUN, MAY 2004

Kudos Bar and Restaurant, which was on Effurun-Sapele Road, was perched comfortably opposite the famous Lord's Nightclub, which was regarded as one of the best nightclubs in the Effurun–Warri axis of Delta State.

Vincent Ubangha came in very early. He carried a rolled umbrella—a habit he'd picked up in England—and, using the umbrella as a walking stick, strolled across the entrance to the main restaurant and situated himself discreetly at the rear.

The day was cold with a hint of rain, and he was dressed for it in a tweed overcoat, a gray bowler hat, and a neat pair of brogues.

He dined alone in the restaurant, and later he relocated to the bar, where he drank half a bottle of Rémy Martin and smoked a Benson & Hedges. From his discreet table, he could observe everyone who came into the bar. He was on edge, waiting for Isaac Wuru and worrying that the boy would not show up.

Everybody in Warri had heard of Isaac Wuru—or Black Wuru, as he was popularly called. He was the most notorious of all the Ijaw youths, and the "bloodiest." His name was in most of the papers reporting the war. But nobody knew anything about him. His name was often mentioned in a tone that was almost reverential in the *ogoro* bars, nightclubs, "jungles," and local *bukas*. To a great many, Wuru was more than a soldier of the Ijaw nation. He was an assassin; he was one of the brightest stars in the gruesome theater of the fratricidal Niger Delta War. There were even some who thought the assassination of Chief Alfred Erewa, an elder statesman and a renowned Itsekiri political chieftain, was carried out by him.

Dr. Vincent Ubangha believed that the young man would carry out the assignment successfully. He knew it. The hatred the young man had for the Itsekiris was something never seen before in the annals of Nigerian tribal wars.

He was sipping from his glass of brandy when Black Wuru came into the bar. He walked to the lecturer's table and sat down.

They regarded each other coldly. Dr. Ubangha looked at his wristwatch. It was ten minutes past the hour of five o'clock.

"You're late," he said quietly, without a hint of anger in his voice, though he meant to be angry.

"I know," Wuru said, curtly. "It's the traffic holdup."

The lecturer smiled. The young man's breath smelled of marijuana. It was a smell he knew very well.

He ordered Guinness stout for Wuru. It was immediately set on the table. Wuru opened the beer himself and drank straight from the bottle. The first gulp finished, he set the bottle down on the table roughly, and the liquid in the bottle quivered. He stared at the door. The lecturer stared at his glass as if looking for something in the bottom of it.

Wuru leisurely went through his shirt pocket and found a cigarette. Then, more leisurely, he proceeded to light it.

"Now I'm here," he said quietly in Izon, amid cigarette smoke. "So what's the gist?"

"He's to be taken next Sunday," the other man replied in the same language.

"It's okay with me. Just take it that he's as good as gone."

The lecturer said nothing. His face was like a sculptured stone.

"Fill me in with the details."

"Yes." The lecturer drained his glass and sighed in silence as he felt the fiery liquid sinking down inside him. "He's a student of the university."

They didn't talk for quite a while. The lecturer watched him light a fresh cigarette and gulped the last of his beer. Wuru signaled the bartender, who came over immediately with a fresh bottle of stout.

Through the louvered window, Wuru watched the sky grow colder and darker. He sighed. *Another bloody rain.*

"Where do you want me to take him?"

"In Lagos. He has an apartment somewhere in Isolo. I've the address here with me."

"Do you have a photograph of him with you?"

The lecturer took out a colored photograph from a smooth-grained leather briefcase beside his chair, studied it for a moment, and then passed it across the table.

"That's the bastard." There's no denying the anger in the lecturer's voice.

Wuru grinned. He was a man who really liked to hear swear words. He studied the picture for a long moment. It was a glossy 15cm × 10cm photo. It was Tosan Mayuku all right.

"It's him."

"Of course it's him," the lecturer said mildly.

For perhaps three minutes, neither of them said a word. Wuru was studying the photograph. The young man in the snapshot was an attractive fellow with a strong, aggressive chin; straight nose; and well-trimmed mustache. He was wearing a baseball cap. Boldly inscribed on the front of the baseball cap was "DALLAS COWBOYS."

'What's he done that you want him wasted?"

Dr. Ubangha shifted uncomfortably and coughed before answering. "What's he done? You tell me your grouse with him; why is he your enemy?"

"He burned down my father's compound." Wuru hadn't meant to speak so loudly, so angrily. "That's the story I heard. Conboye, my best friend, was also killed by his gang. That's why I want him."

The lecturer looked at him for a long moment before he replied, "We're together. In your case, he was with the Warri Vanguard, which razed your family's house. In my case, he ordered people to burn down my house. Though I can't say anybody was killed, that house cost me a fortune. And my four good vehicles were torched. That's why I want him."

"Then he deserves not to live."

"But you'll take care. He is a smart boy—one of the smartest boys on campus."

"He's a cultist?" Wuru's voice was very low.

"He's the leader of the Black Owls," the lecturer said quietly.

Wuru said nothing. The silence lengthened and deepened, the raindrops becoming oppressively loud. He flicked ash off his cigarette, screwing up his lidless eyes as he stared around the room.

A blue Mazda stopped to let out its passengers in the rain—a man and a woman. He watched as they fought their way through the storm and into the next compound. They were soaked through. *Bloody rain.*

"I heard they're one of the most renowned frat groups in this part of the country."

The lecturer nodded. "You're right. In the university, they are the toughest. Tosan is their leader, but that doesn't mean a damn thing. What does matter is that he's got to die."

"I see." Wuru was very quiet. "Is he always in the midst of his cult guys?"

"No. He's not like that. He stays alone. But he's never lonely; he has company all the way. Guys like Tosan are always carrying guns twenty-four hours every day, everywhere. It's natural."

Outside, the wind beat and slapped like a demon, making each casement rattle. Rain slammed onto the roofs and dashed in cascades against the shuddering glass windows.

"How do I get paid?'

"You'll get half payment now."

"And the other half?"

"When he's dead."

Wuru nodded slowly. "Where's the down payment?"

"Here," the lecturer said briefly, and he placed the briefcase on the table. He opened it slightly, and Wuru had a glimpse of neat bundles of naira notes.

Wuru grinned and reached for the briefcase.

The lecturer wrote briefly on a piece of paper and passed it across the table. Wuru took the small paper and read it slowly. He looked up at the lecturer steadily and kept looking for a long time.

"Do you realize that I can just take this money and walk away and not do the job?"

The lecturer smiled faintly. "I know you will not do that. You want him as much as I do, and I'm giving you the opportunity to kill him. I'm also paying you on top of it. I know how desperate you are to nail him. This is your chance. You'll not blow it."

Wuru bit his lip thoughtfully, but he didn't say anything.

The lecturer knew the deal was already sealed.

* * *

Forty minutes later, Black Wuru took an okada to the Creek River Hotel, which was popularly known as Bayelsa. The Creek River Hotel was on Warri-Sapele Road, not far from the NPA yard, overlooking the dirty waters of the Warri River. An Ijaw businessman from Bayelsa State owned it.

The restaurant, bar, and nightclub were all housed in the second floor of the large, spacious, modest, freshly painted, and spotlessly clean four-story building. There was a flower garden in the front yard with a deep blue awning covering it and a small parking lot. In the rear of the four-story building was a parcel of land where the foundation of a house was built.

The Egbesu Boys occupied the left wing of the uppermost floor, and nobody knew what they used it for. Everybody kept clear of it. Even the proprietor and staff never came within reach of it. They avoided it like the plague.

Bayelsa, as it was more becomingly known, was the agora of all Ijaw men and women and their friends. If you were an Ijaw man or woman, it was open for you twenty-four hours. It was a place where you could pop in anytime for a drink, a talk, and a meal. Niger Delta dishes were served at reasonable prices. The owner, Tam, wanted to promote Ijaw culture, and he invited traditional musicians to come and perform Ijaw dance and music once a week. Wrestling matches were held sometimes, and the *Owigiri* girls did their shows every other weekend.

The bar of the hotel was typically filled with people coming and going, particularly oil bunkerers (popularly known as oil-boys), marine tycoons, and prostitutes. It was a landmark and a meeting place of the Ijaw people in Warri and its environs. Sometimes politicians of the Ijaw nation would visit the hotel and give political speeches to their beloved people.

The Egbesu Boys had picked it as their headquarters because of the secret rooms it had underground and its conspicuousness altogether. They wouldn't be noticed easily in the sea of people who thronged it on daily basis. The police had at one time considered closing down the place, but it was said that some powerful palms were greased and the whole proceedings were forgotten. It was all because there were popular rumors that beneath this magnificent building were secret underground rooms where caches of arms and ammunition were stored.

Wuru took the staircase to the fourth floor, walked down the deserted corridor, and rapped on the door, using the usual knock pattern. The door was opened a few inches, and a vicious face peered at him and then flung it wide open for him. He strolled in, shut it, and slammed the bolt home.

Two men sat around a table scattered with playing cards, a loaded tray, wineglasses, and a half-empty bottle of Johnnie Walker. The room was in darkness except for a blue light that fell directly on the table. A smoky haze hung overhead, drifting into the shadows.

Wuru and these two men who sat at the table made up part of the leadership of the Ijaw ethnic militia. They were the brains and skills of the group. A fourth chap, Timi, was sitting in the shadows. Though Wuru couldn't see him, he could smell him. He smelled of books, of learning. He was a gentleman, not yet used to the conscienceless part of war.

Wuru walked into the middle of the room, and slowly he tugged at the light switch. The room was instantly flooded with light. All eyes were on him. He dropped the briefcase on the center of the table, on top of the cards and chips.

"That's the unlucky fellow I've been looking for since God knows when," he said in Ijaw.

One of the two young men reached for the photograph. He was called Lakemfa, but his close friends called him Yellow because of his fair complexion. He studied the photograph for a brief moment and then passed it across to the other fellow at the table.

"It's Tosan Mayuku," he said, his voice an odd mixture of repressed fear and excitement.

Wuru nodded. "It's him."

Manager, the other fellow, smiled at the photograph. Timi came out from the shadows, took the photograph from Manager, and took a long look at it. At last he said in the Ijaw language, "Are we going to kill him?"

Wuru laughed. "What do you think?" was his reply. He was warmed, secretly pleased.

"I think we should just forget it."

"Forget it?" Manager said raising his voice. The other two were equally stunned. They regarded the other chap strangely, as if he'd spoken an unspeakable thing.

"What the hell are you saying, Timi?" said Wuru. "Do you realize that this boy killed Conboye? Do you realize that he's also responsible for my father's burnt-down compound?"

"They're just rumors. We don't really know for sure."

Wuru made a gesture indicating helplessness. "Sometimes I want to believe you have Itsekiri blood in your veins."

"That's your opinion, Wuru," Timi said, smiling. The smile was genuine and friendly. But the others were not smiling. They were staring at Timi strangely, as if he were some kind of alien.

"Timi, this boy killed your father." It was Yellow who said this.

"It's the Warri Vanguard who killed my father," Timi corrected.

"He's one of the founders of the Warri Vanguard," Wuru said.

Timi said nothing. He poured himself some Scotch and looked at Wuru. He strolled to his chair and picked up something.

"This is the picture of the real killer," he said. He held up the paper, an outdated colored magazine, front page forward, displaying the photograph of an unsmiling bespectacled man in a general's uniform. "This man killed Saro-Wiwa. This man turned Ogoniland into a wasteland of blood and bitter hatred. This man killed Kudirat Abiola. This man killed my father. He killed our people. He stole our oil money and stashed it in secrets bank accounts in Switzerland. Why don't we do something about that? Why? Why must we go after a young Itsekiri chap who doesn't really mean any harm?"

Wuru took the paper and looked at the photograph.

"We can't do anything to him," he said softy. "You and I know he's dead."

"But he's the author of our problems."

Fingers drumming on the table, Manager said, "You're damn right there. But the truth is this: we can't fight Abacha. He's dead. And we can't fight the Shege's government. Uncle Shege is not a democrat. Do you remember what he did in Odi? He destroyed the entire town. It's the enemy that we can fight that's who we'll fight. Well, the federal government didn't burn down my father's house; the Itsekiris did. The government did not seize my boats; the Itsekiris did. So what's your point, school boy?"

Timi shrugged. Manager was the chief of staff, which made him the assistant to Wuru. And by designation, he was number two, a squat, dark-complexioned young man in his late twenties with bitter brown eyes. At one time, he was the richest chap among them. That was before the war. He had carved out a comfortable living on the Pessu Market waterfront with three outboard speedboats that raked in over thirty thousand naira daily. But the war came, and all his life's investments were caught up in the inferno. That was when he picked up arms to become a soldier of the Ijaw nation. And since then every decision to him came down to gunshots.

"I agree with you to some extent," Timi said quietly. He regarded Manager as a cold-blooded killer. If there was one thing he would love to do, it would be to dissociate himself from him.

"It's okay," Wuru said, clearing his throat. He was standing in the middle of the room. "We're not going to quarrel over this. Tosan's a bad boy anyway you look at it." He smiled faintly. "He's a cult leader of some secret gang. But that's beside the point. The truth is that I want him. I want him badly. And somebody's provided me with his address, and he's paying me to waste him. Who am I to reject it, then?"

Timi looked at Wuru a long second. "Is he really a cultist?" His voice was anxious. He was the only graduate among them.

Wuru nodded. "He is." He turned to Manager. "We'll take him on Sunday night. I hope it is okay with you?"

Only Lakemfa said it was okay. Manager was silent. His eyes held an expression that promised ill for Timi.

Wuru looked at Timi. Timi was still standing. Whenever he was in the mood of making a point, he preferred standing and pacing. His face was set and sullen. It was as if he were embarrassed that the subject was a cultist.

Timi was a hardworking and brave young man. His bravery and level-headedness had gradually earned the respect of the Ijaw nation. In spite of his knowledge as a holder of a bachelor of science degree, he was neither proud nor arrogant. That was why Wuru liked him greatly.

"Is it okay with you?" Wuru asked him.

Timi sighed and then said, "Actually, no. It's not okay with me. And it'll never be okay with me. Wuru, let's not be fooled. Tosan Mayuku is not the cause of our problem in this country. And he can never be our problem. We've bigger problem than Tosan—or the Itsekiris, for that matter."

"So what's the cause of our problem? And who's our problem?" Yellow asked quietly.

"Yes, tell us," Manager prompted.

Timi began to speak but then stopped himself.

"You're assuming, rightly or wrongly, that Tosan is not the cause of our problem. So tell us what or who is the actual cause of our problems."

"It would be better for me to reserve my comments," Timi replied.

"Are you reserving your comments?" Manager queried. "You can't reserve your comments. Tell us exactly what you feel. It's a free country. Freedom of speech and freedom of expression and all those other freedoms we're told we freely enjoy. Tell us."

Timi began to speak. "Many of us are guided, or rather misguided, by the saying that the Itsekiris are the cause of our problems in this country. But let's be frank with ourselves. Are they really the cause? The most interesting thing here is the great conspiracy by the people in high places to divide and rule us. To plunder our natural resources. Do you know that cabals from other parts of this country are dividing the oil blocs in our communities and allocating them to themselves? Don't you know that the Itsekiris and all other tribes in the Niger Delta are suffering just like us? Do you know that there are cabals in this country who earn millions of dollars everyday from the oil wealth in our backyard and yet we, the indigenes of oil-producing communities, do not have means of sustenance?"

"You're making the whole thing look very confusing," Yellow murmured under his breath.

"Have you finished?" Wuru asked.

"Oh no. I'm just beginning," Timi replied. "Everybody has seen how over twelve billion dollars Gulf War oil windfall revenue went missing in this country during a military regime. It was not the Itsekiris or the Ogonis who squandered that money. Everybody has seen how Abacha mismanaged and siphoned several billion dollars of oil revenue out of this country and into his own private accounts abroad. It was not the Itsekiris who were responsible. We don't even have a share in oil blocs' allocations. What are we fighting for? *Who* are we fighting for? 'Lords of the creeks,' they call us. We kill ourselves; we kill our neighbors, who are not in any way better than us. We kill ourselves, and our environment has been reduced to nothing by this black gold that has darkened our communities, and yet we in no way benefit from it."

Great silence descended on the room.

"Professor Timinimi," Wuru said jokingly. "Have you finished?"

Timi smiled and raised the glass of whiskey he was holding high above his head in mock salutation and said, "This is to the cause—to fight and kill our neighbors who are in such poor, shitty conditions as we are. This is to our generals, retired and untired, the very people who've turned this once great country into this deplorable condition where our creeks are now war colleges, with several lessons to be taught and learned in the new field of warfare called creek-guerrilla war. And this is also to those few men in khaki or *agbada* who are not from our communities yet have made several billion dollars in oil wealth from our communities, and who spend this money they haven't earned in Dubai, Europe, and the Americas to buy houses they don't need, build refineries there that can't employ our teeming graduates, and yet tell us to our collective faces that we're not fit to be called equal citizens of our God-given country. And finally, this is to us, the real generals who don't know the real reason why we're fighting." With that, he drank the whiskey straight down.

"You're drunk," Wuru said.

"It's possible," Timi replied nonchalantly, and he went back to his seat.

Wuru, for no obvious reason, began to smile. "You almost convinced me there. But the truth is that anything you say won't sway me. I want that boy, and I'll get him. Is that clear?"

"Perfectly," Yellow replied.

"Thank you. And you, Manager?"

Manager's face was frozen, expressionless. His eyes were on Timi.

"It's okay."

"On Friday, we'll travel to Lagos. On Saturday, we'll sniff him out. Then, on Sunday night, we'll strike. If all goes according to plan, he will be dead by sundown Sunday evening. Any questions?"

"Yes," Timi said. "Supposing he has friends with him on that night—boyfriends, girlfriends. What do we do? Kill them all?"

"No!" Wuru shook his head decisively. "It's only him we want. But if anybody—boyfriend, girlfriend, or anybody else—tries to be heroic, we'll kill him. That's an order."

"Supposing—"

"Don't suppose!" Wuru's voice was metallic and loud. He was an unsubtle man who, like most Ijaw youth leaders, believed in the utility of force in solving every problem. Timi understood him that much.

"You don't know what I want to say," Timi said slowly and emphatically.

"I don't know, but I can guess. The subject has no soul. His friends would be of the same cast. We'll be doing society a whole world of good if any of them happen to be in our line of fire."

Timi sighed. He felt sad, sick, tired, defenseless, and angry. What could he tell these people about hate—this very inhuman, consuming flame of hatred? Nothing, he knew. Nothing that Wuru wouldn't despise. Nothing Lakemfa wouldn't laugh at. He was a schoolboy. He knew too much. That was his problem. He was a book man. He sighed again, more heavily this time. A book man wasn't supposed to know much about warfare. He wasn't even supposed to suppose.

CHAPTER THREE

JANKARA, JANUARY 2004

Tosan Mayuku lived at no. 17 John Elen Road. His flat was on the top floor of a two-story building. The building was divided into flats; his was the only flat on the second floor, a four-bedroom apartment occupying the entire upper part of the building, while two spacious two-bedroom apartments occupied the first floor.

With the alcohol swimming inside his head, he managed to climb the staircase without breaking his neck. Once inside the flat, he closed the door and looked around him. He loved this apartment. The walls were covered with paintings—his paintings. They rarely pleased those girls who saw them. There was one of a nude girl riding a tiger—a leashed tiger. They hated it so much.

He couldn't bring himself to hate them, though some of his gouaches were bizarre variations of African gods, ghosts, and masquerades. Not many people in Nigeria were brought up to appreciate paintings for all their worth, he knew. Those who appreciated contemporary art were a negligible few in Jankara. Most of his lecturers thought he had a weird talent. To some of them, the word "weird" would have been too mild to qualify his paintings. He studied the paintings. They were nudes, mostly. That was one of his simple pleasures—naked women. One of his classmates had once joked that he painted evil thoughts that conceptualized themselves in his devilish mind.

The paintings were mostly weird, grotesque, and tortured. His subjects were complicated in texture and composition, arrangement and form, balance and personal pleasure. That was what he had in the center of his mind when painting.

An angel in the strong black arms of Jacob stared coldly across the sitting room at him. He had captured the effect correctly. There was that thing in the eyes of the angel that never failed to please him. What was it? Fear? Hopelessness? He could not place it, but he was pleased with himself for creating that expression. In the grotesque clash, it seemed as if Jacob was having a field day as he wrestled fiercely with one of God's own.

He sighed. A double door led to one of the bedrooms—the master bedroom. That was where he slept. One of the bedrooms was his studio. That was where he did his painting. The other one was his study and library; that was where he did his studying. The fourth one was the guest room. He called it the "Guest Palace."

He walked through the double door that led to his bedroom. The bedroom was his private garden—an oven where he baked his ideas and hatched his most secret thoughts. It was a neat room, clean and ordered and beautiful.

It was good that he had come back home. He was not in the mood for partying and shacking up and hustling girls. It was a tedious task, and he was not in the mood tonight. He felt only like painting. Throughout the evening, his mind was involved with the shadowy outline of a picture he wanted to put on canvas. As a man burning with such an idea to paint, he couldn't afford to be held up in a party hall.

It was good to be home, to be back in the comfort of his bedroom, back in the huge king-sized bed with the tapioca-colored bedspread that offered such appealing comfort. His last oil painting hung over the head of the bed. It was the painting of a young girl—a girl in the nude standing in a field in a rich countryside. She held a sickle in her left hand and a flower in her right. A watery yellow sun shone brightly on her innocent nubile figure. There was something warm and beautiful about her. She was a pleasurable treasure to look at: a figure to be cherished—an angel to be dreamed about. He knew it was one of his finest paintings. He had conceived the idea of the painting after reading William Wordsworth's *The Solitary Reaper*. He had dreamed about her, fantasized about her, and loved her, and at long last, he couldn't help it; he had to paint her.

He lay face down in the middle of the bed. There was something so comfy and warm and cool about the bedroom that he found nowhere else—not even in his bedroom in the family house in Koko. The Ijaws had burned that one down. He rose up from the bed. There was a small Sony CD player in the bedroom. He put a Tupac disk in the player. There was a white sheepskin rug that made one want to dance barefoot across the floor. He took off his shoes. There was one soft black chair near the bedroom window. He sat on it, parted the silk curtains, and stared into the night. He wanted to draw inspiration from the darkness.

* * *

Ebi and Mary were both students in the same faculty at the university, and they were staying off campus in the same building. It was a tiny two-story house located on the highway about five kilometers from the university gate.

They were unusual friends, these two girls. Mary was a girl who loved clubbing and partying, but Ebi was not. Mary happened to be one of those "happening" girls in the school. She was a rising model with a top firm in Lagos. She'd done ads for Coca-Cola, MTN, Macclean, and Afprint. Close to the university's gate was a towering billboard with her face on it. It was a Coca-Cola ad in which she posed with two other pretty girls, sipping chilled Cokes.

The difference between the two girls, who were nearly of the same age, was startling. While Mary was the white man's idea of beauty, with her long, straight legs and tiny waist, Ebi was the African's concept of beauty, with her solid hips, well-formed backside, and average bosom.

Mary was interested only in macho guys with connections—guys that paraded fast cars, cruised on power bikes on campus, dressed mostly in jeans, smoked ganja, wore earrings, and plaited their hair like African American music stars. Such guys must have tons of money to spend. Her latest boyfriend was in that league.

Even after two years at the university, Ebi had very few friends, and all of them were on the same level with her. They were not people she could really call friends; they were more like acquaintances. Most girls considered her snobbish because of her air of superiority. It was not her fault, though. Her upbringing in the United States was responsible for that.

Mary was the only girl she could call a friend, because she was the closest person to her. And as for boyfriends, she had none. She was a solitary girl, and in the university community, she was still much at a loss as to how to feel free with her classmates, many of whom she considered socially beneath her. The only male friend she had was an associate professor who was old enough to be her father. If they hadn't had the same fervent interest in paintings, she would not have considered having an affair with him.

She had very few invitations to the parties that were thrown nearly every weekend, and she was glad about that, for she was a shy sort of girl. She never knew what to say to the boys who asked her for a dance. She couldn't flirt freely with them as other girls did, and generally she clammed up around them. Because of her frosty attitude, she discouraged most of the young men who wanted to "toast" and create a kind of romantic relationship with her.

The two girls were unusual friends. Mary was an outdoor girl; Ebi was an indoor girl. Mary liked partying; Ebi liked partying, but she knew she was not in Mary's league. She would never skip lessons in order to travel out of town for one bash or another. When both of them happened to go out together, it was because Ebi allowed herself to be persuaded by Mary's smooth talk.

That was exactly what happened on that fateful night when Ebi attended a party thrown by a frat gang called the Brownstones, popularly known as "the Stones." She knew quite well that Mary's boyfriend was a lord in the Stones, but because she wanted to please her friend, she attended the party. It was a very wild party, as were most parties organized by the Stones. She didn't even know how she managed to stay through the first few hours while the party heated up. Around two o'clock, Mary's boyfriend, Blacky, and his friends decided to leave the party venue earlier than the stipulated closing hour. They all left via the back door and crowded into Blacky's Toyota Pathfinder. There were six of them: three boys and three girls.

It was a beautiful quiet night, with luminous stars bathing the high heavens with shimmering light.

The road was free of traffic, and they had the highway to themselves. Ten minutes of fast driving brought them to Blacky's pad.

They all stumbled out, all of them partially drunk. Blacky was the most serious case. That he was able to drive them all safely to the house by himself was a miracle. In the doorway, he fumbled with his key while the others all crowded around him. A voice called out to them. They all looked up.

"Is that you, Picasso?" Blacky called.

"Yeah, Black," Picasso replied. "Don't tell me you guys want to start another party downstairs?"

There was general laughter and calls of "Correct man Tos," after which Blacky opened the door and put his hand inside.

Bright light came on, illuminating a neat, spacious living room. The walls were covered with colorful posters of rap stars and eminent professional soccer players. Ebi recognized two Notorious B.I.G.s and a larger-than-life full-color poster of Jay

Jay Okocha in pursuit of a spinning ball, approaching the range of eighteen yards to the goal area.

"Come in, everybody," Blacky said, and he walked straight to the CD player mounted on the oaken shelf. He slotted in Biggie's rap disc.

Ebi would have preferred to turn back and go home, but she knew they would not allow her to do so. From the way their conversation was going, she knew they were about to start another party.

She studied the room. It was a fiercely decorated living room with low chairs, a low table, and an oaken shelf carrying a twenty-one-inch color TV set, a VCR, and a CD player. The only light came from a single naked bulb in the center of the high ceiling. The single fan in the room was hanging from the ceiling like the limb of a dead tree. Somebody had turned it on, and it was making whirring sounds like the rotors of a helicopter. The four walls were covered with a dozen posters of gangster rap artistes, soccer stars, and reggae legends. Someone had brought in a bottle of whiskey from the Pathfinder, and there were glasses in everybody's hands.

Biggie's soft rap beautifully filled the room. Someone passed around some joints. Ebi dropped hers in an ashtray, but Mary sucked at hers eagerly as if her life depended on it.

Something told Ebi that she wasn't going to like it in here, and she seriously considered leaving. Mary and Blacky were standing at a corner, her head on his chest, his hand playing with the strands of her brown wig.

She excused her friend to a quiet corner and whispered to her that she felt like leaving, stating that she was not feeling well.

"Go and rest in the guest bedroom," she replied in a low voice. "You'll feel better in a little while."

"I can't do that!" Ebi said, angry and exasperated.

"Then wait until it is daylight." Mary's voice was very low this time. "I'm having a swell time in here."

Ebi said nothing. She knew that her friend was a little bit high. There was no doubt about that. She also knew that if she went into the bedroom, the last fellow in the group who seemed to have no girl friend of his own among the three ladies would steal in after her and possibly harass her. She felt safer in the sitting room.

She withdrew to one of the couches and sat down. Just then, a fellow dropped down close to her. It was the lone fellow who had no girl. And she was the lone lady who had no guy. That made two of them. She studied him. He was a big, gangly, bucket-headed young fellow twice her size, length, and breadth. He was called Ade Lopez.

"Hello, Ebi," he said sweetly. "How are you feeling? Catching the fun?"

"Yeah. I'm cool," she replied, wishing she could think of a smarter reply.

"How do you dig it if we shake the body?"

"I'm sorry, Lopez," Ebi said sincerely. "I'm deadbeat. I just need somewhere right now where I can rest my head and dream of angels."

"Hey, that's not bright talk, baby," the Brownie protested wildly. "Come up off your ass. I'll show you some fine dance steps."

"I already know how to dance," Ebi said flatly.

"I know that," Lopez agreed wryly. "I just want to teach you the latest steps."

"No sir," came her quick reply. "I don't want to dance with you. I'm tired."

Lopez was astounded.

At that moment, the CD player stopped. Blacky said they had run out of "good music." Mary said they'd need blues. The other girl said she'd prefer reggae. Blacky asked whether anybody would go upstairs to borrow some from Picasso. He had barely finished saying what kind of music they would need when Ebi volunteered to run upstairs to get some.

"But you said you're tired," Lopez protested.

"I needed a bit of fresh air," she called back to him.

When she climbed upstairs, she saw that his door was ajar and he was standing, working on the mounted easel. He didn't seem very pleased when he saw her. She had the idea that he was really concentrating on the sketch when she came in unannounced.

He was in his twenties with a rather interesting face. His eyes were deep-set and so arresting that it almost seemed as if they were boring holes into hers. He was wearing sky-blue Pepe jeans and an open-necked screaming blue T-shirt, both of which were ink-spattered.

"What do you people want now?" he inquired immediately, sounding impatient. "Cigarettes or ganja?"

"Some music," she said awkwardly.

He pointed to the shelf where his own CD player sat. "What kind?"

"Reggae. Bob Marley. Cocoa Tea. Gregory Isaac. Peter Tosh. Any of these will do."

"Help yourself. I've got only two Bob Marley CDs and one Peter Tosh. Not a single Cocoa Tea or Gregory Isaac. Take all of them. But make sure you return them yourself or else…" He let his voice trail off, hanging the threat in the air. Threats are always more pronounced when not spelled out.

"Or else what?" she asked.

"Forget it," he said, and he returned to his work.

Ebi went through the collection. It took almost ten minutes because there were so many. She found what she wanted at last.

"I've got them," she said loudly. "Three."

He didn't look up. "I told you that there were three, didn't I?" His voice, she detected, was laced with a finger of annoyance.

As Ebi crossed the room toward the sitting room door, she was startled by a loud hoot from the corner. She turned to see a large silver cage in which a beautiful owl sitting on a loop was regarding her with wide yellow eyes.

Ebi walked to the cage and scratched the silver bars with a manicured fingernail. The owl regarded her suspiciously and then flitted away to the far side.

"You keep an owl?" she called across to him.

"What's the matter if I do?" Tos's reply was curt. Then he paused, and for the first time, he seemed to notice the girl. He looked at her for a long moment.

"What do you know about owls?"

"I just like them, that's all." Ebi's face was expressionless.

Tos smiled faintly. "His name is Scooter. He's part of my family."

There was silence for some time. There was now a puzzled expression on Ebi's face.

"Your family? I don't understand." Ebi scratched the cage again and the bird flitted to another position. "He seems afraid of me."

"Scooter can't be afraid of anybody," Tos said with a little anger.

Ebi was surprised by the tone of his voice. "Oh, I'm sorry. I didn't mean to be unkind."

Something in the girl's voice held Tos. He turned his eyes on her. "Forget it," he said, and he resumed his painting. Ebi was fascinated by what he was doing. She came closer and stood near him, studying his work. All she could see was a nightmare of bright red color, a painful composition of a bleeding beast—something that looked like a centaur. On the easel was blood—*lots* of blood—and a pained, frightful, grotesque monster. A protean monster.

He became aware of her closeness, and he stopped painting.

"Now what do you think you're doing?" he said wrathfully. "Can't you see that I'm busy?"

There was a couple of seconds' silence, and then Ebi bent over, studying the painting closely.

Tos stared at her. He touched her arm.

"Young lady!" His voice was harsh, impatient.

She blinked. Tos's eyes were narrowed, his annoyance barely in check.

"I'm sorry," Ebi's voice was quiet, curiously strained, as if she'd been dazed. "But I must say it's beautiful."

"It's not yet finished."

"I know. But it's going to be a great piece."

"Yeah," Tos said complacently. "But not until it's finished."

They both stared at the painting in silence for a moment, she imagining the creativity, the artistry. She turned and looked at the various paintings hanging on the walls. She'd just noticed them for the first time.

"Are you sure you're the creator of these things?" Her eyes were fixed steadily on him.

Tos smiled noncommittally. Just at that moment, Lopez stuck his head into the room.

"You've taken enough fresh air, baby. Come on out now."

He took the CDs from her and led her downstairs. Tos watched them leave.

In Blacky's apartment, Lopez slotted a Bob Marley disc into the CD player and tried to pull her into the center of the room to dance, but she refused. He followed her to her seat and sat close to her.

"What's biting you? If you don't want to smooch, why did you come here in the first fucking place?" His voice was loud and drew the attention of a boy who was necking his girlfriend. The girl gave her a withering look.

"Be quiet," Ebi said quietly to him.

"Don't tell me you came because you want to see the faces of solid men. Let's see what you've got under those jeans."

"I have the gripes," Ebi said in a small, thin voice. She was trembling visibly.

"That's no cancer, baby. A good, long fuck will take care of it. Trust me."

She winced as if in pain. Then she calculated fast. Before he could say "Wole Soyinka," she had fled quickly out of the room. She reached the door before he knew what she was doing, and he was after her with a dash as fast as lightning.

The light in Tos's sitting room was still on. She almost threw herself against the door blindly and burst inside.

"Help me!" was all she could bring out.

He'd been standing, his head cocked to one side, looking at the mixture of color on the easel. He turned around just as Lopez appeared in the doorway.

"Fucking bitch!" cried Lopez, panting like a dog that had skipped across the Sahara. "You now come out or else I'll force you out."

Tos looked faintly amused. He looked from the panting boy to the frightened girl who was retreating foot by foot farther into the room. He smiled, shook his head knowingly, and walked to Lopez.

"You take it easy, boy. The girl isn't in the mood tonight."

"She's my girlfriend!" Lopez shouted angrily.

"That's a bloody lie," Ebi retorted furiously.

"Ooh lala," Tos said. "Can you hear that from the doll's mouth?"

"She's drunk, man. Crazily drunk. Let me beat the alcohol out of her teeny-weeny ass, and you'll see that she'll tell you different."

Tos shook his head unhappily. "No, boy. This is my pad, my home. And the lady is my guest. I'll tell you two things you can't do in my pad: you don't shout in my pad, and you don't beat my guests. Not even with their permission. Not in my house. You hear that?"

"Are you threatening me?" Lopez shouted.

"Call it what you like, boy. But you don't lay a hand on this girl."

An ugly expression crossed Lopez's face. He considered his appearance. He was tall, big and menacing, a Goliath with a Mike Tyson-like fist. Compared to this punk standing in his way, he was King Kong.

"Who do you think you are?" The words were harsh and loud. "Who the blazing fuck do you think you are, standing there and trying to corner my girl? I've been buying this bitch drinks all night, do you know that?"

"No. I don't know that. But I'll tell you who I am. I am the owner of this apartment and the protector of the lady. If you don't like it, then come and beat her. Then you'll have me to reckon with."

Lopez looked at him, silent, expressionless; looked away; and stared at Ebi for a moment.

"It's okay, Lopez," Blacky said from the doorway. He strolled leisurely into the room and put his hand on Lopez's shoulder. "You don't talk to people anyhow. Tos's a correct man. You hear that? He's a correct man. Apologize to him right now."

Lopez was lost. For ten long seconds, he gazed at Blacky unbelievingly. "Fuck you all," he finally said with fearless anger, and he stormed out of the room.

Blacky frowned worriedly. He was evidently embarrassed. "You see, Tos…" he said, "we have all sorts of characters in this school. Some don't know how to behave. Some don't know when they've sailed too close to the wind or when they have blown their lid. Lopez is one of those boys. I'll talk to him about behaving properly. Kindly accept my apology on his behalf." He reached his hand forward. Tos hesitated, but only briefly. He stretched forth his own hand. It was a firm handshake. "And my young lady too—my apology to you. In case of next time—that is, if there is ever a next time—report to me. I know how to set frayed nerves right. Trust me."

Ebi said okay. Tos smiled good-naturedly, but it wasn't a pleasant smile. It never touched his dark eyes.

"Forget it, Blacky. Forget it. What does it matter? We're good neighbors. We have always been good to each other. But nobody knows what's going to happen to that young man next." The words were innocuous enough, but their tone sent the chill of fear deep into Blacky's mind.

He led Blacky to the door.

"Don't you have a bag or purse you came with?" Tos asked Ebi.

"Yeah. My bag's downstairs."

"Get the bag," Tos said. It was not a request. It was an order.

"I'll get it," Blacky said, and he went downstairs. He came back less than two minutes later with a small black bag. Tos took it from him and nodded his thanks.

When Blacky had gone, he examined the bag. It was one of those luxurious black leather ones with a twenty-four-karat-gold buckle. It was an expensive bag, he knew—more expensive than any bag he'd seen before.

He walked to the girl, placed the bag in her hand and studied her. For thirty seconds, fifty seconds, a whole minute, Tos stared steadily and quietly at her.

"Are you tired of fucking?" he demanded angrily.

She got annoyed, and tears rushed to her eyes.

"Why did you come with them in the first place if not to be laid?"

"I...don't...know!" She sobbed in between the words, and her hands twitched.

Her hair had fallen over her eyes, and she pushed it away, smearing her mascara. It was a proper natural female action. His male reaction was that he immediately felt sorry for her. Just this moment, he looked tough and angry, but when he saw her tears, he softened.

"It's okay. Don't cry," he said gently, trying to make his mood and voice seem sympathetic.

"I'm sorry I had to barge in the way I did," she said, trying to get her handkerchief from her bag. Before she could get it out, he offered his. She hesitantly took it.

He automatically photographed her particulars. She was small, five feet four or a little over, but that was because of the high heels of her stylish soft leather boots. Her tight Wrangler jeans, which were tucked into her boots, hid her slim, straight legs. She had a flat stomach, a narrow waist, and a well-formed backside. She was a fashionable girl. Her blouse's neckline had a low open front, and he could see the tops of her breasts. She had long, jet-black coiffured hair and simple jewelry, and she wore a sophisticated Jean Lassale watch. Her eyes were beautifully, cleverly made up.

She was still drying her tears. He waited, studying her. He liked this girl. She was pretty and extremely attractive and looked every inch like a gentle and brilliant girl. And she spoke English with an accent that was not Nigerian but somewhat American. *Could she be an African American? No.* He could feel his lips stretching into a sneer. *What would an African American be doing in a Nigerian university when they have all those Ivy-League universities?*

"Sit down, miss. You'll feel better in a little while," he said quietly to her.

She nodded unhappily and tried to smile, but the smile was a grimace that flickered only to die the next moment. She looked around. Over half a dozen large oil-on-canvas paintings beautifully adorned the sitting room. There was a thick wall-to-wall Aubusson carpet under her feet. A Sony TV set, a CD player, and a VCR all stood on an oaken shelf. It all blended comfortably with the ugly easy chairs. It was a sharp contrast with the flat downstairs. The only hitch was that it wasn't supposed to be a studio but an exhibition room.

Reluctantly, with a great effort, she dragged herself into one of the ugly chairs. She was really winded and needed to rest.

Tos propped himself up on the settee opposite her. "How old are you, miss?" he asked abruptly.

"I'm twenty-one," she lied. Tos nodded and smiled faintly. He was sure now; her voice had that nice American accent that was common among African Americans.

"Now tell me, what's a twenty-one-year-old girl doing outside her home with a boy who claims he's her boyfriend at this hour of the day? What's wrong with your books? Or don't you know how to read?"

Ebi was very quiet.

"No idea, ma'am?" he asked scathingly.

No reply came from her.

"I think girls under twenty-one should be home and in bed by ten o'clock."

Still there was no reply from Ebi. For a long time, the two young people, the boy and the girl, looked at each other quietly, without expression. After about a minute of silence, it was the boy who broke the silence.

"This is really new to me." He was very blunt. "I've never seen it before. This is Jankara, one of the world's most notorious universities. Out there, this school is known as a war college.

Raping, mugging, cult wars, you name it—it all happens casually here. It's a part of the system. And you know these things. What beats me is what's a twenty-one year old girl doing at this ungodly hour with a Stone? Can you tell me why?"

Ebi shifted uncomfortably on her chair. She said nothing.

For perhaps another one minute, neither of them said a word. Tos looked at her for a long moment.

"What's your name?" he asked abruptly.

"Ebi. Akpoebi Dabiri."

Tos frowned. "You're an Ijaw." It was a statement.

She nodded.

"What course are you studying?"

"I'm in the department of history. I'm majoring in African history."

"What level?"

"This is my second year."

Tos smiled; it was a strange smile. "What state are you from?"

Ebi looked up, amused, curious.

"Delta."

He nodded, but didn't say anything.

"What about you?" she ventured.

"I'm a Deltan. I'm supposed to be your brother."

"What tribe in Delta?"

Tos hesitated. His eyes were dark with remembered horrors. He could see his mother lying in the pool of her own blood, staring sightlessly at the flame licking the building—the family house in Koko.

"I'm an Itsekiri."

Ebi blinked and then recovered quickly. She scarcely heard the words, but she knew what it was all about—pain. She looked deeply at him, faintly astonished. It struck her then and there that he'd been caught in the middle of the crisis that had rocked the oil-rich city of Warri since March 1997.

"It's okay," Tos said gently. "I'm not going to hurt you. You know and I know that even as I'm talking, there's a war going on between our people. It's not supposed to be so, but that's what we're doing. But that doesn't mean we can't talk to each other or assume some civilized conduct of friendship. We must not lose ourselves in the follies of a few misguided individuals."

She averted her eyes from his as she asked a new question. "Did you lose anybody?"

"My beloved mother." The reply was a husky whisper.

"I'm sorry," she said softly." I'm really sorry." She could see the pain in his deep, dark eyes.

"God help us all," he said, and he shook his head. "That boyfriend of yours said earlier that you're drunk. Are you?"

She shook her head. "I'll still say it. He's not my boyfriend."

Tos smiled. "Never mind. Do you care for some wine?"

Ebi shrugged. "I hope it's not—"

"Stay where you are," Tos said, cutting her off, and he rose heavily to his feet. As he walked across the room, she watched him thoughtfully. The glow of the overhead light caught his face. The blue T-shirt and the matching blue jeans fit him beautifully.

When he came back later with a bottle of white French wine, he saw her standing, studying one of his paintings. The picture showed a tiger, realistically drawn; each yellow line was in place, and the mouth was half-open, showing cruel pointed teeth, the tawny eyes alive. It was rearing on its strong hind legs, and its long tail, of an uncommon dark yellow color, hung down taut. Something caught her attention in the painting—the strange detail of the painter's subject matter. A young, naked, but very beautiful girl rode the tiger.

The beautiful angelic face was set in repose, and the girl's small hands held the reins that were fastened to the tiger's mouth. It was a strange, chilling painting, but the artistry, without doubt, was the work of a genius. Each color was specially coordinated, the expressions specifically tailored, the lines professionally blended, all parts of the work in beautiful arrangement.

"Do you like it?" Tos's voice came from the other side of the room.

"It's very beautiful," she said without turning around. She was still studying the painting, her fingers resting on the signature at the edge.

"Your name is Tosan." It was a statement.

"Yeah," Tos said, and he strode across the room toward her. He stood next to her, bending slightly backward, regarding the painting critically.

"Why did you call it *Dance of Death*?"

Tos smiled. He was warmly pleased. She was one of the few strangers who were really interested in his work.

"It just occurred to me while painting it. The girl was riding atop a dangerous animal. There's the grave risk that if anything happens and she chances to fall down, the wild beast will have lunch. It's a death dance."

Ebi didn't move—not even when his shoulder brushed her.

"Where did you learn about painting?" he asked.

"In New York."

"New York?" His voice was sort of funny.

"I was born there, grew up there, and learned about art there..."

His eyes never left her.

"You've heard of Andy Warhol?" Ebi asked suddenly.

"He's one of the best-known American artists," Tos replied.

"Yes. He lived in the neighborhood not fifty yards from where I was born. At a very young age, I learned about his work. The largest public collection of his work is located in New York's City Museum of Modern Art. They are masterpieces. I frequented that place while I was in New York."

Tos looked for a long time into the young lady's face. She was really beautiful. Her dark, coiffured hair was pulled back to the nape of her neck, exposing her heart-shaped face. She had high cheekbones; wide, quiet, confident eyes; and a generous rosy mouth, with full lips painted in attractive colors. He was moved as he hadn't been moved in a long time. He was coming awake. He had a new feeling; the stirring was real.

"Ebi—can I call you Ebi?"

"Sure."

"I must tell you this: you have that rare gift—the ability to make a confident judgment, to distinguish the true worth of a picture. Not many people have that rare talent." With that, he handed her a glass and poured her a drink.

She took a small sip and regarded him coolly.

"You know what, Tosan—I hope you don't mind me calling you Tosan?"

"Not at all."

"You can paint. That's the truth. And believe me, you'll make fortunes from your work."

Tos smiled. "What gave you that idea?"

"This painting," she said softly. "What prompted you to paint this picture?"

"Drinking. I don't normally drink, but anytime I get drunk, I paint. So I did happen to get drunk—very drunk—one Sunday morning, and I painted that picture during my stupor."

Ebi smiled. "You must be joking!"

"Sometimes," Tos said, his voice light. He ran a fingertip round the rim of his wineglass.

A whole minute passed, during which the girl studied the painting and the boy studied the girl.

There was an accord between the tiger and the young girl riding it. It was quietly but beautifully emphasized on the picture. There was softness on the girl's face—a face in repose. The trustful lover was carrying the lady.

Tos drained his glass and refilled it. He cleared his throat noisily. She looked at him.

"What do you think of that picture?" he said, pointing to another painting hanging on the wall.

It was the painting of a very beautiful girl in a flowered miniskirt that was being lifted by the wind. Her private parts were exposed to the world. The wind had bulging eyes that were gazing at the girl's young voluptuous body. The sex organs were clearly and cleanly expressed.

"What do you think?" he asked quietly.

"Why is it that you try to portray sex and sex organs in your work?" She was serious.

Tos hesitated helplessly for a second, and then said,

"I'm not a very good painter. I want to be like Picasso. You know he had the strongest level of feeling. Sexuality. Everything on sensation and sexual desire was his strong point. That's why; I want to paint like him. To me, he's the greatest of the greats."

The thin penciled lines around her eyes rose.

"Is that why you like being called 'Picasso'?"

"I don't like being called 'Picasso'. They call me 'Picasso' simply because they see that I can paint. I can't help it."

She nodded without speaking for some seconds, her eyes already assessing another painting. It was an oil on canvas that captured a burning house, a group of ragtag heavily armed youths cheering in the background, and the inhabitants of the house running away from the scene, dragging along what little of their household property they could carry along with them.

Ebi assessed the painting critically for quite some time. It was an emotive work by a skilled painter. Tosan had caught the frozen action in lucid, vibrant, and exciting colors. The strongest point of the work was the juxtaposition of the use of fluid, happy lines, which made the devilish happiness of the armed youths very vivid, and the anguish visible on the faces of the refugees as they ran, dragging along the few household properties they could salvage, quite touching. It was a sad painting of the impact of war.

"How did you learn to paint so well?" she asked at last.

"It was a gift from God."

"You're good."

It was the truth. He knew it.

"Thank you."

Ebi looked him in the eye. Tos looked at her. He knew then that he liked this girl, and there was something close to admiration in her eyes.

"Come, I want to show you something more," he said quickly, and with his powerful hand on her elbow, he led her into his bedroom. He showed her the painting *The Solitary Reaper*.

"What do you make of that one?"

"Good God!" she said quietly. "It's a great painting!"

Tos grinned to himself.

"Really?" he said casually.

Her eyes were glued to the picture. "Truly!" She sounded clearly enthralled.

Tos smiled faintly, his eyes on the painting. "I entered Wordsworth's innermost sanctum: his dreams, his instincts, his desires, and his thoughts. When I came back, I came back with this piece."

"William Wordsworth's Solitary Reaper was fully clothed when I last heard about her."

Tos nodded. "You're right. She was fully clothed when I met her. But I had to remove the clothes when stealing her. You can deduce that it is all staked on sensation and desire—Picasso's permanent marks on my person."

Ebi carried her wineglass to her lips and drained the last of her wine. "You could sell this one for a fortune."

"Who's going to buy it?"

"Me."

"You want more wine?"

"No. I want this painting."

"Good God! Are you really serious?" He was incredulous.

She scrutinized his lean, dark face. "Do you think I'm joking?"

Tos arched one of his bushy eyebrows. "How can I tell if you're joking?"

"You can tell because I'm not laughing."

Tos nodded. "What are you going to do with the painting of a naïf?" he said, taking the empty wineglass out of her hand.

"Display it in my room. My bedroom, really."

Tos looked at Ebi in slow surprise. "Display it in your bedroom? Is it that good?"

Ebi walked to the side of the bed, reached her hand forward, touched the painting symbolically, smiled tiredly, and turned toward him.

"It's a superb picture. I like it."

Tos watched the young lady a moment. "You really expect me to take all this flattery?"

The lady looked hurt. "I know it's not all that good. But I'll buy it."

He gazed at her, sorry to his heart for disbelieving her professional judgment.

"I'll paint you another one. It's going to be more beautiful than this piece. Believe me."

"What about *Dance of Death*? Are you selling it?"

Tos smiled crookedly. "You want to buy it?"

"I shouldn't be asking if I didn't want to."

"How much can you afford?"

"Should I say one hundred grand?"

For a couple of seconds, Tos stood silent, shocked and unbelieving. He was uncomfortable. A lecturer friend of his had agreed to buy the painting for forty grand. Only last week he had said so. Now this girl was saying she'd buy it for one hundred grand. His last major work had sold for fifty-five grand, and that was a hard bargain.

"Are you serious?" he whispered huskily.

"Of course I'm serious," Ebi replied calmly.

Tos's eyes narrowed. "Now tell me the truth: What do you want to do with these pictures?"

"Never mind," she began, but she checked herself against what she had been about to say. "Okay, I'll come clean with you. I've a friend in New York. He deals in still-lifes, portraits, landscapes and seascapes, and contemporary erotic nude paintings. He has a very big gallery on Madison Avenue. He'll be interested in some of these pictures of yours."

A broad, cheerful grin came near to tearing Tos's face apart.

"We're in business, baby!" he shouted. "We're in cool business."

"Calm down. I feel sleepy already." She stifled a yawn.

Tos closed his eyes for a moment. He was beginning to appreciate the presence of this young lady.

"Tosan!" she called his name quietly.

Tos hardly heard her. His eyes were closed, and he knew he was swaying on his feet.

"Tosan!" This time she shouted into his ear.

"Yes ma'am," he said, opening his eyes with a shock.

"I want to lie down a bit. I'm dead tired."

"Certainly, certainly." His hand gripped her shoulder with a strength that made her wince. "Tomorrow you'll get in touch with this guy. I don't care how; all I care about is that we're in business, okay?"

She nodded sleepily.

"Come, I'll take you to the guestroom." He led her out of the room and into the guest bedroom, a room a little bit smaller than the master bedroom.

"You lie on the bed. Feel at home. I'll wake you at seven, eight—any time you want me to. I'll drive you home if you want me to. Just relax, baby." With that, he impulsively pecked her cheek and stepped back.

She watched him go out, closing the door softly after him, touched her cheek where his lips had brushed her, and wondered why her heart had begun beating differently with the touch of his lips. It was a very strange sensation. It set off something deep inside her heart.

As she was still thinking of him, exhaustion overtook her and she fell asleep, still fully clothed, on top of the bed.

CHAPTER FOUR

Tos woke up late the next morning. He yawned and glanced at his wristwatch lying on the nightstand. It was a quarter past eight. He swore loudly, got to his feet, and walked hurriedly to the guest bedroom. The door was closed. He knocked loudly. There was no response. He knocked again, louder. There was still no response. He twisted the knob, and the door pushed open. There was nobody in the room. The bed was neatly made up. She was gone, he knew. The fragrance of her perfume was what was left.

He frowned. *Where has she gone?* he wondered. He stepped further into the room, and his eyes fell on a small piece of notepaper atop the dressing table. He picked it up and read it out loud: "'Good morning, Tosan. I woke up early. You are still asleep, and I don't want to wake you up. I decided to take my leave. Thanks for the hospitality. You're a very kind person. I want you to meet me at Coke Villa at two o'clock. I owe you at least a lunch. Be seeing you. Ebi.'"

Tos shook his head. The muscles around his mouth formed a smile as he put the notepaper into his jeans pocket. He glanced across the bedroom at the window and the expanse of blue sky outside. It was as blue as crystal. *Woman. She can't even wait for me to prepare at least coffee for her,* he thought.

He went back to his bedroom and shaved. Ten minutes later, he studied his face in the bathroom mirror. It was a lean, clean, handsome face.

"Well, *fashi*," he said, and he turned away from the mirror.

It was a quarter to nine o'clock when he came out.

A fine day, he said to himself as he cut across the staircase and down to the garage. He didn't fancy a dry hot harmattan day, but that was what the day would be later on. He unlocked the door of the black BMW, threw his folder onto the passenger seat, ran the car out, locked the garage door, and then headed along the quiet, deserted street.

It was a few kilometers to the university campus, and he had just fifteen minutes before the day's lecture would begin.

He slowed down at the John Elen intersection, waited for a line of fast cars to pass, and then nosed onto the main highway, which would lead him straight on past the gasoline filling station and toward the school campus. The stream of traffic heading in the direction of the school campus was heavy that morning.

He thought of Ebi. He couldn't think of anything else this morning. He admitted to himself that he was more than a little curious about her.

Driving through the school's main gate, he wound the window all the way down, and the hot, dry air washed in. The trees and bordering hedges around the campus gate wore a bloom of the harmattan dust.

Tos saw the two most imposing billboards in the entire school. They were standing boldly, a bit of distance between them. Painted on the first board in screaming red letters were the words "**SAY NO TO CULTISM—SAY NO TO CAMPUS VIOLENCE.**"

The letters in the second billboard were even bolder and more hysterical: "**THE DEVIL IS THE HEAD OF ALL CULT GROUPS. DO NOT JOIN ANY OF THEM!**"

Tos shook his head. The students felt that the school was under the shackles of the devil, whatever that meant. The religious ones, every last Friday, were in the throes of a great campaign of prayer and fasting. The vice chancellor had given his blessings to all religious groups to organize daytime crusades even when students were preparing for exams. Every morning, in most classrooms, before the commencement of lectures, prayers were offered against violence. During the last major cult clash, the Concerned Christian Students Fellowship had ordered a special weeklong prayer and fasting program. The next week, the violence had stopped; a peace congress had been held, and normal academic activities had resumed. The glory had been given to God.

On the route to his department building, the BMW passed a practice soccer field where some students in blue and yellow jerseys were turning out for a game of soccer.

He pulled into a space in the front parking lot and got out, extracting his folder and activating the alarm button on his key before locking up. He headed for the front door of the neat brick-and-white-stone building that housed the Department of Fine and Visual Arts.

He walked diagonally across the tiny corridor with his powerful strides. The Department of Fine and Visual Arts building had a pleasant entrance lobby, with the walls plastered with artwork of all shades and colors. Two of his paintings were displayed on one part of the wall: a small landscape done in watercolors and an oil painting of a young girl, completely nude. He had titled it *Full Frontal Nudity*. These were some of his early works. He had painted them in his second year. The nude oil painting showed the whole of the girl's body. It was a superb work. Even though they were his own creations, they still gave him a deep thrill of pleasure whenever he looked at them.

He was studying the painting when somebody touched his shoulder lightly.

"We have a class, remember?"

Tos turned around. It was Roland Ibeshi, his classmate. He was also the finest etcher in the department.

"I know. I was just examining this stuff."

"I remember it's your work. Are you thinking of removing it?"

Tos studied him. Roland Ibeshi was a tough-looking, strapping, high-shouldered youth. He was a member of the VVS, one of the

In Turbulent Waters | 57

most violent cult gangs on campus. And from information Tos had gathered, he was their "stirrer," a chieftain.

"What gave you that idea?"

"I don't know. Just a thought, that's all."

"I'm not planning on removing it," Tos said, touching his nose. Ibeshi's cheap eau-de-cologne smelled like a new fence. This was one guy who always used cheap, offensive eau.

"Are we going to class?" Ibeshi asked, glancing at his strap watch.

"We're going to class," Tos said.

* * *

The sun was in the sky, the dry harmattan wind blew mercilessly, and the grass was yellowish green. It was a beautiful day.

In the spacious room of Coke Villa, it was cool and quiet.

"Thanks for coming," Ebi said in a small voice.

"My pleasure," Tos replied quietly. "How was your lecture for the day?"

"Boring but okay. And yours?"

"Cool. Naturally cool."

A girl in a low-cut black blouse and tight blue jeans came to take their orders.

"What'll you have, Picasso?" Ebi asked.

"Give me a big, juicy burger with lettuce, tomato ketchup, mustard, pickles, onions, and a Coke."

The waitress made a note on her notepad and turned her attention to Ebi.

"And you?"

"Fried chicken, red baked beans, rice, and a Coke."

The waitress made some more notes and departed with a self-conscious twist to her movement.

Tos cleared his throat. "To tell you the truth, I'm not really hungry. I came just because I want to see you again."

Ebi smiled faintly. "Really?"

"Yeah. I was very impressed by what you said last night. You have a nice knack for judging a work of art without mincing your words. I believe it's something you know firsthand."

"Thanks. That's a nice thing to say. I guess it was all about my upbringing. I was brought up to appreciate art. I've seen lots of prints, and I know what I was saying last night."

"And talking about last night, what we discussed…Have you given it any more thought?"

"Don't you worry about it. I've made some calls."

"Tell me about them."

"I'm not telling you anything for another twenty-four hours. Do me a favor. Let me run this thing. It's patience that makes things happen."

Tos shrugged. "You're right," he said softly. "You're right." There was no resentment, no annoyance, in his voice.

A few minutes passed in silence. In want of something to say, Tos said, "You're a very lovely girl, Ebi. Do you know that?"

Ebi looked at him for a long moment without speaking.

"Lovely?" she said softly at last.

"Yeah. Lovely. Maybe I've used the wrong adjective. But that's what I really meant to say."

She studied him expressionlessly. There was something about him that she liked. He had an interesting, handsome face and something about his eyes that suggested warmth and coldness. His mouth offered laughter and strength, and his lips, an incredible smile. In a powerful, almost intriguing way, he was very attractive, and she liked him. And she liked the way he was decked out in a red sports shirt, a pair of well-tailored black trousers, black Italian shoes, and a well-tailored blazer.

"You said last night—this morning, to be precise—that you would get in touch with this guy who owns a gallery in New York," Tos said quietly, looking at her hopefully. "Do you think my work will pass muster with him?"

"If your work can make an impact on me, it will definitely make an impact on him; take my word for it."

"Does that mean it's alright?"

"I said you could take my word for it."

He laughed a deep, soft laugh, and she smiled in return.

"So you're telling me that you'll make me a millionaire in a matter of time." It was a statement.

"No sir," she said, trying not to laugh. "Your work is going to make you a millionaire in just a matter of time. Not me."

"But it's your contact."

"It's my contact, but your work will do the homework."

He nodded his assent with a grin.

"When can you get in touch with Mr. Gallery?"

"His name's Reese. Frank Reese. He's among the people I phoned this morning. He'll phone back at five o'clock today. I have to be around."

"Thanks."

"What for?" she asked, matter-of-factly.

"You're a great help."

"One good turn deserves something better."

"I did what anybody might do in similar circumstances."

"You don't fool me. It's only a few people that can do what you did last night. Those guys are Stones. It takes people that are much tougher to stop them. It seems that you're much tougher. Are you an Owlsman?"

Tos looked suddenly embarrassed. "That's a heavy thing to say." His mouth smiled, but his eyes looked serious, almost afraid.

"I'm sorry." She laughed uncomfortably. "I shouldn't have asked. Silly question."

The waitress brought their meals and Cokes. Tos poured his Coke into a tall thin-stemmed glass. Ebi did the same.

"Here's to our health," Tos said, raising his glass and tipping it to his lips.

He concentrated on his lunch. Ebi watched him as he crunched his way through the burger.

"You're not eating," he said, breaking into her thoughts.

"I was just thinking."

"About what?" There was concern in his eyes.

She shifted uncomfortably "Forget it."

"Forget what?"

For perhaps fifty seconds, neither of them said a word. Then she took her time in picking up her knife and fork and attacking her food. He watched her. She wore a dark blue suit of some tweed-like material and a small gold chain. Her lips were only slightly reddened by a dab of lipstick.

There was a wild burst of laughter across the room. Startled, Tos looked around to see Roland Ibeshi and the waitress in a warm embrace. The waitress was giggling.

"Hey, Picasso!" Ibeshi called out loudly. "I can see that you're having a swell time out there."

Tos raised his hand and waved nonchalantly.

"Is he your friend?"

"Not really. Just a classmate, that's it."

"Why don't you invite him over?"

"He's a loudmouth. I don't want to listen to his filthy jokes."

"If you say so," she said demurely, and she concentrated on her meal.

Tos liked this girl. She was so different, so unique—the kind of tiny woman he wanted to toss into the air and catch in his arms.

"Do you really want to know if I'm an Owlsman?" Tos's voice was quiet and soft.

For a couple of seconds, Ebi didn't reply. She dropped her knife and picked up her drink. She just sipped her Coke and watched him.

"Can you fancy me as a cultist?" Tos asked again.

She considered it again for a moment and then nodded imperceptibly.

Tos laughed at her, and for the briefest of moments was about to tell her the truth. She was the sort of girl to whom one gave only the truth. One couldn't get away with less—and wouldn't want to. But he had to be sensible. It would be foolish to open up for a moment of honesty. He thought about telling her but then decided not to; somehow, someday, she'd know by herself.

"I'm a Jew man." He looked over at her with a dubious smile.

She waited a long moment before speaking. "You're really a funny Jew man."

"Just a lily-livered Jew man."

She smiled and watched him quietly.

"Tell me about yourself, Ebi."

"There's not much to tell."

"Just tell it."

"I was born in New York. I've lived most of my life out there. My father's a renowned politician. He was a minister in General Sani Abacha's government. I'm the only child. That's all there's to know."

"What's your father's name?"

"Chief Ezontade Dabiri," Ebi replied.

At the mention of her father's name, a shadow crossed his face.

"You know my father?"

"I know him." The sudden edge of coldness in his voice told her the rest. The truth was that virtually everybody in Warri knew who her father was. And her father had made many enemies since the beginning of the Warri Crisis. Many Itsekiris believed that he was the man interfering with their return to their villages in the riverine areas. The last time he had chanced to come to Warri, an attempt had been made on his life. He had escaped death by the skin of his teeth.

There was a lengthy silence between them.

"Why did you decide to get your degree here?"

She was surprised at the swift change of subject. She suspected that Tos held a personal grudge against her father. He was looking at her with a curious expression on his face.

"It's for a personal reason."

"Are you telling me that there's no good school that teaches African history in the whole of the United States?"

"I said I've got my own reason." Her voice was firm and faintly laced with anger.

Tos looked at her for a long moment and then he broke into a wide grin.

"You've got your own reason. That's fine by me. I won't press it again." He downed the last of his Coke and observed the other diners. He noticed two students—cult lords—who had made their marks on campus. He felt a wave of apprehension. From the way they were dressed, he knew they were members of the Black Panthers, one of the most violent frat gangs on campus.

Tos's gang, the Black Owls, was the university's toughest cult gang. Originally they were called the Outlaws of the Night, or the Night Owls. It was a very tough and particularly well-disciplined gang. The number-one was a guy named Don John Bosco. The term "Don" was a title of leadership preceding the name of the leader of the gang.

Don Bosco was a fine-looking young chap with dark brown eyes, a hawkish nose, and a simian mouth to match. One wet

September night, members of the Black Panthers shot him to death. It was an act that caused great trouble.

With the death of Don Bosco, the gang had been greatly insulted. A week after his death, the Owlsmen took time off to mourn and to plan. In their time of mourning, they choreographed the Panthers' every move; they analyzed the pattern and structure of their organization and plotted every detail of the counterattack. They ran it through a mock exercise, and three weeks later, they struck. It was an action that threw the entire school into a state of chaos.

Tos, who was second in command then, with his men numbering about thirty, stormed the venue of a four-hundred-level political science final examination, calling for the head of the cult lord of the BP. On that fateful day, the examination had just begun when they emerged from the nearby bushes. Without wasting words, they started shooting indiscriminately into the air. They were all dressed in tight-fitting black jeans and black T-shirts with owls embossed boldly in red on the front. All their faces were covered with black cowls, like monks of a secret society. It was their traditional battle gear.

They had positioned themselves strategically around the examination halls, barking out orders and causing one of the greatest commotions ever witnessed inside the university campus. Tos, also masked and dressed in the same outfit, quickly registered his authority by firing a volley of pistol shots into the air. Amid the confusion, he raised a megaphone to his lips and reeled off the purpose of their mission. A King of the Night had been killed, and they had come to avenge his death. He warned all those who valued their lives not to be heroic in any way, because any opposition would be "brutally crushed." "We own this school!" he said loudly and authoritatively. "And we'll take it back. We rule this school, and we'll do anything and everything within our power to protect it, even if that means using and shedding our blood." The operation, which lasted barely thirty minutes, had all the trappings of a well-trained military exercise. They were so many in numbers, all armed with sophisticated weapons, and everybody was terrified.

The boy they were looking for had been fished out from the crowd of students. And with everybody watching, students and lecturers alike, they shot him repeatedly until he was dead. A black owl feather was placed atop his corpse.

The Black Panthers, in order not to be considered weaklings, struck back. It was a clash that sent shock waves of fear through the country's cult-conscious educational system. In its first week, the clash claimed fifteen lives, with thirteen of the dead being Black Panthers. It roused the anger of both the school's administration and the student body, with lecturers boycotting lectures and students demonstrating violently. The student union president declared war against cultism, but barely twenty-four hours after the declaration was made, the president's Peugeot station wagon was machine-gunned by gang butchers. Many students believed the man behind the ruckus was Tosan Mayuku, the new Grand Wizard of the Black Owls.

It was when the death toll was over twenty that a circular bearing the logo of an owl came out, announcing a cease-fire and suing for peace. The peace was negotiated, but by then the Black Panthers had lost their number-one and -two men, and they accounted for about 90 percent of the total casualties. Even after the peace negotiation, a virtual state of war still existed between the Black Panthers and the Owlsmen.

With the appearance of the two cultists, Tos felt apprehensive. *Guys like this could be dangerous,* he thought. *Together these two could take me.* But the two cultists never looked up from their plates of fried rice and braised beef. That eased the tension he felt in the pit of his stomach. But only for a short while.

A shadow fell over the table. Tos looked up. There were three young men. They were Brownies, and they were all decked out in the color of their brotherhood: brown berets, brown clothing, and brown shoes. Tos recognized the fellow in their middle. He was the chap Blacky had called Lopez, the one that had chased Ebi into his flat the night before.

"Do you remember me, Picasso?" Lopez said quietly.

Tos took a bit to reply. "Yeah, I remember you. How do you do?"

"You ran me rough last night because you wanted this bitch for yourself, right?"

Tos arranged a pleasant expression on his face.

"No. I like women to be treated with respect and honor. And that's not what you were doing last night. And that's why I ran you 'rough', to borrow your expression."

Lopez looked at his two companions. They were staring darkly at Tos. A contemptuous smile touched Lopez's mouth. He said, "You're a fucking liar, Picasso. A filthy-minded no-good sonofabitch. You play a hard man rough because you want a taste of the bitch. It's not right. And I don't like it."

"It's not my intention to embarrass you, my friend." Tos's voice was grim and gentle at the same time. "I did what I did because you didn't play the role of a big boy last night. And I must say that I don't owe you any apology."

"Really?" Lopez said easily. "Are you saying I fucked up last night? Is that what you are saying?"

Tos answered in a quiet voice, "Yeah, my friend. You fucked up real good."

"How dare you say I fucked up!" Lopez shouted in a shrill, loud voice as he knocked a chair aside roughly. "How dare you, eh!"

All around them, conversation ceased, and eyes shifted toward their table. Ebi was frozen in place, watching the three Brownies. Roland Ibeshi, hearing every word, was staring at the scene in amusement. The two Black Panthers, drinks in their hands, their faces expressionless, were listening to every word that was being uttered.

Tos rose quietly to his feet and touched Lopez lightly on the shoulder. "You've gone too far this time, my friend. You've really gone too far. You must be very careful, okay. If you have a problem, come to me at a very quiet time, in a very private place, and we'll sort it out man-to-man, one on one. Right now your presence is embarrassing me. Kindly leave now."

"Are you sending me away?" Lopez shouted, his mouth dark and bitter, just like his eyes, which were the color of sour beer.

Tos nodded slowly. Ebi stole a glance at Tos. His face was hard. A look of annoyance she'd seen the night before was there again—a look that could mean nothing but trouble.

"Look, Luger," one of the Brownies said quietly. "Do you want us to tap this guy? If you want us to, say so. Standing here and talking is killing time. We can tap him right here and nothing will happen."

"I think..." Lopez was saying when he became dimly aware of someone leaving his table. He turned in his direction, and his eyes caught sight of a burly, tough-looking guy with a beard who was holding the remnants of a meat pie in his hand, stalking across the restaurant. He carried one of the chairs over, set it down with a thump close to Tos, and lowered himself into it.

"What is it?" the new entrant asked. He then switched his glance from Tos to the three Brownstones. "What's going on here?"

"This guy just insulted me," Lopez said, staring at the stranger, suspecting him to be an Owlsman.

"Did you say 'insulted'?" Tos's voice had hardened. "If anyone's insulted right now, I'm the one."

"It's all right, guys," Roland Ibeshi said, putting the last piece of the meat pie in his mouth. "No need to make trouble. Let's break it up."

Lopez backed off.

"You've not heard the last of me, Picasso."

"What would you do?"

"You've made yourself a big enemy, Picasso. And I swear I'll get my revenge. Nobody treats me the way you've done and gets away with it. Nobody. Ask of me in this school. I'm the one they called Luger. You'll pay for what you've done last night. I swear it." With this, he headed toward the door, his two companions by his side.

Ebi had not felt so cold in her life.

"I'm sorry about that," she said in a small voice.

"Forget it," Tos replied. He turned to Ibeshi. "Thanks for coming around."

"Oh, it's nothing," the VVS chieftain said.

"I hate to say this, Ebi, but I have to go."

"But you've not finished your burger," Ibeshi said.

"I've had enough."

Ebi shrugged and looked at her wristwatch. "I think I should be going too." She opened her handbag and took out some keys and a wad of naira notes. She dropped some of the notes on the table and stood up.

"Thanks for lunching with me."

"I should be thanking you," Tos replied. He shook hands with Roland Ibeshi and led Ebi toward the entrance, opening the door of the restaurant for her.

"I would like to take you out to dinner tonight," he said abruptly as they stepped into the sunshine. "Would you be my guest?"

Ebi smiled faintly. "Dinner? Tonight?"

"Yeah. My treat. Can you make it?"

She detected the seriousness in his voice. "Where will it be?"

"Anywhere of your choice will do just fine."

"Okay. Let's make it Bray's Kitchen. You know it?"

"Do I know it?" Tos said comically. "I own half that joint."

She broke into a wide grin that bordered on laughter. The fiber of this boy intrigued her.

"I'll be there by seven o'clock. Will that be okay with you?"

"I won't disappoint you," she said, and she glanced at him with a look one reserves for a very special friend.

"Want a ride to town?" he asked easily as they walked toward the parking lot.

"No thanks. That's my car over there." She pointed to a cream-colored Porsche 911 Carrera convertible that was gleaming like diamond in the sun.

"Is that your car?" It was obvious that he was stunned.

She nodded quietly. "It's a gift from my father. A birthday present."

"It's a beauty. You're one damn lucky dame."

"I'm not complaining."

She opened the door with her key, got in, and pressed the ignition button.

"You take care. This is one smart car."

She pointedly put the car into gear, and then she took a look at him. "I'm smarter," she said, and she gave him a brief smile. It was a smile that said a million things yet hinted at nothing.

She raised a hand, and the rear wheels spat sand and gravel, and the little creamy car traversed the driveway that led to the main roadway.

Tos watched it drive out of his sight line. He smiled. *This is one smart, nice girl rolling in the lap of luxury.*

"Swell!" he said excitedly as he entered his car. If there was one girl he wanted right now, it was Ebi Dabiri.

He put the car into gear and drove toward the university's gate.

CHAPTER FIVE

Tos arrived at Bray's Kitchen at quarter to seven o'clock. He was on familiar terrain. Bray's Kitchen was his favorite hole, a notable retreat for well-to-do students and businesspeople alike. It had a style of its own with the advantage of allowing two people to talk without sharing their conversation with hovering waitresses and overly inquisitive fellow diners.

He chose a discreet table in a hedged enclosure and sat down. He studied the restaurant, his practiced eyes photographing all the diners. A waitress with a blue beret and pink skirt came for his order. He didn't want anything yet, but he asked for a beer.

His beer arrived, and he took a small sip. Soft music issued from speakers, enveloping the room in warmth and lightheartedness. The setting was designed modestly, with a degree of modernism and romanticism.

He sat alone with his beer, fingering the smooth-grained checkerboard pattern covering the table. Again and again, he checked his watch. 7:05…7:10…7:15…7:20…*Where the fuck is she?* he asked himself.

At seven thirty, he was beginning to grow restless, suspecting that she couldn't make it. He downed the last of his beer and again checked his watch.

"Can you do with some company?"

It was a girl's voice. He knew she was the one. She was the only with that kind of accent.

"You're late," he said. He didn't look at her.

"I know. I'm sorry. Can I sit down?"

He looked at her then and caught his breath. "You look cool," he said. There was no mistaking the admiration in his voice.

"Thanks. Can I sit down?"

"Of course," he said. He then stood up and drew a chair for her. She sat down before he took his seat.

She was wearing a bewitching, sensuous dress that was draped sensationally over her beautiful frame. It was neatly tailored attire with a softened play of color, and the fabric floated with a grace that was irresistible. She looked like an ethereal vision of a goddess, with a golden disk and diamond-like stones bristling at her ears and throat.

Tos watched her. He'd taken some thirty seconds to admire her. She'd noticed his admiration, and her lovely brown eyes flashed.

He noticed the flash in them too and grinned. The beauty of this girl smote him.

"Do you have any idea how beautiful you are?" he said in the softest and most velvety of voices.

Ebi watched him in silence for a moment.

"You must not compliment my beauty to me unless you mean it."

"I mean it," Tos said sincerely. "You should say thank you."

"Thank you."

Tos wasn't going to be put off so easily. "And you're wearing the prettiest dress in town. Do you know that?"

She was delighted; she laughed. "Hogwash."

Tos looked at her soberly. He couldn't keep his eyes from her face. He felt irresistibly pulled into the warmth of her laughter.

"Give me your hand," he commanded. There was something very funny in the command.

She extended her hand to him. Tos caught the hand and lifted it to his lips. The kiss clearly and cleanly caught her off guard. Her gaze shot to his face. What she saw intrigued her.

"What's the meaning of this?" she said foolishly.

Tos was smiling. "I'm trying to tell you in very few words that I'm in the presence of an angel. And I must tell you this: I'll sell my soul to get that angel."

Fire danced in his eyes. His charming, handsome face was close to hers; she could smell the beer on his breath. She thought he was going to kiss her. But she didn't move, and he didn't kiss her either.

"I thought this was a dinner date; aren't we going to order something?"

"Yeah," Tos agreed quietly. "Thanks for reminding me." Her hand trembled in his. He let it go. "Time to take a squint at the menu."

"If you're ready, that is," Ebi said smoothly.

The owner of the restaurant, Boateng Raymond Aggrey Yeboah, a small, thin Ghanaian with a face resembling Nkrumah's, came to their table, another waitress wearing a blue beret and pink skirt trailing behind him.

"It's Don Tos, right?" he said in his heavily accented English.

"It's his brother," Tos replied quietly.

It was their favorite game—an old joke between them whenever he was in the restaurant in the company of a new girl. It wasn't funny anymore, but Bray was still fond of saying it.

"It's Don Tos, right?" Bray repeated, smiling broadly.

"I think so, sir," Ebi answered for him.

"Aren't you making a mistake?" Tos asked.

"Not at all." Ebi smiled.

"Okay. For your sake I'll admit that I'm Don Tos for one day."

"Holy Moses!" Bray shouted. "So you agreed for the sake of this pretty girl? She must be very special then."

"There's nobody more special," Tos said, looking longingly at Ebi. She gave him a huge pantomime grin.

"Where've you been all this while?" the Ghanaian asked.

"Everywhere, I'd say. Studies. Painting. Appointments. All of it."

"We miss you."

"I miss you too, Bray."

"Aren't you going to introduce your angel to me?"

"Not to the devil I know."

Bray slapped his thigh, and his guffaw hit the roof of the restaurant.

Ebi found herself smiling.

"Man, you sounded like a man who's just befriended President Obasanjo's daughter and is afraid he'll lose her to a handsome *bobo* like me. Rest assured, I'm your friend. Your wife is my wife, my wife your wife. My house is still yours; we'll always remain friends, right?"

"Wrong," Tos replied.

Bray seemed comically disappointed.

"Mind if I ask the lady something?" he asked, and he winked discreetly at Ebi.

Tos stared at the restaurateur. "Sure. Go ahead."

"Are you an angel or something?" Bray was staring down at her.

"Something like that," said Tos shortly.

Bray stared at Tos as if he were crazy. "Who's talking to you? At least I know now why you fail those exams."

Tos laughed.

Ebi shook her head. "You're impossible."

"You can say that again, ma'am," Bray replied. For once Ebi knew the Ghanaian was not joking.

"Bray, this is Ebi Dabiri," Tos said quietly. "Ebi, meet Boateng Raymond Aggrey Yeboah. We call him Bray, though. He's the owner of this joint, and he's one of my very good friends. I'm sure you two will like each other."

They shook hands.

"This must be your first visit to Bray's Kitchen, Ebi."

She smiled sweetly. "No. It's my second visit really."

Bray stared at her and then asked, "Was your first visit pleasurable?"

Ebi nodded and Bray smiled, his dark face beaming.

"You're in the right place, Ebi. This is the favorite restaurant in town."

Tos patted the Ghanaian on the back, gesturing at his stomach. "I'm hungry."

"Hah!" snorted Bray. "He's hungry. Hear that? He's hungry, but tell you what, I know how to take good care of my friends. Tos is a correct man. You're on the house. You just name what you want, and you'll have it. It's on the house."

"You don't mean that," Tos objected.

"Of course I do," Bray replied. "You know I'll not deny you anything. A friend is a friend; a brother a brother. If a friend has proven his friendship, showed his mettle, then he becomes a brother. You're one." With that he gestured to the waitresses, patted Tos on the shoulder, and, grinning broadly, sauntered to the next table.

Tos sat in his chair for a long moment and said nothing.

One of the waitresses said, "What will it be, sir?"

Tos looked at Ebi. She was reading the menu. He ordered orange-flavored beef, lemon chicken, and rice sautéed with vegetables.

"And you, miss?"

Ebi looked up. "I'll take the same," she said.

"You'll take the same?" Tos asked, looking at her with slow deliberation.

"There's nothing wrong with that…or is there?"

Tos searched for a rational reply and knew there was only one. "Actually no, but I'd like it if you would settle for something different."

"Thank you, but I'll take the lemon chicken and sautéed rice."

In Turbulent Waters | 77

Neither of them said another word until the two waitresses were gone.

"He's a nice man," Ebi said softly.

"Who?"

"Bray."

Tos nodded his assent. Boateng Raymond Aggrey Yeboah, known in his native Ghana as Kofi but in Jankara as Bray, was a nice man. He had come to Nigeria when he was in his late teens. He had started as a shoeshine boy, going around the streets of Lagos, drumming his wooden toolbox. Now he was the proud owner of the finest eating house in the university town of Jankara and he also owned nearly a dozen eateries in various university communities in Nigeria. And he was not tired. He was always looking to expand. Rumors going around claimed that he was planning to open a similarly themed Bray's Kitchen in the newly-built Kogi State University, to be styled with the same elegance of the original Bray's Kitchen in Jankara.

"Did you hear from Mr. Gallery?" Tos's voice was low, barely a murmur.

"Yeah," Ebi replied matter-of-factly.

"I can't wait to hear the news."

"You'll have to. Dinner first."

"Is it good news?"

"I'll not say."

"I can't wait."

Ebi looked a long time into his face. "Don't be pushy, Tosan. I don't like it."

"I won't crowd you, baby," Tos said.

The waitresses brought their meals, and they waited while the dishes were put in their correct places. Ebi reached over and gouged a sample from Tos's plate. He watched her in amused disbelief as she chewed and then proceeded to attack her own.

"How is it?"

"It's delicious. How's yours?"

"I'm not sure."

"Nuts," Tos replied, and he nibbled at a piece of chicken meat.

They ate in silence. From the concealed speakers, Phil Collins's voice issued out softly.

"You looked cultured," Ebi said.

Tos looked up at her. He detected the trace of admiration in her voice. "Why do say that?"

"You know how to use cutlery and a table napkin. You know how to treat a woman with courtesy and respect. Many guys that have taken me out have embarrassed me with their table manners. It's horrible. But with you it's different."

Tos smiled. "I'm flattered."

"Sorry if I'm flattering you. But it's the truth."

"The truth?" Tos shook his head. "It reminds me of words I've read somewhere: 'Flatter me and I may not believe you—'"

Ebi broke in with a sweet, almost musical voice, like someone reciting a poem: "'Criticize me and I may not like you—'"

"'Ignore me and I may not forgive you—'"

"'Encourage me and I will not forget you.'"

"I believe Williams Arthur Ward said those words," Tos said.

"You're absolutely right," Ebi replied.

"Who is he?" Tos asked.

"I don't know who he is. I came across the line somewhere in *Reader's Digest*, and presto! It's in my head!"

"Good God!" Tos shook his head slowly and looked across at her for a long, speculative moment. "You're impossible."

Ebi looked at him, her face without expression. "Do you believe me now?"

Tos gazed at her through a period of deep silence, dipped his fork into his dish, and nodded his head with a slow movement. Neither of them spoke for a long moment.

Tos finished eating first. He leaned back, his eyes going from table to table as if he was warily in search of an enemy. People were coming and going the whole time. A girl laughed at the next table, happy with the world, happy with her boyfriend. Warri seemed very remote.

"What are you thinking about, Tos?" Her soft voice broke into his train of thought.

"Oh." Tos forced a vague smile.

"What's on your mind?"

"Nothing. Just thinking how nice it would be to be world famous for ten minutes. Just ten minutes."

"You're beginning to talk like Andy Warhol," she said. She put down her knife and fork and regarded him quietly, looking into his saintly long-lashed eyes. They were a rich blend of gray and brown, and they added a special touch to his good looks. "Does that mean so much to you?"

Tos moved his shoulder slightly.

"Yeah. Very much."

"Do you know you're our one new marvelous one hundred percent foolproof Nigerian discovery?"

Tos laughed. The deep, soft laughter rang out from a baritone stream somewhere deep inside his chest.

"You don't believe me?"

"Frank Reese told you that?"

"No. I told myself. Convinced myself."

"What's the gist from Reese, then?"

"His reply was encouraging."

Tos looked at her intently, as though he were trying to see into her innermost heart.

"And?"

"If the paintings were as I'd promised, he would put the sum of two thousand dollars to the first two pieces he would receive. And if the others were as good as the first, then he'd invite the painter to his studio in New York City, where he could paint from live supermodels. Then the young man would start counting real dollars."

Tos was silent for a good moment.

"Did he say that?"

"I just told you."

"What did you tell him for him to make such an offer?"

"I told him that you've got the kind of talent that pays off today. Then he said he'd be delighted to see your paintings."

"Did he believe you?"

"Believe me? I've seen works of art. Picasso. Poussin. Delacroix. They are the greats. You've heard of them. Maybe seen their reproductions. But I've seen their real works. I know what I'm talking about, and Frank Reese knew that I was not blabbing."

Tos dredged a grin from somewhere.

"Do you want some wine?"

Ebi shook her head.

"Nuts!" he said, and he beckoned to a passing waitress. "A bottle of chardonnay, please."

"Who's going to drink that?" she said after the waitress had gone.

Tos gave no sign that he'd heard her. He brought out a packet of cigarettes, fished one out, and fed it to his lips. He lit up. "Let's talk more on this Frank Reese guy. Let's suppose he finds ugliness in my work. What happens then?"

"According to Oscar Wilde, an artist's a maker of beautiful things. It's the corrupt mind that sees ugliness in beautiful things."

Tos found himself smiling.

The waitress came over. She set the bottle of wine on the table; then she took from her colleague a steel server on which sat two tall, thin-stemmed wineglasses. She poured the wine quickly, replaced the bottle on the table and hurried away as if afraid to stay too long in their company.

"We must celebrate my success in advance," Tos said, he picked up his glass, lifted it a little higher. "May you bring me luck," he said softly. He then touched the wineglass to hers and held it to his lips. Ebi watched him without taking a sip from her wineglass.

"Aren't you going to drink with me?"

"Don't count your chickens—"

"Humph," Tos cut in. "I'm not counting any chickens. I'm celebrating my success in advance. And if you don't drink with me, that means I'm doomed to fail. And that's a bad way to start a friendship."

Ebi laughed. "You're nuts."

"I know," Tos agreed quietly. "And thanks for telling me."

There was something in his tone that made Ebi sip from her wineglass. She immediately set the half-empty glass on the table, and Tos lifted the bottle from the table and poured more wine into each of the two glasses.

"It's a French wine," he said, exhaling a thick cloud of smoke.

"I know," she said.

"Don't be annoyed. I was just reminding you." He looked down at his cigarette.

The evening wasn't going too badly at all. She had been fun to have dinner with. She was a highly civilized and charming young lady. And the choice of Bray's Kitchen as the venue of the dinner date was a very wise choice indeed. The wine had been excellent; so had the meal—proper gourmet food exquisitely cooked: A lovely chicken. Even the salad had been outstanding, and the services could be called superb. The restaurateur had been nice and homey and funny. It was lovely.

"Frank Reese is good news and bad news," he said softly. "Good news because he's promised to pay two grand for the first two paintings he'll receive. Bad news if he refuses to pay after getting them."

Ebi shook her head. "Two thousand is peanuts compared to the actual worth of those pieces. But you have to make some sacrifices in the early stages of your career."

Tos nodded slowly without speaking, leaned back in the expensive leather chair, and regarded the lady thoughtfully.

"Excellent speech, Ebi. You have the gift of the gab. Have you considered a future in sales management consultancy?"

Ebi laughed. With the sound of the laughter, the opening up of her facial features transformed her beauty and lit up her face.

"What I said was the truth, and—"

"I know that," Tos interrupted softly. "I'm not contradicting you."

"Then what is it if you're not contradicting me?"

Tos hesitated. "What do you suggest?"

"I'll tell you this in Frank Reese's own words, Tosan: 'Send it over first thing tomorrow morning.'"

"Tomorrow's Sunday."

"Then send it out on Monday morning."

"Sending the stuff either through DHL or UPS will cost good money. And I don't have that kind of money right now."

"I'll lend you the money."

"Interest free?"

"Yeah. Interest free."

Tos smiled wryly. He sat in his chair for a long moment without saying anything. He seemed to be weighing the whole thing with an invisible scale. He took a long last drag of his cigarette, expelled a thick cloud of tangy smoke, and extinguished it on the ashtray.

"Thanks, baby," he said. He hesitated a moment and then added, "I'm indebted."

"Never mind," she replied. He had been told what he wanted to hear at least.

She was sure that his work would sail through. His work had a strong level of feeling conveying tremendous bare force, making one feel the weight he was trying to place on canvas—the force and the tensions, the tonal structure and the melancholic coloration. The most powerful element of his work was sex. The female nude was his obsessive subject. Like Picasso, whom he was obviously aping, his paintings had the same erotic and emotive perspectives, which gave off a wonderful sense of forms. And not only that, but he also imposed on the paintings a load of feelings ranging from dreamy eroticism—as in some of his works, such as *The Solitary Reaper* and *Eyes of the Wind*—to thoughtful and uncomfortable works like *Dance of Death*. He was a genius of talent, this boy. If he could only be connected with those art merchants in New York, a few days in Manhattan would see him producing paintings of considerable power that few young painters could surpass.

"Why don't we go to my pad?" Tos said, breaking into her thoughts. "You can see some of my hidden works—ones that I dare not display for fear of being stoned."

"I'd love to see them," Ebi said softly. "But let's leave it till tomorrow."

He had been looking at her closely for a while as if searching for something. She knew that he fancied her greatly—especially sexually. A familiar mixture of pleasure and curiosity coursed over her.

She looked at the slim gold-and-diamond-studded watch her professor boyfriend had given her—one of his many presents. The time was a little past nine.

"It's getting late, Tosan."

Tos regarded her speculatively. "You came late, remember?"

"I know. I thought you'd forgiven me."

"I have," he said lightly, smiling mysteriously, as if something other than the girl sitting by his side was the reason for his cheerfulness.

"I ought to be home by now."

Tos fingered his glass, his eyes dancing with merriment. This girl had brought something out of him. His mother and Aina were the only people who had the knack of bringing the warmth out of him.

He took her hand and looked at her with deep yearning in his eyes. There was something so warm in the feel of his strong, firm hand against hers, something so natural and intimately affectionate, that she didn't even think of withdrawing it.

"What's before me is a very beautiful girl with formidable qualities."

She smiled. "I'm flattered," she said quietly at last.

Her smile was the most marvelous thing he'd seen. *Good Jesus, if only I could grasp a little of this girl*, he thought.

Judiciously, he took his time. Seconds elapsed. "Ebi…" His thoughts seemed to be stumbling in several directions at once. He said stupidly at last, "Do you have a boyfriend?"

There was a long pause. Neither of them spoke for some time. The question hung over them for eternity.

"Yes," Ebi eventually said. "I have a boyfriend."

"Really?" Tos was genuinely startled, as if he had expected her to say no.

"Yes. But…" she began, faltered, and then started again. "He's not a boy, actually. He's a middle-aged man."

Tos stared across the table at her with a look of incredulity. Ebi reached out her hand and touched his hand.

"I'm not a virgin, Tosan. If you're looking for a virgin, forget it. They don't exist. There are no virgins in New York. And that's where I came from."

"Whatever made you think I'm looking for a virgin?"

"I can think of at least three answers to that question."

"Give me one."

"Forget it."

Tos was speechless for a brief moment. "How long have you known him?"

"Known?"

"Yeah. How long have you both been dating? You and your middle-aged boyfriend?"

"A goodish time."

"Two years?" Something close to resentment had crept into Tos's voice.

"Gosh, no! Just last year."

"Oh fuck!" Tos snapped quietly. He was confused, filled with jealousy.

"What is it?" she asked softly. She could detect the pain etched in his eyes.

"Is he married?"

She shifted uncomfortably but nodded.

Tos pursed his lips, his eyes still bitter.

"What's a girl of your age doing with a middle-aged married man who's old enough to be her father?" He hadn't meant to speak so loudly, so angrily.

"He's a nice man," she said quietly. "He's caring and attentive to my needs. He spoils me with presents. He's deeply in love with me."

Tos nodded slowly. "He comes here to visit weekly, or what?"

"No. He's here. He works here. He lives here."

"He works here and he lives in this town?" Tos said feelingly.

"Yeah." She felt that a bit of a gush was needed. "He's called Dr. Vincent Ubangha. You know him very well."

Tos was visibly bewildered.

"Are you telling me that you're screwing Dikko?"

"Dikko? Is that what he's called?"

Tos didn't answer immediately. He took his time to allow the shock to drain out of his face. When he opened his lips in answer to her question, he made no attempt to disguise his hatred for the man.

"He's the most fucking dirty idiot on campus."

"You make it sound as if I'm sleeping with the former VC."

"The former VC is better than that bastard by far."

"It seems that you hate him."

"Everybody hates him. That's why they called him Dikko—the Nutty Professor."

Ebi stirred uncomfortably. "I've got to go."

Tos didn't look at her. Out of the corner of his eyes, he saw two members of the Black Panthers entering the restaurant. He knew them, and they knew him. *Black Panthers? Again? Is this coincidence?* he wondered. Impulsively reaching downward, he touched the bulge of the handgun tucked in his waistband. Just the feel gave him assurance. The frat guys moved to the other part of the room without so much as glancing at him again.

Ebi wasn't aware of the tension he emitted. This was the weak point of cultism: to find that a sudden coincidence could give one the jitters.

"I want to go home," Ebi said.

Tos signaled to the waitress. She came immediately. He took out his wallet, pulled out a neat wad of hundred-naira notes, and handed them to her.

"It's for the wine," he said softly. "And keep the change."

She wanted to protest, but he silenced her with a wave of his hand. With that, he rose regretfully to his feet and touched Ebi lightly on the shoulder.

"Ready?"

She nodded and stood up.

The night outside was dark. The moon was behind a pocket of clouds, and the streetlights were not working. Starlight twinkled overhead. Tos looked up at the sky. The stars in the pure, sweet darkness above him were bright. The highway was empty. There was not a sound. No single living being, no vehicle, no nothing.

"When can I come over to your place? Or will you come over for the paintings?" Tos asked. They were standing beside her car.

"Why don't you bring them over to my place?"

"That would be nice," he replied with a hint of a smile. "Where's that?"

"Heaven's Gate Lodge."

Tos knew it. It was a popular ultra-posh jewel-box mansion that had been converted into a private girls' hostel. The lodge, as it was today, was made up of about half a dozen two- and three-bedroom flats. The girls in the Lodge owned fridges, PCs, CD players, and air conditioners, and drove flashy cars. Moneyed men (particularly politicians from the state capital) paraded around the place on weekends with all sorts of exotic cars, and most of the girls were branded *pololo*.

"I thought Heaven's Gate Lodge was a denizen of prostitutes."

"Not all of it."

Tos said nothing for a while. "Which particular works do you suggest I bring along?"

"Any of them would do. *Dance of Death, Eyes of the Wind*— any of them would do."

A thin sliver of moon appeared behind some clouds, and the ugly trees at the corner of the road looked beautiful for once, their foliage rustling in the light evening breeze.

"I'll be tied up for most of tomorrow morning. I hope it'd be proper if I checked in, say, in the evening."

"I'll take it," she said in a small, quiet voice.

A car rumbled vaguely in the road, emphasizing the quiet.

Ebi felt Tos's hand on her arm. She didn't draw away, although she knew it wasn't safe. She knew she was inadvertently encouraging him. She liked him. But it was not safe to have an affair with any other guy right now. In spite of his friendly, quiet manners, Dr. Ubangha was a mean man. She remembered that his boys were watching her. His spies were everywhere. He once told her not to misbehave. Not that she loved him—she was only fond of him, though he scared her sometimes.

"I'm sorry about the dirty things I said about your boyfriend," Tos said softly. "Genuinely sorry. I didn't mean to spoil the day."

"It's nothing," she said, smiling. It was a soft, charming smile.

Tos smiled in return and, impulsively reaching forward, touched her on the cheek. When she didn't draw away, he kissed her full on the lips. It was a dry, one-sided kiss. There was no response at all from her.

"I'm sorry," he said crookedly.

"Sorry for what?" Her voice was sharp.

He didn't reply.

She looked up and down the darkened road and climbed behind the wheel.

"You take care," he said.

She switched on the car's lights and started it up.

"Good night," she said, and she ran the small car onto the highway and then headed into the darkness.

Tos watched the taillights for a long moment until they disappeared. He looked at his watch. The time was a few minutes to ten. Time to go home. He headed in the direction of his car. When he was a few feet away from the car, instinct propelled him to look around. Standing in the entrance of the restaurant was a young man with a helmet-like hairdo, wearing a cheap, shapeless gray suit. He was a Panther, no doubt—one of the two Black Panthers he had seen earlier in the restaurant. The man's presence alone sent slivers of apprehension down Tos's spine.

Unhurriedly, he opened the door of his car, started the engine, and drove away.

CHAPTER SIX

He couldn't get her out of his mind.

The previous night's dinner was a meeting of hearts and minds, a date that would always be a part of his life. He would never forget it. All day long, he did nothing but romanced about her beauty, her talents, and the appealing innocence she wore like a neck chain.

On the way to her home, he toyed with the idea of stopping somewhere to smoke ganja. But his better judgment warned him against doing such a reckless thing. Ten minutes' fast driving brought him to the threshold of Heaven's Gate Lodge. It was an old-fashioned but beautifully painted two-story building with a large bay windows and terraces overlooking the expressway.

He lugged a canvas bag and a cardboard box up the staircase to her door. Her apartment was on the second floor. Her name was pinned to the door. He rapped softly and waited. There were some moments of delay. He was about to rap on it again when the door was flung open.

He smiled into her face. "Hello." His voice was husky. He wondered why his heart wouldn't stop beating.

"Hi," she replied.

"Aren't you going to relieve me of my duties?"

"Duties?"

"These loads, of course."

She grinned sympathetically and helped him with the cardboard box.

Tos looked at the young lady. *God! She looks fabulous! Small, smiling, sexy.*

"Come on in," she said.

"Yes ma'am. Right away." Tos hurried into the apartment.

Everything inside the apartment was attraction and distraction, and it all vied for his attention: a patterned leather couch; a small, romantically provocative oil on canvas; a large, ornate etched glass mirror.

"This is cool," he said, surveying the beautifully furnished living room, admiration in his voice.

It was a high-ceilinged spacious living room adorned with carved columns, elegant teak, and walls covered in coarse raw silk, tapestries, and works of art. Persian rugs covered the length and breadth of the room, along with simple furniture and cushions wrapped in beautiful geometric designs. An exquisite giant TV set stood against a far wall. A small white Pekinese was sleeping on the couch. He placed the canvas bag on the couch, bent down, and scratched the dog between its ears.

"What's its name?"

"Canova," Ebi replied softly behind him.

Tos straightened up and took the cardboard box from her. "I've brought you, as compliments of the evening, a bottle of wine." He pulled out the bottle of chardonnay.

She smiled into his face and took the bottle from him. "Can I get you something to drink? A glass of wine or cold beer perhaps?"

"Yeah," Tos replied, and he sat down on the couch close to the dog. "A bottle of beer would do just fine. Stout preferably."

She sauntered away and came back with a server bearing a bottle of chilled stout and a fine cut-glass tumbler. She poured the beer. Tos took a small sip and nodded his satisfaction.

"Truly bitter."

"Have you eaten?"

"I'm not hungry."

"It's no trouble. I can fix you something. I have something in the kitchen, anyway."

"How about some light music?"

"Of course." She went to the shelf, selected a disc, slotted in Whitney Houston, and stepped back, watching him. Whitney's soft, ethereal voice filled the room.

"That's nice." Tos's eyes were on her.

Her face was lightly made up for the evening, a fringe of dark hair set low on her forehead. Her skin, ebony black and smooth, shone beautifully. Her bare feet were small and lithe. They hardly seemed to touch the rug. The housecoat she wore had fallen open when she welcomed him in the doorway. He'd seen the outline of her body as she hastily retied the sash.

The Pekinese was watching him suspiciously, his eyes beady, his head cocked to one side.

"This is my photo album," she said, and she handed him a box of photographs. She sat near him as he flipped through them. Most of them were snapshots taken in the United States: Ebi on a beach in Miami, Ebi on a horse on Madison Avenue, Ebi—a much younger Ebi—as a cheerleader, Ebi coming out of Albert Gompertz showroom on Seventh Avenue, Ebi in cap and gown during matriculation, Ebi with a handsome tapioca-complexioned white boy, standing holding hands, with the Statue of Liberty in the background.

"Is he your boyfriend?"

"That's Roy McGinn. He's a childhood friend."

Tos grunted but said nothing.

Ebi wearing a bikini, sitting on the deck of a luxurious yacht. Ebi on a sailboat.

"Do you sail?"

"Yeah."

"Surf too?"

"Yeah. That's Roy's McGinn's father's boat. That photograph was taken when I spent a few holidays in San Francisco with the

McGinns. They've a house there. Great beach. Beautiful boats. I had lots of fun."

Ebi in Wally Findlay Gallery. Ebi with Henry Howells, the artist. Ebi with Frank Reese. "Do you know who that is?" she said, motioning to the photograph.

"This Reese?" Tos inquired.

"Yeah."

Tos studied the photograph for a long moment. Reese, in the photograph, was a man in his mid-fifties. He was tall and lean, with deep-set blue eyes and fair blond hair that had begun to recede farther up his forehead. He wore an open-collared shirt and simple trousers. Tos liked him in the picture.

"So this is the guy who's going to buy the pictures." It was a statement.

"Yeah."

Tos grinned faintly. "Frank Reese. He's not a bad-looking guy."

"He's a nice man."

"Have you seen the paintings I brought?"

"Which ones did you bring?"

"I'll show you," he said. He dropped the photo album and picked up the large black canvas bag. Slowly he unzipped the bag and laid out eight paintings on the rug with flourish. Both of them bent down and examined them for some time. Actually, it was the girl that studied them while the boy was studying her, looking for any change of expression—anything that would tell him something. But Ebi's face was inscrutable.

She studied the paintings carefully for a long moment, examining each of them thoughtfully. They were all good, very good, she knew. Some of them she'd seen before, like *Dance of Death*, *Eyes of the Wind*, and *The Solitary Reaper*. But there was a particular one that took her breath away. It was an oil on canvas. Ebi stood up, took the painting from the floor, placed it on the glass-topped table in the middle of the room, and examined it closely. She'd not seen this one before. It was a painting of a black woman who stood before a full-length mirror. Her back was painted in such a way that it was facing the observer. Her helmet-like hairdo was tousled and curled. The most interesting thing about the painting was the mirror: reflected in the mirror was the long, curvy body of a white woman. It was the reflection of the black woman's exquisite naked body.

"This, truly, is your best painting ever." Her voice was unusually quiet.

"I hope you're not teasing me?"

"No. These paintings will speak for themselves. My opinion at this point is not important."

He nodded. He'd packed eight of his best works in the large canvas bag. Before the selection, he'd looked long and hard at each of the forty-eight paintings he had at home. He knew he had some talents, but people with tough, independent opinions will always have their own opinions. Frank Reese was a professional gallery owner. He needed to see only the best, and it was his judgment that would count most, not Ebi's.

"*Naked View*. That's what I call it."

"It's much more than that." She regarded the painting much longer. It was an extraordinary painting. "Frank Reese would love it."

"If they're okay, then let's choose the best two."

Ebi shook her head. "We'll send all—all eight of them. Then we'll pray that he accepts them all."

Tos bit his lips thoughtfully. "We'll send them all?" he inquired.

"Yeah."

Tos said nothing. He went back to the couch and resumed flipping through the photo album.

In Turbulent Waters | 97

Ebi, in the arms of the same tall, attractive white man, the two of them sitting on the hood of a red sports car. A radiant Ebi coming down from the cockpit of a private jet. Ebi skating. Ebi skiing. A campus shot of Ebi and her girlfriend, Mary.

"So what about your friend Blacky's girl?"

"Mary? She's fine."

"Are you guys still friends?"

"What we have left is a 'good morning' kind of relationship. We're no longer cool."

"Too bad."

Ebi walked up to him. "Can I get you that something now?"

Tos hesitated briefly. "Yeah. That is if you don't mind."

"I don't mind at all," she replied, and she sauntered toward the kitchen with a provocative sway of her hips.

He followed the motion with an appreciative eye. Her movements were sexually arousing. He rearranged the photographs, downed the last of his beer, and looked around the neat living room, taking in the orderly shelves of books and the landscape painting hanging on the wall.

Atop the TV set, in a heavy silver frame, was a colored photograph of her parents. Her father was a grave middle-aged-looking man; his wife, a well-packaged handsome woman. She was smiling. The man was scowling. He knew that the girl got her beauty from her mother. Even the smile was also borrowed from her mother.

Ebi came back into the room carrying a server. She'd changed into a pair of incredibly provocative sky-blue shorts and a halter-top. She took the plates from the server and set the table in front of him. Then she took the remote control device and reduced the CD player's volume to a background throb. She settled into the couch and curled her legs.

"There's the meal," she said, and she made a lazy motion with her right hand. "My dining table's a bit of a mess right now. I'm doing research on the fall of the Songhai Empire. It's for a class seminar, and I've been chosen as the resource person for my group."

Tos looked toward where she indicated with her hand. A computer with a separate Hewlett Packard printer sat on the dining table. The remaining parts of the tables were occupied by half-opened books and papers. It was really a mess.

"I think I can manage right here."

"Thanks."

She looked slim and beautiful and content with life.

"You look swell in that garb," Tos said.

"Thanks." She smiled faintly. She could sense the chemistry at work between them. The touch of his lips last night had been an incendiary of some sort. It had melted away the layers of ice that had encased her heart for so long.

"Aren't you going to eat?"

Tos studied the table. It was a dish of fried rice, basted chicken with lettuce, and shrimp. A bottle of Ragolis water completed it. He picked up the knife and fork.

"How long have you lived here?"

"Since last year."

"It must be very expensive?" He was eating now.

"Yeah. But I'm the only student here who does not pay rent. The house belongs to a friend of my father. They were classmates back at college."

"So everything here belongs to you?"

She nodded.

"What do you do about these things during the holidays?" He made a sweeping gesture with his knife.

"My father's friend takes care of them. He was a retired chief of police in this district. His boys keep eyes on this place every now and then. It's my father's directive. I'm sort of living in a gilded cage, protected in so many ways."

Tos shook his head. He was really beginning to enjoy the meal. He hadn't known he was this hungry.

It was the truth. She needed to be protected, but not by the police. He knew he was the only one fit to really give her maximum protection.

Ebi rose from the couch and went to the shelf. She turned on the TV set. The face of a woman dressed in colorful African attire appeared on the screen. She was saying something about a famed century-old festival in the Igbo-speaking part of the country. She slotted a disc into the DVD player, took the remote control device, and walked to the couch.

"We're going to Lokoja first thing tomorrow morning," she said.

"Yeah," Tos replied, trying to pay attention to the delicious piece of chicken meat on the dish. She watched him. He caught her gaze, and she turned away quickly, as if afraid to hold his eyes to hers.

She pressed the remote control device, and a picture appeared on the giant screen. A moment later, three words appeared on the screen: "SET IT OFF."

Tos lightly pushed the dishes away from him and ran a piece of very fine linen handkerchief across his lips.

"The tastiest meal I've had in years."

Ebi grinned. "You never were a very good liar, Tosan."

Tos tipped the bottle of Ragolis water over a tall crystal glass. He drank the water in a gulp.

"Delicious meal, cross my heart." He poured out more water again and took another quick gulp as if he was in a hurry.

Ebi cleared the dishes and carried the server. "Care for some wine? It'd be a bit on the cool side now."

Tos nodded. Only one shaded light had been switched on, and her elegant figure blended well with the exotic background of the large living room. She reminded him of Princess Esilokun, a water princess entertaining an important visitor. She was really a perfect hostess, and there was nothing fake about her. She was the sort of girl who wouldn't betray the man she loved. There was only one thing on his mind now—making love to this girl in this apartment, sleeping in her arms, waking up, and making love again when morning came.

"A little wine will do."

Ebi went into the kitchen and came back a short while later with two wineglasses and the bottle of chardonnay. Tos watched her pour the wine. She handed one of the glasses to him.

"Thank you."

She flashed him a smile, her long black lashes curling up.

Tos said slowly and deliberately, "I consider being out here with you my most important accomplishment of these past three hundred and sixty-five days."

Her hand came forward shyly and touched his lips.

"Don't say that. I'm glad I met you on that day. Who knows what must have happened? Thanks for being there on that day."

"Nonsense," Tos replied, and he swallowed his measure of wine in one gulp. He motioned for a refill. She refilled it.

All the lights in the room were out now except the glow from the television set. The blue under curtains of the room were drawn, and the light from the TV set was soft and restful. Tos trifled with his glass, lifted it up, and looked at it through the cathode ray light of the television set. He fingered the glass playfully, lifted it up again, threw back his head, and drank the translucent liquid.

He felt tired, and the low couch lured him to lean back and close his eyes, but for only a brief moment. He had a feeling that he'd just reached a significant turning point in his life. Canova, the Peke, was lying on the couch not far from him. For want of something to do, Tos touched his ear. The dog's tail quivered in response. He continued rubbing his silky head. Canova bared his teeth in an effort to be friendly. Ebi watched them, an amused expression on her face.

The Pekinese put out a paw, and Tos held it. The dog turned its silky head and licked Tos's hand. Tos's other hand was still playing with his ear. Canova rolled over, showing his silky white belly. Tos's finger rubbed the fur softly, and the dog shut his eyes with pleasure.

"You've made a friend of him."

Tos nodded slowly. She had squatted down at his feet and her eyes sparkled in the semidarkness. He stared down at her. It required the artistry of an artist to detect the mix of color in her eyes right now. And he could see two colors in those hazel-brown eyes: the color of love and the color of peace.

He stopped stroking Canova. He knew he was doing the wrong thing with his fingers. This was truly a romantic evening, the adventure scene he had so often dreamed himself into at the movies: the tired, handsome boyfriend enjoying a wonderful evening with his lady. The room was just right. His gaze was transfixed on hers. He hunched his shoulders. This girl fascinated him—her beautiful, hazel brown eyes, the color of her skin, her rosy, tempting lips. Her closeness had set off tiny ripples below the skin of his heart. He was impressed by everything about her: her accent, the room, and the way her lithe, supple body controlled everything in it. He had the feeling he was venturing into a familiar world, a world of beautiful sadness, of delicate feelings—deep emotions that he'd experienced before. He was venturing into a twisted maze, a dangerous terrain. He closed his eyes. Something told him that this beautiful sylph would lead him into trouble, real trouble, and he hadn't been in real trouble for a long time.

On the television screen, Queen Latifah was pressing her gun into Jada Pinkett's face. Tos couldn't make out what they were shouting about. He didn't want to know.

With a slow movement, he lowered himself onto the rug beside her. She studied his weathered face, a face streaked with love and foreboding. He did something she had been expecting, but it surprised her all the same. He put his hand on her shoulder and kissed her. At first, she was rigid, tense. It was only for a brief moment. Then she relaxed, and her lips softened in his. She strained to receive his kiss, letting all her reservation dissolve into desires. The voices from the TV set barely interested them. Tos's tongue seemed to be filling her head. He pulled her down, his free hand fumbling with the strap of her halter. She was losing herself in the pounding filling her head. Her hands fumbled with the buttons of his shirt. He helped her to take off the shirt, and her hand, soft and feathery, caressed the skin of his chest and then moved down his belly, kneading, rubbing. He kissed her cheek, her neck, his fingers light and tender on her breasts. He was breathing hard, her hands like flower petals caressing his naked shoulders.

Perched on the couch was Canova, sleeping peacefully.

On the television screen, Queen Latifah was speaking of another robbery operation. A series of truck noises split the sultry night air.

None of the noises interested the two lovers.

* * *

He must have slept a long while. A grating noise in the street below finally made him stir. He awoke quickly and tensed at once, reality creeping in.

Ebi's head was cradled against his shoulder, her hair soft against his skin. Her breathing was light. Quietly, so as not to wake her up, Tos rolled out of the bed and sidled to the window. He tried to look across. In the dullness of the windowpane, the light coming from the window seemed almost opaque. He couldn't see to any depth beyond the thick slats of the glass. A cock crowed in the distance. He opened one of the windows. Peering down, he noticed that there was a newspaper stand not far from the building. Some workers for the concrete industry and other factories moved briskly, intent on their destinations. Those with a few nairas to spend stopped to buy their choice dailies; those without barely spared the stand a glance. He wondered what the headlines contained this morning.

He went back to the bed. Ebi was still sleeping. He watched her through hungry eyes. Without her clothes, she was a sight to behold. He gazed at her for a long moment. Even gazing at her now, he was stirred. He bent down and kissed her. Her cheek was warm to his lips. The touch roused her. She rolled lazily on her back, the light from outside caressing her nakedness.

"Are you up?" she asked.

"Yeah."

"Enjoyed your sleep?"

"The best night ever."

"How long have you been up?" she said after a brief pause.

He gazed at her for several seconds without speaking. "You're the most beautiful piece of flesh God has ever created," he said at last.

"You're nuts."

"It's the truth," he replied. "Look at you. Your body's perfect. You look wonderful just lying there. I'd love to paint you just as you are."

"I believe you," she said, taking the cloth lying on the bed and covering her nakedness. "Well, not this morning at least. I mean you painting me."

"When are you going to get up?"

"Look, sir," she said quietly. "Why not leave me alone?"

"You know I can't."

"What time is it?"

"Past nine."

She yawned.

"I'm going to take my bath," Tos said. "Where's the bathroom?"

"The room by your left when coming out."

"Are you coming?"

She shook her head.

Tos walked to the chair where he had laid his clothes. He picked up his automatic from among the pile of clothes. She had seen the handgun last night. It had proved the point. *Bloody Jew man indeed!*

He turned around. She was looking at him.

"I'm sorry," he said sincerely.

She got out of the bed, wrapped the cloth around herself like a child, and walked to the window. She opened the window, and a fresh morning breeze washed into the room. Tos joined her at the window and put his arms around her, his lips on her hair.

"Forgive me." His voice was deep and quiet. He pressed a kiss to that tender spot on the back of her neck. "I never thought you'd see the rod. We don't normally discuss such things."

"It doesn't matter anymore," she said. "I've suspected all along."

"I hope you're not mad at me?"

She shook her head.

"I'm sure not going to lie to you again. It's a promise."

She said nothing. He knew she was not happy, and it annoyed him. For a moment he felt a twinge of remorse, but he put the sensation quickly out of his mind.

Fifteen minutes later, he'd finished taking his bath. He was standing naked before the large mirror when the door opened and Ebi came in.

"What are you doing?"

"What do you think I'm doing? I'm admiring my dick."

She looked startled, and then she giggled. "My God!" Her voice was slow, stunned. "Tosan, what's that?"

Tos gave her an odd look. "It's my dick," he said candidly.

She laughed loudly.

"What's so funny?"

Ebi looked at him for a long second. "You're a male chauvinistic pig. And there's going to be no breakfast for you this morning. I must see to it."

Tos smiled, grabbed his clothes, pulled them on, and walked to the living room, leaving Ebi behind to take her bath. He met a woman in the living room, arranging things. *She must be the housekeeper*, he thought.

The housekeeper greeted Tos, and he acknowledged her with a nod of his head. She went straight to the kitchen while Tos took one of the low couches. Soft pop music was issuing from the CD player. He carried the Pekinese into his lap and relaxed his back, playing with the dog's silky hair.

Ebi emerged from the bathroom shortly afterward and dressed in front of him with complete indifference. She put on a sinfully revealing but expensive skirt and blouse, designed by one of Italy's upcoming designers. It was a very sexy outfit that left her arms bare and revealed most of her neat, beautiful legs.

"You look wonderful."

She flattered him with a sexy smile, the likes of which he hadn't seen before.

"Thank you."

"And I'm glad we're doing this thing together."

"I'm glad too."

They had breakfast on the balcony: bacon and eggs, half a dozen slices of buttered toast, and a jug of milk. It was a hurried breakfast. After the meal, Tos collected the black canvas bag, nodded his thanks to Iyabo, the housekeeper, and ran down the staircase.

His BMW was sitting outside just as he had parked it last night.

"We'll use my car," Ebi said when she joined him. She ran the small, bright car out of its garage and motioned Tos to drive the BMW into the Porsche's former space inside the garage.

Tos did as she said; he parked his car in the garage, locked the gate after he was done, took the wheel from her, and then headed along the quiet expressway in the direction of Lokoja.

The sun was just climbing slightly across the roof of the building. It was going to be a sunny day.

* * *

Dr. Vincent Ubangha was an early riser: he had woken at five o' clock. That was his normal waking hour. Now sitting on the balcony of his quiet, two-story mansion, he read the newspaper as the retreating moonlight threw elongated shadows along the highway below.

This was the moment of the day he liked best—the minutes before the noise of the town reached him. Now he sipped at a cup of black coffee and watched the day brighten and the moon vanish, thinking how lovely and beautiful the pockets of fluffy clouds looked over the expanse of the little town. In the last few years, he had found that he enjoyed the town of Jankara. The town was a handsome town, an old town—actually one of the first few clearly defined university communities. And it was the university that had helped to develop it. The various students in the school all came from their respective communities. Some were city dwellers. Some others came from rural communities. They came with different cultural identities, and they had successfully infused these foreign cultures into the town. It had all merged and produced a new kind of culture, and that was the new Jankara image.

The coolness on the balcony, the bitter taste of the coffee, and the whiteness and stretched vastness of the sky, coupled with the peaceful silence of nature and the quietness of the house, made him feel at home with the world.

He took one long, deep drink of unpolluted air and wished Ebi could be here to share these things with him. But his wife, Madam Rachel Ubangha, the first and only iron lady, would have caused brimstone to fall on the earth. She was a very possessive, fiercely jealous wife. That was the reason why he usually spent most of his free time out of the house, away from her.

He took one small sip of bitter black liquid and scanned the newspaper's front page. It was yesterday's edition. It was all focused on Warri. This was how it had been almost every day for the past year. It was always front-page news. The crisis in Warri always caught media attention. The headlines screamed of heavy destruction in some villages along the coastline of the oil city, with X number of Itsekiris and Y number of Ijaws, women, and children having been caught in the fire of the warring youths.

Every now and then, the story out of the oil city was the same. The war in Warri was fratricidal war, a horrible war. There had been more than two dozen villages and towns torched by militant youths. Kidnappings, arson, and stealing were happening more casually in the war-torn city. It was a sad thing to experience.

Dozens of expatriates, particularly Americans, Europeans, and Asians, were targets of kidnappers.

Only last night, another attack had been visited on the city. He was sure that today's newspaper would carry the details on this latest attack. Old wounds had been reopened, old hatreds stirred, and bullets and dynamite were the weapons of mutual destruction.

Dr. Ubangha finished his coffee and dropped the newspaper. He realized that he had a class at nine o'clock. He looked at the tall, stately, Willard grandfather clock in the living room and noted the time. It was just a quarter past seven. Today he would be lecturing to his morning class about the growth and development of cubism and surrealism.

Fifty minutes later, he drove his accustomed route to the university and saw it coming to life in the bright, sunny morning as he walked, briefcase in hand, up the wide stone steps, flanked by the weather-beaten sculptured statues of gowned students of the department. His stride was neat and straight, like that of a much younger man, thanks to the tough cross-country jogging with which he always punished himself.

One of the junior lecturers in the department held the door open for him.

"Good morning, Prof," he said brightly.

He smiled warmly, pleased by the greeting. They always called him "Prof" even though he had not been conferred with full professorship. He was still an associate professor of arts.

"A lovely morning, Cyril. How's it with you?"

"I'm not complaining, sir."

Dr. Ubangha proceeded into the vast lobby. He nodded to a group of students, unaware that their eyes followed him curiously. Dr. Ubangha was a stuffy university lecturer, a man noted for high corruption, course-blocking, and skirt-chasing. He was one of the well-known lecturers noted for demanding bribes before one could score very high in his or her courses. For this reason, the students had nicknamed him "Dikko," after the former minister in President Shagari's cabinet. The senior lecturer, an academic elite, rode in a showy, air-conditioned Toyota Land Cruiser over the university's potholed streets. The latest of his cars had sent tongues wagging. It was a Mercedes M-Class SUV that had been bought, many believed, with students' money.

He walked across the tiled hallway and took the staircase to his office on the second floor.

The reception area was a pleasant spacious room lined with books and furnished with deep easy chairs, watercolor paintings, a wine-red rug, and a large mahogany desk on which stood an IBM portable. His secretary, Mrs. Ehis Osifo, was busy with the typewriter as he entered the reception room.

"Good morning," he said breezily, cheerfully, entering his inner sanctum without breaking his stride. He didn't wait to hear her respond, "Good morning, sir."

In his comfortable, marble-floored office, he sat down and glanced at the orderly presentation of his mail and files. Mrs. Osifo was the best secretary he'd ever known, and by far the most attractive: light complexioned and lively, with lovely brown eyes, charming, radiant smiles, and long, straight, slim legs. Unfortunately, she was married to one of those ugly Lokoja-based businessmen who shipped teenage Nigerian girls to Italy.

He checked his notes on the day's lecture: the growth and development of cubism and surrealism in modern art. It was his first lecture for the day. It was for part-three students. At ten he had a two-hour lecture for final-year students.

Mrs. Osifo knocked on the door and entered with his appointment memo. He went through the notes to get an idea of what his day would look like. He had a meeting at twelve o'clock with Professor Finecountry, the dean of the Faculty of Arts. At one he had another meeting with all lecturers in his department. As head of the department, it was his responsibility to see to their immediate needs. The meeting was going to be a boring one, he knew. He hated the administrative part of his work. Presiding over meaningless meetings. That was the log attached to the perks. At two, he had a lunch date with the head of the department of psychology. At two-thirty he had another seminar with fellow HODs in relevant disciplines in preparation for an art exhibition to be held later in the year. That was all for the day. A heavy day's work ahead. He thanked his secretary and asked her to track down Miss Akpoebi Dabiri for him in the afternoon.

Ten minutes later, he was in the classroom, moving back and forth in the large lecture theater. The auditorium was a large amphitheater built in the shape of a semicircle, and it could hold roughly six hundred students. The long blackboard was soon filled with his neat, clear handwriting and neatly drawn lines exemplifying the discourse on cubism.

The faces of the students watched him as he lectured, making notes as he made points with chalk and emphasized his words with amusing sweeping gestures.

Halfway through the class, the lights were dimmed, and Dr. Ubangha, with the aid of an assistant, illustrated some of the points he was making with slides. He showed different ways that surrealism could be created. The surreal movements of most of the pictures were weird and could be appreciated only by the subconscious mind. It was a bizarre way to produce a picture.

By ten forty-five, he was finished, and he breakfasted on fried chicken and rice. After his last appointment with fellow HODs, he returned to his office. He took a copy of Ernest Hemingway's *Death in the Afternoon* from the desk drawer, opened a marked page, and sat close to the window with the warm rays of the sun falling slightly across his shoulder, carefully going through the pages.

Thirty minutes later, his secretary looked in.

"Professor?"

"Yes?"

"The lady couldn't be found anywhere on campus."

He looked up from the book he was reading.

"Not been found anywhere on campus?" he asked. "Where the hell is she then?"

"That I don't know, sir. I've checked. She was not in class this morning. I went to her class again this afternoon. Nobody has seen her today."

The lecturer frowned. After a while he said, "Okay. You can go. Get in touch with Kraks. You know Kraks?"

"Yes sir."

"Send him to me immediately."

"Yes sir."

She went out. Ten minutes later, Kraks, dressed in black jeans, black beret, and loafers, came into the office. He was in his mid-twenties—a tall, rangy, chap with inquisitive brown eyes, bushy eyebrows, a bulging forehead, and a bulbous nose. During his five years at the university, he had proven himself as a notable sculptor. The HOD liked him and used him.

"Hello, Kraks," the HOD said, motioning toward a chair before his desk. "Come in and sit down."

Kraks settled his lean, brawny frame on the chair.

"How's everything?"

"Cool."

"I've not been seeing you around."

Kraks smiled. "I've been doing some car washing recently and spending the rest of my time in my studies."

"Good. I like that. I like seriousness," Dr. Ubangha said, looking across the desk into the young man's eyes. Both of them knew that it was a lie. Kraks was a naturally endowed sculptor, but he was a very lazy guy when it came to real serious hustling. "Have you been keeping a good eye on my princess?"

"Yeah. Sure."

"She's not in school this morning. Nobody has seen her. Have you seen her lately?"

"I've not seen her today. But I've been keeping a good eye on her."

The lecturer looked at Kraks with a puzzled expression. "Nobody has seen her today. You've not seen her today, and yet you're keeping a good eye on her? What exactly does that mean?"

"Everything's solid, sir. As always. She's only been out of my sight line today."

"You saw her yesterday?"

"Sure."

"What time was that?"

Kraks checked his watch. "I was at her place in the early hours of the evening. And I left very late. Say about eleven-thirty. That's exactly when I left."

"And all through those times you saw her?"

"Yes sir."

"Did she sleep in her apartment?"

"Yes sir."

"Are you sure?"

Kraks said firmly, confidently, "I'm very sure."

"So there's nothing unusual concerning her that you wish to report to me, is there?"

Kraks hesitated briefly. "It might interest you if I say she's taken a fancy to a young chap in this school."

The words seemed to hit the lecturer hard in the face. For almost a minute, he didn't say anything. His eyes were on the boy sitting across from him, and he couldn't seem to look elsewhere.

"Are you sure they're lovers?"

"I have a feeling that they're not just friends. That's judging by what I saw two days ago. And what I've heard."

"Tell me, what did you see? And what did you hear?"

"The princess was with this chap in a very secluded corner in Bray's Kitchen. They were in deep private discussion. Their heads were together. They actually touched. And they were holding hands most of the time. They spent well over two hours in the restaurant. And when they finally came out, I saw them kissing. From the look of things, I believe they're lovers."

"And what have you heard?" the lecturer asked quietly.

"One of the eyes told me that he saw them in Coke Villa. They were also holding hands and whispering to themselves. They also spent close to two hours there."

The lecturer shook his head slowly.

"You have direct supervision over her movements. You could've sent the chap away…had a quiet talk with him."

There was a faint hint of a smile on Kraks's face. He knew that the lecturer was trying to put the blame on him.

"I don't agree, Prof. I've done my duty. My duty is to watch and report, not to interfere. And besides—"

"I just have this feeling that you're not watching her closely enough," the lecturer said, cutting him short. "That's why she's behaving the way she is."

"But, sir, I've done my job. It's not my fault that she's meeting this guy." Kraks was desperately anxious. *The control freak is transferring aggression*, he said to himself.

"You're not smart enough to be working for me."

It was an insult, Kraks knew, but he nodded slowly. Without speaking, he leaned against the back of the chair and looked at the lecturer with what could pass for sadness. "Sir, you don't expect me—"

The lecturer cut him off again. "Who is this boy, really? What's his name?"

"He's called Picasso. But Tosan Mayuku is his real name. He's in this department," Kraks said flatly.

Dr. Vincent Ubangha smiled faintly and placed his hand on the desk before him. He knew the boy. "There's no mistake about this?"

Kraks said nothing for quite some time. "There's no mistake," he said solemnly at last.

Dr. Ubangha picked up a golden pen from his desk, twirled it between his neat fingers, and at the same time regarded the young man thoughtfully. "So she has fallen for one of my students." It was a statement.

Kraks nodded.

"This is very intriguing."

Kraks leaned forward, his eyes shining. "I believe they've been sleeping together. He spent the night at her apartment."

The lecturer looked at Kraks for a long moment. "How long has he been seeing her?"

"I don't know exactly how long. But I started seeing them together on Saturday."

"You're going to keep me informed of the boy's movements. I'll be very interested in whatever he does on and off campus. I want all the info."

"You'll get it," Kraks said quietly.

The lecturer said nothing for about two minutes. He was meditating, trying to bring to his mind's eye the picture of the boy screwing his princess. He knew the boy very well. He was the best painter in the department.

"By the way, is he coded?"

Kraks nodded. "He's coded to the backbone."

Dr. Ubangha made himself smile through tight lips.

"Thanks, Kraks. I believe that will be all for now."

Kraks said nothing. The two of them sat quietly as if in a trance in the quiet office. It was a lengthy silence, both of them in deep thought.

"Well," Kraks sighed. "If you want us to discourage him, it can be done."

Dr. Vincent Ubangha regarded the younger man. "How do you intend to do that?"

"We could pay him off." Kraks's face was quite expressionless. "If the money's okay, we could tell him to back off. From what I know of him, he's a reasonable guy."

Dr. Ubangha smiled faintly. "Don't worry, Kraks. I have a better way of discouraging him." He knew what to do. He'd built up a small team of personal troublemakers who were, as he put it, either "ballplayers" or "eyes." The former were an assortment of forces, and the latter were various informants. Kraks belonged to the spy bracket. But it was the ballplayers he had to rely on.

"I'll leave it to you, then," Kraks said, rising from his seat.

"You do that."

The boy pushed his beret farther down onto his head. "If you want my opinion, sir, I think this Picasso guy can best be discouraged if the money's right."

"Thank you," the lecturer said quickly. "I've heard you. And I think that will be all for today."

The lecturer reopened the book and leaned back in his chair.

Kraks turned in the doorway. Dr. Ubangha looked up.

"You know, sir, when I found your girl with this guy, I remembered what my father told me years ago."

The lecturer's eyebrows climbed up in a straight line. "What did your father tell you?"

"Infidelity is a sad fault in most women. Those were my late father's exact words."

The lecturer was quiet for a moment. "Your father's right. Most women were created with it."

Kraks stood at the door for a few seconds. "I'll still continue watching her. I'll speak to the others about it." He nodded and closed the door softly behind him.

The lecturer sighed. A few minutes passed in silence without him shifting his eyes from the wall. A passion of anger stirred in his heart. This was the moment he had been dreading: the day she'd fall in love with a young person of her liking, someone who'd mesh with her youth, her lifestyle. He had been suspicious of her moves for the past couple of days.

He sat back in the chair, pushed his legs out in a V under the table, and closed his eyes. His thoughts were on her. The event of how he met her forcibly replayed itself before him.

It was a year earlier, and he was in his friend's office. His friend, Professor Boro Finecountry, was the dean of the faculty, and she was his student—the brightest of his students, as he'd told him later. They were discussing Nigerian politics, the dividends of democracy, and the incessant fuel price increment, when a soft knock cut short their discussion. His back was facing the door, so he turned to see a young girl in her twenties come in. She told him some time later that she had yet to celebrate her twentieth birthday.

She was stunningly beautiful. He didn't know anyone could be so beautiful. As soon as she stepped into the office with that short coiffured hair and those straight, slim, beautiful legs, he felt his heart shrink in his chest and thought he was having angina. He discovered to his consternation that it was desire for her, not angina, that had pierced his heart.

She spent well over thirty minutes in the office, joining in the discussion, and she contributed brilliantly like the bright student that she was.

While they were conversing, for obvious reasons, his eyes couldn't focus elsewhere. He noted everything about her: her skirt, her blouse, her jewelry, and her shoes, the voluptuous shape of her breasts, the curve of her hips. The way the tight, short skirt showed off her legs and the white blouse revealed the outline of her breasts was too much for him, and he was forced to ask himself some questions: *Do you really think you'd have a chance with this one?*

He collected her address, and later in the evening he called on her and took her out to dinner at the Dish and Fish Restaurant. That was how he came to know much about her. The discussion particularly dwelled on her and her passion for paintings.

At the end of the dinner, he'd gotten all the information he needed about her. She was a big catch. Her father was a renowned Ijaw chief. He was on the boards of about a dozen giant corporations that operated in a range of sectors, including crude oil, chemicals, and agribusiness. The Dabiri name was a name that had also gathered some connection with the Warri Crisis. And he'd been a face in the political arena. He had been a prominent minister in the Second Republic government, and in 1994, he had taken part in the Constitutional Conference set up by the General Sani Abacha regime. Thereafter he had been made a minister in the same military government. He had served for three years before he had tendered his resignation in order to really monitor his business.

Ebi had been specially raised. Her father's wealth had seen to that. She had been born and had received her elementary and secondary education in New York. Her uncle, Dr. Bolouperemo Dabiri, had one of the biggest private hospitals in New York City. He was the one who had brought her up.

As a young woman, she had stood in much awe of her father's authority and temper. But as his daughter—his only child, for that matter—she was as strong-willed as he was. Because of that, she had a way of getting away with some of her frivolous demands, such as her demand that she get her first degree here in Nigeria.

She was one of the most popular girls on campus, though hers was a different kind of popularity. She was the only American girl on campus and the only girl that drove a cream-colored Porsche. And she had not been having an affair with anybody at that time. That meant the coast was clear. And he was the most eligible man on the grounds.

She'd asked him if he was married, and he had said yes but added quickly that he was working on permanent separation.

They booked a hotel room later that night. It was that night that they became lovers, commencing an intimate relationship. Their rendezvous was Koma Hotels. They had the best suite there reserved for them. And that was where they met twice a week.

It had been a relationship that had no complications then. They normally spent their weekends together at the Dish and Fish Restaurant and Lafia Guest House, and the Koma Hotels. She would not allow him to come over to her place, and he would not allow her to phone his home; but all the same, it was a lovely affair.

Campus Digest, the school's notable unofficial newspaper had serialized the affair two months ago as the hottest romance on campus. His wife had gotten a whiff of it, and it hadn't been an easy war at home. But his wife he could handle. He wasn't so sure about Tosan Mayuku.

It was a fine, long afternoon. *Is it too early to contact the ballplayers?* he wondered.

CHAPTER SEVEN

The moon shone like a night sun in the sky, lighting up the university town of Jankara.

It was a Thursday night, soon after eight o'clock, and Tos and Ebi were sitting on the balcony of her pad, waiting for a call from Frank Reese. Tos was smoking a cigarette so fast that it burned unevenly. Ebi was poring over a *Playboy* magazine, just glaring at the pictures, not bothering to read the lines. She'd carried the living room phone onto the balcony, very close to the couch on which she sat.

There was electric tension between them—tension that was cold and tight. They had sent the paintings to New York first thing on Monday morning. The pictures had arrived there on Wednesday. Later that same day, they had received a fax message from Frank Reese's gallery. He had received the pictures and promised to get word to them on Thursday evening by eight o'clock Nigerian local time.

Tos looked at his watch for the seventh time. Reese had promised that he'd phone at exactly 8:00 p.m. Now it was eight minutes past the hour, and they had yet to hear from him.

"Don't keep looking at your watch," Ebi said mildly. She had just finished looking at her own watch. "Frank isn't like that. He'll call. I know it."

"Fuck! The whole damn thing's getting on my nerves."

Ebi looked for a long second at him. Truly, the whole thing was working on her nerves, but she was not worked up the way Tos was bitching.

"Fuck the bloody hour; it won't work!" he snapped.

Ebi was shocked. For a moment, she couldn't say anything.

"Is that how you feel?" Her tone was crisp and cold with disappointment.

He sensed her coldness. "All right, Mama. I won't get panicky." He was making a strenuous effort to control his patience. "I am sorry to have to be so crude and impatient, but the paintings have been gone for the past four days now—fucking four days. Why can't he just send another fax across simply to tell us how it's all faring? It's high time."

Ebi was mollified by the change in his tone. "You have a point there," she said quietly. "But now I believe he's still assessing it, showing it around, and displaying it. These things take time."

Tos nodded but looked with disgust at his unevenly burning cigarette and threw it into the darkness. Ebi could see the anger in his face.

"Tos, darling. Take it easy. You're working yourself up for nothing."

Tos looked at her and nodded again. "You can say that again. These paintings are terribly important to me. They took me over four months to put on canvas. Sweat and time. No fucking witch bastard's going to con me out of my fucking labor. No-fucking-body!"

"That's out of the question," the girl said. "Nobody's going to con you; you can take my word for it." There was no mistaking the anger in her voice. "If Frank doesn't phone tonight, then tomorrow I will go to the bank and cash you the money. By the way, if you were to put those eight paintings on the market, how much would you sell them for?"

"What kind of question is that?" Tos said cautiously.

"Just answer me. If you were to put those eight paintings on the market, how much would they cost?"

"Look, baby," Tos said quietly, very guardedly. "It has not come to that."

"I'm afraid it has come to that," Ebi said with infinite sadness. "Tell me: How much would they cost?"

Tos stared at her, his face painted with embarrassment. He licked his lips and then said, "Those eight paintings are some of the very best jobs I've done. They could stand for international exhibition. If I were to frame them and put them on the market, they could go for, say, fifty grand apiece, considering the unstable economy."

Ebi stared at him and then began to smile slowly, her face suffused with warm light.

"That would be about four hundred thousand, give or take."

Tos stirred uncomfortably, but he nodded. He knew it was on the high side.

"That's cheap," the girl whispered. "It's very cheap."

"No. No." Tos was instantly friendly. "I'm giving the cheapest price to my dearest friend."

Ebi shook her head. "If Frank doesn't phone before nine o'clock tonight, or even if he does and he doesn't like the pictures, I'll still go to my bank and withdraw the money for you first thing tomorrow morning. Is that okay with you?'

Tos shrugged warily and regarded the lady. He knew he was griping, but he would not take her money. Not if it was her money. *Never*.

"It's okay. It's just that I was fully in a hurry to get some real news. Let's not allow it to sink in between us."

Ebi nodded slowly. "Would you care for something to eat now?" she asked gently. He knew she had softened. "There is some cold turkey in the fridge. Turkey and stout. Is that okay with you?"

Tos wanted to cry out, *That's wonderful!* Instead he said, softly, "That's very thoughtful of you, Mama."

Ebi got out of her chair and went into the living room. She stayed for less than five minutes. When she came back, she was carrying a server bearing a large bottle of Guinness stout and a silver dish. She set it before him and went back to her couch to resume her magazine browsing.

Tos opened the dish. There were three large pieces of very succulent turkey meat arranged beautifully in the dish. He nodded his satisfaction and opened the beer.

"One of these days, I'm going to paint you just as you are, Mama. But you'll be as naked as this beer bottle.

Ebi smiled. "Would you? That would be lovely. When will that be?"

He poured the beer before he replied to her. "Say, next week."

"Am I supposed to book an appointment?"

Tos looked directly at her. She felt her nipples harden under his gaze. He stood up, walked over to her, and dropped onto his knees before her couch. He took her right hand and kissed it softly.

"I love you, Ebi," he said in a husky whisper.

Ebi said nothing but gave him a sweet smile. Tos kissed her smooth bare thighs, the soft flesh that her blue shorts failed to cover.

She looked down into his eyes, her mouth dry, and her body was suddenly awakened with wild sexual awareness. She leaned forward with lips parted and kissed him full on the lips. It was a long, passionate kiss. Tos pushed her silk halter-top upward until her breasts were revealed in their marvelous glory. She was not wearing a bra. He pushed his hands over her smooth, flat stomach, pressed upward, and felt the warmth of her breasts burning his fingers. He fondled, caressed, stroked, and finally moved his head upward and took the nipple of one of her breasts into his mouth, sucking softly like a newborn baby.

She shivered as if cold, her eyes half shut and heat flowing from her body. But she carefully fought to regain her self-control and gently pushed him away.

"Not now," she said. "Maybe later."

Tos nodded, backed away, and took his seat. She knew that if she had not struggled to push him away before it was too late, they would have been making love on the tiled floor in the next few minutes.

"Do I still book an appointment?"

"Appointment for what?"

"For painting me."

"Oh, I'd forgotten. No need for an appointment. You've got a marvelous body. It'll be divine on canvas. To capture the moonlight in your eyes will be divine."

"You're a fuck shit bozo." She had resumed her browsing.

Tos bit into the dark orange flesh of the turkey leg and munched, staring down at the vehicle lights below.

From where he sat, he could make out Blacky's jeep. He was sitting atop the hood, a bottle of beer in his hand. Standing close by was Mary. The moonlight washed over them. Since the night of that incident, Blacky had been anxious, always making inquiries about Ebi's health. He knew already that she was his girl now. And Ebi and Mary had been engulfed in a miniature cold war. That was their business, not his.

"If these first paintings are accepted, I'll give you the treat of your life. How about coming to Lagos with me? We'll spend the weekend painting the town red."

Ebi smiled. "That's the painter talking."

"I'm serious."

"I know. But you'll need your money."

"Of course I'll need my money. But you said the other day that I'm on my way to being a multimillionaire. If all those paintings can give me, say, five thousand dollars, then I'm going to give you an exclusive treat."

"Wait until you hear from Frank."

"You know him very well. Do you think he's going to call?" Tos asked leaning forward.

"Of course I know he's going to phone."

"Then stay cool. I'll give you an angelic treat."

He gnawed at the turkey leg every now and then, laying it down to wipe his fingers on a little tissue paper and then picking it up again.

"Won't you eat something?"

"Not until he calls. I'm perfectly okay."

Tos said nothing. He took a large gulp of the beer. If the American did not phone, then those pictures would be the first and last batch of pictures he'd send across the Atlantic. Zuokumor had told him that there were all sorts of cutthroats out there who did not care about taking one's last dollar. But if he got the money, he knew he could quit his studies and hop to New York. With his kind of talent, he could make real money.

He looked down again onto the streets, and he saw the two lovers. They were now leaning against the door of the jeep. Blacky was kissing Mary, and she was accepting the kiss with equal fervor. He watched them for several seconds and then shook his head. The freshness and newness and mystery of love and lovers were things he would never understand.

Canova came into the balcony, sniffing the air around him. He saw Tos and stood still, observing him questioningly and suspiciously. Then recognition dawned on him, and he walked toward the man. He sat at his feet and gazed at him with jeweled eyes.

In the distance a dog barked. Another nearby howled in response. The tight harmattan wind creaked easily. Canova cocked his tiny, silky head.

At exactly 8:45 p.m., the phone rang.

Tos was bringing the beer to his lips. It was halfway there when the phone rang. He paused, regarded the phone suspiciously, and then set his beer glass on the side table.

Six seconds passed. The phone kept ringing obstinately, incessantly. At fifteen seconds past 8:45p.m., Ebi picked up the receiver.

"Hello," she said softly.

"Miss Dabiri?" The voice was faint but clear. It was free of static. She was glad of that. All she had to do was to strain her ear a little bit.

"Miss Dabiri speaking."

"This is Frank Reese's personal secretary, Miss Tracey Jones…"

"Where's Frank Reese?"

"Mr. Reese? He's traveled to Washington, DC. I'm calling from his New York City Gallery."

"What's he doing in Washington? He promised to call himself." Ebi's voice was loud and annoyed.

"He told me to inform you that the paintings weren't bad—"

"Is that all?" Ebi cut in quickly.

"No, no! Someone has placed a bid for a particular one of them. He said he'll pay ten thousand dollars—"

"Ten thousand dollars, you say?" Ebi's voice was clear, high.

"Yes. But Mr. Reese isn't selling it yet. He's holding out."

"Why's he doing that?"

"He says the work is much better than a ten-thousand-dollar picture. He wants to cut a better deal for your friend."

"Which particular one is the guy interested in?"

"The one called *Naked View*."

Ebi closed her eyes. "What about *The Solitary Reaper*?" she asked at last.

"It's one of the best pictures among the lot. Mr. Reese says he's not going to display that one until the exhibition."

"Truly?"

"Truly. An hour ago, he ordered me to dispatch ten thousand dollars to your friend through Western Union. It's on its way already. It'll reach you tomorrow. You can collect it immediately."

"Is that a partial payment?"

"Not exactly. He said I should inform you that the ten thousand dollars isn't a fee for any of the paintings. It's just a token payment for the artist to buy art materials. And you should tell him not to send any further works to anybody else until he's heard from him."

Ebi raised her beautiful eyebrows, her face expressionless.

"What does that mean?"

"Nothing really. It's just that there's no need for the young man to walk into the wrong hands. The boy should stay put. The ten grand's to make him stay put and work. He's a new talent and still young. Mr. Reese wants to organize an exhibition of some kind. It's going to be for the works of some young Africans. It's designed to expose their work. This boy could be one of the lucky artists. You can see that there's no need for him to muddle the arrangements by peddling his stuff all over the place."

Ebi closed her eyes a second time. She was obviously dazed. Tos walked over to her and held her shoulder. She felt his firm hand gripping her shoulder tightly.

"Miss Dabiri are you there?" Reese's secretary's voice cracked in her ear.

"Yeah, yeah."

"You should be expecting my mail. I've mailed you further interesting messages through DHL. Be expecting them."

"Is that all?"

"Yes, I'm sorry to say. And one more thing: he's extremely sorry that he can't get to you personally. You know—schedule here, there, everywhere. Right now he's in the middle of an art convention in Washington, DC. It's something extremely important. But he promised that he's going to make it up to you when he sees you later this year in New York. He's so sorry. And on a personal note, I'd advise you to keep a tight rein on that boy of yours. He has a rare gift. He paints unlike an African. Much more like a European. Mr. Reese is of the opinion that if all his paintings have the same features—quality, I mean—and all, he'll make him a millionaire in two years."

"In dollars or naira"

"Dollars, of course."

Ebi was too dazed to listen further.

"Are you still with me?'

"Yes." Her voice now was subdued. "You saw the paintings, Miss Jones?"

"Sure."

"Tell me what you personally think about them."

"Between you and me?"

"Yeah. Between you and me."

"Well, I'll tell you what, miss, that boy of yours can paint. He's not the biggest talent yet, but he's cute. He can grow with the tide. The people who saw them on display after they'd been framed were excited. There are possibilities that he can become great with time. Not like *the* greats, but he'll become a household name."

There was a moment of silence. Tos's hand was still resting on her shoulder.

Ebi knew that Miss Jones's suggestion was Reese's opinion. And Reese was a doyen of the New York-based Art Dealers Association of America, a guy always on the lookout for new and raw talents.

"Miss Dabiri, are you still there?" Miss Jones's voice was harsh in her ear.

"Yeah."

"Call me when you've received my mail, okay?"

"Okay," Ebi replied, and the line went dead.

In Turbulent Waters | 131

"Is it a deal?" Tos asked over her shoulder.

For one good minute, Ebi said nothing. She had never felt so drained.

"Give me a cigarette."

Tos took out his pack of cigarettes and lit one. He was surprised at her request, but he didn't hand her the lighted cigarette. "Was it good news?" he asked instead.

Ebi regarded him quietly, and then, smiling, she nodded.

"Well, well, well," Tos said. He was speechless. He just stood there, speechless.

"Y-yes, Tos. You're in money."

He just stared at her. She looked at him, smiling, and her eyes were bright and beautiful.

Tos laughed forcefully. He didn't believe he had heard her right. He looked at the young lady in doubt.

"Ten grand or two grand?" he asked, throwing the cigarette into the night.

"Ten thousand dollars," she said assertively, facing him.

He didn't know whether he should believe or disbelieve her.

"Congrats," she said awkwardly, her brown eyes gazing into his. "This is a great break for you."

"Yeah," he said heavily.

"Congrats" was definitely the right word. He had not been conned out of his painting. Instead he had been presented with the chance of a lifetime.

He took her into his arms and kissed her full on the lips. It was a warm, deep, passionate kiss. And as if from a distance, Tos heard himself say softly, "I love you, baby."

* * *

Outside, the moonlight still held the darkness at a standstill, printing bright light across the glass pane. It fell diagonally across the room, cutting across the figures lying naked on the bed.

Huddled close, her breath warm on his face, Ebi said, "Do you know what I'm thinking, Tos?"

Tos shook his head, running his fingers upon her bare stomach and feeling her back jump with reaction as his fingers traveled downward toward her smooth thigh and into the warm cleft between her legs.

He'd made love hundreds of times since he had been in his teens, but it had never been like this—*real* feelings, this kind of feeling, had never been part of it. He knew he'd fallen in love with the girl. As far as he was concerned, their lives were eternally entwined. Two hearts, two worlds. They were reaching out to each other—blending.

"So tell me what you're thinking."

"I'm thinking how abnormal tonight is for thousands of our people in Warri and its environs. When is it going to be normal for all of us? The madness—when is it going to stop?"

Tos closed his eyes and let the darkness fill his heart. He didn't want to think about it. His mother was dead; the family house had been burnt down. She was now a memory, a bitter memory as vivid and deeply branded as the murders he had committed in her memory. No need for such memories.

Here he was, an Itsekiri chap in bed with an Ijaw dame, while thousands of their people—his people, mostly—were out there, sitting outside their homes, not sleeping, not making love, hearing gunshots, their houses going up in flames, their villages being razed. He didn't want to think about it anymore.

"Tos, are you asleep?"

"Certainly not, Mama," he replied.

She raised her head and looked toward his face. His face was in the part of the shadows where the moonlight couldn't reach.

"What're you thinking about?"

"My future. That's what I'm thinking about."

"Don't think too much about it. Your future is bright."

"I know, baby," he replied quietly. "With you by my side, it couldn't be any brighter."

The room seemed cold suddenly, and Ebi shivered involuntarily. Tos kissed the back of her neck and put his hand on her breasts. She looked more beautiful than ever in the cold light of the moon.

"I love you, Mama," he said, looking into her eyes, enormously moved by the symmetry of her beautiful oval face, wanting like never before to cup it in his hands.

Ebi shut her eyes tight and sighed contentedly. She was happy. Her lecturer boyfriend was thirty some years older than she was. In bed he was no better. Tos was a real treat. She was in love with him. The touch of him, the taste of him, the sheer thrill of being in his arms or even in the same room with him was all magical. But there was only one snag—other women. But she couldn't stop him from carrying other girls when the money started coming in—especially not when she was still having an affair with the man he called Dikko. He was naturally bound to get jealous, like all men.

She knew already what she would do tomorrow.

* * *

The parcel arrived at Ebi's flat that morning. Tos received it. It was a flat white parcel addressed to Ebi from New York. It was simply marked "FRANK REESE GALLERY, NY." He signed for her, collected the parcel, opened the bedroom door, and tossed the parcel onto the sleeping girl.

"Just arrived. DHL from New York."

"It's from Reese," she said, straightening up. She couldn't hide her excitement.

"His name is written on the cover flap."

Ebi opened the parcel and found two separate envelopes. One was addressed to her, and the other to Tos.

"You've got one."

"Let me see."

She handed one of the envelopes to Tos.

He tore the envelope and took out fancy stationery with a letterhead crest. It read as follows:

January 14, 2004

Dear Mr. Mayuku,

I received your paintings. I must commend your talents. You are good, and I am sure your future is very bright. Those works convinced me that you are one of the African talents I'm looking for. Beginning on Wednesday, June 16, I plan to exhibit some selected creative works by three contemporary developing African artists. It is going to be the toast of American art lovers. It is one of the first exhibits of its kind here. I am calling it "Portraits from a Small Part of the World: An Arts and Culture Exhibition." It is going to be here at my gallery, Frank Reese Gallery. I have seen the works of two of the artists. Kwabena Agyemang is an Accra-based sculptor, and Enoch Niyibiriga is a Rwandan painter—but he is based in South Africa. I have penciled down your name as the third artist. The show will run to July 2. I have specifically designed the exhibition as a medium through which the American public can be educated and enlightened as to the artistic creativity present in developing nations. It is really my contribution to the promotion of talented young artists from your part of the world, in various fields of endeavor. This is also an opportunity to visit America. And you could do better here. People always do better here in America. And you would love it here in New York. It is cold sometimes, and it is warm sometimes too. I suppose Miss Dabiri has told you that enough.

The only thing I require of you is this: I still need more paintings from you before you can fully participate in this exhibition, and they must be of the same or better quality. Two dozen paintings at least, and I should get them before the end of May. I would like you to concentrate on nudity; you are good at taking the clothes off women's bodies. And I would also prefer some paintings depicting rural country scenery—typical African village settings. Pictures like semi naked African children in a riverside market, serene primitive environments, and paintings of gods or deities. But they must be good if you expect me to feature your works in this show. If you can deliver these works, then rest assured that I will launch you with this exhibition.

But I must caution you. This, I believe, is your first opportunity to showcase your work in the United States. Do not waste the opportunity; it is the opportunity of a lifetime. You can make the best of your talent. And as for your education, you can complete your studies here in New York. The state of New York has some fine art schools. There is the Pratt Institute, one of America's foremost centers for art. There is also the School of Visual Arts. I could apply to any of these schools on your behalf. And you will also have the opportunity to meet a lot of very important people who could help to advance your career.

Phone or fax your response to me immediately. Do not worry about finances. I will pay for the purchase of your flight ticket and organize your travel papers. You have got talent, and it is no good hiding good talent in the dark. What was it Benjamin Franklin said? "Hide not your talents, they for use were made. What's a sundial in the shade?" And remember this: all art is worthless in the dark. You possess a remarkable talent for painting. You must exhibit it.

I look forward to receiving that reply.

Yours faithfully,
Frank Reese

Tos laughed.

"What does he say?" Ebi asked.

He handed her the letter. "He wants me to come over to New York. He wants me to continue my studies there. And he'll take care of my travel expenses, documents, and all."

Ebi read the letter quickly. A wide smile split her face after she finished reading it.

"You impressed the hell out of him."

Tos nodded and walked to a VOA calendar hanging on the wall. He studied the date slip.

"What're you doing?"

"I have to produce at least twenty-four paintings by the end of May. Do you realize that is only about four months away?"

"I know. But it doesn't matter," she said with warmth in her eyes. "You are a genius. You've got talent. You're always filled with ideas."

"You can humor me any way you like."

She laughed. "You're going, right? You can beat the deadline, can't you?"

"You think I'll not? Do you want to bet on it?"

"No," she said. "I know you're on. And believe me, you'd love New York. It's the coolest city in the world."

"Yeah…the coolest city in the world. It's only an American that can say that," Tos said, smiling as he saw the satisfaction on the girl's face.

"You're wrong, buster. It's the New Yorker talking."

"This whole thing's great. I can use the cash. It'll take care of so many of my problems."

"What about my problems? We're partners, remember?"

Tos nodded. "I know, baby. I know. The cash will solve some of our problems."

"Now you're talking."

"I thought you said earlier that it's my money."

Ebi looked at him for along moment and then said gently, "Do you have a passport?"

"Yes."

"Good. Then we'll fix you a visa."

"Who is he really?"

"Who's who?"

"Frank Reese. What kind of a guy is he?"

"Oh, not an unusual guy. He's just a white male American who truly loves Africa and will kill to get his hands on genuine African art."

"Why is he so interested in African art? Has he ever been to Africa?"

Ebi nodded. "He's been to Africa a number of times." Her voice now was very low, and she was picking her words carefully, her eyes on his face. "He's been to places like Ghana and the Republic of Benin to collect masks and statues of various gods. He's got the largest collection of such items in his gallery—more than any private gallery you can think of. The last time we met—that was about two years ago—he told me he was planning on exhibiting an African project. He said he wanted African paintings by African painters. And he was prepared to pay good money. I think the project is this exhibition he's planning to organize."

Tos said nothing. Thoughts were running through his head. *I'm not afraid of my future. I know I've painted wonderful pictures, and I still have the talent of painting so many more. I have the strength. And I have the inspiration. My strength is my talent. But I have to be determined and smart enough to keep the deadline on this God-given opportunity offered me. I'm already versed in the art and skill of using the marvelous strength God has given me. I'm not the one who really authored my skill; it's God's gift. He's going to see me through this deadline. I must not fail, no matter what.*

"Tos!"

"What's it?"

"I've been calling your name for the past eight seconds."

"I didn't hear you," Tos replied quietly.

"Where have you been?"

Tos blinked. "Something just came into my mind,"

"Remember: we're still going to the bank."

Tos nodded. "For that kind of money, I won't forget."

She regarded him quietly. "You have a distant, faraway look in your eyes. What's the problem?"

"Nothing. I'm just dazed; that's all. The good news just did it."

"Anyway, it makes you look very handsome."

"And you look very, very beautiful, Mama," Tos replied. He took her hand and lifted it to his mouth, the kiss so soft and touching. "You're the most beautiful woman in the world."

Ebi smiled. There was fear and love in her eyes. Tos was the third man in her life, but right now she was afraid because she didn't want her heart to be broken again. She just couldn't cope if Tos should stop loving her.

The housekeeper entered the bedroom then and announced breakfast.

* * *

Dr. Ubangha stood close to the window, his eyes on the street below. There were no clouds, and the sky was a blue that seemed to reflect the endless emptiness of the earth's surface.

He undid the knot of the tasseled belt around his dark blue robe and tied it again. The suite in the Koma Hotels was well furnished—as it should have been at the exorbitant price he was paying. The room was quiet and spacious. An enormous double bed contained the form of a sleeping girl. Close to the shape of the sleeping girl was a slight dent where the lecturer's slim, athletic body had been resting a moment earlier.

Ebi had had time to line up and sort out her thoughts. It was going to end today, right here.

"I don't think I'll be able to come here again," she said softly.

Dr. Ubangha didn't answer. He didn't hear her. He was looking through the window, still deep in thought. This was their first encounter since Kraks had told him about her affair with Tosan, the leader of the Black Owls. What Kraks had reported was the truth. Only this week, she had put him off twice and broken their usual social engagement. He knew that there were only two options left: either she would open up to him or he'd force it out of her.

Ebi was in turmoil. She liked the lecturer in some ways. He'd been a generous and considerate man who'd swept her off her feet. He had taken her out to all of the expensive restaurants in Abuja, Nigeria's capital city, and bought her expensive jewelry. But she didn't love him; that she knew clearly. He was old enough to be her father.

Their affair had been going on for several months, but now the flame was waning. She wanted to be out. Naturally all she had to do was tell him. It was as simple as that. But in reality it would not be easy for her. The man was too powerful for her liking. He was keeping her in the spotlight. He had told her himself that he was having her watched. He'd said he'd done it because he loved her. He was concerned about her safety. The university was a very *rugged* school, and he had no way of knowing whether she was all right or not. One day the idea occurred to him that he should have her followed any time she went out without her knowing, with his guys acting as her protectors. But she knew it was all a smokescreen. He was a very jealous person and a control freak. He wanted to know firsthand how she spent her spare time, the places she went, and what she was doing after class. And he was married, for Christ's sake. He'd told her half a dozen times that he was on the brink of divorcing his wife. But he'd been on that brink for the past eight months.

But now she began to feel a mounting excitement as she was about to tell him. It had to be done, anyhow. She had finally chosen the moment, taken the final decision. But there was a question bothering her: *What if it turns out to be more than I can handle?*

"Vincent." She called his name lightly—far too lightly—and he turned around. He thought he heard something odd in her voice—a hint of indecision, or was it fatigue? That was rare for this beautiful, confident, and brilliant girl.

"Ebi, is everything okay with you?"

"Yeah. Why?" She gave a forced smile. He knew that smile. Her real smile was far more charming and natural. This one was a fake, too automatic. She was about to tell him about the boy now. He could tell from that smile and the incredibly evident note of uncertainty in her voice. He came closer to her.

"Love, whatever it is, just tell me," he said quietly. He sounded patient and concerned. "We'll sort it out together."

"Em…I don't know—"

The lecturer stepped into her front and forced her to face him. "Now cut it! You were about to tell me something. I want it, and I want it now." He hadn't meant to speak so loudly, so harshly.

"Maybe some other time."

"No! Right now," Vincent Ubangha said stiffly, knowing what was coming and conscious of his restricted power.

"Don't sound like a bull, Vince. You're a big boy, remember?"

Dr. Ubangha was a little distracted. No woman other than his wife had spoken to him like that. If Ebi Dabiri had been any other girl, he would have drawn his palm across her face.

"Ebi, will you tell me what's bothering you? I've little patience, you know."

"The truth is that…this…it's the most confusing thing at this moment."

"Go on. What's it?"

"I ran into this guy some time ago. A nice guy, as a matter of fact."

"A guy?" the lecturer asked, his eyes sharp.

"Yeah. He's a student of our school—your department, to be precise."

"Yes. What is it about him?"

"He sort of liked me; he asked me out."

Dr. Ubangha nodded, his face solemn. "Of course, Ebi, you're a very beautiful girl; you're bound to be chased about by boys. Even by my own students. It's natural."

"But this one is different, Vincent. He's a nice guy; he's cool, handsome, good-natured—"

"Oh, stop it. You know how I hate this emotional fussing of yours."

"Really?"

He said nothing.

"Vince, do you ever wonder if…well, if I will stop seeing you because of a younger man?"

"No. Yes. No…I don't really know." He was hesitant, obviously confused. "Well, will you?"

"I don't know. But I want to try it for once. Just for—"

He turned around and faced her. Now this man whom she had been dating for the past eight months was unrecognizable.

"Don't try it!"

"But I—"

"I said don't try it!" His voice was loud and cruel.

"Remember: you're the one who told me to be honest and truthful no matter how much it hurts."

"I didn't say you should hurt me with your silly frankness."

Ebi gnawed at her lip, studying the lecturer quietly.

"This is serious, Vince."

"No, it's not, baby. Remember who I am. I'm the head of his department. I've got everything: wealth, connections, and power. He's got nothing. I can break him. I can affect his papers. I can make him not graduate."

"You can't do a thing like that."

Dr. Ubangha's laugh was short and cruel. "Of course I can, love," he said calmly. "Remember: I own you as surely as your

In Turbulent Waters | 143

father did. Know it and accept it. You're mine—*mine*. Nobody has a right to that beautiful body of yours but me."

Ebi nodded and regarded the lecturer coldly. She had long suspected that he was only interested in her sexually; he only wanted her succulent young body for sexual gratification.

"Do you know what he told me last night?" she said in a low voice. "He told me that he loves me."

"That's madness, and you know it."

Ebi shut her eyes tightly for a moment. "I don't think so," she said softly, opening her eyes. "I think he loves me, and I'm beginning to develop a real liking for him."

Dr. Vincent Ubangha forced a tired smile. "It's time you stopped this nonsense."

"He said he'll take me to Lagos this weekend for a shopping spree. Isn't that romantic?"

"And you said that you'd go with him?" Ubangha's voice was quiet, but his jaw was working.

"I said that I'd think about it."

"Will you?"

"I think it's not a bad idea." She wouldn't look at him.

"You think so?" he whispered to her.

She didn't say anything

The lecturer spoke again: "Did you hear what I just said?"

"What's that?"

"You think it's a good idea to go shopping with this boy?"

She didn't know why, but she couldn't look him in the face.

"Actually, I would love to." Her voice was dull.

The lecturer shook his head. "What's this boy's name?"

"I can't tell you. And I will not tell you."

Dr. Vincent Ubangha laughed. "You think I don't know about your fancy boyfriend?"

Ebi looked at him curiously: "What do you know?"

The lecturer watched the girl's face, looking into her eyes. "You're a fool, my dear girl. A beautiful fool." He laughed sharply. He had humor and gaiety back on his face. "Even Tosan Mayuku knows that."

The girl's eyes narrowed. "So you know his name." It was a statement.

"He's an Itsekiri."

The girl screwed up her eyes. She said indifferently, "Of course he is. What's so strange about that?"

"Everything," the lecturer replied forcefully. "They are our enemies right now. You must not see this boy again. Neither must you accept his invitation to this so-called shopping spree."

"Why not?"

"I said you must not. That's an order."

Ebi licked her lips. She looked at the man thoughtfully. "But I want to. Our tribes may be at war, but personally we're not at war."

"I said you must not go," the lecturer whispered, somewhat angrily.

"You're acting like my father now," the girl said, and she laughed softly. "Papa's a bore sometimes. Just like you."

Dr. Vincent Ubangha drew her closer. "Am I boring you? Tell me, Ebi. Do you feel bored because of me?"

For a couple of seconds she didn't reply.

"Answer me! Am I a bore?" His brown eyes were feverish.

She didn't answer.

"You want to give me up?"

She looked directly into his eyes, into his face. *Jesus Christ, he's dying*, she thought. He was actually dying.

"He's made love to you, Tosan, right." It was a statement.

"Wait a minute. I've never seen you this way before." She was entertained by the way things were going.

"Tell me," he demanded coldly. "You can't keep secrets from me. You know it. Have you slept with him?" His face was dark and rigid as he stood over her.

"He told me that I'm the most beautiful girl he's ever seen. Then he kissed me—against my wish, though. But I sort of enjoyed it."

"You sort of enjoyed it, you say!" the lecturer screamed.

"Vince, lower your voice."

"Fuck my voice! You've slept with him, right?"

"For God's sake, Vince, I'm a woman. I've a right to my feelings."

"You've no right to your fucking feelings, girl. If you must know, I own—"

"I'm a woman! An unmarried woman, for that matter. I can go out with whomever I want to go out with. You can't stop me. I'm not your wife."

"You're sick."

"You're right. I'm lovesick."

"Well, well, well. It's good you're truthful. That's one damn good virtue I respect greatly in you." Breathing hard, he walked aimlessly around the room like a caged animal. She watched him as if he were quite insane. She walked up to him and held his hand.

"I was thinking you would understand," she said. "I really thought you would."

"Understand what? Understand that you're fucking my student and me, is that it? Is that what you want me to understand, eh?" His eyes, normally so filled with warmth and laughter, now were as cold and as bitter as kolanuts.

"That means we've got to end everything. I need some peace and quiet. You know you're too…you're too mature for me. I need something else. Something invigorating."

Dr. Ubangha looked at her fully in the face, his eyes burning hotly. *Oh God, she's very beautiful and tender.* He wanted to strike her beautiful face, but he just couldn't. He loved her too much to hurt her. He didn't even want to think about hurting her.

"I know it hurts, Vince, but we must be realistic." Her voice was pure sugar. "I wouldn't have hurt you for the world. But this was fate or something. It's something I can't interrupt. Something I can't explain. It's something I can't interpret—something I must just let happen."

"I see," the man said coldly. "'Fate.' What a deadly word."

"But you told me that you believe in destiny. In fate. In the workings of the supernatural."

"Don't lecture me, young lady."

There was a long silence. The room was very quiet. It was loaded with tension.

Ebi said, "I've decided. And that decision stands. My life belongs to me. I will do what's best for me." Her voice was soft, almost bantering. "I have been considering all of this for quite some time, and it's the right time to call it quits. I don't mean to break your heart or do anything like that. In my own way, I like you. You can call it love if you like."

"Which one is it? Love me or like me?"

"I don't know."

"Where does that leave me?'

"You have your wife. Go back to her."

"Is that why you did it?" the lecturer said tartly.

Ebi shook her head weakly.

"I'll marry you. Is that what you want? If that's the way you want it, I'll marry you. Is that okay with you?"

"No," Ebi said. "It's not okay with me. I'll not be your spare tire. I'm not going to be anybody's second wife."

"Then I'll get a divorce and I'll marry you, okay?"

"You've been saying that since I knew you."

"You're right there." The lecturer's voice was filled with anxiety now. "But now I'll really get that divorce. I promise you that."

Ebi shook her head. "I'm afraid you won't, Vincent." Her voice was soft. "You don't understand what I need. I know what you need. You need my beautiful young body. And you've had it. Why are you still killing yourself? Why do you still want me? I don't need this relationship anymore. I need a new lease on life. I need to know myself as a young girl enjoying her young life. I don't even need marriage for now. Not until I'm twenty-four. Just you forget about me and look after yourself."

Dr. Ubangha walked away from her and flopped into a chair. "All right. If you want the affair to end right here, then it's fine by me." He exhaled and studied her without saying anything further.

They didn't speak for some time. Ebi walked to where he sat, squatted in front of him, and kissed his cheek mechanically.

"I've meant to tell you this for a long time," she said sincerely. "You're a very rare man. And kind too. I'll always remember you."

He looked into her hazel-brown eyes. *Gosh! She looks so beautiful*, he thought. But he said nothing.

"Goodbye," she said, and she stood up and started gathering her things from the dressing table.

He said her name at last, his mouth bitter. "Ebi. You're endangering your life." When Ebi said nothing, he continued. "Tosan Mayuku's a cultist."

"Thank you for telling me," Ebi said politely.

"His last girlfriend was killed by his enemies—people who want him dead."

Ebi nodded slowly, without speaking, and continued gathering her things.

"You don't believe me?"

She didn't answer him.

"You think I'm lying. You think I'm making it up just to discredit him?"

"I believe you." Her voice was soft and gentle. "Thank you for telling me. And I also believe you've been spying on me. Please remember to tell your boys that it's over between the two of us. There's no need for the hide-and-seek game anymore. Thank you."

"You'll get in trouble, baby."

"That's my pot of soup."

Dr. Ubangha wondered why his heart was beating ever so loudly. *Is it because I've lost her?* he asked himself.

"Goodbye, Vince," she said, hoisting her bag onto her shoulder. When he didn't say anything, she turned away from him and walked quickly out of the room without a backward glance.

Dr. Ubangha closed his eyes for a moment. He was beginning to feel his age, and he didn't like it. Akpoebi Dabiri had gone out of his life. He knew it, but he didn't like it.

The associate professor of arts rose to his feet and slowly paced the room, hands clasped behind his back. He was heartbroken.

CHAPTER EIGHT

Ebi arrived at Tos's apartment in the late afternoon. She found him in his studio, working on a new picture.

"Hi," she greeted him.

"Hello," he replied. "Where've you been? I've been looking for you all day."

"I've been busy with some personal business," she said, and she walked up to him and kissed him on the cheek. "How did your day go?'

"Not very bad."

"What're you doing?"

"I'm trying to make a picture," he said quietly. "You know I've a deadline to meet."

Ebi nodded. Her eye was focused on the canvas. It showed a depiction of three naked women bathing in a pool of blood. What arrested her attention about the painting was the pool, the color of the blood.

"Why's the water like blood?"

Tos smiled softly. "Why did God turn the Nile to blood?" His voice was a husky whisper. "Why did Christ turn water to wine?"

"I don't know. You tell me."

"The nakedness of a woman is the greatest fascination the world has ever experienced. It's the first wonder of the world. Even the devil can't resist it. That's why Adam fell. And hundreds of angels came down from heaven to sleep with the daughters of men."

"What's that got to do with turning the water to blood?"

"Good question," Tos said warmly. He looked at the picture for a long moment, then turned to look at Ebi. "Can't you see it? It's menstruation! Menstruating women bathing in a clean pool of water. The water's got to change color. Women change everything they come in contact with. Don't you know that?"

She elbowed him playfully. "You're impossible, Tosan."

Tos hunched his shoulders. "You like it?"

Ebi said nothing. The painting fascinated her. She stood quietly before it for many minutes. It was warm and elegant, and the natural endowments of the women were skillfully highlighted. The way he had captured their nakedness reminded her of a superb nude painting by a French master that she had seen in Studio 47 Art Gallery in New York.

It was an interesting piece.

"I like it. It's great."

It was as if he hadn't heard her. He was staring at the work critically.

"I said it's great." It was the truth. She liked it.

"Yeah," he replied. "It's great. But not half as great as I wanted it to come out."

"How did you want it to come out?"

"I don't even know," he said sincerely. "But I want it to come out different."

Ebi paused for a moment. She was thinking. She said quietly, "All painters want their works to come out perfect. But there's no such thing as perfect painting. What you can get is close to perfection. Not perfection itself. It doesn't exist. It could exist basically in theory, but not on canvas. To me the painting's great, and Frank Reese will fall for it."

"Do you mean what you've just said?"

"Absolutely," she replied quietly, confidently. She knew what she was saying. Frank Reese had seen in Tos's work a unique style of artistic expression. According to his letter to Ebi, when he'd seen the eight paintings they'd sent to him, he had known at once that the painter was endowed with the blessings of the Muse. To an extent, some of Picasso's values could be seen in the Nigerian's work. *Eyes of the Wind* was an essentially revealing work. *The Solitary Reaper* was an absolute picture of grace and beauty and nature undressed. Tos had invariably shown his deep commitment to unique constructivism: the colors he had employed, the clockwork efficiency with which he had blended the lines, the beauty he had captured, the naturalist talent he had displayed. And part of that talent was very evident in this painting. "This painting's absolutely beautiful. You can quote me if you like."

Tos smiled. The idea amused him. "Yeah. I'll quote you."

Ebi strolled to one of the easy chairs in the studio and sat down.

"Do you fancy a trip to Bray's Kitchen?"

"Bray's Kitchen?" she asked absentmindedly.

"Yeah," Tos said, lighting a cigarette. "I want to show off a little." He drew on the cigarette importantly. He was a goddamn wealthy chap for once. Ten thousand dollars sat comfortably in his bank account. That was how lucky he was. He deserved the best, nothing but the very best. "What do you say to that?"

"Okay. I think I could do with a real dish."

Half an hour later, they sat in the restaurant, at Tos's favorite table. The food they ordered was a wonderful dish of stew flavored with king-sized prawns and duck meat. The rice had an aroma of leek and roasted pepper. The fried plantain was soft and succulent and smelled of garlicked tomato sauce. The duck meat tasted delicious, and it looked as if it had been dipped in Parmesan and sautéed in olive oil. It was accompanied by a bottle of white wine.

"When can I give you the trip I promised you?"

"What trip's that?"

"The Lagos trip."

"Oh. I'd forgotten."

Tos stared at her. "I'm a man of my word."

"Have I disputed that fact?"

"No, Mama. But can you make it to Lagos, say, tomorrow?"

"No," Ebi said, and she tipped the wine bottle over a tall, thin wineglass. "We can take that trip some other time."

Tos shrugged. "If you say so. I'm indebted, though."

They ate in silence. Ebi was not really eating. She was just toying with her dish and sipping her wine.

"You're not eating," Tos said.

Ebi said nothing.

Tos frowned at her plate. "Eat your dinner. That's why we're here."

Ebi took a poke at her sautéed duck. "I'm not hungry."

Tos looked at her. "Oh. You're not hungry." He took a piece of the duck meat from her plate. "It's no good wasting a good part of duck meat."

She laughed heartily, and then she laid down her knife and stared at him straight in the eye.

"Tosan, let's be sincere with ourselves. You've lots of girlfriends, right?"

"Wrong. I've lots of boyfriends. Too many for my liking."

"I'm serious, Tosan."

Tos dropped his knife and fork and regarded her.

"You said we should be sincere with ourselves, right?" he asked.

"That's what I said."

"Okay. I'll tell you this: I love you, baby. I love you so much I'll level with you. I will not fuck around—if that's what you're thinking."

"Is that all?"

"No," he said quietly. "Before I met you, I had gotten lots of women as friends. You could say I was happy and contented and relaxed. Love was for soft people, not for me. Though I had several girlfriends, I didn't have a steady girlfriend. Believe me." He sat back in his chair and took a wary look around. "But now that I've found you, I know what it really is to love."

Ebi said nothing for a while. She regarded him quietly, speculatively. Then abruptly she said, "You forgot to tell me about one of your girls."

"Which one of them."

"Your girlfriend who was killed," she said softly, and she saw sadness creep into his eyes. "Can you tell me how she died?"

"Yeah. I killed her."

"No. You didn't kill her. Your enemies did."

"How did you know about her?"

"It doesn't matter how I know about her. Can you tell me how she died?"

"Yeah." He nodded slowly, closed his eyes, and leaned against the back of the chair. He stayed like that for a long time. When he opened his eyes, there were tears in them. She was touched deeply by the tears. This was a man filled with compassion, and he was still suffering from that loss.

"Are you sure you want to talk about it?"

"Yeah. It's good for you to know." There was an odd note in his voice now. "Her name was Aina. Aina Ribadu—she was the daughter of Professor Alli Ribadu, a member of the school senate. She was a part-two student of sociology. I befriended her in the first semester of her second year. She died in the second semester of that session. She was just twenty years old. She was the only girl I really dated and fell for as a lover. But…" He paused and shut his eyes again.

"But what?"

"But in the end, I killed her. I had her killed because of who I am." His voice was low, soft, and sober.

"Tell me, how did she really die?"

Tos shook his head, and two lone tears slid down his face. She stretched out her hands across the table to him. He took them, and the two sat that way, their hands holding onto each other as if for survival, the tears bright in his eyes. They were also beginning to form in hers.

"Tell me about her," she urged quietly.

"Aina was a nice girl," he said quietly. "Beautiful, intelligent, and very social. I loved her. She was crazy for me. Her father was a very influential man in the school. He was the dean of the engineering faculty. Right from the very beginning, he was against the relationship. But there was nothing he could do to stop us from dating each other. Everybody on campus knew us. Back then I was just making my name as a face in the crowd. Lots of people knew me as a brilliant guy, a talented painter. And that year I'd just won the first prize of the Nigerian National Arts Award organized by the Nigerian Visual Arts Council." He paused and looked at her for a moment. Ebi looked into his eyes, and his voice was soft. "One day, there was a cult clash. My brothers were involved. I was involved, but we took it lightly. It was a common thing in those days. We felt and believed that Owlsmen ruled the school. We carried out a raid against the Brotherhood of the Purebloods one night. We felt that they wouldn't retaliate. But of course, they did. And I was one of the major targets.

"Aina was at my place on that fateful day. She was wearing jeans trousers and one of my shirts. It was a dark night; there was a power outage. They came to look for me. They saw someone sitting on the couch outside my apartment—my old apartment. They assumed it was me, and the cowards opened fire on her. She was killed instantly."

"Oh my God! I'm so sorry."

He nodded quietly and wiped the tears from his eyes. Then he sat back for a moment and watched her. She also watched him, tears bright in her eyes as well. She could feel what he'd gone through—unfathomable pain and sorrow.

"That's how I lost the first love of my life." His voice was a whisper. "And I was almost suspended by the school senate. My mentor and the award I won that year saved my ass. But now things have changed. We now have new rules; Owlsmen rule the school." He smiled faintly. "That was how I lost a gem, and God blessed me with another gem. And I've learned my lessons. But now I care for you more than I've cared for anyone."

Ebi leaned across the table and kissed him quietly. He could still see the tears in her eyes. He dipped his hand into his pocket and held out a white handkerchief.

"I thought you might need this."

"Thanks." She took the handkerchief and dabbed at her eyes.

"Who told you about Aina?"

"Vincent Ubangha."

"Dikko?" There was a look of surprise on his face.

"Yeah."

"What brought it up?"

"It just came up."

Tos looked at her for a long moment without saying anything.

"I broke up with him this afternoon," Ebi said matter-of-factly.

He stared at her quietly, his face expressionless.

"How did he take it?"

"How do you expect he took it?"

"That's a very bad habit. Don't answer questions with questions."

"Okay. I'm sorry," she said softly.

"It's okay," he said. He reached his head forward, took her hand, and kissed it. "I do want to tell you something very personal. I've never met anyone as beautiful as you."

She smiled demurely.

"You believe me, don't you?"

"I believe you," Ebi replied.

Tos sighed and looked away, forcing his interest somewhere else. He saw Bray in the company of some people whom he believed to be a group of radical lecturers. Bray was looking toward Tos's table. Tos nodded imperceptibly to him. Bray returned the greeting with a little nod and a small, meaningless smile.

"What was it like?" Tos said.

"What was what like?"

"New York, the place you ran away from."

Ebi flashed her teeth warmly. "You want to know?" She looked at him steadily.

"Just background information, that's all I want to know."

Ebi sipped her wine, regarding him coolly.

"Are you going to tell me or not?" Tos said, gulping a generous measure of wine. He felt in a good mood to relax. The wine was cool, and it brought out something soft in him. God knew that if he played his cards well, he would be in New York in, say, the next four months. Was this not what the Itsekiris called *esimi*?

Ebi finished her wine, refilled it, and then smiled brightly at him. "Now, exactly what do you want to know?"

"Everything there is to know. The social life particularly."

"You've seen all that on TV."

"I don't watch New York on TV."

"It's the same thing," she said lightly.

"It's not the same thing," Tos countered softly.

"Okay, I'll tell you what I know. New York's the greatest city in the world. New York's the fiercest city in the world. New York's the busiest city in the world. And New York's the most beautiful city in the world. New York's—"

"The dirtiest city in the world," Tos finished for her.

"No. Lagos is the dirtiest city in the world," Ebi said. Her smile was accompanied by a deep-throated laughter.

"If New York's the greatest city in the world, then why did you come to Nigeria to get your degree? Why didn't you get it from Columbia University or New York University or Fordham University? Why?" There was no mistaking the curiosity in Tos's voice.

"I like it here."

"Why here?"

Ebi smiled. "Why do you like painting instead of sculpting?"

There was silence for some time before Tos answered. "I've the yen for painting. Painting's my soul, my life."

"Nigeria's my roots, my blood."

Tos grinned. "I don't envy you at all. Give me the smallest chance or choice to go to school in America, and I'll not hesitate to grab it. Bye-bye to the academic workers' strike, bye-bye to the erratic academic calendar."

Ebi nodded in agreement. "You've a point there. But you asked me why I didn't get my degree in New York, and I will tell you why not. True, New York City has more colleges and universities than any other famous world city I know of. There are over eighty, pricey and ivy-draped—some affordable, some very expensive. But the truth is that I don't want to attend school out there. I want to get my first degree out here, academic workers strike notwithstanding. That's that."

"That's that?" Tos echoed questioningly.

"Yes, that's that," Ebi said. From the expression painted on his face, she knew that he didn't believe her.

"You don't even know how to lie," he said quietly. "Why don't you just tell me the truth? Was it that bad?"

The question was really difficult to skirt around. So she just waited for some minutes, and then said, "All right, love. It was bad. And I'll tell you." There was a hint of sadness in her voice. "His name was Cliff Schafman." Then she told him everything.

She was seventeen when she met Clifford Schafman. It was her first taste of romantic love. Cliff was a very handsome young African American. To her, he was the most handsome man God had ever created. He swept her off her feet with his charm, his easy grace, and his persona. She loved him fiercely and possessively. He was her first man. Naively, she thought it was a relationship that would lead to the altar. But like most beautiful things, it ended abruptly. He left her for a pert Caucasian beauty. Two weeks after she discovered the secret affair going on behind her back, Cliff summoned the courage to tell her he was getting married. That had caused the heartache.

She had asked him why. His reply was straightforward, and she could still remember it: "Monica's father is one of the richest men in New York. He has a private jet. He's well connected. I need his connections. I want to be a part of that dynasty. I hope you'll try to understand."

Of course she understood. A week before the wedding, she had packed her luggage and come to Lagos. She couldn't stand it. That was the reason why she had come back home—to rediscover herself and to find time to heal her wounds.

It wasn't easy, but she tried to forget him, continue with her life, and make something of herself.

"I'm sorry," Tos said when she had finished.

She nodded. "It is part of growing up," she said. "And I can say that I've finally rediscovered myself."

"What's it like?"

"Discovering myself?"

"Yeah."

She didn't answer immediately but quietly looked into his eyes. "It is knowing that you're not a slave to your emotions," she said quietly. Her voice was crisp, and there was something hard in her eyes that made him feel somewhat uncomfortable. She'd been burned; the scar was still visible.

"You know what, baby, when I get to New York, I'll look up this Cliff. Believe me, I'll give him something to remember you by."

Ebi smiled faintly. She knew he was teasing her.

Tos sighed. Things were moving so fast he could hardly breathe. Who'd have thought an art merchant in New York would consider his work? And who'd have thought that he'd become ten thousand dollars richer? This really was a juicy success story. All his life, people outside his ethnic bracket had helped him, particularly the Ijaws and the Urhobos— people at war with his own ethnic group. One of his very good friends, Zuokumor Opubeni was an Ijaw from Bomadi. Zuokumor was a nice guy. The first car he had owned all his life had been a gift from Zuokumor. He had shipped him the car from Germany. Not only that, but Zuokumor sent him dough regularly. Only three weeks ago, he'd sent down five coats, a dozen assorted Diesel T-shirts and seven pairs of Diesel denim jeans, and two beautiful pairs of casual Gucci shoes. The cost, he knew, had been over five thousand dollars. He and Zuokumor had been friends for well over twenty years. They had grown up together in the same neighborhood in Warri. They had attended the same primary and secondary schools. They had been admitted into different tertiary institutions the same year. While Tos had been at Yaba College of Technology, Zuokumor had been at the University of Lagos. But he had spent only two years at the university before he had jumped ship and landed in Germany. Then the first thing Tos received from him was a BMW car. Now it was Ebi, another Ijaw. She had introduced his work to Frank Reese, and in return he had gotten ten thousand dollars in cash and windows of opportunities had been opened to him. And if his *esimi* stayed good, he would be a renowned painter selling his works for thousands of dollars.

"What about going to a nightclub?" he said. "We could knock the town off its spindly legs."

"Nightclub?" Ebi asked. She looked at her watch. "I don't know…" She was not really fond of clubs; she had not gone to many clubs while she had been knocking around with the nightcrawler Cliff Schafman in New York. "Isn't the day too—"

Tos peered at his watch. It was ten minutes past nine o'clock.

"The day's young yet. We could knock it till, say, three o'clock."

"But—"

"No but, darling," Tos said, and he gave her a quick kiss on the cheek. Taking her hand, he added quickly, "Come along. You'll enjoy it."

"Which one are we going to?"

"The Clique, of course. You know it?"

"I think so," she replied with a groan. She knew it. It was really quite expensive. But it was the best.

Tos signaled for the check. An ugly waitress brought it. He peeled the correct notes from his wallet and, adding a large tip, handed them to her.

* * *

It was a dark, moonless night about eight o'clock that same evening as Tos and Ebi were having dinner at Bray's kitchen. But in another part of town, a sinister thing happened.

Ade Lopez and his girlfriend, Tricia, were watching TV at his one-room apartment. They had just finished their supper and were cooling off with an American action movie when they heard pounding on the door. Lopez opened the door and saw a group of about six heavily built men, all of them wearing black hoods to hide their faces. They were all carrying handguns

"What's this?" Lopez asked as a sudden tight ball of fear began to form in his throat.

"We need to talk to you," one of the hooded men said.

"Is there a problem?" he asked hoarsely.

"Come with us."

"No!" Lopez's girl shouted, and she rushed to her boyfriend's side. "He's not going anywhere."

Six pairs of eyes assessed her. She was an extremely attractive girl with luxuriant black hair, curvy hips, and generous breasts.

"Who's this bitch?" another one of the hooded men said.

"She's my girl."

The hooded speaker gestured with his handgun in her direction. "Tell her to keep her dirty mouth shut. Nobody's talking to her. Or do you want us to fuck her right here before your very eyes?"

"Take it easy, men. She's a babe. I guess she's a little jumpy."

"Okay. Come with us."

"Mind if I take a shirt?" He was wearing only a sky-blue undershirt.

"No. We're just taking a short stroll around the neighborhood."

They led him outside. Tricia tried to run after him, but they shoved her roughly back, and she fell hard on the red-carpeted floor.

There was a Toyota Hiace bus waiting in front of the house. They led the Brownstone gangster into the vehicle and then sped away.

Fifteen minutes later, Lopez, now bound hand and foot, was carried like a funeral coffin, three men on each side of him, into an open field. It was a primary school playground. They placed him in the middle of the playground, and right there the beating began. It was six men against one, and they were using all manner of cudgels. Lopez, imprisoned by heavy ropes, was squirming, cursing, trying in vain to free and defend his body. The hooded men just rushed at him maddeningly, kicking, flogging, whipping.

Lopez was screaming, but his screams were only pitiful fowl-like squawks through the rag they had stuffed into his mouth.

They beat him for well over ten minutes before a voice commanded them to stop. It was the voice of someone with authority. He regarded the prisoner coldly. *Does this pig think he can get away with the foolish arrogance of insulting the Don, the king of the entire gangdom?*

"It's okay, guys," he said. "This punishment's to teach the pig a lesson. Make him stand up."

Lopez couldn't move, but pairs of powerful hands held him up. The hooded ringleader bent low to his level and spoke into his ear. "Young man, you don't talk with disrespect to strangers in this school. This lesson's just to make you aware of that. Do you get it?"

Lopez grunted his assent.

"Untie him," the ringleader commanded.

Pairs of hands untied the prisoner and took the rag from his mouth.

"I don't want to hear any sound from you, okay?"

Lopez didn't make a sound; he was busy breathing like a man who had just completed a marathon.

"Next time you meet our Big Eye, remember to stop and apologize for the insult you gave to him the other day, okay?"

A totally repentant Lopez nodded.

At a secret signal from the ringleader, the men again stuffed the rag into Lopez's mouth and lifted him up. A lesson had been taught.

Thirty minutes later, his thoroughly beaten body was thrown out of the moving vehicle in front of his apartment.

* * *

The Clique Nightclub was the university town's hottest watering hole, mostly patronized by frat guys and their girls.

The Clique was not merely a place to dance to blasting music and swill beer. Every weekend, the members of the twenty cult groups of Aliu Zamani University—a mixed group that included members of the Vikings, *Eiye*, Black Axe, Marphites, Black Panthers, Brownstone, V.V.S., Purebloods, Roundheads, Black Owls, Pyrates (Sea Dogs), Buccaneers (Sealords), Jurists, Third Eye, Fliers, Black Cats, Amazons, Black Spider, Daughters of Jezebel, and Trojan Horse—gathered at the club to "mix up" and drink a pint or two.

When the club was founded some five years prior, cult fights were frequent. Fiery cult gangs assaulted one another even for simple reasons, such as a Black Cats guy dancing with a Purebloods man's girl on the floor of the club. In those days a cult war in Jankara had a special quality. It was bloodier and rougher than any other university's cult warfare. The reason was that one of the six major cult gangs was involved. But experience and maturity had changed all that. No cult group took their grievances to the Clique or its environs anymore. No person or cult gang could start a fight in the Clique. It was a no-man's-land, and anybody could walk with confidence on its ground. It was a major shrine, a sacred place.

Tos liked it, as it was now a place where everyone—Owlsmen, Jew men, Axemen, and Marphites—came together in a way unlike anywhere else. The Clique had a powerful energy.

It was almost full when they got there, although it was a few minutes to ten. The bar was jammed, the lights were bright and colorful, feet were shuffling on the dance floor, and the music was blaring. Tos was amused. It was his kind of music in his kind of place.

They got seats at the bar, and Tos ordered beer and cigarettes. *It isn't a bad-looking place*, Ebi thought as she took a sip from her can of beer and assessed the hall. The bar stretched along the

In Turbulent Waters | 167

entire length of one of the walls, with about twenty-five stools for patrons; behind the bar were beautiful-bodied, skimpily dressed girls, serving the customers.

Tos lit a cigarette and smoked in silence for a while. Ebi's eyes were focused on the dance floor. The crowd was young and flashy, decked with the same strong, variegated, multicultic vibes found in most of the university community's clubland.

While Ebi's eyes were focused on the dance floor, Tos's eyes were glancing at something over her shoulder, toward the entranceway.

"Are you expecting someone?" she asked him casually.
"Yeah."
"Who are they?"
"My hatchet men."
She looked at him with a long, slow smile. "That's very interesting. They're coded men, right?"
He shook his head in answer after a long drink of beer.
"Bullshit to that."
"Fowl shit to you."
Ebi laughed good-naturedly. He looked relaxed and easy tonight. There was a new confidence about him now that had been lacking during their first dinner date in Bray's Kitchen. She supposed it was because of the money now sitting comfortably in his bank account.

"What was your mother like, Tos?" she asked suddenly.
"My mother?'
"Yeah. What was she like?"
Tos hesitated. "A wonderful mother," he said quietly at last. "A very beautiful woman, cultured, talented, crazy after me." He shook his head. "She taught me how to paint. I actually inherited it from her." Even sitting here, he could still see some of her paintings. Like the piece she had titled *Esilokun*, a watercolor of a

beached sea goddess, with the goddess's neck adorned with coral beads. Her long, flowing hair was floating, and fishes of various species formed a circle around her. "They killed her."

Ebi felt a twinge of guilt. "What about your father?"

"Died long ago when I was, I think, twelve years old. My mother took care of me. She raised me from nothing, and now at least I'm somebody. I wish I could pay her back."

"Was she very old?"

He shook his head. "Early fifties, that's all. They killed her."

Ebi said nothing. She didn't know what to say.

Tos sighed deeply into his beer, and his eyes traveled around the room casually. He saw the Black Owls' number-two man. He was sitting on a barstool, wearing black jeans and a black leather jacket, his *bololo* haircut shining like an ugly penny. Tos signaled with his finger. Owlsman number two saw him. He slipped off his stool and came over.

"My lord," he said, and he smiled warmly, excitedly.

"Hi, Ovo. I'm glad you could make it."

"I'll always heed the call of my master."

They shook hands, Owlsmen style.

"Ovo, I want you to meet Ebi, my princess. Ebi, this is Ogheneovo. He's my nearest and dearest friend."

"Pleased to meet you, Ebi," Ovo said. He held out his hand, and Ebi met it with hers. As their hands touched, they shared a smile.

"She's my one and only angel and the only princess I know. My heart is her kingdom."

There was a general laugher. Ebi punched Tos lightly on the shoulder. It was a lover's punch.

"What're you drinking, Ovo?" Tos said.

"Stout. As usual."

"Hey—stout please," Tos said loudly.

The waiter brought the drink, a big bottle of Guinness.

Ebi studied Ovo. He was a young man in his late twenties with a clean-shaven head and a dazzling gold earring hanging from his left ear. He cut the picture of a tough guy.

Ovo, in turn, was assessing her. He was trying to work out where he had seen her. He knew that she was not an ordinary girl. He also knew that this was no casual affair. The Big Eye was in love. It was clearly written in his eyes. It was the first time in a long time he had seen Tos with a woman—it had been since the death of Aina. After her death, Tos's relationships with women had been lighthearted flings or one-night stands. The best they could get would be platonic friendship. One never saw him with a woman. Ovo knew this girl must be special. She had a sort of attractive personality, a kind of grace that made her different from all the other women he had seen with the Big Eye.

"What about the others?" Tos asked.

"Some of them have dropped in," Ovo replied, studying the dance floor. "What the hell's happening here? The Clique's full of too many Jew men tonight."

Tos nodded in agreement, his eyes wandering over the crowded dance floor where some Jew men in jeans and T-shirts were dancing away with their girls, mingling freely with the "blended" men. This was the new spirit of the Clique, the clubland he loved so much.

"Where's Christo One Way?" he asked quietly. "Have you seen him tonight?"

"Yeah. Look at him over there," Ovo said pointing into the crowd. "He's coming toward us."

Tos and Ebi turned to see a slim, very dark-skinned handsome chap pushing toward them. He was expensively dressed in a Valentino suit, black Gucci shoes, and a matching bowler hat. Ebi's first reaction was that he looked like an actor.

"My lord," he said, and he took Tos's proffered hand in his, Owlsmen style.

"Thanks for coming in so early," Tos said.

"I'm honored to be here."

"Meet my angel, Ebi Dabiri," Tos said, turning to Ebi. "This is Christopher Edokpolor."

"It's my pleasure knowing you," the newcomer said, and he smiled dully at her. Ebi smiled sweetly in return.

"Hey man, you look subdued. What's the beef?"

Ovo smiled. "I know the reason why he's looking gloomy."

"Mind telling me?"

"Shut up," Christopher Edokpolor said to Ovo, scowling angrily. At that moment, someone else joined them. He was big, the biggest boy Ebi had seen in a very long time.

"I'm so glad to meet you, Ebi," the newcomer said pleasantly after they had been introduced. "I must commend Don Tos's choice," he added comically. "Why don't we get together sometime so that I can tell you about the Don's dirty habit?"

"What the fuck are you trying to do?" Christopher "Christo One Way" Edokpolor asked. "Corner the don's girl? Under his very nose?"

"Is it a bad idea?"

Tos patted the empty cushion closest to him. "Sit down, Kadiri," he commanded quietly. Kadiri quickly, comically, took the chair, and everyone except Christo One Way laughed. He was still wearing the scowl like a mask.

"Why's he not laughing?" Kadiri demanded.

"He's lost again," Ovo replied.

"How much?" Tos asked.

"Seventy-five grand."

"When will you learn, Christo?" Tos said seriously. "This guy here's a crook. By the way, who's the bank manager?"

"Pappy James."

"Ah. You should get your head examined. P. J.'s the boyfriend of Ovo's cousin."

It was common knowledge that Ogheneovo Ikoloba and Christopher Edokpolor, two lucky guys from very rich homes, were always playing Monopoly with real money. That was the only game they both knew how to play. Not chess or Scrabble; just Monopoly. And the stakes were always high. The minimum was fifty grand.

"What fools do with money only God can tell," Kadiri Muazu said bitterly. Unlike Ovo and Christo, he was from a poor background. In him, perpetual poverty had bred a heart of stone that hated wealthy people and respected neither their offspring nor their property.

"You're just looking for trouble this evening," Christo said. "If I decide to play gamble, it's my money. If I lose the money in gambling, it's still my money. What's your problem, Kadiri?"

"My problem is this: If you want to gamble, it's your business. But don't come wearing an ugly face in our midst when you've lost."

Christo was annoyed. "You think I'm broke? Is that what you think?" He placed his hand in his inside pocket and brought out a bundle of two-hundred-naira notes. "Is this not money? Do you think I'm broke like you?"

"Cut the shit right now," Tos said authoritatively. "Enough of this noisemaking."

None of the men said anything for some time. It was as if they were ashamed of each other's presence.

"How's the gig you were commissioned to do?" Tos finally asked, breaking the silence. He didn't direct the question at anybody, but Kadiri Muazu answered him.

"It was a piece of cake. No problem. The guy don collect."

"Good job," Tos said, and he drained the last of his beer. He ordered more beer for everybody and offered a pack of B&H. They all lit up except Ebi. "How long is the pig going to be out of the sidewalk?"

"Can't say for now," Kadiri said ruefully. "But let's say two to four weeks."

"Good job, K. M. One can always trust you with the most delicate operations."

Kadiri Muazu smiled faintly. "I'm at your service, my lord."

Tos nodded. *Serves him right. Little accidents are for those who fail to observe the rules of the system. Big ones are for those who fuck with the system.*

"Look who's bursting in!" Ovo said excitedly. All eyes focused in the direction he was looking.

It was Malik Saleh pushing through the hot crowd to reach them at the bar. Big to the point of obesity, with a full-bearded face, and dressed in a black T-shirt adorned with shiny skulls and crossbones and black baggy shorts, complete with open-toe sandals, he was not the most attractive of men. But he was one of the most hardhearted students the school had ever had the bad luck of admitting. He was swigging from a bottle of Ponche. It was his favorite drink. Malik Saleh was a heavy drinker, but he was a very steady man.

After the handshakes and greetings and introduction were done, it was Kadiri Muazu that first attacked the newcomer.

"Malik—there's a rumor flying around that you're fucking one of your female lecturers—the one that teaches statistics."

"Me?" Malik was taken aback. "Me have an affair with Ms. Ikuomola?"

"Yes, of course," Ovo replied.

"Rumor's wrong. I would rather shag a dog than Ms. Ikuomola. By the way, who told you?"

There was general laughter.

"You're an asshole," Malik said, feigning annoyance, but beneath his dark scowl, it was obvious that he understood the joke.

"But I'm dead serious," Kadiri Muazu said.

"What do you want to do now?" Christo One Way cut in. "Are you trying to persuade Malik by saying he's having a sexual relationship with the ugliest and the most wicked female lecturer in his department? Is that what you're trying to do?"

"Look at this pig," Kadiri said heatedly. "What the fuck are you trying to imply?"

"Hey, hey. There's no need to be offensive, Kadiri," Ovo said, touching him on the shoulders.

"But this fucker's trying to—"

"Nobody's trying to do anything," Tos broke in. "Kadiri was just making a joke. Christo One Way's equally trying to prolong the joke. If anybody says Malik's having an affair with Ms. Ikuomola, then that's his or her own private, very private, opinion. No reasonable guy will believe it."

"I do believe it, though." Kadiri's voice was barely a whisper, but he said it with a smile.

"Fuck you," Malik whispered fiercely.

"Fuck you too," Kadiri replied.

"Do me a favor, guys. For God's sake, my princess is here."

"We're sorry, princess," Ovo said. He dipped his head low in greeting, and raised his beer glass to his lips.

There was silence for some moments, every one of them drinking his beer and focusing his attention on the dance floor.

"Where's Max?" Tos asked no one in particular. "Have any of you seen Max around here this evening?"

"Due to an unfortunate circumstance, Max can't be with us," Malik said.

"What happened?" Ovo asked.

"I was with him this afternoon," Malik replied. "He got a message; his mother's terribly sick. He rushed down home to check on her."

Tos nodded. Max "Paxman" Osuagwu was the Kwill of the Black Owls. That made him Owlsman number three. Malik Saleh was his deputy, and he was number four.

"The news from home—is it very serious?"

"The guy that came said the mother doesn't look too pretty. Could be worse. Nobody knows. Messengers like that usually couch the bitter truth."

"Let's hope it's not something serious."

"Yeah."

Ovo saw Owlsman number five. He was at the far end of the room, chatting with two well-dressed girls.

"That's Keme," Ovo said over the blare of Tupac's rap, pointing his cigarette in the direction.

"Always with women, that one," Kadiri said.

"They keep him going," Christo One Way countered.

"Hey fucker, you come over here!" Malik shouted above the din.

Keme saw them and shambled unhurriedly toward them. Tos and the others watched him as he made his way toward them with his long-legged, fluid movement.

"I hail the Don!" Keme, the number-five, said. He stood at attention, military-style, and the tips of his fingers touched his forehead.

"All hail the Don!" the others chorused, raising their beer bottles.

"You're late," Tos said.

"It's the female holdup," Keme replied with a smile.

"You could've taken a shorter route," Ovo said.

"That's the suicide route. It's not for me."

Tos turned to Ebi, who had been silent all this while. "Keme—this is Ebi Dabiri. She's your sister. But she's the very soul of my world."

Keme looked at the girl. "So this is the soul of my king, huh? You're so beautiful, Ebi." He took Ebi's hand in both of his and kissed it tenderly. Ebi grinned self-consciously, looking into his face. Tos knew she liked him right away.

"I'm glad to meet you," Ebi said.

"Don't mention it. The pleasure's all mine."

"I suppose you're going to take two hours to shake her hand," Kadiri said jokingly.

Keme ignored him. "I didn't know the king had a queen as beautiful as this. Please pardon me if I'm embarrassing you, my lady."

"It's no problem."

"So you're really my sister?"

Ebi nodded.

Keme looked at Tos. "You lucky son of a gun; I did not know you had a girl as sweet as this. She's by far the most beautiful girl in Ijawland."

"You're drunk, man. You're fucking drunk," Kadiri said.

Keme ignored him again. He said to Tos, "My lord, do you mind if I give Ebi a brotherly Ijaw kiss?" He didn't wait for Tos's response before he kissed Ebi on the forehead. Everybody laughed. Ebi was very moved by all this attention.

"His full name's Ebikeme Doutimiye," Tos said. "But he's also known as Al-Mustafa."

Keme was still holding Ebi's hand, and Tos was now saying something about retiring into the Blue Room, where the meeting would be held. Kadiri's eyes were watching their hands—Ebi's long, tapered well-varnished fingers in Keme's lean hand.

"When a handshake's well over ten minutes, know that it has become something else," Kadiri said jokingly.

"Why can't this guy mind his own business?" Keme complained.

"I'll mind my business. But only if your hands are back in your pockets."

There was general laughter, and boy and girl were forced to break the handshake. But she couldn't keep her eyes off the boy.

"Now let's get down to the Blue Room," Tos said after Keme had collected his Gulder. "We've lots of things to talk about." He signaled the bartender who had attended to them, handed him a wad of naira notes, and the man gave him a key. Then, as if on cue, they all stood. "Malik, you stay behind for some time and keep Ebi company. If any of the guys come around, bring them upstairs."

Malik nodded.

"Excuse me briefly, my lady," Tos said, and he planted a kiss on Ebi's lips. "I'll be back shortly." With that he cut across the crowd, and the others followed him across the hall toward the staircase.

They stopped at a door while Tos dipped his key to the lock and twisted it slightly. He pushed the door open, and they all stepped inside. The room was large and opulent, with teakwood paneling and beautiful blue draperies covering the window. The major color in the room was blue. The furnishings were blue; they had given the room its name.

"Everybody sit down," Tos said. "I've booked this place for this gathering, all expenses paid." He pointed to the elaborate minibar with neatly arranged bottles of exotic wines. "Help yourself if you feel like it. It's well stocked."

"Well, if you don't mind," Keme said, he and walked to the bar. He took a bottle of Rémy Martin cognac champagne, sniffed it appreciatively, and poured a generous measure. He tasted it and looked a bit awed. "This is the real thing."

"Yeah. Do you like it?"

"Yeah. Yeah. It's great. Wait a minute. This place costs plenty. Who's paying for it?"

Tos smiled and looked directly at Keme. "My girl's paying for it."

Ovo had settled himself in a small chair close to Tos. The chairs were arranged in a half-moon circle. "That girl of yours is one in a million."

"Yeah. She's classy. But you guys should take your seats."

Keme joined the others and sat down, placing the bottle of Rémy Martin atop the table. Tos brought about half a dozen wineglasses and placed them on the table, walked to the door, twisted the key to the lock position, and returned to the table.

"Now, gentlemen, let's get down to business," he said after the seated men had all poured themselves drinks. "I've chosen a date for the Grand Wizard's Night."

There was a moment of silence. None of the men said anything. They just sat there clutching their drinks in their hands, eyes fixed on each other.

Ovo ventured the first question. "What day have you fixed?"

"The thirty-first of this month."

The other four men exchanged rapid looks. "It's too close," Ovo said slowly, shaking his head. "And I don't think we'll be able to raise that kind of money."

Tos smiled faintly. "I'll bankroll it."

"You'll bankroll it?" All four pairs of eyes were fixed suspiciously on him.

Tos nodded. "This is no bullshit."

"So where do we start from?" Kadiri asked.

"Let's begin by making a list of things that will have to be done," Tos said quietly.

Christopher "Christo One Way" Edokpolor took a fountain pen from his inside pocket, turned over the cover of his writing pad, and waited to write down the required items.

"I like style. Real style," Tos began. "I want to use this place as the venue."

"You want to use here?" Ovo demanded quietly. "You're really shitting us. Booking the Clique will cost good money."

"I've got the money. The venue's here."

Christo wrote "The Clique" under the column he had marked "Venue."

"How many guests are we going to put on the guest list?" Kadiri asked.

"Maximum five hundred."

"That's not enough," Ovo said. "We're talking about the Grand Wizard's Night, not some small-scale social function. Five hundred is a small number."

The others nodded their agreement. The Black Owls' Grand Wizard's Night, otherwise known as the Big Eye's Night, was an annual ritual held to honor the reigning grand wizard. Any graduated or undergraduate Owlsman at any tertiary institution was eligible to attend by right. It was a tradition that had been in existence since the formation of the gang.

Tos knew that his Grand Wizard's Night would witness a record turnout. The problem lay in entertaining all the invited Owlsmen.

"We can't invite everybody," he said quietly.

"There are sure going to be a lot of feathered chieftains—feathers that will need no ruffling," Ovo said.

"Let's look at it from this view," Keme stated. "Everyone who's anyone, so far he's an Owlsman, will expect to be invited. Now how many people can this club hold?"

"A thousand, roughly," Christo volunteered.

"Two thousand if stretched."

"We'll use the space outside."

"That will take another five hundred people."

"How much budget are we working with?"

"Half a million naira."

"Half a million naira?" Ovo asked. He looked at Tos strangely.

"Is it too small?" Tos replied.

"Do you have that kind of money?"

"Don't worry about the money. It's with me, and that's the money I'm prepared to spend for the Grand Wizard's Night. If it will only take care of five hundred guests, then only five hundred guests will be invited."

Ovo drained his glass, refilled it, and looked squarely into Tos's eyes.

"The guest list will cause a small problem. Nearly every member of the family will want to be on ground on that day."

"It's not a matter of whether they would like to be on ground. It's my night; I'll choose what I want and how I want it, and how much I'm prepared to spend."

There was a long, intense silence between them. He was right, of course. Many graduated Big Eyes had spent less than one hundred thousand naira to organize their Grand Wizard's Night, and they had all been successful.

Christo One Way's voice broke the silence. "I would support the Big Eye with one hundred grand." All eyes turned on him.

"Did you say one hundred thousand naira?" Kadiri asked.

"Yeah. That's what I just said," Christo replied, smiling self-consciously. "It's my token contribution."

"You're a very nice guy after all," Kadiri murmured. After all, he was the Bill Gates of the Black Owls. He was the only Owlsman in the entire school that owned a Rolex and drove three cars, all owned by him. All he spent his money on was designer clothing, girls, gambling, electronics, and, of course, showing off. *Sons of rich men often view money as easy to come by and easier to spend,* Kadiri thought.

"Thank you Christo," Tos said. "That will help a lot."

At that moment, there was a tap at the door. Ovo signaled Kadiri toward the door. When he opened it, four men entered the room. One of them was Malik.

"All hail the Don!" they greeted loudly in one voice.

"You're terribly late guys." Tos's voice was angry.

"Forgive us, Don Tos. It's due to unforeseen circumstances," one of the new entrants said, and they walked quickly to the table. "I hope some little devil's piss is still left in this bottle." He shook the bottle and tipped it into one of the used crystal glasses.

"Sit down, guys. We're in a middle of a meeting," Ovo said.

"But this is not an official meeting," one of the newcomers said.

"But it's still a meeting," Kadiri replied.

"It's okay. Find somewhere to fold yourselves in."

Three of the Owlsmen managed to find themselves seats, but one of the men remained standing. He was the one who had just poured himself a drink.

"Why don't you look for somewhere to sit?" Tos asked him.

"I'll stand."

"No, you won't."

The chap nodded and walked to the window. He rested his back on the wall, close to the window. Everybody stared at him. He was roughly six feet tall and had dark, restless eyes. His face was an unmistakably Warri face—the type of face that could be traced from Ajamimogha to Ugbolokposo. It was a stubborn face. His head was shaved, and his eyes were a dark tobacco brown and looked fascinating in his weathered feline face.

His nickname (many students didn't know his real name) was Black Mamba. Everybody in the university had heard that name many times. Black Mamba was also known as Black Prelude. He was one smart boy on campus. He owned a Kenwood stereo and drove a charcoal-black Honda Prelude—the reason his sobriquet became Black Prelude. He was a cool guy—*ajebutter,* some might say, but very brutal when it came to violence. He was the son of a Port Harcourt–based oil-and-banking magnate, and his father, it was rumored, regularly send him a check of eighty grand on monthly basis, as pocket money. That was more than five times what some of his classmates got throughout a semester. Sometimes he drove to school in his father's Toyota Land Cruiser. His relatively wealthy background was nothing new in Jankara, but still he stood out. He was the number seven in the Black Owls' Wizards Council.

The Black Owls were named after the mysterious bird with big eyes. In the very beginning, the cultists in this gang had used the name as a cryptic symbol to conceal their nocturnal identities and to hide their existence from their perceived enemies. Aliu Zamani University, Jankara, was where the Black Owls had been founded, but now the gang had spread to well over twenty-five universities, sixteen polytechnics, and twelve colleges of education in the country. They also had zones beyond the shores of Nigeria. They called their leader on campus "Don" or "Big Eye," their zonal or state leader "Grand Eye" or "Grand Wizard," and the national leader "Supreme Eye" or "Supreme Wizard." And their overall world leader was known as the "Ultimate Eye" or the "Ultimate Wizard."

Over the years, Owlsmen (a.k.a. Nightmen) had grown so powerful, well connected, and fearless that they had become bold enough in public to adopt the name openly and use the black feather of the owl as their emblem. Many members now wore tattoos of the owl or feather on their bodies. Some others had live owls at homes. Others wore neck chains with owl pendants, while still others had owl-shaped lighters.

As a warning sign, Owlsmen would leave the feather of an owl on the doorway of the home of a person who had wronged them or on the corpse of one of their victims. Any time an intended victim came across a feather, any feather, he knew that trouble was waiting for him.

Owlsmen used that system of sending an owl's feather so efficiently that it became a myth. A feather dipped in blood and attached to one's doorway was a sign of death, particularly by shooting, stabbing, or lynching. A white feather was a sign of peace. But when a black feather was attached to a door or a windowsill, it was a sign of warning. Nightmen did not warn twice. A burned feather was a sign that the victim was going to be burned or roasted alive. The Black Owls were not a cult gang for the fainthearted. It was for guys with edge and balls.

The feather system was what made Owlsmen what they were. The sending of a feather had been so efficiently exploited that they had used it to rake in money and to create a legend. Many times, a single feather was all that was needed to make a victim pay a huge sum of money. It had made Nightmen become bold, organized, and mythologized.

But there was more to the Black Owls' mystery. It was a cult with distinction. There was secrecy inside secrecy—a cell within a cell. The first cell was general membership. The second cell was the *serious* membership. They were the people with feathers—the real chieftains.

The Black Owls' leadership divided the gang into two groups—the feathered and the unfeathered groups. The feathered group were called "masters." The unfeathered group were called "minions." There were fifty-four feathered members. A feathered member was a chieftain; he was a lord. They were also known as Wisemen. A member must have "plucked" a minimum of two feathers before he would be designated a lord; and to be regarded as a Wizard, he must have plucked at least five feathers. A minimum of seven feathers plucked was required before one could be considered for the position of Grand Wizard. The feather depended on the member's level of commitment. A feather represented a life taken. The least one could do in order to achieve a feather was to kill for the gang. An Owlsman who had "wetted his beak" with blood would be a likely candidate to pluck a feather. But it did not usually end in a single killing. It meant killings and dedication and finally, the Second Initiation, or SI.

The fifty-four chieftains were regarded as men of secrets. Not only did other unfeathered members not know their full identities, but they didn't always meet them on a daily basis. The reason for this was quite simple in the Black Owls' circle. Owlsmen were paranoid about secrecy and betrayal. The feathered members were people who were secretly and seriously connected to the tenets of the gang. In past days, security agents had caught members, and they had spilled all their knowledge to the police, the church, and the general public. The cloud of secrecy had been introduced to check this "unwholesome" trend. For one to be a candidate for feathering, he had to pass through some rigorous training and the Second Initiation. After the Second Initiation, one could be regarded as a feathered member. Lots of people had tried the SI, but the majority of them didn't survive it. Owlsmen, if they died, were said to have been "swallowed by the Owl."

Owlsmen leadership believed that the less the general membership knew about the gang, the better for them. It was common knowledge that one could not betray what or whom one did not know.

The added advantage of passing the First and Second Initiations was that anybody who succeeded at the second initiation, upon graduation, was rewarded with automatic employment by the economic networks of Owlsmen in the society. This could include public or private service in the oil industry, the banking and shipping industries, insurance, the military—you name it. Graduated Owlsmen working in these places had great plans for their feathered brethren still on campus. And that was what the Owlsmen were told before initiation.

Graduated Owlsmen constituted a large part of the tycoon cartel, which owned and controlled a very large segment of the economy and the government. These Owlsmen were people who'd graduated from different tertiary institutions, but they belonged to the same brotherhood. Such brotherhood controlled most sectors of the economy, including commerce and industry. Most of the money used to sponsor campus violence came from these Owlsmen, and after graduation, cultism opened the door through which most of these graduates came to good-paying employment.

These dons imprisoned all sectors of the economy. Campus fraternities opened the magic door to the boardroom of good employment, insofar as one was "blended" in his student days.

The Black Owls leadership had also divided the feathered group into two—an inner and outer core—handing control of major issues to the inner core and leaving the outer core and the unfeathered members with the choice of putting up or shutting up. This method neatly centralized power with the twelve principal officers of the Black Owls. These twelve men made up the Council of Wizards. And out of these twelve men, nine were presents in the Blue Room of the Clique Nightclub tonight.

The Black Owls were different from other frat gangs in terms of organizational structure. They had a leadership of six men picked according to their abilities. Each of these men had a deputy.

The six men and their deputies made up the Supreme Council, a.k.a. the Council of Wizards. It was the highest decision-making body of the Black Owls in the university.

The head of the Supreme Council of the Black Owls on campus was labeled "Number One," but they also called him the "Big Eye" or the "Grand Eye." His function was to preside over meetings and the general administration of the gang. He was the Don. His deputy was Number Two by numerical designation. He was also known as the Evil Eye or the Vee-Eye.

Number Three was known as the Kwill. As may be imagined, Number Three's functions were purely secretarial and clerical matters. His deputy, designated as Number Four, was also dubbed "the Klerk."

Number Five and Number Six, which began as the operational arms of the gang, were called "Defense Chief" and "Hammer," respectively. They were also called the "Klaws"—"Klaws I" and "Klaws II." Their offices concerned themselves with the security of the gang. Security in this sense implied military-like operations and organization of hits, robberies, and other operations. There was nothing that people in this department would not do to protect the gang.

Number Seven and Number Eight handled recruitment (initiations), information, and welfare operations and made recommendations for the promotions and demotions ("unfeathering") of feathered chiefs. Their official titles were "Town Krier" and "Hooter."

Number Nine and Number Ten concerned themselves with finances. Their offices covered raising funds and operational expenses. There was nothing that these two people and the men under them would not do for money. They collected fines and dues from members and protection money from nonmembers who required protection; they robbed if they had to (though they did not call it "armed robbery," but "tapping"), and they would assassinate if they must. Their official titles were "K1" and "K2"—"Kashier I" and "Kashier II."

Number Eleven and Number Twelve were known to be surveillance officers. They were the intelligence officers. They took care of all matters of field investigation, compilation of information, and other related functions. This group devoted its personnel to the considerable task of keeping track of the huge number of cult groups that operated in the institution, and they tried to compile information about these groups and how their existence affected the security of Owlsmen. Their official titles were "Moscow I" and "Moscow II," or "M1" and "M2" for short.

As an Owlsman, once initiated, one was expected to join one of the four committees that made up the operations of the Black Owls. Every member had to fulfill a role that was exactly defined as to both position and function. It was more or less a divine order.

Tos surveyed the eight men quietly for a long time. These men made up his regime. They were his Knights of the Round Table. His MOT—men of trust. As a group, they were clearly the most influential force within the Black Owls' gang. They were Owlsmen loyal to the death.

"What about live band?" the Vee-Eye asked. "We need the best, remember."

"You're damn right. We need a live band," Keme, the Defense Chief added.

"I'll handle that one," one of the new arrivals said. He was called Morgan Akumagba. He was Kashier II and Number Ten by designation. "The Black Shadows Blast Band from Warri will do just fine. I have their number. I'll phone their manager to see if we can book them for that night."

"Good. Do that," Tos said. He hesitated. "I leave you to deal with the details on that one. Christo, put it down under entertainment. Now, the major problem's how to provide enough shacks for everybody. That's the one area where I envisage some problems."

"How many guests do we have in mind?"

"Let's say about three thousand persons, give or take," the Vee-Eye replied.

Tos shook his head. "That's too many. By far too many."

"What about two thousand persons?" Keme asked.

Tos considered this for a moment and again shook his head. "Still too many."

There was a moment's silence.

"I'll support in the area of drinks," Number Seven, the Krier, said, and the room was filled with the excited hooting that was common among Owlsmen.

After the excitement had died down, Malik said, "We don't know how many cartons of beer he's promised. Our major problems will still be the drinks. The last Wizard's Night, we'd emptied all the drinks before the party started proper. That's because the guests outnumbered the drinks."

"How many cartons of beer can you volunteer?" the Vee-Eye asked Black Mamba.

"How many cartons do we need?"

"As many as possible."

"I'll support in that area," Black Mamba said.

"Will you?" There was no mistaking the amusement in Tos's voice.

"Yeah, my lord."

"Do we have specifics of what and what?" the Vee-Eye asked.

"No. I'll let you guys know when it's ready."

"We'll need the specifics," Christo said.

"Okay. I'll contribute fifty cartons of canned beer. Heineken."

"Good. Christo, take note of it," Tos said.

Christo turned over a fresh page of his writing pad and continued writing.

"What about security?" somebody asked.

"Forget security," Keme replied. "Nightmen are security."

"Food," Kadiri said. "What do we do about chewables?"

"I knew you'd be the one to mention food," Christo said with a satirical laugh.

Kadiri looked at Christo briefly but shook his head knowingly.

"Hooter's right," Keme said. "We'll need real food. This is no *isi-ewu* or *burukutu* party. This is the real thing."

"I'd prefer takeaways," Christo said, looking up from his notes.

"Talking about food, who's going to do the cooking?" Number Six, the Hammer, asked.

"We'll contract it to a caterer."

"That's going to cost us extra dough. And we're trying to cut costs here."

"How about if we get our girls together and tell them what to do."

"Fine talk."

"That's a very good idea."

By now Christo was on the fourth page in his writing pad.

"What's the name of that band again?" he asked, looking from his notepad.

"The Black Shadows Blast Band. They are a bunch of new guys."

"Are they very good?"

"They're the best in the Niger Delta."

"They'd better be, because I don't want that una Warri *gbas kelele* stuff o!"

"But you suppose know say Warri nor dey carry last na."

There was general laughter.

Tos studied all of them carefully. They all had one thing in common: mixed childishness and seriousness. And it was securely wrapped in warm friendship.

For the next hour, all the men went over any problems that might arise during the party, down to the most peculiar.

CHAPTER NINE

A VERY BEAUTIFUL AKPOEBI DABIRI STOOD AT THE SECOND entranceway of the Clique Nightclub beside Don Tos to greet the guests as they were introduced by the young MC. Ebi was a little nervous, but Tos seemed totally in charge here. His bearing was elegant, intense, and yet polite. In his beautifully cut black Valentino suit (he was the only one allowed by convention to wear an all-black outfit tonight), he stood in the entranceway like a Catholic priest, greeting the guests—the feathered guests—as they filed into the hall. It was the tradition. All titled men must shake his hand, see his face, and listen to the impressive Owlsman's expected words of welcome. He was almost a kind of a god tonight. And the air was charged with his special kind of presence.

One by one, the feathered men shook hands first with him in the traditional cultic fashion and then with the girl beside him, whom they believed to be his girlfriend.

"Don Apalla?" Tos shook the hand of UniLag's Big Eye. "What a pleasure."

"The pleasure is mine, my lord," Don Apalla said warmly. Tos patted him on the back as he moved on.

"Holy Owl! Who am I seeing?"

"Nobody but old me."

"It's Don Tobino!" Tos said, and he reached to embrace the guy in a quick hug.

Don Alexander Tobino was a former president of the National Association of Nigerian Students (NANS). He was one of the most notable student leaders in recent times—a guy whose name had once been on the Abacha government's Most Wanted List. He had made his name a week after Ken Saro-Wiwa was killed. Back then he had been a part-three law student at the University of Port Harcourt, and true to his image as the number-one student in the Federal Republic of Nigeria, he had led a massive demonstration of thousands of Nigerian students through the streets of Port Harcourt to protest the killings. The protesting students had attacked the military governor's office with rocks and broken bottles, and had shut down Shell's office in the oil city. As the students' leader, Tobino had been interviewed by CNN. From that moment, he had been hounded, almost assassinated, arrested, and imprisoned for nine months. Finally he had been released at the behest of a notable member of the brass in the Nigerian Army who was an Owlsman. From then, his name had become a household name. Today he was a practicing barrister with a prestigious law firm in Lagos and a nationally recognized human rights activist.

"Would you mind if I don't stay for refreshment?" the activist asked. "I'm supposed to be in Makurdi for a NANS-sponsored seminar. I'm expected to deliver some lectures."

"Not on my night."

"I know, my lord. That's why I'm here."

"You've not changed one damn bit. You're still the *aluta* choirmaster."

Don Tobino laughed at the joke. "I'm trying to maintain the image."

"Okay. This is what you'll do: you'll stay only for two hours. Then you can be on your way. But first you must break bread with me."

"You've not changed, either," Don Tobino replied, and they both laughed.

The next entrant was a man Tos hadn't met, but the chap recognized him at once. Tos was the most famous Owlsman he had ever met. When they were introduced, the man made the Owlsmen's most honorable gesture of brotherhood, the "I'll die for you" symbol, with his left hand crossing his chest and his right hand touching Tos on the left shoulders. Tos did the same to him.

"M'lurdy, this is a pleasure—a great honor. You won't believe this, but you've been an inspiration to Owlsmen everywhere."

Tos nodded solemnly. "That's very nice of you to say, Lord Akatakpo." And so it continued.

Any party organized by the Owlsmen was always an event. The Grand Wizard's Night was the highlight of the year in the university community, and Owlsmen came from all the surrounding universities and polytechnics to participate. The venue was the town's hottest watering hole. The yard in the back of the building was tented for the occasion. The elegant open interior of the immense building looked its best, with beautiful chandeliers glittering with lights, balloons floating in the air, and flowers everywhere. All the windows were opened to the yard, wherein the management had laced fairy lights through the branches of the trees. The powerful lights from the clubroom spilled onto the lawn and made brilliant, blazing blue colors on the neatly trimmed flowers in their tubs.

Colorful plastic tables and chairs on the terrace made a fabulous place to sit out between dances.

The theme for all Owlsmen's parties was B&W—black trousers and white shirts. This was no exception. It was an ancient tradition in the history of the frat gang. The tough and not-so-tough Owlsmen, all of them in their customary black-and-white garb, walked with noticeable swagger.

All the girls wore jeans. Ebi also was in jeans—good original black Levi's with a white body-hugging shirt with a flirtatious, feminine, and smartly styled décolleté design.

"THE GRAND WIZARD'S NIGHT" read the banner fluttering above the bandstand. Below the banner, the five-piece live band invited from Warri began to play dance music softly. The party had begun.

Sighing, Tos looked at Ebi, his eyes soft.

"How lovely you're looking tonight," he said. It was the second time he had said these words to her this evening.

"Really?"

"Yes, of course. Or don't you enjoy looking nice and being told so?"

Ebi laughed. "I like being told that I'm looking nice," she said. "But you flatter me too much."

Tos shook his head. "Not at all, baby. I love you."

There was no need for him to say it. She knew it. She looked lovingly and adoringly at him. She felt comfortable and safe with him.

Tos took up one of her strong, well-shaped hands.

"Come and let's dance," he said, and he led her through the crowd. As he mounted the dance floor, there was a thunderous shout of "Don Tos!"

Tos was not much of a dancer, but he managed well with Ebi for about forty minutes. When he was beginning to tire out, he handed her over to Don Alex Tobino and retreated to a quiet corner. He lit a cigarette, took a glass of Canadian Mist from a hovering wine waitress, and started circulating the party ground.

He swept his eyes around the area. He was pleased with what he saw. He had never seen many of these people before, and yet he had always known them. They were all his men—tough men like him: The "Feather 'n' Bloods," the "Eyes of the Night," "Kiki de Lion," the "Caves of the Dead," the "Zuma Pillars." They were proud frat men—good people. They were always on hand to back up their brethren. And they did it right. It was an institution to them—a ritual—a great tradition that must be adhered to. Tos loved it. Real friends must be like this. These unloved outlaws of the night banded together and formed a world of their own, an establishment of their own, to give each other hope and courage and strength.

This was his place: a powerful fortress—his world—a world of brothers and friendship. It was true what they said: men don't need friendship; men need brotherhood. He hadn't expected a turnout this large. All Owlsmen wanted to grace the party—Owlsmen from far and near. He couldn't help it. With a solid reputation, he ruled his cult empire with fear and fire. His own men feared him, and his enemies feared him more. None of his men wanted to be in his bad books, so they all came in their hundreds. Though many had not been formally invited, still they came in droves. But the thanks were to his principal officers, men like Number Two, Number Seven, and Number Eight.

Ovo alone had bought ten cartons of Crown Royal blended Canadian whiskey and five cartons of Chivas Regal blended Scotch whiskey—his "miserly contribution," he called it. Black Mamba had sent in a contribution of five cartons of Seagram's Extra Dry Gin and fifty cartons of canned beer. Malik had contributed twenty-four bottles of Martell cognac. Christo One Way had assisted him with two hundred grand, doubling his earlier pledge. But it was Ebi who had done the most. She had bought him the suit he was wearing tonight, paid for the venue, contributed thirty cases of Rémy Martin cognac champagne and fifty cases of Heineken canned beer, and supplied the non-nouvelle beef, chicken, and turkey. He was not going to forget these things in a hurry.

"Lord of the Night Don Tos."

Tos turned to see a young woman in her mid-twenties in a tight body-hugging white shirt and crotch-clutching black jeans.

"Cleopatra," he said, smiling. "I didn't expect you to grace my night. I don't remember sending you an invitation"

"It doesn't matter. I don't even need it." She was attractive, very attractive, with the sort of wild good looks that can be found only in Africa.

"Where've you been these past few weeks?"

"I've been doing some traveling recently. I came back two days ago."

"That's great. Traveling looks good on you. You're becoming more beautiful."

"Well, thanks. And you too. You look very handsome."

"Thanks. But I mean what I just said."

Cleopatra smiled. "You're lying. I don't look the least beautiful. My hair is a mess, and you don't give me the room to really put on a party dress. Black happens to be the color I hate most."

"Too bad, my dear. Too bad." He pulled his cigarette pack from his pocket.

"Care for a cigarette?"

She shook her head. Tos lit a fresh cigarette for himself and smoked quietly for a minute or two.

Cleo had been his first girlfriend when he had come to the university. She was now a final-year student of sociology and a notable member of the Daughters of Jezebel, the second female gang trying to make its mark on campus.

"I heard you now have a new BMW."

Tos tried to look annoyed but just couldn't quite succeed. Not with Cleopatra.

"It's not a new BMW. Her name's Ebi Dabiri."

Cleopatra smiled. "Darling Tos, tell me everything. Is she a good lay?"

"Why are you asking?" It was common knowledge that Cleopatra was a bisexual bitch. She sucked up anything in boxer shorts, cunt and dick alike. She was always described in *Campus Digest* as "Viva," which meant "gay." "I'll not have you ask me such questions on my night."

"I don't understand myself sometimes," she said, and she sighed. "I heard that she was Dikko's girl once. Is that true?"

"Is it your business?"

"Yeah, it is, because I'm fond of you. Dikko's a very dark character. He'd probably kill the man who looked sideways at her."

"I don't want to talk about Dikko."

"Are you in love with her?"

Tos warmed to that question. "Yeah," he said softly, his eyes on the most beautiful girl in his life. She was dancing in the middle of the dance floor, her body scarcely moving in the new dance style that was now very popular. Her hips moved seductively, her legs hardly at all. She seemed to be enjoying herself. Her eyes were closed as the music blasted and swam around her. She seemed to be in a kind of peculiar personal communion with the music.

"She's beautiful," Cleopatra said, smiling.

Tos didn't smile back. He was studying Ebi, a faraway look in his eyes.

Ebi saw Tos watching her from across the dance floor. He made a motion with his eyes. She excused herself from her partner and made her way toward him.

"I think you deserve a drink after dancing about like that," he said, handing her his wineglass.

"Oh, Tos," she said sulkily. "Is that why you cut my dance short?"

The way she said it made him smile. "Baby, I want you to meet a friend of mine. Cleo, meet Ebi Dabiri. Ebi, this is Cleopatra Gyamfi."

The two women looked at each other for a second or two before they both pitched forward and touched cheeks.

"It's my pleasure, Ebi," Cleopatra said in a smoky, velvety voice.

"Mine too, Cleopatra," Ebi replied.

"I hope lover boy's not been mean on you."

Ebi shook her head. "So far so good, Tos is a correct man." He had not given her sleepless nights.

"If he does, let me know. I know how to handle him."

Ebi nodded, smiling; her expression was one of amused irony.

"Cleo's the only person who can guarantee that," Tos said, amusement written all over his face.

"That's the problem with you, Tosan. Any time I say anything serious, it's something funny to you."

Tos shook his head. "I know you meant what you just said." She looked at him, and he at her. Ebi observed the look that passed between them.

"Come on, baby; let's get on the dance floor and let the good music roll." Cleo took hold of one of Ebi's hands and led her onto the floor. The live band was now playing a popular song—"Yellow Fever" by Fela. Tos watched the two girls. They were both beautiful in their own ways.

The night was filled with smiles, and the music was jazzy. The foreign Owlsmen mingled with their Jankara brethren as one smooth, thick crowd, swaying to the heavy beat of the music. Tos moved among them like Caesar among his praetorian guards, accepting the recognition due to him, shaking hands, kissing cheeks, and giving meaningless speeches. The aromas of basted meat and alcoholic beverages, mixed with the smell of marijuana, assailed the air.

When the music changed to blues, it took Ebi less than ten minutes to break up her dance with Cleopatra.

"She's a lesbian," she said to Tos when she found him.

"I'm afraid she is, Ebi."

"You mean you knew!" The words burst from Ebi with a kind of surprise.

"Everybody knows that Cleo's gay."

Ebi was sickened. "I hated her almost immediately."

Tos didn't reply.

"She was squeezing my breasts and caressing my ass. She said I should enjoy it."

Tos smiled. "She's not a bad girl. Only a sick little beautiful girl."

"She was once your girlfriend."

"She told you that?"

"Yeah."

Tos looked at the throng of people on the dance floor. Cleopatra had found another partner.

"Yes, she was once my girl. But we broke up long ago. Come." He led her around until they found a secluded corner from which they could watch the dance floor comfortably. Not a minute later, a group of his men came over to pay their homage. They brought with them an assortment of gift items. Tos was effusive in his appreciation.

Ebi hovered around the rim of the congregation as they clustered around him.

She let her eyes comb the throng of people, screening the faces. They were all there. Some of the faces she knew; many she didn't.

In another corner of the great hall was clustered a small group of men, Jankara's own group of feathered Wizards. Every one of them seemed to be having a fun time.

"Christ—doesn't everybody look cute in their B and W?" Kadiri Muazu said, a glass of wine in his hand.

"What do you expect?" Christo One Way replied. "It's Don Tos's night."

"Yeah, it is Don Tos's night, and I'm fucking thirsty," Malik said angrily. "Don't they serve drinks at this party?"

"They do," Black Mamba said. He caught the eye of a passing waitress and signaled to her. She came over immediately. Malik ordered for a full bottle of Canadian Mist.

"Are you sure you want to take that thing alone?" Morgan Akumagba asked.

"You never said you were thirsty."

"You'll get drunk," Christo said.

"I won't, and don't blackmail me. I'm not sharing it. You can order your own. This is a free party."

"I don't know when I've had so much fun," Paxman, Owlsman Number Three, said softly. "So many beautiful people—boys and girls, *capons* and dons, black lords and beautiful jezebels—all in one hall. This is cute, man."

"Yeah, it's cute," Malik sneered. "Go and write a poem about it."

Paxman nodded. "I think that's what I would do next."

"Just look at you two," Christo said. "Drunkards."

Malik rounded on him. "How dare you call me a drunkard?"

Christo, his eyes bright with excitement, said quietly, "Malik, you're really a stupid drunkard. But don't turn around. Your girlfriend's here."

"What do you mean? I don't have a girlfriend."

"I know, but that girl you're dying for—the one you toasted in the Vee-Eye's party last time."

There was a short pause while Malik digested this. "Are you serious, Christo?"

"I mean it. She's here in person—flesh, blood, and all—and she's been here for the past two hours."

Malik turned around, and his eyes searched the crowd.

"Where is she? I can't find her."

"Over there, on the barstool. The one with the brown wig and big breasts."

"Fuck you. That's not the girl, damn you. Do you think I'm that drunk?"

Every one of them burst into laughter.

"But don't you like her?" Morgan asked.

Malik was still staring at the girl, his tongue visible on his lips. "She's not bad. I mean, her breasts are not bad."

"But are you seeing what's written there?"

Still looking at the girl, Malik replied, "What's written there? I'm not sure I can see it clearly."

"Let me see," Morgan said, and after a pause he added, "Cross my tits and prepare to die."

"You mean—" Malik looked in amazement. "You mean that's what's written across those breasts?"

All the Wizards nodded as if on cue.

"Then I think—" Malik's voice scraped—"I don't like girls with big breasts."

"What kinds of girls do you like, then?" Black Mamba asked.

"Sweet, sexy, owlishly big-eyed, big-assed beauties. No big breasts for me. But they must be bad. Excuse me guys; I think my drink's here." He collected the bottle of drink from the girl, poured a generous measure for himself, tasted it, and nodded his satisfaction. "Excuse me, guys; this place is pretty damn hot. I want to take some air outside."

After he was gone, Paxman said, "I think he wants to drink that thing all by himself."

"I think that's a foolish idea," Morgan said. "He'll end up with the mother of all hangovers."

"There are too many people at this party," Black Mamba said.

"Tos is too damn popular, that's why."

"Where's that tray of peanuts?" Kadiri asked.

"Over there," Morgan replied.

"Damn. Call her. I could do with some peanuts."

Morgan signaled the waiter and mimed his needs. The jacketed male waiter nodded and was lost in the crowd.

"Has anybody seen Al-Mustafa? I've not seen him all evening," Paxman said.

"I saw him earlier in the evening," Christo replied. "He's somewhere with a girl, I believe."

"Anybody want more drinks?" Black Mamba asked.

"I sure would like a nice, cold big bottle of Guinness right now," Christo said.

"Me, too," Morgan added.

"A Budweiser for me," Paxman said.

"Heineken for me," Kadiri said. "It's high time I switch to beer."

Black Mamba nodded. "I'll get them. I'm sure I would like a nice, cold big bottle of Guinness myself," he said, and he left. He spent a short time away and came back in the company of Frank White, Owlsman Number Six, (the Hammer), and a wine steward. The drinks were distributed, and the peanuts shared among them.

"Have you seen Linda?" Frank White asked Morgan. Frank White wasn't his real name. It was Franklin Akuwa. But "Frank White" was what they popularly called him, though some people referred to him as Frankie Pentangeli (after Mario Puzo's Mafia character); but the great majority called him Frank White. And the name stuck to him. In the Black Owls, when they gave their members such a nickname, it was a kind of acknowledgment in a great way. A special honor.

"For Christ's sake, is Linda here?" Morgan cried.

"Yeah."

"Fuck shit. Who invited her?"

"I did, man," Frank said quietly. "I told her to bring some of her girlfriends to add color to the groove, and true to type, she did. And not just her friends here, but some of her friends over from UniBen. I never thought she would."

"Why the fuck did you do such a damn fool thing?" Morgan wailed.

All the other Wizards were watching him, and they were all enjoying his discomfort.

Frank grasped his arm firmly. "Hey, cool your voice down. I think she's coming right over."

Morgan turned around and saw the slim, wide-hipped pretty girl walking toward them. There was a small smile on her lips.

"Hi," she greeted them all with a charming smile.

"Hi," Morgan said, trying to avoid looking at her.

"Aren't you happy to see me, Morgan?"

His gaze rested on her eyes. "I'm mightily glad."

"No, you're not," she said quietly, almost casually. "It seems I'm no longer attractive in your eyes."

Morgan sighed. "No, you're still the most beautiful woman in the school. In this gathering, you're the most attractive. You're by far more beautiful than the Grand Wizard's girlfriend."

Linda smiled. "You're not convincing anymore, Morgan. You despise me. I know. I can feel it. I can see it in your eyes."

Morgan shook his head. "You're impossible."

"It's the truth. Don't deny it. Say it. It doesn't matter."

She was once a girl he had pined for, a long time ago. Most of the Wizards still had the fresh recollection of the time and devotion he had wasted on her. But things hadn't worked out. And that was because another brother, who had been Number Three then, had been interested in her. One of the Black Owls' cardinal rules was this: "Brothers don't chase the same girl." As a junior member, he had been forced to step down. And not because he hadn't had all it would take to win her, but because a superior brother was involved.

"I brought some of my friends. There's a very nice girl I've reserved for you. I'm sure you'll like her."

Morgan listened, looking straight ahead.

"Her name is Gladys."

"I don't need her," Morgan said coldly. "I'm not looking for a girl. I can—"

"Is she beautiful?" Kadiri cut in.

"Yeah. Very beautiful."

"If Morgan doesn't want her, I do. I'm free, available, single, and still searching," Kadiri said with all the excitement and wonder of a ten-year-old.

"Shit. I don't think I want to hear this," Morgan said with a small smile.

Keme joined them at that instant.

"So this is where you guys are all hiding," he said, shaking hands all around.

"Linda here's got a date for Morgan, and he's groaning like he's got the gripes."

"Where is she?"

"Over there."

"Point her out to me. If she's okay, I'll convince Morgan to talk to her and probably take her seriously. But if she's not, I'll send her home immediately."

"You won't dare," Linda said with sure confidence. But all the same, she raised her hand and signaled to a group of girls. A girl broke out of the group and came over.

"Hello," Keme said and shook her hand warmly. "This here's my brother. I think he wants to meet you."

The girl looked at Morgan, and the Owlsman let his face register a smile of welcome.

"Lady, let me introduce myself properly. My name's Morgan. What's your name?"

The girl smiled shyly. "My name's Gladys."

They eyed each other for a brief moment. The others had formed a circle around them.

"It's good of you to grace our party, Gladys."

"I'm honored to be here."

"Gladys," Keme said quickly "This guy here's been dying to meet you. I think he likes you. In fact, he wants to ask you to dance with him. How about that? Would you like to dance with him?"

The boy and the girl gazed at each other wordlessly. Everybody, as if commanded by a secret signal, burst into laughter.

At last Morgan turned to the girl. "I'm sure I would like to dance with you, Gladys, but I think my brother has had too much to drink right now, and he's not on his best behavior. Can I get you a drink?"

"If it's not too much trouble."

"No, it's not," Morgan said, and he took hold of her hand. As he was leading her away, Kadiri said loudly enough for both of them to hear, "I said I'm free, available, and still searching. Gladys, don't you like single guys?"

But the boy and the girl ignored him.

The MC said something just then, and as if from little children, shrill whistling, clapping, and deafening owl-like hooting echoed across the great hall as over one thousand Owlsmen—the feathered and the unfeathered, the deadly and the harmless—gave Don Tos the traditional Owlsman's greetings.

While the men were still clapping and hooting, Ovo climbed the platform where the MC stood, took the mike from him, and raised his hand for silence. It was a few minutes later that the great hall became silent.

Without preamble, Ovo addressed the crowd. "A good leader is an asset to an association that always wants to put its members' minds at rest. In the person of Don Tos, we have found such a leader." Ovo paused for a moment and gave Tos a frank and level look. "He's reliable and experienced. He's the bedrock of our strength in this school. He's the biggest *factor*." The last word was pronounced meaningfully.

There was a thunderous applause and deafening owl-like hooting.

In the quiet corner where he sat with Ebi, Tos smiled and whispered something to her. She elbowed him playfully.

The hall was silent again. Ovo resumed: "Here in Jankara, we call him Picasso. We call him so because leadership, to him, is like a work of art. It's all about beauty and style and coordination. We owe a great deal to him. I present to you the greatest authority outside the school authority."

The ovation swelled into the night, two miles in all directions. Ovo stepped off the platform, placed the mike in Tos's hand, and led him back to the stage. The Owlsmen were all screaming and chanting and clapping.

Don Tos looked at them but did not speak. He waited three minutes before the hall was silent again. All pairs of eyes were focused on him in quiet wonderment. Next to the late Don Bosco, he was the greatest figure in the cultic history of Owlsmen.

"This is a great family with a great history," he said, and he smiled at them paternally.

"Hear! Hear!" chorused the audience.

"And I'm proud to be a part of this great family."

"I too!" shouted an unfamiliar voice, and everybody laughed good-naturedly.

"And I must say this: I'm a proud Owlsman. And I'll always be an Owlsman first, last, and forever."

There was a great applause that lasted for two minutes. He continued.

"Owlsmen—there's nothing I would not do to prevent any further suffering or intimidation of my brethren."

A voice in the crowd yelled, "You've done it before! You'll do it again!"

Tos smiled. "Yes. I would do it again. The Great Owl knows I would."

There was loud cheering for the next five minutes. Tos held up his hand for quiet, and there was silence. "Any hand raised against any Owlsman is raised against every Owlsman in this school. Not only Owlsmen in this zone, but Owlsmen everywhere. And as Owlsmen, we will defend our own any time, any day. I have spoken."

One of the most excited Owlsmen, who was evidently drunk and could not curtail his emotion, ran onto the raised platform and kissed Tos's shoes. "M'lurd, I'll defend you with every breath of my life."

Tos smiled, bent low, and patted the man's shoulder. "You're an Owlsman indeed." He paused. His charisma was electrifying. "My personal ambition is for the Black Owls to become the most sought-after fraternity in the whole of Africa. I believe it can be done. But the only way to do this is to consolidate our positions in our respective schools. If you can hold onto your school and I hold mine, I don't see why it can't be done."

In the quiet corner where she sat, Ebi assessed the faces of the Owlsmen. They all seemed to be hanging on every word that was issuing from Tos's mouth.

"He's good, isn't he?" a voice whispered close to her ear. She turned, and her eyes fell on Keme.

"Keme," she said softly.

His hard, dark eyes took in a long and frankly appreciative appraisal of her figure in the black-and-white outfit.

"Are you having a good time?"

"Yes. And you?"

"I'm not complaining."

Ebi looked at him but did not speak. She was vaguely aware of an odd note in Keme's voice.

He was looking at her with something close to flirtatious, open admiration.

"What're they doing up there?"

Keme half-turned and looked at the platform. "It looks like a toast."

"Oh. And I don't even have a drink."

"Don't worry," he said. He strolled to the nearby table and confiscated a half bottle of Rémy Martin and two glasses.

"A toast," said Ovo, and he raised his glass. All the men and ladies in the room raised their glasses. Ebi and Keme raised their glasses also. "We give you a toast, Big Eye Don Tos. To the strength of the brotherhood. Cheers!"

They all chorused "Cheers!" and drank as one.

CHAPTER TEN

Two days later, the news was all over the campus and the university town that Don Tos and Akpoebi Dabiri were now the hottest couple on campus.

On that fateful day, a Monday in early February a few days after the Grand Wizard's Night, Dr. Ubangha sent word to Tos to see him in his office at ten o' clock in the morning. Tos was a little worried when he got the message.

He came to the office at a quarter past ten, right after his first class of the day. There he met Mrs. Osifo. She told him that the lecturer was in the inner sanctum.

Tos took the polished brass knocker, designed in the shape of a human hand, and tapped loudly. He waited a few moments and tapped again.

"Yes?" a soft voice answered from within.

"It's me, Tosan Mayuku."

"Oh, come in."

Tos opened the door, stepped inside, and nearly stumbled. The lecturer's long arm shot out and steadied him.

"Good day, sir," Tos said.

"Good day. You're Tosan Mayuku?"

"I'm Tosan," Tos replied.

"Then come in and sit down."

There was a profusion of leather furniture, couches, and easy chairs. Tos took one of the armchairs, which was apparently made of some excellent cowhide.

"What can I get you, Tosan—spirits, mineral water, wine? You name it."

What can he get me? Tos thought. *The last I came here, I was not even offered the hospitality of resting my ass, not to talk of light refreshment. Ebi must be something very special to him.*

"Nothing, thank you."

"Really?" The lecturer took on a fatherly, all-embracing air.

"Yeah. Nothing," Tos replied, and he sat back, seemingly satisfied.

The lecturer went behind the huge desk and sat down heavily. Framed behind him was a large picture of a much younger Vincent Ubangha in a convocation gown.

"How's your day, Tosan?" the lecturer asked, looking at Tos with bright, hawk-like eyes.

"It's okay."

The lecturer cleared his throat.

"Tosan, tell me, what do you know about Miss Akpoebi Dabiri?"

Tos spread his long, powerful hands. His brown eyes gleamed, and there seemed to be a slight movement in the corner of his cheek.

"She's my friend."

"Just a friend, right?"

"No. She's my girlfriend. My lover."

The lecturer nodded, and his eyelids dropped as he looked away from Tos's dark face. "Is there any other thing you might want to tell me about her?"

"Nothing," Tos said. "Except that I happened to see in the current edition of *Campus Digest* that it was rumored you had a kind of relationship with her once."

"Is that all?"

Tos stretched out his long legs. "That's all."

The lecturer nodded again, and they were silent for a moment. Then he said quietly, as if he were talking to himself, "Ebi's a very decent girl."

"You're quite right, sir."

The lecturer nodded and gazed at him for a long time.

"I've investigated, Tosan, and I found out that you're a bright boy." Tos listened to what the man said but made no comment. The lecturer continued. "But I would keep to the point. We're talking about Ebi. And I think you ought to know that I loved that girl. I love her very much. We broke up over nothing. It was a terrible loss to me. But it's a loss I'm prepared to get back." The lecturer got up and walked over to Tos and patted him affectionately on his shoulder.

"I heard that you're her new boyfriend. But not to worry; I'm prepared to compensate you for the inconvenience." He pointed at a small parcel on top of a filing cabinet close to his chair. "That's fifty grand. You can take it and forget about the girl."

The room was silent.

Tos half-closed his eyes and breathed out sharply. "Is this the point of my coming in here?" he asked softly.

"There's no other reason, boy."

"I see," Tos said. Gravely, he regarded the lecturer. "So the idea's to cut a deal with you and forgo the girl, right?"

"You're on the point."

Tos looked at the lecturer with something close to contempt.

"You really went for this one, sir."

"Yeah. I love the girl."

"It's hard to believe," Tos said in a low voice.

"Believe it."

Tos laughed and then looked at the lecturer fixedly.

"You have a reputation in this school with the girls. Not many of them would believe you if you would say you loved them."

The lecturer moved slowly back to his part of the table. He sat down. "Should I increase the ante—say, eighty grand?"

"This isn't a game, sir," Tos replied.

"If it's not a game, then what do you propose we call it?"

Tos said nothing. Eighty grand. *Sweet hot pie.* He could simply collect the money and still end up dating the girl. There was nothing the lecturer or anybody could do about it. She was his woman. She loved him.

"You're too talented a young man," Dr. Ubangha said and leaned back, crossing one slim leg over the other. "The world needs you. Needs your talent greatly."

Tos showed his teeth in what could pass for a smile. "What has talent got to do with the conversation?"

"I wouldn't like anything to distract you from your chosen course in life." He paused for a brief moment and then continued. "In this life, we must believe that we're gifted for something—for a particular field of expertise—and this field must be attained at whatever cost. I want you to get used to that idea. Don't let the girls of this world distract you."

"Is that a threat or advice?"

"Interpret it any way you like. It's for your own good."

"Okay. I love the girl. She's the love of my life."

The lecturer's lips parted in a smile. "I'll up the ante. A hundred thousand and a two-one degree. Is it okay now?"

Tos closed his eyes. The HOD waited while he thought.

Dr. Vincent Ubangha, when he chose to be, had the charm of Bill Clinton. He was always sleeping with his female students and victimizing their boyfriends. He could hypnotize most girls into believing every word he said and discourage their boyfriends from going out with them. It was a gift he used efficiently. He was completely crazy when women were concerned. If he suspected that a certain boy was going out with a certain girl for whom he had the yen, he'd invite the young man to his office. Then he'd ask mild questions and look at the young man's face and dig about in the endless chain of interrogation, probing. But his eyes would always remain quiet, and his voice soft, and his manner Clintonian. In doing this, he spent money like water. He was romantic, but he was also shrewd. He'd buy the boyfriend off (if he was willing to be bought) or threaten him (if he was a weakling and able to be threatened), and then he'd spoil the girls with expensive gift items. He had the power of making every woman he met into his property, and their boyfriends into his enemies.

"Are you playing?"

Tos said nothing.

The lecturer looked at him, surprised. "You've never had an offer like this before in your life, have you? Not even for your paintings. How can you possibly turn it down? One hundred thousand—what're you thinking?"

Tos grinned. "I've had better deals. The National Visual Arts Council's prize was five hundred grand. I earned it. It's a fine deal. There's no catch to it."

The lecturer's eyelids lowered as though he was contemplating something. "You're right there. But it won't guarantee you a two-one degree. If you take this deal, I might be able to recommend your work for the upcoming International Foundation of African Students' Arts Competition."

Tos took a deep breath. The IFASA's awards were an opportunity for every art student to expose his work and explore the works of other gifted artists from every country in Africa. Most students would fall over themselves to have their work endorsed by their school. He shook his head. "I'm not interested in this talk." The softness of his words and the way he said them, revealed the serene confidence of a man who had worked through the mathematics and seen the solutions.

The lecturer looked at him significantly. "Boy, let me talk to you man to a man. Whether you like it or not, I want that girl."

Tos looked at him quietly. Dr. Ubangha was using a tone of voice that smelled of violence.

"Give her the money," he said with a shrug. "Maybe she'll change her mind."

"She doesn't care about my money—or anybody's money, for that matter."

"Then what do you want me to do?"

"It's simple. Tell her you're no longer interested in the relationship—at all. If you can do that, it'll shatter her. She'll come to her senses. She'll come back to me."

Tos stared intently at the lecturer's face. "I'm sorry. I can't help you, sir."

"I want her back." The lecturer's hostility was unmistakable. "If you don't release her, I'll finish you up in the gutter, whether you like it or not. I'll string you up one way or the other."

Tos studied the lecturer curiously. *What's the point of all this talk?* he asked himself. *What can Dikko do? He might set a couple of toughs after me—and that's the worst he can do. And what's that? What would it amount to if they ever found me: lynching? Or a knife stuck in my gut?* He shook his head knowingly. He was not afraid of a crowd. He could always look after himself.

A whole minute passed before either of them spoke again. It was the lecturer who broke the silence.

"Do we understand ourselves, boy?"

Tos smiled. "I'm afraid not, sir."

Dr. Vincent Ubangha was annoyed. "I hope you know the consequence of what you're doing."

Tos's voice was cool, almost mocking, when he said, "I know what I'm doing."

Vincent Ubangha stared at the boy across from him. He was annoyed and charmed at the same time by the courage and coolness of the young man.

"Then you're not afraid of dying, young man," he said meaningfully.

The young man blinked, his eyes narrowed. Carefully he said, "Let me get this straight: Am I to take it that you represent a threat to my personal safety?"

The older man grinned, showing a flash of strong white teeth. "If you've not done anything wrong, then you've nothing to worry about."

Tos nodded understandingly. "Believe me, I'm not remotely worried. I can take care of myself."

"I'm sure you can, young man, but what really concerns me is the fact that you can't predict when and how you'll die."

"You don't really imagine I'm in any danger, do you, sir?"

The lecturer eyed him for some time and then shrugged. "Are you afraid to die?"

Tos listened to the silence that followed the question.

"I can take care of myself. Don't try anything funny. Don't forget who I am."

"Tosan, you have no idea just how serious I am."

The young man mooned about this for a while, his eyes clouded with thoughts. "Does she know about this meeting?"

"Not yet."

"I'll let her know you're still crazy for her."

"Nothing's going to stop me from having her."

"I'll let her know about that also." Tos stood up stiffly. "I have to leave now."

"Sure." Vincent Ubangha climbed awkwardly to his feet as if climbing out of a bathtub. "Think over what we've just discussed." He led Tos to the door. "There's one thing I should like you to consider seriously. Some people die recklessly for no just reason." His tone was casual. With that, he swung open the door and motioned the young man to leave.

Tos knew by the tone of voice that he was not simply talking for talking's sake. *Could he really arrange to kill me?* he thought. A cold fear chilled his insides. For the first time in his life, he felt intimidated by somebody on the school campus. "You can't do anything to me," he said quietly. "Don't forget who I am. I have friends in very important positions inside and outside this school, in the corridors of power and in the dark parts of the forests. Don't do anything funny unless you want this school to be razed to the ground…unless you want to gamble with your life."

"Deep waters are for those who can swim. Don't get beyond your depth. Remember that always. Now get out of my office."

Tos nodded and stepped out of the office. He controlled his smile until he was well down the corridor. It was time he should be watching his back more closely.

Dr. Ubangha closed the door angrily. His face was a death mask. He stepped out from the doorway and started wandering about the room, his thoughts far away. He mumbled incoherently to himself. *Nonsense! Ebi made a poor choice. A very poor choice. An Itsekiri student, that's who she fell for. It's too bad. There must be a solution to the whole sordid mess. What am I going to do to this boy?* Tos was an Itsekiri. The Ijaws hated the Itsekiris. They would kill them whenever they had the chance. In the crisis in the creeks, Dr. Ubangha had heard of Ijaw fathers killing their own children because they resembled their Itsekiri wives. Today, if you give an Ijaw man a hundred grand to waste an Itsekiri man, he will worship you. He will even bankroll his ballplayers. Dr. Ubangha knew the ballplayers would do the job. They'd do it well. If they couldn't do it, then he was going to invite the Egbesu Boys. That was it. That would be the final step.

Dr. Ubangha knew Tosan must be stopped at all costs.

CHAPTER ELEVEN

"He offered you money?" Ebi asked. A look of surprise and incredulity was on her face.

Tos nodded. "A hundred grand."

"A hundred grand." Ebi had to laugh. "You must be joking."

"I wish I was joking, baby. He literally said he's going to kill me."

Tos heard an intake of breath from her.

"I think we should have a quiet talk, Ebi."

It was as if she didn't hear him. "Vincent won't do a thing like that, Tos."

"That's what you say. He's threatening me."

Ebi shrugged. "He's jealous."

"Yeah, he's jealous. That's why it's dangerous." Tos's tight-lipped expression was an ugly sight. "If he's jealous, then he might do something really stupid."

Ebi said nothing. She was conscious of one fact: jealousy builds the fastest of bridges between pure enmity and dark hatred. Many times it fuses the two diseased reasons. A man can do anything when under the spell of jealousy.

"What do we do now?" Ebi finally asked.

"I'm looking for some information about him."

"What kind of information?"

A muscle twitched in Don Tos's dark cheek, and his voice, when he spoke, was cold. "Like if he's affiliated with any of the campus frat gangs, if he's a sponsor of any of the groups—things like that."

"I don't know. All I know is that he has spies everywhere."

"Do you know any of his spies?"

"I can't say I do. But I know he was spying on me while we were still dating."

"And you don't know any of his boys."

"I know two of them. Facially. I don't know their names—not even their departments."

There was a short silence. "I could guess who his boys are," Tos said quietly.

"Could you?"

He nodded. Ebi thought about this for a moment.

"Then what's going to happen?" Her tone betrayed her state of mind.

"I'll advise them not to do anything stupid."

Ebi looked at him tensely, an unspoken question in her mind.

"I hope you're not going to get into a cult fight because of me?"

Tos hesitated. She had been bold enough to come right to the point.

"No, baby. It'll not come to that."

"Is that a promise?"

"Yeah. I promise that I'll not again get into a cult fight," he said, and he put his arms around her.

They heard the front door open. It was the housekeeper. She greeted both of them and went straight to the kitchen.

"I've got some business to undertake. Are you coming with me?"

"Where's that?"

"Downtown. I have to see some of my men."

"I'll help prepare dinner."

"Suit yourself. I might eat outside though."

"Okay. I'm coming with you."

"Then tell the cook that we won't be home for dinner."

Ebi nodded and went to the kitchen. She came out almost immediately.

"Can we go now?"

"Yes." Tos's answer came slowly. He shepherded her out of the room.

By seven o'clock they were in the heart of the town. The men with whom Tos chatted on the steps of the Clique were his gang members. They stood close together in a tight circle. They spoke for only ten minutes, and Tos said good night to them in his usual quiet manner, using the sparsest of words. His men watched him climb gently down the steps and cross the forecourt.

Ebi's Porsche waited for him. He got behind the wheel, and the small car disappeared smoothly in the direction of the village.

Tos drove for five minutes without saying a word. At last Ebi said, "Where are we going?"

"Bray's Kitchen." Tos's voice was subdued.

"What are you planning on doing next?"

"Nothing." The reply was curt.

"I hope I've not offended you in any way?" She was worried, he knew. This whole business with Vincent Ubangha had her caught up in a whirlwind. She knew it was all her fault.

"No, baby, you've not offended me in any way." He suddenly reached over with his free hand and took her hand.

As the car sped along the major highway that cut across the town toward the village, Tos thought about his talk with the HOD. He'd thought of the whole thing over and over again. The lecturer could be a bad guy. There was always an element of risk, no matter how infinitesimal. He had made his own assessment of it and come to the conclusion that the lecturer could pay other people to waste him—maybe not around the school environment, but they would gun for him all the same.

At the restaurant, a cheerful waitress greeted them. She ushered them to Tos's favorite table. Tos ordered *egusi* soup with assorted bush meat and *eba*. Ebi ordered Mexican chicken with vegetable fried rice and Russian salad. Before the meals were served, Bray came over to pay his homage. He and Tos shared two jokes before he left them alone.

"I have something for you," Tos said after he was gone.

"What is it?" Ebi replied.

"A small surprise," he said, and he unceremoniously pushed a small black box into her hand. "Open it."

She held it as if it contained a strange insect.

"Go on, open it," he prodded. There was an urgency in his voice she had never heard before.

She sprung the box open and stared at a small, beautiful ring with a glittering white stone.

"Wow!" she exclaimed. "It's beautiful."

"I knew you'd like it," Tos said quietly.

"Oh, Tos…it's too expensive."

"Forget about the cost. Put it on," he commanded.

She did so. It suited her finger beautifully. He took her hand and stared at the ring for a brief moment, and then his eyes rested on hers.

"Five thousand miles from this place, I guess, is a city you Americans call the Big Apple. If we get there, will you marry me?"

Ebi's eyes widened. Stunned, she couldn't say a thing. She sat there staring into his face, into his eyes. There was something in his eyes she hadn't seen before.

She nodded at last, unable to utter a word.

"Say it. I want to hear it."

Ebi's eyes closed momentarily and then stared squarely at him. "I'll marry you if we get to New York."

Tos nodded and pressed her finger to his lips.

At that moment, their order was placed before them. Tos was hungry, and he attacked the meal immediately after the waiter removed the covers. Ebi was not eating. She was studying the ring on her middle finger. With a feeling of love, she smiled to herself. This was an engagement. Tos had really shown that he loved her—that he cared for her and appreciated her. She was happy.

"Eat up," he commanded, half of the *eba* dish already gone. "We're going to the newest pub in town to celebrate."

Ebi wasn't in the mood to eat. She was just over the moon with happiness. But obediently, she ate half her dinner. The food, so professionally prepared by the seasoned cooks in Brays Kitchen, was bland and tasteless on her tongue.

After dinner, she offered to drive them to the new joint. It was on a small street near the old local government secretariat, a stone's throw from Vincent Ubangha's residence. It was a busy street with many shops and blocks of residential flats built some thirty years ago. She parked the car and followed Tos into the spacious interior.

It was called the Greenhouse Restaurant and Wine Bar, a neoclassic bar a little bigger than the average millionaire's dining room, with three tiers and a fanciful alfresco dining area outside. The interior was airy with a lovers' atmosphere, with wooden tables, fresh flowers, fancy ceiling fans, and dimly lit neon. On the walls hung delicate nude paintings and exquisite framed petit point designs.

"What a charming place," Ebi said.

Tos nodded, looking around. "It's cute, isn't it?" he said, holding a chair for her.

"Yeah. I like it."

They were seated now. Gentle jazz played in the background.

A competent-looking, beautifully uniformed waitress came to take their order. Tos ordered champagne and roasted chicken.

"Where's your boss?" he asked when the lady had brought their order.

"He's upstairs."

"Tell him his boss is here."

Tos poured the wine, and they toasted. They were on their second refill when someone coughed respectfully near their table. Tos turned and looked up into the handsome face of Tombrifa Opubeni.

"Don Tos! I can't believe it. I'm happy to see you." They shook hands.

"I'm glad to see you too, Tom."

"You're looking well."

"So are you. How's life?"

"Life's cool, brother. Cool. Long time, no see."

"That's life."

They broke the handshake. For the first time, he noticed Tos's companion.

"This is my woman—Ebi Dabiri. Ebi, this is Tombrifa Opubeni. He's the immediate younger brother of Zuokumor, the fellow I was telling you about the other day."

"I remember," Ebi said. "I'm glad to meet you."

"Me too," Tom said. There was nothing but pleasure in his face as he reached out and took both her hands in his. "You must be my sister from another mother."

"I didn't know I had a brother," Ebi said, smiling.

He smiled with her. "You've known him tonight." He drew out a chair and sat down. "So what's between both of you, if I may ask?"

"Ebi and I were in the mood of celebrating our engagement. What better place to do it than her brother's joint? What do you think?"

Tombrifa Opubeni looked comically stricken.

"You mean you're engaged to this ugly chap?"

Ebi laughed easily. "Yeah."

"Do you know that he's an Itsekiri?"

Ebi nodded. "He told me."

Tom made a face. "And you still love him?"

Ebi looked at the engagement ring on her finger and nodded again.

"Are you serious?"

"Of course, yes." There was a faint smile on Ebi's face.

"And you want to marry him?"

"Is that inconceivable?"

Tom was silent for a moment. He shook his head.

"We're engaged; we love each other," Ebi said seriously.

"I'm sorry, guys," Tom said." I didn't mean to make you both uncomfortable."

"It's okay, Tom. Remember: I'm a thick-skinned chap."

"You're a tough guy, all right," Tom said, and he looked at them gravely. "The stories from Warri are not encouraging. You're engaged at the wrong time. Emotions are still very high, and parents are apt to ask. Besides, you're on the list."

Ebi blinked, not quite understanding what Tom's last sentence meant.

Tos drew a deep breath and exhaled slowly. He was fed up with the story of Warri. The oil city was falling into very grave disorder, and he knew that if the violent trends were not checked, the city would remain in that state for a long time. The inaction of the federal government was the most painful part of the whole madness. Itsekiris were killed everywhere—in their homes—outside their homes. Over thirty of their communities had been torched, and some of them illegally and forcefully occupied. They had become refugees in their own homeland. Yet they believed it was the duty of the Nigerian government to restore law and order. And the violence continued. All over the riverine communities, there were scores of attacks on the homes of Itsekiri people. Villages were wiped out. Businesses were crippled. Lots of companies, such as Shell and Chevron and Total, had closed shop in the area. Unemployment had become widespread. Bitter-looking and discontented youths from the Escravos area flooded the streets of Warri. The Nigerian government and its security agents were not overly bothered.

Then his mother had been brutally killed. And that was what had gotten him actively involved in the crisis.

There were two ethnic forces at war with the Itsekiris. First there were the Urhobos (Warri Urhobos) on the Warri mainland and the Ijaws on the waterways. Tos knew there and then that if they were to regain lost ground, the two forces would have to be repelled. That was when he, together with some of the oil-producing communities' youth leaders had called a secret congress of Itsekiri youths. A good many other community youth leaders had attended. Many of these youth leaders were passionate and hotheaded. Wealthy businessmen and contractors were there. Even redundant youths who had been laid off unceremoniously by these oil companies had attended. Itsekiri student and graduate associations had been ably represented. They all had been determined to draw up a master plan of counterattack. The idea had excited them. Donations had been made freely. At the end of the day, it had run into millions of naira. And at first, it was what provided the youths with valuable and dangerous weapons. And that night, they had created the Warri Vanguard. It was a volunteer effort—a body of very angry youths, midway between militia and guerilla, Itsekiris armed and hastily organized for the defense of the lives, towns, and properties of the Itsekiri people. And they were led, if they could be said to be led by anybody, by him, Don Tos. That was what had created his image in Warri and put his name on the wanted list of the Ijaws. It was also the cause of the quarrel he had with Keme. It was Keme's belief that Tos had utilized Owlsmen's resources in fighting against the Ijaw people.

Tos had been popular at first, but his popularity had declined rapidly. He was sidelined by the more radical elements, the Agbukumasa and Jenekpo Boys factions of the Warri Vanguard and the consequences of their actions had become too much for him to bear. He'd had to resign and return to campus. But his name still topped the wanted list Tombrifa referred to.

"The crisis will soon end," Tos said at last.

"You're the greatest optimist I've met this year," Tom said somberly. "The crisis is the oldest crisis in the country."

"I heard there's some kind of peace talk going on. That's why it'll soon end."

"What peace talk is that?" Tombrifa said quickly. "Don't believe whatever those politicians are saying on TV." His voice was gloomy. "Ijaws and Itsekiris have been holding peace meetings since the crisis began several years ago. Between you and me, we know peace talks are not leading us anywhere. Ijaws are still killing Itsekiris, and Itsekiris are still killing Ijaws."

There was some moment of silence.

"What a charming place you have here," Ebi said, trying to divert the conversation.

Tombrifa smiled. "You like it?"

"It's beautiful."

Tom nodded, his eyes going around the bar room. It was almost filled with people. The music issuing from the concealed sound system was cool and soothing.

"Your boyfriend's very talented," Tom said, and he pointed to the walls. "He did those paintings and those other designs himself." He spoke quietly, but there was an undercurrent of real reverence in his voice. "He has great talent. He did these things free of charge. Imagine that—beautiful paintings like these, free of charge."

Tos smiled weakly and then shook his head. "You're a pot of shit, Tom."

"What a charming picture of Tombrifa Opubeni."

"By the way, have you heard from Zuokumor lately?" The question was meant to divert the discussion.

"Yeah, he phoned last week."

"When is he coming home?"

Tom shook his head. "Zuokumor's firmly settled that he's not even contemplating coming back home. He's planning on marrying a German lady—Helga Halfman or something."

"Helga Kaufman. He told me the last time I phoned him." There was an awkward pause. "I want to ask you a few questions."

Tom looked at him, halfway between curiosity and suspicion. "What do you want to know?"

"Do you know Dikko?"

"Sure."

"I heard he dines here regularly."

"Sometimes."

"Do you know anything about his eyes?"

Tom looked at Tos, stone-faced. He understood. "What's this all about?"

Tos didn't take his eyes off him.

"I want a word with his eyes. I was told that he uses here as a meeting point or something."

Tom shook his head. "I don't know anything about that."

"You know, Tom. Give me their names. I only want their names. And I want them now." Tos's voice and manner had changed. What he'd just said was no request. It was an order, and Tombrifa was conscious of it.

He looked straight at Tos. *No names,* he wanted to say. By tradition, he should not give away such information. What the patrons of his restaurant did within the walls of the restaurant was confidential. But he knew he couldn't refuse. This was a man who had risked his life for Zuokumor once. For a brief, awkward moment, he was tongue-tied.

"If you want to protect them, good for you."

It was a threat. Tom knew it. He managed a weak, embarrassed laugh. "You know I can't give this information."

Tos inclined his head to one side. "You can't, or won't? Which one is it?"

Tom's mind raced. He knew he was boxed in. "Okay, I'll tell you. Who exactly are you looking for?"

"Three names will do."

Tom hesitated for a brief moment, but finally he said, "There's Kelly Okoro, Oje Ehime, and Kraks Idonije. Kelly's a Brownie, Oje's a PB, and Kraks is a Roundhead. Kraks, I believe, is in your department. Ehime's in Biochem—"

"Thank you," Tos said. He'd gotten what he wanted.

"I'll leave you two to your privacy now," Tom said, and he stood up.

"Yeah."

"Bye, Ebi. And thank you, Don Tos—for bringing her here. I'd love to have her here more often."

Tos nodded and waved him away.

* * *

"I need another drink."

Ebi didn't answer. They had been in the bar for close to two hours now, and Tos was already drunk.

"I said I need another drink, babe."

"Come on, Tos," she said quietly. "You're drunk already."

"Who told you I'm drunk? I am as conscious as everybody in this hellhole."

"I know, but you're drunk all the same."

"You should not be talking as to what I must drink."

"There's nothing to be upset about," Ebi said pleasantly.

"Really?" Tos was staring at her. "You're denying me my drink, and yet there's nothing to get upset about? I think your imagination is running away with you."

Ebi shook her head and sighed. "Tos, this is our evening. Do you want to spoil it or what?"

Tos smiled reassuringly. "I'll not spoil it, angel. Trust me."

Ebi stared at him for a long moment.

"What's the matter with you, woman? You don't believe me?"

Ebi tried to think how to answer question without annoying him. "I'm all right. And I believe you."

Tos nodded and said quietly, "Can I get that drink now?"

Ebi regarded him and chuckled.

"Why are you laughing?"

"How I wish you could see your ugly horse face."

For a moment, Tos screwed up his eyes and opened them, as if unsure of the lady sitting opposite him.

"Me. Resemble a horse, eh?"

"No, you resemble an artist."

"No. A painter, that's who I am. A painter. A famous painter. Picasso's kinsman."

His voice was very loud. It attracted the couple sitting at the next table.

Ebi leaned across the table and lowered her voice. "You're making an ass of yourself."

"An ass is a kind of stupid animal. Even stupider than a goat."

Ebi hurriedly glanced around. A few people were looking at them, listening. The others managed the right attitude of indifference. Tombrifa was nowhere in sight. She lowered her voice further.

"Tos, it's time for us to go."

"Go? Go where?"

"Home, of course."

"I…what's wrong with you? You want to jilt me because I drank a couple glasses of wine?"

Ebi moaned as if in physical pain.

Tos learned over and stroked her hair. "Mama, cool it. All I need is just a little drink. I know what I'm doing."

"You're drunk," she said angrily.

"It's not as bad as you think."

"Drinks are dangerous; do you know that?" Ebi's voice was soft and soothing now. "With your talent, you don't need alcohol. It'll rob you of your brain."

Tos laughed. "You're wrong. It inspires me. That's what it does to me."

Ebi's eyes made a slow assessment of all the other patrons of the bar. Most of them were furtively looking at them now.

"You're making a scene. Do you know that?" The cold way she said these words cut through Tos.

"Hey guys," he announced loudly. "I never argue with this lady. She's my mama. If she says it's time to go home, then it's time to go home."

They left the bar at a quarter past eleven. Ebi started him up and led him into the night. With half his weight on her, his arm around her waist, his steps weren't quite a stagger. She steered him through the partial darkness and into her car.

"Please, sweetheart," Tos said in his drunken stupor. "Drive slowly."

"Don't worry. I'll get you home safe and sound," Ebi said reassuringly.

Tos took a compact disc from the glove compartment and punched it into the car stereo. Then he rolled down the window, and cold air blasted his face. The car vibrated. Tupac's voice filled the car at maximum volume.

"We gonna get all you, motherfucker! All you motherfuckers, fuck you!" Tos sang at the top of his voice. Ebi looked at him from the corner of her eyes, but she said nothing.

He continued singing: "We'll make sure all your kids don't grow!"

But he fell asleep before they arrived at her apartment. She woke him up with him murmuring incoherently. "Can't you let a man have a moment of rest?" He cocked his head to one side. "What's happened to my music?"

"It played itself out."

"Oh gosh."

"Can we go in now?"

"Wait a minute; is it raining?"

The February night was cold, but it was the harmattan; there was not even a drop of rain.

"I thought it was raining," he said, and he opened the car door. Across the compound, a large black Mercedes-Benz was parked half on the street, half on the sidewalk. "Now who owns this swell *kyab*?"

Ebi barely listened. She didn't even spare the *kyab* a glance.

"Now would you please get down so that I can get this car into the garage?"

He gave her a tragic smile. The alcohol was really eating into him. It seemed to be swimming all over his face in a dark, ugly way.

"I need your assistance to get out of this car," he said.

Ebi stared at him for a moment and then shook her head meaningfully. She got out of the car, helped him to his feet, and led him into the dim hallway.

CHAPTER TWELVE

"So you're going out with that young man?" It was an accusation.

Ebi looked at her mother without expression.

"Yes."

Her mother looked at her for a long moment.

"Is he one of us?" Her voice was deceptively gentle.

"One of us? I don't think I understand that, Mom."

"Don't pretend ignorance, Akpos. You know what I mean."

"What do you mean, Mom?" Ebi asked quietly.

"I mean, is he an Ijaw man?"

There was a pause, and then the young girl said, "No."

"He's not an Ijaw man." It was not her mother who had spoken. It was her aunt. Her voice was laced with annoyance. "What is he, then?"

Swallowing hard and holding her breath, Ebi said, "He's an Itsekiri man."

"What?" Her mother was open-mouthed. Her aunt was staring at her in horror.

"He's an Itsekiri man," Ebi said. She knew it was an inadequate remark, but the expression on her mother's face was frightening.

"What on earth made you do such a damn fool thing?" Her aunt's voice was clearly angry, and she regarded her niece quizzically.

"Auntie Seyeifa, what is it? What have I done?"

"Akpos, don't you understand? He's an Itsekiri. Itsekiri! Why did you decide to go out with him in the first place? Are there no other eligible men in this school of yours? Don't you realize how embarrassing this could be for all of us? My God, do you have any idea the trouble this action of yours could cause us—cause the whole family?"

Ebi touched her dry lips with her tongue but said nothing.

"Akpos, why did you do it?" Auntie Seyeifa asked.

"I love him."

The answer was so unexpected that the two women looked at each other immediately, and then at the girl strangely.

Ebi stared at her aunt. She was afraid to look at her mother, who was watching her angrily. Her aunt was fiftyish, very well preserved, and extremely well dressed in expensive lace attire, with a hard businesswoman's face. She looked what she was—a Nigerian woman of means.

"Aunt Seyeifa, Tosan isn't as bad as you may think," she said quietly.

"How do you know what we think, Ebi?"

"It's not exactly bad that the two of us are going out. We are adults; we can make decisions for ourselves."

"Girl, you're still a baby. You don't know the impact of what you're doing."

Ebi was getting annoyed now. Her head was throbbing from the alcohol. She was no better than Tos, only she knew how to control herself. All she needed now was to get some sleep. Her mother and Aunt Seyeifa were the last people she had been expecting to see tonight.

When she had parked the car, she'd rushed to her room only to find her aunt and mother tongue-lashing Tos. He was just standing there, speechless, swaying drunkenly on his feet. It was then that it had dawned on her. The black Mercedes parked in the front of her residence was one of her mother's latest cars. She hadn't been expecting her mother, though.

"Akpos, do you know why we came down here?" her mother asked quietly, as if reading her daughter's thoughts.

There was a moment of silence, and then at last Ebi said, "No."

"It was to confirm what we've just seen."

"So you know?" There was an edge to Ebi's voice.

"You'd like to hear the whole story, wouldn't you?" Mrs. Dabiri said, looking at her sister for support.

Aunt Seyeifa nodded.

"We all heard the news from a man who said he knows you. Young-Green or something. He claimed to be a friend of yours."

For a moment Ebi couldn't remember who Young-Green was, but then she recalled one evening with Dr. Ubangha at a restaurant when a stranger had walked up to their table and addressed the lecturer as Young-Green. He had told her later that the man had been his colleague at college and that "Young-Green" had been his college moniker.

"I know him, Mother. He's a lecturer at my school."

"He lives in town here, right?"

"It seems so," Ebi said slowly.

Mrs. Dabiri gave her daughter a sudden searching glance. "He claimed to be one of us. He said he knows your father—that he admires your father greatly and all that. He sent the current edition of *Campus Digest* to us and told us how you were living a bad life, mixing with cult boys and all that. He says Tosan, who's your current boyfriend, is a cult boy, a murderer. And because of him, you no longer attend lectures. When other students are in school, you go to wine bars and disco halls with him. We are deeply concerned, Akpos. It got us worried. Your father could've been here, but I promised him that everything would be all right and I'd see to it myself."

Ebi looked annoyed. "A man who calls himself Young-Green told you all this?"

"Yes. He phoned last week and we received your school magazine yesterday. You're all over the front page, all over the good-for-nothing bastard. It's truly annoying. Just think of what people would say."

"All right, Mother. I'm going to tell you something you and Papa didn't know about Young-Green. He's a fifty-something-year-old man, almost as old as Papa himself. He's a senior lecturer; he's the head of the Department of Fine and Visual Arts. Tosan's a student of that department. And Young-Green's my ex-boyfriend. Or do I call him my ex–old man friend?"

The two women were momentarily taken aback by her outburst.

"You're lying, Ebi!" her mother countered.

Ebi smiled her I-don't-give-a-damn smile. "I'm not finished, Mother. He's a married man, married to a woman almost your age. I left him because I didn't want to spoil his marriage and probably bring shame on the golden family name. That's who Young-Green is."

Aunt Seyeifa stared at her, open-mouthed. "You're trying to cover up your tracks, Akpoebi. You know it."

Ebi ignored her aunt.

"Maybe he's your ex-lover. But is he the one who wrote those bad write-ups about your boyfriend?"

Ebi took a deep breath. "You're not counting on a dirty news rag like *CD* to give you a true news story, are you, Mom? That's a storybook grapevine rag. Nobody buys it these days."

"The young man we saw was no different from what the magazine said he was."

"We went out celebrating, Mom, and Tosan was bombed out. He's not a bad boy, actually." There was a touch of righteous indignation in Ebi's voice.

Mrs. Adaka Dabiri shook her head.

"No matter what you say, Akpos, you must get that young man out of this house. Get him out of your life—out of our family."

Ebi stared at her mother squarely in the face. There was no need for the outburst. Tos was already in Mary's apartment, probably sleeping. She had had no choice but to take him down there. It had been very kind of Mary to let him in without asking questions. That was one thing she liked about Mary; one could count on her in times of emergency. But what was her mother griping about? Tos had not even come to see her father for his blessing, yet she was already on the edge of breaking an artery. What if he came? What would it look like then?

"Aren't you going to offer us something, Akpos?" Aunt Seyeifa said, breaking the silence.

"Forgive me, auntie," Ebi replied. "All this haranguing tired me out. I believe there's something in the fridge." She walked into the kitchen, leaving both women in the living room.

"The gods aren't too favorably disposed to your husband right now," Aunt Seyeifa said solemnly.

Mrs. Dabiri nodded. "I still find it difficult to believe. He looked so much like Etan. What kind of fate is this?"

"I thought he looked so much like the mother—Eyitemi."

Mrs. Dabiri thought about this for some time. "You're right. He's got his mother's eyes and talents. But he's unmistakably Etan's son. The height and the complexion, no doubt."

There was a moment silence.

"Tosan is Eyitemi's only child, right?"

Mrs. Adaka Dabiri nodded again. "As you know, she died in the crisis. Etan died over ten years ago, I believe, in a ghastly motor accident. The poor boy's an orphan."

Aunt Seyeifa lifted her shoulder. "It's not anybody's fault."

"It's not anybody's fault," Mrs. Dabiri repeated. Her tone, as well as her expression, was both uneasy and somber. "I've a gut feeling that this whole thing has the workings of the supernatural." She looked about her, aware that this was her second contact with her daughter's private life in the university. *This is where she lives,* she thought. *This is where she spends her studying hours with her Itsekiri boyfriend.*

She wandered around the room, touching the expensive furniture and examining the paintings hanging on the walls. A particular one caught her attention. It was a huge oil-on-canvas portrait of her daughter. Inscribed neatly at the bottom were the words "I have found her, the Queen of my Heart. Tosan."

She was so absorbed in the painting that she didn't hear her daughter come into the room. She almost jumped when Ebi spoke to her.

"Do you like it?"

"Who did it?"

"Tosan."

Her mother studied the painting for a long moment. The portrait was painted in unique primary colors of blue, red, and yellow, and Ebi's beauty beamed out with such presence that it was almost lifelike. She feared that her daughter's image might wink at any moment.

"It's beautiful," her mother said quietly.

Ebi nodded. "Would you care for fruit juice, Mom?"

"No, thank you."

Aunt Seyeifa was already devouring her fried chicken with a packet of fresh fruit juice. Mrs. Adaka Dabiri joined her on the couch and regarded her daughter quietly.

"We've not finished our discussion," she said at last.

Ebi clenched her teeth. "Oh no, Mother! How can I make you understand?"

"You've got it wrong. What does it take to get *you* to understand that we don't want you to date an Itsekiri man?"

Ebi felt an anger that was difficult to control. "This is absurd, Mom. I mean it's appalling. True, he's an Itsekiri man, but he's a human being—a decent man. Besides, he didn't choose his tribe, and I didn't choose mine either. God, in His divine wisdom, created us so. And please, for Christ's sake, let's stop this talk. I'm sick and tired of it."

Her mother and Aunt Seyeifa sat together on the couch, surveying her.

"You liberated young American-born women of today, you're really something," Aunt Seyeifa said quietly. "You ought to be more respectful."

"Forgive me, Aunt Seyeifa, but I have not been disrespectful in any way. I mean, what do you want me to do?" Ebi was on the verge of tears.

Her mother was unruffled. "You're ending this affair today."

"I can't, Mom."

"Yes you can."

"I'll tell you something, Mother. This is my life we're discussing, not somebody else's. I'm entitled to live my life. I'll soon be twenty-one years old, and nobody tells me what I'll do and what I'll not do. I want to live my life the way I want it. Take a look at this; we're engaged." She displayed her beringed finger proudly.

"Engaged?" her mother said breathlessly.

"We are. That's why we went out celebrating and stayed late."

Aunt Seyeifa, surprised, opened her mouth to speak but then closed it again. *It's none of my business*, she thought. *The girl's a grown woman now. Twenty-one years no be joke, abi.*

"I hope you're joking."

"How could I joke about such a thing, Mother?"

There was a long pause. "Do you know anything about his family background?"

Ebi frowned. "Not too much. His mother died last year, in the crisis. She was a painter. His father was a businessman. He died a long time ago. He said it was a motor accident. He didn't tell me much about his family background."

"Did he tell you that he took part in the fight in Warri?"

Ebi nodded. "He said he only fought to avenge his mother's death and to defend his homeland. Nothing more. He's not a part of the senseless killings."

Aunt Seyeifa eyed her young niece carefully, criticism rich on her mind. She said quietly, "Did he tell you he was declared wanted by Ijaw youths? Did he tell you his name was number one on their list?"

Ebi was startled. It was evident in her eyes. "Why would they declare him wanted? What has he done?"

Aunt Seyeifa hesitated and then said, "He was said to have led Itsekiri youths to an Ijaw community, sacked the village, killed about eight people, and abducted a dozen others. It was not the first mission he'd done. He has been seen during various flashpoints of the crisis. He's their leader."

Ebi shook her head. "I don't believe it." There were tears gathering deep in her eyes. Her own mother shook her head sorrowfully, tears rolling down her cheek, one hand clutching the loose end of her wrapper.

"Oh my God," Mrs. Adaka Dabiri gasped. "What would our enemy say? This is the work of the devil."

Ebi stared at her mother wildly. Tears were flowing freely down her cheeks now. Her mother's tears were the cause of her own tears. Her aunt was wrapping her hand around her mother's shoulder, consoling her.

"Take it easy, Ada," Aunt Seyeifa said softly "It's going to be all right."

Mrs. Dabiri covered her face with her hand and began to sob.

"I'll arrest that young man."

"You can't do that," Ebi answered.

"Oh yes I can. We'll send him to prison. That's where he belongs."

"Don't you understand, Mom? I love him. He loves me. We're engaged. Tosan's incapable of doing what they said he's done. I believe he's—"

"Shut up!" Mrs. Dabiri cried angrily.

"I know it hurts, Mom, but this is my life. Give me the chance to do what I want for a change."

"And what exactly are you planning to do? Get married immediately?" Her mother was much calmer now, but that was on the surface. She was dying inside. Listening to her daughter talk this way was a cut to the core of her heart.

"We plan to, but not just immediately. Probably when he's in New York later in the year."

"New York?" her mother asked. "Are you planning on eloping?"

"No. A friend of mine in New York has seen Tosan's paintings, and he's interested in them. He's invited him over to the United States."

There was silence in the room for a long moment. Mrs. Dabiri dried her eyes and studied her daughter closely. There was a fire in her rich brown eyes. Barely twenty-one, she was now inevitably a burden on her shoulders—a burden that had become heavier because of that Itsekiri boy. At first it had been the issue of her education. She had attended a very fine secondary school in New York. When it came time for her to further her studies at a university, Mrs. Dabiri had thought that schools like Harvard, Yale, Howard, Tallahassee, and all those pricey American universities would suit Ebi. And what had happened? She had shocked the whole family by telling them that she wanted to come home to Nigeria to obtain her first degree. Her father had been adamant, but she was stubborn. At last her father had shifted ground when he had seen that she was relentless. Again she shocked the family by insisting that it would be the Aliu Zamani University at Jankara or no other school. Her father had no choice. After all, she had inherited his resilient strength. In the end, she got her way and entered the university, which was regarded as the most notorious in secret cult activities throughout the nation.

What pained her mother was all the money that had been lavished on her, all that effort that had been made to make her an American citizen, all the money and training that had gone into making her somebody unique. Now what was the result? Rebellion. They had no choice. They couldn't just wash their hands of her affairs. She was their only child. They still needed to protect her.

Aunt Seyeifa finished the last drop of her fruit drink.

"Akpos, can you get me another juice?"

"I'll get it, Auntie," Ebi said. She was almost at the doorway of the kitchen when she stopped and said to her mother, "Would you care for something now, Mom?"

Again Adaku Dabiri answered, "Of course not, dear. It's late. Hardly the eating hour for me."

Ebi disappeared into the kitchen. She knew her mother would not forgive her this one so easily.

* * *

In the morning, Tos was bewildered to find himself in a strange bedroom. At first he couldn't remember where he was. Outside, the sun was burning, and its harsh light was pouring through the window like a bucketful of warm water. He discovered that he was naked, save for his underwear.

There was a dull ache in his head. It was a mild hangover, and it disturbed him. He closed his eyes and slowly tried to remember where he was. It was almost thirty seconds later that he remembered where he was. He was in Mary Oloyi's flat, in her bed. He knew this only because he saw her photograph on the nightstand.

There was a slight knock on the door, and it opened without his consent. Tos turned his head quickly. Mary came into the room and crossed to the bed. Tos groped for the bedsheets and pulled them across his naked body. But the girl had already seen him.

"How did I get here?"

"Picasso, I believe you were plastered last night, and Ebi's mother almost had you for supper. That's how you got here."

"Really?" he asked. He sounded as though he didn't believe her.

"Yeah."

Tos was silent for a moment, his eyes tightly shut, lost in contemplation as if he was fitting together the pieces of the puzzle of how he had found himself half naked in Mary's bed.

He knew they had come home the worse for drink. He remembered meeting two women in the living room, and they'd nearly finished him with their mouths. That was where he met the brick wall. He didn't remember how he had ended up in Mary's bed. The little he could remember was the tone of the women's voices as they shouted, screamed, and cursed. It was not at all welcoming.

He opened his eyes. "I feel very old this morning."

"You've been overdrinking."

There was a short silence. He watched the sun outside the windows. The girl watched him.

"Want to take a bath?"

He shook his head.

"Coffee?"

He could taste stale beer on his breath, and his skin smelled of cigar smoke. What he really wanted was cold water on his skin and nothing else.

"You want coffee?" the girl asked again.

Tos looked at her closely now. She was an attractive girl with wide-set brown eyes, prominent cheekbones, and generous lips, slightly reddened. She was wearing a soft sky-blue nightgown. It made her look very sexy.

"Can you get me my clothes?" he said abruptly.

The girl regarded him for a moment without moving. Her eyes undressed him and caressed him, and without warning, she reached out her hand, and her delicate fingers touched his face, probing his lips, his cheeks.

Tos was stirred. There was something more than admiration in Mary's eyes. Behind those eyes, something like sexual hunger was clearly written. *Have we already done it?* he wondered. Panic gripped him at the realization that something like this might have taken place.

"Stop it!"

The force of his voice made her stiffen. Her hands stopped their tender excursion of his flesh.

"I want my clothes. And I want them now." Tos's voice was matter-of-fact.

The girl nodded and left the room.

Ten minutes later, he departed her flat. When he came downstairs, the black Mercedes-Benz car was still there. He was sure it was Ebi's mother's car that was parked awkwardly in the compound.

He took an *okada* to his residence and was able to shave and have breakfast in peace. After his morning meal, he found a clean pair of jeans and his favorite T-shirt, a Tommy Hilfiger. He had just finished dressing when his doorbell rang. He peeked from behind a curtain before he went to open the door. One of the Owlsmen had just arrived. It was Christopher "Christo One Way" Edokpolor.

He opened the door and looked into Christo's impassive face.

"Yeah, Don Tos. I got your message. What's it all about?"

"Come on in," Tos said, and he led the way into the sitting room. He pointed to a chair, and Christo sat down. He offered his visitor a can of beer and his pack of B&H, and they both lit up.

"So now, tell me. What's it all about?"

"You remember Ebi?"

Christo puffed quietly for a moment before he answered. "Your woman, right?"

Tos nodded.

Christo nodded also. "I've heard. The word around town's that Dikko's making threats against you because of her. Am I correct?"

"Dikko wants to play me rough because of her."

Smoke wandered from Christo's mouth across his face. "I think we should cool it with him. The guy's dangerous."

"That's why I called this meeting."

"Must there be a meeting before we settle a threat of this nature?"

Tos nodded. He knew Christo One Way. He was a one-way thinker and an impatient fellow. He had a belligerent attitude. To him, obstacles were not insurmountable. The official route was the wrong route. He hated the idea of debate—especially when it involved violence. He hated meetings. And that was why Don Bosco had him suspended for twelve months.

One wet April night, Christo had found a note on his Range Rover's windshield. The note had simply said, "If you come to Vik's place again. I'll kill you. You know me, so watch out for me." And they'd destroyed his windshield and slashed all four tires.

Of course, Christo knew the guy. They were both hustling the same chick. The girl was a big chick. Christo didn't take the matter to the Council of Wizards. What he did was simple. He and a few feathered men had driven to the guy's pad and knocked on his door, and the guy that opened the door had received undiluted acid full on the face. It was an unlucky day for the guy who was bathed with the acid, as it was a case of mistaken identity. They had been looking for his cousin, but he was the one who had received the treatment. If Christo had taken the case to the Council, they probably would not have gotten the wrong guy. He had been suspended for one session, and his feather was withdrawn. But that had been under Don Bosco's leadership. When Tos had come on board as the new Grand Wizard, he had had Christo pardoned and refeathered. Since then, he had been a good boy, but the old violent streak was still in him.

"I want the Council to make a decision."

Christo smiled bleakly. "Then there will be an investigation, right?"

Tos didn't answer immediately. The doorbell was ringing. He went to the window. Five other Wizards had arrived. Ovo and Keme came in Number Two's brand-new Jaguar XJ Sports 3.2, and they left the car beside Christo's Range Rover. The others came in Black Mamba's Honda Prelude.

He opened the door, and the five men came into the room.

"Grab your seats," he said.

Ovo's body filled Tos's favorite chair, and Keme took the couch facing Christo One Way. Black Mamba, Malik, and Frank White folded themselves into a single long sofa.

Tos was about to open the discussion again when the sound of tires on gravel announced the arrival of more Wizards. The newcomers were Max "Paxman" Osuagwu, Kadiri Muazu, Morgan Akumagba, Elvis Kabaka, and Bolo Araba-Benson. All the people who made up the Council of Wizards were present in the room.

Tos asked them if they would care for some beer.

"Of course I care. If any of them don't care, then that's their problem," Malik said, and there was a general riffle of laughter.

Tos stood up and disappeared into the kitchen. When he came back, he was carrying a case of Budweiser. He distributed the beer to each of his guests in turn.

"What about smokes?" somebody asked.

He fetched a pack of B&H and, like the beer, distributed it to those who wished to smoke. When the rings were ripped, the tips of their cigarettes were glowing red, and every man was leaning back in his chair, Tos cleared his throat for silence.

"Councilors," he began in a very quiet voice. All eyes were watching him. "Yesterday, I was invited by my HOD to his office. I spent forty-five minutes with him. We discussed nothing but Ebi. For forty-five minutes, we discussed only my girl, and nothing more."

Ovo lifted his canned beer and sipped it. "Are there any special details about your discussion?"

"Dikko advised me to give up on the girl. He wants to pay a price. He offered me money. About one hundred grand. It's an offer I refused. Thereafter, he bluntly told me to leave the girl."

"What if you don't?" The question was from Kadiri Muazu.

"I can't predict when and how I'll die."

There was a collective sigh. They all knew that this was the traditional declaration of war. If anybody says you can't predict when and how you'll die, it meant he was going to "arrange your death," in cultic parlance.

Black Mamba spoke through a cloud of Benson & Hedges: "This is not an empty threat."

"It's about bloody time somebody crates this Dikko just like General Idiagbon did the other Dikko," Elvis Kabaka said, laughing mirthlessly. Elvis was nineteen years old. He was by four years the youngest member of the Council of Wizards.

Nobody laughed with him, but most of them agreed with him in their hearts. Not many of them liked lecturers who slept with their female students. Dikko had a reputation. Everyone on campus knew him to be a randy old goat.

"So, gentlemen, this is why I called the gathering—to sample everyone's opinions."

There was an awkward silence. Every one of them was thinking, analyzing the whole thing in their minds.

"My lord. What d'you want us to do? Kill him or talk to him?" Christo One Way asked.

Tos learned forward in his chair. "That's why I called this meeting. I'm not supposed to do all the talking. I want different opinions."

"As for me," said Morgan Akumagba, "this is no idle threat. This is a crisis in our hands. I think we'll have to visit Dikko and have a quiet talk with him. Reason with him. He's a family man. He'll backpedal."

Tos nodded. "What about you, Black Mamba?"

"I'd like to knife that creep," Black Mamba said angrily.

Tos smiled. "Thanks for that opinion. Can we hear your opinion, Kadiri?"

Kadiri Muazu said nothing for some time. He was the oldest Owlsman in the Council of Wizards. Born in 1967, the son of an army captain who had butchered innocent Igbo civilians during the Nigerian Civil War, Kadiri was an apostle of violence.

"We'll burn one of his cars and claim responsibility. That way he'll know that he's playing with the big boys."

Tos gave him a broad smile. "Another fine opinion. What about you, Christo—what's on your mind?"

Christo One Way shook his head. "This is no thinly veiled threat. This whole episode's something beyond a harmless nutty professor trying to play the role of a connected man. He's a *connected* man. Dikko's a dangerous man. If we need to deal with him, we'll need to send the fear of death into his household, into his family."

Tos looked over at Keme. It was his turn to wade in. He could predict what was on his mind.

"Keme, what do you think? You think this is an idle threat?"

Keme didn't say anything for a while. He knew the import of the question. In cultic circles, threats against lords were considered as real threats. The repercussion could be death. That was even without overt moves to carry them out.

He chose his words carefully. "With all due respect, I must say I don't totally agree with the earlier speakers. As I see it, Dikko's threat is more like a harmless threat. I don't think he has boys to pull any stunt."

"That's bullshit!" Christo One Way said angrily. "Dikko threatened the Grand Wizard. Do any of you know what that means?"

A brief period of silence greeted his words. They all knew what it meant.

"We've got no other option than to put the fear of death into his dirty, lecherous heart," Christo continued, pausing for effect. "To me, that's the only option."

"And you, Ovo?"

Number Two's bushy eyebrows shot up. The glowing cigarette hung in his limp hand.

"I agree with Christo," he said. "Dikko's a dangerous character. And I think we can assume that he's the financier of our archrivals. If that's so, traditionally, he'll get in touch with them within the next few days. It wouldn't be a bad idea to put people on his trail so that we know the kind of people he dines with, drinks with, and the lot. What do you think, Keme?"

Keme made a face. "You have a point, Vee-Eye, but I don't see this thing as a problem at all. In a nutshell, I agree with you. We can have him watched and wait to see what he can do. At least for a few days."

Christo One Way shook his head. He was still angry. "We can't wait. It's too damn risky. This, in my own opinion, is what we'll do. We'll waste him before he wastes the BE. There's no better option. We'll kill him. That's it."

There was an uneasy silence—silence accentuated by the traffic movement outside.

"Christo, my dear," Tos said quietly, his eyes fastened on Christo's. "I don't want another bloodbath. We had enough of it last year." His eyes were looking deep into Christo, as if peering into his soul.

"But—" Christo began.

"No buts," said Tos. "I want Dikko to have a rethink. That can be done without spilling a drop of blood. Am I making a point?" Tos looked at each and every one of them in turn now, a serious expression on his face. He wanted to see that they'd grasped the import of what he had just said. Some of them nodded, but others just stared at him.

Christo looked at Tos as though a part of his face had caved in. *Is Don Tos growing soft?* he wondered.

"I'm sorry, my lord," he said coldly. "But there's no way to make that bastard have a rethink without sending him to his grave."

Tos listened to the cold, cruel worlds quietly. He stared knowingly at Number Nine, who sat comfortably enjoying his cigarette yet spoiling for war.

"Don't worry, Christo," Tos said quietly. "I've got other plans."

Keme, smiling mysteriously, shook his head. The differences of opinion between him and Don Tos were legendary. Many believed this was not unconnected to the Warri Crisis. When Tos had traveled out of town several months prior to take part in the Warri Crisis, it had been Keme who had challenged him on his return. He had accused Tos of using the resources of the Black Owls to wage a private war. That had been the beginning of their cold relationship. Now Tos had showed another of his cunning Itsekiri skills. He wanted all of them to say what was on their minds, whereas he had his own game plan.

"What kind of plan have you got?" Keme asked, looking him straight in the eye. "Can we hear it?"

Tos knew he was suspicious, but he chose to ignore him. Rather, he focused his eyes on Christo. "I'd be the happiest man on God's earth if Dikko could be wasted immediately. But that's not what I've got in mind."

Christo ripped off the ring of another canned beer, tossed a fresh cigarette to his lips, and produced a small owl-shaped lighter. The flame it produced poured from its tight little mouth neatly and torched the tip of the cigarette.

"If we don't visit Dikko," Ovo said, "if we don't do anything, what effect is it going to have on us—in terms of status damage?"

"That's what I've been meaning to ask," Kadiri Muazu said seriously.

"If we don't act, they'll act," Black Mamba said. "If he's really a sponsor of one or two of our rivals, then we should expect trouble, because they will try to do something funny. And I must say it's going to be rough for us."

"If that's the case, then let's *gbege* him," Frank White said, speaking for the first time.

All eyes in the room settled on him. Frank White was a butcher's son. To him, all meat looked alike when it came to killing. Tos, Keme, and Frank White were the three most hard-hearted men in the Council of Wizards. Tos was Don Corleone, Keme was Luca Brasi, and Frank White was Frank Pentangeli—the three wise men.

"Can I ask a question?" Bolo Araba-Benson said. By designation, he was Number Twelve, a taciturn fellow.

"Yeah. Sure," Tos replied.

"My question is this: Is this issue worth fighting for?"

Christo One Way frowned; most of the others gave Araba-Benson dirty looks. Keme was smiling. But it was Black Mamba who answered him.

"Anything worth having is worth fighting for, Bolo. Ebi's worth fighting for. If Dikko takes Ebi today, he's taken her not only from the Big Eye but from each and every one of us present in this room. And that includes you."

There was dead silence for some time.

"So what do you suggest now?" Keme said. He was talking to Tos. "You're the Big Eye; you're the boss." The message was clear.

Tos nodded and looked at Elvis Kabaka and Bolo Araba-Benson.

"We'll need the services of our Moscow."

The two young men who were the intelligence chieftains looked at each other and then at Tos. "We're ready," Kabaka said.

"Dikko's got some boys that work for him. His *eyes*, I heard he calls them?"

"I've heard about them," Elvis Kabaka said.

"What about his ballplayers?" Malik asked.

"Ballplayers—who are they?" Kadiri asked.

Nobody answered him. Tos looked at them, one after the other. "Paxman—any idea?"

Paxman shrugged. He had been silent since the beginning of the discussion, his eyes assessing every speaker. To him, silence was golden. Most times in their midst he would sit, bide his time, and listen to the others, never talking, watching, noting—the proper scribe.

"Do you have any idea who the ballplayers are?" Tos repeated.

"They're his hired guns—so I heard," Paxman said. "But nobody seems to know them."

Keme looked at the ceiling. There was an almost audible groan from him.

"Moscow Two—what can you tell us about these guys, the ballplayers?"

All eyes in the room focused on Number Twelve.

"Nothing," he said. "The only people who can possibly tell us anything are his eyes."

"Do you know any of them?"

He shrugged. "Some of them."

"Can you give us names and addresses?" Ovo asked.

"There's this guy called Kelly Okoro. He's a Brownie. He's a part-three business economics student. He lives in town." He gave the name of the guy's hostel. "Another, I think another of his eyes, is Oje Ehime. He's a Purebloodsman." He gave another address in town. "Oje's in the natural science faculty. I'm not sure about the exact department or his level. Then there's this other guy—Kraks. Kraks is in your department, my lord. He's a Roundhead."

Tos nodded. "Speed is of essence here," he said. "Elvis, I want you to put together a small group of men within your department. I want it very small—not more than ten guys. I want to know what Dikko's up to, day in and day out—who he meets, the kind of students he parleys with. I need this info as soon as possible. Frank White will assist you. Any questions?"

There was no question from Elvis, but Bolo Araba-Benson had a question: "What about the eyes?"

"You can handle them, can't you?"

"Of course we can handle them. But how do you want us to handle them?"

"Have them kidnapped, blindfolded, and taken to the arena. Work them over; persuade them to answer a few questions. I want to know what Dikko's up to—what he's going to spring, the kind of people he'll try to use. I want to know. I want to know in a week."

Elvis and Bolo nodded.

"It's done," Elvis said.

"It really must be done quickly," Tos said.

Elvis smiled. "I said it's done. Trust me, my lord."

Tos nodded. Elvis Kabaka was young for the job of the Black Owls' most notorious spymaster. As head of their intelligence efforts, he was subtle, experienced, and very reliable—a guy held in high regard by all wizards.

"Is there any other question?" Tos asked, his eyes scanning the faces of his men.

There was no question. The meeting ended on that note. Ten minutes later, Tos dismissed the others but told Ovo, Frank White, Keme, and Christo One Way to stay behind.

"I hope this won't take too long," Christo said. "I'm supposed to be in Abuja by four o'clock. I'm traveling out of the country for the weekend."

Tos nodded.

"What time does your plane leave?"

"Eleven o'clock."

"Relax. You'll catch your plane in good time."

Christo again folded himself into his chair, lit a cigarette, and crossed one long leg over the other.

Tos looked at all of them approvingly. These were people he respected and trusted.

"We're listening," Keme said.

"It's more important than this Dikko's issue. That's why I want you guys to be the first to know."

They all looked very interested now.

"I'm calling the Council into session on the twentieth of April. I'll announce to the family my decision to step down into retirement at the end of that month. Then, on the fourth of May, we'll have a new Grand Wizard."

For the next minute, there was taut silence.

"Are you guys surprised?"

Keme nodded. "That's an understatement. We're dumbstruck."

Christo was looking at Tos strangely. "The Council will not be convened until the twenty-second of September," he said quietly.

"I know," Tos said quietly. "There's a project I'm working on right now. It's going to take all of my time. That's why I want to be relieved of my duties. It's actually the major reason why I called this meeting. I'm ready to retire. I've served the brotherhood, commanded this great gang, and done my work. But now I want to quit the stage. I want to focus on the project I'm working on. It'll take most, if not the whole, of my time."

"You can delegate." This came from Ovo.

They all looked at Ovo. He was the highest on the seniority ladder. If Tos should delegate, then leadership would automatically fall into his lap.

"I'm not delegating," Tos said.

"Then what's on your mind?" Christo asked.

Tos nodded and looked at every one of them in turn, a mischievous expression lurking in his eyes.

"I want the new Grand Wizard to be Ogheneovo."

There was a moment of silence as his words sank in.

"Any dissenting voice?"

There was none. Traditionally, it was normally his decision, going by the constitution, to delegate responsibility. It was also allowed by the law of the Council for him to nominate his successor. It was not something that required consultation. Though the Assembly of Feathered Men could nominate somebody else, popular vote would usher in the new Grand Eye.

"I've been the Grand Eye for two years. It's enough time for me to bow out. You guys need a change in terms of leadership. Ovo's a good man. He'll make a good Grand Eye. But as traditions demand, I'll still ask him. Are you ready to take it?"

All eyes were on the Number Two. They could see in his eyes the quest for power. But he hesitated for only an instant. Then he touched his heart and his lips in the traditional Owlsmen's gesture of acceptance.

"I have confidence in his abilities. He can take care of things." Tos looked at Keme. "Keme, I'll nominate you as the new Vee-Eye to keep an eye on the Grand Eye. And Frank White, you're the new Klaws I—you'll replace your boss and give them strength. Christo—" His eyes were boring into Christo's eyes. "You'll be the new Kwill. All of you guys will hold the family together. Be prepared to do a good job. Do we have an understanding?"

As one, they all nodded.

CHAPTER THIRTEEN

The dry, cold harmattan breeze of the early March evening blew across the state and swept over the town of Jankara and into the balcony, then through the french windows of Akpoebi Dabiri's bedroom.

Tos sat with his back to the balcony and the wind, concentrating on the copy of *Ebony* in which he was reading about successful African Americans who had made their mark on the American nation.

He looked at Ebi, who was lying on the bed in simple light blue shorts and bra, her stomach and shoulders bare. She was reading a voluminous book on African history.

"What's this?" Tos said loudly. "There's so much wealth displayed in this magazine."

Ebi laughed. "They are Americans. They've the right to be wealthy."

Tos stared at her. "They've the right to be wealthy?"

"That's it," Ebi replied.

"Why can't Nigerians be something like this?"

"It's probably because Nigeria is suffering from a heavenly curse or Nigerians are too timid to stand up and hold their government accountable."

Tos stood up. "I don't want to get involved in Nigeria's politics. It's very annoying what the political class has done with this great nation." He was walking toward the kitchen. "I think I need a beer. Can I get you one?"

Ebi shook her head. Tos strolled leisurely out of the bedroom and came back a short while later with a can of Heineken. He eased into the chair where he had been sitting earlier and lit a cigarette. His manner had changed. It was as if there was something disturbing him. Ebi detected the faraway look in his eyes.

"Is anything the matter, Picasso?"

He smiled, but his eyes were cold. "My name's Tosan."

"Hey, lighten up. We all know it's just a nickname."

"I know. But when I'm with you, try to call me by my legal name."

Ebi nodded, but she was looking at him curiously. "Something is bothering you, Tosan. I'm your girl. Tell me what's bothering you."

Tos shook his head, but she was still staring at him curiously, her face wearing the mask a mother wears when her beloved son is in trouble.

Tos forced a smile to his lips. "Nothing is bothering me."

"You can do better than that," she replied quietly.

Tos regarded her for some time. It was true. Something was disturbing him. Actually, he had every reason to be disturbed. A tiny twinge of guilt nipped his conscience. He knew he ought to tell her. But *how* would he tell her?

What will her reaction be?

"Am I right in thinking that, after I was chased out the other day, you talked about me? You and your mother?"

Ebi didn't reply immediately. There were a few seconds of silence, in one of those awkward moments between lovers when the truth is laying an ambush.

"Is that why you're disturbed?" She was guessing.

"Just tell me whether you discussed me or not."

"Yeah. We discussed you. Partly—but of course we discussed other things."

"What exactly did your mother say about me?"

"Everything an Ijaw woman would say about her daughter dating an Itsekiri boy in the heat of the crisis."

"What about my parents? Did she say anything about my parents?"

Ebi looked at him like, *What's this all about?* "My mom doesn't know your parents. Or does she?"

Tos was silent for a moment, his brown eyes on her with an expression in them that was hard to interpret.

"No, forget it."

She knew it was his way of ending an unpleasant conversation. But she was not yet through with this discussion. She sat in silence for a long time, recalling the discussion she'd had with her mother and Aunt Seyeifa. Since that night, this was the first time Tos had been in her apartment, and she was sensitive enough to detect that he was not his usual self.

"Tosan," she called quietly. "My mom and Aunt Seyeifa told me to quit this relationship. But there's something I want to tell you." She left the bed and sat on the floor close to his chair. "I love you, Tosan. Nobody's going to stop me from loving you. You ought to know that by now."

"Not even your parents?"

She shook her head. "Not even my parents."

Tos patted her lightly on the cheek. "You don't need to say it if you don't mean it."

She smiled. Impulsively, she reached out to him and kissed him. "Has that answered your question?"

Tos hesitated a moment. *Can this thing wait?* he wondered. Something told him that he should not tell her yet. It was a very small part of him that said this, but a very influential part of him. He knew he was scared of talking, and it was because of the Frank Reese business. The opportunity was very important to him. But either way, he knew he would tell her at a more convenient time.

He nodded, but she waited for him to say something.

"Ebi—I'm scared." The unsure tone of his voice and the vacant expression in his eyes gave her some satisfaction.

"What are you scared of, darling?"

For Tos, it was a cinch. He would say something, anything, to divert her attention for the time being.

"I'm afraid of this Frank Reese project. I'm afraid I'm not up to the task. And the money he wants to pay me is too good to be true. I'm not a professional. I'm an amateur. I thought what I would get would be something very comfortable. I didn't expect what I got. Ebi, I'm scared."

Ebi smiled weakly. "Do you believe in yourself, Tosan? And in those paintings?"

"Of course I do."

She nodded. "Then let me be honest with you. Don't be scared. You're a very good painter. Tomorrow you'll continue from where you stopped. This is what you want. Don't tell me you can't do it. That's bullshit. You're the best, youngest painter I've met personally. And I've met a handful."

"But Ebi—"

"I don't want to hear another word. Tomorrow we'll shop for art materials. Where's that Iyabo? She should have announced dinner half an hour ago."

"Not until I've finished with you first," Tos said, and he carried her to the bed.

* * *

That same evening, while Tos was at Ebi's flat, Dr. Vincent Ubangha made his way into the Pinkwater Restaurant, his favorite eating joint. He had barely settled down to place his order when three young men came to his table and sat down.

"Shall we have beer?" he asked.

The three young men nodded. Dr. Ubangha signaled the waitress and ordered Heineken canned beers for everybody. When the waitress had placed the drinks before them and returned to her counter, he broke the silence.

"This is a business discussion. You're going to take care of a pig for me."

"That's why we're here," one of the young men said. He was called Osaro, Osas for short; he was a three-hundred-level biochemistry student and a member of the Black Panthers.

"Who's he?" the tallest of the three young men asked. He was called Nosa Akhimien, a member of the Brotherhood of the Purebloods.

The lecturer pushed an envelope across the table. Nosa took the envelope and quietly studied the colored, glossy print that was in the envelope.

"Let me see it," the third fellow said eagerly. Nosa handed him the envelope. He took it quietly, wordlessly, and studied with an impassive professional air the picture of Tos's dark face.

"This is Don Tos," he said last.

"Yeah," Nosa replied thickly.

Vincent Ubangha sat back in his chair. "What about him?" he asked quietly.

"This boy's trouble," the third fellow, Mike, said.

"Let me see the print," Osas said. Mike handed the photograph over to him.

"What do you think, Osas?" the lecturer asked after some minutes' silence. The boy didn't answer immediately. He was studying the close-up of Don Tos.

"I hope you can take him, Osaro?"

Osaro's reply came quicker this time. "I can't touch him. He's a bunch of trouble."

The lecturer nodded. "What about you, Nosa? You can take him, right?"

Nosa looked up. His eyes had widened with fear and apprehension. "Take him?" he asked. "I don't think I can do that, sir. The guy's too tight for me."

"But you're a pro, aren't you?"

"Of course I'm a pro, but he's a tougher guy. I'm sorry, sir. I can't do this unless you have another assignment for me."

There was a moment of silence. The lecturer used the moment to assess the third ballplayer. He wore a black beret and a pair of black jeans, and he had three-day stubble on his mean, ugly face.

"If we'll take him, we'll take him. But that's if the pay's cool." Mike's voice was cold. He didn't look at the lecturer or the two other boys but at the beer can sitting in front of him.

"I said I wouldn't do it," Nosa said emphatically, turning his massive neck and looking at Mike as if he were a man dancing on the edge of lunacy. "Guy, what are you trying to do?"

There was a pause. The lecturer cashed in on the silence. "Mike, I know you can do it."

"Yeah," Mike replied slowly, confidently.

He's confident; by God, he can do it! Dr. Ubangha thought excitedly.

"You're not just being brave, are you, Mike?" Nosa asked quietly.

Mike's liquid brown eyes flashed angrily. "I said we'll do it."

"We will or you will?" Nosa was getting angry now. The whole idea struck him as crazy. Screwing up with Don Tos, the Black Owls' Number One, simply wasn't worth the money the lecturer would pay them.

Mike's lip parted in the imitation of a smile. "Nosa, it's high time we all team up and get the fucking guy out of the way. Once Don Tos is out of the way, the structure of the Black Owls will crumble. That way, we'll all have peace of mind."

Nosa was shaking his head. "No," he said in a cold whisper. "The school will not know peace. I can't stand that. No decent person will stand that."

The lecturer let the bitterness free in his voice. "What sort of decent pig are you?"

Nosa turned toward him, and his cold eyes grew even chillier. "I don't want innocent people to die for a fight that doesn't concern them. That's the sort of decent pig I am."

"I thought you were really a good ballplayer."

"I play a different kind of ball game, sir. I won't allow innocent people to die because you have a crush on one little damsel. She's not worth the trouble. No woman's ever worth such trouble."

The lecturer felt the heat rising in him, the muscles in his chest tightening, and the beer congealing inside his stomach.

"What have you just said?" he asked quietly.

"I said the truth. The whole school's talking about the whole thing now—Don Tos and your little American-bred siren in a sizzling hot romance. If anything bad at all happens to Don Tos, heads are surely going to roll. I don't want mine included."

The lecturer breathed out. The breath took several seconds and seemed to take all the air out of his body. When he spoke, his voice was low and precise. "Leave us." It was all he could do to stop himself from smashing his fist into the young man's face.

"You don't understand. I think—"

"I said *leave us!*" Vincent Ubangha snapped.

Nosa stood up. He looked at Mike. "Don't do this. Walk away from it. I know you're about to start some real big trouble around here. Believe me; nobody's going to like the outcome."

Mike shrugged. "Don't sweat over it."

Nosa was not misled by Mike's casual tone. "Don't engage yourself in a fight you know you can't win."

Mike laughed. It was a hollow laugh. "I don't make futile battles, my friend."

Nosa nodded, smiled good-naturedly, stepped around Mike, and walked out of the restaurant.

"What about you Osas—do you want to leave us too?" Dr. Ubangha asked.

Osas shook his head. There was something about the lecturer that brought him over. Money. He's free with money—good money. It wouldn't be a good thing to break contact with him no matter how sick in the head he might be. If Mike can do it as he said, they'll pluck some cool cash from this operation.

"Why don't you leave with the pig?"

Osas chose his words carefully. "If Mike says he'll do it, then he'll do it. I'll assist him."

"Is it okay with you, Mike?"

"It's okay with me," Mike replied.

Dr. Ubangha was satisfied with what he saw in the boy. He recognized the signs of professionalism. This boy was hard, solid, and reliable. Like Tos, he was a cult lord. The only thing against him was that while Tos could command a battalion, Mike couldn't. But that was no big problem. Anybody with confidence on his side could take Tos anytime, any day. And this boy had enough of it.

"Now let's talk money. How much are you asking for this job?"

Mike looked him in the eyes.

"Half a million naira will do just fine."

The lecturer nodded. It was on the high side, but not bad. "I'll send Kraks with the down payment Saturday evening. You know Kraks?"

He nodded.

"Where can he get you?"

Mike wrote something on the envelope and pushed it to the lecturer. The lecturer read it and nodded.

"Can he be trusted with that kind of money?" Osas asked.

"Yes."

"What about Nosa—can he also be trusted?" Osas asked again.

Dr. Ubangha was thoughtful for a moment. The boy had asked a very disturbing question. Normally between him and his ballplayers, secrets were well kept. But he was not sure about Nosa now.

But it was Mike who answered the question.

"Don't worry about that. I'll take care of him."

Osas's Adam's apple bounced as he swallowed. He didn't relish the job he had landed himself this time.

* * *

Tos went out shopping with Ebi the next morning. They bought lots of working materials: gesso boards, acrylics, canvas boards, oils, brushes, watercolor sets, pads, and canvases.

That same day, in the evening, he started three paintings simultaneously. He poured all his enthusiasm into the works. He worked feverishly both day and night, missed classes, ignored all the usual distractions, and lost himself in a world of paint and canvas boards, covering naked canvas upon naked canvas with creative ideas.

If it hadn't been for Ebi, he wouldn't have been able to get himself straightened out for the job. For the first time in a long time, he spent a whole five days confined to his room. She encouraged him to maintain this strict regimen. It was done in order to avoid contact with his men and concentrate on his work. He also stayed away from Bray's Kitchen, the Greenhouse Bar and Restaurant, and the Clique Nightclub.

He had made a pledge that he would finish the paintings before May 15. By Thursday afternoon (March 11), he had done six multipane acrylics, two watercolors and one oil painting, and he busied himself with the second oil painting he was working on in the past fifty-four hours, creating distinct images on the canvas board. At a quarter past four, he stood back to admire the latest oil, his last handwork before the break for the day.

Something in him told him that this last oil painting was the best work he had done in the past five days. A shape had emerged from the easels where this morning there had been simply a featureless square of canvas. Ebi, lying on the chair watching him work, could now see creatively painted people and objects.

Tos had now assumed another position to assess the work, to get a different view. The direct light of the sun streaking across the room revealed the works as the extraordinary compositions of a very talented painter.

"Princess, come over here," he called.

Ebi stood up and joined him.

"What do you think?"

Ebi stared at the painting. The technique was violent and ornately real, like a living picture.

"So what do you think?" Tos repeated.

"It's raw," Ebi said with sincerity.

Tos studied the painting for some time. "The idea occurred to me three days ago. I was afraid I wouldn't be able to capture the mood right. This is the best I could come up with. Do you think this work would cut it with Reese?"

Ebi's expression did not change. "The style's a bit raw, but it's okay."

Tos's smile was slow. He walked close to the painting and stared at it closely.

"I deliberately took off their clothes, exposed their nakedness. I hoped Reese would fall for it."

"Would you have clothed them even if Reese told you to?"

Tos's eyes lit up. "Probably. I would have clothed them."

Ebi laughed. "You've painted what your mind told you to paint. It's not a sin to paint naked women. Nude paintings, in most cases, capture the elegant innocence of the female body. It's the warped mind that sees it differently. Besides, you have the freedom to create your image."

Tos nodded. "You're right on that score. The artist has freedom to create his images the way he wishes. It's left for the viewers to accept or reject them. You know, the ideas of the mind are very influential. We're nothing but pawns in their grips."

Ebi nodded too. "Trust your work," she said softly, seriously.

"You're my strength."

Ebi touched his arm and squeezed lightly. "God's your strength. Don't forget that, Picasso." Her tone was serious.

"Maybe that's blasphemy. I'm sorry. God will understand."

Ebi nodded, but she was still studying the painting, deep in thought. Tos thought he saw her shiver. He was almost sure. But he knew it could also have been his imagination.

There was moment of silence. Then Ebi said, "You're a talented painter. You are made of the great stuff that geniuses are made of."

Tos laughed without mirth. "You flatter me too much."

Ebi looked at him. "It's not flattery, Tosan. You're very good. Very talented."

"How good?"

"As good as good could be."

Tos smiled. "The term 'good' is a relative term. It's a deceptive word."

"But you're still a genius."

His eyes met hers with only a hint of mockery. Tos knew she was serious.

"When a girl calls her lover a genius, know that the world's about to come to an end."

Ebi shook her head. "That's very funny," she said.

"I'm not joking," Tos replied. He spread his hands, displaying his seriousness.

"Let me get you a bottle of wine. This is a pure work of art. It will hang in one of those notable galleries very soon."

"God, this girl is really a saleswoman. Baby, I'll make you my manager. It's high time you started looking after my investments."

"I'm serious, Picasso."

Tos patted her shoulder reverently. "I know that, baby. I trust you. Now, can I get that wine?"

It took Ebi four minutes to get the wine. She poured him a glassful of the French red. Tos took the first sip with a light mind. He knew he was experiencing a lucky streak.

"Come on, drink with me, my princess," he said, smiling broadly.

* * *

It was nearly 4.00 p.m. on that same Thursday afternoon. The Faculy of Arts building was quiet at this time of the day. Dr. Vincent Ubangha left his office and walked down the corridor of the faculty building. He stopped in the front of an impressive walnut door with plastic lettering that read, "PROF. BORO FINECOUNTRY, DEAN." He knocked boldly on the door, and a voice from inside told him to come right in.

"Vincent," the dean said when he saw who was at the door. "How nice of you to drop in." There was a warm smile on the dean's face as they shook hands. "Please sit down."

Dr. Ubangha took one of the leather chairs and looked around the office. It was a spacious but very quiet air-conditioned office. Hanging on one part of the wall was a large death mask. It was a beautifully carved work with a calm, mysterious face, the eternal image of everlasting rest. There was also an oil painting of the professor on the other part of the wall. It was an elegant painting. The artist had captured, skillfully, the distinct serenity of the dean's face. In Aliu Zamani University, Professor Boro

Finecountry was the patron saint of fine and visual arts—a man respected greatly in art circles and popular among the students.

The professor studied the HOD curiously. Ever since he'd called that morning, asking to see him by four in the evening, he had been wondering what it was he wanted to see him about.

"Can I get you anything, Vincent?" The professor pointed to the fridge at the corner of the office. They were on first-name terms.

Vincent Ubangha looked up. "No thank you, Boro."

"So what brings you to my office?"

Vincent Ubangha nodded. This was a man not known for wasting time on small talk. He came right to the point: "One of our students has been nominated for the International Foundation of African Students' Arts competition."

Professor Finecountry nodded slowly. "His name is Tosan Mayuku. He's a final-year student of your department."

"Yes. I want to ask a simple favor."

The professor stared at the HOD. "What's it?"

Vincent Ubangha's face was deadpan. "I want to withdraw his nomination. I want this boy's name taken off the list."

"Why should I do such a thing?" the dean asked quietly.

"One, it is unrealistic for us to expect that he'll win the prestigious prize."

The dean could see how carefully the lie was phrased. The young man had won almost every major visual art award during the past two years. His paintings had caused quite a stir throughout the university. He was the best painter the school had produced so far. He was the school's best chance of winning the competition.

"I don't like this, Vincent," he said suddenly. "Tosan Mayuku deserves the award. And it would be a triumph for this school as a whole if he won it. He's our only chance of winning this competition."

The HOD shook his head. "You may be right, Boro. But I don't want him."

For a moment, the dean couldn't speak. Actually, the nomination usually came from the head of the department of the contestant. His job was to append his signature, indicating that he supported the department's choice. It wasn't actually his job; nor was it his territory.

He finally found his voice. "You have a candidate?"

Vincent Ubangha nodded.

"What if this candidate of yours doesn't get the award?" The prize of the award in question was $50,000.

"What's the guarantee that this Tosan Mayuku will?" the HOD asked shrewdly.

Professor Boro Finecountry stared at Dr. Vincent Ubangha speculatively. He knew Tosan. Tosan was his own protégé. Removing his name from the nomination list would be doing the unthinkable. The boy was a genius. He was a metaphor of creativity in the genre of painting in the country. Wasn't he the winner of the National Visual Arts Council prize? Ever since the dean had wooed him over to the university, he'd personally watched him grow. Finecountry loved his works, particularly his still lifes, his sketches, and his tempera-on-canvas works. He did structured, measured, powerful drawings, whereas other students were drawing dust-covered withered trees and dry school buildings. Some of his most elegant drawings were proudly displayed in his country home in Port Harcourt.

"What's your second reason why you want his name canceled from the list?"

"He's a cultist."

Professor Finecountry waved his hand. "Who's not in this school?"

The HOD nodded. "I'm not concerned about other students. I'm concerned about the image of the candidate that will represent my department—this school and this country. It's not a personal grudge or anything like that."

Ten minutes later, Professor Finecountry watched the HOD leave the office. He pondered what they'd just discussed. He knew there was a catch somewhere. And he didn't like it.

* * *

The early-morning sun bathed the entire town with blessedly hot, harsh light. Three days ago, it had rained incessantly and had made everybody in the community wish for the hot sun.

Tos was in an excellent mood. He'd painted four other major oil paintings Ebi had described as "original, honest, and highly forceful." And Frank Reese had called him the night before. He promised to call regularly to check on his progress. They'd agreed to the terms of the exhibition. The American would take 70 percent of the cut from every picture sold during exhibition, and Tos would collect the remainder. So far as Reese was concerned, work had started on the project the moment Tos had collected the money from Western Union and appended his signature on the contract papers. It was not a bad deal. Ebi had said this arrangement was because Tos was new on the game, stating that things were always rough at the beginning of such things. But all in all, it was not a bad deal.

Frank Reese had also informed him that he was processing his travel papers and that he had commenced contact with the American Embassy in Lagos. Pratt Institute had also corresponded with him. All he needed to do right now was to send the transcript of his academic records. And that's exactly what he planned to do within the week. The agreed date of his traveling to New York was pegged on May 31, just a week after the first semester exams. To Tos, this was good news. All he really needed to do now was to paint more paintings and find a little time to prepare for the exams. And that was not a problem. As far as he was concerned, he was about to start a new life in New York. There was really nothing like the coming to fruition of one's dream.

He dropped his brown Samsonite suitcase in the center of the room. He was traveling to Lagos this morning to see an official of the American Embassy in view of his visa, to go to his former school to collect his transcripts, and to send a dozen more paintings to Frank Reese.

"Hey baby, I'm set!" he called out loudly.

"I'm coming," Ebi replied from the bedroom. "Just a moment."

Just a moment was another thirty minutes. But Tos wasn't in the mood to complain this morning. She had insisted on traveling with him to Lagos. Who was he to refuse?

When she came out of the bedroom, he was thrilled by her appearance. She looked tremendously lovely in a tailored black-and-white Bandini cocktail suit with matching brimmed hat.

"Assess me; how do I look?" she asked, swirling around.

There was a long moment of silence before Tos found his tongue.

"You look great."

Ebi smiled at him. She knew Tos didn't know that the pantsuit was custom-made by Bandini, right out of the couture.

"Can we go now?"

"No, I'll be back in a minute," she said, and she dashed into the bedroom.

"We're killing time."

"I'm looking for my car keys."

"They are here, baby."

"It's okay; I'm coming now."

Iyabo, the housekeeper, and Canova stood in the front of the house and waved goodbye to them ten minutes later.

The journey from Jankara to Lagos took all but eight hours. When they got to the city, Tos assured Ebi that there would be plenty of time to go shopping before their trip to New York, and he drove straight to his family compound in Isolo.

He nosed the Porsche into the space marked "parking lot" and killed the engine.

"We're home," he said quietly. It had been a long day, and he was worn out.

Ebi said nothing. She was looking around. The neighborhood was quiet. It was also a little bit clean. And the house was neatly concealed in row of old-fashioned houses on Mureni Street—a street that led off toward Isolo Road.

"Is this where you live?"

"Were you expecting something cuter, grander?"

She smiled at the question. She knew he was teasing her. He was not from a moneyed family. He was just an up-and-coming painter. She didn't expect him to have an apartment in Victoria Island.

"This is okay, Tos," she said quietly. "I know you're not a minister's son."

Tos reached out and pulled her against him almost violently. "I'm going to do better than a minister's son in the next six months," he whispered, and he kissed her roughly.

"You're a goon," she said, touching her lipsticked mouth in the side mirror. "Fiend."

"You want me to give you another tongue twister?" Tos said, making another move toward her.

"Don't dare," she said, and she pulled away from his reach.

He laughed. "Afraid of your fiend?"

"Are we going to stay here all day or what?"

Tos got out of the car. She followed suit. She studied the building closely for the first time. It was a big house, newly whitewashed, with aluminum roofing sheets.

Tos, standing beside her, was also staring at the building. *This is home*, he was thinking. His mother had been the sole heir of her parents' landed property. Now she was dead, and this house automatically belonged to him. If he traveled to New York, Auntie Yemi would inherit it. Auntie Yemi was his mother's only surviving sister. She was actually a half-sister. She was also a widow with four children: two sons and two daughters. But the children were all grown up, much older than Tos, and were all respectably married. The eldest son was with the Lagos State Civil Service, and the other son was an accountant, a branch manager of First Bank Nigeria Plc. somewhere in Ikeja. One of the daughters was married to a popular Christian minister. The last one was married to a *danfo* driver.

His mother's maiden name was Olajire. It was one of the oldest families in Isolo. They were not a family with fortune, but at least they were not starving. The maternal grandfather, when he died, had left the modest house to his only surviving child, Eyitemi Mayuku *nee* Olajire.

Where the hell's Auntie Yemi? Tos wondered. *Probably she's gone to the market.* She had a large superstore in Isolo Market where she sold beverages and provisions and assorted wines.

The atmosphere in the hallway was rancid. Tos took the staircase leading to the top floor. Ebi followed him closely. He opened the door on the top floor and led her into a comfortably furnished living room. A door led to the balcony. Ebi walked around the room, studying the old-fashioned furniture, an old TV set, an ancient radio, a telephone, and some framed photographs. She dropped her bag in one of the chairs, walked to the curtained window, and pulled back the curtains. Fresh air flowed unhindered into the room.

"This is home," Tos said. It was a statement. "Are you tired?"

"No." She turned away from the window and studied the room again. Close by was a colored oil painting of a naked girl framed in black passe-partout. She went to it and examined it closely.

"It's your work." It was another statement.

"Yeah. My early work."

She looked around. Surprisingly, there were no other works hanging around. "Where do those doors lead?"

"The kitchen's over there. Bathroom's the room to the left, and that one is my mother's bedroom." Sitting on a deep, ugly chair, Tos watched her.

"Where's your bedroom?"

Tos pointed to another door. She walked toward it, opened the door, and stared inside. She didn't go in.

"Do you like it?" She heard his voice from behind her.

"It's not bad," she replied, and she made for the kitchen. It was very spacious and cool. There was an old model gas cooker and a large kerosene stove, as well as a rack bearing dishes and saucers. Standing quietly in a discreet corner was a tall, imposing fridge. She walked to it and opened it. It was empty. From the kitchen, she went to his mother's bedroom. It was also a spacious room, the floor carpeted with a wine-red rug. A king-size bed and an equally large closet dominated the other part of the room. There were about six paintings of various sizes and shades in the room. Two caught her attention. One was a large oil-on-canvas portrait of a seemingly handsome man.

The handsome, bold, intelligent face of Etan Mayuku stared straight at her from the canvas. He was decked out in *kemeje*, a traditional Itsekiri dress, and had on great magenta-colored beads around his neck. The deep brown eyes stared unflinchingly at her from beneath dark, bushy eyebrows, and she detected a trace of laughter, something like humor, in his open yet bold face.

"That's my father." Tos's voice made her turn around.

"I know," she said, and she returned to the painting. The painting was true to life and closely resembled the photo of him Tos had showed her once. "You have his eyes and forehead."

"Really? Well, that painting was done by my mother."

The funny tone in his voice surprised her, and she turned around and regarded him quietly for a while, an amused expression on her face.

"You never tell me anything about your father."

"You never ask."

"I'm asking now."

Tos lifted his shoulders. "My father was the late Etan Mayuku. He was a self-made industrialist. Some people who knew him well said he was a good man. But things got worse, and as I heard, he made enemies in his business. Things got so bad that finally his business folded. A few years later, he died in an auto crash."

"I'm so sorry to hear that," Ebi said softly.

"My mother raised me. God rest her soul. I was her only child. She believed I was gifted to be an artist like her, and she encouraged me to paint. She was my inspiration. It was her belief that her son should be better than herself. I don't know yet if I'm better than she was." He paused. She was looking at him. He was unaware of how self-revealing the pause was. "I think she was a wonderful painter and a very good mother. In my heart, I know I can't be as good as she was."

Ebi nodded in understanding. "She was very good."

Tos smiled. "Thank you for saying that."

"But the good news," Ebi said brightly, "is that you're on your way to going to the United States. It's something that would make your mother proud wherever she is right now."

Tos nodded.

She was staring at the second painting. "Is that her work also?"

"Ah, yes. One of her works I've refused to sell."

Ebi tilted her head to one side, assessing the painting. It was also oil on canvas, titled *Esilokun*, and it depicted a beached water goddess. It was an extraordinary paintwork, so rich in detail that it looked real. The mermaid was skillfully painted and the mix of colors made her compellingly real, like living flesh. The background, which was the sea, was an endless blue that reflected the mystery of the mermaid world.

"You could take this painting to Reese?"

Tos shook his head. "I'm taking this one to New York. But I'm definitely not selling it."

"Why not?"

"It's my mascot," he said quietly. From the tone of his voice, she knew the discussion on the painting was over. He led her out of the room.

All in all, she saw that Tos's family home was impressive. The balcony was spacious and looked out over a part of the town. The floor was parquet, and the furniture ugly and outdated. Ebi liked what she saw. It gave her a feeling of peace and homeliness, and it was something her father's sybaritic mansion in Victoria Island lacked.

She went out into the balcony and saw that there was an octagonal table and some easy chairs.

"What do you make of it?"

"It's beautiful. I like it."

He put his arms around her, his fingers cupping her breasts. He kissed her lightly on the nape of her neck.

"You really like it?" His voice was filled with the smell of anticipation.

"It's cool. But it could be cooler if we repainted it and brought in some little things."

"Things like what?"

"New set of curtains, quilts, tablecloths, and all that."

Tos disengaged himself from her and wandered back into the living room.

"You're right. We'll do it the day after tomorrow. Tomorrow's going to be a heavy day for me."

"It's fine by me." She joined him in the living room. "Is there any food in this house?"

"I don't think there is. Are you hungry?"

"Yeah."

"Me too."

"I think there's a market somewhere around here."

"Yeah. I'll rush down and get something for dinner. But first let me get your things from the car."

"That can wait. We'll go to the market first."

"If you insist."

Together they drove to Isolo Market. The first thing they did was locate his aunt's shop. She had a large supermarket in the middle of the market. Tos introduced Ebi to her, and she approved of the young girl immediately. She was a woman in her late fifties with a well-fed round face and hair turning gray but carefully arranged down to the last strand. In her shop, they collected two crates of eggs, some peaches, Indian herbs and spices, corned beef, custard, butter, milk, whipped cream, apple juice, Kugelhof coffee, fresh bread, and three bottles of expensive white wine. In the nearby open-air shops, they wandered amid the delicious smell of onions and tomatoes. They bought white asparagus and cheese, tomatoes, hot peppers, onion fritters, garden vegetables, and refrigerated chicken. An hour later, they were back at the apartment, exhausted. But it had all been worth the effort.

"Now hurry up, baby," Tos said. "I'm starving."

One hour later, they ate on the balcony and watched the golden disk of the sun going gently down and the glittering lights of the community coming up.

Tos poured more wine for her. It was a romantic evening, with a delicious meal, an exotic wine, and a very beautiful girl on a quiet evening.

"Do you want to go out for the evening?"

"Should we?"

Tos nodded.

"I thought you said earlier on that we should spend the evening all by ourselves and not go out tonight."

"You're right. That was what I said in the market. But what do we do all evening? Watch TV?"

"No, make love."

Tos smiled. "You're a spoiled child."

"Are you not the one who spoiled me?"

"Okay, let's be serious. What do you have in mind?"

"No. You tell me what you have in mind."

"How about going to a nightclub to do some wining and dancing? I used to know a nice little place that's reasonable."

"Okay, we'll go then."

After clearing away the dishes, Ebi went to the bedroom to change. She put on a simple short dress that set off her figure, combed and brushed her hair into place, and sprayed herself with an expensive Paris perfume. When she came out, Tos was already waiting for her. He looked very handsome in a dark blue Valentino suit. It had been one of her presents to him for the Grand Wizard's Night.

"Are we ready?" he asked her.

"If you are."

* * *

Jasper Aziken was an Owlsman of marginal ability. And he was scared this evening. He was scared because he was involved in an operation—the abduction of the rival gang member.

For the past three days, Jasper and his colleagues had been on the guy's tail. Every day, they followed him to school in a different car and followed him home. They'd twice followed him to his girlfriend's place. They didn't mind the waiting. It had been part of their job.

Jasper scratched his ear and wondered about the abduction operation. Frank White, Klaws II, had told him that the operation was a very simple one. Their work was to nab the fella, and that would be all. But Aziken knew things would not be that simple in a real kidnap situation. He'd learned that again and again. And he also knew that inasmuch as the operation involved the abduction of a rival cultist, things wouldn't be easy. Who knew—maybe the guy was packing steel.

He chanced a look at the guy sitting beside him. It was Klaws II. And he was dozing. Aziken's mouth tightened. Here he was, frightened to his toenails, and Frank White was sleeping peacefully. How he envied him. Frank White was one of the most fearless men in the gang, and clearly one of the most ruthlessly efficient men Jasper had ever known. It was a blessing that they were brothers. He'd hate to have the Hammer as an enemy.

Jasper looked at the backseat of the car. He could tell Chux Arowolo was not dozing. Chux was a big boy, built like an iroko tree with a massive chest, evenly spread out in his black T-shirt and huge thighs. He was actually a 220-pound man. Many unfeathered Owlsmen believed Chux was a dangerous man. But for all his ruthlessness, he had yet to kill a man. He'd only been involved in knife fights and had not yet bloodied his beak. Jasper knew he was dying to pluck a feather.

"What's the time?" Chux asked quietly.

Jasper peered at the dashboard clock.

"Fifteen minutes past nine," he replied, his voice hoarse. This was the first real operation he'd been involved in as a member of the Black Owls, and by God, he sounded frightened.

"I think somebody's coming out of the building," Chux said.

Jasper suddenly felt sweat trickling down his face. He saw the guy all right. It was Kraks. There was no mistake about it. He wore a dark blue lightweight jean jacket and a blue baseball cap. He was carrying a small bag that was slung across his shoulders.

Chux and Jasper watched him quietly. Kraks came out of the little courtyard of his hostel building and walked onto the sidewalk. The moon dimly lighted the path. He was staring at his watch.

Obviously he was waiting for an *okada*. The small gray Toyota Carina where the Owlsmen were sitting was parked not more than thirty yards away from where Kraks was standing.

The guy's activities this morning had raised the alarm and alerted the Owlsmen. Chux had sworn that he had seen him enter Dikko's office and that he had spent well over forty minutes inside. And when he came out of the office, he'd taken a bike home, changed his clothes, and come out of his hostel with a Jimtex bag. He had taken another *okada* to the center of town, and from a discreet distance they had seen him enter a bank. He came out an hour later.

The bank thing was what alarmed the three Owlsmen. Obviously, Kraks was on a kind of secret mission. *Has he been sent to waste the Don?* Jasper wondered.

Chux touched Frank White lightly on the shoulder. He opened his eyes.

"What is it?"

"The guy's out," Chux whispered.

Frank looked through the window. He saw Kraks, and then he looked at Jasper. "Are you ready?" Jasper nodded. He seemed nervous. Frank White could tell. "Take off your seat belt. We're not traveling to Abuja."

Jasper nodded again and unclasped the belt. He wiped the sweat from his face. He felt his heart begin to pound. God, he wanted this thing to be over quickly. He wasn't in a hurry to pluck a feather.

At exactly nine-thirty, Kraks flagged down an *okada*. The *okada* rider reversed at his instructions and headed across the town toward the village.

Jasper started the car, accelerated fast at Frank's insistence, and dashed into the darkness after the quickly vanishing *okada*.

The evening was cold, and the traffic was light. Jasper kept a good distance between the motorbike and the car. They'd all received their instructions clearly: Watch him closely for a couple of days, and when he began to act suspicious, grab him, attracting the least attention possible—no gun-toting and whistle-blowing stuff.

"Give me the dog," Frank White said, looking through the window. The chap called Chux sitting in the rear seat brought out a small snub-nosed semiautomatic and passed it to the Klaws.

Frank White checked it to see whether it was ready for use. Satisfied, he laid the gun on his lap. Out of the corner of his eye, Jasper noticed it. He was tensed up, and his heart was beating unevenly. God, how he envied Frank White. The Klaws was as cool as a cucumber. He just sat there confidently, humming to himself, his bejeaned legs apart, one hand in his lap, covering the gun, with fingers resting lightly on the trigger guard and the other hand hanging on the window.

An enormous Mack truck pulling an equally enormous trailer zoomed past them, blasting its horn. Jasper's little dark eyes were fixed on the *okada* and its passenger, which were maintaining a good lead ahead.

"Frank—what's the line of action?"

"Have him taken. That's it."

Chux nodded.

"Are you prepared?"

"I'm cool."

"What about you, Jasper?"

The driver nodded.

"How do we take him?" Chux asked.

"We wait until he gets to his destination; then we'll crowd him," Frank said, and he wiped the back of his neck with his handkerchief. "Get the bigger dog. That's what we'll use."

Chux reached across the seat, threw a dark blanket aside, and brought out a short-barreled pump-action shotgun. He placed it between his legs.

Ten minutes later, the motorbike stopped and Kraks climbed down. He paid the bikeman his fare and looked around him. It was a quiet area. There was no electric light anywhere. A small black cloud had drifted across the face of the moon, and all around was partial darkness. Ahead of him was a narrow dirt road. It was a shortcut that led to the next street. The next street was also a narrow cul-de-sac. And that was where he was heading.

He was just beginning to fade into the dark pathway when the Toyota came to a silent halt.

"Stay here. Don't run away no matter what happens," Frank White whispered to Jasper before he opened the door and hopped out. Chux followed suit. Without bothering to shut the doors of the car, they dashed quickly into the bushes. Frank White kept well to the bushy pathway after Kraks, bending low as he ran, the 9 mm semiautomatic held firmly by his side. Chux, with one arm in front of his face to protect him from the thick vegetation, slipped quietly into the thick bush and cut hurriedly but quietly through the heavy, damp foliage.

Frank White was in time to see Dikko's errand boy cutting through the darkness.

"Hey Kraks," he called. "Wait a minute." It was just a trick to halt the guy.

Kraks stopped as if he had run into a brick wall. He spun around, trying to see who had called his name in the darkness. It was a mistake.

"Is that you, Miko?"

"Yeah," Frank replied.

Kraks tilted his head to one side, trying to process the voice. At that moment, Chux was waiting just behind a tree, out of sight, his clothing blending beautifully with the surrounding bushes. He could see the Roundheadsman.

"I don't think I know you," Kraks said, stepping backward. He could make out the other guy.

Frank White saw him take something out of his jacket. It glittered dully in the dim light.

Chux raised the short-barreled gun as if it were a club and came quietly from behind the tree. Kraks had made up his mind. He whipped around, but he was some seconds too late. The weight of the gun struck him on the back of the head. The sound was like that of pestle hitting mortar. Kraks fell slowly, heavily, his legs folding onto the damp ground.

"I've got him," Chux called.

Frank White materialized from the darkness. He pocketed his gun when he saw the body lying grotesquely on the pathway.

"I hope you didn't break his neck."

"I don't think so."

They stood over the unconscious boy.

"Where's the bag?"

"It's over here," Chux said, and he picked up the bag. Then they half-carried and half-dragged the unconscious boy through the darkness toward their car.

Chapter Fourteen

Tos left the apartment very early the next morning for the American Embassy. The house felt acutely empty when he had gone. After some moments of idleness, Ebi told herself to do something constructive, such as take her bath. And that she did. Later she dressed in tight blue jeans and a white T-shirt, and then she made a trip to her father's residence.

She arrived at her father's house on Bishop Aboyade Cole Street at about eleven o'clock. She had never liked the house. She never looked at it quite as a home. But it was a three-story dwelling of red granite and glass with twelve exclusive bedrooms, a tiled driveway, a water fountain, nineteen-foot floor-to-ceiling windows, and an Olympic-sized swimming pool.

She stopped her car before the imposing gate and tapped her horn three times loudly.

"I dey come oh!" shouted the *maiguard* from his security hut. With eyes glued to the discreet spy-hole, he spied the car. Recognizing the car, he shouted, "Madam! Abeg, I dey come now, now."

She heard him unlocking the gate and rushing to the car.

"Welcome, madam."

"Thank you, Musa. It's been a long time."

"No be small o, Madam. We miss you well well o."

Ebi smiled. Musa was her parents' *maiguard*. He'd spent fifteen years on the post.

"I miss you too, Musa."

"Wetin you buy for Musa now, madam?"

"Don't worry. I'll send it down in a short while," Ebi replied. She drove up the long driveway and parked near the short stone steps leading to the house. For a moment, she gazed at the house. It was a house of power and wealth.

She got out of the car, and as she made for the steps, the front door was pushed open and the youngest housemaid came rushing down the steps.

"Auntie Akpos! Auntie Akpos!" She hugged Ebi so tightly that both of them almost fell down the stairs. "Welcome, Auntie."

"How are you, Agnes?"

"I'm fine. You too dey fine well, well this morning, Auntie," Agnes said sweetly. "But you comot weit small, cha. But I like your hair like that."

Ebi smiled. "Stop flattering me, Agnes."

"I no sabi flatter, Auntie. I dey talk the true."

"It's okay. It's good to see you."

"We happy to see you too," the young girl said with a giddy smile. "I hope bread dey?"

Ebi laughed. It was really because of the simple people like Agnes and Musa that she sometimes felt homesick for this house.

"Don't worry. I bought you people some gifts." She handed the maid the car keys. "I've got some things in the car. Take them to my room."

"Yes, Auntie," the maid replied obediently. She was about Ebi's age, and they were very fond of each other. She was more or less Ebi's personal maid.

"What about my mother?" she asked as she climbed up the stairs.

"Madam has gone to the cloth market at Ikorodu."

"And Papa?"

"He dey upstairs. He just came back never long. He dey sleep now." The maid opened the car's trunk and carried out two large bags. "Make I go wake am?"

"No! Let him rest. I'm dead tired myself. It has been a long day. If he wakes up, tell him I'm in my room."

"Yes, Auntie."

Ebi left her there, passed through the spacious entryway, and walked straight to her quarters. She really was not in the mood to see anybody right now. She wanted to be alone for a while. The two-hour-and-thirty-minute drive from Tos's pad had been stressful—Lagos traffic and all that, as well as the heat—the roasting, headache-inducing heat!

She peeled off her clothes and entered the bathroom. She stood under the cold shower for twenty minutes. By the time she came out, her bags were already in the room. She opened them, sorted out the various gift items she'd bought for the entire household, climbed into bed, and curled up like a child. Sleep did not take long to sweep over her.

When she woke up, it was already dark. She rolled out of the bed and walked into the spacious living room. Nobody was there. She looked around. It was professionally clean and depressingly quiet. She could tell the furniture had been changed recently. The nineteenth-century Persian rug covering the dramatic black-bordered white marble floor was new. The soaring coiffered wood ceiling and the elegant piano were new. The chairs and tables were of high quality.

It was truly an opulent, elegant room. She heard voices talking on the balcony. *It must be Papa*, she thought. *Papa and whom?* They were talking in hushed tones. *It must be Papa and Mom.* They had allowed her to sleep, probably knowing that she needed the rest. She suspected they were talking about her.

She walked quietly to the balcony. Both her parents were there. When they saw her, they immediately stopped talking.

"Akpos—you're awake?" her mother asked.

"My sweetheart—you're welcome home. How's your school?"

"School's fine, Papa," Ebi replied quietly.

"How was your journey?" It was her mother who spoke.

"It was hitch free, Mom."

It was her traditional way of addressing them. Her father was "Papa" and her mother was "Mom"—not that there was great disparity in their ages.

"Did you sleep well?" It was her father who asked.

"Yes, Father."

"Are you hungry now? I've prepared your favorite dish."

"I'm not hungry, Mom. Not now. Maybe later. Thank you very much."

Her father studied her "We've just been talking about you, Akpos. Me and your mother."

Ebi glanced at her mother with curiosity in her eyes.

"Excuse me," her mother said. "I must see what's happening in the kitchen."

There was an awkward pause as her mother departed. Her father turned his attention on his daughter, his only child. Yes, she was still only a child.

"So tell me. How are your studies going?"

"Studies are going well, Papa."

"I missed you so much, child. Aren't you going to give your pappy a good girl's kiss?"

Ebi laughed. "I missed you dearly, Papa," she said, and she planted a kiss on his cheek.

"I'm sure you must be enjoying Jankara."

She held her breath. *Is Papa going to play out these games of his?* she thought.

"Come on. Let's go inside. The cold is already eating into my system," Chief Ezontade Dabiri said, and he stood up. Ebi led the way into the living room. Her father took the big armchair and sat down heavily. *Possibly his latest favorite*, thought Ebi.

Ebi loved her father in her own peculiar way. He was a tough old bird. He never denied her whatever she wanted, especially regarding material needs. The brand-new Porsche, the expensive clothes, and the jewelry were all physical evidence of that benevolence. Even when he kept her on a tight leash, he still created an atmosphere of freedom for her.

Her father looked older and more tired than she had ever seen him look before.

"It seems as though you've been working too hard, Papa," she said quietly.

Chief Dabiri searched her face quietly as he settled himself more comfortably in the chair. She looked simply exquisite and very fetching in a $300 silk caftan. She was more of a woman than the last time he'd seen her, and probably thinner.

He nodded his head to her question. "It's just simple work, my child. Nothing else but simple work."

Ebi raised an eyebrow. He had not been very healthy recently and shouldn't have even contemplated work for the next couple of months. He shouldn't be far from his doctor. His heart needed a lot of attention. It had all began after the failed attempt on his life in Warri.

She knew her father. He was a very stubborn man. He would always claim that he was in very fine condition and that his energy would shame many young men.

"You ought to make it a point not to do any work at all. Not the simplest work, even. You'll get yourself worked up. Do you understand, Papa?"

He didn't answer immediately, but his eyes were quietly assessing her.

"What about you? You've lost weight, my child." It was a fatherly accusation.

"Really?"

"Really." She heard the certainty in his voice. "Are you watching your weight or something?" She looked really chipper, though, and more beautiful. "Akpos, you ought to eat well. Eat well so that you can read well."

Ebi smiled.

Chief Dabiri studied her somberly. He was deeply troubled by the story her mother had brought him about her. Even thinking of it made him realize that he just couldn't bring himself to accept such a nonsensical coincidence woven by fate. It could happen only in beautiful fiction. It couldn't happen in real life.

"You were in town yesterday. You didn't come home. Would you mind telling me why?"

There was a pause. Ebi was surprised by the question.

"Who said I was in town?"

"They saw your car. My boys. They saw your car. They know your car."

Ebi sighed. She was quiet for a very brief moment to sort out her thoughts. She knew her father's spies permeated every layer of Lagos society and every corner of Ijawland, from the Forcados Terminal to the creeks and islands in the Niger Delta, down to the docks of Apapa. She believed that they were even more numerous than the late General Abacha's own network of spies had been during the dark days of his draconian regime.

"It's true. I was in town," she said quietly, without remorse.

"Why didn't you make it home?"

"We came to town for something. It was a kind of rush thing. And I felt I shouldn't breeze in just like that. After all, we'll be traveling back to campus in two days' time."

"Who's 'we'?"

"Me and Tosan, my boyfriend."

Her father looked at her as if she had completely gone mad.

"So you've been lodging at that drunken riffraff's house, eh?"

"You're not being fair, Papa. You don't know Tosan. You've not met him."

Her father stared at her. *Christ! What's wrong with female children? A man spends all he's got to build up an empire and a good life for his family, but because she's the only child, she falls for the first idiot that comes her way preaching love.*

"Young-Green's a sick man, Papa. He's jealous." There was no need for her to paint a graphic picture of him to her father.

"Why did you bother to come here?" Chief Dabiri said bluntly. The anger in him was blinding him, and the irony of it made him sick. "Is it to change your clothes or to announce your engagement? Which one is it?"

"I came because this is my home." Ebi's tone was equally blunt.

"No. You came to announce your engagement. You've let your mother in on it; aren't you going to let your father in on it too?"

Ebi said nothing. She was staring at the engagement ring on her finger.

"Do you have to engage yourself to this boy, Akpos?" Her father's voice had softened. He knew his daughter very well. She had taken a step into herself somehow now. The usually cheerful face was expressionless, and she was staring at him dully. *I know that look*, he thought. *It says this discussion's pointless.*

"I love him dearly, Papa."

He was silent for a moment.

"Tell me about him. What's he like?"

"I'd say he's very talented. Gifted. And nice too."

"And he's a member of a secret cult."

"No he's not," she said quickly—too quickly.

"He's a cultist," her father said, as if he'd not heard her. "He drinks human blood; he kills people. That's what *Campus Digest* says about him."

Ebi laughed. Then she shook her head. "That can't be true, Papa. Tosan's not that sort of man."

"If he's not a cultist, who the hell is he then?"

"An intelligent, brilliant artist. He's totally devoted to his work. Frank Reese has seen his work, and he was impressed with what he saw. There's an extremely good opportunity for him to travel to New York and develop his talents. Frank has invited him over. That's why we came to Lagos—in view of his visa."

Chief Dabiri knew Reese, the moneyed American art dealer. He'd bought a Poussin and a Chagall from him only the previous year.

"You helped him get in contact with Reese?" *Like I helped his mother get in contact with the wife of the American ambassador—thirty years ago.*

Ebi nodded.

"And he's planning on traveling to New York?"

Ebi nodded again.

Her father shook his head. *This really is supreme nonsense,* he thought. *Can you imagine that! Tosan Mayuku, Etan's son, sleeping with my daughter. God, how can this kind of thing be happening to me? There must be something wrong somewhere.* He took a deep breath, lifted his eyes, and met Ebi's gaze squarely.

"The boy's an Itsekiri, Akpos," he said softly but with deadly emphasis. "And you just can't date him. It's a problem."

"Everybody has got to belong to an ethnic group, Papa," Ebi said pointedly. "Tosan didn't chose his tribe; neither did I." She was clearly angry now. "Every person is best judged by his or her personal conduct. We're all human beings. If only we could start speaking of good and bad human beings and not good and bad tribes. There's no bad tribe. What we may have are bad individuals. And Tosan's not a bad individual. I can assure you of that, Papa."

Chief Dabiri studied his daughter thoughtfully. He knew she had inherited his strength. She wasn't even troubled by what her parents thought of her affair with her "gifted" boyfriend. She had not lied to him to please him. She was already sleeping with him.

She was even engaged to him. The next thing would be marriage. That was certain from her tone of voice. Then what would his people say? That he was a Janus-faced bastard providing the arms and sending other people's children to fight the Itsekiris while allowing his only child to date one. Was that not treachery? Or was there any other name for it? What about the other factor? He was Etan Mayuku's son—his only child. It was coincidental. They were both only children. Ebi was an only child, beautiful and intelligent. The boy, too, was an only child, talented, but a cultist and a rebel. The truth was that twenty-six years had not eased his hatred for Etan Mayuku.

"Let me tell you this, love: you're far too pretty and far too young to waste yourself on a two-bit brush-and-paint artist-student."

Ebi came to her feet in a fluid movement and positioned herself on the arm of his chair, wrapping one of her hands across his shoulder.

"I don't mind about that, Papa. I'd still be engaged to him even if he was the ugliest, the poorest, and the least educated person on planet Earth."

"Remember what happened in Warri," he said calmly. "My convoy was attacked. I was almost assassinated. Your cousin wasn't so lucky. I hope you've not forgotten your cousin Ebakumor. This boy's people killed him. They killed him in coldblood. That's my nephew I'm talking about. Your cousin. Your boy's people killed him. Do you think I'll forget about that so easily? Do you?"

She looked at her father for a long time, her face an impassive mask. Then she carefully removed her hand from his shoulders. She said nothing for a long moment.

"Tosan's mother was also killed in the crisis, Papa," she said at last, her eyes moist. "We're not the only ones who've lost somebody. Everybody's lost somebody or something, one way or the other." The tears were now running down her face. She pressed her mouth against the side of his face. "I don't want you to dwell on it, Papa. It's in our best interests if we just forget about the wounds and think of building more bridges, more relationships."

The chief stood up, moved away from his young daughter reluctantly, and stood by the window.

"I know this: we've only ever wanted the best for you." His back was turned to her. "We don't want you to get connected to the wrong people in the wrong area. Try to see the whole thing from our point of view. Your mother and I grew up in Nigeria. It's a different world entirely from what you've experienced in the States. We don't have the civilized advantages you had as a teenager. Ours is a rough environment. It's tribalism all the way—primal rivalries of tribe against tribe. That's how it is. True, the content of one's character is by far the most important thing, but here in Nigeria it's practically not so. Tribal and primordial affiliation is by far the most important thing. That's what I want you to understand." He turned around and faced her.

Ebi had listened intently to all he'd said. Now she gave him a quiet, straightforward look.

"Papa—have you ever fallen in love?"

Chief Ezontade Dabiri hesitated, unaware of how self-revealing the pause was.

"What's that?"

"Have you ever fallen really in love?"

The man regarded his daughter closely, quietly. There was an odd look in his eyes, as if the question had touched him in a place he had not expected. "Yes. Your mother's the most beautiful and wonderful woman in the whole world. And I love her deeply."

An expression of triumph showed itself on Ebi's face.

"Would you consider leaving my mother if your own father told you to do so simply because Mom belonged to an ethnic group other than your own?"

Chief Dabiri took a deep breath. "It depends."

"It depends?" The expression of triumph vanished from Ebi's face now. "Papa, answer my question—yes or no."

Her father gave her a scathing look. "Listen, girl. What I'm trying to say is that you're a special gift. God gave us something unique. You're that wonderful gift. We love you. We want the best for you."

Ebi laughed mirthlessly. "Love me? Do you think so, Papa?" She shook her head. "If you love me, you'll let me enjoy my life, be who I want to be, choose whom I want to go out with. If you actually love me, you'll let me do these things."

Chief Dabiri shook his head gently.

"You're a pretty girl, Akpos, but you're just as stubborn as I was when I was about your age. I suggest that you travel back to the States for vacation—say, during the holiday. See much of that white boy—McGinn or whatever his name was."

"I can't, Papa. If I do go, then it's with Tosan. If he is in the bargain, then I'm on it. But if not, then forget it."

Oh God, this is going to be one of those days when her face looks exactly like mine.

"You can't be serious, child."

"I've got a choice, Papa."

Something told him she had made up her mind. This was his daughter, young, clean-faced, free, honest, American-bred, unburdened, and unbothered by the laws that regulated people like him. He had grown up with a taboo, an ethnic-based law in an ethnicity-based tribally divided country called Nigeria.

For a moment he tried to imagine his people's reactions if the news had already gotten to them. It was going to cause a great sensation. He knew that. Back home, so many people knew quite well that he was the most important financier of the Ijaw cause. Over the past five years, he had steadily supplied automatic weapons to the EBA. He had always been the man with the plan. Even at the height of the war, he had commanded their line of action and told them what to do. For that alone, he was respected—even by those people who didn't totally agree with him—and loved by those uneducated, unemployed youths who appreciated his blunt talks, his adhesive criticism of both the state and federal governments, and his refusal to compromise his tough ideas on the Ijaw agenda in the Niger Delta. His residential compound was one of the council offices of the EBA. For the past five years, he'd encouraged the violence in Warri and its environs. In a famous speech he had delivered in the Creek River Hotel in Warri, he had been more vocal when he'd warned Ijaws to "beware of Itsekiris." And he had been more explicit when he had added, "If we must fight to get back what belongs to us, then we must fight because violence is the only thing we can use to achieve our objective in this country." That statement had popularized his name.

"Look, Akpos," Chief Dabiri said quietly at last. "I'm not going to pretend that I like the boy when I don't like the boy. But if you insist that this Tosan's the boy you want—the boy you're sure can bring you happiness and peace—then it's good for you. But don't ask for my blessing. You won't get it. Not on my grave."

Ebi looked straight at her father. "There's a stage in every young woman's life when she has to choose between her family and the man she loves. That time, I think, is not too far off, Papa. The time's not too far off now."

"I hope you're not going to do anything foolish."

"It's my business, Papa."

The chief's almost colorless eyes glinted angrily as he studied his daughter. "Akpos, I won't have you disgrace this family."

Ebi was looking him straight in the eye. "My life's my business, Papa. I can take care of it. I always have and always will. You should not be worrying about me."

"Nothing changes with you, does it, Akpos? Always the stubborn girl, right?"

"You're certainly right about that, Papa. We're in love. We're going away together. When we get to New York, we'll get married." She paused. "He's the only man I've ever truly loved. We're going to be happy together. We'll even give you beautiful grandchildren in the not-too-distant future."

"Enough!" Chief Dabiri said quietly, fiercely. "Enough of this nonsense." His teeth were clenched in rage. "Leave my presence immediately. Now!"

He stood staring at the door after she had taken her leave. He was really angry now. He began to pace the room, cursing quietly. Ebi wasn't the target of the venomous barbed arrow shot from the bow of his wounded pride. *This is shit! An insult! Very soon, the story will come out—that is if it's not out already—and everyone will be talking about it. About me!*

His major fear was from his enemies within Ijawland. Lots of people were waiting for an opportunity like this to wrestle the leadership from his grasp. That's what they'd been praying for.

Why in hell would Akpos let this happen now? Just when everything was going so wonderfully and perfectly. Akpos, why must you do this to your family? To us? The school magazine, *Campus Digest*, had painted an ugly, graphic picture of them. The bold headline ran thus: "**THE ITSEKIRI CHIEF AND HIS IJAW PRINCESS**." The article stated the following:

> Well-known final-year art student and National Visual Arts Council award winner Tosan Mayuku is deeply in love with flamboyant Akpoebi Dabiri, sophomore history student and American-bred daughter of ex-Transport and Industry minister Chief Ezontade Dabiri. The sizzling romance is the

hottest thing that has ever happened on campus. CD authoritatively gathered that the two lovebirds are planning on getting married at a time when their respective ethnic groups are enveloped in the fiercest, bloodiest, cruelest, and most prolonged ethnic war ever witnessed in the federation of Nigeria ..."

Chief Dabiri sat down and stared at the ceiling for a long time. This was clearly not a fate that he had intended for himself.

* * *

Kelly Okoro's eyes snapped open, dull in the half-light. It was 4:43 a.m. Wednesday morning—the morning the day after Kraks had been kidnapped. Kelly was yet to know, though. If he'd woken up an hour later than that, it would have meant a struggle for space among two hundred students in a dilapidated one-hundred-seat lecture hall. And he would have had to copy from a blackboard about thirty meters away. He didn't want to do that, so he hurriedly rolled out of bed and groped his way down to the makeshift bamboo- and zinc-fenced bathroom.

Thirty minutes later, he left his room, hurrying out of the compound into the dewy half light of the retreating darkness. At that hour, he was able to catch a campus shuttle bus to school and fight for a seat with a good vantage point.

At nine o'clock, he was comfortably seated in the lecture auditorium, receiving his third lecture of the day. All this while he was oblivious of one thing—he didn't know he was being followed and closely watched. He didn't even suspect a thing.

It was two o'clock when Kelly decided to go home. He was really hungry, not having taken a meal since the day began. At home, all he would need to do was to heat water for *eba*. His vegetable soup was only a day old. Just the thought of it made him salivate.

When he had just finished his last class for the day, he stumbled to his feet, collected his writing materials, and made out of the classroom with two of his classmates.

The three business economics students made for the campus shuttle bus-stop. In his faded blue jeans and white T-shirt, Kelly looked as inconspicuous as his two companions did. But the two Owlsmen in the dark green Mitsubishi Galant picked him out easily. They had already perfected their plans. Over forty-eight hours spent shadowing the "Stone" was more than enough. They had made up their minds to pick him up at the slightest opening.

They watched him and his companions cross the road toward the bus-stop terminal building.

"It's now," the driver said quietly to his companion. His companion was called Charles Afara, a.k.a. Charlisco. He was a skinny young chap with a quiet bearing—what many people call a good Christian look.

"Wait a minute," Charlisco said. "I know when we'll take him. We're not going to rush him. Just trust me."

The driver, who went by the name Pappy James, gave him a look that said, "I hope you know what you're doing."

Charlisco was a friendly sort of fellow. Few of his friends would have believed he was an Owlsman. He was not a very popular face on campus. But the truth was that he was a feathered Owlsman, though he was more of a backroom operator, largely unnoticed among the gang's more fiery and charismatic leaders.

Pappy James drove the car across the road and slowed close to Kelly and his two companions, who were about to enter the terminal building.

"Hey, my G! Wait a minute."

The three business economics students stopped. They were surprised, and they stared at the car suspiciously.

Charlisco was leaning out the window.

"Who's Kelly Okoro?" he asked. It was a clear question.

The three business economics students exchanged glances.

"Who's looking for him?" one of them asked.

"Dr. Ubangha—HOD, Fine Arts Department, that's who," Charlisco Afara said, smiling.

Kelly tried to get a better look at the two occupants of the car. The driver was a nondescript man a little bit older than the guy sitting beside him. The companion that had called his name had an open, friendly face. He was still grinning amiably. There seemed to be no malice or guile in his face or the grin.

"The HOD wants me?" he asked. His voice was not sure, questioning.

Charlisco looked at him as if he were not sure of the person talking.

"Are you Kelly Okoro?"

Kelly nodded. On another day, with another fellow, he would have shaken his head, but this guy seemed innocent.

"Hop in, then. The HOD sent us to get you. He wants to see you right away. He said we should take you to the Greenhouse Restaurant. He's waiting right now."

Kelly didn't reply immediately. He again exchanged a glance with his two companions.

"Is it so urgent?" one of his friends said. Behind the question was a quantum of suspicion.

"Yeah. The lecturer's waiting as I'm talking to you. You want a ride, or do you want to take a bus?"

The eye considered the option briefly. Taking the bus would take more time, would be less comfortable, and in the end would cost him a fare. *Who knows*, he thought, *maybe the prof will buy me lunch.*

"But I'll want to get home and change into something—"

Charlisco didn't allow him to finish. "Do I pass that message on to the lecturer?" Pappy James had already set the car rolling, bit by bit.

"Wait!" Kelly said quickly, thinking they were about to drive away.

"Are you coming or not?" Charlisco said impatiently, the grin already gone from his face.

"I'm coming," Kelly said, and he shook hands hurriedly with his two companions. "Catch you guys later," he said to them.

Charlisco opened the rear door. Kelly dropped into the comfortable plush seat. Pappy James engaged gear and drove fast over the roughly tarred road in the direction of the school gate.

Kelly's two companions looked at the car as it disappeared and then shrugged simultaneously and joined the line to wait for the ramshackle buses.

CHAPTER FIFTEEN

AT EXACTLY THE TIME KELLY OKORO WAS BEING LOCKED UP in the Devil's Arena, Tos arrived at Chief Ezontade Dabiri's residence. He came in a chartered taxi. Ebi had given him the address three days before. When she hadn't come back the day before as she'd promised, he felt he should visit her instead of calling her phone. He really missed her. He knew she would be shocked when she saw him.

When he saw the house, his eyes nearly bulged out of his head. So this was the famous Chief Dabiri's Victoria Island house. Tos had heard how magnificent the lovely mansion was. The picture of it was on the Lagos State tourist guide.

The *maiguard* allowed him in only when Tos convinced him that he was Akpoebi Dabiri's colleague at the university. That was only after the guard had phoned the madam and was told by Ebi to let him in. And before he was finally allowed in, he had to fill out a form and register the purpose of his visit.

While Tos waited for her, he took his time in studying the immense, expensive house. It was a unique upscale building loaded with luxurious ambience. The city guide stated that an Italian engineer had constructed the swimming pool and that the side chairs, tables, and umbrellas had been imported from France. The building itself boasted an enormous, constantly replenished inventory of choice English furniture and an assortment of quality antique pieces from Europe, especially France. A high-flying botanist under contract from a federal university professionally and regularly maintained the flowers.

From where he sat, he could see the garage. He recognized Ebi's Porsche. He also saw a Mercedes-Benz E-class, a Vitra jeep, an M-class Benz jeep, a Benz S-600, and a Cadillac limousine. They were all garishly displayed in the sheltered garage.

Tos shook his head enviously. *The money these people spend*, he thought with envy. They just dished out cool millions of dollars to erect buildings that looked as if they had been imported.

Ebi joined him later, and they embraced tightly, ignoring the *maiguard*, who was smiling foolishly, revealing kolanut-stained teeth. Their first wild, passionate greeting over, Tos drew Ebi beside him on the leather couch where he was sitting and held her close. He began to talk.

"There was a message from school. It was from Ovo. It's very important."

"Message?" Ebi asked quickly. "What message?"

The news of the capture of two of Dikko's eyes had just reached him. In the message, they had told him to return to Jankara immediately.

"What's the hurry?"

"I don't know yet. That's why I'm traveling down tonight."

"What about your visa stuff?"

"Not ready yet. Reese will handle it." He had been to the American Embassy twice already, and he had been discouraged by the line. He had tried to wangle his way in, but to no avail. Most of the people he met there had waited all night; some had spent well over three days waiting. He knew that if he decided to join them, he'd spend a week there. And he didn't have that time. That was why he had phoned Reese, and the American had said he would do something about it.

"What about the paintings?"

"I mailed them this morning."

"So what's up in Jankara that's so important that you can't wait?" She was very curious.

"Nothing I can think of."

"But you're sure everything's okay."

"As okay as the word itself."

Ebi was silent for a moment.

"Are you coming with me or what?"

"I've got to tell my father first."

Tos nodded. "Yes, of course. Do that."

Ebi stood up and returned to the house. She met her father on the airy balcony at the side of the building, where he was reading a newspaper.

"Papa," she called hesitantly.

Chief Dabiri looked up. "What's the matter?"

"Tosan's here. We've had a change of plans. We've decided to travel back to school tonight."

Chief Dabiri studied his daughter closely.

"Tosan? Your boyfriend?"

Ebi nodded.

"Where is he?"

She sucked in her breath. "He's downstairs. By the gatehouse."

Chief Dabiri dropped his newspaper, got to his feet, and walked into the living room with a slow gait that reminded Ebi of a cat. She heard him speaking on the phone in that deep politician's voice of his.

"Musa? Tell that young man out there to come up." He returned to the balcony.

Five minutes later, Tos appeared on the balcony. The young man made an impact on the chief immediately. He was immaculate in a nicely tailored navy-blue suit, Hermes tie, and Bally shoes. He was a very handsome man. And he looked just like his father. But he had something else: something his father had lacked—something that hinted of strength laced with a hidden amount of violence.

"You're Tosan Mayuku?"

"Yes sir," Tos replied promptly.

"Come, let's go inside," the chief said, and he led the way into the living room. Tos and Ebi followed him quietly. "Take a seat; make yourself comfortable."

Tos took an antique side chair covered in an expensive black-and-white fabric. Ebi sat close to him. The chief was sitting across from them in an expensive African-print coat and was still holding the newspaper.

Tos was looking at the house. The chief was looking at him.

"You've a very fine place here, sir," Tos said quietly. He was awed by the dignity of this beautiful house. Chief Dabiri had great taste. The antique furniture, Oriental rugs, Ming vases, and power paintings were real. All of it was evidence of oil money. The money these guys were making was enough to support a small African country.

Chief Dabiri nodded. He was used to this reaction from people on their first visits to his house.

Ebi had told Tos so much about her father's house and his priceless works of art. Seeing them firsthand now, Tos admitted the chief's taste in excellent artwork.

"Ebi told me you're a lover of art."

"Just a simple habit," Chief Dabiri said briefly.

Tos nodded.

"So you're the famous Tosan Mayuku." Chief Dabiri regarded him thoughtfully, unsmiling.

Tos nodded again.

"My daughter has been telling me about you."

"My pleasure, sir."

"Would you like a drink?"

Tos shook his head. "No thank you, sir."

Chief Dabiri nodded slowly and regarded the young man coldly. It was very obvious that he didn't like this boy and never would. *He is Etan Mayuku's son.* If Etan were still alive, he would be fifty-nine years old now. And if Eyitemi had not died in the crisis in Warri, she would still be beautiful and healthy and he would still hate her and she would continue to haunt him, even from her grave. His entire married life to his wife, Ada, had been a union to conceal the pain in his heart. Eyitemi was dead—gone from his life forever. But she was here again to torment him, through her son. It made him furious and sick to the pit of his stomach.

He still could not fathom it. On that day some twenty-six years ago, a child was born. His name was Tosan Mayuku. The name of the child's father was Etan, and that of his mother was Eyitemi Olajire; paternally she was Yoruba, but maternally she was Itsekiri. And to Chief Dabiri, both of them were Itsekiris. Etan had once been his best friend. Eyitemi had once been his girlfriend. She had actually been his fiancée. But they had both cheated on him and gotten married and left him to heal his pain. Then the bastard had become a threat to his business, using the Nigerian Navy to harass his boats and arrest his workers. "Such is life," people had told him. "A man's best friend can also be a man's worst enemy."

Then God had blessed him with a beautiful baby girl—his little princess. Now Tosan had emerged from nowhere, ignored the millions of girls in the world, and settled for his daughter, and the world again expected him to be the one to lose out. No, he wouldn't. She would never answer that Itsekiri name. *Never.*

"So you're an art student?"

"Yes sir."

They regarded each other for a moment, and then the old man stroked the side of his jaw with his thumb. He could see that the boy was wary of him and not totally at ease.

"And some nut in the United States has promised to make money off of you, right?"

"Yes sir." Tos laughed and turned to Ebi. "It's thanks to your lovely daughter."

Ebi waved her hand casually. "I only made a recommendation, nothing really worth mentioning."

Tos patted her hand; she in return squeezed his shoulder. Chief Dabiri could see the depth of their friendship.

"Let's talk men's talk." The chief's voice was cool. "My daughter gave me the general outline about you. Now, I want you to tell me the details." He leaned back on the chair and crossed his legs, his eyes fixed steadily on the boy.

"Details? What kind of details, sir?" Tos stared at Chief Dabiri with an expression that conferred unspoken respect upon the chief. But there was something hard in the old man's eyes that he couldn't decode. It made him feel uncomfortable. Actually, he felt a feeling he knew very well: fear. He was scared of the chief, very scared, and he was trying his best not to show it.

"Akpos—leave us for a moment."

Ebi frowned. "But Papa—"

"I said leave us for a moment." It was an order.

Ebi's frown deepened. She dipped her head so that her mouth was close to Tos's ear and whispered, "Don't let him stampede you, love. I know he'll try to chew on you. But be yourself." She patted his shoulder gently and strode out of the room. She would have loved to hang around and eavesdrop on their discussion, but she knew it would be unnecessary. Tos would surely tell her everything later. She instead made her way upstairs to her room.

"You're sure you really don't need a drink?"

Tos shook his head.

"My daughter told me that you're engaged to be married. Is that right?"

"That's the truth, sir."

The chief nodded. "Do you love her well enough to bind yourself with a promise to marry her?"

"I'm crazy about her, sir."

The chief studied him for a moment, and then shook his head. "Hold on a moment. 'Crazy'? Isn't that a rather strong word?"

"It's the mildest word I can use right now to qualify my affection for your lovely daughter."

Chief Dabiri frowned. The boy was being bold; he had spirit and a sense of humor. A thought hit him. Wouldn't it be a great joke, a sacrilegious joke, if he happened to die and will all his family wealth to this young man courtesy of his daughter? He could almost see the look of horror on his kinsmen's faces.

"Do you know that she's my only daughter?"

"Yes sir. She told me."

"And you still love her?"

"Of course."

"How can you prove that?"

Tos was silent. *I must tread carefully*, he told himself. *How can I prove that? Is it by simply saying that I love her, that I'm crazy about her, that if God recreated the world ten times over, I would still search her out and befriend her ten times over?* He knew he couldn't prove it. Not in words, at least.

"She completes me," he said slowly. "That's the only proof I've got. I don't expect you to believe me, though."

Chief Dabiri couldn't help laughing.

"How can that be possible? How can an Ijaw girl complete an Itsekiri boy? You know it's just not possible. There's just no way an Itsekiri boy can complete anything." There was a note of contempt in the last sentence—ethnic-based contempt.

Tos couldn't help feeling hot under the collar.

Then Chief Dabiri threw back his head and laughed deeply. It was a deep, rich laugh that unsettled Tos and made him frown.

"Look, young man," Chief Dabiri said at last. "I know who you are. You also know who I am. Don't you?"

The question hung implicit in the silence for almost a minute. Tos was staring at the chief, and he didn't like the look on the old man's face.

"Tell me. You know who I am, don't you?"

Tos's voice failed him. He just looked at the old man and nodded.

"Your old man and me…we were once friends. Solid friends. We went through some rough times together back in the old days. We did business together for some solid good years. I made him. Structured him. But he fucked me up."

Tos listened, frightened now.

"I heard he died about twelve, fifteen years ago."

Still tongue-tied, Tos nodded again.

"What about your mother? I also heard she was killed in the crisis?"

Tos nodded absently. *Killed by the guns you supplied to the EBA.*

"Life's full of irony," Chief Dabiri said quietly. "Way back, I never thought I'd have a cause to hate your father or your mother. We were the best of friends. Your mother particularly. I made her who she was, but she allowed herself to be impregnated by him. You're the outcome of that one-year romantic fling." The word "romantic" sounded in his mouth like some dreaded disease.

"Sir, I loved my parents—"

"Yeah. I can understand that. Your father was a romantic man, Tosan. You're just like him. That's how he got your mother hooked. It seems you've inherited this romantic trait from him." The chief paused, and suddenly he sat on the edge of the chair, staring angrily at the boy. "You've hooked my daughter with it." His voice dropped to a deadly whisper. "Your father took Eyitemi away from me. Now you want to take my only daughter away from me. Do you really think I'll sit down quietly and allow it to happen?"

Tos's face had grown stiff with anger, but he said nothing.

"For five years, I dated your mother. Trained her. I gave her all the links, the contacts. But she betrayed me. Now— today—my daughter, too, has given you the link to better your lot. How am I sure you're not going to betray her?"

"I love Ebi." Tos's voice was quiet.

Chief Dabiri's face was rigid with anger. "Tell me what you know about love."

Tos was frozen into deep silence. He just stared at the chief for well over thirty seconds before he answered. "It's when somebody who's not remotely connected to you comes into your life and completes a vacuum that God has put inside of you. That's what I call love."

Chief Dabiri rose slowly, painfully, to his feet. Tos's eyes were on him. The old man was deep in thought, his eyes vacant, but Tos felt his power. And the aura was intimidating. He had met other men who had the same *odidi* about them, but none of them had exuded this unmistakable impression of devilish ruthlessness.

"Listen, young man. My little girl may love you. I don't know if you love her. And I don't care." Chief Dabiri had stopped pacing. He was standing in the middle of the room, his eyes boring holes into the young man. "I don't give a damn if she falls in love with an illiterate bastard. But I bloody care if she falls in love with Etan Mayuku's son. I represent the Ijaw nation. It would be a slight on my person if people came to hear that my daughter, my only child, is frolicking with the enemy of my people. I won't take it, and I won't allow it. Not while I'm alive."

Tos was speechless. He just sat there, sweat feeding his face, his heart thumping, his half-opened mouth dry.

"I've been checking on your track record, and everything is wrong about you. You're an Itsekiri, and not only that, you're Etan Mayuku's son. And again, you're a cultist—a cultist to the backbone of your ass. You're the head of a devilish cult group in your school. Do you know what I think of cultists, young man?"

Tos didn't answer.

"Cultists are vagabonds of the lowest backgrounds. You're an artist. You're supposed to know." The old man smiled ruefully, his eyes still locked on the boy's. "You really like to live dangerously, don't you, young man?"

Tos took a deep breath. "I don't know what you mean, sir."

Chief Ezontade Dabiri sighed. "Don't feign ignorance, boy. In Warri, you're in the Warri Vanguard. In that school of yours, you're the chief cultist. In your little world, you think you're all-powerful, a legend. Untouchable. They even call you 'General' back home. My daughter isn't going to fuck around with a fucking cult boy and a rebel who has killed Ijaw people—her *own* people."

Ah, Tos thought. *This really is very interesting.* He could visualize the faces of Itsekiri old men, women, and children murdered and several Itsekiri riverine oil-producing communities invaded and burned down by militant Ijaw youths—an unprovoked attack orchestrated by some Ijaw leaders like Chief Dabiri himself. Some of these Itsekiri communities were forcibly and illegally occupied, even right under the nose of security operatives, mostly soldiers and navy, deployed to guard oil facilities in Itsekiriland. Yet this same man who encouraged the violence, who supplied the Ijaw youths with the tools to carry out the dirty job, didn't like cultists.

"I've already gotten a replacement for you," Chief Dabiri said, easily breaking into his thoughts.

Tos just looked at him.

"His name's McGinn. His name's coupled with hers back in the US. They used to be an item. He's called several times. He loves her; he's even planning on coming out here on a visit."

Tos said nothing for a while. But when he pulled himself to his feet, the anger was clearly etched on his face.

"Sir, with all due respect to you, I'll take my leave." His voice was quiet but carried well. "I would be a fool not to tell you this. I love Ebi. And in my heart I believe she's got feelings for me. Nobody can take that away from us. The crisis in Warri didn't have anything to do with us, and whatever you and my father did twenty some years ago is your business. The responsibility for those actions is not ours to bear. What Ebi and I are doing today is our business. We can live without one bit of the enmity our parents—our people—carried with them."

Tos had reached the door when the chief's voice caused him to pause, his hand already on the doorknob.

"I bet the name Isaac Wuru isn't a strange name to you—or is it?"

Tos didn't say anything. He just stared at the old man. Yes. He knew Wuru. His name was coupled with the Egbesu Boys. They said he was their leader. And the rumor going around the streets of the Niger Delta was that he was all-powerful, indestructible, another rebel in the making. His friend and lieutenant, a guy called Conboye, was also indestructible, but a few months before, the WV cornered this Conboye chap and simply but brutally killed him. Then, a week later, the EBA had brought out a list of WV members penned down for elimination. Tos's name was number one on the list.

"You're a dangerous man. Wuru's a dangerous man. And he's looking for you."

Tos shrugged. "It's quite all right. I can take care of myself." With that, he walked out of the room.

Chief Ezontade Dabiri was thoughtful for a long moment. He tried to resist the temptation, resist the idea jelling in his mind. He would do anything to save face. *Anything*. Even waste his daughter's lover. Paranoid though the idea may have seemed to his better self, he knew it was the only solution. *I must do what I have to do to stop this nonsense before it goes too far. The sudden and painful death of the boy would end the whole nightmare.*

He knew what to do.

He stared at the ceiling and thought of the idea. He would simply have a contract put out on the goddamned boy and end the whole thing quietly. It could be arranged so neatly that it would pass for a cult killing. *Yes! That's the idea. Wuru will move swiftly and silently and expeditiously to get rid of the bastard. He'll be overjoyed to do it.* The boy was a threat to his well-orchestrated future. Murder was the answer. The plan was formed. Ebi was his only child. She would inherit his wealth—his estate. He didn't want to leave his wealth or his daughter to the bastard.

Ebi came into the living room then.

"Where's Tosan, Papa?" she asked quietly.

Chief Dabiri looked her in the eyes. His dark eyes were as piercing as a detective's.

"We've finished our discussion. I sent him away."

"You did what?" The words slipped out of Ebi's lips unconsciously, automatically.

"I sent the boy away," said her father without enthusiasm. "That's what I did."

"Oh, damn!" Ebi moaned, stamping her feet hard. "I'm out of this place." She dashed toward her living quarters.

"Akpos! Akpos! Don't do anything foolish," he called after her. It was a useless effort. She was already out of earshot.

She came out about thirty minutes later, carrying a Gokey leather travel bag. "I'm off to school, Papa." That was all she said, and then she disappeared downstairs.

Chief Dabiri waited for the heavy mahogany door below to open and close. He heard her car start up and drive out of the compound.

He felt as if his heart were bleeding, as if something in the innermost part of his being were slowly being squeezed to death. And it was all because of one stupid prick of a boy. Despite his differences with his only child, he loved her very much. His sufferings were caused because of that love, and he was totally at her mercy.

It was an hour before he moved from his chair, went straight to the sideboard, picked up the phone, and began to dial. It was not her fault. He'd spoilt her, treated her as though she were a fragile relic from Shakespeare's century. It was now time to put a stop to this nonsense.

* * *

It was almost ten o'clock when Tos arrived at Jankara. He arrived in a chartered interstate cab. The first thing he did when he arrived was check on Christopher Edokpolor as planned. He met Christo One Way at home, and he used Christo's cell phone to tell the Evil Eye that he was in Jankara and already on his way to the Devil's Arena.

Ten minutes later, in Christo's jeep, they set out from town. Their destination was a tiny village called Ukpabunoh. It was midnight when they entered the village; the villagers, as expected, were already asleep. The village itself was made up of only a hundred colorless ramshackle houses painted with dust and darkness. There wasn't a single light left burning anywhere. Virtually everybody was in bed at that hour. And it wasn't a very dark night.

They parked the car at the outskirts of the village and walked into the forest.

It was, in fact, a long walk to the arena. Most of the way, no meaningful conversation passed between the two Owlsmen. Tos mostly ignored Christo One Way's attempt at banter.

Tos was in a pensive mood. The conversation he had had with the chief had depressed him. Chief Dabiri obviously hated him. Even now he couldn't believe what the old man had said to him. But one thing he was very sure of was this: There was nothing anybody could do about his relationship with Ebi. That he was very, very sure of.

After about fifteen minutes of trekking, they were stopped by the shouts of various men:

"Halt!"

"Don't move!"

"Identify yourselves!" a disembodied voice said from the darkness.

"The cleanest conscience is not afraid of a bullet," Christo One Way said quietly.

"Are you alone?" Tos recognized Morgan Akumagba's cold voice.

"I'm with him," Tos said. The jerking beams of flashlights fell on them immediately.

"It's the Don," Morgan said, and they turned off the lights.

Tos and Christo followed the path that led to the entrance of the arena. Actually, it was a farmhouse on what was more or less an abandoned farmstead, a fenced piece of farmland once inhabited by goats and hens, and at the back of the house itself was built an attempt at a barn. The farm building was built of concrete; obscured moonlight made it looked like an oversized rabbit hutch. The farmhouse was situated well inside the forest so that easy access to it from the main highway was cut off. It was initially the Owlsmen's initiation ground, which had now been converted into an informal agora where they performed all sorts of criminal activities. Its main use now was as a jail for prisoners—people who had offended Owlsmen.

As Tos and Christo climbed the wooden steps, the front door swung open and Ovo came out.

"You're late," he said quietly.

"I'm here," Tos replied.

"In my message, I said it was urgent."

Tos nodded, holding Number Two's eyes with his own. "You'd said so on the phone," he said matter-of-factly.

Ovo had started back into the house. Tos and Christo followed him quickly into the almost dark hall-like room, turned right, and walked through a heavy wooden doorway. About three hurricane lamps that hung on the walls cast grotesque shadows on the floor. Some six Owlsmen were on guard here. Two of them were carrying shotguns, and the others Kalashnikov rifles. They saluted the new entrants as corporals might salute a general. Tos acknowledged them with a wave of the hand as he went by. In the wide corridor, Ovo held up his hand as he stopped outside a heavy door. Tos also stopped and leaned close to the wooden panel that made up the walls of the room. He could hear voices on the other side of the wall—above all, that of Kraks, high-pitched and pleading. There were other voices he detected to be Owlsmen's.

"You'll need this," Ovo said, and he handed Tos a black cloth.

Tos took it and pulled it over his head. It was a cowl mask with only little slits for eyes, nose, and mouth. Ovo and Christo were already masked.

"I don't know anything," Kraks's high-pitched voice protested eerily from within. "Please spare me the pain, please."

"You've not seen anything yet; I'll kill you." It was Keme's voice, cold and furious. It was followed by an ear-splitting scream.

Tos pushed down the door handle and swung open the door. Together he, Ovo, and Christo walked into the room. All eyes within the room turned on them.

The room was lit by a dim oil lamp and smelled of urine and vomit. The lamp was burning steadily and threw grotesque shadows on the walls and ceiling. Kraks was sitting on a high-backed chair. He was tied to the chair. Tos could see that he was worn out and looking ill. His face was gleaming with sweat, and one eye was partly closed as a result of what must have been a savage blow. He was not wearing a shirt, and except for faded blue jean shorts, he was practically naked. His flesh was raw with wounds, his lower body bathed in sweat. Near his left pectoral muscle was a small, neat tattoo of a knife. Standing near him was the masked Keme, a.k.a. Al-Mustafa. Tos recognized him by identifying two things: his shoes first and foremost, and secondly, his body. He was bare-chested, and scar marks ran down his chest like weird tattoos. In the middle of his stomach, just a few inches above his navel, was a very visible tattoo of an owl with extended wings. He was holding a large club spiked with nails, which he had been using to punish the prisoner. Kraks had been under this kind of punishment for the last two days. He had been told directly that he was in deep trouble and that unless he talked, he would not leave the room alive.

Since the day he was kidnapped, Kraks had not seen the light of day. He remembered being attacked some three nights ago. When he had come to, he was in darkness. He was seated, his hands tied behind his back and his entire body tied to a chair. His head ached badly, and his body was alive with burning pain. He'd tried to move, but couldn't. A masked fellow had materialized from the darkness and told him that he had been kidnapped and was really in big trouble. That was how his nightmare had begun. They had showed him the money and asked him who had given it to him. He'd lied that it was his Christian campus fellowship money and that, as the treasurer, he had been charged to keep it. The blow he'd received for telling that lie had nearly burst his eyes.

Kraks's first reaction when he saw the newcomer was to turn to him pleadingly.

"Who sent you with the money?" Tos whispered harshly.

"Nobody sent me. It belongs to—"

"Listen," Ovo cut in. "No need to lie. We've got Kelly Okoro too. I believe he's your colleague."

There was something like a gasp from the prisoner. It had slipped out of his throat unconsciously. He understood the meaning of what the fellow had just said. If they had Kelly, then it was over. Kelly was not built tough. He'd crack under the first heat.

"Kelly? Who's he?"

Tos inched forward and slapped the prisoner hard on the face. Tied strongly, Kraks didn't have enough room to swerve his head. Tos's hand immediately connected with his face, a bright spurt of light burst into his eyes, and he shut them in pain. His nose began to bleed.

"Listen," Tos said, "Lie as much as you can. But it won't save you. Nothing can save you except the truth." The words were spoken in a cold whisper.

"But I'm—"

Tos slapped him again, harder. Kraks's vision swam dizzily. A series of lights floated across his brain. Involuntarily, he sucked in a fast, deep breath.

"Are you talking or not?" Tos knew he had to be rough and tough, and he couldn't afford to let down his guard in front of his men. They would say he was softening. He knew he didn't need it.

"What do you want from me, for God's sake?"

"Just tell us the truth."

"What truth?"

Tos slapped him a third time, the hardest yet. The blood was dripping down from Kraks's nostrils in streams now.

"Please stop," he cried out weakly.

"I'll not stop unless you tell me the truth—the *whole* truth—about the money: who sent you to deliver it, to whom it's being delivered, and what it's meant for. I want to know everything. Tell me everything."

Kraks hesitated. Blood was still rolling slowly down each corner of his mouth before sliding down to his chin and neck. His defense was slackening, he knew. He was at the breaking point. He knew he couldn't endure the torture anymore.

"Are you talking or you are not talking?"

"All right. Don't hit me. I'll talk."

"Good. I like a chap who tells the truth when he's asked. He's a foolish chap who tells lies when he knows that he should be telling the truth."

"One lecturer sent me with the money; that's all I know."

Tos looked down at the prisoner, his classmate, who was an abused mess now. When released, Kraks would surely need to see a doctor about the eye.

"What did you just say?"

"That's all I know—"

"No," interrupted Tos. "Before that. Who's the person who sent you with the money?"

"He's a lecturer."

"What's his name?"

"Dr. Ubangha—Vincent Ubangha. He's my HOD."

Tos nodded as he exchanged glances with Number Two, Number Five, and Christo, who was just standing in the background. One question answered. At least five more questions left.

"Who're you sending the money to?"

Tos knew Kraks wasn't hot enough to collect a contract for a hit. He was from a shallow house.

"Who're you sending the money to?"

"He told me that I should take the bag to a joint called the Congo and somebody would come for it. That's all I know."

Tos listened to the prisoner's words, looking for an inconsistency.

"What's the person's name?" His voice had almost lost its threatening note.

"I don't know the person; I'm simply just delivering a bag. The person, I believe, will know me."

"Answer this question yes or no: Are you one of his eyes?"

Kraks hesitated for the merest moment. "I don't know what you mean."

"Remember: you're a prisoner," Tos reminded him quietly. "And I can force it out of you."

"All right, I'll tell you. Yes. I'm one of his eyes."

"Very well," Tos said, and with his left hand, he pulled the black hood from his head. Kraks found himself staring at the man he knew so well. The nut-brown eyes were without warmth.

"You know me. And that's what saved you from being killed," Tos said softly, and then he pulled a handkerchief from his pocket and wiped Kraks's face with it. "Bring in the next chap." He directed the words to Keme. Keme went out and came back a short while later with a blindfolded young man. "Take off the cloth."

Number Five took off the prisoner's blindfold and shoved the chap roughly onto the floor. It was Kelly Okoro, and he didn't particularly look himself tonight. For the past three days, he'd been kidnapped and kept a prisoner. He had not bathed for those three days, and his clothes already smelled.

Tos studied the young man as he was made to fall on his knees before him. He was the most frightened young man Tos had seen for a long time. He was not fit to be a *solid man*. He had no guts, and right now he was nearly over the edge with what was happening to him.

"What's your name?"

"Kelly Okoro."

"Good. What frat gang do you belong to?"

The boy didn't answer immediately. The blood oath he had taken during initiation was too strong for him to break.

"What's the name of your frat gang?" Tos repeated gently.

Kelly made no response.

Tos reached down to touch the boy's ear.

"Is something wrong with your ear?"

"No," the boy muttered, not looking at him.

Then Tos noticed that he was wearing a green plastic rosary around his neck

"Are you a Catholic?"

The boy nodded.

"Catholicism and cultism—a very bad combination. By the way, have you prayed the rosary today?"

Kelly didn't answer.

Tos took hold of the rosary and tore it from the boy's neck.

"You don't need a rosary. What you need is a hangman's noose around your neck."

Kelly looked at Tos quietly, his expression pleading.

Tos looked at Ovo. "What do you suggest we do with this dung?"

Ovo Two shrugged. "What do we do with fuckers? We kill them."

Tos grinned ruefully, then said, "Go ahead. Kill him."

Ovo pulled out a black .38 semiautomatic, dragged the chap forward, trapped his head between his knees and stuck the pistol into his mouth, the cold steel touching his teeth.

"I'll talk. I'll tell everything. Don't kill me!" Kelly muttered. The words were barely decipherable. He was breathing fast and hard, sweating now, looking obviously frightened.

Tos nodded. "Are you sure you want to talk?"

"Please, I'll talk. Don't kill me." The bundled boy tried to edge away from the heavy weight atop him.

"Release him a bit, and let's hear what he's got to say."

Ovo did as he was told, but the gun was still making contact with the boy's head.

Taking a few deep breaths to steady himself, Kelly said quietly, "What do you want to know?"

"What gang do you belong to?"

There was a momentary hesitation, and then Elvis said, "I'm a Stone."

"Are you one of Dikko's eyes?"

The boy was silent for a moment, and then he said, "Yes."

Tos smiled. "I want the names and addresses of his ballplayers."

Kelly gulped. Sweating with fright, he stared transfixed at the gun in Ovo's hand. For the first time in his life, he knew terror.

"There're only three of them," he said hoarsely.

"Come on," Tos said. He was no longer smiling. "This is no time for games. Give me their names. And be fast with it."

Kelly pursed his thick lips, squinted at Tos, and then sighed as he said quietly, "One of them is Michael Imoni. He's a Stone. He's a three-hundred-level geophysics student. The other one's Osaro; he's a Panther. He's a three-hundred-level biochem student. The last one's called Nosa. He's a PB. He's in the department of psychology. That's just it."

Tos knew them all. They were all troublemakers on campus.

"Give me their addresses."

"I only know where Nosa stays. He's a resident of Queen Amina Hostel on Mission Road. As for the other two, I don't know where they're staying. That's the truth. I swear to God."

Tos turned to Ovo. "What do you think?"

Ovo gave a short, nasty laugh. "I think we should go and dive the bastard."

* * *

The next morning, Mike, bespectacled, and Osas, bejeaned, were ushered into the HOD's office. The lecturer greeted them at the door and motioned them to take up seats.

"What's the problem?"

"'Problem' isn't the right word, sir," Osas said quickly.

The lecturer frowned. "What, then, is the right word?"

"'Trouble,'" snapped the boy. "Real deep shit." His tone was nervous.

"What the hell do you mean by that?"

Osas got up and began pacing aimlessly around the spacious office.

The lecturer looked at him questioningly. "Will somebody tell me what the hell the trouble is?"

"All right. All right. I'll tell you what's been happening." Osas had stopped before the desk, his fingers resting on the edge of his chair. "We didn't receive the money. That's the first hitch. We came out here to inquire why, but your sec told us that you'd traveled to Port Harcourt—"

"Is that all?" Vincent Ubangha interrupted.

"That's not all. When we left here, we went to Kraks's pad—at least to inquire if you'd given him the money. His neighbors told us that he had not been seen for the past two days. Another guy added that the last time he had been seen, he said something about going down to the Congo to take care of some business. But that was over three days ago."

"Is that all?" the lecturer asked again.

"That's the first part of the trouble. Yesterday we went to his pad again to check him out. It was still the same story. Nobody seems to have seen him. He's not in school; he's not anywhere anybody knows. We went to your place again. We met your wife, and she told us that you were not yet back, though you had called and promised to come back yesterday afternoon at the latest."

"I came back last night"

"We said we would check on you this morning," Osas continued, as if the lecturer had not broken into his rambling. "On our way coming here, we dropped by at Kraks's place. He was not yet back. Mike said we should check on Nosa before coming to school to check if you were back. On getting to Nosa's place, the whole neighborhood was in turbulence. We were told that two Mercedes-Benz cars had arrived at his hostel block early this morning, with guys suspected to be Owlsmen disturbing the peace of the neighborhood with gunfire. Nosa, we were told, was practically forced into one of the cars and whisked away. Nobody knows where."

"You mean he was kidnapped?" the lecturer asked at last.

"Yeah," Osas said with a note of finality. "And that's where the trouble lies. Believe me, it's real trouble."

"What about Kraks—does anybody know his whereabouts?"

Osas shook his head.

Mike's voice cut in like a knife blade. "Did you give Kraks the money?"

"I gave him the check to cash the money about five days ago. I even called the bank to inquire, and they reassured me that he'd cashed the check for two hundred fifty thousand naira."

"Can he be trusted with that kind of money?"

That got to the lecturer. His eyes narrowed with thought. The question implied that Kraks had probably taken to his heels with the money. But that was unthinkable. Two hundred fifty grand was peanuts. Kraks had handled much bigger amounts of money than two hundred fifty grand.

"I can trust him," the lecturer said finally.

"How well?"

"Completely. Like a son."

A slow smile spread over Mike's face. It started out like a proper smile but then changed into an ugly grimace. "If my suspicion is correct, then allow me to say this: Kraks has been kidnapped. Just like Nosa."

The lecturer's eyes had darkened. He was visibly disturbed. "Kidnapped? By whom?" It was a foolish question.

Mike said nothing. It was Osas who answered the question.

"Owlsmen, of course. Who else do you think? They've blown the game; they've let the cat out of the bag."

"You mean they've got Kraks and Nosa?"

Osas moved back to his seat and sat down. "You should understand me, sir. Since I've been in this office, I've not spoken in tongues—or have I?"

Mike chuckled.

The lecturer was thoughtful for a moment. It looked as though he had reached the end of his life. Even Mike was chuckling easily, as if he were enjoying the way things were turning out, making him feel very much alone and unprotected, as well as in a very messy situation.

"What must we do now?"

"Of course nothing." Osas's reply was loud. "They'll talk. The fucking bastards will talk. Oh my God—what have I done? I've spent the last year avoiding Owlsmen."

"Hold it, Osaro. Kraks can be trusted. He'll not crack. He's the most reliable eye I've got. That chap can conceal secrets."

"I'm not going to bet my last kobo on it. Anybody—everybody—inasmuch as they're in the Owlsmen's net, will talk. They'll threaten him with acid. They'll shove a gun up his ass."

"I think you're overestimating this whole thing. Kraks will not talk."

"What about Nosa? Do you think he'll hold out?"

"Yeah."

"No. He'll squeal. Remember: you called him a pig!"

This time Mike spoke up. "Let him talk." He was no longer chuckling. He was staring at Osas, his face deadpan.

"What're you saying, Mike?"

"I said let them talk. We've not fucked up yet."

"What about the money?" It was the lecturer who had spoken. "Do you think the money was with Kraks when they came to get him?"

Mike said nothing.

"They must have taken it," Osas replied. "They'll use it to buy weapons. This is trouble. This is war. What do you say, Mike?"

Mike looked at his companion as if he was embarrassed by his presence. Osas had the look of a man ready to surrender.

"It's not over unless it's really over," he said philosophically.

"I'm afraid, Mike. I can see no escape."

Mike looked at him in disbelief. "Are you scared? Boy, let's give them hell. This is a dream come true. I want to hit those Owlsmen where it hurts."

Osas couldn't believe what he was hearing. He looked at Mike as if he had gone quite mad.

"What are you saying?"

Mike's smile was quiet and easy. "Let's fight this battle."

Osas stared at him. "Fight what battle? I'm planning on traveling to Abuja to hide my ass, and you're telling me to fight a battle. What kind of nonsense talk is that?"

Mike was still smiling easily, and there was no change of tone in his voice as he said, "Only this one battle. The only way to clear away the impediment the Owlsmen represent is to eliminate their head man. Don Tos is the impediment. He and his number men."

"Owlsmen alone represent about fifteen percent of the cult population in this school. And we have nineteen or more cult gangs in this school. Do you know that?"

"Yeah. And we'll make use of the remaining eighty-five percent."

Osas hesitated. He opened his mouth to speak. Mike knew what his protest would be and cut him off. "I know we're not as equipped as they are, but the best form of defense is still attack. We'll utilize speed and use all frat gangs against them. We can do it. Our boss here can sponsor it. Or would you rather not, sir?"

Vincent Ubangha's hurried head-nodding indicated agreement.

"You see—we're on."

Osas regarded Mike. There was an electric sense of possibility in his expression. He was not satisfied with it, though. With that sure instinct of a little animal smelling out a baited trap, he knew that once he allowed himself to be swayed by Mike's confidence, he would never again be free.

Beyond that, he knew that if anything happened to Don Tos, Owlsmen would go for other cult gangs' hitmen's throats again. And it would bring to the surface the traditional old frat conflicts of blood and steel. The only bright spot in this very gloomy scheme of things was that they could back out now, while there was still ample time to do so. The operation was blown already. His better judgment was telling him that once an operation was blown as badly as this one, it became imperative that every man must be for himself.

"Not me, Mike," he said quietly. "I'm out."

The incredulous expression on Mike's face was an ugly sight.

"I guess there's no way I can convince you. If you don't want to fight, then you don't want to fight. But I'll give you two hours to clear out of town. Get lost. You've graduated. You're forever banished from this school—and from this town. Don't ever come back here again. If you do, I'll personally kill you."

Osas couldn't conceal his anger. Without thinking, he touched the bulge in his waistband that was the small semiautomatic he always carried.

"You don't talk to me that way, Miko." His voice was one of mechanized anger. "If you want to be eliminated, then go and die a fool's death. I'm not ready to be eliminated yet. And you should mind the way you talk to me."

"I talk to you the way I like; you're no longer a solid man. You're a cheap *mugu*."

"Who the fuck do you think you're talking to? Are you trying to run me around or what? Tell me: Is that what you're trying to do?" Osas tried to disengage the small black handgun from the waistband of his jeans, but the calm, composed Mike already had his out.

"If you don't keep out of town—out of this school—then consider yourself dead meat, Osas. Remember that."

"Keep that thing out of sight," the lecturer said quietly. He didn't blink when he saw the weapon. Being armed was a way of life in the university. His grouse was with their displaying it in his office. Anybody could walk in and see them pointing guns at one another.

It was as if Mike didn't hear him. His eyes were fastened on Osas. The lecturer stumbled quickly to his feet and took the handgun from Mike.

"This isn't the best place to display this kind of thing," he said angrily.

Osas was still sitting down; his eyes fastened on Mike with unmasked anger. He stood up quietly and grinned, but Mike noticed the coldness in his eyes.

"It's a pity you're not going to come out of this alive. I would've loved to see your face when I came back." He didn't wait to hear Mike's reply before he made his exit. He closed the heavy oaken door gently behind him.

It was almost three minutes before either of them spoke.

"He's quite a boy."

Mike stared at the lecturer. "I'm going to see this thing through."

"How do you intend to do that?"

"I've got it fairly well-planned in my own mind. If I've got the money, I'll send the word out to all top number men of every gang that's against the authority of Owlsmen. Then we'll hold a meeting. In that meeting, we'll discuss the modalities of how we'll strike. We'll order our men to break and scatter and go underground as far as possible, as deep as they can. Then we'll arrange a strike force encompassing all hit men in the various gangs. Even top hit men from other schools will be invited to assist in dethroning the most peculiarly atrocious and demonically evil cult gang in the history of this school. It's going to be explosive. It's going to be tough. It will only cost extra money."

"Remember: I've paid two hundred fifty thousand—"

"We—I—never received it. The Owlsmen have it."

"Where the hell do you expect me to raise extra cash?"

"If you don't want to pay, then I won't play." Mike stood up, collected his pistol, and chucked it into his pocket.

"Wait a minute."

Mike paused.

The lecturer debated with himself briefly. "You think you can get this boy?"

"I'll do my damnedest."

"How much are we talking about now?"

"Just another five hundred grand. I'll give you until tomorrow evening to raise half of the dough. I'm going to wage a war—the kind of war this school has not experienced before."

Vincent Ubangha said nothing. There was nothing more to say. He was getting a little tired of the whole thing now. It was as if Mike had a personal score to settle with Don Tos.

"Why are you doing this? Aren't you afraid for your life?"

Mike laughed. "I'm keyed to action. And I like taking risks. It's my only vicarious pleasure."

"Okay," the lecturer growled. "You'll get part of the money this evening. Meet me at the Greenhouse Restaurant, say, five o'clock."

"I'll be there."

"One more thing."

Mike had already reached the door. "What is it?"

"I'll need protection. Myself and my family."

The ballplayer grimaced in thought, trying to think of something.

"It's possible, isn't it?"

"Why's it so special? You've got a guard already. I heard he's armed."

The lecturer came from behind his desk and stood facing the boy. "Don Tos will know that I'm Kraks's master and the owner of the money—that is if the money was with Kraks when they came for him. Nosa also will talk. They'll come for me." His words were just above a whisper. "I'll not be safe. I'm afraid one night guard will not be enough to protect me. You must know that."

The tall, rugged ballplayer shook his head. "Why don't you look at it this way?" he said, also in a whisper. "Take a short vacation, say, for three weeks. Don't tell anybody where you're going. Just for a little while, until this whole thing is over. It'll be over in a short while."

The lecturer nodded. What the boy had just said was a good idea.

"I'll just travel out of town, right?"

Mike's reply was automatic. "You need not even tell me."

Chapter Sixteen

CHUX WAS DOING THE DRIVING. HIS EXPRESSION WAS practically deadpan. Christo One Way was sitting beside him, a black beret covering his closely shaved head. Every now and then, Chux cast a quick look his way. He could tell Christo was in a sour mood.

In the rear seat of the Mazda were Don Tos and the Vee-Eye. A second car, a gray Mercedes-Benz 280 with four heavily armed Owlsmen in it, was following the Mazda closely.

Traffic was light because it was getting late in the night, and the few trucks they passed were those of criminal loggers who illegally felled lumber and used the cover of darkness to smuggle it to neighboring states.

It was the same evening of the day they'd nabbed Nosa. They had worked the ballplayer over, and he had cooperated quite readily.

In the Mercedes were Frank White, who was driving; Keme, who was sitting beside him; and Charles Afara and Kadiri Muazu in the rear seat. The four of them sat quietly in the stolen car. Together with Christo One Way, they were the ones who had carried out the interrogation, and from what Nosa had revealed, there was the smell of a hit. And it worried all of them. What worried them even more was the way the Don was taking the whole thing. A unanimous voice vote had been taken that Dikko should be wasted tonight, but Don Tos had had his own plans. He had said earlier, "The Black Owls fraternity is a wonderful hammer; I intend to use it when and if necessary to waste a few lives and knock a few heads, in order to make people leave people alone. But there's no way I'll use that hammer unjustly." From those quietly spoken words, it seemed that to him wasting the lecturer without confronting him with the facts was an unjust act. And the Don had vowed that he would not consent to it.

"What do you want us to do to him?" Ovo said to the Don. "Are we going for the kill or not?"

Tos brooded for a moment, staring at the road, dark and sinuous in the headlights.

"You leave it to me," he said quietly. "I know what to do."

"But this is supposed to be a kill mission," Ovo protested. He had pulled his .38 semiautomatic from the inside of his coat and was turning it in his hands.

"It's supposed to be a kill mission. But I don't want any more killings. This is a social call. We're not going to do anything bloody. We'll just advise him to call off his thugs."

"What about if he refuses?" The question came from Christo One Way.

"Then we'll burn his house. We'll burn his cars. No matter how much money he's got, no matter how connected he is, he can't deal with Owlsmen. We'll emphasize it; we'll tell him that if he makes any further move, any silly move, then we'll kill him."

Christo One Way shook his head. It seemed incongruous that a man like Don Tos, who in the last clash with the Black Panthers had been treated like a god, had now grown soft and weak. It must be the influence of that girl. Only a woman could soften a man in such a short time.

"Instead of driving this far to visit him, why don't we just call him on phone and tell him that we know what his game plan is? That would be the best thing to do, I think." There was a sneering note in Christo's voice.

"Christo, don't." Tos's voice was clearly angry.

"Yeah, my lord," Christo said, staring into the darkness.

Nobody said anything after that. They drove in deep silence. Above, the moon had swung around the pocket of dark cloud, whitewashing the road.

But Tos was in deep thought. Christo's words were really quite disturbing. *Am I losing my personality?* He wondered. *Am I growing soft? Am I losing my toughness, my violent streak, and my godfather identity?* The realization worried him.

*   *   *

The guard sat in the hut. He was smoking alone in the hut. This week he was on night duty. Outside, the night was dark and quiet and very still. Big black clouds looking like bags of rainwater hung threateningly low in the distant sky. The yellow face of a partially concealed full moon glowed white, just hanging over the black trees. It appeared to be just within the reach of a hand.

His mind bored, the guard sat quietly, smoking peacefully. The red end of his cheap cigarette was bright in the deep darkness of the gatehouse. He wanted it that way. People wouldn't believe that he was sitting in the darkness with a double-barreled shotgun and two cases of shells. With this new trick, he had spoiled the previous burglary operation. He had even been publicly commended for it by the local police chief.

A big lorry flashed past in the street. It carried with it dust and darkness. Onah, for that was the guard's name, was startled by the noise the powerful truck had made. It interrupted his line of thinking. But when the silence of the night returned, he returned to his reverie.

The Mazda slowed onto the side of the road a few hundred yards from the gatehouse. Chux professionally parked it under the clump of mango trees and turned off the lights. The Mercedes following it did the same. The guy sitting beside Frank White leaped from his seat and closed the door softly. He was Keme, and he was the OIC (Owlsman-in-charge) of the operation. The other three men in the car also came out, guns drawn. Keme gave instructions, and they all nodded. Then he walked to the Mazda.

"There's a guard out there in the gateway," Ovo told him through the window.

"I know."

"He's armed."

Keme nodded. "I'll take him out quietly," he said. He signaled the three other boys, and they all walked toward the fenced compound. Walking on the green grass bordering the road and the compound, the four of them approached the compound quietly. They all had their guns out now and were ready for any unwanted hindrance.

Vincent Ubangha's compound was fenced in, and the security post stood right by the gate. The hut was in darkness, but they were not fooled. They could make out the guard's burning cigarette. Keme was in the lead. He glanced to his right. As expected, there was no one in the street.

Keme turned to his left and walked along the edge of the fence toward the gatehouse. The three others followed him closely. They kept well into the shadows; it was easy to do so because the tall, gigantic security lights above the gate had been shorted out. Silently moving their feet with care, they approached the hut's iron-barred window. Keme motioned Frank White to go ahead and take the initiative. Frank placed his fingers on the window ledge and pulled himself up quietly and slowly. The guard was sitting quite close to the window, smoking his cigarette in silence. He was alone, as far as Frank could tell. He was supposed to be alone. The one working the day shift ought to have gone home by now.

Frank waited a minute, feeling his heart beating jerkily against his ribcage. The moon rode high above the tall trees, its beautiful yellow face still partly obscured by heavy clouds. The wind rustled the leaves and the flower shrubs, and the night was suddenly alive with whispered sounds. The air carried fine, aromatic smells and the scent of insects.

He rapped on the window ledge softly with his knuckles and whispered sounds out of sight. The guard immediately came over to the window and peered out into the darkness. His body was pressed to the bars. The only thing holding him inside were the iron bars used as protection against burglary. Frank reached out and gripped Onah's shirt and dug the cold muzzle of his gun into his neck. "I want the keys now!" he snarled.

The other three men came out of hiding, and while Kadiri Muazu also trained his gun at Onah's clearly frightened face, Keme scaled the fence quite easily. He entered the hut hurriedly, collected the guard's shotgun lying on the table at the far end of the room, and then, with a quick, savage swing, struck the guard behind the back of his head with the stock of the gun.

Onah went down like a sack of onions.

"You've killed him," Frank White said.

Keme looked down at the guard and shook his head. "He'll only sleep for a while. He'll need some stitches later, though." He bent down, searched the guard, found the keys, and went out to open the small side entrance gate. Only Frank White and Kadiri Muazu came in. Charles Afara had gone back to notify the others.

While he was away, Keme looked toward the house. A bright light was burning in the downstairs apartment. Dikko was in. His regular car, the Mercedes jeep, testified to it.

It was less than ten minutes later that the Mazda pulled up outside the gate. Frank opened the big iron gate, and Chux drove the car into the compound.

Tos and Ovo came out of the car. They stood and stared at the house. It was an off-white, uniquely built two-story mansion that had been designed with an easy, upscale, graceful style. It stood there, an elegant, impressive symbol of wealth.

Tos motioned to Keme and the others. "You guys should keep your eyes open," he warned. "I don't want any trouble down here." With that said, he and Ovo walked up the short gravel pathway and stood outside the outer screen door. Ovo pulled at the bell. They heard it ring somewhere within the house.

Tos looked around. He saw six cars parked neatly in rows. There was a BMW 7 series, a BMW 5 series, a Mercedes-Benz S-600, a Renault Laguna, a Toyota Calibra, and an M-Class Benz jeep—the latter being the latest of his collection and his favorite.

Ovo pulled at the bell again. Behind the blinds, yellow light gleamed dully. Dikko was not yet in bed. Through the screen door, they could see his wife coming. Tos knew her. Her name was Rachel. He had met her twice. The first time had been at the last art exhibition organized by the department. In that exhibition, Dikko had milked and fleeced them all. She did not know him, though.

He nodded to Ovo and chucked his hands into the pockets of his coat. His expression was featureless. His right finger touched the trigger of the .22 caliber automatic.

The screen door opened outward, and Rachel stood in the doorway, looking at them both with an open expression. It was not a very strange thing. Sometimes they received late callers. It was not even ten yet.

"What can I do for you, gentlemen?"

Tos stepped back a little and studied her. She was buxom and plain looking. He put her age at fifty or thereabout. Her body was covered with an expensive wrap, the ends of it touching the floor. Her voice was cordial, and it showed her education. She was the director of a private school somewhere across the town. It was the lecturer's own little private investment.

"Is the doctor in?" It was Ovo who spoke.

The lady nodded. "He's sleeping. Who are you people?" Her eyes dropped to the bag in Ovo's hand suspiciously.

"We're his students," Tos said, and he took a step forward, forcing her back into the house. Followed closely by the Vee-Eye, he walked confidently into the house. For a moment, there was something close to fear in the woman's eyes.

"Who are you people? You can't come bursting in like this."

Tos had been in the house once. He knew his way. The living room, kitchen, and dining room were downstairs. The library, bedrooms, art studio, and recreational rooms were upstairs. He walked into the living room.

The living room was lavishly furnished and thickly carpeted from wall to wall. A giant Sony TV set sat proudly on a polished cabinet that contained a high-powered sound system. On the wall hung a split-unit air-conditioning system. Portraits of Dikko and his wife adorned part of the walls. The atmosphere was evocative of a romantic love nest, decorated quietly in plush taupe and coral colors, and embellished with beautiful floral arrangements, gilt-framed watercolors, and Léger and Lichtenstein paintings.

The lecturer was lying on a couch, a remote control device in his right hand. His attention was glued to the TV set. On the nearby couch, a child was sleeping peacefully.

Tos coughed loudly. The lecturer turned around. He pushed to his feet quickly when he saw who it was. It was obvious that he was startled.

"What do you want?" he asked quickly and quietly. He was the man of the house. He wasn't going to lose his head.

Tos smiled. "I came in here to see you."

"But you can't come in here like this."

"I can come in here any way I like."

The woman brushed past Tos and ran over to her husband. She was badly frightened of the two black-bereted young men. She knew now that they were cultists.

"What do you want?"

"Get your woman out of here. I want to talk to you alone."

The lecturer looked at his wife and said, "Rachel, take the child and go to bed."

The woman looked at her husband briefly. His eyes were dark but not scared.

"Go," the lecturer said again.

The woman carried the baby off the couch and went out without a word.

"Now, what is it you want to talk to me about?" he said when she was gone.

Tos let the words hang in the air. He was staring at the tube.

"It's Sinbaaaaaaaad!" somebody shouted from the TV set. Vincent Ubangha looked at the television. It was the VibeTV show, and Sinbad was doing his thing: the stage funny walk. *Is this prancing or sashaying?* Tos wondered. He was wearing a beautiful black leather suit. The crowd was laughing and shouting. He was shaking their hands. They loved him passionately. Tos had watched it many times, and it was always the same: the same crowd, the same trick, and the same screaming by the same people. He reached over, took the remote control device from the table where the lecturer had dropped it, and turned down the volume.

"You said you want to talk. Let's talk."

For a moment, Tos didn't say anything. He just stood there staring at the lecturer.

"I've got two of your eyes. And one of your ballplayers. That's why I'm here."

The lecturer stood very still. "What the hell are you talking about?" His voice was loud.

Tos didn't say anything. He went to the couch and sat down. Ovo stood close to the door, watching the TV set. Sinbad was holding up a hand. He was smiling mischievously, like an overexcited child. The audience cracked up at that funny, lazy smile of his. Tos pushed button after button until the television set switched off.

"You know what the hell I'm talking about, Dikko," he said gently. "I'm simply here to advise you. You're going to run into a lot of trouble if you don't tell Mike and Osas to back off."

"Are you threatening me?" Annoyance was clearly in the lecturer's voice.

"Am I in a threatening mood, Dikko? I'm simply advising you—stay off my back."

The lecturer's expression went a shade uglier. "I'll call security if you two boys don't get out right now."

"You call them and see what good that'll get you."

Vincent Ubangha said nothing for a while. His mind was mostly blank. He'd just returned about four hours prior from his meeting with Mike at the Greenhouse Restaurant. He had given him the money—half of the said amount, as arranged. Mike had assured him that he would set everything in motion. The wheel would soon start spinning. *Can I get Mike to drop action?* he wondered. That was unlikely. Mike had even said he would travel out of town immediately. *What am I to do now?*

His wife came and joined them. Her eyes looked deeply at her husband.

"What's this all about, Vincent?"

The lecturer didn't say anything, but she didn't take her eyes off him.

"Tell me, what's this all about?" she repeated.

"He paid some cultists so much money to waste me. Exactly two hundred fifty thousand naira. I've gotten hold of the boys and the money. They've given him up. That's why we're here."

Rachel Ubangha's eyes went wild. "Vincent—is it the truth?"

Vincent Ubangha's expression didn't change. "I don't know what he's saying."

Tos pointed to Ovo. "That's the money."

The woman looked at the Jimtex bag in Ovo's hand and then once again shot a glance at her husband. "For God's sake Vincent, tell me what's going on."

"What do you mean by 'what's going on'? Can't you see that this is a setup?"

"You want to feign ignorance of your scheme?" Tos asked.

"I don't know what you are talking about, young man. I would really appreciate it if you would leave me and my family alone."

Tos turned his attention to the woman. "I want to make this point clear to your husband that I'm not a troublemaker. We're already aware of his plans to have me killed. I'm only here to advise your husband to call his gunmen off my back. If he doesn't, I'll not hesitate to do something really bad—something like killing a loved one in front of loved ones. Killing is nothing strange to me. I've done some terrible things in this school. You must have heard of me. I'm the head of the most powerful cult gang in this school. I'm Picasso. Ask around; those who know will tell you more about me."

Mrs. Ubangha turned her head and looked at her husband slowly. She appeared dazed and couldn't believe what she was hearing. It seemed an eternity before the words escaped from her lips.

"So you sponsor cultists, Vincent." It was an accusatory statement.

The lecturer licked his dry lips. He was pathetically ashamed of the situation.

"Tell me, young man, why would my husband want you dead?"

There was a pause, and then Tos said, "Madam, it's for a reason you won't believe."

"Tell me," Rachel Ubangha said tightly.

Tos nodded. "It's because of a girl. His former girlfriend. He wants her back. I'm the rival standing in his way. He wants to take care of the rival so that he can get her back."

Rachel Ubangha put her hand on her husband's arm. Her throat was tight, but she kept her voice light. "Tell me he's lying, Vincent."

"He's lying!" the lecturer shouted savagely. His face was drawn, his eyes hard. "He's lying. You don't believe him, do you?"

The woman said nothing. From her husband's expression, she knew he was the one who was lying.

"I don't know what to believe, Vincent."

"Believe me, madam. This whole thing's right here on tape," Tos said, and he signaled to Ovo, who stepped forward, took a small tape player from his jacket, placed it atop the table, and pressed one of its buttons. Nosa's voice filled the room.

"…He showed us a photograph of the guy. It was Picasso's picture. I know him very well. What he represents in this school. There and then I told him my mind."

There was a pause. "Did he mention money?" It was Keme's voice.

"I didn't wait for the discussion to get to that stage. Dikko—that's Dr. Ubangha—was annoyed with me. He sent me away. But I told him that I didn't want anything to do with the job."

Rachel Ubangha barely listened. She was trembling so much that she couldn't speak. Ovo let the tape play itself out before picking the recorder up from the table.

"So, madam," Tos said painfully. "That's the reason why we're here. Your husband actually discussed having me wasted. But he forgot something. He forgot that Owlsmen's eyes are wide open. He forgot that we're mafia—that we're different from every other cult gang in this school. We're already aware of his plans, and right now his name is number one on our death list. If any Owlsman is killed, your family will face our wrath. Are we clear?"

The lecturer kept his mouth shut. The information from the tape had been the last blow that punctured his air of innocence. He had been disgraced before his wife. For want of something to do, he made a move toward her, but she pushed herself away from his reach, and almost immediately, she began to cry. It was an annoying little sniveling sound.

"It's been a real pleasure to come to this house," Tos said. He nodded stiffly to the lecturer and rose to his feet. "I'll leave you people now. Madam, I'd advise you to advise your husband not to do anything stupid. He's got a lovely wife and, I believe, lovely children. They should grow up to see their father. I'm not so bad a boy to kill women and children—but if your husband doesn't behave himself, then the big owl will perch on this house. Remember: the owl's eyes are wide open."

Mrs. Ubangha slipped to her knees before Tos, trying to touch his feet, Indian-style, but the boy pushed himself from her reach. "We'll take our leave. But I want to register this: If I so much as perceive a threat to my person or any of my brothers, the world's ended for you, Dikko." He stood like that for a long time until the words became a threat ten times over. Then he jerked his hand in the direction of Ovo. "That's my deputy. He's Number Two. He controls the mob. He's more or less the leader now. I'm almost out of the system. If anything happens to me, he knows what to do. I brought him here to introduce him to the family. Deep waters are for those who can swim—you remember that, sir? Don't go beyond your depth. That's what you said the other day. If I were you, I'd heed my own advice." He nodded his head at Ovo, and together the two boys in black leather jackets and black berets walked to the door. The taller one opened the door for the other one, and they walked out of the room and into the night, leaving husband and wife alone, one crying on the floor, the other standing beside the couch for a long time, thinking of so many things all at the same time.

* * *

"Mount Kilimanjaro" was situated in the deep forests of Jankara. It was a log cabin deeply isolated, with no other house within a mile in any direction. Electricity was nonexistent there, and the only accessible road leading to it was a farmer's track: a tiny, well-beaten, leaf-strewn road. The cabin belonged to a farmer who'd died about four years prior. He had been childless, and no relative of his had laid claim to the cabin since his death. Some of the university's cult gangs had discovered it, and they'd used it a number of times as a "safe house"—a negotiation ground. It was picked simply for a single reason: it was situated miles from civilization and was beyond the reach of everyday society.

They all sat in the open clearing in the front yard of the cabin and waited for the Brownie to come. The moon that had just appeared above the pocket of dark clouds threw disjointed white light beams everywhere. They were all there. Each gang had come with eight reps, and the five most violent gangs were all represented.

The meeting was supposed to have started at twelve midnight, but it was almost a quarter past twelve.

The circular had been specifically clear:

All Five Top Gang Members Should Converge for a Dikodikoko

Date: Midnight Tonight
Venue: Mount Kilimanjaro
Reps: Eight: Three Titled Men, Five Durojaiyes

It had been signed in brown ink, with the symbol of the Brownstone.

It was now fifteen minutes past midnight, and yet there had been no sign of the convener of the meeting. It was not that they were frightened. Each of the represented five gangs had their gunmen—*durojaiyes*—posted around the safe house in case of any eventuality. Each *durojaiye* was well armed. Their primary job was to direct members to the meeting ground and, at the same time, ward off intruders.

"What the hell's happening?" A titled man, a member of the Roundheads' team, threw out the question. "I thought the circular said twelve midnight."

"That's the time," the head of the VVS reps replied. In his brotherhood, he was the Big Eye, which made him Number One. The VVS—*Vy Vato Sakelika* ("strong and hard like stone and iron") was originally a Madagascan secret society formed in 1913 by seven medical students, mainly organized to resist the spread of European culture. Ironically, seven medical students of diverse ethnic nationalities at the Aliu Zamani University had copied it in Nigeria in 1983. They had announced in their fliers that it was formed for "themselves to sacrifice themselves for themselves so that they could pursue their academic work in freedom, peace, and dignity." The major reason for the formation of this gang had been to fight against the negative tendencies of tribalism that were very rampant in the school at that time and to protect the weak from oppression of the more powerful elements on campus. Today in AZU, the VVS was one of the most notable cult gangs with a strong culture of violence.

The Killer and Maker of Soul of the Roundheads said from his quiet corner, "If they are not here by twelve thirty, then we are out of this place." He was the assistant leader of the representatives of his gang, and that was clearly the position of the gang.

Most students were not precisely sure what the Purebloods were. In 1986, a very visionary member of the VVS broke away from that gang and founded the Brotherhood of the Purebloods, known popularly as the PB. The PB, at its inception, was not a cult gang. Its members did not swear any oath of secrecy; nor did they bind themselves with blood oaths. In most cases in those days, they held public seminars and outings in which they paraded along the streets of the campus in broad daylight, protesting against unfair school rules like the sales of handouts, the "no payment of fees, no exams" policy, and the non-indigenes' discrimination. The school authorities then knew the identities of the PB's members. But all that changed in 1990.

Now they were interested, it seemed, in little else but campus violence. They roamed the university community with their faces hooded with white cowls, a bold letter *P* emblazoned across the hoods. They seemed more interested in crimes than causes and left terror and sometimes death in their wake. Like the VVS, they were one of the most violent cult gangs in the school.

"Probably they are testing our patience to see—" somebody was saying.

But the leader of the Black Panthers cut him off. "They've got no right to test anybody. If they're not here by twelve thirty, then we all should leave this place."

"Nobody's leaving," a voice said from the darkness.

The twelve young men sat still, their fingers unconsciously touching their weapons, their eyes photographing the bushes surrounding them.

Out of the darkness, Mike came up to the open clearing. If he hadn't spoken up, they might not have seen or heard his approach. He came into the middle of the gathering, his two companions hanging just behind him.

A guy got to his feet. "You kept us waiting. We'd like to know why."

Mike looked at the guy. He was the Stirrer of the Purebloods. He was Number Two by designation and the leader of his team. Mike knew him very well, a guy of distinction who had no qualms about firing a gun into a crowded classroom or knifing a classmate. He might have ignored him if the fellow hadn't possessed a remarkable track record.

"I had a hard time convincing some bigwigs—my financiers. I apologize to you all."

The chap studied Mike for a brief moment, shrugged his angular shoulders, and sat down. His name was Abel Udoh.

"Can we start now?" somebody said.

"We have started already," Mike said, reaching into his pocket for a cigarette. "We're gathered here for a simple reason. For the past four years, a group of persons who call themselves the Black Owls have ruled this school, and they're still ruling it with an iron grip. They've got great guns, and they've got great guys—just like every other frat gang on campus. But the bitter truth is that they've oppressed everybody, ourselves included, and they're still oppressing us this very moment. Some time ago, they abducted one Ade Lopez and beat him to a pulp. The guy was a Stone. And only last week, our oppressors abused our collective strength and went on a muscle-flexing spree. They abducted one Kelly Okoro. The guy's a PB. They disregarded his person; they disrespected what he stood for on campus, and took him somewhere and lynched the living daylight out of him. And as if that's not enough, they rounded up two other guys. One of them was Nosa Akhimien—he's a VVS. The other was Kraks Idonije, he's a Roundheadsman. They beat them, and when they were satisfied with what they'd done, they released them. But they threatened them not to talk—not even to us, their brethren. With that action, Owlsmen have proved once again that this institution belongs to them. And everybody's mighty pleased. That's the essence of this meeting."

A heavy silence fell on the gathering. What he had said was not far from the truth. They'd been humiliated by Owlsmen. Students who were known as *civilians* and *Jew men* were now making a mockery of other cultists. The Owlsmen were having a field day on campus right now. And if it continued, then the Black Owls would consider colonizing all other frat gangs' territories.

"What do you suggest we do?" The question was from the Stirrer of the Black Panthers.

"Supposing we killed some of the top Owlsmen."

Most of the representatives' eyes widened with disbelief.

"This is crazy," Abel Udoh said quickly. "Killing an Owlsman is the last thing I'd do in this school."

"Killing Owlsmen will start another wide-scale cult war," Roland Ibeshi said quietly. "I don't think any gang present here can afford it right now."

"If we don't strike back, then we've lost something," Mike said suddenly. "Can't any of you guys see that?"

"What have we lost?" somebody demanded.

"Power. Each time Owlsmen molest one of our own and we do nothing, their power is enforced."

"But using violence on violence will not solve the problem."

"Then what's going to solve it?" Mike demanded from Roland Ibeshi.

"I don't know," Ibeshi replied. "But to me and my brethren, war's not an option."

Mike lit the cigarette he was holding, his eyes, like the weather, cold. "There's no alternative to this nonsense," he said after expelling a thick cloud of smoke from his mouth. "We've all been insulted—you included. If not directly, then indirectly. Death—the violent deaths of Don Tos, Ovo, Keme, Christo One Way, Black Mamba, and Frank White is the solution to this nonsense. If we can get these men, then forget it. The Black Owls' camp will crumble."

There was silence for a moment, with all the gang leaders deep in thought. The arrogance of the Owlsmen was a terrible scourge upon them all. Not a single gang was safe from the intimidation.

The Black Panthers' gang leader shook his head. Only a fool or very brave men would challenge Owlsmen.

"My friend, don't get carried away by what happened a few days ago," he said casually, speaking for the first time. "We're students of this university, and we all know what's happening in this school. An enemy like Don Tos is a big risk. I don't think we can afford to cross him right now. I'd advise that we leave the issue alone. It's too risky."

"Risky?" Mike's voice was loud, and the anger in it very clear. "We take risks every day of our lives. All of us who're strongmen take risks every day. The risk of dying's not a strange thing to us. You know it. We all know it. It's not new."

"It's not new, but there's an adage in this school: 'Don't fight Owlsmen. You can't win.'"

"You can't be saying this, Lord Opanka," Mike said angrily. "You're the last person in the world that I would ever expect to hear say those words."

Ikpoko Opanka, the Black Panthers' High Priest, stared at Mike in amazement. It was true that the Panthers were the most powerful of the five gangs present. And it seemed that the

Brownstone chap was counting heavily on his support. But the truth was that cult wars were never really pretty.

The Black Panthers so far had been the only cult gang of consequence to declare outright war on the Black Owls. They had been defeated, but losing that fight had been like winning a war. It had boosted the members' morale. But right now, they were not in a hurry to antagonize Don Tos and his bunch of madmen.

"The issue before us, gentlemen," he said with magisterial calmness, "is frightening. If not handled with reasonableness, it will lead to dangerous consequences."

There was a general murmur of assent.

Mike looked at High Priest Opanka in amazement. Then, quite suddenly, a strangely slow smile came to his lips. "You're dead right, Lord Opanka. The issue before us is frightening. There was a time when the Black Panthers were the rave in this school. There was also a time when the Brownstones ruled this campus. But now what do we have? We collectively are now in awe of Owlsmen. Why? Is it because they have guys like Don Tos, Ovo, Keme, and a few fearless madmen with machine guns? No! They are powerful because you and I let them be powerful. Now they've cornered all the pretty girls. They walk with swagger on campus. Presently they rule six of the eleven villages that make up Jankara. We respect them. We tried to be like them. We begged to exercise some authority—some prestige like them. But they wouldn't let us. And even when they did, they made it embarrassingly clear that the school is theirs. And the only amount of influence we've got is that which they've kindly bestowed on us. Under the leadership of Don Tos and the misbehavior of Ovo, Christo, Black Mamba, Frank White and Keme, they've made all of us look like spineless old men. That's why it's frightening. And that's why it must stop. As gang lords, we've got our strengths. Our guns. And our philosophy. We're prepared for buckets of blood anytime.

"Today we're pissed on and we pretend that all's well, when what we really want is complete command of authority—respect from bloody Jew men. But look at us now. Owlsmen have been generally dubbed the most powerful cult gang on campus, possibly in Nigeria. Meanwhile, we're here—all of us are here, watching. Our fuckup is the greatest fuckup ever imagined. Personally, Owlsmen have wounded my pride by kidnapping my brother—by torturing a strong man. Yesterday it was Ade Lopez, Kraks, and a host of other guys. Tomorrow it may be you or me."

There was a deep silence for a moment. Some of them were beginning to catch some of Mike's confidence.

"Our people are oppressed," said the assistant to the Black Panthers' High Priest. "And the more we tolerate it, the worse it will become. I believe Mike's got a very good point. Delay is dangerous."

Roland Ibeshi shook his head. These guys were taking this thing too seriously. Oppression from Owlsmen was nothing new in Jankara. The things Mike said were pretty good reasons why they shouldn't allow this bullshit to continue. But it was something they had to live with.

"With all due respect, gentlemen, I think we should forget that this meeting ever took place."

There was stunned silence in the whole assembly of gang leaders. At that moment, he commanded the complete attention of everybody.

"What did you say?" Mike asked quietly.

Roland Ibeshi shrugged. "I believe there are over two thousand Owlsmen in this school. They're better organized. They've got more money. If we go ahead and declare war, it could go either of these two ways. We could succeed. But, of course, we all know the tendency toward failure is there. And if we happen to fail, God forbid, Owlsmen would be right up our collective asses. And there would be no protection for us. Let's not make the wrong move, I beg of you guys."

Some people nodded. He had a point there. But another fellow cut in.

"It's the truth that we're talking about the greatest power on campus. No other gang in this school has the kind of powers Owlsmen have. And they've abused those powers countless times. The question, then, is this: Are we supposed to sit by and let this shit continue? What Mike said is the naked truth. We've been undermined. We've been insulted. And it's not going to end there. I've been watching Don Tos for quite some time now. The way he and his men act, it's as if they're untouchables. And they're delighted in making enemies everywhere. It's got to stop."

"Do you think the death of Don Tos and some of his titled men will end this insult?" Roland Ibeshi demanded.

"Of course, yes," the previous speaker replied to him.

"Wrong, my friend. It will not. Do you remember Don Bosco?"

All eyes in the gathering fixed on the VVS Stirrer. Every one of them in the gathering knew who Don Bosco was. He was Don Tos's predecessor. His regime, compared to Don Tos's, had been relatively peaceful. He had lacked the color and terror and power of Don Tos's style of leadership. His style of intimidation had not been of the same texture as Don Tos's Black Owls; his terror had had none of Tos's brutality. He had been a decent don. He'd had all the virtue of a good cultist. But the Panthers had gone ahead and killed him, hoping that by killing him they would serve their interests and the generality of other cult gangs' interests. But, of course, that action had disturbed the hornets' nest. Now the Black Owls were left with a new leader, and the university with a new Black Owls. Today Don Tos was a man of headier vintage than the man he replaced had been—a much more violent man. Now everybody was suffering the consequences.

"I know your thoughts on the Don Bosco affair," High Priest Opanka said. He had been in his second year when Don Bosco was killed. It was an affair that a Panther would remember with little joy. In that episode, the Black Panthers had lost over twenty men, including their number one and number two. "But I think this Don Tos issue must be tackled differently—that is, if it must be done at all. There's some kind of sickness behind his arrogance. I really think that's why we must stop him."

Roland Ibeshi swallowed. He didn't say anything. There was something wrong about this setup. The truth was that in every cult gang there was always a group of men—extremists, fanatics, and zealots—who were convinced of the use of violence in solving every day's problems. All such men had in common was the eight-letter word 'violence'. But Ibeshi knew in his mind that this was not what he wanted and not what any of them really needed. Once started, a fight of this nature would be like the Liberian War—easier to get into than to get out of.

"Let me make this clear," Mike, said at last. "We're gathered here of our own free will. And anyone can leave if he so desires. At the end of tonight's meeting, we'll reach an agreement, and a contract to that effect will be drawn up. And we'll sign it—and that's only if we agree to topple the leadership of the Black Owls. That agreement, once made and signed by any one gang here, is irrevocable and binding; we can never be free of that contract until we've achieved our aims."

Some of the young men nodded their heads in understanding. But as was to be expected, only one voice broke the silence.

"And after that, what next?"

"Of course, we'll go back to what we obtained before the dictatorship of Don Bosco and install the cultic culture," Mike replied.

Once again, more heads nodded. Mike's reply made good sense. All of them knew what the cultic culture meant on campus. It was a state in which cult members, irrespective of which cult gang they belonged to, were equal to the members of another cult gang, and members were free to act as they thought fit within the respective bounds of that cult gang's law. But it was not freedom and equality for every student. It was only for cultic elements.

There were some people in the gathering who believed that the cultic culture was a utopian idea and could never be attained. A cult gang was bound by natural inclination to oppose or intimidate another cult gang. It was very certain. It had to be expected.

Ibeshi suppressed a smile. He knew that the desire of any gang's action was to replace the Black Owls as the most powerful gang on campus. No cult gang wanted to be under a cult gang superpower, but every gang wanted to be a superpower on campus over the other gangs. They wanted a kind of power that would enable their members to do whatever they wanted, so long as that behavior was not incompatible with the law of that gang. So after the fall of the Black Owls, who was going to be the next super cult gang?

"If anybody or any gangs want to leave, they're free to leave now. This is when we separate the boys from the men." Mike looked at the men one after the other. Twelve pairs of eyes focused pointedly and unemotionally on him.

Thomas Dakyap, Stirrer of the Roundheads, a proud, solidly built chap with hard eyes, got slowly to his feet. He looked at Mike squarely for close to twenty seconds before he spoke.

"I think it's better if we confer among ourselves before we decide on this thing." These were the magical words in the minds of many of the men.

Mike nodded. "I agree with you. It's a very logical thing to do before commitment."

The groups broke up into three each, and there was hushed, albeit heated, discussion by gang brothers for some twenty minutes. When they came back to the meeting ground and again took up their seats on the felled trees, it was Mike who broke the silence.

"Have we reached an agreement?" His voice was soft, but there was an urgent edge to it.

Thomas Dakyap once again rose to his feet. All eyes in the gathering were fastened on him. He said in a careful, quiet tone of voice. "The Roundheads have conferred, and we've agreed that we need to do something. As a cult gang, we have to emphasize our sovereignty, and we've got to stop this nonsense. This is the time to fight back to take back our sovereignty. Owlsmen will not give it to us on a platter of gold. We've got to kill to get it. We're for this battle. That's the position of the Roundheads."

The gathering was silent for the next one minute. Mike's dark brown eyes surveyed the meeting ground.

"We're waiting for the next gang to declare its position."

Abel Udoh of the Purebloods stood up stiffly and said quietly. "The Purebloods have resolved that a little physical violence is necessary. It breeds respect. It's time to fight and remove this obstacle once and for all. We're for this battle."

Mike nodded with satisfaction. Two were already in the bag. The VVS and the Black Panthers were the only two gangs left.

"Do we have other supporters?" His voice was patient.

The chap who stood to his feet was tall and thin, with a long chin beard. He was wearing black from head to toe. It was the trademark of the Black Panthers. He said slowly, "There's no power gained without bloodshed. Panthers have resolved. Absolute power demands the blood of Don Tos and his titled men. We'll devote our energies to it. That's our position. We're for this battle."

Roland Ibeshi shook his head. It seemed that virtually all of them were prepared for war.

Mike was grinning. "We've still got a gang left to decide. What's your position?"

Every one of them in the gathering was looking expectantly at the members of the VVS, particularly Roland Ibeshi.

Ibeshi stood up at last and said, "Revenge is the catalyst that stirs us into battle. But the truth is that most of the bloodshed that revenge draws us into is not worthy of our blood—"

Mike's voice cut in smoothly. "Are the VVS for battle or not?"

The VVS Stirrer ignored him. "Last time, it didn't work. The Panthers thought it was Don Bosco. 'Let's kill Don Bosco,' they said. They killed Don Bosco. It didn't resolve the problem. Instead it made things worse. Personally, it's not my wish to be a part of the repeat of the Bloody September episode. But as a member of the VVS, I have an obligation to my family."

"Obligation?" Mike said. "What obligation? Please just tell us the position of your gang."

For a brief moment, Ibeshi looked embarrassed. Then he said with a sad smile, "We're for battle."

Mike nodded. There was a satisfied smile on his lips. "'Battle.' I like the sound of that word."

The word "battle" was repeated round the gathering. Mike continued after the noise had subsided. "We can do it. All of us can do it. But that's only if we really want to do it."

High Priest Opanka nodded. "I'm one hundred percent behind this thing. But I want outsiders to carry it out."

"That's a good point," Abel Udoh said.

Mike said, "You must leave it to me. I've taken big trouble to arrange this thing. I can move in men from other institutions if I have the money. And if it must be done, then it must be done the right way. Owlsmen are notorious for their never ending inquiries and their spy network in this school. We don't want to take the chance of allowing too many ears to hear about this."

"Let's assume it could be done and that you could bring it about. How much do you have in mind?"

Mike looked at the guy who'd spoken. It was the VVS Stirrer.

"A good question. The sponsors of my outfit sprang a hundred fifty grand for this operation. Don't ask me to reveal their identities. I won't." He signaled to one of his men. The chap came forward. He threw open the black Jimtex bag he was carrying and displayed crisp bundles of neatly stacked bills. Satisfied that they'd all seen the contents, he zipped up the bag and retreated to his quiet corner. Mike continued, "I'll still need at least eight hundred fifty thousand to complete the fund. If we can get that, then we're on."

Roland Ibeshi shook his head. "That's a big amount of money. And speaking of money, we don't have that kind of money." His face was gloomy. "This is what I'm trying to say. There's no way we can raise such money. We know it. But Owlsmen, they've got more than enough money to fight us. What have we got in return? Almost nothing. They'll take us. They'll kick the shit out of us."

Mike made a noise like a bullfrog. His patience with this guy was wearing thin. Some of the other guys were shifting uncomfortably in their places.

"That's the more reason why we've got to fight this thing," he said patiently. "To radically and violently change the system."

There was some silence now. Most of them were deep in thought. Mike watched them as some of them sized him up speculatively. They were strong men—men who always went about with guns, guys who had used their guns to kill and would do so again if the opportunity arose. Some of them were already lost in the brutal and ruthless vortex of cultism. They were not in the least comfortable with even sitting in the same gathering. Each gang was a potential threat, an enemy, and a symbol of danger to the other. Since the last major clash between Panthers and Owlsmen, every major cult figure now carried at least a 9 mm handgun.

"But the money—" someone said.

Mike cut him short. "It's a large sum of money, I know. But if you can only allow your mind to dwell on what it's going to be used for, then you must agree with me that it's peanuts."

The others, except the VVS Stirrer, nodded their agreement.

Not to be left out, Roland Ibeshi said, "Maybe you're right."

"He's right," Thomas Dakyap said quickly. "Within ourselves, we can spring the cash—say two hundred grand apiece. How about it, gentlemen?"

"You may trust him. I'm not sure I do yet." Ibeshi was at it again.

"May I ask why?" Mike asked quietly, his eyes boring straight into Ibeshi's.

"This is money we're talking about."

"And so?"

"What's going to stop you, after collecting the money, from disappearing with it?"

It was the Black Panthers' High Priest who replied to him. "We would reach him. No matter where or how long he'd hide, we'd certainly reach him. There are no two ways about that. Or what do you think, gentlemen?"

Mike looked at the others. There was a general nodding of heads. Then he looked at Ibeshi. "Are you satisfied now?"

Ibeshi had no answer.

"How soon do you need the money?" someone asked instead.

"Two days at the most. I'm traveling out of town immediately. The speed factor's very important."

"Okay. We'll meet here tomorrow, same time, with the dough. Is it okay by us?"

There were unanimous ayes. Ibeshi didn't answer, though.

"The ayes have it, then," High Priest Opanka said.

"Can such a group—the outsiders we're talking about—be relied on to carry out the hit without any fuckup?" It was a member of the Roundheads who asked the question. All eyes turned in his direction.

Mike showed his teeth and looked at the guy. "Maybe you'd really like to know one more thing about me. Don't worry. I've done this kind of thing before. What we need to do this job is an exclusive execution team, totally dissociated from this school. Most probably, we'll draw from the various gangs represented in this gathering—men from outside this institution. But I won't do that. I know what to do. Just trust me. With the money, I'll raise a good team—an execution squad of no less than seven and no more than ten men. It will be their operations, but under my supervision. And it's going to be unique. Nothing like this has ever happened in this school before. But it will be made; the execution can be guaranteed. I can assure that."

The representatives all but looked at themselves. It was obvious that Mike had convinced them wholeheartedly.

The Purebloods' Number Four said, "We'll raise the money."

All the other reps echoed the same thing.

The meeting was over, and the cultists were soon in various stages of leaving.

"Thanks, gentlemen, for coming," Mike commented at last.

Ibeshi cut in abruptly. "Under the circumstances, I believe there's no need to thank anybody just yet. We can do that after Don Tos and his chieftains are dead."

"Thanks anyway," Mike replied to him. He shook hands with most of the men, and then he disappeared with his two companions into the darkness.

The battle line with the Black Owls had been drawn.

CHAPTER SEVENTEEN

Tos walked down the third-floor hallway of the Faculty of Arts building. It was a long, tiled corridor with fluorescent lighting. He was not alone. As usual these days, he was always in the company of three men. They were his personal guards. One stayed by the head of the staircase as they appeared in the corridor, and the other two, one on each side of him, walked him to a door bearing a simple nameplate that read, "PROF. BORO FINECOUNTRY (DEAN)." The two gunmen waited outside, and Tos walked straight ahead. It was their duty to keep an eye on the Grand Wizard. Whatever weapons they carried under their jean jackets were well concealed but within easy reach.

"Ah Tosan, you received my message," the professor said. "Come in and sit down. We've got some things to talk about."

"That's what I heard," Tos said, and he sat down across the huge desk from the lecturer, close to the window. From his seat, he commanded a good view. Outside, below, a mammoth yellow bulldozer was knocking over some of the ancient trees in preparation for the new graphic arts building.

"The governor means business on this new structure."

The professor nodded. "He's trying. He's the best governor so far in the history of this state."

"I hope they equip it immediately after construction."

"Yes. I hope he'll remember to do that," the professor said. He sat down and regarded the young man quietly. Tos had taken a cigarette packet from his shirt pocket and was fumbling for his lighter.

"No smoking here." The lecturer pointed to a No Smoking sticker attached to the desk. "Dangerous to the health."

Tos smiled knowingly and put the cigarette away.

"You must have guessed why I sent for you, son." It was a statement.

Tos shook his head, a sign of surprise flickering on his face.

"By the way, how's your project work going?"

"I've not really started."

"Who's your supervisor?"

"Dr. Dennis Jamaho."

"He's a good man."

Tos looked out the window at the gigantic instrument of destruction chewing up nature's perfect landscape and leaving in its wake nothing but red soil. The artist in him was already trying to create a surrealist idea from the scene.

"Tell me, son, what's your relationship with your HOD like?"

"Amicable," Tos replied carefully.

"Is that all?"

"Yes sir." Tos's voice was strangely soft.

Professor Finecountry shook his head. "There's no evidence whatsoever to support what you've just said."

Tos said nothing. He stared quietly at the professor. He didn't want to lie to this erudite man. His fortune of knowing this great man and being very close to him was a regular source of joy and an inspiration to him.

"Look, son. I've been doing my own investigation. I've been hearing stories about you. Ugly stories. And I don't like it. Dr. Ubangha's got connections, and he hates your guts. Anybody who's got connections and hates your guts can do you great harm. Do know that?"

Tos smiled. "That's right, sir."

"So tell me, what's the problem between the two of you?"

"I don't think there's really any problem, sir."

The lecturer regarded him closely for some time. "Look, son. Since I've started teaching in this school, the scales have dropped from my eyes. I know what's going on in this school, particularly in this faculty: the cheating that's going on, lecturers sleeping with their female students, the prostitution—it's even more sinful than the activities of the girls standing on our major streets, looking for men—and, of course, cultism, the greatest vice trapped inside the walls of our school. I heard that you're a cultist."

The last sentence was a statement, pure and simple. And Tos was taken aback by the directness of it.

"No sir."

"The last time you were in trouble because of that girl that was killed, you said you were not involved in cult activities. But I've heard from a very reliable source that you're a cultist."

Tos shook his head. The last time he had been in trouble was when his girlfriend, Aina Ribadu had been killed. The panel that had been set up to investigate him had quizzed him for well over a week. But at the end of the day, all the charges against him had been dropped. It was not because he was innocent; it was simply because there was no strong proof to link him to any of the various cult gangs. And the professor had been one of the few individuals who had stood by him then. He was naturally like that—an ever-present help in times of trouble. Tos really didn't want to lie to this very decent man, but it was best that he didn't know.

"So you're not a cultist?"

Tos shook his head.

The lecturer tried to see whether the boy was lying. Tos's face was expressionless.

"If you're not a cultist, what then is the problem between you and your HOD?"

"I don't know if I have any problem with him."

"Don't give me that look, boy. You're the best student in this faculty, and you're among the best three in the entire school. You're first-class material. I know your worth. But when your lecturer hates you, it diminishes your worth."

"You're right, sir."

"I've been wondering why your name was removed from the IFASA competition. I'm curious in knowing why the best student's work is not recognized in his department, in his immediate constituency."

"It's all part of the institutional corruption you're talking about, sir."

The lecturer shook his head sadly. "I know what the problem is. It's not corruption. It's more or less a vendetta against you personally. You're fucking one of his girls, yes?"

Tos looked at the man in surprise. Obviously the language the lecturer had used shocked him. He'd never before heard the man speak like this.

"Sir, what makes you think it's because of a girl?"

"It's just a hunch. You're sleeping with his favorite girl. And he's not at all happy about it."

"Okay. You're right. I'm having an affair with one of his former girls."

The lecturer looked at him curiously. "Do you know that she's his favorite girlfriend?"

"Yes sir. And I also know that he's had other girls. More beautiful girls."

"Beauty's not the issue here."

"What's the issue, sir?"

The professor looked at him doubtfully over his glasses and sighed. "You're in trouble," he said quietly. "Do you know that?"

Tos shook his head.

"Dr. Ubangha's one mean lecturer in this school. Women are his weak point. If you want to get in his bad books, go after his women and he'll come after you. But what you've just done is not only go after one of his women, you've slept with the favorite one. And that, to him, is like breaking the greatest of his commandments. And he'll take, as was his tradition, the pis aller."

"And what's that?"

"The last and only resort left for him to take. And that's your life."

Tos held his breath for a long moment. He looked through the window. The huge machine was still destroying nature. He let out his breath. Professor Finecountry was a very brilliant lecturer. He had been educated at both the Sorbonne and Oxford. He'd had a clean 2.1 from that prestigious, ancient British university. He was a very fine man. But in the very violent commonplace existence of Aliu Zamani University, he was a gentleman. He didn't sleep with his female students. He didn't collect *egunje*, otherwise known as "blocking." A man of spartan discipline, he neither drank nor smoked; nor did he succumb to the sin of the flesh. He was the type of college professor who always stayed behind his desk, enmeshed in volumes of paperwork, and kept well out of everybody's way. There were few art lecturers in the entire country who knew more about visual arts than this simple man. Tos felt for him sometimes. He had been elected to the position of the dean of the faculty because he had an impeccable academic record. The Faculty of Arts in Aliu Zamani University had seven departments—African History, Music, Modern Languages, Fine and Visual Arts, English and Literary Studies, Architecture, and Theater Arts. It was his astute and credible administration that saw the faculty graduating some students who later gained local and international reputations as lecturers, writers, painters, sculptors, architects, and actors, most of them excelling in several endeavors. The faculty was one of the most creditable faculties in the entire school, and there were hundreds of consummate geniuses studying in it.

Tos's first encounter with Professor Finecountry had taken place in 1998, when he was a student at Yaba College of Technology. The professor had been invited by the Department of Fine Arts as a guest lecturer during an exhibition of the finest works of the department's best brains.

A great number of YabaTech students had heard so much about the man, just as so many English and literature students had heard of Kongi. He was a pioneering art lecturer of the AZU art school. He was the second Nigerian to acquire a doctorate degree in art education, and the first professor of art in Nigeria—a man who had gained an international reputation as a philosopher, a painter, a sculptor and a lecturer on the esthetic values of artwork. His contemporaries included great names like Professor Solomon Irein Wangboje (the late master printmaker and visual arts scholar of the University of Benin) and Dr. Bruce Onobrakpeya.

Initially Tos had been unable to believe that the impressive credentials belonged to this simple man who looked then like a native doctor in his Senegalese kaftan.

Out of the many art students who met with the professor later on the day of the lecture, one left an indelible impression on him. It was Tosan Mayuku. Tos's HOD had personally introduced Tos to the erudite scholar as his protégé and the creator of the work Professor Finecountry had earlier admired in the HOD's office. The guest professor had been impressed. And before he finally left later that night, he said to Tos in his quiet, gentle voice that the boy should see art as a discipline that offers limitless opportunities in life and that if Tos should think of pursuing further studies after his diploma program, he should come to AZU to pick up a degree.

The professor became Tos's mentor and guardian when he finally got admitted into the university sometime later. But Tos had already been a *strong man* in his former school. The next twenty-four months had seen him climbing the rungs of power until he finally became the Grand Eye and spiritual head of the association known as the Order of the Black Owls in AZU. And it was something his mentor was ignorant of.

"Do you know that Dr. Ubangha finances musclemen?"

"By musclemen, do you mean cultists?"

"Yes."

"I've heard something like that," Tos said.

The dean was silent for a whole minute. He sighed and said softly, "I never would've raised this subject except out of deep concern for your future. Dr. Ubangha is a pleasant enough man. But where women are concerned, he's a dangerous man."

"How dangerous?"

"He finances musclemen. And he smokes."

"He smokes?"

"I'm not talking about cigarettes. I'm talking about marijuana. Ganja." The word "ganja" was spat out as if it were a dreaded disease. "You can imagine that—a ganja smoker with a deep appetite for his female students. It's not right for a lecturer to be smoking ganja and fucking his girls."

Tos laughed. He didn't mean to. The sound just came out easily and unconsciously.

"Why are you laughing? Do you think this is a laughing matter?"

"No," Tos said lightly. "It's just that I can't comprehend or picture Dr. Ubangha smoking ganja."

"Let me tell you a story, young man," the lecturer said seriously. "Some few years ago, there was a very brilliant student in this faculty. He was a wizard on canvas, this boy. You might have heard of him. His name was Osigwe Ajado. The boy was multitalented. And he was very good-looking, and girls liked him. It happened, unfortunately, that this boy and Dr. Ubangha were both having an affair with a law student. Dikko—as you young people so disrespectfully call him—was really going for this girl. But it was obvious that the girl preferred the young chap. Dikko, being a very cunning man who was madly in love with this girl, decided to set this chap up."

Tos's eyes narrowed. "How did it happen?"

The professor waved his hand. "We never knew how it happened, but it just happened. And it was bizarre."

"How bizarre?"

"One day we heard that the cops had arrested this boy. The police, without a warrant, came to the boy's apartment and searched everywhere, and they found a human skull and an automatic handgun. That was it. They said the boy was a cultist and took him away. We couldn't comprehend it. The boy was too damn gentle to be involved in such a satanic exercise. The girl at the center of the whole thing was very loyal to her lover. She went to the police station in the company of some of the student union leaders. They all believed the boy had been framed. The next morning, when the girl went to the station, the police took her to the morgue and showed her the corpse of her boyfriend. The girl went mad. The story was that the boy had been killed by an overzealous police officer. The police said the boy had attempted to escape, and in their bid to stop him, he had collected a bullet in the back. And he died on the way to the hospital. You know our police. Nobody believed them. The station would have been burned down if not for the quick intervention of the VC, the governor, and all other top personalities in the state. But that was the end of the young man's life and his talents, just like that—simply because he was vying with somebody for the affection of a woman."

Tos looked sad now. "That's a hell of a way to die."

"Yes. It's a very horrible way to die. You know some men feel very deeply about women. They can kill because of women. I don't understand it, but it's true. That's why you must be careful. Your

HOD is shameless in his love for this girl. He met her right here in this office, and since then he's been telling me how much he loves her and the plans he's making to make her his second wife. From those spontaneous discussions, I gathered bits of intelligence—what she meant to him and things like that."

Tos nodded. It had been three days since they'd paid the visit to Dikko, three nights since they'd told the lecturer to get off his back. Nothing unusual had happened since then. He was convinced Dikko wouldn't do anything stupid. He had a family to protect, so Tos felt he'd better not do anything stupid.

"Sir, what do you think I should do?" Tos's voice was low and intense.

"You know what I think? I think you're in for a rotten time. Dr. Ubangha's an unforgiving man. But if am I to say what's on my mind, I'd say you should continue having a nice time with the girl, and Dikko can go to hell. But that's not the best thing. The best thing is this: What should be of interest to you right now are your studies, and all your efforts should be geared toward your final exams. Give up on the girl."

Tos leaned back in the chair and regarded his mentor thoughtfully. "Sir, you want me to give up on the girl?" he asked quietly.

The lecturer nodded.

"Dikko's not a forgiving man—that's what you've just said. If I give up on the girl, he could still find an excuse to do me harm. If I don't give up on the girl, he has an excuse to do me harm. In that case, I'm keeping the girl."

The professor stared at him. There was something close to sadness in his eyes. "I've told you the story of Osigwe."

Tos nodded. "Sir, I appreciate your concern. I smell blood. But it's not my blood. If Dikko wants blood, then that's what he'll get. I'm not frightened of his musclemen." Tos got to his feet.

"Thanks for the advice, sir. From now on, I think I'll keep taking more interest in my surroundings. And I'll always remember your kindness."

The dean got to his feet. "Be careful," he said, giving Tos a sympathetic look.

"Yes sir," Tos replied dryly.

"It's wise men who listen to the counsel of wiser men."

Tos smiled and nodded. "I understand," he said slowly, looking at the professor respectfully. They shook hands warmly, and Tos let himself quietly out of the office.

The lecturer sat back in his easy chair, deep in thought. Talent was the greatest gift God had bestowed on man from birth. But it was something that had to be defined, nurtured, protected, and used as leverage for the actualization of dreams. Tosan Mayuku, like Osigwe Ajado, was very talented—even more talented than Ajado. Tosan was living talent, a walking genius. Like Ajado, he must not allow himself to be swayed by the beauty of a girl. The lecturer had really investigated her. She was a very beautiful girl, well brought up, and had attended the right schools abroad. And her father, the Ijaw chief, was very popular and stupendously wealthy. What Tosan must know was that the girl was unattainable, firstly because of Dr. Ubangha, and secondly because of his ethnic background—Chief Dabiri was not the type of father who would comfortably receive a boy like Tosan when he was presented as a suitor.

It had been a long time since he'd thought of Osigwe Ajado, and the creative connection between the two talented young men made him uneasy He couldn't comprehend the monstrous things people did in the guise of love, in bids to protect their love. Who could understand such a diabolical force that drove men to do such things as killing a fellow man? He knew he'd tried his best.

There was nothing more he could do. He could only watch and pray.

*   *   *

When he left Jankara that morning, Mike Osueke Imoni was aware of the growing enthusiasm of the League of Five (as the coalition of the five gangs had become secretly known) and of the rapidly accumulating forces against Owlsmen. He was aware that a brutal, bloody fight was the solution to the insult they had all received and that only victory on their part could secure their power in either AZU or any other university where the Black Owls had control. And victory could be achieved only by the death of Don Tos and his titled men.

The day before, each of the respective gangs—the League of Five—had received a white status letter from the Black Owls. In that letter, the Black Owls' scribe, Max "Paxman" Osuagwu, had explained in clear terms why Owlsmen had done what they had done a few days ago, and he had emphasized the point that their action had not been meant as a slight in any way on the respective gangs whose men had been abducted. And he had advised that, in the interest of peace, no gang should take advantage of the situation to do "anything foolhardy." The letter further stated that if any of the gang felt insulted, they should wait until a peace congress was convened and all grievances should be forwarded to the floor of the congress. The Kwill had promised that the Black Owls would address all the issues concerning the ill treatment they had "unintentionally meted out to all members of the respective gangs."

The letter, when they had received it, had caused a little furor. Two of the gangs, the VVS and the Roundheads, had wanted to opt out of the proposed plan to strike. Roland Ibeshi acted as their chief spokesman and tried his persuasive best to dissuade the others, but in the long run, the majority had agreed that the letter was belated. Mike had been able to convince them that the Owlsmen were using the letter as a momentary truce to buy time because they knew they couldn't withstand the full pressure of the combined five gangs. Finally, the League of Five had agreed with Mike's earlier plan to carry out the mission and reach out to other institutions in the South.

And they'd covered their tracks well. First they had sworn an oath of loyalty, "blood for blood," and then the oath of secrecy. No one outside the respective gangs' number men was to be told of the operation. Success depended upon Mike's sudden disappearance; total secrecy was the code to be maintained.

That was what Mike had done. He had arrived at Lagos around two o'clock. From the motor park, he took a chartered taxi to University Road, Akoka, Yaba. The taxicab dropped him off at the gate of a popular restaurant some two kilometers away from the school's main gate. He'd been there before. It was a large restaurant—one of the largest in the area.

It was called Jimoni's Lodge Restaurant. It was one of the priciest restaurants in the entire area, and one of the most patronized. James "Jimoni" Adebayo owned the restaurant. He was a soft-spoken thirty-some-year-old man, a product of the university. He was a graduate with an MSc degree in economics. He had nursed this vision of owning a business enterprise. Today he was commercially dug into the university community, his restaurant elegant and strategically located. And he made tons of money from it, living the life of a successful businessman. Already he was the local organizer of one of the thirty political parties trying to wriggle their way into the tightly controlled southwestern part of the country.

Jimoni's Lodge was enjoying a bit of good business at that hour. It was almost filled with bejeaned undergraduates. Mike pushed his way through a thick crowd near the door and stood for a moment, trying to orient himself to his surroundings. Ahead inside the very spacious rooms were tables with clean linen draped over them. Each of the tables was graced with fresh flowers. About two dozen students, boys and girls, were sitting at various tables. The students near him were speaking Yoruba in loud, raucous voices.

Mike made his way across the crowded eating section, moving through blue curls of cigarette smoke spiraling the air. He located a solitary table and sat down, placing his bag near his feet. A male waiter, his manners identifying him as obviously an undergraduate, decked out in clean blue jeans, a black sweatshirt, and casual loafers, came to take his order. He ordered two bottles of Guinness stout and a breast of chicken.

While he waited for his order, Mike took his time to study the restaurant. On the walls hung beautiful paintings with riverside themes. A well-concealed CD player was issuing soft Afrobeat music. More students had come into the room. Some who sat at tables close to his were singing in loud, coarse voices. He knew they were quite drunk.

The waiter brought Mike's beers and his chicken. He took a long swallow and discovered that the waiter was waiting for him.

"What is it?"

"Cash. We collect money immediately after service," the chap said.

"Oh," Mike replied. He looked at the tiny slip of paper on the table and handed the boy the correct notes. Just when the waiter was about to go, he called him back. "I'm looking for Jimoni."

"Who wants him?"

"Tell him it's Miko."

The boy nodded and walked away.

Mike concentrated on his chicken and beer. He had finished the first bottle and was midway into the second when someone called his name. He turned around before he saw who it was. It was James "Jimoni" Adebayo, a fair-complexioned five-foot-five chap wearing a red nylon jacket with an indecipherable foreign crest, a white denim shirt, black trousers, and black loafers.

"It's lucky of you to have come early," Jimoni said and sat down. "I'm about to travel out of town."

"I'm one lucky chap in the family," Mike replied, taking the other's outstretched hand.

"What brought you here?"

"It's a long story. But first have a beer."

"I'll take a malt drink instead."

"That's okay with me," Mike said, and he signaled to the waiter.

"I suppose it's no big problem."

Mike laughed without malice. "Why do you always think it's a problem that usually brings me here?"

Jimoni shrugged. "I'm just trying to predict you."

"Then let's say it's a problem."

Jimoni nodded. "There's no problem without a solution."

The waiter brought Jimoni's malt. But this time he did not wait to collect money.

Jimoni took a small sip and regarded the boy from AZU quietly. James "Jimoni" Adebayo had once been the Big Eye, otherwise known as big brother number one, of the university's branch of the Brotherhood of the Roundheads. With his skull-cut haircut, quiet manners, and slow, steady innocent smile, no one would believe he was once the numero uno of the Roundheads.

"So what's the problem?"

Mike laid his right hand on Jimoni's arm. "I need some men," he said quietly.

Jimoni studied his cousin, his face inscrutable. "Men? What do you need men for?"

"It's for a job I'm involved in."

"A job?"

"Yeah. A job."

"Are you in trouble?"

"Something like that."

"I'm sorry, Miko. I'm willing to help you. But I can't without knowing what exactly this whole thing is all about."

Mike pulled out a packet of cigarettes from his shirt pocket. He offered the pack to his cousin, who shook his head. He lit one for himself and blew a cloud of smoke rings into the air.

"Let's just say there's a clash of interests in my school right now. And I'm in the thick of it." Mike had lowered his voice significantly.

Jimoni sighed. "Is that all?"

"It's against the Black Owls." His voice was now a whisper.

Again the restaurateur's face darkened, and he shifted uncomfortably in his chair. It was clear that he was uncomfortable.

"That's Tosan and his gang."

"Unfortunately, yes."

Jimoni frowned and studied his cousin. "What actually happened?"

"That's not the issue right now. It has happened. And I'm here to raise a team to solve this problem."

Jimoni glared at the man in front of him. If not for the blood relation, he'd have told him to fuck off. But how could he? It was Mike's mother, his auntie, who had raised him up after his own mother had died during childbirth—his birth. He had grown to regard that very special woman as his own mother. How could he then turn down her son, his cousin, when he needed his help, after all the kindness and love that very special woman had shown him?

But they were not from the same camp. Mike was a member of the Brownstones, a rival frat gang.

"Come; let's get out of here. This is not the place to discuss this kind of thing." Jimoni grabbed the bottle of malt drink and downed it in a gulp. Mike did the same and followed his cousin outside. Jimoni led him to a maroon Audi.

"So this is the car?"

Jimoni smiled proudly. "Just the small toy I'm using right now. It's part of the image I'm cultivating—the big boy with fancy clothes, owner of the fancy restaurant, cruising around in the fancy car. Do you like it?"

Mike walked around the car, touching as if rubbing his fingers along the naked body of a beautiful girl.

"It's beautiful," he said at last.

"I knew you would like it," Jimoni said, and he opened the door. "Come on; get in and let's go."

The car eased down the ever-busy street. Fifteen minutes later, he parked outside a cream-colored bungalow. Jimoni locked up and led his cousin into the house. It was a very spacious house, and its dark, quiet luxury was impressive. Mike took one of the twin leather couches, and Jimoni sat across from him.

"So tell me everything," he said quietly.

Mike did so while Jimoni listened attentively. After he was finished, Jimoni thought about what he'd been told for several minutes. At last he sighed heavily and said, "I don't want to be involved in this thing."

Mike was silent for a moment. Then he said, "Can you tell me why?"

"Forget the why. You're interfering, Miko. Get out of this thing. Leave Owlsmen alone."

Mike laughed. It was not a nice laugh. "Do you know why I'm laughing?"

Jimoni shook his head.

"Some time ago, when I told people at parties that I was a Stone, they used to bow down before me. And even the few hard ones ran out of my path. Back then I felt like Mike Tyson. Now if I tell people that I'm a Stone, they look at me as if I'm a shitface—as if I'm a stinking Jew man. Owlsmen have cornered all the respect, and more and more people are running into their fold. Believe me; at the next initiation, anybody wanting to blend into any of the gangs in my school except the Black Owls would be regarded as a madman."

"I understand your point, and I admire your courage," Jimoni said quietly. "But still I'll advise you as my brother. Walk away from this thing."

"Why the hell's everybody saying that?" Mike was clearly annoyed. "Who the hell created this myth?"

Jimoni shrugged. "They are Owlsmen. And the man you wanted to kill is not just an ordinary Owlsman. He's their leader. If you want to know the force of his name, come and I'll drive you straight to the school campus and I'll ask you to insult the first ten students you'll meet. I bet if you mention that you're Don Tos, all of them will simply apologize and run out of your way. Everybody's heard of him. He's a dangerous fellow."

Mike nodded. "We're saying the same thing. Cultism isn't just a place of shelter for the unprotected anymore. It's now where many of us bask in insult. Cultism breeds respect, I was told during my initiation. But today, what do we have? The process that helps shape our identities, our machismo, is now being taken away gradually. But the truth is that I'll not sit around and do nothing. I've made a deal to take Don Tos and his top men out. And that's what I'm going to do."

Jimoni looked a long time at Mike's face. He saw the determination. It was clearly etched in that bold, hard countenance.

At last he said, "Mike, I've been in the system. I've witnessed over a dozen cult fights. And I can tell you that it's not a pretty thing to experience. Go back to that school of yours and forget this whole thing."

Mike reflected for a while. "It's too late, brother. I've been committed to this thing."

Jimoni sighed. "Okay I'll give you a letter to some guys in Calamity."

"A letter? I thought you could do more than that."

"I have my reasons. Owlsmen know more about our operations than any other frat gang does. They know about our tactics; they'll recognize our operations. If a team is organized from here, word will get out. This is not our scene. If you really want to make history, then you have no choice but to take the letter. It's your only chance to be a hero. Is it okay?"

"Let me get something right. Why Calamity?"

"It's the only school that's under our control right now. I know plenty of reliable guys out there. I'm very sure they'll help."

Mike looked closely at Jimoni to see whether he meant what he'd just said. What he saw on his cousin's face told him the guy was serious. He leaned forward in his chair, his eyes staring pointedly at the restaurateur. "I want to tell you something I've never told you. I also have some letters on me. One of those letters is from your brotherhood in my school. All the major gangs in my school have resolved to gang up against the dictatorship of Don Tos and his men. That was why I became involved. Jankara's Brotherhood of the Roundheads is equally involved. And I have their letter right here with me. This is not a bucket of blood. This is the real thing—the mother of all cult wars."

Jimoni was thinking. Traditionally, when two gangs met and they got themselves involved in a blood fight, such a confrontation was known as a "bucket of blood" on campus. But now a group of the major gangs was up against a single gang, and now the violence that was sure to follow would sound more like a river of blood.

Actually, he didn't want to get involved. Because had experienced it before, he could predict Owlsmen's wrath with some level of confidence. It was still the best-organized and most *secret* secret cult gang—and by far the most violent. The Roundheads and the Black Owls had clashed once, on his own turf, and other Owlsmen from AZU had been invited in by their brethren to intervene. That was the only time they had clashed. The one-week war had been a riot of fierce gun battles and battle-ax encounters so fiery that it was a miracle the campus had not gone up in flames. It had been a terrible experience.

"Mike, listen to me." Jimoni's voice was calm. "Let's reason together. I've dealt with Owlsmen before. I know it's no big deal to you, but if you kill a single Owlsman, the best you'll get is public recognition. That's all. But Owlsmen will work round the clock to find the killer of their own. They are like the Israelis. They'll not rest. And that school of yours will not know peace. I know what I'm talking about. Are you prepared to take that risk?"

Mike smiled grimly. "That's why I traveled this far."

Jimoni sighed for the fourth time. He knew there was no way that he would not give his cousin cooperation. His only benefit would be the fall of Don Tos and his key men.

"I think I need that beer now," he said, and he got to his feet and walked to the kitchen, where the fridge was. He came back a minute later with two bottles of beer.

"How many men can you promise me?" Mike asked after the drinks had been opened.

"I have access to some forces in Calamity: good people—men who are more than willing to fight this kind of fight. But it's only a question of money. They'll come in their own spare time and execute the job."

"How many men will I get here?"

Jimoni was thoughtful for a while. "The Roundheads have some very reliable men," he said at last. "I can only promise you three such men. And that's after due consultation with my topnotch men."

Mike nodded. It was what he wanted to hear. The whole operation would cost him less money, particularly now that his cousin had promised him three men.

"Who are they?"

Jimoni paused, his Guinness stout short of his mouth, and looked at his cousin closely. "Sixqo, Vissalo, and Gordons." Obviously, from the manner in which he spoke the names, Mike was sure the names meant a lot to the former Big Eye. But they meant nothing to him. The name "Vissalo" seemed familiar, but he could not put his finger on it.

"Are they good?"

Jimoni shrugged. "Let's just say that they're some of our best butchers."

"That's great."

Later that day, about five o'clock, Mike was taken to another part of town where he met the three Roundheads—Sixqo Adedeji, Vissalo Apatira, and Gordons Inupa. He assessed them and was impressed by them. Jimoni proudly told him they were members of the butchers, the hit squad. They had done this kind of operation before and had partaken in different missions in various schools, with the sole purpose of the elimination of the hit men of other rival gangs.

Sixqo Adedeji was a slender, wiry chap with a very conspicuous tattoo on his biceps; Vissalo Apatira was a bulky sour-faced guy with a full beard cheek and a slight resemblance to Dr. Philip Emeagwali; and Gordons Inupa, the oldest of the three, was lean and square shouldered. But they were all fighting men. Even in the short session that they had shared after being introduced, Mike had discovered that they were all packing guns. It was a symbol of professionalism. But what he didn't know was that the three young men were no longer students of the university. Two of them were students who had graduated some two years prior, and the third one, Vissalo, had been advised over two years before to withdraw from the institution. But he was still seen on daily a basis prowling around the school community, causing trouble.

The next morning, Jimoni put several wheels in motion, one after the other. After breakfast of *jollof* rice with salad and cowtail, he drove Mike to the parking lot, where he chartered an unmarked sedan to continue his journey to another university in the South, where he hoped to gather about five other hit men to complement the three Roundheads' butchers. And on his way back, they would converge at Jimoni's Lodge to map out plans and modes of operation.

* * *

It was a moonlit Friday evening in late April. A week had passed since Tos had visited Professor Finecountry. In those times, he had completed the remaining paintings. He had only needed some more time to focus on his project and then relax a little and take time to prepare for his exams. He had sent all the paintings to Reese. There were eight of them. Frank Reese had phoned him immediately to acknowledge that he'd received them. He had commented that the works, though very creative, showed a slight deviation from his earlier works.

One of the paintings was a forest picture. The forest was delicately outlined in lively colors, and animals of all shapes and sizes dominated the background. In some of the trees hung monkeys and birds. This was one of the paintings that impressed Reese.

Another of the pictures that interested the American was one of a very thin, ugly fisherman throwing nets into syrupy water, while in the background there was what at first seemed to be a gigantic crocodile. But a close look at it revealed what it really was. It was a huge tank farm, and some of the things that were falling out of the crocodile's mouth were suspended barrels of oils, limp fishes, and what could pass for bloated human corpses. The meaning of this picture was well concealed, but with concentrated attention the meaning became clearer. The overwhelming mood of this particular picture was one of loneliness and the sufferings endured by the oil-producing riverside communities. He had titled the painting *Bateren Creek*. It was a picture set against the backdrop of the great forces that had driven the region into poverty, crisis, and despair.

Another was an evocative oil of lean men riding limp bicycles and half-naked ugly women with large bundles of firewood and precious cargo of varied farm produce on their heads and lean babies tied to their backs with rags. On the side of the road were ugly, lean, idle men playing a game of checkers. It was a painting that defined the lives of peasant farmers, set against a backdrop of great poverty and idleness. It was a painting properly painted.

The other "stimulating" painting was the one he called *Benin River*. It was a picture of a traditional war boat floating on turbulent dark waters. The side of the boat was brimming with cannons and dozens of men on the side holding paddles and ancient rifles. The four other paintings were pictures of gods and African deities. On the whole, the American had commended Tos's talent, and he believed that the exhibition would stimulate great interest in the Nigerian's work. But Tos know that it was better not to be too optimistic.

Another good piece of news was that Pratt Institute, one of America's foremost centers for art and architecture studies, had accepted his application. And Frank Reese had promised him a nice apartment in Brooklyn and a car of his own. Life would be very good in New York, with all the luxury Uncle Sam could offer.

On this very evening, they were in Ebi's flat, and Tos was lying on the bed, his eyes following Ebi, who'd just come out of the bathroom. She was drying herself. Since they had returned from Lagos, they had seemed inseparable. It was as if they had a mutual desire to defy her father. Tos hardly spent the night in his apartment anymore. Her apartment was their mutual lovenest. They had been together every night. Sometimes they went to Bray's Kitchen; at other times, they would visit the Greenhouse Bar and Restaurant. But they always did so in the company of Tos's three bodyguards.

Tos liked watching her from the bed, especially when she had just come out of the bathroom and was toweling her lovely figure. He loved those moments. He liked observing her nakedness, pointedly, the artist in him creating a picture of her in his mind. He had painted a tempera-on-canvas of her stark naked. She was very pleased about it, and she'd hung it close to her bed. She loved posing nude for him. All in all, he had painted three pictures of her—paintings she adored greatly.

Ebi was the best thing that had ever happened to him in all his twenty-six years. She fascinated him like no other girl. With her he had come to understand the meaning of living and loving; he had come to appreciate the untainted joy of living with another human being. He loved the personality of her person, which he saw closely as her lover. He liked to come to her apartment and lie down on her bed, doing nothing, just smelling that peculiar smell that was associated with and natural to her, listening to her voice. He loved her fiercely.

"Can I get you something, Tosan?" She asked. Anytime she used his name, the magic was always there.

"Um," Tos murmured.

"Is that a yes or no?"

From where he lay, Tos could see her boobs clearly. They were beautiful to behold. They thrilled him—the sight of them alone. They were of average size and proud with pale, hard nipples.

"Drop that towel and fetch yourself here," Tos said, patting the bed for emphasis.

"You're a leech," she said. "Sometimes I hate the sight of you."

Tos smiled easily, the lines at the corner of his eyes crinkling with boyish charm.

"The trouble is we can't resist each other."

"Try me if you think I can't."

"Come on over here," Tos ordered.

Ebi smiled and waved a beautiful manicured hand in the air. "You can do better than that, lover boy."

"Are you coming or not?"

She shook her head coquettishly.

Without effort from where he was lying, he could define the texture of her hair and the smoothness of her soft ebony skin. He knew her inside out now, including things like the small mole on the inside of her thigh and the delicate whorl of her tiny navel. Love truly is a privileged condition—an opportunity to know another person inside out.

"I'm going to count to three, and if you're not here before I finish counting, then know that you're in trouble. One!"

Ebi grinned. She was enjoying this.

"Two!"

She chewed her lower lip, watching him and still grinning mischievously.

"Th—"

"Okay!" she interjected, and she approached the bed. She gave him a long look from under her lashes. He reached up and pulled her down into the bed roughly. "Oh my God!" she exclaimed.

"Now put your ass in gear," he commanded. He pulled her atop him, and they both laughed as she straddled him with her straight, beautiful legs. He liked her atop him sometimes. It changed the rhythm of their lovemaking.

Ebi traced a line across his bare chest. It was a trick he found amusing. She had the most beautiful hips and neatly sculpted breasts that thrilled him by mere naked contact.

He stretched out beneath her, feeling himself drifting into that perfect island where lovers always find solace at the end of rapturous lovemaking. He ran his fingers across her bare bottom lightly, and she bit his nipple, pressing her supple young body into his own, imprisoning him with her body.

"The crazy nymphet."

"The crazy artist," she replied, biting him lightly on the soft part of his ear.

"Cannibal."

"Cannibal. Is that what I am?"

"Fiend. That's what you are."

She laughed. There was genuine merriment in her voice.

"I dreamed about you last night," he said abruptly after some silence.

She raised her eyebrows. "About me? Well, I shall be interested to hear about it. Tell me," she said sweetly. She now sat upright, straddling him, her breasts swinging in the dim light of the room, hanging temptingly above him like fruits.

Tos averted his gaze and looked through the window. The moon was out. It was a big, clear, clean yellow moon. It hung so low in the sky.

"Aren't you going to tell me about your dream?"

Tos said nothing. He listened to the silence that followed her question.

"Tosan?"

"May I help you?" Tos took this as a joke.

"Haven't you made up your mind?"

Tos let his gaze settle on her face. "Oh, fucking shit. I shouldn't have mentioned it. You'll think I'm going crazy or something. So let's just forget it."

She arched her eyebrow, touching his face softly with her fingers. "You'll tell."

Tos shook his head. "I said forget it."

"Okay. I think I can handle you," Ebi said, and she swung her body around, her face to his groin, and took him gently in her mouth. Tos felt as if all the electric current in the whole building were connected directly to his body. He moaned, his fingers gripping the bedsheets tightly. When she'd worked him to the edge of explosion, she rolled away from him, but Tos wouldn't let her go.

"Now you'll tell me," Ebi said quietly.

"Yeah," Tos agreed. He reached for a cigarette and lit it, and the fire of the light dimly illuminated his face. He was a very handsome man, with his wonderfully straight jawline, well-shaped mouth, and high cheekbones that gave his face strength.

"So tell me, sir."

"What's that?" Tos asked, feigning ignorance.

She raised her eyebrows. He knew she didn't take it as a joke.

"Okay. I'm sorry. I remember now." He gave her a reassuring smile. "You want to hear the dream."

She nodded quietly.

"Well, I dreamed last night. It was a horrible dream. It was all about death. It's got to do with that painting *Dance of Death*. In the dream, you were the girl riding the tiger. Both of you went for a ride.

It was a dark night, sort of, with only a small light illuminating you and the beast. The tiger was running fast through the bushes when a gunshot sounded, ringing loud and clear. The tiger went down with you. You fell off her. The animal was bleeding profusely. There was another shot. The tiger was hit again. This time it lay motionless. Like I said before, you were the girl riding the beast. You screamed twice. It was ear-splitting. Then three men emerged out of the darkness. They were clutching automatic weapons." Tos paused here.

"Then what happened next?" Ebi asked quickly.

"I'm not saying," Tos replied, blowing smoke rings.

"Tell me what happened next," Ebi insisted.

Tos hesitated. "You want to hear everything?"

"Yeah, I want to hear everything," she replied coolly. "Tell me everything."

"Okay. This is what happened. They took a shot at you."

"They took a shot at me?" There was unmistakable surprise in Ebi's voice.

Tos nodded. "Yeah."

"So what happened next?"

He shook his head and continued, quite as if she had not spoken. Now his voice was somber.

"You went down silently. From where I stood observing the whole thing, no one saw me. Not any one of them. The three men came forward, examined the effect of their work, and walked away. Obviously, they were satisfied with what they had done. I hurried to where you and the beast lay. Guess what I saw?" He was staring at her.

"You tell me."

Tos smiled slightly. "You were there, of course. But the beast was no longer the beast. It was me, in yellow-striped clothing. I was staring at my own lifeless body."

"The tiger—you!" Ebi exclaimed. She was stunned.

"Yeah. It's me."

She shivered slightly but seemed unaware of it.

"You're shivering," Tos said, watching her closely. "I felt it."

"Me?"

"Yeah. Are you scared?"

She shook her head. Remembering his ability to read her face, she summoned up her best expression and said coolly, "It's only a dream. I'm not supposed to let it frighten me."

"But some dreams do come true."

"Do yours?"

"Some of them."

She blinked her eyes. "Let me get this straight. Do you mean we're going to be killed?"

"I've not said that." He stubbed out his cigarette.

"You know something, Tosan. You're joking. You didn't dream any dream. You've conned me just to let me make love to you." She was laughing. She had one of those rich fruit-juice laughs that radiated warmth, and it changed the temperature of the room like fine music.

"You think so?" Tos asked. "I don't think it's funny."

"But it's the truth," she said, and she nudged him with an elbow.

Tos nodded. "I'd like to think so," he said quietly, and he peered at the moonlight that shone against the window, thrown on the glass by a faraway yellow moon. He felt both comfortable and secure with this lovely girl at his side. She completed a part of him that had been missing these past years.

"What a dreadful thing to do, Tosan," she said playfully, throwing her arms around him in a display of warm affection. But he was not there. She could sense it. "What's the matter?"

"Nothing." He abruptly got out of the bed and went into the kitchen. She heard the fridge open and close. When he came back, he was carrying a can of cold water. He drank from it, set the can atop the small sideboard attached to the bed, and slipped under the sheets beside her.

"You're worried," she said.

"Yeah," he acknowledged regretfully.

"Is it because of the dream?"

He nodded. The girl pressed her face into his shoulders, her damp lips against his naked skin. His story about the dream had changed the romantic atmosphere of the room in the space of a few minutes. The funny thing was that in Africa people placed much emphasis on dreams and witchcraft, anything and everything superstitious.

"I'm sorry," she said.

"For what?"

She shrugged. "I don't know. Maybe for making you tell your dream."

He propped himself up on one elbow. He stroked the side of her face with his other hand.

"The truth is that my dreams more often than not come true."

"True?" She blurted out, startled by the tone with which he had said it.

"Yeah. Two weeks before my mother met her death, I dreamed about it. I didn't believe it then. Two weeks later, she was killed."

"Oh my God!" Ebi muttered, but the words were muffled by Tos's hand.

"You need not worry," he said, stroking her hair. "The only hitch is that I hate to lose you to death or anybody."

She sighed.

"You know something, sweetheart? Don't stake your smallest penny on this one. It's not worth it."

She laughed. It was best that way. It was best to keep everything at a level of playfulness that she could deal with and that he could handle. He was staring at the moonlit window. The silence of the moon beyond the window was frightening, impenetrable, as if everybody on the face of the earth had been raptured.

He moved his body close to her, holding her. For some reason, he felt a throbbing, deep urgency for sex. The softness of the girl's body and the warmth it generated to his loins was unbearable. He ran his hand across her flat stomach, tracing downward until he found the center of her gravity, and ever so gently, he began to stroke. She closed her eyes and clung to him tightly.

"Please, Tosan, don't," she whispered against his ear. But it was as if he didn't hear her. Gently he held her legs apart, entered her, and rode her until they were both tired and satisfied and weak in the legs.

"Let's go down to Bray's Kitchen," Tos said at last.

"What about if I fix something for dinner?"

"No need to. My guys are hosting me."

"Oh, I've forgotten," she said, and she leaned across and kissed him.

"Come," Tos said, rolling out of bed. "Let's take a bath together."

Ebi leaped out of bed, and hand in hand, they strolled naked into the bathroom.

* * *

The five of them entered the restaurant just after eight later that evening. Bray's Kitchen was enjoying a bit of good business at that hour. A group of tables booked for the evening were set together, close to the wall. The Owlsmen were already seated and waiting for Tos. It was Christo who first saw him. He stood up and shouted loudly for all to hear, "I hail the Don!"

The other Owlsmen stood up as one and echoed the greeting.

Several heads turned to see what the fuss was about. Several cultists in other gangs stared in envy and embarrassment. Among the other diners who were conversant with the happenings in the school cultdom, there was a whispered, "That's Tos—Owlsman Number One."

Owlsmen occupied many of the tables. But a particular table was conspicuously vacant. Tos knew that was his table. He shook hands with all those around, Owlsmen style, hand raised high and touching the wrist of each of the brothers in turn. He was a legend among them, the greatest living cult personality. Many of them knew that the gang would find it difficult to enjoy the leadership of another like Don Tos.

A few tables away, a boy whispered to his friend, "They treat him like a king."

"He's sort of like a king in this school," the other boy replied, eyeing Tos enviously.

"We've been waiting for quite some time," Ovo said.

Tos looked at his watch. It was getting near eight thirty. "I'm sorry, guys. I was delayed. Now, what are we eating?"

"We're waiting for you," Christo replied.

Tos picked up the menu in front of him and studied it briefly. "I think I'll take the Mexican chicken with vegetable fried rice and Russian salad."

Ebi grinned. "I prefer the American beef sauté, oriental rice, and cabbage. Try it. You'll like it."

Tos smiled. "Do I have a choice?" Every one of them laughed. Then they all ordered their choice of meals.

Tos knew that today's dinner date was an all-hail-the-king-let's-drink-champagne event.

"Where's Frank White?" he asked.

"Couldn't make it. He called a few minutes ago. He said he's traveling to Okene," Kadiri Muazu said.

Tos nodded and leaned back against the chair. Several of the Owlsmen were smoking now, and discussion was casual. He watched the other tables. He recognized some Roundheads and Panthers. They were watching him curiously. Tos pretended not to see them.

After a while, a file of jacketed waiters and waitresses came to serve them. The one who served Tos, after arranging his dish, reached into his vest pocket and brought out a piece of paper with a brief message written on it. He didn't look at it but quietly slipped it to Tos, who took it and digested its contents with a quick glance. He then proceeded to attack his meal. But it was all a charade. He didn't eat much. His mind was not on the meal. Ebi took one meaningful look at him and suspected that something was wrong.

"What is it?" she demanded quietly.

Tos shrugged. "Don't know yet." He toyed with his meal for another two minutes, and then he excused himself and stood up. Automatically, as if from some secret signal, his three guards stood up.

"Where are you going?" Ovo asked.

"I want to pee and check on Bray," Tos replied. He nodded to the others and threaded his way through the tables toward the door, the three guards following closely behind. Eyes followed them as they went out through the side door.

Once outside, Tos walked hurriedly, a little unsteadily, the note crumpled in his hand. Before he entered the office, he told the three gunmen to keep their eyes open. With that, he knocked gently on the door, opened it, and entered the office.

* * *

"Does it make sense to you?" the Ghanaian restaurateur said quietly to Tos.

"I don't know what to say. But is this info genuine?"

Bray rolled his eyes upward. "You don't believe me." It was an accusative statement.

Tos sat back in the heavy office chair, looking a little too carelessly at Bray, trying to assess the situation. After a short while, he said softly, "Where did you get the information from?"

"You think I'm goofing?" Bray said.

"No. I don't think you're goofing, Bray," Tos replied quietly. "It's just that I'm trying to analyze the situation."

The Ghanaian regarded the boy for a while and shifted his weight in his chair. "Look, my friend," he said softly. "What I've told you is what I've heard. It could be rumor, but there could be an element of truth in it. There are strangers in this town. What could be their mission? I don't know. You can figure that out for yourself."

Tos studied the Ghanaian's face. In all the years they'd known each other, he'd never seen the restaurateur so troubled.

"Do you think they're out for a hit?"

"I don't know; I can't say for sure. But there are rumors floating around."

"Bray, I know this info is very important. But it's not very clear. It's just fragments of what people are whispering. Titbits. I need something that I can rationally analyze and that makes sense to me."

Bray placed both his hands on the desk and leaned forward in his chair. His voice when he spoke was a little above a whisper. "I'm a restaurant owner, and I mingle with people—all sorts of people. And I hear things—all sorts of things. For the past few days, I've been hearing some info: fragments about some strange faces in town—people probably contracted for a hit. I can't say for sure, and I don't know if my deduction is rational or logical. You're the biggest boy around the block, and I heard that recently you've stepped on certain toes. It all means that certain men want you dead. They've said to all who care to hear that you're too arrogant, too powerful. And inasmuch as you're head of the Black Owls, the gang that has effectively rendered all other cult groups irrelevant, you're a threat to peace. And you must be dispensed with. My advice to you, therefore, is this: Leave the restaurant immediately. And don't go home tonight. Don't even sleep at your girl's place. It's a target. Get out of this town for a few days."

Tos smiled with a touch of humor. "You mean I should take off?"

"Just get out of town for a while. The last thing this school needs is a gang war, and it would be bad for business."

Tos was silent for a moment, deep in thought. "Jankara's my domain. A king who can't stay in his kingdom when trouble comes is not fit to rule."

"Oh, come on, Don Tos," Bray said quickly, seeing the stubborn streak in the boy. "Don't get me wrong. I know quite well that you're fearless and all that, but the best thing to do right now is to get out of town for a while—lie low. I've kept some very tough guys informed about trouble that's brewing, but because of their very large egos, they disregarded my advice. At the end of the day, they were the ones who ended up in grief. I like you, Don Tos. Take my advice and leave town tonight. You, your girl, and your men."

"I'm not a weakling, Bray. I just can't leave town."

"I'm not saying that you are. I must tell you this: lots of bad guys are in town. Some of them are guys I know personally. Vissalo—you might have heard of him. He's a Roundheads butcher from a university in the West. Sixqo—he's also another butcher from the same school. These guys are dangerous characters. Do you think any of them are in town just because they want to fuck the girls in this school?"

Tos fingered the heavy buckle of his belt, opened his mouth, and then closed it again.

"I know I'm a Jew man when it comes to a lot of this *secret* secret cult business. But I've been around some university communities, and I happen to know some dark characters, just as I have come to know and respect you. I'm not telling you this because I like your gang. I'm telling you because I like you and that girl of yours. Already the rumor has reached my ear that some gangs are preparing for a major gang war. It would be wicked of me not to pass along this info to you."

Tos nodded. He didn't want to say anything more. This was serious business. He actually didn't want Bray to get himself involved in a cloak-and-dagger cult *wahala*. He had come to Bray's Kitchen to be hosted by his men, but now he realized that he had gotten more than a dull hosting, and his entire gang had gotten more than their money's worth. It was better, as it was, to play it the Ghanaian's way.

He stood up. "I appreciate everything, Bray," he said quietly. "Thanks. I think I'll act at once."

"Do that, my friend," Bray said and shifted uneasily in his seat. "But try to keep me out of the picture."

Tos found himself smiling. "Don't worry. If you can trust me to tell me, you can trust me to keep it secret. And I appreciate your letting me know this."

"I'm happy you're interested," Bray replied, and he stood up. Then they shook hands. Tos walked to the door. "Wait a minute." Tos paused. Bray walked up to him. "I just want to tell you this: No man is a hero to his grave. Don't forget to take my advice. You must get out of town tonight."

Tos nodded and, without speaking, left the office.

Bray wiped his forehead with his bright blue handkerchief and returned to his seat. *This is nonsense. Cult wars accomplish nothing. They spoil a business; that is their only accomplishment.*

* * *

When Tos returned to his table, the others watched him curiously, but his expression was inscrutable.

"Come on, guys, let's drink," he said easily.

Fresh drinks were placed before them.

"Let's toast the Don," Ovo said. His glass was already filled. "Fill up, guys." All of them at the table filled their glasses. Ovo ambled to his feet. He surveyed the table, and his eyes traveled around the restaurant, assessing the other diners, who were pretending not to see him.

Suddenly music blared over the restaurant's music box. It was a Ghanaian number.

"Turn that blasted music down!" Ovo shouted.

The music was lowered instantly. "Do you think you're in Ghana?" Keme queried. Nobody replied to him.

"It's okay," Tos said.

Ovo nodded. He commanded everyone's attention now.

"To a great Owlsman," he said loudly. "To someone we all respect and love to emulate." He paused, and his eyes rested squarely on Tos. "To someone we will all miss so greatly. To Don Tos—the legend among us. Cheers!"

"Cheers!" the others chorused, and all downed their drinks.

Tos looked at Ebi. She was smiling. Tos shook his head and took a deep breath.

"My lord, say something," Ovo urged.

Tos shrugged. "What can I say?"

"Anything," Keme said.

Tos nodded and then rose to his feet. He let his eyes sweep over the faces of his brethren. Finally they rested on Ovo.

"I must say that I'm flattered and proud to be associated with you guys," he said quietly. He didn't take his eyes from Ovo as he spoke. "Thanks for hosting me and my princess with this expensive dinner. It's good to have such good people like you around me. It makes me feel really important. Thank you all."

Every one of them laughed.

"When are you two off to America?" Keme asked.

"End of next month," Tos replied as he took his seat.

"Blast it, man. You're one lucky don, my lord." It was Kadiri that said this.

Tos grinned. "You could still be lucky. Play the DV Visa Lottery. It could get you to America."

"I've played it four consecutive times and no hope," Kadiri replied.

"Continue playing it. You'll win one day."

"Are you quitting studies?" It was Paxman that asked this.

"What studies am I still doing in this school? I'm already a graduate. I just have this final exam to write, and that's all. Have you been there before, Christo?"

Christo shook his head. "Why did you choose to go to America?" he asked.

"It was Ebi's idea. She said I could begin a new life in New York. She said everything's new in New York."

"Well, I envy you, my lord" Paxman said.

"It's all right."

"We'll miss you," Christo said.

"I'll miss you guys too."

"You'll send me postcards," Kadiri Muazu said.

"I'll send you dollars."

This got a good laugh.

"Don't forget us!" Ovo's girl said. Tos beamed at them.

"A thousand dollars each for you girls if I get there," he said gently, and the girls giggled.

After dinner, all of them stood up one after the other, and the bodyguards pushed open the door and led the way as they filed through the doorway, heading toward the parking lot. When they came to Tos's car, the guards formed a protective ring around them.

"You can tell us now, my lord. What's it all about?" Ovo said quietly, looking pointedly at him.

Tos told them of the Ghanaian's warning.

"I don't believe it," Keme said after he'd finished. "They can't do anything stupid. They'd be dealt with in a matter of days."

"Bray said Jankara's crawling with strangers. It's obvious that somebody's planning a hit, and they are using outside force."

"Is this info for real?" Christo asked.

"Bray's absolutely cast-iron sure."

Kadiri Muazu nodded. "It makes sense to me. Remember: they failed to honor our white status letter. This could be the reason why they failed to answer that letter."

"But this is crazy," Keme said. "First, we know the identities of the various gangs behind this thing. We have the names of their chief butchers on our list. Therefore, it's stupid for them to declare war on us."

"You have a point there," Ovo said, rubbing his chin reflectively. "But it is common knowledge that most cult fights arise out of stupidity."

There was some silence, with many of them remaining deep in thought.

Tos was glad of the silence. It made all of them reflective. He said at last, "Araba-Benson, since Black Mamba is not around to disseminate the information, your task is to send out the word. I know these guys would not do anything stupid, but it's better to be cautious. And I also believe that Bray can't be lying. There's no reason for him to tell me lies. My orders are these: All feathered men should converge in Featherland, and all unfeathered brethren should retire to the Owls' Nest. Is that okay?"

Most of them nodded.

Keme shook his head. "Nobody in his right mind would want to fight Owlsmen. We're too close-knit. We're too dangerous."

"I know what's on your mind, Keme," Tos said patiently. "But before it's twelve midnight, I want all Owlsmen to vacate this town. Get the word around town. I repeat: everybody should keep away from this town for now. Is that okay?"

They all nodded this time.

"Chisto—get some men, smell around, and find out what they are up to. I want a fast job. We want info. Is that okay?"

They all nodded.

"Good. I'll see you guys tomorrow," Tos said, and he entered his car. One of his guards was already sitting in the driver's seat. Another took the passenger seat beside him. Tos took Ebi's hand and let his eyes sweep over his men as they hurriedly made for their respective cars.

A minute later, the guard under the wheel engaged gears, turned the powerful car around, and headed toward John Elen Road. Later that night, some twenty-five feathered men and over three hundred unfeathered men packed a few things and flew out of town.

CHAPTER EIGHTEEN

GAFARU TAIRU WAS AWAKENED BY WHAT HE DIDN'T KNOW. He peered at the luminous bedside clock. It was a quarter past 4:00 a.m. He looked at Fatoki Ganiyu, his co-guard. The guy was snoring softly; one of his hands was resting on his cheek. He touched him lightly, and the snoring stopped, but the boy didn't wake up. He decided not to wake him. Instead he got up from the bed, leaving the other boy to sleep peacefully.

It took a moment before his eyes could adjust to the dimness. He made his way to the living room. It was dark like the guest bedroom, and the last chap who was supposed to be on guard was lying on one of the ugly couches, snoring loudly. Gafaru couldn't see him, but he knew exactly where the guy was sleeping. The guy's name was Taojeek Kakawa, and he was the one that had drawn night watch tonight. And the fucker was sleeping peacefully.

Gafaru didn't bother to turn on the light, though the darkness disturbed him somewhat. But he was actually bothered by something else. He didn't know what. For almost three minutes he stood in the middle of the living room motionless, as if he was meditating.

Something compelled him to the barred window that overlooked John Elen Road. He parted the heavy curtains slightly and looked out, his eyes photographing the surroundings with professional interest. All he could see was parked cars and a soulless, deserted street. Yet he felt disturbed. Just then a black cat with white stripes dashed across the road, and the boy followed it with his eyes until it disappeared into the next compound. The boy didn't know why, but he felt more restless, and a cold shiver cut across his heart.

He scanned the street carefully again, as if he were searching for something or somebody. Then he saw something.

He knew something was not right in the street below. Now he'd seen it. It was a black-suited figure. The figure had materialized from the shadows and was standing near a street lamppost, watching the building. It was as if he was looking right at Gafaru.

Gafaru knew he was standing in the shadows and the guy couldn't see him.

The full impact of who the guy could be registered immediately on Gafaru when he remembered the Big Eye's warning from a few hours prior.

For several minutes, Ganiyu watched, completely bewildered. His heart was beating furiously like a kettledrum. He wondered if the black-suited figure could see him. He doubted it, yet he felt a trembling within his body. Quickly, as if in panic, he turned away from the window. His mind was now keyed to action. He walked to his sleeping colleague, very gently woke him up, and quietly told him to be on the alert and to stay away from the window and the light switches. Then he walked straight into the master bedroom.

Tos's eyes snapped open at the first cold touch, and he regarded Gafaru closely, his eyes totally on alert.

"What is it?" he whispered.

"I think birds of prey have come to visit us in the dead of the night," Gafaru whispered in return.

Tos spun out of bed, his movement fluid, and his hand gripped the automatic handgun from the bedside chest. The suddenness of the move attracted the girl sleeping by his side.

"What is it?" she asked, taking in the situation at once.

"We've got company. I think Bray was right after all," Tos whispered.

She stared at him for a moment, her brown eyes bewildered. He motioned for her to stay where she was, then quietly and smoothly he followed Gafaru into the dark living room.

Taojeek Kakawa and Fatoki Ganiyu were crouching close to the window. Tos and Gafaru took up positions beside them.

Ganiyu parted the curtains slightly, and Tos peered into the street below. He saw two men. When Gafaru had gone to call him, another black-suited chap had joined the first one.

Tos knew this was trouble. There was no doubt that he was looking at the butchers sent to kill him—the very people Bray had warned him about. The two fellows were looking at the building, obviously at his apartment.

Just then a large green van turned the dark corner quietly and stopped right in front of the two men. Two other guys stepped out of the van. More butchers, Tos knew. The two guys that had just arrived were carrying rifles. Tos recognized the rifles. They were Kalashnikov automatic rifles—the famous Russian rifles that could take out a dozen men in less than twelve seconds. It was a gun popularly known in the streets of Warri as "Kalashi." He'd handled one during the crisis. And they also had plenty of them in their armory, right in Featherland.

"What are we going to do, my lord?" Gafaru whispered.

"Wait till I give the order," Tos whispered back, and crouching low, he tiptoed to the bedroom. Ebi was sitting on the bed, her eyes looking worried.

"What is it, Tosan?"

Tos didn't reply immediately. Instead he signaled her to get under the bed, and when she was safely out of sight, he took out his cell phone and punched in a number he knew by heart.

"Hello," Ovo's voice replied.

"Where are you?"

"I'm at my girl's place. In bed. Where are you?"

"I'm at my pad. Can you guess what I'm doing?"

"No, my lord."

"I'm standing very close to my window."

"What's the meaning of that?"

"Bray was right. I'm standing near my window, and some groups of guys in black are outside my pad right now. They're watching my apartment. They're carrying Kalashi. It's obvious that they are planning on invading my apartment right now. That's why I'm watching from two hundred yards away through my window."

"Fuck!"

"Don't say that word. Get out off the phone now and get some of the boys. I want you guys here in two minutes. Get it? Two minutes or I'll seize your feather."

"I'll be there."

Tos made another call, this one to Black Mamba, but he couldn't get him. He tried Keme's number, but he couldn't get him either. He tried Paxman, and when he couldn't raise him, he tried Christo's number. He got him and told him that his house would be under attack within the next few minutes. Christo, being his characteristic self, said he was already on his way.

Tos returned to the living room and crouched low beside the guards who had already drawn their guns. Everything was as he had left it some three minutes ago.

"What do you suggest we do?" he whispered to the nearest guard.

"We take the first shot," Gafaru replied.

Tos took a deep breath. "We'll do it together then. But on my signal."

Gafaru nodded and crept forward into a strategic position. He pulled the slide window frame gently to one side, leant his gun on the ledge, and took a steady aim. He got the target he wanted first. It was the easiest one.

The men were in a tight conference, standing in a group. It was as if they were taking last-minute instructions.

The figure he had in his gun's sights had his back to him. The guy was carrying a Kalashi. His name was Gordons Inupa.

Tos had signaled the other two guards to take up positions in the next window while he joined Gafaru and laid his handgun on the ledge, its muzzle trained on the bus.

"Ready?" he whispered.

The boy nodded.

"Let it off."

Simultaneously, they pulled their triggers. At that distance, in the dead of the night, the pistol shots sounded like machine gun fire. Tos's first five shots were lucky deadly shots. The first two caught the passenger sitting close to the driver in the chest, leaving him slumped in the chair; the next two caught the driver in the shoulder, and the fifth buried itself harmlessly in the leather seat.

Gafaru's target collected a bullet in the back. As he fell, he screamed. The group had broken up quickly, and the gunmen were sheltering behind the van and any other available defense shields they could lay their eyes on. The other two guards were shooting sporadically, making their targets hide their heads.

After a few minutes, the reply that came from the streets was rapid. The men sprayed the building with their assault rifles. All the windows were shattered. But before then, Tos and his guards had fallen flat on their stomachs and hugged themselves to the floor. They felt bullets twisting and wreaking havoc on the air above their heads.

Tos knew he had killed one of the two occupants of the van, though he was not sure whether he had killed the other. The only sound they could hear now was the unceasing singing tune of bullets connecting, bouncing, and burying themselves in the building.

For the next five minutes, there was steady, concentrated shooting from outside the building. The four Owlsmen dared not raise their heads or change positions.

Ten minutes later, another volley of gunfire interfered with the ones that had dominated the airwaves for such a long time. It came from far off and was drawing nearer inch by fiery inch.

Tos looked at the three guards and said, "I think our guys are coming now."

"Thank God for that," Gafaru said.

"It's good that they got here on time. I don't think I have the stamina to listen to this shooting anymore," Taojeek Kakawa said.

Outside, counter fire raked the streets around the van. The gunfire was coming from a dilapidated, smoke-belching Peugeot sedan that was tearing down the street like a bat out of hell. Two of the Owlsmen were leaning out the windows on both sides of the vehicle, submachine guns in their hands. They were squeezing the triggers, and the streams of bullets were pouring out like water out of fire hoses.

The assassins, seeing superior firepower coming from the other side of the street, knew then that their operation was botched. Hurriedly cutting a retreat, they carried their wounded and the body of Gordons Inupa and were in time to dash into the security of their van as more slugs embedded themselves in the bodywork of the vehicle.

The driver, with blood on his shoulder, changed gear and sped out of the area with screaming tires.

From where he crouched, Tos watched the van wheeling down the road in a shameful retreat.

Immediately after the firing stopped, Tos opened the front door of his apartment as a group of five Owlsmen came out of the Peugeot, all of them bearing arms. They moved to the foot of the staircase and looked up at the figure at the head of the staircase.

Tos and the three guards looked down into the hard faces of his men, and for the first time he could clearly see Christo One Way.

"There you are," he said. "I said five minutes. What is it by your time?"

Christo looked at his watch with the aid of the moonlight. "I'm sorry, my lord," he said apologetically as he began to climb the staircase. "It took me quite some time to gather the boys." Before he entered the apartment, he turned around and directed instruction to the men who had come with him to stay in the darkness but to keep their eyes focused should any of the attackers come back to again fire on the apartment.

Tos switched on the living room light. Miraculously, it came on. Virtually everything in the living room was a mess. Bullets had perforated most of the paintings hanging on the walls. The television set had been pierced by bullets from different guns. The birdcage was lying on the floor.

"Christ!" Tos shouted. "The damn fuckers killed Scooter." He fell on his knees. There were a few feathers about. He reached into the cage and gently took out the bird. There was miserable expression on Tos's face. He held the bird gently in his hand. His cold hard eyes were fastened on the bundle of feathers in his hands.

"Where's Ebi?" Christo said from behind him.

Tos looked up, his eyes red. "In the bedroom."

"My lord, get her and let's get the hell out of this place."

Tos nodded. He stood up and walked into the bedroom. Ebi was sitting on the edge of the bed, her eyes wide with fear.

"Ebi, we're moving out of here," he said, walking past her toward the closet.

"Moving? Aren't you going to notify the police?"

"What police?" Tos's voice was dark and heavy and cracked with anger. "We're not calling any police. This is not a police thing. This is a cult war!" He picked up a shirt hanging on the closet door and slipped it on. Then he took a hold-all bag and stuffed a few clothes into it. "Don't stand there staring at me. Pack something, and let's get the fucking hell out of here."

Ebi jumped out of the bed, took one of her bags and started collecting some of her personal effects.

"Where are we going?"

"Have you read the novel *The Godfather*?"

"No."

"Have you watched the movie?"

"Yes."

Tos turned and faced her. "It's time to go to the mattresses."

"I don't think I understand what that means"

"Come on. You won't understand, but don't worry. All's well. Nobody's dead yet."

"When are we coming back?"

"Not for a couple of days."

Fifteen minutes later, a dilapidated smoke-belching Peugeot sedan, a Jaguar, and a black BMW quietly left the sleeping town of Jankara.

* * *

At exactly the time Tos was talking to the Vee-Eye eye on the phone, an Owlsman came out of Osazuna Tavern, a quiet, beautiful drinking clubhouse in the village. He stood in the doorway for a brief moment to light a cigarette. After a second drag, he turned and walked toward his car. The Owlsman was the Town Krier of the Black Owls, Number Seven by designation. His name was Black Mamba, a.k.a. Black Prelude.

His vehicle, a black Honda Prelude, was parked some three electric poles away from the restaurant, as the closer parking spaces had all been occupied. He didn't mind the distance. The night, though very cold, was not rainy. It was pleasant enough for the beginning of the rainy season. He'd had a wonderful evening with his colleagues; many of them were his classmates, and none were Owlsmen. That was why he had been unable to grace the dinner date hosted by the Councilors for Don Tos. The hosting had actually been the planning of Christo One Way, and that was one of the reasons why he had decided not to attend.

He was partially drunk, and that was why he failed to see the three figures across the street, standing not fifty yards from his car. They were watching him.

He crossed the street and stood before his car. There he fumbled for car keys, having trouble finding them. That was when he heard the scuttling of feet behind him. He half-turned, his other hand going for the gun in his waistband.

A hand that struck at him was tightly holding a knife. The blow hit the side of his body, and the blade of the knife was lost in soft human flesh. He screamed once with an agonized animal-like wail. The second knife blow was struck by another fellow. It was a forceful stab that sunk deep into his throat, cutting one of his arteries. He went down in a heap as the life began to ebb gently out of his body.

They dragged his body into a tangle of nearby bushes and in the darkness began to strip him of his valuable items. They took his watch, his gun, and his wallet, and one of the guys was just taking his Nokia cell phone when it rang. The guy switched it off and melted into the darkness. The call was from Tos.

It was nearly dawn before his body was found. He had been dead for at least three hours. He was the first victim of *Operation Anaconda*.

* * *

It was 4:15 a.m., and all was dark and quiet in Jankara. At Apia, a university community within trekking distance of the university campus, everybody was fast asleep, and most of the houses were in darkness. NEPA had cut the electrical supply to the area because of a faulty transformer. But on the first-floor apartment of an unfenced private hostel, a lone light was on. One student was bent over his table, his face a few inches away from the rechargeable lantern he was using. He was going through a legal journal. He was a four-hundred level law student, and he was cramming for a test he had the next morning.

From the window, the sleeping community looked like an irregular collection of discarded old brick buildings of riotous browns, greens, blues, and yellows.

It looked deceptively peaceful. But not far from the window were bushes, and unknown to him, two men were crouching there. They were both clutching handguns by their sides.

In the room, Yakubu Ayu—for that was the Owlsman's name—was not alone. His roommate was snoring loudly, and Yakubu himself battled with sleep. He wanted just thirty minutes more.

It was ten minutes later that the two gunmen crept silently to the window, pushed their guns forward until they touched the mosquito netting, and shot the boy point-blank in the face. And like ghosts, they melted into the darkness.

It was less than two hours until the break of dawn, and *Operation Anaconda* had just claimed its second victim.

* * *

The fourth assault was on Frank White's residence. It was about 4:25 a.m. A gray Nissan pulled up to the security post of the compound. Four gunmen disembarked from the car, brandishing their weapons. In the next minute, they entered the compound, and the security men were rounded up and all beaten badly. But it was unnecessary. Frank White had traveled out of town.

Another group struck later that night. The assault was at Ogheneovo Ikoloba's apartment. The gunmen forced their way into the compound, fired some gunshots carelessly everywhere, and came out some ten minutes later, looking visibly disappointed. The Vee-Eye was nowhere to be found.

At about five o'clock, the same group of men that had stormed Frank White's apartment arrived at Keme's apartment. Keme's apartment was in a private residential hostel called Eagles Lodge. The area was clearly an Owlsmen-controlled zone of the town. What the men did was quite simple. They parked their car a few yards away from the hostel gate and waited in the darkness.

Keme and Malik Saleh had gone to the Clique Nightclub. Malik dropped Keme in front of his hostel at about 5:15. The four men in the Nissan spotted Keme immediately as he got out of Malik's Mercedes. Upon sighting the Owlsmen, the Nissan's doors swung open and the men started toward the Owlsmen. Malik stepped on the accelerator and sped from the scene in the Mercedes.

Keme, unable to get back into the car, decided upon the only other alternative left for him. He took to his heels. The four men dashed after him, shooting at him as they ran.

On this particular night, Keme was not carrying a gun. The only thing he had on him was an African juju he was wearing around his waist like a belt. It was a native protective charm he had gotten from a very powerful traditional medicine man from Ijebu. It was for safety and security. It held a very mysterious force that could make the wearer appear and disappear at will. If the wearer, for example, found himself swamped by armed attackers, all he needed to do was run to the nearest wall or tree and mutter a few incantations. As he did this, he would disappear mysteriously, only to reappear in a safe place many kilometers away.

Running fast, with his assailants hot on his heels, Keme saw a fence and dashed toward it. When he was very close to it, he stopped, turned around, and faced his assailants. The four men had likewise stopped running. They walked warily toward the Owlsman. Keme stepped backward until his back touched the cold fence. He leaned against it and began to recite the mysterious incantations. He didn't disappear. One of the gunmen went to him, pointed the gun at his knees and squeezed the trigger.

Keme screamed, and the scream filled the night. The other gunmen came forward; they shot him several times, lifted his body, and walked hurriedly toward their car, which was already driving toward them.

* * *

Aliu Zamani University was shaken to its very foundations with the news of the killings.

By the dawn of the following day, Keme's corpse was delivered to the residence of his girlfriend. The time was around 5:24 a.m.—exactly twenty-four hours after he had been shot. Keme's girlfriend had already traveled out of town, and it was a friend of hers who had discovered the body. She had yelled, and within ten minutes, people had crowded around. Word got around, and less than thirty minutes later, Owlsmen, all hooded in black and carrying assault weapons, came and moved the body. They took the body to Featherland, just as they had done earlier with the two other bodies.

Keme's corpse was a sickening sight. His men recognized him only by his clothing and the tattoos on his body. There was nothing left of his face. The killers had bloodied it beyond recognition. They had plucked out his eyes, and the empty sockets stared sightlessly at his colleagues. There were also bullet holes in his neck and body, and splotches of dried blood and red dust covered him.

Tos had rolled him onto his stomach, and they had all seen the fresh axe wounds on his back. And attached to his body was a note held in place by a nail driven into his chest, the words written in clumsy block letters: "This is just the beginning. Others will go just like him." It was signed with the colors and insignia of the five gangs that now called themselves the L5.

The Owlsmen knew that those who had killed Keme were trying to tell them that they had punished him before they finally had him killed.

Killing was nothing new to Tos. He knew this was really just the beginning.

The decision to waste the three Owlsmen had been the most ill-advised action ever taken by any gang in recent times. They had forced issues by their action. Keme's corpse and the note attached to his body provoked Owlsmen all over and beyond Jankara. The Owlsmen in Jankara were boiling with anger and dying to strike the next day. But going by convention, that was not the gang's style. That notwithstanding, unless vengeance was wreaked, Aliu Zamani University would know no peace. Every Owlsman had a duty to see to it. Apart from the killing itself, which was bad as it was, the note attached to Number Five's body was the official declaration of war. And more lives would be lost, just as they had predicted.

The objective of the killing was simple: top titled men had to be killed so that Owlsmen would learn the importance and dignity of other gangs.

The League of Five had understood the furor their action would cause. They knew that the deaths of the three Owlsmen and the note attached to Number Five's corpse would provoke Owlsmen. But to the Owlsmen, the consequences of what would follow that brutal act could better be imagined. There would be a fierce cult war.

Tos knew that he had done his best. Only the week before, he had sent emissaries with letters to the various gangs to which Kraks, Kelly, and Nosa belonged, and in those letters, which were signed by Paxman, he had explained why they did what they had done. He had emphasized that what Owlsmen had done had not been carried out in view of ridiculing or disregarding all the various frat gangs, but rather it that it should be seen as a personal score that had needed personal settlement between himself and the people that were abducted. Then he had added that should any of the gangs feel their sanctity violated or slighted by the Black Owls' actions, they should patiently stay action until a way was prepared for a general peace meeting—as was generally the tradition. But none of the gangs had given an inkling that they were preparing for a bucket of blood.

Tos knew he had stepped on toes, but he hadn't really believed it would lead to a full-scale cult war. He was not daunted, though. Even as the five gangs had teamed up together against the Black Owls, the fiery gang he had headed for close to two years now would still come out as the most powerful cult gang in any Nigerian university.

Four days had passed since the day of violence—three days since the body of Keme had been deposited at the Black Owls' territory. Throughout those times, Tos and his men had been reflective of what had happened.

The Wizards' deaths had been a professional concept. The strategy was classic. The three chieftains who had died in that violence had clearly been marked out, and their tracks had been clearly defined for the kill. The method utilized was the zenith of killing tricks. Most of them had been done, Tos believed, by outsiders. They were butchers from other schools. There had been nothing like this before in the history of cult warfare in Jankara.

One thing was certain now: Mike and Osas were not acting alone. After all, they were from different houses. Their gangs were acting in concert with other gangs; they were projecting and protecting the interests of the various gangs. The five insignias clearly proved that the five major cult gangs in the school were clearly against the superiority of the Black Owls. It was the only explanation. Otherwise, there would've been no conflict.

Tos had the gut instinct that he was right in thinking along this line. His instinct had never failed him before. It would not fail him now. He trusted it absolutely.

Revenge would take only a matter of days, perhaps weeks. But it was certain that Owlsmen would fight back. And who in the whole of Jankara could stand the vengeance of Owlsmen? This was not the first time Owlsmen had been targets of factions distinct from each other. They had dealt with opposing broad based frat gangs before. They could do it again.

The first few days after the hit were a time of depression and self-pity for the Owlsmen. But as Number One, Tos knew he was the ultimate target. He had escaped death by sheer luck. They had prepared and visited his apartment in the dead of the night with submachine guns. But God, through Bray and the intuition of his guards, had allowed him to escape death by a whisker's breadth. Now everything depended on his coolheadedness. He knew that if he acted immediately, he would be caught on the wrong foot of violence and more souls would be foolishly lost. Therefore he called for caution—at least to allow passion to cool down and professionalism to takeover.

In that vein, he declared a week of mourning.

* * *

Featherland was a haunt of feathered men who wished to have a sheltered haven from the violent heat in Jankara. Six hours prior, the first gunshot had started the gang war; and by 8:00 a.m. the next morning, over thirty-five wizards had flown to the farm. By noon of that same day, it was totally crowded with feathered Owlsmen.

Featherland was situated in the middle of a lovely expanse of very green forests, a rich verdure of fertile land approximately thirty miles from Jankara. They called it Featherland because only titled men had the privilege of taking shelter within its walls. But the property belonged to all Owlsmen. It had been built with Owlsmen's money and equipped with Owlsmen's money. Keeping and maintaining this piece of property was not cheap. It included the use of about a dozen motorcycles (the only means of transportation to and from the nearest town, which was about fifteen miles away), the fueling of the diesel-powered generator, the feeding and keeping of the poultry and farm animals, which included chickens and goats, and the upkeep of the Fulani herdsman, who together with his family stayed on the farm all through the year. Then came the cost of arms and ammunitions. Generally, it cost them almost two million naira a year to keep the farm functional.

By students' standards, Featherland was without doubt a compound of abundance. In every major crisis period, as part of the preparations for staying there for several days, Owlsmen flooded the farm with all sorts of luxuries: canned foods, toilet papers, bags of rice, beverages, soap and toiletries, packets of cigarettes, canned beers, secondhand clothing—you name it. But they only brought in these items during very serious war situations, like the one they were encountering at the moment.

Featherland was the real headquarters of the Order of the Black Owls. It was here that men were given their second birth, the Second Initiation. It was here that they planned strategies, and it was here they retreated to after major strikes. But in truth, only a very few Owlsmen knew of its existence.

The area of the farmstead was in the middle of a deep forest. No actual farmland lay within ten miles in any direction—no rice paddies and no modern human cultivation of any sort. All around it were just sun-baked yellow hills and very tall trees. It was a perfect hideout. Nobody would possibly want to go there.

The Owlsmen, of course, delighted in their privacy, and every now and then they would send armed men to look around. The weapons used to guard the farmstead were SMGs, and there were over a dozen such deadly weapons in Featherland.

A tribe called Mokanah inhabited the distant mountains and forests around the farmstead. They were a primitive, partially naked people who looked like the cousins of the Koma people of Adamawa. The Owlsmen called them "Bushmen." And the name stuck to them, not without some justification.

The Bushmen were the only immediate next-door neighbors to the farmstead. They did not speak or understand English. Their mode of dress was the Stone Age type—simple loincloths—and they usually wore animals' teeth around their necks. They had a strange religion. They worshipped stones, which they placed atop one another until they looked like totems. They were a short-statured, dark-skinned people with matted, wooly hair. The women lived by picking fruits, and the men were hunters. Their instruments of hunting were crudely constructed bows and arrows and a funny type of bamboo rod that shot darts made of heat-treated bamboo slivers laced with snake venom.

They kept to themselves, and the Owlsmen likewise kept to themselves. But generally they were very good neighbors.

The forest all around the farmstead was peaceful. There was really no enemy activity within the nearest thirty miles; that could come only from Jankara.

The farmhouse itself was a large, quiet wooden house. Inside there were a dozen rooms called "joints." The joints were nothing more than large empty spaces with family-sized mattresses laid on the bare floor. The furniture—what little there was—was spartan, with quilted cushions, and black curtains covered each of the entranceways of these rooms. All the windows had mosquito netting over them, and all the rooms were connected to a large, spacious hall. At the back was an airy kitchen. A few yards from the house was a walled wooden enclosure. It contained the shower stalls—twenty of them in all.

The eating hall attached to the kitchen was like an officers' mess hall, with amateurishly built wooden seats and tables. The assembly hall was like a secondary school hall, but it was a neat and good-natured place.

Featherland was heavily populated at that moment. The crisis on the ground made it so. About half of the Owlsmen seeking shelter there came with their girls. Most of the girls that came with their men were girls who were well known to be connected to gang members.

Don Tos had a joint to himself in the house. He shared it with Ebi. (Ebi was one of the twenty-two girls on the farm. Ovo's girlfriend, a dark, lovely girl called Tracy, was there; Paxman's girl also was there.) But truly, rank had its privilege. Don Tos, as the Number One, had a joint to himself.

Initially, Ebi was not comfortable with the situation on the farm. But once they had settled in, she had no choice but to adjust.

The food was terrible. Every day's breakfast, according to the roster, was tea, loaf (which ran out after the third day), and corned beef. Lunch was white rice and goat meat stew. Ebi, who hated goat meat, was forced to blend in. She had little choice. Such meals were usually accompanied with fruit juice or real fruits, such as oranges or papaya. But they had beans and yam porridge for supper. To Ebi, it was the worst meal on the roster. This was because the beans were terribly cooked. Each food cooked on the farm was a new little adventure. But whenever she was faced with beans or any kind of strange cooking, she always opted for canned food.

Life on the farm was quite interesting at first. Those first few days were sunny, open, and quiet. But as the days of mourning wore on, it became oppressively boring. All they had to do was to watch the sun rise in the morning; then they would have breakfast, play cards (or Scrabble or chess, and sometimes Monopoly, as the case may be), eat lunch, take siestas, play more games, and consider the threat that lay ahead. When the sun went down, it was Howling Hour, or the Hour of the Owls. So they would rush through supper, and after supper they would start a large fire burning in the middle of the compound.

In the middle of the night, the Owlsmen would gather around the great fire to *sallay. Sallaying* was a mad moment of fearful, eerie crying, hooting, and ghoulish dancing around the ever-burning fire, accompanied by feverish drumming.

The sallaying in the center of the compound stopped when the rain came. It started with a mild shower on the third night. Then they formed a circle around the fire and began chanting terribly loud cultic songs that were corrupted versions of good Christian songs. But the rain came, and the Owlsmen lost control of the weather.

It rained heavily for the next three days; it was as if the heavens were taking the side of the Owlsmen in mourning their dead.

On the seventh night after the violence, with the rain still drizzling lightly, Ebi was sleeping in Tos's joint. It was a quiet and very cold night. The time was about 11:15 p.m. She woke up with a start. There was heavy silence around her. It was an eerie, frightening silence that, in fact, was the thing that had awakened her. Featherland, at any time of the day, was an unlikely place to experience that kind of silence. She got off the mattress. As she walked soundlessly toward the doorway, she heard noises. She paused and cocked her head, listening. The joint was in darkness. As silently as she could manage, she edged forward carefully, opened the black curtains slowly, and peered into the hallway. At first she could not see clearly until her eyes adjusted to the dimness of the hall. The fluorescent light had been deliberately shorted. Dozens of black and red candles were positioned strategically, their orange flames creating frightening shadows everywhere.

It seemed as if a sort of cultic ceremony was going on. She saw Tos. He was obviously the one in charge of the ceremony. There were over forty men in the hall. They wore only black loincloths—like the Bushmen—and all their black cult marks were clearly visible. Tos wore a red toga with a black owl emblazoned boldly across the front.

An arrangement of the forty-odd men in two lines had been formed, leaving a wide aisle that led to the Grand Wizard. In front of him lay three coffins. They were real coffins with real corpses inside. She couldn't believe what she was seeing. The longer she looked, the clearer and more bizarre the whole scene appeared before her eyes.

She just stood in the doorframe in a black slip and watched them.

Keme's coffin was the one nearest Tos. It was partially open; his body, crudely embalmed with formaldehyde but already starting to decay, was visible to her. Blood had been spilled around and on the sides of the coffins. Red and black candles, placed atop green beer bottles, were positioned on the edges of the coffins.

Close to Keme's coffin was a very low table—a table as low as the ugly wooden coffins. On the center of the table was laid the cult idol. Surrounding the idol were over two dozen ugly tumblers, shining dully where the yellow light touched them. Dominating the table was a great brown calabash, and near the calabash was a small, very brown clay server bearing lobes of what looked like kolanuts and kaolin. Next to the server was a skull that Ebi perceived to be human—though she couldn't be completely sure.

Tos towered over them. That was because he was standing on a little raised platform.

"O Kirinja!" he shouted loudly.

"O-hoooo!" the group of wizards replied strongly.

Tos picked up the cult idol. He stood transfixed as he contemplated the heavy black woodwork tied with strings of cowries and shrouded in red cloth.

"O Kirinja!" he screamed again.

"O-hoooo!" the wizards replied strongly, and then, as one body, they all fell on their knees.

"Kirinja—you are the god of the forests, the controller of the night. We cry out to you because we are grieved. Death is everywhere. Our enemies have come out boldly to declare war on us. Your apostles were slain. Your servants were killed. Your worshippers were humiliated." At this point Tos paused and fell on his knees. "I am your high priest, the vessel through which your orders are passed on to your worshippers. Tonight we come before you so that we shall all be protected. Feather, on whom we wholly depend, we greet you with a great chant."

There was a resounding general chant. It lasted for about a minute, and then it stopped suddenly.

"There is blood on the face of the earth. It is the blood of your servants. For that, we ask that you clothe us with the toga of invincibility so we can take back our pound of flesh. This is your fight. Give us strength to prosecute it. Let the moon rise, and let the sun hide. The light of the moon is our hope. So let the light of the moon cover the land, and let our enemies show themselves. One by one, let them fall. For that we chant for you."

For what seemed like two minutes, another thundering chant filled the hall, and then it stopped simultaneously and the men stared at their high priest, the expressions on their faces difficult to fathom.

Tos continued in the same tone of voice. "The light of the moon is the power of the night. O Kirinja, you are the king of the night. Clothe us with the power of the night so that when the battle is over, no matter how many deaths shall be reported, there shall be no loss among us. For that, Owlsmen howl for you."

All the Owlsmen howled as one. The echo of that great shout raced into the night.

"Black Owl—clothe us with the night. The safest place is your shadow. With your decree, the sun will not show. The forces of Darkness will strengthen us. May the stream of the blood of our enemies flow in Jankara. And let the whole of the town wear sad faces. Tomorrow when the story shall be told, the death of a single Nightman shall not be reported. For that, we howl for you."

This shout was the loudest but the briefest. After it had stopped, Tos bowed his head and replaced the idol on the center of the low table. As he did so, he picked up something and stood up. Now he had a black cock in his left hand and a machete of menacing sharpness in his right.

He stood with his back still to them, muttering some incantations, directing the words toward the cult idol and the large painting of a man wrestling fiercely with a man-sized owl. Twelve giant red candles and a cloud of the cock's feathers surrounded the platform on which he stood. He held the black bird firmly, wings, feet, and all. Bright blood dripped down his arms.

With a deep, macabre chant that enveloped the air in the hall, Tos made the forty-plus bare-chested figures rise. The hall was filled with the aroma of fresh blood and sweat, and the solemnity of the rock-faced cultists made the oblation more frightening. Tos uttered a muted chant, and they took up the chanting in low tones. He gave a command with a wave of the machete, and the Owlsmen stretched out their hands and laced fingers. He raised the chant louder, and they replied to him more loudly.

He started the Owlsmen's dance, the cock feathers billowing all around him. The others followed suit. It was weird: Owlsmen, all wielding axes and handguns now, swarmed like fireflies around the hall. In the delirium of the oblation, they hooted and howled like hyenas, gyrated and snarled excitedly like wildcats.

Tos, his dancing fervent, looking like an *Ifa* priest with juju and cowries dangling around his waist, became a stranger to Ebi. He looked now like someone possessed by demons.

When they had danced for well over ten minutes, he gave a command and they all knelt again as a body. But he remained standing. He waved the cock in the air and displayed the knife with a flourish. Its sharp edge glittered evilly in the muted light. He said something in cultic patois, and one of the bare-chested figures stood up. It was Ovo. His body was shiny with sweat, and on his neck and arms were strings of cowries and assorted charms.

Trembling slightly, Ovo touched his lips to the machete, and in a tone of deep-throated vehemence, he swore an oath of allegiance to the Brotherhood of the Black Owls.

After the oath, Ovo broke into a powerful chant that the others picked up excitedly. When he stopped, the others also stopped, all of them sweating profusely in the hot, airless hall. Ovo took a tumbler from the table and measured a dark liquid from the calabash. He drank it in a gulp and set the tumbler gently on the table. He then took a lobe of what looked like kolanut and popped it into his mouth as if it were popcorn. In the same deep-throated, resonant voice, he said he vowed this night to be an instrument of murder, to fight against the murderers of the three Owlsmen, to kick against oppression and intimidation no matter from what quarter it came, and to always respond to the call "to pick up beak." He promised to live and die a committed Owlsman and said that if he should betray any of his brothers, he should die before graduation. He ended by saying, "May the kokoma squeeze the life out of me the moment I break any of the oaths I am making tonight."

After the declaration, he fell on his knees again. The next fellow, Owlsman Number Three, was Max "Paxman" Osuagwu. He took his oath, drank from the portion in the calabash, and knelt. Malik Saleh, Owlsman Number Four, was next. He took his oath vehemently and completed the exercise by brandishing a revolver. The fourth chap was Frank White. His oath was very brief. The fifth chap was Kadiri Muazu. Like Frank, his oath also was very brief. The sixth chap was Christo One Way. He swore his allegiance in an uncommonly loud voice.

The ceremony proceeded until all the forty-eight wizards—they were forty-eight in number with the exclusion of Tos—had taken their oaths. After the declaration, Tos raised his right arm, which held a machete full of a million reflections. The others chanted a chorus, and the machete descended and swiftly slashed the cock's head. The headless cock fought vainly in his hand. It twitched in its death throes, and its blood splattered on their bodies.

The cock's head that landed on the table looked like kolanut. Ebi placed her hand on her lips to stop herself from screaming. The Owlsmen, one after the other, drank again. She noticed that Tos had directed the stream of the bird's blood into the calabash.

They danced feverishly for another long moment before Tos stopped them with a command and motioned toward the three coffins with the remains of the dead cock. Paxman, Morgan, Frank White, and Malik came forward and lifted Keme's coffin. Other wizards lifted the other two coffins. As they filed out with Tos in the lead, they raised a subdued song of mourning and made their way out of the hall and into the dark, drizzling night as quietly as possible, as if they were afraid of waking the inhabitants of the house.

They sang quietly until they were high and deep into the far side of the farm, where they stood on the edge of three freshly dug graves.

Tos performed the graveside ceremony. Ten minutes later, twenty-one rifles faced the heavens and emitted sounds. It was the gun salute for fallen chieftains.

* * *

When silence descended on the house, Ebi crept back into bed. In her heart was black grief, in her eyes dark anger. Keme had been killed because of her. The three of them were dead because of her.

She thought back to the Clique Nightclub. That was the very first time she had met Keme. She blamed herself for their deaths; she blamed herself for becoming involved with Dr. Ubangha.

Only a few days ago, they had all been in Bray's Kitchen, laughing and joking. But all they had of them now were embalmed corpses that they were returning to the earth.

The sounds of short wooden African drums beating out there in the cold, rainy darkness reached her. The sorrowful sound of the Owlsmen chanting their weird cult dirge made her shudder with fright. Thereafter, the loud report of twenty-one gunshots punctured the night. The drumming and the shooting continued for a long time.

CHAPTER NINETEEN

Ebi was relieved the next morning when Tos ordered her to go back to Lagos. She protested convincingly, of course; she even cried. But in the depth of her heart, that was what she really wanted. The atmosphere on the farm was beginning to tire her. She longed for fresher air. She longed for her bedroom; she longed for the feel of the clean bedspread against her skin. She missed her apartment—the only place where she could bathe in clean water and eat good food.

When she was gone, Tos called a war council meeting.

The meeting began at exactly 12.00 p.m. He found himself seated at the head of the roughly hewn, seven-foot-long, unvarnished conference table, looking at the deadpan faces of his nine *eclassia* members: the inner circle—the final authority of the gang.

Up the table to his immediate right was Ogheneovo Ikoloba, the Evil Eye. On his immediate left was Max "Paxman" Osuagwu. Next to Ovo was seated Frank White, the former assistant chief security officer, or Klaws II, but automatically the CSO, or Klaws I, after Keme's death.

Frank White's dark eyes, Tos could see, were red from ganja smoke. He was dying for revenge. He knew they all needed blood. Anything short of that would lead to mutiny. Friends had died; brothers had been brutally, fearlessly killed.

Tos thoughtfully studied his men one after the other as he decided what to say.

They were all looking coldly at him. The whole thing was entirely his fault, he knew. They were all mad at him, though none of them was bold enough to voice it within his hearing. He was still the Don, a man of action and fierce temper and violence. He had only been momentarily weakened by the love of a woman. He was still the hero of over a dozen cult fights. He was still the Don.

The truth was that he had possessed the information at his fingertips. He had had only one choice and that had been to mount a series of preemptive strikes on the five major gangs at the moment they least expected it. But he had blown the opportunity, and now the war had been declared by the coalition of these gangs.

Tos couldn't understand it at all—not any of it. It was unbelievable. It was appalling. But it was real. The problem before them had only one solution—a declaration of war. Owlsmen were facing a challenge from a league of incomparable gangs—smaller rival gangs. And three of his chieftains had been canceled out, unbelievably gunned down. For that alone, darkness and desolation would descend on Jankara. Like a shadow from the grave, death and catastrophe would visit all those men who had connections with the deaths of the wizards. Human beings would be killed like dogs. The university would be transformed into a killing field. The blood of the guilty would flow. The blood of innocents also would flow.

Tos remembered the chant at the second initiation ceremony:

> Black as the Owl,
> Blacker than the Night;
> Shrouded by the Cowl,
> Surrounded by the Night.
> Baked in the Womb,
> Bigger than the Tomb;
> A Lord of the Night,
> Is bigger than Death.

He remembered also the vow during the Second Birth: "If we must die, let it not be by guns. Let no machete cut us, and let no battleaxe hack us. If we must die, let Kirinja swallow us. And let our spirits go the way of all Owlsmen. That had been long ago, at the initiation. He'd thought the rituals would shelter them from guns and knives and battleaxes. What about the charms and the rituals?

It was very annoying. Keme was dead, killed by cultists' guns. *If Keme and the two other strong men had to die, must cultists' guns have killed them?* Tos wondered. *Where was Kirinja, the great protector who is supposed to swallow death and protect the ordinary Owlsman? Instead they were killed, sent to their early graves. And instead of going in peace, swallowed by Kirinja, they were cold-bloodedly murdered, their lives taken forcibly, unbelievably, in the night. All this happened when the whole world was sleeping, and the great Kirinja, the protector of the night, also slept. How could the king of the night have slept and allowed this to happen?* He felt anger at himself as much as anyone did. It was his fault. Kirinja must not be blamed for his indifference when they had failed on their part to do their homework. He should have dealt seriously with the threat Dikko represented. But all the same, everything was still under control. The previous night, all wizards had sworn the oath of vengeance. Now they must talk.

"Before the commencement of this meeting, let's bow our heads and pray," Tos said quietly.

All the ten feathered chiefs bowed their heads over the table. It was a three-minute cultic prayer, and Tos's loud voice rang clearly over the table.

He was the first to lift up his head, and he looked around uneasily. His eyes were tired from lack of sleep.

"Aye," he said. "All feathered heads up."

All those present raised their heads, and nine pairs of eyes assessed him pointedly.

"The first item on the agenda is to maintain a minute's silence for our slain brothers. The second item is the only other item on the agenda. And this"—he paused deliberately—"is picking up beak. Every one of us present here this afternoon will say a word on it. Then we'll know the method we should employ. But first, a minute's silence."

The whole assembly of ten men remained silent for over two minutes.

At last Tos raised his eyes and surveyed the table. All the men's eyes were on him. He studied them quietly, deep in his own personal thoughts. He had presided over war council meetings before. This wasn't the first one, and he was not disturbed over the problem this one presented. War council meetings tended to be rare, but rather formal. The Number One traditionally was the chairman. The first war council meeting he had presided over had been immediately after the Don Bosco affair. Since then, he had presided over four others ones in Jankara and had attended six others in other institutions. In this case, however, he knew the situation was much more serious. The Black Owls were up against a league of five gangs, and there was no time for filibustering.

The killings had affected them all, and Tos knew there would be a unanimous blood judgment on all the gangs involved in this thing.

"Brothers," Tos began quietly, "We all know why we are here: to look at the chances of finding out and destroying these people who have inflicted these pains—these unimaginable crimes—on us. What I want to know from you Wisemen is this: What do we do to take back our pound of flesh, and what security measures do we take to prevent this kind of thing from happening again? How many heads do we need to cancel our loss? I want every one of us to react and bring out ideas."

It was Ovo who first reacted. "Great blows have been rained on us," he began in a heavy voice. "Uncountable bullets have been spent. Three lives were cold-bloodedly taken. In the cause of justice and vengeance, I suggest we take fifteen lives."

"Not at all," Frank White said, and he laughed without malice. "It's my boss who was killed. For me, twenty lives is what I suggest."

"Twenty lives?" Christo One Way said. "Why are we so merciful? What's the matter with us? Three chieftains were murdered. Two of them were members of this inner circle, and yet we're showing mercy? It could've been you or me. Or the Don. I say we should bulldoze the entire town. If it comes to a vote, I'll vote that fifty pigs be wasted. Fifty bloody pig heads. Or have we forgotten our twelfth commandment?"

Tos shook his head as if to clear water from his eyes. He remembered the twelfth commandment as well as the other commandments. The twelfth commandments said, "Forget the smell of mercy when dealing with your enemies."

"Does anybody have any contrary view?"

"Yeah." It was Bolo Araba-Benson, Owlsman Number Twelve. "I say we double the number of our victims."

"That would be six, right?" Ovo asked.

"Yeah."

"That's not enough," Ovo said, shaking his head.

Tos nodded solemnly and looked at each of the chieftains in turn.

"Is there any other contrary viewpoint?"

After a while, all the young men shook their heads.

Tos took a deep breath. "Wisemen, I have no illusion about what we're up against. We all recognize the threat, but I tried to logicize it. I let myself down. I let you guys down, and for that I'm sorry. I promise to correct this error and avenge our slain brethren. But in doing that, we should not let our emotions run away with us. I asked a question: How many heads do we need to cancel out our loss? It's a practical question and not an emotional one. I need a practical answer. We've lost three good men. What do we do to regain our self-worth? Our value? Our respect? I'm not talking about mindless, stupid killings. I'm talking about meaningful, strategic killings. I don't want the deaths of innocent people. If you ask me how many heads I want, I, like Christo, would say fifty pigs heads and then deploy butchers to the streets of Jankara to effect the demand. But that's being emotional. If I'm to be a professional —which I am—I'd say we need to get the chieftains of all the gangs involved in the killings of our brothers. But unfortunately we can't get all of them, because most of them have traveled out of town. Since this incident happened, the only people who have sent us condolence messages are the less-violent gangs. To me personally, that shows that all who refuse to mourn with us are involved in these killings. Am I making sense?"

"Yeah," most of them replied.

"This whole thing's straightforward. We know the gangs who pulled this stunt. The problem is how to reach them and effect the greatest damage. So what do you guys think?" Up till this very moment, only five persons had made suggestions. Tos was surprised when Morgan Akumagba, hard-bitten chieftain Number Ten, spoke up.

"My lord, this is not really a big problem if you imagine it from my point of view. There are, as you know, five renowned gangs leagued against us. They are solid as a league. And they've scored the first point. What I advise we do instead of rushing into war, wasting more lives, and short-circuiting our future, is to call a peace meeting."

"A peace meeting?" Tos was puzzled. Somebody laughed.

"Yes."

Tos studied Morgan carefully, but he detected no jest in his voice.

"Nothing's worthless, Councilor. Go on."

Morgan nodded. All eyes in the gathering were looking at him with interest.

"Our intelligence men believe that there are six venues that have been used for peace meetings since the beginning of peace conferences in this school. The only one that I attended that was held outside this town occurred when Owlsmen in this zone got involved in another zone's affair, and that was only because the particular incident took place in another zone. The tendency that one of these six venues would be used is very high. If this were so, then the operation would be an easy one. We would make sure the various gangs involved in the killings of our brothers would be present at the meeting. After the meeting commenced, our gunmen would simply come in and get out with no problem, and be home ten minutes later. By then we'd already have taken our revenge."

There was no immediate response from the others. The silence in the gathering said more than a gasp or a sudden sharp intake of breath.

Tos dwelled on these words thoughtfully and regarded Morgan speculatively.

"Tell us more. How do we do it?"

Morgan shrugged. "I'll wager that they won't change the way we normally organize peace meetings. There are exactly six venues where we normally hold these types of meetings. It's going to be a very neat job—that is, if our gunmen can be relied on. We'll insert our best gunmen into the ceiling of each venue of the meeting hall. These men would be well armed, of course. While the meeting progresses, the chosen gunmen would interrupt and do the damage."

There was stunned silence after he had finished speaking. Those people who had scoffed at him when he first made his point were now looking at him with something close to respect in their eyes. He actually commanded the attention of all the men.

"They're not stupid," Christo said. "They'll see it as bait. They won't even accept our peace offer."

"There's no other way around this thing," Morgan said quickly. "Of course they'll suspect foul play. But I believe they'll suspect anything at this moment. Even a genuine peace conference would still be highly suspect. But this thing is straightforward. And there're no two ways about it. There are only six venues. Hours—or even better, days—before the acceptance of our peace offer, we'll have our men in place."

"It's risky," Paxman said quietly. "Even if they were to accept the peace offer, the venue would be heavily guarded. The hit men that pull the job would be exposing themselves to great risks. It's a suicide mission."

"I think you have a point there," Tos said. "But even if we try the bait of suing for peace, what will we put in the white status letter to convince them that it's genuine peace we are seeking?"

Morgan looked steadily at Tos. "Maybe we should tell them that the university community, the families of our slain brothers, and the school management are all tired of the bloodshed. In some ways, we could convince them that they want to assist us to wrap up our differences. Even the VC is a major stakeholder in this whole thing. The school authorities could be told that we're seeking measures to end the violence. They could even assist by giving some compensation to the families of our slain brothers. In some ways, it could convince them."

"It's not good enough. Try again," Christo said.

"I think I'm at my wits' end," Morgan replied.

Tos regarded the men quietly for a while. "What do you think, Ovo? Is it feasible?"

Ovo nodded. "It's cool thinking, my lord. If I understand Morgan very well, we could set them up smooth and solid. We could get the VC to authenticate the peace initiative. And like he said, there are six places that all gangs normally use for peace meetings. We'll let them pick any one of these venues. But if I understand him very well, we'll case all the joints before coming out with our white flag. Then, as the meeting progresses, our hit man will do the damage inside, and at the same time, our men can storm the building from the outside. It's a very good plan. We could clean them out before they know what hit them."

Tos waited for a counterview. When none was forthcoming, he told Morgan to give more details about his plan.

Quietly and clearly, Morgan explained the details. By the time he finished speaking, Tos had made up his mind.

He stared down the table. "We'll put it to a voice vote. To me, it's a good plan." He paused for a moment. "If you're for Morgan's plan, please say aye."

"Aye," about six members said in unison.

"Anybody against it?"

"I'm against it," Paxman said.

"Me too," Kadiri Muazu also said.

"May I ask why?" Tos asked.

Paxman said, "First, it's too risky. And besides, people will think it's not a good thing to kill in a peace meeting. It's a tradition. I think we should respect it."

"I don't give a flying fuck what people think," Tos said angrily. "All I want is revenge. Before they killed our men, we sent a white status letter, but they rejected it and went ahead to kill our brothers. This is our turn to reject laid-down conventions." He faced Kadiri now. "What's your excuse?"

"I've changed my mind," Kadiri said.

Tos smiled. "Thank you."

"So we'll wait to see if they accept our peace offer?" Christo asked.

Tos nodded. "We'll swallow our pride, pretend to forget our loss and do everything possible to make sure that they agree to peace. We'll be as meek as lambs. We'll reach the VC; we'll send out the word suing for peace. Whatever names they call us, we will not be provoked. We will not react to it. But meanwhile we'll have our own agenda. How about it?"

"Some will call this cowardice," Kabaka said.

Tos nodded. "Kabaka—don't you see what we're trying to do? We're employing a different tactic. I'll call it Morgan's Tactic. Our primary objective is to gather them in one place and do a clean job. This is the best and only way to do it. And we can only do it under the cover of a peace meeting. If they continue to provoke us, we'll still act as though our mission is indeed peaceful. At the last minute, our guys will storm the meeting ground and go for the kill. That's how the Mafia arranges it. Are we ready for Morgan's Plan?"

They all nodded as one.

Tos let his eyes sweep over their faces. He was pleased with what he saw—utter concentration.

"Now, Councilors, let's fine-tune Morgan's Plan. I'll need everyone to bring in his own special ideas. I want a foolproof plan."

* * *

Mrs. Adaka Dabiri had just finished lunch, and one of the maids was clearing away the dishes when another maid came into the dining room.

"Madam, telephone for you." Madam Adaka Dabiri looked puzzled. She was not expecting a call right now.

"Who's on the line?"

"It's small, madam," the maid said quickly.

Adaka Dabiri sighed with relief. The prodigal daughter was calling. She stood up and walked hurriedly into the living room.

Across the very spacious room, on an elegant three-legged table bearing an impressive porcelain figurine sculpture, sat the cream-colored telephone, its receiver off the cradle and lying on its side. She put the receiver to her ear and heard her daughter's voice among the crackling sound of the static.

"Akpos, are you there?"

"Mom?" Ebi's anxious voice replied questioningly.

"Where are you? We've looked for you all over Jankara. Where've you been?"

"I'm all right, Mom."

"Are you quite sure, my darling?"

The voice that came back over the line was hesitant, almost nervous. "I'm all right, Mom. It's just that there's been a little accident out in my school."

"It wasn't a 'little accident,' Akpos. It was a very serious and a major accident. The police said ten people were killed. The papers said fifteen or more people died. We don't know what or whom to believe. It has us worried. You shouldn't have left the way you did, without telling me. You got me worried."

"I know, Mom. I'm very sorry." Ebi kept her voice light, but she meant it.

"Before you left, we could have settled everything, talked things over. You know, like mother and daughter."

"I said I'm very sorry, Mom." Ebi's voice was a few inches away from anger. "Tosan said I was wrong to leave home the way I did."

"Is he there with you?"

Ebi hesitated briefly. "No."

"Is he all right?"

Ebi smiled into the phone. *Can my mother really be concerned about Tosan's well-being?*

"Don't worry, Mom. He's okay. Tos is a big boy. He can take care of himself."

"Where are you, honey?"

Ebi paused for a fraction of a second. "I'm in a hotel."

"In a hotel? In Jankara?" Her mother's voice was incredulous.

"No," Ebi replied softly. "I'm right here in Lagos. How's Papa?"

"He just left for Apapa. He'll be thrilled you called." There was a pause that lasted for a few seconds. "When are you coming over?"

"Coming home, you mean?"

"That's right."

Ebi paused. "I'll come over, say, tomorrow—if that's all right with Papa. I behaved badly the last time I was with him. Do you think he'll forgive me?"

"Don't you worry about your father right now." Mrs. Dabiri gave the automatic motherly response. "You're always welcome in this house. It's your house. It's your home. Just get yourself safely here, okay?"

"I will, Mom. Bye."

After she hung up the phone, Mrs. Dabiri stared into space for some time. When they had heard that a very violent cult clash had happened in Jankara, she and her husband had rushed to the university town, as most parents who had wards there had done. But it had been a futile trip. There had been no sign of their beloved daughter. They had visited the police station in the company of her husband's old friend, a retired police boss. The high-ranking police officer who was in charge of the case had assured them that the girl was safe wherever she might be, and this he was very sure of because there had been no female victims in the clash. Her husband had looked grim, but he had nodded as if to say he believed all that they'd been told and had shaken hands with the police officer. Finally they had returned to Lagos.

It had been over three weeks since Ebi had traveled back to school, in which time she had not communicated with her family.

Even though her husband had not spoken about their daughter's disappearance, Mrs. Dabiri could tell that he was deeply troubled by it. Every day, she had phoned Ebi's apartment, but the girl never answered the phone. It was only Iyabo, the housekeeper, who answered the phone, and she had always reassured her that Ebi was doing fine. Then they had heard the news about the killings. The newspapers' accounts had them shaken. They were not yet reconciled to the fact that their daughter was connected with a boy who was heavily connected with secret cult activities. Mrs. Dabiri believed that being a cultist was one of the lowest and dirtiest things a human being could stoop to, and she just couldn't believe that Tosan, such a gifted soul, could be involved in it. Even though the newspapers hadn't mentioned his name, they knew he was the one they were talking about. The connection was that his department had been mentioned. The newspapers all had agreed in their reports that a final-year student of the Department of Fine and Visual Arts had almost been killed when his apartment had been machine-gunned. And a girl, it was believed, had been living with the boy at the time of the attack. But since the incident, the young man and his girlfriend had not been seen. The newspapers even had displayed a photograph of the building, showing shattered windows and bullets holes in the walls. Adaka Dabiri and her husband had deduced that it was Tosan's apartment and that their daughter had been living with him at the time his apartment had been stormed.

Now deep in thought, she wished Ebi would just go back to America. If she wanted to make mischief over there, that was her own cup of tea. *Wouldn't it be better that way instead of endangering her life over here?*

* * *

Mike Imoni had spent the past week after the hit at the Beefeater Motel, just outside Jankara. He had paid in advance for the two weeks he planned to stay. He passed the days holed up in his room, watching TV and listening to the news broadcast. He also paid to have newspapers brought up to his room, and he smoked at least a pack of cigarettes per day. His meals consisted of bread, egg rolls, sandwiches, and beefsteak. He always ate in his room, never visiting the public dining room. When darkness came, he would slip into the night, take a cab, and visit the nearby whorehouse to meet with his favorite whore. Sometimes he would slip into Jankara to get news of what was happening in the town.

The past week had been enough for him to replay the whole exercise over and over in his mind, and he was beginning to understand what he was in for. *Operation Anaconda* had failed; they had succeeded in eliminating only three notable Owlsmen instead of the eight men targeted for the kill. The effort had been a waste. Now there was terrible heat on the whole of Jankara. The fiery, palpable tension and the pressure of the counterattack that was bound to come were frightening

The post-strike tension and the very danger he had exposed himself to had completely unnerved him. Roland Ibeshi had been right; Operation Anaconda, right from the very first meeting, had been a very bad idea. Now what would it cost in terms of damage analysis?

On that very night, just before nine o'clock, Mike came out of his room, slipped into the night, and boarded a taxi heading in the direction of Lokoja.

* * *

At exactly 11.50 a.m., Akpoebi Dabiri parked her car in her father's elegant compound. The polished oak doors pushed open, and her mother strode down the front steps. It was obvious that she had been looking out for her car all day.

"My baby, you look dead tired," said Adaka, standing back from the warm embrace with which she had welcomed her daughter.

Ebi couldn't help smiling. Once again the awesome beauty and vastness of the house struck her. And she was also flattered by the love expressed by her mother in welcoming her.

"You look lean and worn out, sweetheart."

Ebi nodded. "That's the least of my worries right now, Mom."

Adaka Dabiri raised her eyebrows. "What's the first of your worries?"

Ebi didn't answer that one. "It's lovely to be home," she said instead as her mother led her into the house. "Where's Papa?" she asked, following her mother through the living room toward the dining section.

"He went to play golf with the governor," her mother said, smiling. "But don't worry. Let's get something inside you first. I've prepared your favorite dish."

There was a place laid at the dining table, and her mother took one of the seats close to the window. Ebi sat down across from her mother. She raised her eyebrows and said quietly, "Roast duck in raspberry sauce?"

"Yes."

"Thanks, Mom, but I'd rather have plain snacks if I want to be faithful to myself."

"Never, my dear. You deserve a real treat, and that's what you'll get." She called the maids. Two of them came in a rush of excitement and greeted Ebi warmly.

"Bring the dishes from the oven, and be quick about it," said Ebi's mother.

There was a flurry of activity as the maids busied themselves.

"Now tell me, how's your friend?"

"Tosan?"

"Yes."

"He's fine." There was a moment of silence—a moment that the girl used to look at her mother steadily. "Mom, what do you really think of Tosan?" Ebi's voice was quiet, and her eyes were serious.

"You know I don't really know him," Adaka replied tactfully.

"But you've met him."

The older woman hesitated a moment "Yes, I've met him. But it wasn't the best of circumstances. He was drunk when I first met him. Do you want me to judge him by that first impression?"

For a moment or two, Ebi looked at her mother reflectively without saying anything.

"You've seen his work." It was a statement.

"Yes. I've seen his works. And from what I saw I think he's very talented. But as for his character, it's hard for me to say. I don't know him in the real sense. He's a cultist, that is for sure. He's a heavy drinker, also. But generally there's little I know of his other side."

Ebi gave her mother her radiant, fascinating smile.

"You'll love him, Mom," she said. "Tosan's not like any of the boys I've met here. As for his drinking, he'll get over it."

"So what's his other side like?"

"Deep inside, he's kindhearted, understanding, and wonderfully agreeable. He's devoted to me. You know it flatters a girl to have a man who worships the ground she walks on."

Adaka Dabiri smiled lightly. She knew her daughter was madly in love with the boy. Obviously, God had made it so. To be young and in love. *Tare* was what the Ijaws called love. It warmed something inside her, too.

"You must love him, then."

"Very much, Mom."

When the maids had finished delivering the dishes and were gone, mother and daughter attacked the meals silently. While they ate, they never said a word. They just concentrated on the meal, all further discussion relegated to the background. Less than thirty minutes after they started, lunch was over.

The maids came, and there was a brisk, brief rattle as they cleared away the dishes. Adaka led her daughter to the vast living room. There was a place by a large window where they would get a good view of the water fountain. They sat down there.

Adaka looked at her daughter quietly for a long time, her eyes troubled.

"I thought I'd better tell you why your father doesn't want you to have anything to do with the boy."

"I think I know it all. It's because of his tribe."

Adaka Dabiri shook her head.

"You're partly right," she said seriously.

Ebi saw a change in her mother's attitude. *What's up?* she wondered.

"But it has more to do with Tosan's name than his tribe."

"His name?" Ebi opened her eyes wide in surprise.

Her mother nodded. She knew that her daughter didn't know the full story of what was involved in the whole sordid affair.

"I'll tell you a story. There was a time when one Etan Mayuku was your father's dearest friend. Your father attended a business seminar in Lagos—that was where he met Etan, a brilliant man who worked for UAC as marketing manager. They sat together during the seminar. They sized each other up and saw the same thing in each other: fierce determination and ambition. Etan Mayuku was an Itsekiri and lived and worked in Warri. Your father was an Ijaw. He also lived and worked in Warri. They struck up a friendship and decided to team up and float a company together. But I'll tell you that I'm probably one of the few persons alive today who actually knew the strength of their friendship, the company they floated, the intrigues involved, and how everything broke up."

"Just a minute, Mom. Suppose you let me fix us something to drink. It seems this story of yours is a long one."

Adaka nodded. "Yes, of course."

Ebi went to the bar at the end of room and brought a bottle of champagne and two glasses. She poured the drinks liberally and handed one glass to her mother.

Adaka thanked her and took a large swallow.

"So tell me the story, Mom," Ebi said after a small sip.

Adaka nodded amiably. "One thing I want you to know is that I'm not against your relationship with Tosan in the real sense of the word. If you love the boy, then it's okay with me. It's your father I'm concerned about. He won't accept it. He'll do anything, everything, to put a stop to it. One of the reasons is because of his position, but that could be arranged quietly. Both of you can travel out of the country and get married in the United States. That's what rich people like us do in situations like this. But the truth is that your father does not want his daughter to get married to Tosan. He doesn't want you to bear that name."

Ebi fixed her mother with quiet hazel-brown eyes.

"Tell me what happened between Etan Mayuku and Papa."

Adaka looked at her daughter's innocent, smooth oval face, unmarked by poverty or want. She obviously had no idea what she was dealing with. Adaka let out a deep breath. She said, "I daresay there was a very great affection between your father and Etan Mayuku." She sat back and looked through the window at the water fountain. "Well, like I said before, they met at a business seminar, and thereafter they floated a construction company together. It was a good business venture. They managed it efficiently and it grew reasonably well. It was the era of the oil boom at that time and their business diversified into shipping, and they bought a couple of barges, fishing trawlers, and other oceangoing sea vessels. They were among the few Nigerian businessmen who could afford to buy these boats in those days. And business was good."

Ebi said, "I fear the worst. Etan Mayuku defrauded my father and claimed the company for himself, right?" She was intrigued.

"No," Adaka said, shaking her head. "But I must say, you're partly on track. Your father was the chairman of the company—of course, that was understandable, as he had the largest percentage of the shares. Etan Mayuku was the group-managing director of the entire company, and he had some forty-six percent of the total shares. You father wanted him to have that much because he wanted him to put his best into the company. And he did, truth be told. But for Etan Mayuku's great business acumen and handiwork, the business would have foundered."

"So what happened?"

Adaka did not reply immediately. She gazed out the window, seeing nothing but the beautiful sea of white clouds.

"So what happened?" Ebi repeated.

"The usual thing. The business grew larger and Etan Mayuku worked hard for it, and things went along fine for some time. Then Eyitemi stepped into the picture."

"Who's Eyitemi?"

"Tosan's mother."

"Tell me about her."

Adaka refilled her glass before she replied. "Eyitemi Olajire—that was her maiden name—was a woman blessed with uncanny artistic skill. It was a rare gift, and she utilized it efficiently. She was not only blessed with the gift of the arts; she was blessed also with a wonderful face and a desirable figure." She paused and regarded her daughter quietly. "How could any man resist a woman so beautiful, someone so alluring that other women paled into insignificance beside her? Well, nobody could blame your father. He met her, and he was taken in by her. And that was many years before he met Etan Mayuku." Her mother stopped talking suddenly, as if somebody had told her to shut up.

Ebi learned forward. "What happened next, Mom?"

Adaka Dabiri spoke without looking at her daughter. "The impact of her beauty on your father was really frightening. I cannot blame your father. Eyitemi had this attraction that made even the strongest of men's heads swoon with so much as a smile from her. Well, your father fell in love with her, and they started dating within a week of their meeting each other. Before your father met her, he was a womanizer, a lover of beautiful women. But Eyitemi changed all that. She was poised, elegant, clever—a girl with that elusive indefinable quality of feminine mystique. And he loved her. I know all this because I was her confidante. I knew everything that was going on. Our friendship went back several years. Both of us had attended the same college. And she was the one who introduced me to your father and made it possible for me to secure a job as his secretary."

"What really happened after that?"

Adaka stared straight at her daughter now. "I'll tell you. Your father's relationship with Eyitemi went smoothly until Etan Mayuku entered his life. By the time he met Etan, he had already sent Eyitemi to Europe to further her education. All your father ever wanted was to give her the best advantage as a woman. All the time she was away—she spent about three years abroad—he always traveled to Germany once a month to be with her. And back home, Etan Mayuku was handling the company well. Business was going well, and they were making fortunes. And everybody was happy."

"Tell me more about Etan Mayuku."

"Well, he was the most incredible, sensual man I'd ever met."

"Is that all?"

"No," Adaka replied stiffly. "He was a very handsome man—charming to the women and gracious to the men, and very gentlemanly to the clients. He was more popular in the company than your father was. Virtually all the women working in the company fell in love with him. And I was no exception."

Ebi lifted an eyebrow. "Really, Mom?"

Adaka nodded. "It is the truth. Everybody in the company liked him. In so many ways, he was a likable man. He had one of those charming, sexy smiles and an easygoing, good-natured attitude. People invariably liked him at once—women especially. They listened when he talked, partly because he was witty and partly because he had a voice that came out like a baritone, beautifully and delicately modulated. When he talked, you listened. I knew several girls who almost killed themselves just to get his attention. But he never dated any of them. And another thing was that he was a natty dresser. It did not matter what he wore—European suits or indigenous attire or a simple shirt over a pair of jean trousers—Etan always looked good. He was what we, the female staff, called a 'quintessential gentleman' in those days.

"Then Eyitemi came back from Europe, and your father threw a large welcome party for her. That was when Etan and Eyitemi met. Etan was obviously smitten by her beauty; and Eyitemi, by his virility. And that was the beginning of the end of your father's relationship with Etan."

"But Etan was my father's best friend, wasn't he?"

"Yes," Adaka said quietly. "Your father was in love with Eyitemi, but it was Etan Mayuku she admired. Your father focused all his attention on her, but she in turn focused all her attention on Etan, wanting always to be in his company."

"Did my father not suspect anything?"

Adaka considered the question briefly. "A man in love can't see or think straight," she said quietly. "Your father thought they were merely friends. He proposed to Eyitemi. It took her some time before she finally agreed to marry him. But she said she must be twenty-eight years old before a date would be fixed for the marriage. Your father accepted. At that time, Eyitemi and I were staying together. Since I was her best friend, she was complaining bitterly to me that your father wasn't spending quality time with her. I was always listening to her complaints, day in, day out. She was not the understanding type. She didn't want to agree that the company was growing, that your father was making tons of money, and that the business was really taking his time and energy. Your father couldn't have been more engaged. The company was at its highest growth level. They had contracts everywhere. Your father would leave his home at seven each morning and not finish until quite late in the evening. And sometimes he would travel out of town for days.

"It was obvious that he drove her mad with this workaholic habit. But as a man in love, he would always apologize to her and bring her flowers and expensive gifts, take her to exotic restaurants, and promise her that when he became more established, he wouldn't have to work so hard or travel so much. But the truth was that, as the company became more and more established, he just worked harder and harder. She wanted more of his attention, but he wasn't there for her. And Etan Mayuku, who was supposed to be doing the actual work, started taking time off from the office to visit her. And you know people are never what they are expected to be." Her mother became silent for a brief second.

"So Etan Mayuku started sleeping with her, right?"

Adaka nodded "Etan Mayuku and Eyitemi Olajire were not total strangers, as your father thought they were. They had been lovers briefly, both of them having met originally when they had attended the same small college some years a long way back. Your father was fooled into thinking that they were meeting for the first time when he introduced them at the welcome party he threw for her.

"But everything appeared to run smoothly until, quite unexpectedly, it was discovered that she was pregnant. Your father thought he was the one responsible for the pregnancy. But she shocked everybody by saying that Etan was responsible."

"How did Papa take it?"

"You know him. He was overwhelmed with rage, shame, guilt, embarrassment, and self-directed anger. Being a very emotional man, he started drinking. His confidence and self-esteem suffered greatly. During that time, about two months later, Etan and Eyitemi got married. It was a very big marriage ceremony. I attended. Most of the company staff attended. Your father felt betrayed and sacked virtually all of them. I'm not talking about small-time workers; I'm talking about heads of departments, executive managers, and such. But curiously, I was not sacked. I became his confidential secretary—somebody he could talk to and confide in. I was practically running the company then, also doubling as his best friend. I encouraged him to put the whole thing behind him and to move on with his life. And, of course, he did. But before then, the company broke up. Etan took the construction section, and your father took the marine department. Both of them went their separate ways; then Etan Mayuku reemployed all those people your father had sacked, they coupled their respective companies together, and he became a major rival of your father in the industry."

Ebi sighed. "Mom—this is one hell of a story," she said in a thick voice.

Adaka hesitated and then nodded. "It didn't end there. It was the same Etan Mayuku who destroyed your father's business in Warri."

"How did he do it?" Ebi asked quickly.

"At first, after the breakup, Etan's business flourished and expanded while your father's was in shambles. Etan's popularity increased. But after a while, your father put himself together and made a startling comeback. His business doubled, and he started entering Etan's business space. This led to a game of sabotage between them. For years, not one of your father's barges ever returned to Warri. They were either confiscated by the navy or hijacked by pirates. It was Etan Mayuku who made all of this possible. He had the navy in his pocket. When your father couldn't match him in this systematic way of sabotage, he had to relocate to Lagos. For more than seven years, the boy's father destroyed your father's business in the Niger Delta."

Tears sprang to Ebi's eyes. "So that's the reason behind the whole thing."

"Yes," Adaka replied gently. "Your father has never forgiven Etan Mayuku. Your father had planned to destroy him, but Etan Mayuku died before the plan could be actualized. So when he heard that one Tosan Mayuku was playing around with his daughter, he was enraged. Then he had his second angina pectoris and was hospitalized for two days. That was why I came to Jankara the other day to confirm the whole thing."

Ebi shook her head. Tears were now streaming down her cheeks. She did not want to cry, but she couldn't stop the tears from flowing. *Poor Papa, he must have gone through a pretty rough time.* And her befriending Tosan hadn't really helped matters at all.

"Don't cry, my baby," Adaka said gently. "Life's a terrible place. Perhaps you should stop seeing the boy. It's not good for your father's health. If you can do it, then we will all be happy."

"But I can't, Mom," Ebi said quietly. "What would I tell him? Tell me what I would tell him."

"Tell him the truth. Tell him about the hatred your father has for his mother and his late father."

Ebi shook her head. "I can't, Mom." She paused and regarded her mother thoughtfully. "Are you sure Tosan even knows about all this?"

"Even if he knows, he won't tell you. He'll hide it from you."

Ebi shook her head again. "I don't think so, Mom. He'll tell me. He loves me. And I trust him."

"Don't be silly, child. Your father trusted his mother and his father. But the truth is that people aren't really what they seem to be. They betrayed that trust, and your father's still carrying the pain to date."

"Christ!" Ebi sobbed.

Tears were now shimmering in Adaka's eyes. She knew what her daughter was going through. Ebi's relationship with Tosan had been a complicated one right from the very beginning. But as a woman filled with emotion, she hated to see people suffer, especially her beloved husband and her lovely young daughter. Any way this thing would end, she believed one of them was going to suffer.

Her daughter, she knew, had a very compassionate nature and wouldn't want to break off the relationship because of sins the boy hadn't committed himself. And if she, as a mother, should say what was on her mind, she would say it was better for Ebi to make the decision according to the dictate of her heart. If she should be forced to make any decision that was not in line with her conscience, it would leave her unfulfilled for the rest of her life. It was true what she had said some time ago—the first time she had confronted her with the information from the lecturer who called himself Young-Green: a man doesn't get to choose his parents. One's parentage or one's family name is a thing one is born with. No one chooses where or by whom he or she is born. As humans, we have no control over lots of things that happen in life. We don't select the tribe, town, location, or circumstances of our births or upbringings. Such things are far beyond our control. The boy didn't ask to be born an Itsekiri, but his father happened to be one. And even more disturbing was that he had been born by Eyitemi and fathered by Etan Mayuku. Should the two young people suffer for a crime they didn't commit?

"Mom," Ebi said suddenly. "How did you and Papa know that Tosan is Etan Mayuku's son?"

"His picture was on the cover of the *Weekend Vanguard*. He had just won the National Visual Arts Council's award then, and the paper carried everything about him. Everything: his full history, his mother's and father's names, the school he attended, the school he's presently attending, and all else there is to know about a new celebrity. So when we received a copy of *Campus Digest* with your picture and his on the front page, your father immediately connected it and got the whole picture."

There was noise outside. Adaka gazed out the window and saw her husband's car drive into the compound.

"Your father's back."

When Chief Ezontade Dabiri strolled leisurely into the living room about five minutes later, he was surprised to find his daughter and his wife crying and clinging to each other as if they were drowning in a sea of despair.

"Hey!" he said in alarm "Has anybody died?"

"No," Adaka said softly. "Ebi's just crying for leaving home the way she did."

Chief Dabiri held up his hand. His voice held a hint of annoyance.

"The trouble with only children is that they always feel indispensable. Aren't you going to give your old man a welcome smile?"

Ebi stood up slowly and entered his open arms. He crushed her in a bear hug and whispered in her ear, "Welcome home, my princess."

Adaka, watching them, felt the tears welling up again in her eyes.

* * *

It was almost closing time at Daddy Alhaji's Place, a shabby tavern on the Jankara-Lokoja highway a ten-minute drive from the capital city. In the back fenced-in booth, well out of earshot of other customers, a group of young men were in a whispered conference. They were the same people who had held a similar meeting three weeks prior deep in the woods of Jankara at a place called Mount Kilimanjaro.

The young man doing most of the talking was Mike Imoni. Since the hit that had led to the deaths of the three Owlsmen and two innocent students killed by stray bullets, this was the second time the League of Five had met. The first meeting was postponed because most of the gang leaders had traveled out of town immediately after the attack. They were all certain that the Owlsmen would soon be picking up beak. Picking up beak was a call to arms. But instead what they had heard were rumors of a peace meeting to end the crisis, and the rumors had finally been confirmed when the League of Five received white status letters with enclosed white feathers, calling for a peace meeting.

"I don't understand this at all," Mike Imoni was saying. He was visibly angry. "This is unlike the Black Owls. Normally Owlsmen would strike back. But now they're suing for peace. Gentlemen, what do you make of it?"

One of the fellows, the Killer and Maker of Soul of his own gang, spoke: "It could be they're frightened. What we did was a shocker." The guy was obviously pleased with himself.

"Frightened?" Mike kept the disappointment out of his voice. "Don Tos is not frightened. I can tell you that. His type is not easily frightened. And to me this whole thing seems like a sham."

Thomas Dakyap, the Stirrer of the Purebloods, picked dirt from between his teeth with a matchstick and stared coldly across the table at Mike. His beady, cunning eyes were fixed steadily on the Brownstone hit man.

"You initiated the hit," he said quietly. "You sold us the idea. Tell us what to do. I honestly think we'll do it."

Mike made a gesture of annoyance. "This is an issue of life and death, guys. And it won't do to let me do all the thinking and all the planning and all the talking. It's a matter of what we do collectively now. It's not a matter of me telling people what to do. The issue's beyond that now."

For a long moment, Roland Ibeshi was watching Mike. His eyes were ugly, and his face tight with anger. The Stirrer of the VVS was lost in his own thoughts, drinking occasionally from the beer mug in front of him and at the same time regarding Mike with his dark eyes.

"We've miscalculated, gentlemen," Mike said. "But that's by the wayside."

"That's not by the wayside," somebody replied to him heatedly. "I believe we've all been too hasty from the beginning. Now they've sued for peace after the deaths of five souls, and this could've been easily avoided if we had accepted their first letter that sued for peace. At least the whole thing would've been straightened out. Now we're discussing it. It's stupid if you ask me."

"We've not accepted yet. And we won't accept it." Mike kept his voice calm.

"Who's 'we'? I advise you to speak on behalf of your gang," Thomas Dakyap said. "The issue is that Owlsmen have sued for peace, and in my own candid opinion—and I'm speaking for my gang—I think we should honor it. I'm sure there's going to be no trouble. And if there were any trouble at all, which I sincerely doubt, it wouldn't lead to death. If, unfortunately, it does, it would destroy the tradition of suing for peace. And that's an ancient tradition."

Mike banged his beer mug on the table loudly. Dealing with men such as this could be so extremely trying. He gave the Purebloodsman one swift, meaningful glance and made a face. These guys weren't even intelligent enough to make intelligent suggestions.

All of them had lusted for the final defeat of Don Tos and his numbered men. Since that victory had eluded them, they had all turned their grievances against Mike, the man who had sold them on the idea and hadn't been able to deliver them complete victory. But the truth was that he needed these men for survival in defeat—particularly if Owlsmen decided to strike back with full measure of violence. He needed as many men as he could get to watch his back. *But can these guys be relied on?* he wondered.

"Gentlemen, I must register this," Mike said gently and patiently. "I don't trust these guys. This is a trap. I'm sure some of you guys don't trust them either. Don Tos is a fiery element. He's never been like this before, and I strongly believe this is a trap to get us all killed. He could be working on a counterattack. No cult gang that has all the resources to fight would willingly shy away from such a fight. A fighter who knows he has the chance of winning a fight does not give up such a fight willingly. Don Tos is playing a new kind of ballgame, and I don't like it. Who knows—maybe he has arranged for help from other schools controlled by Owlsmen and has actually begun communication with their hit men. We must give the most serious consideration to this peace initiative before we commit ourselves. To me it looks like a strategy to get us disorganized and possibly killed. And the best way to seize the offered opportunity for peace is to reject it. We want peace, but not at all costs. Or even if we so desire it, we can sue for it in, say, two or three weeks' time, on our own terms."

There was a highly troubling silence for a moment. They knew he had a point there. But right now, peace as a concept was more appealing than war. And most of them were in a hurry to wrap up the whole thing by any reasonable peaceful method.

"What you've just said is very convincing," Thomas Dakyap said. "It's a very persuasive theory. But what I want now is a chance to graduate peacefully from this school. If Owlsmen are asking for peace, the Brotherhood of the Purebloods will accept it."

Opanka, the High Priest of the Black Panthers, spoke for the first time. "Is there any middle way?"

"No," someone replied. "There are only two choices: war and peace. And peace looks more attractive to me."

Mike looked at the chap who had just spoken. "My friends, there's a great deal at stake here. For once, let us think very deeply. Three Owlsmen were brutally murdered, and Owlsmen are suing for peace. Think about it. Isn't it too generous of them? What do you think, Opanka?" He was looking at the Black Panthers' leader, but the guy avoided meeting his eyes and avoided even commenting.

Roland Ibeshi shook his head and said quietly, "In the very beginning, I said it was a very big risk to declare war against Owlsmen. But you told us that you had figured out—"

Mike cut in. "If you put it that way, yeah. I'd figured out everything at the beginning. It was just a little bad luck that spoiled everything at the end."

Roland Ibeshi regarded the Brownstone hit man coldly. "The Yorubas have a saying: 'If you attack a king, you must kill him.' But in this case, you attacked the king and couldn't kill him. Now the king has sent you a letter asking you to meet with him so that both of you can iron out your differences, and you're fidgeting. Don't you think this is an opportunity to kill this king?"

Mike looked insulted by the question. "I can't blame you guys for blaming me. I fucked up. But I want us to be reasonable about this whole peace offer. I don't think it's genuine."

"The leadership of the Black Owls are reasonable people," Roland Ibeshi said. "I've known Don Tos for quite some time now. And I—"

"Don Tos has no reputation for mercy," Mike replied heatedly. "If you know him as you claim you do, you ought to know that also. The last clash between Owlsmen and Panthers led to the death of Don Bosco. In revenge, seventeen Panthers died that I know of. You surely must know of others who died. Do you consider that kind of guy reasonable or merciful?"

Roland Ibeshi gave the slightest hint of a smile. Half of the people at the table knew he was in the same class with Don Tos, and they probably suspected that he was sort of a friend of his. But Ibeshi had told them what they truthfully knew.

"In that clash, if I remember correctly, it was the Owlsmen who sued for peace, even though they had the upper hand. High Priest Opanka is here. He can tell us, if he so wishes, exactly what happened, how the peace initiative came about."

Mike scratched his ten-day-old beard. He couldn't make sense of this whole discussion. Things were getting out of hand. He knew it. He felt it right in his gut.

"Lord Opanka, I must say that you're a fearless gang leader. And because of that, I'll ask you to weigh this thing and tell us exactly what you feel."

The Black Panthers' High Priest hesitated. The peace initiative was a temptation; he had no desire of running all around various towns, for safety reasons—not at his age.

"Mike, I think there's a great deal at stake here," he began carefully. "This isn't just our lives we're talking about. It's equally about the life of our great school. Let us for once consider very seriously the status and authenticity of their letter and accept it conditionally. We can tell them the venue we're going to use. We can meet them at The Grillo or Balbina or the Jucee Motel. These are quiet meeting points. We've held peace meetings in these places before. Each gang can have three to five representatives. We can talk there and make peace. I think it's worth trying."

"You never can trust Owlsmen," Mike said feelingly. "They may have the idea of storming the meeting ground."

"Nobody has stormed a meeting ground before," Ibeshi replied to him.

"There's always a first time."

"Not this one," Dakyap said. "Besides, it would be extremely risky to do so. Don Tos must attend the meeting. That should be one of the conditions. With two of his high-ranking officials. We'll make sure the place is heavily guarded. And if there's any foul play, then they won't leave the meeting ground alive."

Mike was thoughtful for some time, and then he shot a hard glance at the Black Panthers' Number One.

"This thing stinks," he said quietly.

Roland Ibeshi looked caught between amusement and irritation. "You should've known that this thing stunk before you brought the dumb idea forward and made the bloody attempt." He was looking at Mike with undisguised contempt now. "You brought us the idea from day one; you said you would clean out Don Tos and his titled men. We trusted you, believed you, but now we all know it was all empty talk. The guy's still alive and fully in charge of his gang. What do you have to say now for your failure?"

Mike's face tightened angrily, but the VVS Stirrer looked at him without flinching. He then continued, "We gave you over half a million naira to waste them, but you succeeded in killing only three of them and losing other innocent souls. That's failure to me, and to the others who contributed their money to this project. All failures have their price."

Mike was looking at him with fire in his eyes, but he couldn't utter a word. It was the Black Panthers' Number One who went to his rescue.

"Cut it out, Ibeshi. It's not fair. Mike has actually done the hit. It's unfortunate that Don Tos and some of his chiefs escaped unhurt."

"So much for the half-a-million-naira contract," Ibeshi said. "We should be thanking our God that they're suing for peace. At least it shows that we're heading somewhere."

Mike shook his head weakly. He had launched his anti-Owlsmen campaign to prove he was a factor in the traditional cultic mold, but unfortunately his plans had folded like a house of cards. His plan had been to waste Don Tos, Ovo, Paxman, Christo One Way, Frank White, Keme, Black Mamba, and Morgan Akumagba. With these eight men out of the way, the chances were that there would have been no fight. The others, he knew, lacked leadership power. No fighting meant no further deaths, and the entire gangdom would have come out of it the better. He didn't like the way things had gone now. His entire plan from the very beginning had been to strike fast and hard and wipe out the entire Warri clique. Then it would've been merely another unsolved mystery of cult killings in Jankara.

"Roland Ibeshi was right," he said quietly. "He's always right about shit like this. It's unfortunate we didn't succeed one hundred percent. So where does that leave us? In the middle of nowhere. Then out of the blue came this letter suing for peace. And you guys want us to blindly accept it? Believe me, I'm confused."

"They want to deescalate the war," Dakyap said.

"You can deescalate a cult war *only* if nobody's seriously wounded in the initial stage. You're supposed to know that."

"So are you telling us to continue the bloodletting?" The question was from High Priest Opanka.

"Continue? Of course yes. We have a contract—a mission to fulfill. We haven't accomplished half of it, and we're already talking of quitting. What are we afraid of? They've got guns and we've got guns. We've killed three of their solid men, and they haven't even taken any of our men. Let's fucking fight this fight to the finish."

High Priest Opanka looked at Mike. A look of surprise was etched on his face. He said, "Let me affirm what Roland Ibeshi said a few minutes ago. When Owlsmen and Panthers clashed the last time, twenty-two Panthers were killed. That was in answer to the five Owlsmen, who I believed, lost their lives. But it was also the Owlsmen who sued for peace even when they still had the stamina and the resources to continue the bloodletting. They sent us a white status letter. Of course, we accepted. The meeting took place, and in the long run we deescalated the violence. I still think we can accept this letter of peace, and it would in the long run also deescalate this violence."

Mike leaned back in his chair and regarded the BP chieftain thoughtfully. He hated him even worse than he hated Roland Ibeshi now.

"So we should accept their peace initiative?" Mike asked resignedly.

"Certainly," Dakyap said.

"Don Tos wants settlement for tactical reasons." Ibeshi added. "I heard from a reliable source that he's planning on traveling to the United States—possibly he's afraid of dying just now."

Mike smiled at that piece of information. It was clear that Roland Ibeshi had come to this meeting prepared with facts.

"Okay, guys," he said. "Let's discuss this peace idea of theirs a little further."

CHAPTER TWENTY

THE KANGAROO TAVERN WAS IN OKENE. THE TAVERN BOASTED two elegant dining rooms, tiny rooms upstairs in the modest frame house where travelers could spend the night, and a spectacular courtyard adjacent to a magnificent garden where dozens of plastic chairs were arranged neatly and the smell of the flowers was simply magical.

It was a cold, chilly night with the moon playing hide-and-seek with the clouds. There was a hint of rain in the air, and lots of people were drinking in the open courtyard. Generally, it was a pleasant evening.

Outside the limestone house, a Mercedes-Benz jeep pulled up to a corner streetlight pole. Dr. Vincent Ubangha got out, looked around carefully, and then went into the restaurant.

Inside one of the dining rooms, at a discreet table by the rear near the window, Mike was drinking a bottle of Star lager.

A waiter came up about a minute after the lecturer had sat down. He asked him whether he would like a drink or food. The lecturer ordered beer, and when the waiter had gone, he rested his back against the straight-backed chair and regarded the boy quietly. His face was dark and bitter. His hard black eyes were sweeping the dining room, restlessly assessing everything in the large room except the lecturer.

Dr. Ubangha guessed that something was bothering the boy.

"What's on your mind, Mike?"

Mike put his hands flat on the table. He said quietly, "They've called a peace meeting."

"Who's called a peace meeting?"

"Owlsmen."

"Oh," the lecturer said with annoyance. "Has a date been fixed yet?"

"Not yet."

There was some silence. The waiter came and placed a bottle of Star in front of the lecturer. When the waiter had gone, Vincent Ubangha poured out a large glass of the beer and swallowed more than half of it. Then he wiped his mouth with a white napkin and regarded the boy thoughtfully. This was the second time they had met after the hit.

When he had commissioned Mike with the job, it had been out of a need to do something, anything, to stop Tos from getting the girl. It had been to prove to the boy that he had some control, some measure of power. But right now, he had lost the control he so desperately sought. He was scared now. Even meeting this boy here wasn't something he enjoyed.

"How's your family?"

"They are fine."

A few days ago, he had deposited his wife and his son at an old friend's place in Okene, a comfortable distance from Jankara. They were safe, he knew. *But for how long?* he wondered.

He had been smart enough to move his family out of town before the hit. His wife was already calling for divorce. She had said she would never set foot in Jankara again. And that meant she would close down the school and travel to another town to start all over.

"What about your properties?"

"I took all my valuables, all my relevant documents, all my expensive paintings. But I couldn't get all the cars out. I'm not worried about the cars. My major concern is the house. My prayer is that the house should be spared."

"Let's hope it won't cross their minds."

For a while they were silent, both of them deep in thought.

"You must not go to that meeting," the lecturer said abruptly.

Mike shook his head sadly. "They'll look upon me as a turncoat. It's too dangerous. It'll make me attract too many enemies. It's too risky."

"Why don't you travel out of town?"

Mike shook his head. The lecturer was not impressed. He wondered whether the boy knew the risks of what he was doing. He should run now that there was ample time left to do so.

As if reading his thoughts, Mike said, "I'm a hit man, sir. If I made the mistake of traveling, then I would have two forces on my heels. I've got no option other than to see this thing through to the end. My prayer is that this peace meeting will bring about the desired peace."

The lecturer was silent. He knew the boy was right.

"So what are you going to do?" Mike asked.

"I'm making some plans."

Mike nodded, but inwardly he wondered what sort of plans Dikko might be planning.

Is he quitting the school or what? he wondered.

* * *

Everything was quiet in the university town of Jankara. Two whole weeks had passed without a killing. The students and townsfolk alike, knowing their university and their community, were not in the least fooled by this calmness. Many students, cultists and Jew men alike, had fled the town. They had long known that a bloodbath would soon swallow the town.

But some of them with "liver" stayed; they had resigned themselves to the inevitable. Some of them, particularly the final-year students, were praying to God to quicken their graduation day. Others were praying and fasting for the day when the situation would be back to normal.

It was unbelievable. Fourteen days without a deadly gun battle had built a fiery, mounting tension that was becoming more frightening than the expected gunfight. "What are Owlsmen up to?" some asked. "Or are they weakening?" In the old days, if an Owlsman happened to die at the hands of a rival cult gang, what would follow was killing every day, what was popularly known as a bucket of blood. And now, with the deaths of Keme, a.k.a. Al-Mustafa, and Black Mamba, two men who had killed over a dozen students between them, who would be next? And who was safe?

The students discussed it, thought about it, and dreamed about it. A majority of the students were of one mind: Owlsmen will go for vengeance. It was the only logical thing to do.

So for fourteen whole days, tension sat over the town and the university like a vampire watching its prey.

On the fifteenth day, three students, Alexander Odita, Abudu Maitama, and Masha Ikoya, all engineering students, were drinking beers and discussing the situation in a seedy tavern outside the university campus.

"I wish it would just happen and be done with," Masha Ikoya said quietly. "God, I hate the tension."

His friends were of the same thought with him. And the irony was that the VC did not bother to postpone the examination or close down the school as advised by well-meaning individuals in the state. The circular that came out insisted that the examination would take place as planned.

"I heard that there's going to be a peace meeting between the various gangs." Alexander Odita said. "And the VC's strongly in support of it. I believe that's the reason why the exams have not been shifted."

"I don't believe that," Abudu Maitama said.

"Believe it," Odita said. "The information is from reliable source."

Abudu Maitama didn't say anything. In Jankara, every "reliable source" was generally more accurate than CNN.

Masha Ikoya, like Abudu, was not convinced. He said in a low voice, "I do not believe it. Owlsmen won't sue for peace. Remember: they lost seven men, including Don Tos, Black Mamba, and Al-Mustafa, who you all know was their strongest butcher. They'll avenge the deaths of these men before they'll even consider it."

"My source is reliable," Odita said confidently.

"Is he an Owlsman then?" Abudu Maitama asked in a very low voice.

Odita looked behind him and around himself and then said, "He's a Purebloodsman."

Masha Ikoya shook his head. "I still don't believe it. They said Don Tos was dead, but somebody said the guy's alive. And if that guy is alive, believe me, he will not sue for peace."

"But Don Tos's dead," insisted Odita. And so on the discussion went.

At first the rumor had been that Tos was dead. When neither Tos nor any of his chieftains had put in any appearance at any of the melting pots frequented by strong men, the rumor had gained traction and spread around the university town like a bonfire. Reliable information had "confirmed" it. Don Tos, Ovo, Al-Mustafa, Black Mamba, and Frank White were all dead and buried in God-knows-where. The news had engulfed the school in unparalleled excitement. News traveled fast in a small town like Jankara. Apart from the news of the deaths of the Owlsmen, other news concerning a proposed peace meeting among the school's various cult gangs also filtered to every part of the town. Some of the stories peddled around said that Owlsmen were suing for peace and that the various gangs concerned had rejected the offer.

Professor Jinadu Azeez Abubakar, the fifty-six-year-old vice chancellor of the university, was troubled by the news of the killings and the rumors that the news had generated. Some national newspapers had come out with reports that sixteen students of the institution had lost their lives in the shootout between the rival cult gangs. But the VC, in a state television interview, had denied the reports of the newspapers and had maintained the official position of AZU that five people had been killed, and that of the five only two had been bona fide students of the university. The police had also reiterated that only five people had died and that only two corpses had been seen so far.

Professor Abubakar, when he had received news of a peace meeting between the gangs, had quickly issued a memo summoning the gang leaders to a secret meeting.

Present at the meeting were the vice chancellor, other high-ranking officials of the institution, representatives of the six warring cult gangs, Black Omaha, a.k.a. Makepeace (a student, a cult leader, and an adviser to the VC on cult-related issues), and leaders of the eleven off-campus university communities. At the meeting, the six Number Ones of all six gangs were noticeably absent. The Kwill, Max "Paxman" Osuagwu, represented the Black Owls.

But that notwithstanding, the VC made it known to them all that their personal vendetta could create untold problems for the school. The communities' leaders also condemned the violent activities of the cultists and other criminal-minded individuals who had turned their communities into killing fields. The representatives of the gangs themselves condemned the recent incidents that had led to the deaths of the five students and said they believed that the perpetrators had come from neighboring schools and had attacked the innocent students. They were all finally made to sign conciliation forms promising in the future to eschew violence and to utilize the tool of dialogue to settle all their differences. The meeting, to the many observers, was successful.

A similar incident in the past was what had motivated Professor Abubakar to summon the cult gangs to the secret meeting. He didn't want a repeat of what had happened during the tenure of his predecessor, Professor I. Adisa.

Jinadu Azeez Abubakar was a professor of biochemistry. He had succeeded Professor Issa Adisa, the fifty-nine-year-old sociologist who had been shamelessly sent packing less than two years before. Professor I. Adisa's tenure had been the bloodiest in the history of the school. As the school administrator, Professor Adisa tried to rid the school of the various gangs that held the institution in a chokehold. He declared war on cultism. The student union leadership also declared war on cultism. It was the worst mistake they made. He sent a seven-day ultimatum to the various cult gangs asking for "renunciation," threatening "unpleasant circumstances" for noncompliance. After it had expired, the gangs in turn sent a strongly worded letter to him, saying, "You should start your war. And we'll finish it for you."

Of course the VC had been serious, and the cultists had been equally serious. Shortly afterward, over one hundred students were arrested by security forces in a one-day raid. That same week, another sixty-eight were arrested. But it was after a team of mobile policemen (MoPol) arrested the don of a powerhouse gang that had operated violently in the university for many years that everyone knew that the war had really started.

The next day, the VC's lodge was burned down and the registrar was abducted. It could have been worse on that day because Professor Adisa was number one on the target list, and Dr. Lawal, the registrar, was a likable man, and his name was not even on the target list. But being a suave administrator who could smell danger from anywhere within a hundred-mile radius, Professor Adisa had taken to his heels from the heavily protected vice chancellor's lodge before the boys had time to get there. All the same, Dr. Lawal was held hostage, and three days later he was exchanged for the "kidnapped" Don Bosco. All the other arrested cultists were eventually released on the excuse that the charges against them had not been properly investigated.

From that day onward, the state government doubled the security network in the school. Professor Adisa's family started enjoying the protection of police security to and from school. The campus violence, usually regarded as just skirmishes that were normal in the Nigerian university system, graduated into full-blown war. Over the whole session, AZU experienced five very violent clashes among the gangs themselves and between the gangs and security operatives. The various stakeholders finally initiated a peace meeting. All the gangs gave only one condition for peace: Professor Issa Adisa must leave the school. The reasons were that he had unofficially sanctioned unbridled corruption and that his tenure so far had been synchronous with the academic decay the school was now popularly known for. And that had ended Professor Adisa's tall ambition to rid Aliu Zamani University of its violent criminal elements. His tenure was supposed to end in 2004.

The new VC, Professor Abubakar, knew that for peace to reign, he had to deal in a gentlemanly fashion with the various gangs. He knew that if he acted otherwise, he would have many battles ahead of him. And that was something he could not afford, because apart from violent tendencies of the cult gangs, they had some very key and influential personalities in positions of authority. And in Nigeria, that was what counted.

Professor Abubakar's gentleman's strategy of achieving peace through "meaningful dialogue" had worked in the past. Over the past two years, it had brought so many crises under control. It was his prayer that it would put a stop to this current one.

* * *

"This thing's too risky, my lord," Ovo complained.

"We'll have to chance it," Tos replied mildly. They were in Ovo's apartment. Tos was lying down on a reclining chair, reading a glossy magazine. About four other Owlsmen were in the room. The sun outside was bright, and the entire street was swarming with heavily armed Owlsmen.

"Do you really think this meeting will hold?" Kadiri Muaza asked. It was his fourth time asking this question.

"I'm sure it will hold," Tos said without looking up from the magazine.

Ovo made a face. "They should've phoned by now if they really want it to hold."

Tos didn't reply. Ovo's dark eyes moved questioningly over Tos's face. "Talk to me, my lord," he said angrily.

Tos laid the paper down and studied his deputy. "Stay cool, man. They said they would phone by twelve to let us know. It's not too late yet."

"But it's past twelve," Max "Paxman" Osuagwu said.

Tos looked briefly at his watch. "You're right. It's past twelve. But there's something called African man's time. Let's wait till that time."

"What if they don't call?" The question was from Adams Banjoko.

Tos looked at the guy. He was the Klaws I of UniPort's branch of the Black Owls. He was no common errand boy. He was one of the most highly placed and reliable Owlsmen from that zone.

"Joko, they'll call. Count on it."

"If you say so," the guy said.

"Yeah. I've said so." Tos picked up the magazine again. "You guys should stay calm," he said from behind the magazine. "They will take the bait, and within a matter of hours, tomorrow at most, our mission will be completed."

"I wish I had your confidence," Ovo said.

"Don't be a fucker, Ovo," Tos said. "You're good. You're the backbone of this thing when I'm gone. Stay cool, and we'll play it cool. We cannot fail this time."

"Yeah, I'll play it cool. Just like you. But for Christ's sake, there'll be shooting—lots of shooting."

Tos nodded. "And don't forget that we'll be doing the first shooting." Without looking further at Ovo, he went back to his reading.

There was a brief silence in the room. Ovo was not happy as the events of the past few days began to take shape before his very eyes. He was beginning to see that the whole affair looked risky—really suicidal. And he was going to play a significant role in it.

"I dreamed a bad dream last night." The tone of his voice made everyone stare at him.

"You're always dreaming," Tos said indifferently. "Particularly these past few days."

Kadiri Muazu laughed, but the look from Ovo caused him to convert the laugh to a cough.

Ovo let his chair tip forward. He put his right hand on Tos's chair. "It was about you, my lord."

"Me. In your dream?"

"Yeah."

There was a moment of silence. Then Tos said, "What was I doing in your dream?"

"You were shot. I don't know by whom. There was blood all over your body. Even on your head. I tried to talk to you, but it looked as if you were dead. Long dead. You didn't move."

Tos smiled wearily. "Then what did you do?"

"I tried to get help. But nobody would help me. When I came back, I saw your body on fire."

Everybody in the room, as if from some secret signal, burst into laughter.

"Oghenovo Ikoloba, what a bloody ugly liar you are." Tos was laughing loudly now. "You didn't dream anything. You're tensed up."

Ovo shrugged and made a little move of annoyance. "I guess everybody here thinks I'm joking."

"Take a nap, and we'll talk about it later when this whole business is over."

"It's okay," Ovo said. He pushed back his chair and stood up. "I'm not going to take a nap. I'm going to the toilet." With that, he walked out of the room. Tos and the others watched him go, and immediately after the toilet door was closed, they all laughed boisterously.

Five days earlier, the Owlsmen had come out of Featherland and the Owls' Nest. The first thing Tos had done was visit his apartment. He was shocked at what he saw. The front of the house was pocked with submachine gun bullets, and the casement windows had been torn to shreds. A team of mobile policemen had cordoned the house off, and some cultists living in the neighborhood had been arrested. The police had also arrested and detained the leaders of some minor gangs. But Tos and some of his men, in the company of a retired brigadier general and a political bigwig, had driven to the police station.

Tos knew the crisis on ground wasn't something he could handle with small fry, so he had invited some national leaders of the Order of the Black Owls. Upon getting to the station, the officer in charge of the case had told them that it was beyond his power to release the detained cultists or to call off the police guarding Tos and his titled men's residences. The police officer, who was an assistant commissioner of police, had said that Abuja, which meant Nigeria Police Force Headquarters, was involved in the issue. The retired army general had then made some calls, and less than thirty minutes later, the order had come for the withdrawal of the police officers and the release of the cultists. The students were told to go home and not disturb the public peace again.

Since then, the Owlsmen had gone about their normal businesses, waiting for replies from their enemies. Tos knew that if the L5 accepted their letter asking for peace, the rest would be easy. They had gone over the plan again and again. There were only six very likely places that could be used for a meeting of that nature. What they had done was quite simple. They had withdrawn a good amount of money from the gang's dedicated account and had sent for twenty solid men from schools under the control of the Black Owls. They had chosen the best six of these guys and had booked each one of them in the motels that could be the likely venue of the meeting. If the L5 happened to choose any of these meeting grounds, all they had to do was call and activate the guy covering that particular meeting ground to be on the alert. Since this was the cell phone age, the plan was perfect. They had gone over the exercise twice before they had issued the white status letters.

In any of the probable meeting grounds, a man planted inside could do a lot of havoc. The butcher would penetrate the conference room and make the attack from the ceilinged enclosure. It was a good plan, concocted by Morgan Akumagba. But that was if it could be done.

The Owlsmen intelligence crew had been working around the clock to perfect the strike, and the League of Five chieftains were keeping their plans very secret. When Owlsmen had first mooted the peace conference, little chance had been given of an acceptance. Owlsmen had waited for four days before a reply was given by the L5. Even then it had been a tentative reply. They had agreed to send a small participant group to represent the various gangs that had leagued themselves, and they would pick the venue and the number of delegates to represent the Black Owls, even down to the names of the delegates.

On the day that they had received the reply, the Owlsmen had already been losing hope in the whole initiative. Two street urchins had come down to the Black Owls' secretariat with the secretly worded letter. It ran thus:

> To: ____The Big Eye, Brotherhood of the Black Owls
>
> From: ____The Central Working Committee, the Union of the League of Five
>
> Subject: ____Re: White Status Letter

> The Union of the League of Five has tentatively agreed to your letter suing for peace. We accept because we know that this is a serious *dikodikoko*. We believe that the mystery of the masquerade will soon be solved, and tomorrow is a long way to go. In the interests of peace and security, we will holla you the name of the venue, and the network man will spread the nets, and the others will follow the ropes.
>
> But note: We are watching every bit of your movements. We are already aware of your plans to storm the meeting ground. And a word of advice for your storm troopers: Three of their most reliable leaders will be inside the meeting hall. If anything

happens from outside, they will be killed from inside. You must remember that …

The letter was signed with the symbols of each of the five gangs. On the back was a list of the three Owlsmen they wanted in attendance: Big Eye Don Tos, Vee-Eye Ogheneovo Ikoloba, and Klaws II Frank Akuwa. A terse warning in cultic vernacular followed it: "No man can destroy a house that is firmly established. The Black Owls' tyrannical reign must end. For that we shall shed the blood of all our brudahs. But first we shall sup. But remember: the table must remain harmless. They who defile the supper shall have no food. Wait for Greenwich. The signal is there."

Tos and his men knew that the L5 were holding their cards close to their chests. It was exactly what they needed. They needed the L5 to make all the moves and convince themselves that all was going according to their plans. It would make them lower their guard. The meeting ground was still going to be the battleground, but knowing it would be the problem. The job profile was simple in concept, but the truth was that it was going to be difficult in execution.

The L5 were really trying to be smart. First they had tried to disarm the Owlsmen by saying that they were aware of the plan to storm the meeting ground. Secondly they were using the Big Eye of the Black Spiders as a chairman and arbiter to settle the dispute. Tos wondered if the amiable marketing student would be in the way of his men's fire.

Ovo came into the room, drying his hands with a blue towel.

"Have they called yet?" he asked, resuming his seat again.

Tos shook his head.

Just then the kitchen door opened and Christo One Way came in. He had been in the kitchen for the past hour. He bore a tray of fried chicken and cucumber salad that he placed on the table before Tos.

"It's ready," he said.

"Thanks," Tos replied. He then gestured toward Ovo. "You might as well join me."

Ovo looked longingly at the chicken, and he settled for one of the pieces. Kadiri Muazu rose from his chair and took one also.

"Bring more cutlery and a bowl of water," Tos said, and he offered the dish to the guy from Port Harcourt. Christo nodded and left for the kitchen.

The front door opened at that moment, and Frank White came in. "Hey, you guys are doing it big here."

"You're free to join the party," Tos replied.

Frank White went to the table and took a piece of the meat. Christo came with another tray and a set of cutlery. He placed the tray on the table and distributed the cutlery.

"What are we celebrating?" Frank White asked, settling on a vacant chair.

"The last supper," Ovo said with a laugh.

"That's not funny," Tos said.

Christo One Way went to the reading table at one corner of the room. On the table was a brown paper bag of marijuana. He took the bag and started putting a joint together.

After a short while, he lit up and took a long drag. From behind the thick cloud of smoke, he watched the other boys devouring the chicken. He was hooked on the stuff, and from the manner with which he was drawing smoke into his lungs, it was obvious that he wanted to get really high. Intoxication always hardened him. There was a job to be done, and he needed his eyes to shine.

"Frank, are you ready for this job?" he asked.

"I'm always ready for them," Frank White replied as he washed his hands in the large plastic bowl. He dried his hands with the towel Ovo had used some moments prior and threw it to Adams Banjoko. Then he leaned back in the chair, his hands clasped behind his head. His jacket rode up, and the others could see the .38 semiautomatic tucked into his waistband.

"I don't know why my name was omitted from the letter," Christo said as he took a big hit.

"Then let's trade places," Ovo said with a smile.

At that moment, the phone rang. Christo was the first to reach it. He plucked the receiver from its cradle.

"Hello?"

"I wish to speak personally to the Grand Wizard of the Black Owls," the disembodied voice said.

"Very well," Christo said. "Hold on a minute for him." He beckoned to Tos. "My lord, it's for you."

Tos snatched the towel from the table, wiped his hands hurriedly, and took the phone from Christo. "Hello," he said quietly.

"This is Thomas Dakyap speaking. I'm the spokesman of the League of Five. I want to speak personally to the Grand Wizard of the Black Owls."

"Yes, Thomas. I'm Don Tos—I'm the Grand Wizard of the Black Owls. I'm listening."

"Good. I'm speaking on behalf of the five gangs. Please don't interrupt, and listen very carefully. This is what we've decided: The venue of the meeting is the Jucee Motel—"

"The Jucee Motel—" Tos's voice was sharp.

"Please don't interrupt. The Jucee Motel's the meeting ground. And I must inform you that if there's any attempt to storm the venue of the meeting by armed men, the meeting will automatically be aborted and there will be immediate reprisal. Either the three reps you present will kill fifteen others or they will be killed. You and your men must not do anything stupid. There will be enough of our men outside to absorb the shock of an attack. Is that understood?"

"Yes. Is there anything else?"

"Yes," the disembodied voice said. "We're not going to contact you again until an hour to the meeting time. That's when we'll give you the password. The password is the key that will admit you into the venue. If we don't call, know then that the meeting has been postponed temporarily. And we'll give you guys a new date and venue. If we give you the password, that means we'll proceed with the meeting. That's all for now." There was a sharp click, and the line was off.

Tos looked at Christo One Way and then at Ovo as if they were the reason why the guy had hung up. He said, "The Jucee Motel's the killing ground. But they won't reveal the time yet."

"What do we do now?" Kadiri Muaza asked.

"We'll inform the guy in the Jucee Motel," Frank White said.

"Who's our guy there?"

Adams Banjoko consulted a list in his hands. "It's Billy Akatakpo."

Tos turned the name over in his mind. "Who's he?"

"He's Zone B's best butcher," Banjoko said. "He was the last guy chosen from the twenty. In Zone B, they called him Al-Assassin. He's an Owlsman of great repute. He's the zone's answer to the late Al-Mustafa."

Tos remembered the guy now. He had personally chosen him. There had been something about the guy that had brought him over.

"That makes it easier," Tos said, and he began punching numbers into his cell phone.

Ovo was grinning. "It is not so bad, then."

"Hello," a thin, flat voice replied to Tos's call.

"The mystery of the masquerade has been revealed."

"They who defile the night will never see the light of day."

Tos smiled. "The match will take place in your territory. But the time could be anytime from the next one or two hours."

"So they've really decided to play?"

"Yeah. But you must not fuck up."

"No *yawa*, capo. It'll be clean."

"May your blood clot if you fail."

There was theatrical laughter from the other end. "There's no failure here, my lord. The fickle-minded enemies of the Owls are in the hall of Al-Assassin. And there's no mistake about it." The sentence was followed by a macabre laugh, and then the line went dead.

It was really what Tos had needed. Knowing where the meeting would be held was what was really important. He began to punch numbers into his cell phone again. Now was the time to make all the necessary arrangements.

* * *

The Jucee Motel was located on the ever-busy Lokoja–Ajaokuta federal highway. The motel was a stone's throw away from the Ajaokuta Town Elite Club, the place where Professor Lateef Nasiru, AZU's onetime deputy vice chancellor (academics) had been shot to death by a masked gunman three years ago.

The Jucee boasted eighteen chalet-like rooms, two a la carte dining rooms, an impressive conference room, and a spectacular courtyard adjacent to a magnificent garden. A former chairman of the local council owned the place.

In one of the very private motel rooms, a young man was drinking a bottle of stout by himself. He was of medium height, a twenty-something-year-old man with a face like an ancient Benin mask, simple round eyes, and plenty of rainforest-Afro hairstyle, with hairs standing out like those on a wig. He was wearing dark blue jeans and a black T-shirt with "SATAN's GAME" emblazoned boldly in white. He was known simply as Billy Akatakpo, a.k.a. Al-Assassin. He was a notorious Owlsman.

To kill a bunch of bastards seemed simple enough to this young man. He knew this was one job that promised action and excitement. That was why he had gotten himself initiated into cultism in the first place—to be a part of the action and to enjoy the excitement.

The plan was simple, and the method of the hit had been programmed. He would climb right into the ceiling with loaded weapons. Nobody would know he was there at first. And then, from a height of about twelve feet up, he would do the damage.

At fifteen minutes past seven o'clock, he downed the last of his stout, and then he went to the door and bolted it securely from within. On the other side of the door was a locked padlock. It showed that the room was not occupied. The booking register had already showed that room number 15 was unoccupied but reserved. The motel management had been well paid in advance.

Akatakpo took a small leather bag from atop the little desk built into the wall and hung it across his shoulders. Then he climbed the bed and carefully pried open the ceiling board. He pushed it aside. It took him nearly ten minutes to hoist himself through the passage he had created into the ceiling. All around him was total darkness. It took him another five minutes before his eyes became adjusted to the inky blackness. He could make out the thick timbers rising in an L shape from the ceiling to the zinc overhead. He repositioned the displaced ceiling board and began his journey into the bowels of the ceiling chamber. There was hardly any air at all in this darkened vault, and in no time he was sweating and breathing heavily. The trouble made him curse all Owlsmen, but Tos in particular. This was supposed to be Zone

A's baby, but here he was climbing into a motel roof in another town, doing Zone A's dirty work.

He fished out a tiny pocket-sized torchlight and flicked it on. The wooden beams supporting the roof of the building were solid like stone, and they rose to a vault about three feet above the ceiling. With the tiny beam of light from the flashlight, he made out the stone walls separating each of the rooms from the other. He wriggled into the nearest one and started creeping forward. Everywhere he turned his light, there were blankets of dust, layers of filth, and entombed heat.

He crept across about four rooms before he detected a change in the building's structure. The roof height here was lower and was supported by a much thicker wooden pole that rose through the brickwork in the dust-covered, asbestos-ceilinged floor. He tried his weight on the pole; it was strong. Gently, he crossed over. The place into which he had crossed to was the motel's conference room. He knew because he had cased it before. As he remembered it from his earlier excursion, there was a better vantage angle where his crouch would be more comfortable. He searched for it in the gloom.

After a while without seeming to locate it, it occurred to him that he should scout for another place. He felt along the edge of the wooden beam for a good handhold, and when he located one, he swung over to the next ledge. He lowered himself very carefully, his feet flying over the asbestos board to find the next foothold. It was an awkward move, and he lost his balance. He would have fallen down but for his quick reflexes. He landed with his hand desperately and powerfully grabbing another handhold and at the same time suspending his weight from pressing down on the dry ceiling board. He had to stop for breath before he continued. When it came, he repositioned himself and crouched in the darkness. When he felt comfortable enough, he dropped the leather bag he was carrying with him and brought out some things. Among them were some ammunition clips, a file, a chisel, and a pair of pincers.

With the pincers, he set to work pulling out the rusted nails holding the ceiling beams together. When he was satisfied with his progress, he stopped and listened for quite some time. When he couldn't detect any noise, he started boring holes into the ceiling beams as carefully as he could. The noise he was making was no louder than an excessive amount of lizard-like scratching.

By the time he was finished, there were a good number of punctured holes through which he could see into the conference room below.

He lay on his belly, his head and shoulders supported by the wooden beam, and peered through the tiny holes he had created. The long conference table was clearly below him. The chairs had all been neatly arranged. There was nobody in the room. He surveyed the breadth and width of the room, his eyes photographing all that he saw. At last, he sighed and resumed his normal sitting position. He took the .38 automatic and examined it in the torchlight. It was a handgun of high velocity and great penetrating power—the type of gun that would cause considerable damage on impact. He had killed with this gun before. It was his favorite tool. It was a highly accurate precision piece. He took out the magazine, examined it closely in the light, and, satisfied with it, slipped it back into the weapon's grip. He took out some shells from the bag, picked up the other handgun, and began to load it. When he had finished, he looked at his watch. It was fifteen minutes to eight o'clock. He decided that he had all the time in the world, so he removed a cellophane parcel from the small leather bag, extracted a large meat pie, and took a delicate bite from it. As he chewed, he thought of the people who had arranged the meeting. They would be thinking that they had gone the extra mile and taken the extra trouble to set this meeting up in foolproof fashion. But there was nothing like foolproof in any arrangement. Anything foolproof always has a flaw somewhere. All that it really takes to spoil a foolproof plan is an object reflex and a profound imagination.

He felt at home in the darkness as he waited for his victims.

* * *

It was a dark night with just a tiny crescent of a moon hanging shyly in the sky as if it were ashamed to make its presence felt. The stars were deceptively low and bright.

It was almost twelve o'clock midnight when the dark blue Mazda bearing the Owlsmen arrived at the Jucee Motel. Ovo was behind the steering wheel. He parked the car near an electrical pole. There were about seven cars already parked at the roadside. Among these cars was a navy-blue Mercedes with a Lagos license plate. Tos knew the car. The three of them got out of their car and walked over to the Mercedes. Attached boldly to the windshield was a black sticker bearing neat, spidery script that read, "I'm proud to be a Spider man. By my fingers you shall know me."

"This must be Omaha's car," Frank White said.

Tos nodded. "He's already here." He looked around but couldn't see much—just thick, heavy shadows covering a deserted street. Apart from the empty shadows and the unoccupied cars, there was nothing of further suspicion. Everything was calm and still.

"Let's go into the lion's den," Tos whispered near Ovo's ear, and then he chuckled and patted his back as they mounted the steps leading to the door. "No matter what happens, don't panic, guys. Let's stay cool and get this business over with."

"It's going to be a meeting of the giants," Ovo replied. "God, I need a cigarette badly."

"Forget a cigarette for now," Tos said.

"But it's good for cooling the tension," Frank White said.

"Illusion," Tos replied.

Ahead of them five armed men stood ready. They were standing in the doorway, staring at them.

Tos, Ovo, and Frank White stopped at the head of the steps. The five armed men at the other end didn't move an inch toward them. They just stood in the doorway, blocking it and staring at them.

Tos decided to take the initiative. "The hour of midnight is the meeting point of titled men," he said quietly.

"Their only agenda will be peace," one of the men said.

"And it will be honored by all men."

The men looked at each other. Then one of them stepped forward.

"What's the password?"

"The dogs have not eaten up the cat," Tos replied.

"You're welcome," a disembodied voice said suddenly from the darkness.

The three Owlsmen turned around. The owner of the voice stepped out of the shadow at the end of hall. He was a tall, heavily built chap in all-denim apparel.

"I'll take you guys to the meeting hall. But first you must show that you are not armed."

Tos shook his head. Ovo touched his lips with the tip of his tongue and looked at Tos and then at Frank White.

"What? You want to take our arms?" This was from Frank. His tone was low and quite angry. He wanted to push forward, but Tos stopped him.

"We'll not part with our arms," Tos said quietly. "All peace meetings have rules. It's the tradition. One of the rules is that one is free to be armed if he feels he's not secure. I trust that the others are also armed."

The tall, heavily built fellow looked from the Owlsmen to the other five armed men. He said, "You wait here. I'll have to go inside and confirm." With that, he melted into the shadows. He spent less than three minutes inside. When he came back, he said, "Follow me."

The conference room was already packed with the representatives of each of the five gangs. It was a large, spacious room, and the long conference table was the only furniture. A few extra chairs were set against the wall. Three men whom Tos suspected to be Spidermen sat on these chairs. Obviously, they were Black Omaha's guards. At the head of the elliptical conference table was Black Omaha. There were only three unoccupied chairs. Tos and his two companions went to them and sat down quietly.

The atmosphere was heavy with tension. Tos knew that everybody in the hall was packing weapons. It was to be expected, and it didn't bother him.

He looked around the large room. It was a simple and elegant room, totally devoid of any furniture except for the long conference table and the chairs surrounding it. There were six large, uncurtained windows, but they were all sealed off because of the meeting. Tos was satisfied with what he saw. It was a beautiful hall and an ideal place for men to die.

Tos looked at Black Omaha. The presiding chairman acknowledged him with a slight nod of the head. He peered at his watch. He seemed to be satisfied with the time. His eyes acknowledged the presence of everybody in the room quietly. The men, in turn, looked at him respectfully.

That they were there was due chiefly to Black Omaha, a.k.a. Makepeace. Of all the cult elements in the school, he was the most respected. While it could be said that Don Tos was the most feared, Omaha was deeply respected by all—even by Tos. There was never a man in Jankara who didn't like him.

Thirty years old, short, and gentle-looking, Black Omaha was a preeminent gang leader. He was the Big Eye of the Black Spiders. In some ways, he looked like a reverend. He had one of those happy faces with laugh lines, and bright light in his nut-brown eyes. People liked the sincerity in those eyes. When he spoke, they listened—not because he was a factor, but because of two other things. One was that he looked like a priest, exuding confidence, a peaceful mien, sincerity, and humanity—something that many believed was in terribly short supply at the university and its environs. And the second was because he had a great voice; it was similar to Ron Kenoly's. It was delicately modulated and emerged from somewhere deep inside him and sprang forth with a glorious combination of overtones and coordination. When he talked, nobody else talked. He was renowned and greatly respected by all gangs and their leaders. Because of this, he had been known as a peacemaker, a mediator between rival cult groups in times of crisis, always helping to create peace on campus. At the same time, he worked as an informal "private adviser" to the VC on cult-related issues. And over the years this had helped built his reputation as a factor. In the last major clash between the Black Owls and the Black Panthers, he was the one who had brokered the peace deal that ended that weeklong firefight.

Black Omaha cleared his throat and glanced at the leader of the Black Owls. Their gazes held fractionally longer than convention warranted.

With everyone now seated, Black Omaha opened the meeting.

"Gentlemen—I'm using the word 'gentlemen' because I believe that we are all gentle, mature, and very respectable people. We are all here for one purpose, and that's to put an end to the violence that took place recently. This university is an important institution in this country. As the chairman of this meeting, I think it's in everyone's best interest if we stop this violence—this war. I believe that everybody in this hall knows me. I've chaired several peace meetings, and they've all been fruitful. It's my prayer that this one will be successful.

"At present there are more than one hundred gun-toting law enforcement officers guarding our school. Aliu Zamani University is under siege. That's the appropriate word. The siege is not from external forces. The student body of our great school is the cause of it. Now the full resources of the state have been committed because of the violence that shook the university community a few days ago.

"This morning we're meeting here to de-emphasize the violence." Over eighteen pairs of eyes were boring into Black Omaha's as the attendees listened to the deep baritone issuing from him. "Aliu Zamani University is a major university in this country. But with our hands, we're killing it. What has happened is in all the national dailies. We're always on the news—and mostly on the negative side of the news. It's a shame. It's my sincere hope that we'll iron out our differences and bring back the glory of AZU." He paused here and assessed the men again. All the men at the conference table were gang leaders. They were the men behind the Jankara myths, the faces behind the masks, the lives behind the names, the actual legends behind the events that had made the school so infamous and famous. Because of them, the school's motto had been changed from "The citadel where tomorrow's leaders are molded" to "The place where tomorrow's leaders are murdered."

"It has been agreed that one man shall speak on behalf of each gang," Omaha continued. "The speakers elected to represent their gangs know themselves, I believe. And anybody can ask questions that concern his fraternity. But a question may not be answered if it is too controversial, if I may use that expression.

"Before we begin, I should make it plain that our conversation has to be couched with utmost civility. This is a peace meeting. We're here to settle our differences, not to aggravate them. Is that okay by us?"

All the men nodded.

"Don Tos, you called this meeting, so tell us what you have to say."

Tos looked at the table in sullen silence. He had been preparing himself for this meeting for a couple of days now.

"I'm Tosan Mayuku," he said quietly at last. His voice was cool and smooth. "In my brotherhood, they all call me Don Tos." He touched Ovo's shoulder. "And this is Ogheneovo Ikoloba. He's my deputy." He paused and touched Frank White on the shoulder. "And I believe you all must know my new defense chief, Franklin Akuwa."

"We know all of you," the presiding chairman said. "So let's go on with it."

"Before I say anything further, can I ask for something?"

Black Omaha hesitated. He didn't know what was on Don Tos's mind, and his instinct warned him that whatever the Owlsman was going to say might produce protest.

"Sure. Go ahead."

"Before we say whatsoever we want to say here tonight, I would like us to maintain a minute's silence in respect for my slain colleagues."

"Objection!" Mike replied immediately. "I reject that suggestion. Don Tos should know that we will not accept this kind of suggestion."

Black Omaha cleared his throat. His voice was firm when he spoke. "I'm sorry to say that at this early point of this meeting, it's not very appropriate to maintain a minute of silence. But it's my

In Turbulent Waters | 513

hope that it's something we'll do before the close of the meeting. But for now, let's settle the problem before us."

Tos nodded. The merest hint of a smile lifted the corner of his lips at the chairman's words. Wise words they were to him.

Mike, however, was surprised at how calmly he took it. This was unlike Don Tos. But the look Tos shot him was more than the look of a hunter toward the hunted. Mike saw the cold, cruel hatred in that glance.

"I'm glad to meet you all," Tos said. The words came out smoothly to the ordinary observer, but to him they came out with difficulty. "Most especially all gang leaders for honoring our white letters. But first and foremost, I would like to thank most deeply Black Omaha, or Makepeace, and other members of this gathering for the tremendous effort and expense they've incurred in organizing this meeting. I come with greetings and pleadings. I ask for peace. That's the reason why we're here. It's only peace I come to ask for. It's a small word, but it's a very important word. It's more important than bloodshed. It's more potent than love. Our founding fathers and their fathers before them knew that peace is what makes our campus what it is today. But peace has its price. It's not an expensive item. The rich can afford it. All present here today can afford it. It's only with peace that we can continue our stay in this school. I come in peace, and it's my sincere wish that we'll get the peace we so deserve."

There was a great silence for some time. Then, as if from some hidden cue, Mike was the one who asked the first question.

"What informed this change of mind, this change of heart? You've been known on campus not as an apostle of peace, but as a very violent and vengeful man. You're supposed to be mad with the death of your colleagues, not preaching peace."

Tos had expected this kind of question. He began his answer quietly. "My friend, I'm mad as hell. We've lost men—good men.

Personally, I'd love to fight back. But of course, my men want peace. Our primary objective in this institution is to be graduates. If we continue to fight at every provocation, then we'll all die before the expiration of our studies. We'll only kill each other." He paused and stared at Mike. "Or would you prefer that, my friend? What do you expect that sort of action would lead us to? A circle of violence, of course. The university would be closed down indefinitely. Indefinitely could be a year or more. Don't you see, gentlemen? By suing for peace, my men and I have swallowed our pride. We came here as men of peace. Whatever deduction you make is up to you."

Mike was not as enthusiastic as the others were. Most of them nodded, obviously carried away by the Owlsman's quiet tone and reflective mood. But Mike knew something was not right. He was studying Don Tos as he spoke. He harbored deep suspicions that the Owlsman was playing his hand with one more trump card still up his sleeve, something he was keeping very close to his chest. As things stood, it was, as it is called in the game of chess, a gambit. And he didn't like it. In cultic chess, one had to conduct one's moves in ways that were obscure to onlookers as well as to one's opponents. *Is that the Owlsman's game?* But commonsense told him that a sudden mess of killing at a peace meeting could create untold problems for all of them that wouldn't benefit anybody.

Roland Ibeshi of the VVS said, "I think that if Owlsmen want peace, the VVS also want peace. That's the way we see it. But the thing is, we hope it's not a graveyard kind of peace."

Somebody raised his hand. Black Omaha acknowledged him. It was Thomas Dakyap, the Stirrer of the Roundheads.

"I want to say here to everybody present in this gathering that whatever might have happened three weeks ago happened because of certain issues. Strong men are not respected. We all know that most students get initiated into frat gangs because of the prestige, security, and respect they get as members of these gangs. As ganglords, you must also know that students sense this security in the quality of the gangs' strengths on campus. But Owlsmen came along and started pushing everybody around like people without a brotherhood. So tell us, Don Tos, since you are asking for peace from us, are you going to give us back what you took from us—the privileged position we're entitled to as solid men? Our security and respect? Will you?"

Tos took the question. "Before the whole thing developed into the killing of my men, we sent out a white status letter. We sued for peace. That was our intention then—to give every gang on campus the respect they deserve. That's our intention now. It's unfortunate that our first letters were rejected."

"We don't believe in your white status letters," Mike said quickly. "And besides, we never rejected your white status letters. We received them late. You should've informed us before you abducted our men. That way this bloodshed could've been avoided. But you went ahead to insult our men without informing us. Then, after insulting us, you sent us a letter explaining to us why you did what you did. Even that's enough reason not to believe in your white letters."

Tos took a deep breath. "By refusing to attend the peace congress, you equally insulted us. Not only that, but you insulted us with your deed—our dead."

"What did you expect? Anyone who continues oppressing people must one day expect trouble," Mike said, staring directly into Tos's brown eyes. "And of course, trouble came, and you lost a few men. Good men they may have seemed to you. But I must tell you this: On campus, all cult men are sacred. Every cultist is a divine being. After all, we are all descended from one heaven— one cultic divine institution."

There was silence for a moment. Attending a peace meeting was a terrifying thing. It was a terrible experience. Even for those guys who had participated fully in the first League of Five meeting at Mount Kilimanjaro and who had been very vocal against Owlsmen's power on campus, sitting face-to-face with the Owlsmen now was a terrifying moment for them.

Tos broke the silence. "Three good men were killed."

"It's quite an unfortunate situation," Mike replied to him. "It's unfortunate that people have to die. People will always die. It's the law of life."

Tos's face darkened. He gave Mike a dangerous look. *This must be the guy who killed Keme*, he thought. There was no doubt about that now. Mike's eyes were sharp and bitter, authenticating the picture of a killer.

"I have a question for you, Mike," he said, his voice calm and even.

"Go ahead with it," Mike said dramatically, pushing his chair forward.

"I'll ask it once."

Black Omaha was shaking his head. He had been watching both of them while they talked and had seen the expression of deep hatred in the eyes of both men. "What's this all about?" he said

"Let him ask it," Mike said. He was obviously enjoying himself.

Tos looked straight into Mike's eyes as if searching for something. Then he said quietly, "Mike Imoni—for the good of this meeting, I want you to answer this question truthfully."

Mike gathered himself and looked at the presiding chairman. Black Omaha signaled him not to answer it. The Brownstone hit man instead nodded his head, an insolent grin planted on his face. He said, "Okay. Let me have the question."

"Are you the one who killed my chief security officer, Keme Doutimiye?"

There was a heavy silence in the hall. Tos was studying Mike closely, his eyes searching the boy's face as if trying to read the answer before it was spoken.

"You know I can't answer that question, Mr. Chairman," Mike said at last. His voice was calm and reasonable. "This kind of question is not supposed to come up. This is a peace meeting. And I believe our aim of coming here was to talk settlement."

"I want the truth," Tos said quietly.

"I won't answer it," Mike said. He was smiling, but it was a smile that never reached his eyes. Seated at the conference table, he felt himself protected—a diplomat on the negotiation table, with immunity from war crimes.

High Priest Opanka of the Black Panthers spoke for the first time since the meeting began.

"Don Tos, tell us what you really want."

Tos repeated thoughtfully, "What I really want?" For a while he made his eyes go around the table. They finally settled for a long moment on High Priest Opanka. Tos was wondering how many students had died in front of his pistol. A dozen, perhaps. When he spoke again, there was anger in his voice. "I want the men who killed my men. If it was only one man who did the act, I want that man. If there were ten men, I want those ten men. And if the men responsible for the deaths of my men can't be provided, then I demand an apology written in blood and a hundred million naira as damage. That's the only basis for peace to reign in this great school. A hundred million as a bargaining chip, or I want the men responsible for the deaths of my brothers. And if neither, then no deal for peace. And we'll all go back to the trenches, and nobody should hold me responsible for whatever happens thereafter."

Everybody looked at him uncomfortably.

"We don't welcome war, but we don't fear it either," Mike said quietly.

"It has not come to that," the presiding chairman cut in severely.

"I bet it has," Tos said quietly. There was no longer anger in his voice now, but the others knew it had to be there. "A society in which a dog kills a tiger is unsafe to live in. You will not find peace in that society. I've spoken. A hundred million or we go back to the trenches."

Black Omaha hesitated. He realized that the meeting was souring by the minute. He knew he had to do something.

"Don Tos, I think we understand how you feel," he said in his very deep, resounding voice. "But let's not stir things up. Let's think of things that will settle this thing."

"What's this?" Tos said. His voice was loud and hard. "Do you guys expect me to accept the loss of three good men with an assurance that it won't happen again? Is that all you can say? Is that what this meeting's all about?" He shook his head sadly. "We all want an end to the violence. But I'm primarily concerned about the people responsible for the deaths of my brethren. My demands are as follows: That this meeting tell me those persons who killed my men. Why were those particular men killed? And I want to claim damage for the loss of those lives. That's the only way for peace to reign."

The message was clear. The Owlsmen were demanding a hundred million naira for damages and an apology written in blood. Mike shook his head. Nobody would entertain this condition for peace. It was absurd.

From the beginning, he had not seen this issue as a case susceptible to settlement by mere discussion. This was a case that demanded settlement by bloodshed. Sitting here and discussing this thing was a waste of time. *I told them, but the stupid fools wouldn't listen. Now this is what this meeting's all about.*

"We've come to this meeting of our free will," Roland Ibeshi said carefully. He was sweating, knowing that the Owlsmen might cause trouble and that Mike and the others would certainly oblige them. And he didn't want that. He was torn between fear of what Tos and Mike might do. "It's a big risk even to be here in the first place. Please, gentlemen, let's not make it any worse."

"Roland Ibeshi, put yourself in my place. I'm a gang leader. Three of my very loyal men were killed. I could easily declare war to avenge the deaths of my men. But instead of doing that, I decided to call for a peace meeting. And that's my second time calling for peace in thirty days. If I understand the traditional pattern of meetings of this nature, I should say we should tell the truth, pay some damages, and then eschew hostility. Personally, I've got nothing against anybody. We should not allow our nuances to becloud our sense of judgment. We are all mature minds here, and issues like this must be handled maturely. My colleagues and I sued for peace because we want peace. This meeting and the manner of some people attending it will determine whether there will be peace or not."

There was palpable tension in the hall now. The atmosphere was electric.

* * *

Akatakpo was surrounded by the river he called silence. Leaning on a timber beam twelve feet above the tiled conference room below, he listened to the discussion going on. Most of the time, his eyes were peering through the tiny punctured holes. He was a patient man. Most of his killings were actualized because he was a patient man.

For the better part of an hour, he had leaned motionlessly in the deep darkness of the vaulted ceiling while the men below had talked. From his position, he could see well what was happening below. Tos had skillfully zeroed in on the key target, drawing him out from among all the other men seated at the table. Though the guy had not openly confessed to killing Keme and the other Owlsmen, it was obvious that he had personally taken part in the killings. Most of the conversation below was between Don Tos and Mike Imoni. It was as if they were the only two people in the hall.

The major target was dressed in all brown denim, save for his baseball cap, which was black. He presented a very good target. Akatakpo's gun was aimed directly at the small of his back.

He had done a lot of jobs from rooftops, but this was the first one he was going to do from inside the ceiling in the same building with the targets. This was a job he must do successfully.

Oh God, let me not fail, he thought. He took a deep breath and looked again at the target. It was a good scenario below. The key target was still sitting in the same position. There was no indication that any of them were alerted yet to the presence of a gunman in the ceiling. But what bothered Akatakpo was the concern for the safety of his brethren. There were about fifteen targets. The chances were slim that he could take out more than five men before the others would start pulling their weapons. If only he could neutralize, say, seven of them, then he knew that Tos and the two others would be able to clean up the remainder before they knew what had hit them.

The only consolation, he knew, was that Tos wouldn't mind an open gunfight so long as the first three targets were neutralized. And this was something he had to do. He shut his mind to all other thoughts, peered through the tiny cracks, and listened to what the "peacemakers" were saying.

* * *

"I fucking said it!" Mike shouted at the top of his voice, at the same time making a move to stand up. "I warned you guys that coming to this meeting would be a waste of our precious time. We can't arrive at a compromise."

Black Omaha looked at him, an angry expression on his face. "Sit down," he said quietly.

Mike sensed danger in the presiding chairman's tone. He settled back into his chair grudgingly but turned his body sideways, as if to avoid looking at Tos directly. Unbeknownst to him, he presented a beautiful target to the unseen gunman in the ceiling.

"Don Tos," Omaha said quietly. "I want you to do a rethink. We can still salvage the situation. Paying a hundred million naira or writing an apology in blood is not the solution to this thing. We can have dialogue and come to an amicable resolution to these senseless killings."

Tos shook his head. "You know me, Mr. Chairman," he said with a tired sigh. "I've always admired you and the rest of the gentlemen seated at this table. I bore nobody any ill will. I know that we all came to this meeting on our own volition. But I also want us to leave here the same way we all came in. And let me quickly make one thing absolutely clear. There's a price for everything we do in life." He paused and looked directly at Mike. But the Brownstone hit man wouldn't look at him. "If you fuck anybody up, believe me, there's always a guy out there who'll be waiting to fuck you up. It's God's law, and there's no partiality in it. You guys have fucked us up real good. We've paid a dear price for small sins. I want to ask: Is a hundred million naira and an apology written in blood equal to the lives of three renowned Owlsmen, brutally and cold-bloodedly murdered? Or are the deaths of three notable Owlsmen equal to a little slight committed in ignorance? Can any reasonable person among us equate such a small sin to the killing of my men?" He paused here and leaned forward in his chair. "If I must suffer for the offenses that I personally committed, it's just. But if innocent Owlsmen were killed for a sin they knew nothing about, it's unjust. People in this gathering killed my men. We've named a price to save more lives, and it's non-negotiable. We're trying to play it down and move on with our lives, but the killers of my men are sitting at this table and making nonsense of our efforts. It's not right. It's not just. A man's head is equal to a man's head. It's a cultic tradition, and we must respect it."

Black Omaha pursed his lips and nodded, his eyes going round the table. After some minutes' silence, he said, "Gentlemen, we have to remember that Don Tos and his men are mourning. We have to appreciate the tremendously brave thing they are trying to do by asking for peace. What's good is what we want. I'll ask everyone present here tonight to know that peace has no close substitute. You're either for war or for peace. A poor man who has peace is greater than a man who has all the wealth in the world but is without peace. Money can't buy peace. That's my belief. But common sense can. Our parents sent us to school with so much money and material things invested in our heads. And not just money, but so many prayers. But without peace, those prayers are useless. Today, some students sent to school who were not even cultists were slain by people among us here. We're all guilty of such sins. But the bottom line is this: are we prepared for peace, or for the continuation of the violence? If we don't agree to peace tonight, then we're all doomed, because more lives will definitely be lost, our school will surely be closed down for a long time, and we'll be forced to go home without graduating. Then we'll all be the losers for it because our mates from other schools will graduate on time and secure the few available jobs while we'll be held back of our own free will. The bloody everyday violence that exists in our school reveals a total betrayal of what cultism stands for. I believe that authentic cultism has abandoned us. What we have today on campus is the direct opposite of what cultism stands for. And nobody is happy about it." He sounded pained.

"I have the greatest respect for the Big Eye of the Black Owls," the Black Panthers' High Priest said quietly. "What inspired the killings a couple of days ago was the high-handedness of Owlsmen. Personally, to me, the killings are regrettable. But I must say this: Eating everything alone is bad eating. That's an Igbo proverb. And that's what caused this whole thing. I suggest that we forget about paying any money for peace. Like the presiding chairman said, money can't buy peace. Besides, where does Don Tos want us to raise that kind of money? Robbery? With the kind of security in this town right now, I don't think Panthers would take part in any tapping operation."

Tos looked at the guy who had just spoken. *He, too, is surely going to be cut down like Mike. He'll soon join Keme. I'll personally see to that,* he thought.

"I'll remember your words," he said quietly.

Mike started to open his mouth to speak, but Black Omaha cut him off.

"Hold your peace, Mike."

Mike nodded and kept quiet. It was Roland Ibeshi who spoke instead.

"We're all cultists. We're all birds of the same feathers. We're supposed to respect each other and oppress those guys out there who're civilians. Instead, what are we doing? We're killing ourselves! Can anyone tell me anything that's stupider than that?"

Nobody answered the question.

"As for me and my family," Ibeshi continued, "peace is what we want. Negotiated peace."

Tos looked at Ibeshi and smiled. It was a cold, cruel smile, and it was frighteningly inhuman.

"I propose that we turn this whole thing into a vote," Abel Udoh of the Roundheads said. "That way we'll know those for peace and those against peace."

Black Omaha frowned. "I don't think that's a very wise idea. I'd prefer everybody here subscribe to a peace deal—a negotiated and generally accepted peace deal."

Tos closed his eyes and dragged a long, deep breath. He knew none of them had any inkling of what was about to happen.

He opened his eyes and surveyed all the cult chiefs sitting at the table.

"I think I'll subscribe to us putting this thing to a vote," he said steadily, keeping the excitement out of his voice. "That way we'll know where we stand on this issue."

"I don't know what to say," Black Omaha said hesitantly.

"You're the chairman of these proceedings," Tos said easily. "The yam and the knife are in your hands. Tell us what you want and what to do. We'll do it."

"Yeah, but—" Black Omaha began hesitantly again. "I don't think it's right to put this thing to a vote."

"Give me a cigarette," Tos said quietly. Ovo was holding a packet of Benson & Hedges in his hand. He handed it to Tos. The Grand Wizard of the Black Owls took a cigarette lighter from his shirt pocket. That was the signal: the lighting of the cigarette.

Mike Imoni was saying something. "Presiding chairman, I won't accept this kind of—"

Those were the last words he uttered before he died. There was a loud report. Then another. Then three others, successively. The first bullet tore a gaping hole in his neck and killed him instantly.

Except for the three Owlsmen, at first nobody knew where the shots were coming from. It happened so quickly that the men in the room looked dazed. Before the most composed men at the table could pull out their weapons, the three Owlsmen already had theirs out, covering every one of them in the room.

"The game is over," Tos said. There was no immediate counterpoint.

Outside, the hidden Owlsmen reacted immediately when they heard the shooting from inside. The entire din of the world seemed to be concentrated outside the building as the guns on both sides started flashing. The Owlsmen had the advantage of numbers, the element of surprise, and plenty of sophisticated instruments of destruction. Skills and hatred fused at that moment. Bullets knocked down men, peeled away the paintwork of the building, and punctured the windows, tires, and chassis of the nearby vehicles.

In the first thirty seconds of the shooting, the Owlsmen dropped three of the armed men guarding the first entranceway, and the others, seeing the full weight of the assault and the futility of withstanding the pressure of that kind of shooting, began to retreat inch by inch.

It was the perfect picture of the Black Owls' fighting men in action. They were all working in perfect unison, their hands pressing and squeezing, pumping triggers with studied intensity, pouring bullets into the building with a frenzy. As soon as they emptied their magazines, they would automatically slam in new ones before rolling along the ground, firing more shots, and taking positions.

From the staccato, yammering crash of steady gunfire outside, Tos knew his men were storming the building and that the gunmen outside were defending it. But just at that moment, something happened. To his right, Thomas Dakyap jerked backward in one swift movement, pulling out his gun.

Frank White's movement was one swift fluid motion—swifter by some five seconds. He pulled the trigger and shot the Purebloodsman in the chest region, between the collarbones. Dakyap howled like a dog, dropped his gun, grabbed his chest, fell to his knees, and then toppled to his side.

Another two guys jumped to their feet, drawing their guns. Frank White saw them and reacted immediately, training his gun on them.

"Don't be stupid, guys!" he shouted.

But the two VVS gunmen were either very stupid or they didn't hear him. Frank White's two shots took the two chaps by surprise. They were dead before they hit the floor. All the men in the room saw the Owlsman in action. He was very fast, very calm, and very deadly.

Tos asked, "Who wants to die next? Who wants to take the next chance at being a hero?"

None of the men answered him.

Frank White said, "Now let's see all your dogs on the table."

All the remaining men looked among themselves, and then, very slowly, they took out their guns and lay them on the table. The three men who had come with the presiding chairman and who had not moved since the meeting had begun also gently laid their guns on the floor.

There were about eleven guns in all. Ovo grabbed the guns and emptied them of their shells.

There were six dead men on the floor, along with Thomas Dakyap, who was grievously injured. He was sitting in a puddle of his bright red blood. Mike's corpse was doubled up near him, dead—very dead.

There was so much blood everywhere. Black Omaha, now standing on his feet, his heart beating like a kettledrum, was staring open-mouthed at the dead men on the floor—men who a few minutes prior had been living people. In his life as a mediator at peace meetings, he had never seen anything like this.

Outside, the yammering sound of machine gun fire had receded. At that moment, there was a gentle pounding on the door. Ovo opened the door, and a rough-looking Owlsman stepped into the hall and nodded at the Owlsmen. He was decked out in faded black jeans; dark stubble covered his cheeks, and he was carrying a Kalashnikov.

"What's the situation report outside?" Tos asked him.

"We've taken everywhere and secured the area," the chap replied, his eyes on the dead men on the floor. "The pigs were not much up for a fight. The coast is clear."

"What's the casualty ratio out there?"

"Two of our brothers were killed," the boy replied. "There were about six or seven dead pigs out there."

Tos swore under his breath. *Two other brothers killed.*

"Okay, Azenge. Take care of these guys."

The boy nodded briskly, stepping further into the room. "Lace your fingers behind your head," he commanded the prisoners. "Right now. Move it!"

The unarmed men did as they were ordered. Four other Owlsmen came into the hall: Kadiri Muazu, Christo One Way, Morgan Akumagba, and Banjoko. They were also armed with submachine guns. They picked up all the guns on the table and packed them into a jute bag.

"A well-played setup," High Priest Opanka of the Black Panthers said. His eyes were cold and hard and utterly without warmth.

"Yes." Tos's voice was equally as cold as his was. "Don't you guys admire my ingenuity? You know it's not every day that you hide men in ceilings with handguns up their sleeves."

"This was supposed to be a peace meeting," Abel Udoh said. "But we all know now that it was a clear setup."

"It was supposed to be a peace meeting," Tos said, smiling pleasantly. "My men were killed when we sued for peace. It was a well-planned setup. But I'd advise you guys not to do anything stupid. It's in your own interests."

The oddest smile flitted across Opanka's face as he said, "What will you do with us now?"

Tos hesitated briefly and then said, "Tell me, how does it feel to be at the mercy of your enemy when you know that the final and ultimate victory, your very life, lies in that enemy's hands? With just a word, it could be over."

A great, ominous silence greeted his words. All the unarmed men were staring at him. He was a different man now. There was no pity in his eyes. Of course, he was brilliant, and he was also a strategist. He had all the aces now; there was no question about it.

Black Omaha finally spoke, his voice almost a whisper. "You're the man in charge now, Don Tos. What do you want to do to these men?"

Tos turned his head slightly so that he was staring fully at the presiding chairman.

"There's supposed to be a vote—peace on campus or terror on campus. But for peace to be there, there first must be terror. At least that's why this meeting took place—to create terror. As the American president said after terrorists struck the World Trade Center, 'The only way to pursue peace is to pursue those who threaten it.' But I really think that the best way to pursue peace is to *kill* those who threaten it." He paused and smiled, obviously enjoying himself. "But the truth is that unlike President Bush, I'm a democrat. So I'll put it to a vote. But mind you—if the result's not favorable to me, I'm free to rig or annul the election. That's the Nigerian way, after all, so don't blame me thereafter. Now, gentlemen, let us vote. Who wants war? Let me see your hands in the air."

Not a single hand was raised.

"It's a peace congress." Black Omaha's voice was firm and without fear. "There were supposed to be no killings. Now you've killed a tradition."

Tos smiled tolerantly. "You're free to say anything you want to say, Mr. Chairman. But the truth is that tradition is made for man, and not man for tradition. And as for these men, they'll soon know the punishment that befits those pigs who fuck with Owlsmen."

"I have a favor to ask," Omaha said quietly.

Tos made an elaborate, comical bow. "You've but to ask it, Mr. Chairman."

"Spare these men."

"Is that all?"

"Yes. That's all."

"Must you be so classically forgiving to forget that I'm here to seek revenge?"

"You've got nothing to lose if you let these men go free."

"Damn!" Tos shouted. He was no longer smiling. "Out there, two Owlsmen were killed! A fortnight ago, three of my chiefs were brutally killed. And you want me to forgive? Were another man to ask that favor, I would shoot him."

Black Omaha nodded. He understood everything, and there was nothing he could do at this moment or at any other moment.

He could only save himself and his three bodyguards, and nobody else.

Roland Ibeshi, who was listening with a dazed expression on his face like the others, said, "Don Tos, I didn't take part in the killings of your men. I swear to my God."

Tos stared at Ibeshi, his classmate. It was as if he was remembering something that had happened a long time ago.

"Who killed my Klaws?"

Roland Ibeshi saw hope in the question. In love for his life, he would do anything to save his skin, to keep himself alive.

"It was Mike who organized the hit," he said in a strong, controlled voice. "He started the whole thing. He was the one who personally killed Keme."

Tos looked at him coldly. "It doesn't matter. What does matter is that you had a hand in the death of my brethren. And that's the worst sin anybody can commit against me." His voice was harsh and cruel, leaving no doubt of his feelings in Ibeshi's or the other unarmed men's minds.

Roland Ibeshi swore, and tears started running down his cheeks. This was it. This could be nothing else but death. He knew it. In a few minutes more he would be dead; they would all be dead. *Oh my God! It's my birthday tomorrow. And tonight I'm going to die a cultist death!*

"Don Tos, please spare my life. Tomorrow's my birthday. I want to be twenty-eight."

Tos shook his head and laughed his well-known, devilish, I-don't-give-a-damn-about-the-consequences laugh of a cult don. "I thought you were born in September."

"I was born in May," Ibeshi replied desperately. "I swear to my God."

Tos ignored him and looked at Black Omaha. He said, "Mr. Chairman, you're free to go. You and your guards. They'll give you your dogs and escort you out of the building to your car. Leave immediately. But remember this: You never saw anything. You didn't even attend this meeting. Are we cool?"

The Black Spiders' leader nodded.

"Kadiri, see that they get their tools."

Kadiri Muazu nodded and said, "Follow me."

They were almost at the door when Tos said, "Wait a minute."

They stopped. "I've a gift for you," Tos said, looking at Roland Ibeshi. "You have my permission to leave."

Roland Ibeshi closed his eyes. He couldn't believe what he had just heard. *I'm being told to go. That means God isn't done with me yet.*

Hurriedly he walked toward the other men at the door.

"Wait!"

He stopped, his heart beating like a drum.

"I don't want to hear about what happened here from anybody. Is that clear?"

Roland Ibeshi nodded and left the conference room. He didn't look back once at the men he was leaving behind.

There was not a sound in the room after they were gone. Tos walked down the table and stood close to where Mike's lifeless body lay. He looked down at it thoughtfully for some time, and his mouth curled into a tight, bitter smile.

"This fucking pig did a very bad thing trying to prove that he was a factor," he said loudly. "Just look at him now. He's dead meat." He turned and faced the disarmed men. "Gentlemen, the battle's over. Peace has finally returned to Jankara. Look at you people now; you're all dead men. Dead as in D-E-A-D. My men and I, we live, we win. You're all losers."

The disarmed men didn't reply to him. They were all lost in their own panicked, furious thoughts.

Thomas Dakyap was hurt deeply and was still bleeding. The bullet had entered his chest and fractured a collarbone. That was not what frightened him. Given time, and with luck, he knew such an injury could be treated. What troubled him was not that he was injured. It was that he was captured and certain death was staring him in the face. That made him helpless. And being helpless is not something one wants to experience in a peace meeting.

As for High Priest Opanka, he was not frightened of his fate. He had killed before, and he had known one day it would be his turn to be killed. He knew he was deeply committed to the world of cultism, as Don Tos was. This large conference room with bloodstains on the elliptical table might be the end of him, but it would never be the end of cultism.

In his own personal thoughts, Abel Udoh hadn't seriously considered dying before. *What will Don Tos do to us?* he wondered. *Take us out in a group to the bush to be shot?*

Billy Akatakpo swept into the hall then. He walked straight to Don Tos, and they stood facing each other like two gladiators squaring up for a fight. Tos studied him for some time without speaking.

Because of this boy, history had been made tonight. Tos knew the Akatakpo name was already a legend. His record in cult history had been secured. He would no longer fall into obscurity. He would be remembered and known in the Black Owls' history as the brother who had secretly burrowed into a ceiling to waste enemies of the brotherhood. And he would become popular, like Don Tos and the late Don Bosco. At the very least, it would give generations of students yet unborn something to gossip about for years to come.

"Thank you Akatakpo," Tos said warmly. "You did an excellent job." He held out his hand.

Akatakpo smiled, dipped his head in greeting, and shook the hand solemnly. He felt pretty damn good.

"What are you going to do with these men?" he asked, looking around the hall. All the disarmed men were looking back at him. He was thinking that they seemed so young and so frightened.

"I've got some very good plans for them," Tos replied. He then signaled Ovo and Frank White to come forward. They did. He held a whispered conference with them. After the hushed discussion, Ovo broke the silence.

"Come, gentlemen. Let's go for a walk."

The disarmed men were rounded up and led roughly out of the hall.

* * *

At almost exactly the time the Owlsmen were storming the conference hall of the Jucee Motel, three dark, gleaming cars drew to a smooth stop in front of Dr. Vincent Ubangha's house. About eight young men, all of them masked, wearing dark clothing, and carrying handguns and jerrycans of gasoline, leaped out of the cars. Unhurriedly, they approached the tall, imposing gate. Two of them produced hacksaws and went to work on the two large padlocks that were securing the gate.

Onah, the security man, had resigned after the last attack on his person, so the coast was clear for the young men. In less than ten minutes, the padlocks had been sawed off, and the young men entered the compound. They went straight to the garage, doused all four cars with gasoline, and then proceeded to the house and forced their way into the apartment. Unhurriedly, they poured the fuel onto everything they saw, and when they were satisfied, they came out and tossed a matchstick in a wastebasket near the garage. They left as quietly as they had come in. The only thing they left behind were the burned feathers of an owl, which they scattered at the entranceway to the compound.

Two hours later, Vincent Ubangha's tastefully furnished and extremely expensive two-story building was burned down to a blackened skeleton. All four exotic vehicles in the garage were also burned to cinders. Nobody could rescue anything. The local firefighters didn't even bother to come. Their vehicles had been grounded for the past five years.

* * *

The lights of Jankara faded away behind them as the four vehicles dashed along the highway surrounded on either side by low hills and tall dark trees. The Mazda was in front, the Mitsubishi and Audi in the middle, and the Mercedes in the rear.

The four vehicles dashed down the ancient highway. It was a long, deserted road leading into darkness and treacherous hills. Tos was sitting beside Ovo, who was driving the Mazda. In the rear seat were Akatakpo and Frank White. Leaving the Jucee Motel was like leaving a battlefield. The motel's entrance was a mess. Hundreds of bullets had shattered the front of the building and punctured the windshields and chassis of the cars. There was blood and broken glass everywhere.

They had been driving for the past thirty minutes with no other vehicles on the highway—just a dark ribbon of a road meandering between hills. It was a quiet night, and they drove in silence, as quiet as strangers, yet as close as friends. There was one last job to do. And until the job was done, there was going to be no rest for them—and no easy conversation, either.

Ovo drove the Mazda between two hills. The road bisected them. Ten minutes later, he pulled into a tiny dirt road and drove on another mile or two before stopping. The other vehicles also stopped a good distance away.

"Ovo, you stay right here," Tos said as he yanked the seatbelt off and opened the door. His heavy boots hit the ground. Slowly he walked toward the other vehicles. The three other vehicles were a Mitsubishi bus, an Audi sedan, and a Mercedes-Benz jeep. An Owlsman had opened the trunk of the Audi and lifted out a twenty-liter jerrycan. When he brought the can to Tos and opened it, the smell of gasoline filled the air.

Tos walked very close to the bus and looked inside. All the prisoners were tied with thick ropes, and they were piled atop one another, grotesquely, on the floor of the vehicle. He surveyed them for some time. They were so young, and there were so many of them. And, of course, they were very, very frightened. It was not a job he relished doing, but it was something that must be done—a thing that would be a lesson for those who interfered with the Black Owls.

Tos motioned to the driver. The driver, Kadiri Muazu, knew the sign. He climbed out of the vehicle and walked toward the other group of Owlsmen

Tos looked around him. Apart from the headlights of the four vehicles, the entire scene was in total darkness. He nodded his satisfaction. It was the perfect place.

He peered into the bus again. In the middle of the bed of the vehicle were seven boys heaped atop one another. He recognized High Priest Opanka. He was staring at Tos with eyes pleading for mercy—eyes that were saying, "You just can't waste us!"

Tos felt, just for a moment, a twinge of pity for all of them. He shook his head as if to clear his brain. He could not undo the damage that had been done. It would not change anything. The original plan was clear about it. *The only thing that'll keep the prisoners from getting shot to death is their getting burned to death.* That was the game plan—death by burning. This was the night of death, and the god of death would get his full due.

He stepped away from the vehicle and motioned the Owlsman carrying the jerrycan to come forward. The chap came forward and lifted the heavy can with the aid of another chap, and they poured the contents into the vehicle. The air filled with fumes as the chilly liquid splashed on the tied boys. They soon were all doused.

"Let's get the hell out of here," Tos said. The others clambered into the Audi, the Mercedes, and the Mazda. The engines of the three cars started simultaneously, and they drove a safe distance away. Tos walked slowly toward them. When he climbed into the passenger seat of the Mazda, Frank White brought out a beer bottle. It was a crude Molotov cocktail with a very thick cloth wick that he immediately torched with a cigarette lighter. As the flame caught the wick, he stepped forward and threw the bottle toward the bus.

The sound of shattering glass and a powerful whoosh of flame split the night in one powerful pyrotechnicolor blast, and the Owlsmen, in their respective cars some eighty yards away, shielded their eyes with their arms.

The men in the three cars waited only five minutes before they drove away from the scene, leaving behind the frame of a Mitsubishi bus that was burning like a college bonfire on Riot Day.

CHAPTER TWENTY-ONE

It seemed as though the slaughter at the Jucee Motel had been the signal for a fresh upsurge of hostility and violence throughout Jankara. Twelve students were brutally killed the next day.

The killings took place inside the university community and two other neighboring communities with high student populations.

Faruk Galadima and Gbenga Omotayo, two final-year students who had gone to the school earlier to read, were the first victims. The school compound had a standby power generation plant that supplied uninterrupted power, and the two young men were coming back in the early morning hours when they were ambushed by a group of five heavily armed men. The gunmen, all Brownstone hit men, didn't wait to figure out what cult gangs the two boys belonged to. They just shot them at close range and disappeared into the bushes. That was the first counter-killing, and within hours, wheels within wheels whirred and spun webs of more violence. Strange gunmen from other schools poured into Jankara, all of them wanting to take part in the killing spree. Strong men and Jew men, lecturers, and local indigenes began to panic.

The third victim was Samson Duru, a three-hundred-level law student. The baby-faced twenty-three-year-old student was in his room sleeping when they came for him. They tore the door of his room to shreds, took him outside, and macheted him to death. The people who carried out the act were dressed in the colors of the Brotherhood of the Purebloods. And as with the first two killings, Samson Duru was an innocent student who didn't know why he was being killed. It was his misfortune that his cousin was an Owlsman.

The fourth killing was that of a nineteen-year-old English student who had come out of his apartment to pee in the nearby bushes. Moments later he was lying at the corner of a bush, his zipper opened, his penis exposed, and a bullet in his brain. Members of the VVS who had suspected him to be a new initiate of the Black Owls had killed him.

In less than two hours after the fourth killing, the campus was taken over by heavily armed mobile policemen at the insistence of the VC. But unfortunately, their presence did not stop further killings in the two nearby off-campus communities or stop the exodus of students fleeing the school.

The next day, when the authorities saw that the cultists were growing bolder in their killing spree, the presence of security men notwithstanding, the school was declared closed indefinitely.

The police also found the burned Mitsubishi bus. It was actually a local farmer, an old man with a hoe slung over his shoulder while wheeling a bicycle, who found the bus, and he was quick to report it to the police. The local police made an appearance at the scene a few hours later, but there was nothing they could do. The identities of the burned corpses couldn't even be ascertained. The local police reported the incident to the Jankara Divisional Police HQ, who linked the recent killings in the university community to the burned vehicle. They knew it was a cult case, but that was all. Investigation was underway. Of course there would be an intensive investigation, but the majority of people knew the police would never find the perpetrators of the crimes.

It was really not the fault of the police. The police force was a bloated behemoth, corrupt and disreputable, an emblem of everything wrong with Nigerian society.

* * *

Don Tos had scheduled the Congress of Wizards for the third Sunday of May. The meeting of the feathered men was held in the main hall in Featherland.

All the new men who had plucked their feathers and wetted their beaks were present in the large conference room. The meeting had only two items on the agenda: Don Tos's retirement as the Grand Wizard and the nomination and selection of a successor.

Standing on a raised platform in front of a red banner with an outsized owl painted in the middle, Tos made his last speech before the congregation of titled men as the leader of the most powerful cult gang in Aliu Zamani University.

He started by outlining the danger that had faced their fraternity since his induction as the Grand Wizard. He painted the whole picture, from the day Don Bosco had been brutally killed to how he himself had been selected.

When Don Bosco was killed in the Bloody September Crisis, the Council of Wizards waited four days to name his successor. But thank God, he, Don Tos, was alive and happy in their midst to participate in the selection of a new Grand Wizard. He reminded them that all of them present there in the hall, alongside their unfeathered brethren, had fought tooth and nail, had risked all they had, to avenge the deaths of their brothers and to recover the campus and the glory of the brotherhood.

He paused and regarded the assembly of feathered men and those Owlsmen who had just recently wetted their beaks. He knew they regarded him as their idol. He was the don who was about to retire and give control to somebody else.

As far as the brotherhood was concerned, Don Tos was a good leader. After all, he was the mirror in which Owlsmen always found themselves faithfully reflected. As a don, he was modest, affable, and unpretending. He had all the virtues of a good leader; he was dignified, courageous, and blessed with a profound mind and penetrating reasoning. Virtually all Owlsmen appreciated his leadership. If Owlsmen were Frenchmen, he would have been their Napoleon. If Owlsmen were Chinese men, he would have been their Mao Zedong. If Owlsmen were South Africans, he would have been their Nelson Mandela. If Owlsmen were Americans, he would have been their George Washington. He had a leader's strong conviction and sturdy common sense. And he was highly respected.

They all watched him with deep concentration, hanging on every word issuing from his lips. He was handsome, though wicked-looking, and he was beautiful in the black Valentino suit—the image of the brotherhood he had inspired to a new level. About 95 percent of the people present in the hall tonight were decked out like him, in black suits and ties. This was becoming known as Don Tos's image.

As he spoke, he brought before their very eyes the brilliant feats of his regime and the unfortunate incident that had led to Keme's, Black Mamba's, and Ayu's deaths and the deaths of the two others that had taken place when they stormed the venue of the peace meeting. But thanks to his leadership, the Black Owls had once again avenged those deaths like they had avenged Don Bosco's death, at a very minimal cost to the brotherhood. It had all been possible because of his iron nerves and the unswerving and uncompromising support of all the Owlsmen. For that, he received a standing ovation that lasted for about three minutes.

When the excitement had died down, he continued in a more somber tone. He once again reminded them of the gang's rallying cry: "One for all, all for One." The spirit should not be weakened. It should instead be strengthened, because the battle is not yet over. There is danger ahead, and there will always be danger.

He reminded them of the constant danger that would be posed by the more ambitious, more aggressive, and overly angered members of the other five most violent gangs. Owlsmen could survive such attacks only if they continued to stick to the gang's principles. And the principles were determination, devotion, and dedication. There was too much to lose if the Black Owls' myth was broken. It had to be protected. It had to be maintained no matter what. If it meant sacrificing campus peace to maintain it, then so be it.

He received a thunderous ovation again. Every one of them knew he was speaking his mind and the minds of most Owlsmen.

He was actually a ruthless leader. His methods, without doubt, were those of a vicious leader. But they were necessary if Owlsmen wanted really to suppress all opposition, particularly that of cult gangs like the Black Panthers, the Brotherhood of the Purebloods, the Brownstones, the VVS, and, of course, the Roundheads—the other violent gangs that wanted supreme power on campus. But all in all, he was the single most powerful Grand Wizard who had strengthened the brotherhood and had given his brethren—the feathered and the unfeathered—greater power, more prestige, and better security than any Owlsman from Jankara or any other institution had ever enjoyed. And he had transformed the Order of the Black Owls into a formidable cult gang that was free from intimidation or molestation for the first time since its inception.

In the face of campus-wide opposition, he had introduced wide, sweeping reforms, dealing ruthlessly with all the Black Owls' opponents, one after the other. Some of his greatest achievements included the complete overhaul of the gang's leadership, the introduction and enforcement of the feather system of communication and intimidation, the improvement of the initiation method, the collection of finances, and the creation of a new identity for Owlsmen. But they knew his greatest and most symbolic achievement had been the creation of Featherland, the headquarters of the gang.

Tos glanced down the length and breadth of the hall, his eyes resting on everyone. It was as if he were counting the number of people in the room. He had enjoyed his stint as the Big Eye. It had been stimulating and exciting, and he had reveled in the power and the envy his name had commanded. Leaders of other gangs envied and feared him. That alone was nothing else but prestige. In Jankara, no cultist's name could have been bigger than Don Tos's.

He continued in his strong, commanding voice. "Now that those evil, overambitious men who killed Keme, Black Mamba, Yakubu Ayu, and all the other staunch Owlsmen have been uncovered and killed, for perhaps the next two or three sessions, the university campus will know peace. But peace can only be maintained by eternal vigilance." There was another round of thunderous applause.

Tos waited for the ovation to die down before he spoke again. "I've served this great family with every bit of strength at my disposal. As one of the apostles said in the Bible, I have fought a good fight, I have finished my course, I have kept the faith, and today I can proudly say that I have not failed. But now the time has come for me to depart. I believe I've done all I could as an Owlsman, as a feathered man, and as a Grand Wizard. I know that my retirement date's supposed to be in September—a few months away—but I wish to retire this month. And what the family needs now is a new leader—a vigorous man, an Owlsman loyal to death. That's the kind of man I want to succeed me. And who could that man be? That's the major reason I called this meeting."

There was stunned silence now.

On the platform, Tos studied the faces of all the assembled Owlsmen. He continued quietly. During his regime, he told them, a very good man had ably assisted him. "Some of you have worked with him. He's a good man. He's a man of strength and vision, a

Wizard who has proved himself in the heat of violence, a man who's been very visible throughout the past crises we've faced. This man, I know, will add some juice to the family. I'm proud to nominate to the highest leadership position in the family the incumbent Vee-Eye. I nominate Ogheneovo Ikoloba to succeed me. I know he'll give the family quality leadership."

The nomination, or rather selection, of the Evil Eye was just an official announcement.

The Number Two had given every impression of being an ideal replacement for Don Tos. He was handsome, vicious in nature, popular in the Council of Wizards, and moneyed. He spoke with a light and even humorous touch, and as the Evil Eye, he had shown real interest in the office of the Big Eye.

His nomination was unanimously adopted, and he became the twelfth Grand Wizard, a.k.a. Big Eye, of the Order of the Black Owls.

* * *

It had been two weeks since the university was closed down and exactly a week since Tos had traveled back to Lagos.

On that day, at exactly twelve midday, Tos was in a telephone conversation with Frank Reese.

"I've just checked with the American Embassy," Frank Reese was saying. "They told me you've collected your visa."

"Yes, I did. Collected it yesterday."

"That's very good. Are you having any problems? Is there anything I can do for you?"

"No sir."

"In about five days' time, you'll be in America. I've done everything here to make you as comfortable as possible."

"I appreciate it, sir."

"Remember that I promised to take care of your flight. My secretary will book it tomorrow. You're flying first class, and I'll have a man here in John F. Kennedy Airport to meet you. Is that okay by you?"

Tos smiled. *Is that okay by me?* "Why not? I'd like that."

"Tell me: How did you find the catalog?"

Tos turned around, and his eyes fell on the glossy catalog lying on the table. On the front were reproductions of three pictures, *The Solitary Reaper* and two others. Obviously, they were works of the other two artists. The headline was bold: "PORTRAITS FROM A SMALL PART OF THE WORLD: AN ARTS AND CULTURE EXHIBITION." Below it were the dates and the venue of the event.

"It's wonderful. I like it."

"I'm glad to hear that," the American's disembodied voice replied. "I hope to see you on the thirty-first."

"Yeah."

"Send Ebi my regards."

"I will."

Tos dropped the phone. He was still smiling. The last time he had called, Reese had complimented him, saying that he had done a most complete job. He had even called him a genius. And now he had received three copies of the catalogs and three hand-signed copies of the invitations for the opening, just in case he wanted some of his lecturers or friends to attend.

He knew two of his friends would've loved to attend: Ovo and Christo. And Professor Finecountry also would've loved to be there, the distance notwithstanding. But the recent happenings in Jankara dissuaded him from telling them.

He walked to the calendar hanging on the wall. There he counted the days with his eyes. There were just about four remaining.

Things were working as planned. Tosan Mayuku was a man of the future. In about a hundred hours more, he would be out of this country for good. That was a future. But just then he frowned. *Ebi.* He had tried impatiently for over a week to raise her on the phone, but he hadn't been able to get through. He knew the reason why. It was because of her father.

He checked his watch. It was some twenty-five minutes past midday. He knew Chief Dabiri's home number and Ebi's personal mobile number by rote. But it seemed that Ebi's phone was frozen. He had tried it several times without success. And the last time he had gone to her house, the warning he had gotten was an earful. After that warning, he felt just a little hesitant about calling the house. But right now the temptation was just too much for him. He wanted to break the news to the girl who had given him the big break.

He picked up the phone and dialed the house number.

"Chief Dabiri's residence," a female voice answered.

"Yes. I want to speak with Ebi, please."

"Ebi?" The voice asked.

"Yeah. Please tell her it's very important."

"Who should I say is calling her?"

"Tell her a friend of hers from the university."

There was a moment of silence. Then he heard, "I'm sorry, sir. Ebi's not at home right now," and the line went dead.

Tos raised an eyebrow, and then he dialed the number again.

"Chief Dabiri's residence." It was the same voice.

"Please don't hang up on me. I really want to speak with Ebi."

There was a long pause. It was as if somebody was talking in the room. After a while, the next voice that came on the line was a man's voice.

"Who's on the line?"

"Uh…sir…Chief…uh…"

"I said who's on the line?"

"Chief, this is Tosan."

There was a moment of silence.

"What do you want, young man?"

Tos frowned. He looked at the window. He said softly, "Sir, I want a word with Ebi."

"Ebi doesn't want anything to do with you," came the reply, and the line went dead.

Tos looked at his bare feet in dismay. He dropped the phone gently, walked to the deep, ugly chair, and sat down heavily. He had been treated this way for the past few days. Immediately after he had come back from Jankara, he had driven to her place with the gift he had bought for her—long-stemmed roses, a big box of candy, and a bottle of her favorite perfume—Chanel No. 5. At the gate, they had embarrassed him. And since then, he had not received any word from her.

He couldn't accept what her father had said on the phone. He had to see her somehow. She was the love of his life, and he had to see her.

For the past couple of days, he hadn't been able to get the image of her beautiful face out of his mind. He missed her so much that it hurt him.

Could it really be that she is angry with me? he wondered. *Does she know?* He had promised himself that if he made it to New York, he would tell her the truth about himself. He would not hide anything from her. He would be a fool not to tell her the truth.

His mind flooded with the plans they had made for the future. He remembered what she had told him the very night Keme had been killed. She'd said that if they made it to New York, she would take him to see the Statue of Liberty. And not only that, but she would take him to see the Empire State Building, and then they would visit Ground Zero—the former site of the World Trade

Center. And they would take a boat ride around the Hudson River. Of course, she had said she would take him to visit the New York Museum of Modern Art.

He believed that his relationship with Ebi was inevitable—perhaps more than inevitable. It was something destined to be—something preordained even before he was birthed. With that thought in his mind, he stood up and went into the bathroom. Fifteen minutes later, he stepped out clean and fresh. He went into his bedroom to dress. It took him another twenty minutes to do that.

By the time he finished and assessed himself in the full-length mirror, he was satisfied with the image he cut. He looked truly smashing in a well-fitted suede jacket and a stylish black beret.

When he came out, he remembered that he had forgotten something. He dashed back into the bedroom to get his car keys but then stopped, eyeing the small cabinet beside his bed. He walked over to it, yanked the bottom drawer open, and grabbed his .38 semiautomatic handgun. He checked it with the hand of a professional and then put it in his coat pocket. Now he could do with some protection. The two Owlsmen downstairs delegated to guard him were very good gunmen, but that notwithstanding, he still needed his own gun.

Ten minutes later, he drove out of the compound in the company of his two guards.

* * *

The black BMW drew to a smooth stop in front of Chief Dabiri's house. Tos leaped out of the car and started toward the tall, heavy metal gates. He banged on them loudly, and they were opened immediately. It was as if they were expecting him. Musa, the *maiguard*, and two black-suited security men stood in the entranceway, and they were staring at him strangely.

"What do you want?" One of the security men demanded.

"I want to see Ebi," Tos replied. "I called a few minutes ago. She's expecting me."

"That's a lie," the other security man said. "Ebi's not at home. She has traveled out of the country."

"That, my friend, is the real lie," Tos said. "What's the big deal? I just want a word with her."

The two security men said nothing; Musa, the *maiguard*, shrugged and said, "You no sabi oyibo? Madam no dey house."

"Fuck you," Tos said in an agitated voice, and he pushed forward as if to walk right past the three men. The two black-suited men blocked his path. Musa was already making as if to lock the gate. He knew he was seeing a repeat of what the boy had done a couple of days ago.

"Ebi! Ebi!" Tos was shouting over the shoulders of the two security men. "Ebi, will you come out and talk to me!"

"I'll tell you something, boy," one of the security men said. "I don't think she'll answer you even if she hears you."

Tos grabbed the man's shoulder and tried to push past him. What he received instead was a sledgehammer blow to his face. He found himself on all fours. He was dazed for a few seconds. It was with the aid of Ganiyu and Gafaru, his two bodyguards, that he was able to make it to his feet. There was blood on the corner of his lips. He could taste it.

"My lord, do you want us to *nack* these guys?" Gafaru asked, angry that the security man had had the gut to pull a sucker punch on the Don.

Tos ignored the question. Instead he touched his mouth.

"Ganiyu, Gafaru—keep out of this," he said at last. "I think I can handle this." He studied the man who had knocked him down. He was a bearded, heavily-built middle-aged man. He addressed him. "Is this how you want to play it, eh?"

"It's your choice," the man said.

"You think so?" There was fire in Tos's eyes as he said these words. "Are you guys sure you want some rough play?"

"Get the hell out of here, otherwise you'll get hurt."

Tos pulled the gun from his pocket. He leveled it at the two men. "Tell me, who is going to get hurt—me or you?"

The two men stiffened. Both of them said nothing, but their stunned faces said everything.

"Now can I come in?"

Musa, seeing the gun, had taken flight.

"Now can I come in?"

The two men surrendered. "Sure, you can come in," one of them said as he opened the gate. "Come in."

"You go in first," Tos commanded. Gafaru and Ganiyu had also pulled out their guns from their pockets, and they pushed the men through the gate. As they entered the compound, they came face-to-face with Chief Dabiri, who obviously had been called by Musa.

"Good morning, sir," Tos began.

Chief Dabiri walked up to them. He showed no interest in the guns in the young men's hands.

"So you have the boldness to come to my house with your cult gangs and guns, eh?" he said quietly.

Tos lowered his gun. He smiled and laughed a little, hoping it would help diffuse the tension the presence of the guns had caused.

"I'm sorry, sir. I don't mean any harm. I just want a word with Ebi, and that's all."

Chief Dabiri looked at the young man for a long moment; it was as if looking might make him understand that he was not wanted in the compound.

"Get out of here," the chief said.

"Sir, I can explain what just happened. Believe me."

"I said get the hell out of here."

"But, sir—this is not the way to treat your future son-in-law."

Chief Dabiri was shouting now. "Get the hell out of here before I call the police!"

Tos nodded, looked at the gun in his hand and walked toward the two security men. He said to the bearded man, "I think you owe me something." With that, he aimed a blow with the butt of the gun at the man's face.

The impeccably black-suited, heavily-built man hit the ground with a thud.

"That's fair enough," Tos said, and he walked unhurriedly to the car. Gafaru was already behind the steering wheel. He did a swift U-turn and zoomed off.

* * *

In the upstairs room, standing near the window, Ebi watched them drive off. There were tears in her eyes as she turned away. She flopped on the bed, and her eyes rolled shut. She remained like that for a long time, deep in thought. She was thinking of Tos. She had not been able to think of anything else. She felt very lonely and lost.

If she ever came face-to-face with Tos, how could she explain this thing to him? How could she tell him the depth of the hatred her father bore for him—the man she loved wholeheartedly? It was hatred transferred from father to son, something about the sins of the father being visited on the son.

And because of that, she was beginning to develop a dislike for her parents, particularly for her father. She felt he should forget about the past and move on with his life.

The whole thing was weighing her down. Walking into the dining room and having dinner with them was a huge effort. Listening to their boring conversation was another huge effort.

Don't they realize they are killing me slowly? Don't they realize that I love the boy and there's nothing any of them can do about it?

The image of his face was on her mind all the time, and in her heart she knew she had to see him. And seeing him this afternoon had intensified the hunger eating away at her heart.

The last couple of days had been nightmare days for her. They were days she would not forget in a hurry. She was practically grounded. She had no leisure, no pleasure, and, worst of all, no freedom. She was literally caged inside the gilded compound. The other painful aspect was the "communication break," as her father chose to call it. Her cell phone was withdrawn, her bedroom phone was disconnected, and all the other phones in the house were off-limits for her. And the security men were specifically ordered not to let her out of the compound.

Today she had seen him and she had heard his voice. She must see him again. She opened her eyes. Already she had made a plan in her mind. She stood up, walked up to the closet, and picked up one of her bags. She dipped her hand into it and came out with a billfold. She opened it and took out some dollar bills. She counted them and nodded her head. It would do.

CHAPTER TWENTY-TWO

WARRI, MAY 2004

IT WAS AN EXCEPTIONALLY BRIGHT, MOONLIT NIGHT IN THE oil-rich city of Warri. It was nearing midnight in the Bunker, the nondescript apartment block on the nondescript street. The snack meal had been cleared away. The four young men sat in the darkened living room of the Bunker watching satellite TV. The four of them were deeply engrossed in what they were seeing on the television set, and their hardened faces were lit by the bluish glow of the television tube. It was a Western movie featuring Clint Eastwood.

After watching two or three movies, as was their tradition every night, they would take turns bathing in the single bathroom, and then three of them would go to bed while one of them would keep watch over the others. That was what they normally did every night. It was a tradition.

Three weeks after the killings of the seven oil workers, the young men had moved out of the Creek River Hotel, a.k.a. Bayelsa, and were now installed in the Bunker, a set of secured flats in another part of Warri.

The Benin River killing of the expatriate workers had been a major mistake on the part of the fighting youths. That was when they had seen, firsthand, the determination of the government. It was obvious that the killings of the two Americans had put real diplomatic pressure on Aso Rock, and now heavily armed squads of the combined military patrolled the major streets and highways of Warri. Hundreds of secret service agents and CIDs, all decked out in mufti, eavesdropped on conversations and infiltrated all the major bars and restaurants in the various ethnic enclaves, listening for hints as to where the youth leaders were hiding. Any time a hint was dropped, the security agents would swoop on a particular bar, arresting the man who had dropped the hint and every known or suspected youth leader on both sides of the warring parties. What had saved Isaac Wuru and three of his colleagues was that there had been a security leak. Ten minutes was what had saved them from the violent arrest.

On the NTA's monthly media show (the four of them actually watched it), the president of the federal republic had maintained, when answering a question, that "the youths in the Niger Delta have gone too far. And no respectable government would condone such acts of criminal violence as the ones they've been committing for the past year. And in light of the continuing atrocities being perpetrated in the name of ethnic wars, the government has ordered hundreds of well-trained, well-equipped military forces, comprising the army, the navy, the air force, and mobile policemen, into the area. Their mission is to put a stop to the senseless killings there. I know this may seem draconian to some section of the people, especially to the press, but allowing the piracy, the rape, the pipeline vandalization, and the slaughter of innocent oil workers and citizens to continue would be even worse. I think it is healthy and normal in a democracy for a group or a tribe of people to express their dissatisfaction with the government or with one another. But such expressions of dissatisfaction should follow the line of legal agitation. Using violence as an instrument to call the government's attention to your grievances is bad, and anybody or any group of persons who does that will likewise be stopped violently..."

Nigerians took divergent views on the matter. Those who supported the government's action saw it as the only way to solve the *abiku*esque problem called "senseless violence" in the Niger Delta. And those who were against the action, particularly those from the Niger Delta region, viewed the decision to militarize Warri and the entire Niger Delta region as ill-advised. Their belief was that sending thousands of heavily armed military personnel into Warri and its environs would not solve the problem.

But the government was not to be dissuaded. The military and other security agents had attacked scores of villages and islands used by the youths as bases of operations. Casualty figures were running into the hundreds. But most of the victims, as in all war situations, were women, children, and the aged. The heavily armed youths had retreated well into the treacherous creeks and had taken over most of the deserted communities. The military were having a hard time fighting in the inaccessible creeks and swampy islands. After the president's appearance on the NTA show, more contingents of the military were drafted into the war zones. Within a week, no fewer than five Ijaw militant camps had been completely razed, and several Itsekiri villages had been forcibly occupied by the military forces.

Three weeks after the killings, the federal government, started abducting youth leaders. In some cases, aged community leaders were invited for questioning and subsequently detained for days.

On the twenty-fifth of May, that was exactly a month and two days after the Olero Oil Field killings and a day after Wuru had finished his discussion with the lecturer about the contract to kill Tos, the security agents arrested one James Maimai. Maimai was an Ijaw youth leader. He was caught on a tiny island near Burutu. During a lengthy interrogation, the young man made some useful confessional statements. Parts of his statement indicated that he had participated in a process that had resulted in the recent killings of some white men. He actually admitted to having taken part in the mission and said that his "commander" was one Isaac Wuru, and his "chief of staff" was one Manager Akimi.

The joint task force overseeing the security situation in the Niger Delta, led by a brigadier-general, swung into action. They raided the Creek River Hotel, but neither of two young men named as commander and chief of staff were in the hotel at the time of the raid. Feeling outmaneuvered by the youth leaders, the brigadier general ordered the arrest of everybody in the hotel at that time. The action was meant to teach the people the lesson of their lives. The next day, the military general was quick to announce to the listening public that the number of arrested armed youths had risen to 415 from last week's 272, and that some of these "sea pirates" were the people who had attacked the seven oil workers at Olero Oil Field.

Isaac Wuru, commander; Manager Akimi, his chief of staff (Number Two by designation); Timi Pereweibina, secretary general; and Yellow were now hiding in the Bunker until tension cooled down. With James Maimai and the others behind bars, they knew the situation would soon calm. The army did not patrol and control the city effectively enough, nor did the navy patrol and control the waterways firmly enough, to halt the legendary lawlessness. Piracy, though in small quantity, was still going on.

Wuru and the others believed that these criminal pirates, masquerading as fighters for the cause, had carried out the killings of the two Americans. He knew James Maimai. The boy was the head of the Ijaw Salvation Army, a rogue splinter group of the Egbesu. He was surprised when he heard that the boy had been captured at a small island base near Burutu. The military had told newsmen that at the time James Maimai and his boys were captured, a medium-sized barge had just deposited boxes of arms and ammunitions. A well-known baron owned the barge. The barge had been actively involved in the oil bunkering business. Wuru knew nothing would be done to the baron. These bunkerers had a great deal of influence on the machinery of the government. The politicians out there in Abuja knew exactly what was happening in the creeks.

Wuru was even more surprised when he heard that he himself was said to have been the main instigator of the now infamous mission. He suspected that James had made those confessions under duress. The boy must have been subjected to cruel, inhuman, degrading torture. There was no way such a confession could stand the full scrutiny of seasoned lawyers in a court of law.

But the government was not interested in lawyers and their courtroom theatrics. The crackdown on criminality and piracy on the Niger Delta waterways was the only thing that concerned them, and now they were trying to run everybody aground. The consolation was that there were lots of places to get lost in Warri. Though the military proudly claimed that they had arrested about 80 percent of the troublemakers in the creeks, the truth was that many others had gone into hiding, and the military couldn't yet pin down the locations of these hiding places. The Warri waterfront area, for example, was a rabbit warren of little streets and slum quarters, all twisted about like a maze. The majority of the houses there were unlisted and without plans. And the army couldn't be called to invade the houses of honest people or to arrest everyone living in the slums.

The four young men knew that before their hideout could be stormed, their informants would give them a hint, and they would make good their escape easily before the arrival of government security forces. The Bunker was not defensible; it was only a place with hundreds of escape routes—a place easy to get into and easy to get out of.

On this very night, after they had taken their baths and were preparing to turn in, the phone in the room rang. It was a very private line, and only a few people knew its number. And they would not call unless it was very important. Yellow walked across the room and picked up the phone.

"Hello," he said softly.

"Hello," the voice at the other end replied to him.

"Who's on the line?"

"The Ginger Man."

A startled exclamation escaped the boy. He couldn't believe his ear. This was Chief 'Tade Dabiri—the big chief in Lagos. He was utterly speechless.

"Hello, are you there?"

"Y-yessir."

"Get Wuru on the line immediately."

"Y-yes sir," Yellow stammered. Covering the mouthpiece with his fingers, he motioned for Wuru to come and answer the call.

"Who is it?" Wuru asked, coming over.

"Chief 'Tade Dabiri."

"Really?"

"Nobody else."

Wuru snatched the receiver from Timi's hand. "Good evening, sir. This is Wuru."

"Wuru?"

"Yes sir."

"Good. I want you here in Lagos as soon as possible." The words were spoken clearly.

"Lagos?"

"Yes."

"As soon as possible?"

"Yes."

Wuru made a mental calculation. Security men were looking for them in Warri. Only three days ago, a man had given him money to go to Lagos to waste Tosan. Now Chief 'Tade Dabiri also wanted him in Lagos. *How am I going to arrange this?* he wondered.

"You know my place in Victoria Island." It was a statement.

"Yes sir."

"I want you to be here tomorrow or the day after. Can you make it?"

"I think so."

"Good. I want you to come clean. Take one or two of your boys, but no tools. Make no mistake about that."

"If you say so, sir."

"Okay. See you then." The chief hung up.

Wuru looked at the silent phone. Like Yellow, he was clearly speechless. He could not believe his ears. *The great Chief Ezontade Dabiri! What could be on the Chief's mind? Probably he wants me to supervise the tapping and siphoning and delivery of his crude onto the ship that is bound for the United States.*

It was always Wuru's job to see that the crude got to the high seas.

* * *

It was six o'clock the following morning when Isaac Wuru and the three other boys got into his Toyota Camry and began the journey to Lagos. It was one of those wet mornings in May, the watery sun trying to be brave, fighting the dark clouds, vainly trying to make an appearance. Obviously, it would rain later in the day.

The drive from Warri to Lagos would ordinarily take six hours in a fast car, but if one took into account the three dozen military checkpoints in the highway (six were on the Warri Federal highway alone); the bumpy, rutted roads; and the traffic jams along the way, then one would see it would take roughly ten hours. All the same, they hoped to get to the chief's house by a little after four o'clock. That would give them enough daylight to sight-see in a little part of the former federal capital.

Wuru was the only one among them who had visited Lagos, and he knew the state like the back of his hand. As he drove, he gave them an informative tour of the state.

They entered Lagos at about three o'clock and encountered a traffic jam on Ikorodu Road. On both sides of the highway, they could see lots of uniformed security men.

"It's a police checkpoint," Timi, who was sitting beside Wuru, said.

"It's the thirtieth military point," Yellow said from behind them.

"Are you counting them?" Wuru asked.

"Yeah."

"It looks like they're searching the vehicles," Manager said.

All the other checkpoints they had passed had been smooth sailing for them. Not one of the police officers on duty had waved them out of the line of cars to do a body search on them. Decked out in three-piece suits and ties with matching wide-brimmed hats, they cut the image of respectable people. Anyone would have taken the four of them for lawyers or perhaps bankers or big-time businessmen. And that was the secret to being casually waved through. They understood the rules of the game. If you dressed respectably, the public would treat you respectably. Even the police and soldiers mounting roadblocks on the highway were duty-bound to treat you with deference. For that reason, they were treated with respect and waved through.

"You guys should leave the questions to me," Wuru said.

"Won't they search us?" Manager asked again. "They're searching the other cars."

"Are you tooled?" Wuru was looking at him.

"Yeah."

"Oh my God!" Wuru exclaimed. "Are you joking?"

"I'm not joking."

"But I said no tools!" Wuru said angrily, looking at him in the rearview mirror. Obviously, he looked suspicious. "What were you thinking?"

Manager shrugged. "I guess I didn't hear you."

"Let's hope they won't search us," Yellow said calmly. "We should just relax."

Wuru cursed. Timi looked sideways at him. He wasn't certain whether fear or excitement contributed most to the tension clutching his heart.

"Oh my God! What do we do now?" Timi said in a shaky voice.

The vehicle in front of theirs was now being searched.

"You must not look frightened, Timi," Manager said from the rear seat.

"You're telling me!" Timi hissed. "You must not look frightened too."

"This is stupid," Wuru said, and he dangled one of his arms through the window, and drummed his fingers lightly against the car's bodywork. From the rearview mirror, he could see Manager fumbling as if he was hiding the handgun.

The vehicle in front of them, a Volvo, was let through, and Wuru pushed the car forward a little.

When the car stopped in front of the MoPol clutching an AK-47, Timi felt his heart cause him actual physical pain. He was immediately of one mind—making a bolt for it. But the snag was that there was a group of heavily armed policemen on either side of the road. An armored personnel carrier and two antiriot vehicles were parked not twenty yards ahead; all of them partially blocked the road.

"Good afternoon, officer," Wuru said pleasantly.

"Good afternoon," the officer said quietly, and he gestured for all the rolled-up windows to come down. Wuru touched a button inside the car, and all the windows rolled down noiselessly. All the other officers were training their weapons, though casually, on the car.

"Where from, sir?"

"Benin," Wuru lied. He knew if he said Warri, more attention would be focused on the car and its occupants. The war in Warri and the recent killings of the oil workers had not helped the image of the town.

"Your ID, please."

Wuru whipped out his ID card and quickly hand it to the officer. The officer examined it closely. On the ID, he actually looked cool and more like an oil and gas junior staffer than a jobless, violent youth leader embroiled in the crisis and wanted by the military. The officer gave him back the ID card.

"What's in your trunk?"

Aware that all the security men were watching them, Wuru shrugged in a carefree manner.

"There's nothing in my trunk."

"Can I see it?"

Wuru hesitated. He caught the eye of some of the officers sitting inside the rear of the black painted personnel carrier. They were young, about his age, decked out in bulletproof vests, their hands loosely clutching their SMGs.

"Can I see your trunk?" another voice demanded. The voice belonged to another officer—a sergeant, going by the insignia on his uniform. He was a much older man. He had just joined the pleasant-faced younger officer, and unlike the younger man, he was not smiling.

Wuru came out and opened the trunk of the car. The young officer searched it under the watchful eye of the sergeant. He didn't find anything.

The sergeant walked to the other side of the car.

"Your ID, please," he said to Timi.

Timi dug his hand into his jacket and pulled out a wallet, flipped it open, and, like Wuru, displayed his artfully forged

Halliburton ID card. The police officer examined it closely and, after some seconds, nodded. The wallet snapped shut.

"Is this your car?" The question was directed at Wuru.

"Yeah."

"Your driver's license, please."

Wuru produced it. It was genuine. The sergeant inspected it for another two minutes. It still had some six months before expiration.

"Who're these?" the sergeant said after handing back the driver's license. He was staring into the rear seat of the car.

"My colleagues."

"Let me see their IDs."

Wuru nodded and told Manager and Yellow to bring out their ID cards. The two ID cards appeared simultaneously. Like Wuru's and Timi's, these two cards were also forged, and the forgery was of exceptional quality.

"Tell them to come out."

The three men came out. The officer stared at them one after the other, matching their faces with the photos on the IDs. They were all the same people, but he had to do his job. He had instructions from his superiors; all vehicles going into or coming out of state must be searched. There were too many cases of armed robbery in Lagos these days. This was one of the ways to curb their easy mobility in the state.

"You can go, gentlemen," the sergeant said. "And sorry for the inconvenience."

Wuru smiled as he got behind the wheel. "You're doing your job, officer." His voice was friendly. He started the car, and they continued their journey as the sergeant waved the next car to a halt.

"That was close," Timi said. Sweat was still rolling down his forehead.

"Yeah. But we're clear," Manager said.

Wuru said nothing. They drove in silence for some minutes. On City Way, a siren wailed and they were forced to clear out of the way as a black MoPol truck swung in front of them. Over two dozen stone-faced mobile policemen in their antiriot gear sat in the tarpaulin-covered truck. The four young men could see their guns and boots.

"What do you think is happening?" Yellow asked.

"Yabatech students are rioting," Wuru said. "It was on the news this morning. It seems they've taken over Aggrey Road and Herbert Macauley Road."

"What's Yabatech?" Manager asked.

"It's a school. Just like a university," Timi replied.

"This is stupid," Manager said angrily. "They send police to stop the problem in Lagos, but they would send the army to Warri. Who's the government deceiving?"

"Manager—the government can't send in the army to stop protesting students. Protesting students are not carrying guns," Timi said patiently.

"But they're burning cars and destroying houses. What does the government think we're doing in Warri? Are we not protesting? They should send in the police, not the army. The army should be sent to Liberia and Sierra Leone."

"That's enough!" Wuru said angrily.

The others fell silent. They drove the remaining distance in silence until they parked in the parking lot of the expensive Banana Hotel on Nnamdi Azikiwe Street. They booked two separate rooms, but because they were not in a hurry to check in until later in the day, and that only after they had seen the chief, they came out of the hotel, climbed back into the car, and drove out of the city toward Victoria Island.

An hour later, they were seated in Chief Dabiri's study. It was a spacious room on the second floor with overstuffed chairs and shelves of books taking up two of the walls. Timi could see that some of the books were on politics and history, some were manuals on petroleum and crude oil minerals, and some others were law books and classic novels.

On the other part of the wall was a large map of all the oil-producing states of Nigeria. Every oil-producing community was clearly indicated, every oil well neatly marked. In red was every flow station, in black every tank farm, in green every well and the networks of the oil exploration pipelines. In Chief Dabiri's view, it was the right of every Niger Deltan to burst pipe and siphon crude. Anybody who was taking oil, so far as he was from an oil-producing community, was not a criminal. He called it "self-help." After all, the money from the region was being used not to develop the region but to develop other parts of the country, while the people in the region were the ones who suffered the adverse effects of the oil exploration activities.

Chief Dabiri, resplendent in a sky-blue Senegalese kaftan and seated in one of the oversized stuffed chairs, regarded the four young men quietly. Despite his chronic heart problem of the past few months, he looked strong and healthy.

The boys had fed him the situation report from the creeks. The heat in creeks was becoming unbearable. He knew it was all the government's master plan to silence the people in the area to ensure the free flow of oil. The military were no longer content capturing the fighters; they were also beginning to arrest and interrogate chiefs and other community leaders.

"The reason why I invited you people here is to take care of a small problem," Chief Dabiri said quietly. "It's a personal problem, and I want you boys to handle it with dispatch."

There was no reaction from the four young men. They regarded the chief quietly, with a mixture of fear and reverence. This man, they knew, ruled the Ijaw nation. He was the greatest of the Ijaw chiefs and had made the noblest contributions any man could make for the struggle of the Ijaw nation. From his youth, he had identified with the people. The creek of Ijawland was his country, and most of the young Ijaw men fighting the Itsekiris in Warri looked up to him. He was like a king to them. In fact, he was respected even more than a king. His chieftaincy title was *Izonebidowei*; loosely translated, it meant "he who seeks the good of the Izon people." That title alone soothed pains. And his words were his bond, his oaths revered more than oracle, his love for his people clear, his thoughts "Ijaw-rized," his tears genuine messages coming from his heart. And his heart was in Kaiama, the birthplace of Isaac Boro and the neo-spiritual heartland of the Ijaw nation.

His voice was the loudest in the resource control agitation, and the vision he had for his native country was a Niger Delta republic comprising all six oil-producing South-South states, with Ijaw as the dominant ethnic group that would call the shots. He believed that Nigeria was an "enormous colonial mistake" and that one day that mistake would be corrected.

Back home, Chief Dabiri had been roundly applauded as one of the most honorable sons of Ijawland. The previous year, in the thick of the bloody war between Ijaw and Itsekiri youths, his oil bunkering company, Ginger Man, Inc., had sent in twelve hundred automatic rifles, twelve machine guns, and thirty-six submachine guns. To the Egbesu Boys, he was the most consistent, the most powerful, and the most connected man, and that made him the most reliable of all the Ijaw leaders. The SEA—Supreme Egbesu Assembly—had much confidence in him.

Any time he chanced to come to Warri to deliver speeches, particularly at the Creek River Hotel (he was a frequent visitor to the hotel), his theme was always the same and carried the loudest ovation: the Niger Delta and Ijawland, again, again, and again. He would blast the federal government that had raped Ijawland and brought the entire Niger Delta region to her knees. The Niger Delta, he'd always remind them, was the home of 100 percent of Nigeria's oil wealth. From such speeches, it had been suggested that the Niger Delta and the Ijaw nation were one and the same thing. He would say that the solution to the Niger Delta Crisis was one of autonomy and control over the proceeds of their own wealth. In other words, it was a matter of resource control. Of all the various tribes in the Niger Delta, he arrogantly maintained, the Ijaws were the largest. Their population alone was about half of the entire area. The population of all other tribes—Itsekiris, Binis, Urhobos, Isokos, Ogonis, Ibibios, Efiks, Ikwerres, Ilajes, etc.—was just a tiny fraction of the region. And their land was an infinitesimal geographical space in the oil-producing area called the Niger Delta region.

He had educated them that the Niger Delta region was the most inhospitable region in the Nigerian federation and was also the wealthiest region. But the central government, because of its political and economic wickedness, had squandered the region's resources, and the people living in the oil-producing region were deprived of all the good things of life. As a seasoned politician, he played upon the growing despair of the people, who were mostly uneducated and economically disadvantaged. He cried out for justice for them and promised them the heavens. The poor, downtrodden people would one day control their God-given resources.

For the jobless Ijaw man, there would be gainful employment. For the fishermen, there would be enough fresh fish in pollution-free waters. For those in the agricultural sector, the land would be assisted with fertilizers, and there would be enough food on the table and dignity for them all. Most of the time, he brought his listeners to their feet with his passionate and charismatic aura, and even his greatest skeptics knew he was telling the people the *truth*. But the few enlightened ones always took his words with a pinch of salt. Those few knew that "in times of war," as the Churchillian phrase goes, "truth is so sacred that it has to be accompanied always by a bodyguard of lies." To be economical with the truth was the in thing in the brand of politics that was being played in Nigeria at the moment.

Timi was among those few enlightened men wielding guns for him. He knew the chief was not the messiah the Ijaw nation was looking for. Ijawland for a long time now had lacked a truly popular, charismatic leader. To some people, the presence and the aura of Chief Dabiri was the sure sign that their prayer had been answered. But the question on Timi's mind was "Can a truly charismatic national leader be among the clique of the criminal profiteers and oil bunkerers who get what, when, and how from the Niger Delta Crisis?"

"Tell us about the problem, sir," Wuru said, breaking the silence that had enveloped the room for the past few minutes. "We'll handle it."

Chief Dabiri nodded. "I will, Wuru," he said gently. Secretly, the chief admired Wuru. The young man was the most stable, hard-driving youth leader, and he was the commander of the much-talked-about Egbesu Boys, the ethnic militia that had etched the Ijaw name on the world map.

Wuru, as a youth leader, was reputed to be merciless. He had been in most of the fights between the Ijaws and her neighbors. Both the Aladja/Diebiri/Ogbe-Ijaw Crisis of 1995 and the Aladja/Ogbe-Ijaw Crisis of 1996 saw him engaged in action.

On the twenty-fourth of May 1997, Benneth Island, an Itsekiri community, was sacked. He was the one who had led militant youths to the island. For the past seven years, the boy had headed the security unit of Ginger Man Inc., which was one of the largest and most prosperous chains of crude oil smugglers in the Niger Delta creeks. These creeks, which were difficult to police, were the home of lots of the criminal bunkerers and smugglers who used their heavy barges to carry the crude oil out of the country.

But he had actually made his name when he led a group of some thirty heavily armed men and violently seized a Shell oil platform in the creek, preventing the company from carrying out their operations. The incident had been relayed by CNN. A team of naval and army personnel in six gunboats had stormed the platform and rescued the hostages. But he had held the platform hostage for about two weeks.

"The boy's name is Tosan Mayuku," Chief Dabiri said quietly. "He's the bastard behind the attack on my convoy in Warri."

Uneasily, the four young men looked at one another. Timi frowned and then shook his head. He couldn't believe any of this. There were simply too many loose ends, too many coincidences, and too many assumptions. Wuru said he was the one who had killed Conboye. The university teacher said he was the one who burned down his house. Now Chief Dabiri had just said he had been the one behind the attempt on his life. *Could only one man be responsible for all these things mentioned?* he wondered.

The rumors making rounds in Warri were that Chief Aghomi was the man who wanted Chief Dabiri killed. Chief Aghomi was an Itsekiri, but that was not why he had made an attempt on the *Izonebidowei's* life. It was actually because they were both oil bunkerers, and the death of one would make way for the other to fully control the entire network of waterways.

"What do you want us to do with him?" Wuru asked, chewing on his thick lips.

The chief simply said, "Kill him."

The four young men looked at the chief soberly, without comment. But after some minutes of silence, Wuru said, "The man you want us to take, do you have a photograph of him?"

"Yes. I have a photograph of him." The chief reached in an envelope atop the reading desk. He pulled out a photograph. It was actually a passport that had been enlarged.

"This is it."

The four men studied the photograph one after the other. It was unmistakable. It was Tosan, the same person they had been commissioned to kill. And there was no way any of them could know that the photograph was a passport photo stolen from the boy's school file and blown up to a large size.

"You'll be supplied with another photograph before you leave," the older man said quietly. "It's a five by seven and much clearer. I don't want you to hit the wrong man. The right man's what we want."

"Don't worry, sir," Wuru said with a predatory smile. "We already know the bastard. We've been looking for him for the past eight months."

"That's wonderful," the chief said with a roguish twinkle in his brown eyes.

There was silence for a moment.

Suddenly, as if bitten by an insect, Timi stood up and walked away from the others as if he wanted no part of the discussion. From the casual way they were talking, they might have been discussing the sale of a pig or a sheep—anything except the prelude to murder. He absentmindedly fingered the books on the shelf as if looking for a particular volume.

There was a baffling avoidance in his manner. It was detectable. The chief could feel it. The others already knew it. Something was bothering him, and Chief Dabiri could sense it.

"What's the problem with him?"

Wuru shrugged. "Probably the situation in Warri's worrying him."

Chief Dabiri nodded. "Oh, that."

Timi was now standing by the window, a book in his hand. Outside, the immense sky was surprisingly warm and was still looking beautiful, like warm, deep seawater. He knew they were watching him strangely.

"Are you afraid?" The voice was very close to him. Timi turned around and found Chief Dabiri standing not two feet away from him.

"Pardon me, sir. I didn't hear what you just said."

The chief looked deeply at him—read him. In the studied casualness, he saw Timi's fear. "Are you afraid?" he asked again.

Timi shrugged. "Afraid? I don't know." It was the best answer he could come out with. It was not a lie, but neither was it the truth.

"Do you think you can go ahead with this job?"

Timi looked past the chief at Wuru. The commander was looking at him with dark, ugly eyes. He turned to the other two boys. They were also staring at him coldly. He knew he had no choice.

With the appropriate warmth, he said, "I think I can go ahead with it."

He saw the relief in the chief's eyes. He had to disarm whatever suspicion the chief might have about him.

Chief Dabiri walked back to his chair. "What about you, son? Can you do it?" The question was directed at Yellow. Timi knew the chief was asking the question for his benefit.

"It's already done, sir," Yellow replied quietly. He sounded like a model soldier dutifully reacting to the orders of his superior. "The guy's already gone."

The chief nodded. He liked this one; he had nerves of marble and the feel of a killer.

Wuru looked at his watch. "When do you want us to hit him?"

"Not today," Chief Dabiri said slowly. "Not even tomorrow. I want you people to take your time. First get to know where he stays and familiarize yourselves with the area."

"What's the address?"

Chief Dabiri reached into one of the open drawers on the desk and pulled out a small notepad and a tiny stub of a pencil. He scribbled something and handed the piece of paper to Wuru.

"Take this to my aide, Friday. He lives in Lagos Island. My driver will take you boys to him. He knows what to do immediately when he sees it."

"What about tools?"

"Just get in touch with him. He'll provide all that you'll need: the address, the tools, and the car. Even the driver. But the action will be your job."

Wuru nodded.

"You can't afford to fail," the chief said softly. "At the most, he must be wasted by Sunday night. Any questions?"

They all shook their heads except Wuru, who said, "I think I have a question."

"What is it?"

"We don't need a driver. He should just get us the car, the tools, and the address. I think that's all we need."

Chief Dabiri looked at him. Timi also looked at him, but differently. To the chief, he seemed a cold, ruthless man, perfectly prepared to do the job. But Timi was overwhelmed by the sadistic expression of pleasure on his face. A shudder racked his shoulders. The commander was a menace.

"Then you'll case the apartment yourself. My driver will drive you to my boy Friday's place."

"As you say, sir."

The meeting was over. The four young men and the chief stood up. He shook hands with every one of them and escorted them out of the study. In the corridor, they met Ebi. She barely glanced at them. It was Wuru, the man in the rear, who really took a close look at her face and figure. He had seen her before. She was the chief's famous only child. *Such a beautiful girl*, he mused.

Ten minutes later, the four young men stepped out into the hot, silent day.

* * *

Leaving Chief Dabiri's house, the four young men in the Toyota Camry followed the Chief's driver in his Mercedes to Friday's place in Lagos Island. The aide, after he had seen the note, understood everything. He quickly supplied them with the right tools and a navy-blue Audi with all the papers presented. Timi knew it was a stolen car.

It was late when they returned to their hotel in the two separate cars. Immediately when they got to the hotel, they went to their separate rooms. Black Wuru and Timi were sharing a suite, while Yellow and Manager were sharing the room next door.

Half an hour later, Manager and Yellow came to suite 46 and found the two occupants in a heated discussion.

"It's not enough reason," Timi was saying.

"It's a good enough reason!" Wuru yelled in return.

"The Chief's got no reason!" Timi shouted.

"There are so many reasons," Wuru replied. "The lecturer said he was the one who burned down his house. Chief said he was the one who made an attempt on his life. And he's also the one who killed Conboye."

Timi paused for a long time, thinking about what Wuru had just said.

"I'm not sure of any of these. There're no witnesses."

"That's what you say," Wuru said. "Everybody back home knows he was the one who killed Conboye."

"You can't be too sure."

"I don't need to be too sure. I have to make sure that I kill him."

Timi mumbled something incoherent, grinding his teeth.

"What did you say?"

"Madness—that's what I just said. And we don't know our right from our left."

A minute passed in silence. None of the four men said anything. Timi could see Manager's eyes on him. It made him feel uncomfortable. Timi groaned inwardly and turned away from Manager, who now sat on a thin, skeletal chair.

"What's the quarrel about?" Manager asked.

"He says the Chief's lying and that we should forget about the assignment," Wuru said, red-eyed and tired. "And besides that, he said something terrible will happen to us if we go ahead with it."

"Is that what you said, Timi?" Manager demanded.

"Yeah," Timi snapped. "That's what I said."

"Are you saying Chief Dabiri's lying?" Manager's voice was deceptively soft. Like Wuru, he was an ardent admirer of the chief.

Timi nodded.

"Why?"

Timi said angrily, "Here we fight, while the big men live in Abuja and Lagos, our major capital cities, with their families, hundreds of miles away from the violence. But we are the youths. We're the ones with blood on our hands, no money in our pockets, yet daggers drawn at each other's throats. But the *gboguns*, they live in exotic houses, feed on sumptuous meals, drive the most expensive cars—eight hundred miles away from the killing field. They're the ones living fat on the wealth from the land. My friends, what are we fighting for? Who are we fighting for? We're not bunkerers; we don't have vast receipts to carry oil. We're not oil contractors, we're not given multibillion-naira contracts to carry crude oil or tar roads or build bridges that are never completed. By fighting and killing each other, we only assist them in making more money. And what do we get from all this? Just the crumbs that fall off their tables. The government will come and dish out billions of nairas to pacify the elite, but we're too far from the seat of power to get anything. It's those chiefs, those *gboguns* who get everything—by telling us bloody lies, by providing us those bloody tools—while innocent men die in the creeks and on the streets. And we're arrested and accused of the crimes they send us to do, and yet they'll be given national honors, awards, and honorary degrees. We rot in prison cells, yet the *gboguns* are left free to dialogue with the government on our behalf and feed fat on the oil wealth. Brothers, will the creeks of the Niger Delta run endlessly with rivers of blood? Shall we always resort to violence at the slightest provocation—and swallow all the misinformation— continue to burn down our own houses and our own communities, and allow men from Abuja to harvest our wealth? If this is revolution, Wuru, then it's okay. But this is no revolution. This is misinformation. It's madness, and it's clearly branded across the sky. You don't need education to see the sky. You don't need education to understand it. It's madness."

There was deep silence after he had finished speaking. The three boys looked at him oddly.

"Are you really saying the Chief's lying?" Manager asked again.

"What I believe is what I've just said. From most of the information I've heard, it is Chief Aghomi who wanted Chief

Dabiri dead. And we all know the reason. It's because he wants to control the waterways and the entire bunkering business, right down to the Forcados and Escravos areas. So he attacked Chief Dabiri to get him out of the way."

"Maybe Chief Aghomi used Tosan to pull the job," Yellow said.

Timi looked quickly at him. "But you know that's not true. Tosan is no longer in control of the Warri Vanguard. The boy's gone back to school."

The four of them fell silent. It was a long silence that stretched for well over two minutes.

"But you didn't say the Chief was lying when he gave you an opportunity to better your life," Manager said with sarcasm. "When you graduated long ago and there was no job and you were almost starving, you never said he was lying. Now, all of a sudden, you're saying he's lying after he's kept you in work and receiving good money."

Timi chose to ignore him.

But Wuru rose from his chair, came within a foot of Timi, and said, "To tell you the truth, I don't care whether the Chief is telling the truth or not. But I don't believe Tosan is innocent of Conboye's death. And I don't believe he's innocent of all those killings in that school of his. Anyway you look at it, the boy's not a saint. And it's my job to waste him. If not for any other reason, at least for Conboye's death."

Timi shrugged. "You're the commander, so you have to do what you have to do. But the bottom line is that, one, I'm not a hundred percent certain that the boy was behind the assassination attempt. Two, I believe there's more to this thing that we don't really know of. The coincidence is just too damn close."

"You could be right," Yellow said, regarding Timi with a small smile on his lips. He knew that behind that small head of his was an intelligent brain. That was why he was the secretary. But it was becoming obvious that Timi was no longer interested in fighting in the crisis. Maybe it was because they had been declared wanted by security agents and he was afraid for his life.

But the truth was that Chief Dabiri never would have given them this assignment unless he had a very good reason to kill the boy.

"So where do we go from here?" Manager said.

"Where do you think?" Wuru replied. "We're going to the boy's apartment first thing tomorrow morning."

Manager nodded slowly, his small rat-like eyes narrow in what seemed to be silent laughter.

Timi said nothing, but Wuru saw something odd in his eyes. *Is Timi scared?* he wondered. But he doubted it.

Timi was one of millions of Nigerian male graduates caught up in the unemployment bracket. He had graduated and done his national youth service some eight years ago, and since his graduation, he had not gotten a job. He found it difficult to believe that this could be happening to him, a citizen of a country so blessed with the black gold, yet economically and politically mismanaged—a country where able-bodied young men trudged the streets in search of anything to keep them alive. In his own case, he had hustled and written over a hundred employment applications until he stopped counting. He had scouted for jobs in the banks (he had a bachelor of science degree in economics with a good second-class upper-division grade), the civil service, the oil industry, and all other places with no success. Then he had taken up part-time employment with Ginger Man, Inc., the bunkering arm of Chief Dabiri's businesses. At that point Chief Dabiri had been the most powerful oil bunkerer in the Niger Delta. His myriad illegal business activities cut across all the major creeks in the Niger Delta coastline. Back then, Chief

Aghomi hadn't made his mark in the business, and Chief Dabiri had been the major baron—very wealthy, well protected, and also connected with the military government. Then, in March 1997, the Warri Crisis had broken out, the military had sealed the waterways, and it had become too hot for the bunkerers to operate. Unable to get another job that would fetch him the kind of money he was earning in Ginger Man, Inc., Timi had decided to join the newly formed Egbesu Boys of Africa—the red-eyed Ijaw militant youths who were paid as much as fifty thousand naira per trip to enter waterways and raid the riverine Itsekiri communities.

As an idle man, Timi had been fascinated by the job, and the opportunity presented him his first block of five hundred thousand naira cash. The risk was there, but he was more prepared to face it than to stay hungry. As days rolled into weeks, weeks into months, and months into years, Timi had becomes so completely soaked in this new employment that he was traveling across dangerous rivers and deep seas to hijack boats, invade flow stations, and escort oil tankers. And in three years' time, he had become irredeemably initiated into the new spirit of the Niger Delta river, piracy, and the possibilities and wealth that this risky job presented him.

Then, in August 2003, tragedy struck when the WV, in about a dozen speed boats mounted with machine guns, had invaded his village. It was a tiny community in the Benin River area. Sixteen people had been killed. His father was among those who lost their lives. He was devastated. It was then that it had dawned on him what those people must have felt when they lost loved ones in the war. Since then he had become a changed man.

"Timi, we came here to do a job," Wuru said at last. "And we must do it no matter what it takes. The lecturer has his reasons for wanting the guy killed. Chief 'Tade also has his reasons for making sure that he's killed. Personally, I think the guy is responsible for Conboye's death. The young man stinks. I want him, and nothing will stop me from taking him."

"I'm not surprised at anything anymore," Timi said. He walked to the window and looked out into the darkness. "But everything in me tells me that this will be the last job we'll pull together."

"What does that mean?" Wuru said coldly.

Timi considered the question for a while, shrugged, and then said, "You don't see this thing the way I see it. You won't understand."

The others didn't say anything.

That night it rained heavily, and the next morning was chilly and terribly cold. The four young men left the hotel very early in the morning. Wuru drove them in the Toyota. The morning's job was to case the whole of Isolo in search of Tos's apartment. Thereafter they would return with their tools to pull the jobs.

It was about 12:24 p.m. when they finally located the compound. Wuru managed to park the car a few blocks away from the compound. For a long time they studied the compound. When it was a quarter past two, they drove to an upscale restaurant on Sangobiyi Street. It was a quiet street a short distance away. In the restaurant, they took their first meal of the day; and after the meal, well-fed, relaxed, and comfortable, they returned to their hotel, collected their tools, put them in the trunk of the Audi and the Toyota Camry, and began the journey back to Isolo.

By 5:40 p.m. they had secreted the Toyota, their getaway car, on Chesebrough Way, a busy area in Isolo, and forty minutes later they had parked the "borrowed" Audi on Mureni Street. There was a strategic reason for parking the Toyota so far from the premises of the hit. In the next couple of days, there would be frequent changes of cars for feeling out the territory and studying and observing their target.

A few meters ahead of them was parked an old tarpaulin-covered Peugeot station wagon. On the left of the station wagon, around a hundred yards away, stood the two-story brownstone house, quiet in the now-warm evening, freshly painted in cream and white, its windows covered in green-colored glass and orange curtains.

All around, the little town of Isolo spread in all directions, busy and lovely in the evening light. It was a very beautiful May evening. The area, though overly busy, looked very safe and ideal for the job.

The four young men sat in the car, their eyes directed at the house. They were in no hurry. They were willing to wait for a long time.

* * *

It was getting near seven o'clock the next day when Ebi was awakened, and she sat up with a start, an uneasy coldness blanketing her. For quite some time now, she hadn't been able to get a good sleep. She couldn't even coordinate her thoughts. Every day of the past week, she had been thinking of only one thing: Tosan. She wanted to see him. She needed his presence much more than anyone could imagine. The thought of not seeing him again was like the thrust of a knife into her heart.

She closed her eyes and imagined him in the room. She imagined him in the bed. His fingers were caressing her, gently running erotically over her breasts, and her supple young body was responding. Her body was warm. Suddenly it was no longer her imagination. Suddenly he was very real. He was in the bed.

He was kissing her, and she was enjoying every bit of it. Then he stopped. Then he was gone. The room was again empty. She opened her eyes reluctantly. She knew it had been her imagination. He had never been in the room. She really wanted to see him. She wanted to travel with him, or at least say goodbye to him before his traveling.

She stared quietly around the luxuriously appointed bedroom with dark, empty eyes. She was unhappy. Her mood was not helped by the fact that in a few hours' time, Tos would be traveling out of the country. And that was what was disturbing her.

That was part of what had woken her from sleep. It also seemed that she was disturbed by something else. It seemed that her fright was a presentiment of danger. *Is Tosan in danger?* she wondered. *No. Tosan can't be in danger,* she reassured herself. *Tosan's in his apartment. And by tomorrow he'll be in New York.*

She lay on the bed for quite some time, watching the dusk creeping into darkness, and then suddenly she got out of the bed, slipped on a flowered wrap, and went to the large Lalique window. The estate was spread out magnificently before her. Immediately below her was the flower garden, and a little beyond was a terrace where she could see some of her father's security guards. They were pacing to and fro, rifles slung across their shoulders.

She stood in the bedroom window for a long time, drenched in the perfumed fragrance emanating from the garden below her. She had perfected her plans. Already Agnes had spirited her travel bag out of the compound to her cousin's friend's place. Musa, the *maiguard*, was in the know. They all knew that the "small madam," the bird in the gilded cage, was dying inside the cage, and they were willing to help her, even when they knew that their actions could cost them their jobs. But Ebi had made available a handsome amount of money to take care of their immediate financial needs in case they were let go for helping her.

She turned away from the window and went straight to the closet, and in less than fifteen minutes she was fully clothed. She went back to the window and stared into the darkness. She saw one of the guards light a cigarette and pass something, probably a lighter, to his colleague, who also lit a cigarette. She could see about half a dozen of them—all of them uniformed in black and khaki attire, and well armed. They were in the compound to protect her father from another assassination attempt. When Chief Bola Ige had been killed, he had contracted two men to guard him. When Harry Marshall also had been killed, he had doubled the security men to four. Then an attempt had been made on his life in Warri. That was when he had contracted the private security company to arrange for another twenty men around him. If a justice minister and other top politicians could be killed like *okada* riders, then nobody was safe in the country.

Already she had seen the commander of the security men. She had given him an envelope containing four thousand dollars, and another envelope containing twenty one-hundred-dollar bills would follow later. With the falling rate of the naira, that would be some cool cash for them. It was enough motivation, for that they would allow her to take a short stroll out of the compound. That was what she had told them. They were not aware that Agnes and Musa had ferried some of her things out of the compound.

It seemed that the men were in dire need of money, and going by the exchange rate, the six thousand dollars was a wee bit juicy. The plan was to get her out of the compound so that she could spend a few hours with her lover, who was traveling to America the next day. Two of the security men would escort her to the house they planned to use as the meeting place. And later in the morning, at about 5:00a.m., they would come back to collect her.

She needed to get out of the compound. She knew that if she stayed there another day longer, she would go quite crazy.

She heard a sound just then. It startled her, startled the darkness and quietness around her. It was his bird—darkness bird. An owl. Tos's mascot. *What's an owl doing in my father's compound?* she wondered. *Or does it mean that it's time for me to go?*

She turned away from the window, and when she stared at the bedroom clock, she saw it was a quarter past seven.

When it was a quarter past eight, she left her room and as quickly as possible made her way downstairs.

* * *

It was a warm May night with a bright moon in the sky overhead. The four men sat huddled inside the car. Every half hour for the past four hours, one of them would leave the car and, after a while, return. The message he would relay was always the same: "Not yet back." And they would all sit in the darkness, waiting patiently.

For over thirty-eight hours, they had staked out the building, particularly during the early hours of the morning and late at night. Thrice tonight Manager and Yellow had strolled past house number 37, observing it closely. Timi had refused to leave the car.

They all knew the job would not prove difficult. Police patrol of the area was routine, and the young men actually appreciated it that way. The compound did not have a fence, and the area didn't have the vigilante groups that guarded most areas these days. Tosan would be taken easily.

Six times in the past forty-eight hours, they had spotted him leaving the compound in company of two other boys. Each of those times, they had been tempted to pull the job, but Wuru had restrained them. He said he was not in a hurry. He said he wanted the meeting between him and Tosan to be face-to-face.

Tedious as it was, they had spent the last couple of days observing the area. Every five hours, they had switched positions as carefully and as casually as they could. The Toyota would stay for around three hours, and then it would disappear. Some five hours later, the Audi would appear and park on another part of the street, observing, and sometimes they would drive casually around the area, observing things.

They knew the area in and out now. They knew who went where. They knew who the early risers were. They knew who the late risers were. They knew who came and left immediately and who lingered behind.

Most of all, they had created a pattern about Tos. He was always in the company of the two young men. He never went anywhere without them. From the way they were behaving, it was obvious that they were his friends from the university.

This night there was little movement in the street—an occasional *okada*, a bicycle, and a handful of people walking by—mostly men hurrying home from late work or unfaithful husbands returning home from their girlfriends' places. A few lovers were holding hands and necking in dark corners. A dog barked periodically from the rail-fenced compound a few yards away.

At exactly the time Ebi was changing her clothes that evening, Aunt Yemi arrived at the compound. They all watched her with interest as she locked her car, a red Nissan Bluebird, and entered the compound in the company of a little boy.

"What do you think?" Manager asked.

"We'll wait for another thirty minutes. Then one of us will go in and pretend that he's Tosan's friend from the university—a guy who came from a very faraway place and does not have a place to stay or money to transport himself back."

"You're a genius, Wuru," Yellow said.

"I've planned everything in my mind."

They waited in the darkness for another thirty minutes. The inside of the car was getting hot, and the wait quite boring.

Timi was sweating slightly, his face grim but set. The others had told him to learn to hate. *But how could I?* he wondered. Hatred, he knew, is a disease. It eats away the sanity of a man, it disfigures the way a man shapes his thought, it cripples the direction of his rationality, and then it ends it and finally destroys the individual.

"It's time to go," Wuru said.

"Who'll handle it?" Yellow asked.

"Can't you do it?" Manager asked.

There was a pause. "Timi should do it instead. He's the educated one." It was Yellow who said this.

"I'm not going to do it," Timi said quickly.

"I'll do it then," Manager said.

"No. Lakemfa should do it."

Yellow briefly considered what the commander had just said and then shrugged.

"Good. Are you set?"

Yellow nodded.

"Now listen very carefully. Don't rush it. Go in quietly, convincingly, as a friend of Tosan. Try as much as possible to win her trust. I suspect that Tosan will not be back until sometime later. Are you set?"

Yellow nodded again, opened the door, and disappeared into the compound.

* * *

Yellow punched the doorbell again and waited. He had been punching it for the past two minutes, but nobody had answered him. He could see light inside the sitting room.

Just as he was about to punch it again, from somewhere in the house he heard a strong, loud female voice.

"Who's there?" the voice queried.

"It's somebody…please."

Aunt Yemi threw the door open. "So you're the one who's been disturbing my bell. Do you want to ruin it?"

Yellow smiled and nodded as if he found what she had just said funny.

"What do you want?" Aunt Yemi demanded. It was obvious that she was not in a smiling mood.

"I'm a friend of Tosan. I need to see him."

"You're from where?"

"I came from Jankara, I mean the university, and now it seems that he's not around."

"This is an odd hour to call on somebody. This area is not too friendly right now."

"I'm sorry, Madam. Nightfall met me in town, and I don't even have extra cash on me to take me to my destination. I thought I would see Tosan here and spend the night with him."

"Tosan will be back soon. I believe he just went for a stroll. You can hang around."

"Can I come in and wait for him?"

The old woman gazed at the boy, eyeing him suspiciously. "Wait for him? Here?"

Yellow nodded and stared around him helplessly. "I don't know anywhere else to go. I can't go back to the university. The school has been closed down, and I don't know anybody around here that'll shelter me for the night."

Aunt Yemi nodded. Everybody who had been following the news was aware of the heavy fight that had taken place in the university town of Jankara recently. The university was closed down. That was the reason why her nephew had come back early from school.

She looked closely at the boy. He looked every inch like a student. He was well dressed in neat trousers, a well-pressed shirt, a large jacket, and a nice tie. It didn't occur to her that the boy was not carrying a bag.

"Since you said you've come from that long distance, you had better come inside."

Five minutes later, she opened the burglary-proofed entrance protection gate and allowed the boy to enter her sitting room.

"Sit down. Make yourself comfortable."

Yellow nodded and took one of the soft easy chairs. He looked around him. The room was large, cool, and quiet, save for the soft music issuing from the TV set. There was a profusion of good quality furniture and high-class electronic appliances, and green carpet cut in a thick vegetation pattern. The walls were adorned with numerous framed photographs and three paintings of varied shades.

From somewhere inside the house, Yellow heard the sound of a boy's voice.

Aunt Yemi was staring at him. Her mind was working. He was handsome. He had a nice, open face.

"Can I get you something?"

"A glass of cold water, if you don't mind."

"No. I don't mind at all," Aunt Yemi said, and she walked out of the room.

When she came back a few minutes later, Yellow was looking at the TV set. She handed the glass to him, and he thanked her courteously.

Yellow downed the water. It was cool on his thirsty tongue. He set the now empty, steaming glass on the coffee table.

"What really happened at that school of yours?" Aunt Yemi asked casually.

Yellow sighed and crossed his legs in a casual fashion.

"It was some useless people. Cultists. They were fighting themselves and killing people. And the—"

"Who's killing people?"

Yellow stopped. He looked toward the voice, startled. A small boy had entered the room and was staring at him. He was about ten years old.

"Who's killing people?" the boy repeated.

Yellow smiled good-naturedly. "Good question. Some bad people are killing themselves."

"Is my Uncle Tos a bad people?" the boy asked innocently.

Yellow still kept smiling at the boy. "No. Your uncle's a very good person." He paused. "What's your name?"

"Kola," the boy said, smiling broadly. "And what's yours?"

"William," Yellow lied smoothly.

Aunt Yemi smiled apologetically and said, "Kola, go and do your homework."

It was as if the boy didn't hear her. He had stepped forward a little.

"My Uncle Tos is a good person," he said. "And he's a wonderful painter."

"Yeah," Yellow agreed, not knowing what he was agreeing to.

"And he's going to America tomorrow," the little boy said with the proper pride of a youngster whose relative had been given the opportunity to travel to God's own country.

"Really?" Yellow asked quietly.

"Didn't you know?" Aunt Yemi asked immediately.

The directness of the question at first seemed to unsettle Yellow. But it was only for a brief moment.

"Yeah. I remember now. He did mention it. I didn't know it was this soon."

Aunt Yemi looked at Yellow quietly. The way the boy had answered the question had stirred something inside of her. Even Yellow caught a fleeting sign of caution.

"Come and see that picture," Kola said and pointed to a sofa-size framed canvas hanging on the wall. "My Uncle Tos painted it. But he gave it to me as a gift."

Yellow stood up and walked across the room toward the painting. When he was within a foot of it, he stopped and observed it.

He studied the picture for a moment while the two other people in the room—the little boy and the woman—stared at him quietly.

Yellow, despite himself, was impressed. This was the first time in his life he had seen an original painting by an original painter. It was real. He really didn't know what a good picture looked like. But all his instincts told him this one must be it.

The coastal scene depicted in the picture looked familiar. It was as if the spirit of some strange force was lurking behind each neatly drawn line.

He turned away from the picture. "Are you sure your Uncle Tosan's the one who painted this picture?" He had bent over at the waist to bring his face to Kola's level.

The boy nodded.

Yellow shook his head as if he couldn't quite believe him.

"Are you sure?"

"His name's written on the bottom." The little boy's voice was strong and proud.

Yellow looked closely again at the painting and saw the name. It was signed neatly in deep black ink.

He seemed to gather himself before he spoke again, and the words were directed at the little boy.

"Your Uncle Tosan's a very good painter."

Kola smiled. It was a very broad smile.

"So you didn't know your friend's a painter, too?" Aunt Yemi asked. Her voice was not very friendly this time. It was curious, suspicious. The boy's behavior had abruptly stirred some element of suspicion in her.

Yellow didn't reply. He was staring at the little boy. He didn't know how he felt about the boy. There was something precocious about the little imp—something like awareness and enlightenment. He couldn't be more than ten years old. Perhaps twelve years, but not a day older. He was very precocious and brilliant, and heartbreakingly innocent.

"Is he your son?" Yellow's voice was not friendly now.

Strangely, Aunt Yemi had an inkling that the inquiry was really about Tosan, not Kola.

"He's my grandson."

"He's a very lovely boy," Yellow said, his eyes focused on the painting.

Aunt Yemi was flattered. "He's actually a naughty boy." And abruptly she said rather sternly to the little boy, "Kola, go and do your homework."

The boy nodded and dashed out of the room.

"Tosan's a very good painter," Yellow said, and he went back to his seat.

Aunt Yemi knew the boy was hiding something. He was leading her on. But she nodded and smiled briefly.

"Tosan's highly talented. And we're very proud of him."

There was a moment of uneasy silence.

"You haven't answered my question," Aunt Yemi said pointedly.

"What question?" Yellow asked quietly.

"You said you're Tosan's friend from the university, but it's as if you didn't know he's a painter."

Yellow didn't seem disturbed by the question. His voice was controlled when he said, "The picture reveals another creative aspect of Tosan's talents."

Aunt Yemi didn't say anything for a while. She wanted the boy to believe he had made a fool of her.

"Can I get you something to eat?"

Yellow shook his head. "Thank you. I'm not hungry. I ate something on the way before getting here."

Aunt Yemi stood up. "Excuse me, then. Let me fetch something in the kitchen."

Immediately after she was out of sight, Yellow stood up abruptly and went to the window. He stood like that, looking outside. The street was dark. He could see the car, their car, but he couldn't see inside it.

Aunt Yemi silently came back into the room.

"What are you doing?"

Yellow abruptly whipped around and pulled a gun out from the roomy pocket of his jacket.

"*Egbami* o!" Aunt Yemi screamed.

Infuriated, Yellow covered the distance between them, slapped her hard in the face, and ordered her not to make any noise.

Though she was stunned, she nodded. She was stunned not because of the slap but more because of the gun. She couldn't believe it. *A gun!* She had never seen a gun in the hand of a civilian before in her life. But the boy was carrying one, and he was pointing it carelessly at her. She wanted to scream again, but she knew she couldn't. She wouldn't. It would only worsen everything. She was practically trapped.

On hearing his grandmother's scream, Kola dashed into the living room. He saw his granny lying on the floor and the boy with the gun standing over her. *This must be a bad person*, he thought. Kola, small as he was, rushed maddeningly at the assailant. He really had so much energy packed inside his small frame. He collapsed into Yellow, screaming, pinching, biting. Yellow managed to subdue him by giving him a very violent slap on the right cheek. The force of the slap caused one of the boy's teeth to fall out of his mouth.

Wuru and the others in the car also heard the scream. It came once. They had heard it because all their attention was focused on the apartment. Wuru and Manager came out of the car at once and quickly and quietly sneaked into the compound. Ten minutes later, Yellow opened the burglary-proofed entrance protection gate, and they both entered the apartment.

The woman was still lying on the floor, her grandson's head lying on her lap. Wuru took in the situation. He was satisfied. Yellow had handled it pretty well. There hadn't been much of a scuffle. After he had satisfied himself that all was well, he ordered Yellow to go back to the car to relieve Timi. He didn't trust Timi out there alone.

Yellow nodded and left the apartment quickly. Ten minutes later, Timi entered the apartment, and Manager locked the burglary-proofed door.

Alone in the car with an AK-47, a Colt M-16A2 American automatic rifle, and a Heckler & Koch G3 rifle, all of them fully loaded, Yellow was equipped to handle the entire area in case of any violent surprises.

* * *

At exactly the time the drama was playing itself out in Aunt Yemi's living room, Tos was in a wine bar and restaurant with his two companions, the two armed men who were staying with him until he traveled. They were drinking Baileys Irish Cream and discussing in hushed tones. They were companionable drunks, his two bodyguards. This would be their last night together, and they had decided to drink themselves stupid, go home, and sleep till morning.

* * *

Ebi ordered the driver of the taxicab to drop her off at Mureni Street, in front of Tos's residence. She paid him his fare, crossed the street, and entered the compound. She walked right past the borrowed Audi. From inside the car, Yellow watched her enter the compound. He punched a few numbers into his cell phone and said, "A girl has just entered the building."

"Don't worry. We've seen her" was Wuru's reply.

Ebi had opened the steel outer hallway door with the spare key Tos had given her. She shut it. Fatigue flowed through her so that she leaned back against the cold steel door and closed her eyes. Weariness, like vapor, drained out of her. She had managed to lug her bag up the staircase. She had seen the light in Aunt Yemi's apartment, but she had decided not to disturb the poor lady.

When she entered Tos's apartment, she pushed the bag inside and looked around her. It had been a long time since she had been in the room. It was neat and tidy, and very empty of human presence. Tos wasn't at home. She had not seen his car. *Or could he have sold it?* she wondered. He had told her that he just might leave it to his cousin, the banker.

She knew Tos wouldn't be home for at least another hour. He was a night owl. She suspected that he had gone to a wine bar or a nightclub somewhere, drinking flagrantly expensive wine.

She flicked on the TV set. The *Super Story* program was on. She lowered the volume, went to the bedroom, quickly took off her clothes, and went straight to the bathroom. She spent some twenty minutes there, and later she dried herself with Tos's well-used towel and slipped on one of his clean striped shirts.

Her coming here had been one hell of a game. The two security men had dropped her, as planned, at the apartment in Lagos Island. They had even entered the apartment just to be sure that she had entered one of the rooms. The apartment belonged to a friend of a cousin of Agnes. The guy even hugged her in the doorway just to convince the security men who were watching that he was indeed her lover. Immediately after they were gone, the guy had called a taxicab for her, and that was how she had made it to Tos's apartment.

On the television set, a late-night movie was playing. Because she was not interested, she didn't bother to increase the volume. She looked out the window, looking for Tos. She had warned him about this night habit of his. At least he had to be home before nine o'clock. But the Tos she knew had once told her to mind her own business because he was a big boy who could take care of himself.

She was hungry, so she went to the kitchen and began to put a simple meal together. It would be two hours later that three figures in jeans and loafers would drive into the compound. And one of the occupants of the car would be Tos.

* * *

The black BMW drove into the compound, parked beside Aunt Yemi's car, and three people exited it. Tos rested for a moment on the door of the car. He was weaving. The last bottle of the malt whiskey they had shared was beginning to get to his head, to his soul, lifting his spirit higher than ever before, transporting him to new level. He thought of the phone conversation he had had with Frank Reese. Everything was set. There had been only a minor adjustment to the plan. Instead of arriving through John F. Kennedy International Airport, he would now arrive through Newark Liberty International Airport. Newark was just some fifteen miles from Midtown, and some seventeen miles away from

Kennedy International. So the plans, more or less, remained the same. It was only left for him now to board the plane the next day. That alone could give one a heady high. That alone was life—and he was prepared to soak it up, taste it, feel it, and eat it. *I feel good!* he wanted to scream like James Brown, but he was too drunk even to scream.

By God, he wanted to say. *I'm going to strike it rich in America. I want to make my first million in dollars.*

He could feel it now: the godlike satisfaction of seeing his future. It was a powerful pleasure, a unique feeling of knowing where he would be in the next twenty-four hours. Already he could see New York. Within his mind's sight was a gigantic city with gigantic superstructures, broad superhighways, and busy, overfed, well-dressed Americans. For the moment, he tried to find the right Itsekiri word for this feeling of lightheartedness, but he couldn't. Instead he thought of Ebi. It was a pity he would not be able to say goodbye to her. She was temporarily gone from his life. It was really sad. She had been a great help. He remembered the discussion they had had some time back in his apartment. He had said, "Do you know the first words I'll say if I get off the plane in New York?"

Ebi had said, "No. You tell me."

"I'll say, Okay New York, you've just swallowed another artistic and creative talent from Naija. But I hope you'll let me rule Madison Avenue; allow me to display my work in the Museum of the City of New York and the Metropolitan Museum of Art."

"Why do you think New York has swallowed Nigerian talents?"

"Have you not heard? It's a cliché. Brain drain. There are more Nigerian writers in America than there are in Nigeria. There are more Nigerian doctors in New York than there are in the whole of Nigeria. And of course they have a valid reason for being there.

But the consolation is this: one day they're going to rule America; they'll put somebody there in the White House. It'll be beautiful."

Ebi had laughed then. "When hell's frozen," she had said.

Tos looked around him. That had been some weeks ago. But this was the present. And everywhere was in partial darkness. The cool naturalness of the star-filled night flooded his soul. The wind was chilly, and he inhaled the unpolluted fresh air deeply, taking in more than his fair share of it. He stared at the sky. This was Nigeria. *And it's a wonder that I'm still alive and kicking after all that I've been through. It's my esimi. God! How beautiful life is. How close the moon is, and the stars looking like jeweled specks in the sky.* Staring at nature, feeling it—it all gave him a sense of weightlessness, peacefulness, and lightheartedness. He closed the car's door and slowly, as if counting his steps, walked into the hallway and closed the heavy steel door behind him. The other two boys were already climbing the staircase. He took hold of the handrail and carefully began to climb after them.

*   *   *

In Aunt Yemi's apartment downstairs, the three young men were standing close to the window. They had seen the car drive into the compound, and Wuru had had his first very close sight of Tosan for a long time. He found himself swooning. The sight of him alone fired his anger, and it made him nurse the hatred, letting it gather momentum. He drew on it to drug his heart. The unrelenting fury burned like coal within his chest. It was great self-control that stopped him from squeezing the trigger. The truth was that he wanted to see Tosan eyeball-to-eyeball. He wanted to ask him the singular question, Are you the one who killed Conboye? And he wanted to see the fear in his eyes. He wanted him to be aware—to know that he was about to die.

He left the window, went back to the chair, and sat down. He didn't say anything for a while.

When he finally raised his head, he was surprised to see Timi still standing in front of the painting as if in a trance.

"What's Timi doing?" Wuru asked carefully.

Manager shrugged. Like Wuru, he was intrigued by the intensity of Timi's interest in the picture—a painting that was nothing more than an evocative, unpretentious large oil of a town's coastal scene. He couldn't understand how a mere picture could evoke such a feeling in the observer.

Wuru stood up abruptly and walked up to Timi. He stood just a little behind him, and he, too, stared at the painting.

Timi moved closer, as if to see something that was not clear in the painting. Wuru stared at him, and Manager stared at both of them. Only Wuru could see Timi's face. It was a face that was deeply enthralled by the painting he was observing. Wuru knew that Timi was a lover of art and that he had the eye of a professional curator.

To say the painting enraptured Timi was an understatement. It was the first thing he had seen when he had stepped foot in the apartment. It was the most vivid painting he had ever seen in his entire life. It was executed with psychedelic, bold force so that it looked as if a great master had painted it. The colors were neatly organized and exquisitely blended, and there was no object in the picture that lacked depth or distance. It was a complex picture, technically painted. It was obviously the best picture in the room, and Timi was surprised by his own response to it.

"What's so special in this picture that you seem lost in it?"

Timi jumped, obviously jerked from his trance by Wuru's voice.

"What did you say?" Timi asked.

Wuru spoke in Ijaw. "What's so special about this picture?"

"It's a picture of Warri," Timi replied in English.

"Warri?" Wuru asked doubtfully.

"Yes. It's the Alderstown area," Timi said quietly. "Look, see here." He touched the picture. "This was my family's house." He indicated one of six or seven large houses strung out along the deep black line of a wide river. "This was my home." He tapped the house symbolically. "This was Chief Pessu's compound, and this one,"—he touched another ancient-looking house—"was Prince Atsemudiara's house. It used to be the first and best house in this entire area several years back. This was Mallori's house. This should be Obahor's house. And this was Chief Dore's house. And this was the Aladura church my family used to attend."

Wuru stared at the painting. He still couldn't fathom the object of Timi's deep concentration.

"These are Itsekiri houses," he said at last.

"But this is Obahor's house, and this is my father's house," Timi insisted. "Obahor is Urhobo."

"But your father's house is no longer there," Wuru countered. "It's been destroyed. And I doubt if Obahor's house still exists."

Timi didn't answer him. All his focus was still on the painting. He had been unprepared for the powerful feeling the picture had aroused in him. He believed it was what the French called déjà vu.

He stared closely at the church building with the large white cross on the roof. He knew every inch of that church. It was the only church he knew. It was the church he had grown up in. It was the church where he had been christened and baptized. He knew every secret corner, every secret entranceway of that church. As a child growing up in Warri, that very old church in Market Road, that old whitewashed block edifice, had been his major playground. It was well over four years since he had set foot in this part of Warri, and seeing it in a painting now made him look like a little boy. It was so strange, and he was so surprised to see his birthplace on canvas. Looking at it now, emotion washed over him.

The painting was alive. The heavily emphasized familiar buildings were bold and colorful; their roofs, painted in deep brown ink, depicted the harsh African sun. The people were artfully drawn. It was a superb painting, a picture that seemed to speak one word—"peace," a distinct word trying to make an impression on the minds of the inhabitants of a violent city.

The Warri River was well illustrated, with local boats floating on the still waters. This was the river where, as little children, they used to fish and swim—youths of all ethnic nationalities swimming and fishing together.

He knew every inch of that area. Chief Pessu's house was that white one with the brown roof on the sharp corner of Market Road. Timi's own father's house was a few blocks away. Timi's family, the Pereweibinas, was well integrated, like most of the old families of the area they now called Old Warri. The family house had been built long before Delta State was created. It was one of the first modern houses in that part of the oil city. But it was no more. It was one of the hundreds of choice properties that had been caught up in the war. Now there was not a single Ijaw family living in the area.

But all the same, he knew the painting was speaking of a time when no house was marked with the signpost of false ethnic identification. *Or were they?* he wondered.

He searched for an ethnic identification. There was none. There were no Ijaw or Itsekiri or Urhobo houses. It was simply Old Warri before the crisis—a land of peace. That should have been what the signpost read; that was the only guide for the oil city to march forward, to press on toward its future. Timi smiled. This picture was a chart toward that direction. It was a pity that

Wuru and Manager did not know the import of this painting—its meaning and significance.

"Why are you smiling?" Manager said.

"You wouldn't understand," Timi replied, his voice laced with the tinge of nostalgia. It was the truth. Wuru and Manager would not understand the sudden wave of longing this painting had inspired in him. Though Timi conceded that it was partly out of context, the painter had tried his best to express his own perception of the area.

"I think you like it because your home was painted in the picture," Manager said.

Timi smiled weakly. "I think I like it for other reasons," he replied.

"Did the artist do justice to it?" This was from Wuru.

Timi considered the question for a moment; then he studied the painting again, looking at the familiar houses. He was deep in thought. After a long while he said,

"I think artistically it was beautifully done. I guess it was painted before the war. The area, I am told, is different today. My father's house is no longer there. And the painter, I guess, took certain liberties. But it's a great picture. It's really an original work. And I commend the painter's attention to the small details, as well as the overarching vision." He shook his head as if to clear his thoughts. "Christ! To have such talent! Where did you buy this picture?" The question was directed at Aunt Yemi.

The old woman ignored him.

Timi walked to where she was lying. He studied her quietly for a whole minute, and then he said, almost in a whisper, "I don't want to force it out of you, madam, but can you tell me where you bought this painting?"

Aunt Yemi considered the question for a few seconds, and then she said, "I didn't buy it. My nephew painted it."

"Your nephew? Who's your nephew?"

"Tosan."

"Tosan?"

She nodded.

Timi was surprised. This piece of information overwhelmed his mind. He looked first at Manager, then at Wuru. The commander shrugged and then said, "If you like it, you can take it."

Timi hesitated.

"Don't you want to take it?" Manager prompted.

Timi was tempted. The painting was magnificent. To own such a piece of artwork, such a force on canvas! It was something he would have loved to own.

But he shook his head instead, smiled regretfully, walked to one of the low, comfortable armchairs, and lowered himself into it and stretched out his legs. He glanced quietly at the prisoners. He felt a cold shiver run through him. With consciousness of mind, he had engaged himself in this madness. An assignment, they had called it. But madness he knew it to be. He wanted the whole affair to be over as quickly as possible. He didn't consider himself a part of it.

He looked at Wuru. The commander's face was very still, an ebony mask. He wondered what thought lay under that mask. There was something chilly and distant about Wuru now. Clearly he was obsessed with the spirit of vengeance.

Timi glanced furtively at Manager. The chief of staff's face was imponderably blank. He was sitting across from them. He carried the only big weapon in the room. It was a G3 rifle. He held it casually but possessively with both hands, so that it was resting on his knee. In that casual stance, he looked every inch like a soldier. His head was held high, and a meaningless smile was playing pranks with his lips. The feel of the gun intoxicated him.

Everything about him seemed organized and energized by the feel of the gun. He was ready for action and wanted it now.

* * *

"Is this the ideal time to come home, Picasso?"

Tos and his two bodyguards stood in the doorway, staring unbelievingly at the girl.

"Boy oh boy! Now this is one beautiful female I really needed to see," Tos said, and he stood there grinning that silly, meaningless grin of his. "Come on, sweetheart. Come on, give your old man a kiss."

Ebi rushed into his arms, her arms holding tight to his wide shoulders.

"I miss you terribly, baby," Tos groaned, his hands moving all over her body like tree limbs, squeezing her and pressing himself into her.

Ganiyu and Gafaru were watching them, smiling stupidly.

Tos broke the embrace and let his eyes run up and down Ebi's beautiful figure. She was the last person he had been expecting to see tonight. She had really been in his arms when he had embraced her. He had thought he was imagining things.

He just stood there, staring unbelievingly at her.

She stared back at him. She hadn't realized how much she had missed him—his touch, and especially that sweet, sexy smile of his that set her heart on fire. She knew she could not deceive herself. She loved him like crazy. She couldn't stay here in Nigeria after he had gone.

"Is this what we're going to do all night, Picasso," she said lightly, "stare at each other?"

"No, baby," Tos replied. He swept her off her feet and kissed her hungrily. She was wearing her favorite perfume. He remembered the fragrance clearly.

She knew he was drunk. He smelled of alcohol. He was always drinking. But she was not going to complain tonight.

"Sorry guys. My lady's around, so I'll leave the sitting room to you gentlemen. Good night." Stepping inside the bedroom and still holding onto Ebi, Tos kicked the door shut with his foot and placed her right down in the middle of the bed.

Ten minutes later, they were making love, as in the days when they had lived in her apartment in Jankara. And that had been many weeks ago.

* * *

It was a quarter past midnight when Wuru stood up suddenly. He took out a heavy handgun and walked to where the woman and the child were sitting.

"Do you realize what this is?" he asked the woman.

Aunt Yemi didn't reply. She was staring at him, frightened.

"Don't be scared. You're free to speak. Tell me the name of the thing in my hand."

In a faint voice, the woman said, "It's a gun."

"Good," Wuru said in his thick, heavy voice. "Now listen carefully. This gun is fully loaded, and from here or anywhere around here, I can't miss. Do you understand that?"

The woman nodded.

"We're not here to harm you. There's a boy living right now in this house. He has an apartment upstairs. That's who we're looking for."

"Who?" Aunt Yemi asked dully.

"Your nephew Tosan."

Aunt Yemi swallowed.

"I want you to go upstairs and bring him down here."

"I don't think I can do—"

"Look, madam, we've come a long way to do the job. We've seen you with him a couple of times. And you just told us he's your nephew. I know you can bring him here to us. But if you think we're playing—"

"But I cannot bring —"

"This is no child's play," Wuru warned.

"I know, but I cannot bring him here. I cannot force him downstairs."

Wuru moved away from her a little. "You won't force him. Simply tell him that your little boy here is sick or dying and you need Tosan's help to take him to the hospital. He's a nice boy. He'll follow you downstairs."

Aunt Yemi thought about what he had said for a whole minute, but her mind was working haphazardly. Finally she shook her head. "I don't think I can bring him down."

Wuru glanced at Manager and said something to him, a stream of hurried words falling over each other. It was the language she had heard them speak several times.

Manager stepped forward, lowered the barrel of his gun at the little boy, and said: "If you don't do as you're told, I'll shoot him dead." He didn't say the words loudly, but the threat was clearly spelled out. He wanted her to know that he was a different cast of character than Wuru, that he was not ashamed to be pointing his gun at the little boy, and that he was capable of pulling the trigger.

The little boy broke into tears.

Aunt Yemi glanced at her grandchild and then at Manager. She sensed that he meant what he had said. She dreaded him more than the one who appeared to be their leader. And he was the one carrying the biggest gun. The other one, who had spent some time studying the picture, looked as if he was not part of the whole episode.

"Don't shoot him," she said. Her words felt empty even to her own hearing. "I'll get him."

Wuru smiled a cold smile. "Thank you. I can see that now you're using your head." Oddly, from the way he said the words, it was as if there were some measure of sadness and kindness in him.

Aunt Yemi stood up and glanced sideways at her grandchild. Then, turning to walk away, she said over her shoulder, "Please do not hurt my grandson."

The three boys watched her leave the apartment without answering.

* * *

A sharp, insistent rapping came on the iron door. After about two minutes, a rough male voice said, "Who's there?"

"Aunt Yemi—I'm the landlady."

The heavy iron door was pushed open, and Gafaru stood there.

"Sorry to bother you, but I want to see Tosan." Aunt Yemi's voice was small and weak.

"Tosan? At this hour?" Gafaru looked at his wristwatch in the poor light of the hallway. "Madam, do you know what the time is?"

Aunt Yemi nodded. The hallway was filled with the strong, acrid smell of marijuana. "I know. I just want to see him quickly. I *must* see him quickly."

"Tosan's sleeping," another voice said from the dark hallway. It was Ganiyu's voice.

"I thought you boys were aware that Tosan is my nephew. I'm more or less a mother to him. And I want to see my son. It's urgent."

Gafaru looked at Ganiyu, and Ganiyu looked at Gafaru.

"Very well then," Gafaru said at last. "Come right in." He opened the door wide for the woman, and Ganiyu guided her up the staircase with Gafaru following closely behind. Immediately when they entered the sitting room, Ganiyu went straight toward Tos's bedroom.

In the darkness, Tos and Ebi lay stark naked on the large bed. Ebi's head was lying on his shoulder. They were still trying to get back their energy after the steamy round of sex they had had. Through the heavy oak door came a loud, embarrassed cough. Then there was quiet knocking.

"Who's out there?" Tos called loudly from the bed.

"It's me, my lord." Tos recognized the voice. It was Ganiyu's loud, rough voice.

"Is anything the problem, Ganiyu?"

"Yeah. I think the landlady wants a word with you. She says it's urgent."

Tos sprang from the bed, pulled on his jeans, zipped up carelessly, and threw a red T-shirt across his shoulders.

He opened the door and found Ganiyu resting against the wall.

"What is it?"

Ganiyu did not say a word. Instead he pointed to the lady standing in the middle of the sitting room. Tos came out of the bedroom, shutting the door behind him. He walked to his aunt, placed his hand across her shoulders, led her to a chair, and sat across from her.

"What's the matter, Auntie?" he asked promptly.

"Nothing," came the quick reply. Tos knew the reply was too quick, and it posed more questions than it had answered.

"But you were crying. Your eyes are red."

"I'm just tired; that is all."

Tos stared at her. *This is odd*, he was thinking. "I hope you're not weeping because of this traveling business of mine."

Aunt Yemi shook her head.

"Where's Kola?"

Aunt Yemi hesitated briefly. "He is downstairs. He's sleeping."

Tos looked suspiciously at her. The other two boys were staring at the woman strangely.

Just then Ebi came out of the bedroom. Over her beautiful figure she wore a cerulean terrycloth robe tied at the waist. Even through the roomy robe, her derriere was sensually pronounced.

She took a seat near the one on which Tos was sitting and placed one of her hands on his lap.

Tos was still staring at his aunt, his expression one of total bewilderment.

"Auntie," he said gently. "You don't look well. Will you please tell me what exactly the matter is?"

That was when the dam broke and hot tears, like flowing lava from a volcanic eruption, broke free and spoke the pains of her heart.

Oddly, Tos did not utter a word. He waited until she had emptied the tears swimming in the surface of her heart and the moment of crying had subsided before he uttered the simple question "What exactly is the problem?"

Auntie Yemi replied, "It's some people—tall, dark strangers. They are in my apartment. They want to see you."

"See me?"

Aunt Yemi, her tears gone now but replaced with fear, nodded. "They are carrying guns. Big guns."

A look of fear flitted over Tos's handsome, dark features. "Men with guns looking for me?" He spoke the words subconsciously.

Aunt Yemi looked helplessly at her nephew, at the boy who was going to be one of the most important artists in the country, the boy who was going to be a rich man in America, the boy whom she was very proud of.

"Tosan, please let me warn you. I think they want to kill you."

Ebi was shocked at the last sentence, and she looked it. Ganiyu and Gafaru, with drawn guns, had inched toward the door leading to the staircase.

Tos was thinking, *I wonder who these guys could be. Panthers or Brownies?* He said instead, "Are they robbers?"

"I do not think so."

Tos took a deep breath, held it for some seconds, and let it out finally as a sigh. He stared at Ebi, who was looking as if she would faint in the next minute.

"Why did they say they want to see me?" Tos knew it was a stupid question, but he asked it anyway.

"I do not know. But I'm sure they are not armed robbers."

Tos nodded. "And they say you must bring me?"

Aunt Yemi nodded. "Kola is with them."

Tos could see the whole setup. Aunt Yemi was just a pawn, and if she didn't return with the target, they would kill the little boy. It was a dangerous situation, and he hated it.

"So what are we going to do?" he asked no one in particular. He knew his enemies were a million people; trying to figure out who and from where these men were would be a fruitless effort. "Excuse me," he said suddenly, and he disappeared into the bedroom. When he came out some two minutes later, he was carrying a handgun. Aunt Yemi stared first at the gun in her nephew's hand and then at his face. His face was dark and stormy, and there was sadness in his eyes. It was as though he regretted bringing trouble to his beloved aunt.

"Auntie, I want you to tell me precisely how many they are and what exactly they said about me. And what was your first impression of them?"

Aunt Yemi was silent for a moment, and then she finally said, "They are four in number. Three of them are in my sitting room right now. I believe they are not armed robbers. Whenever they are talking to themselves, they are speaking a kind of language. It sounds like Ijaw. It's Ijaw."

It happened so fast that everybody in the room was shocked. Tos did not even know what he was doing. His decision had been made instantly and without any real thought. He was pounding down the stairs, Aunt Yemi crying and running after him.

Ebi, thinking panicked thoughts, with fear clearly and dramatically sketched on her face, ran after them.

Gafaru and Ganiyu were nearly caught napping. Seeing their don running and the other two women running after him, they instantly reacted and joined the trio.

Manager was standing near the entranceway when Tos, gun in hand, pushed open the heavy iron door. Aunt Yemi and Ebi were a step or two behind him.

"Come in, Tosan," he said with a smile. "You can lock the door."

"Not this door," Gafaru said, and he forcefully entered the room with Ganiyu just a shade behind him, both of them holding heavy automatic guns in their hands.

Yellow, from his vantage point in the car, saw Tos, Auntie Yemi, Ebi, and the two other boys running toward the flat. He couldn't believe it. There was no way he could send a signal to his colleagues inside the flat. He had seen their guns and knew that it was time for trouble. He had to make decision, and make it fast.

As they entered the apartment, Wuru shook his head and smiled evilly. Here indeed was Tosan Mayuku—the Itsekiri whose incredible exploits and boldness had earned him a reputation in the Warri War. He was the boy whose daring had made him both feared and hated but equally respected by the Ijaws, his enemies.

"Oh my God, it's Wuru," Tos muttered under his breath.

"Tosan," Wuru said quietly, his gun pointed at Tos. "I'm glad that you were kind enough to come down. You're really a brave man. Timi, Manager—what do you think? Hasn't it been quite some time since we last saw our fellow warrior here?"

"Sure," Manager replied. "Tosan, it would be wise if you and your guys would drop your guns."

Before Tos could reply to him, Gafaru said loudly from the doorway, "Not on your life! You drop your gun." He used his rough voice—the voice that had put the fear of death into the hearts of some of the toughest and roughest cultists in the country.

Wuru was still smiling. *Tos's companion has plenty of guts*, he thought. He couldn't help but admire his boldness. At this close range, he knew he could simply pull the trigger and kill Tos and his two companions. And he also knew that there was the possibility that Tos and his two gun-toting companions at this close range could easily pull the triggers of their guns and kill him, too. So they didn't want to waste each other, so what?

"Tosan, it's been a long time since we last saw you, and we concluded that you had neglected us. That's why we came looking for you."

Tos walked a little further into the room so that he was standing a few feet away from Wuru. His outstretched gun-wielding hand was rock steady, and from the expression on his face, Wuru knew he was prepared for trouble.

Wuru was thinking, *Am I to kill or not to kill?*

Timi's flesh crawled. Like Wuru, he was thinking, *God, what's the commander going to do to this talented painter?*

Tos also was thinking, *I'm not planning to kill again. But if these guys give me the reason, I might just be forced to kill.*

"For a long time now, Tosan, you've been a thorn in our flesh," Wuru said in a thick, heavy voice. "You and the Warri Vanguard. I heard that you're their chief strategist. You've always plotted their plans of assault. You killed Conboye. Conboye was my best friend. He was a very loyal member of the Egbesu. And you killed him."

Tos was silent, but his eyes were on Wuru. As always, his superb brain was functioning, and like the educated young man that he was, he was thinking ahead. He tried to control the anger burning in his eyes. The alcohol in him had no effect whatsoever now. He was expecting to hear a burst of gunfire at any moment, and already he could feel the bullets pumping into his body. It wasn't a nice feeling at all.

"Self-control," he muttered under his breath. "Self-control." After a moment of silence, he asked quietly, "Have you finished?"

But before Wuru could reply, a voice said firmly from the doorway, "I want all you guys to put your guns gently on the floor."

Tos and his two gun-toting companions didn't turn around immediately. The one who finally did so was Ganiyu. When he turned around, he saw a tall, fair-complexioned young man standing in the doorway. The new entrant was carrying an AK-47 rifle, and the assault weapon was covering every one of them in the room.

Casually, Ganiyu walked up to the newcomer and pointed his gun in his face. Yellow was shocked. The expression in the boy's eyes was as cold as Yellow's.

By Egbesu! What nerve! This was not how he had expected any of the boys to react. He expected to see fear, surprise. He expected them to jump confusedly on their feet. But he saw determination and death, and he didn't like it. He could easily squeeze the trigger of the rifle he was carrying, but he refrained from doing so—not because he did not want to kill the young man pointing a handgun at his face, but because he knew that if he started shooting, Manager and Wuru would be in his line of fire. And their deaths would be on his hands.

"Who's going to start the shooting?" Timi asked no one in particular. Of all the young men in the room he was the only one carrying a gun but not pointing it at anybody in particular. It was as if he were a silent observer analyzing the whole scenario. He glanced at Wuru. Wuru's face was a death mask. He glanced at Tosan. Tos's face was inscrutable.

"If nobody's prepared to start shooting, then I think you guys should simply drop your weapons, and let's get the hell out of here and allow the poor woman to go to bed."

Wuru shifted his eyes from Tos to Timi and back to Tos again. His face began to swell with surprise and rage. *What's Timi up to?* he wondered.

Ebi was staring helplessly at Tos. She saw her lover, the painter, the cultist, the famed former leader of the Warri Vanguard, change under her eyes; she saw the tightening of those lips she loved to kiss, the hardening of the deep-set, fierce, and fearless eyes. She also saw something else. She saw ethnic pride so deep and potent that it troubled her. It was extraordinary how tension could express the inexpressible and change a man within the twinkle of an eye.

Timi stood up then and took a step toward the commander of the Egbesu.

"Are you going to take the first shot?" he asked innocently.

Wuru did not answer him. He stared into the muzzle of the gun in front of his face and surveyed Tos's face with his black and bitter eyes. He had always wondered about the feelings of men when faced with imminent death. *What does it feel like?* It did not feel like anything that could be explained. It was just one of those things one had to experience to really know what it felt like.

He looked briefly at Timi and pondered the boy's question.

What's wrong with Timi? he wondered. *Why is he always coming at me?*

Sometimes in the past few days, he hadn't been able to tell whose side the boy was on. His reasoning these days, as far as the Ijaw–Itsekiri bloodletting was concerned, was illogical and judgmental.

Tos stared briefly at Timi. "So where do you stand on this matter?"

Timi shuffled his feet, his face deep in thought, aware of the significance of his answer.

"As warring youths, hostility is our collective motto. What's wrong with unity? What's wrong with peace? To answer your question, I'm on the side of reason. I'm on the side of peace—that is, if there was ever any such side."

"You fool! You stupid damn…" the commander broke off, muttering, and glared at Timi. The next words he spoke to Timi were spoken in a tongue that Tos was very familiar with: Izon. When he had finished speaking in his language, he glared at Tos.

"We can cut a deal and—" Timi was saying when Tos cut him short.

"I'm not making any deal with any of you guys." Tos's voice was steeped in confidence.

"That's good news," Wuru said, and Tos laughed with gusty, gutsy good humor, given the circumstance.

The others looked at him strangely. It was as if he had lost his mind.

"Why are you laughing?" Timi asked him.

Tos shook his head as if to clear his thoughts. "How's this," he replied after a short while. "'I have never made but one prayer to God, a very short one: "O Lord, make my enemies ridiculous." And God granted it.' But mark you, those are not my words."

"How do you mean?" Wuru asked.

It was Timi who was laughing now. "He's waxing philosophic," he said at last amid laughter. "That is, if I remember reading Voltaire correctly."

"You're a good student," Tos said. "You're not doing badly at all."

Wuru was still puzzled. "I still don't get you."

"You wouldn't understand," Timi replied. "It's book talk."

"Let me help you," Tos said gently. "What we're doing with these dangerous weapons is ridiculous. We all know it. We're never going to shoot ourselves. The moment to do so has eluded us, and we can never recapture it tonight. And I pray we never recapture it again."

Wuru understood now. He closed his eyes and saw Conboye dead on the sidewalk, his huge beady eyes open in death. He opened his own eyes and stared unblinkingly at Tos. This was their third confrontation. It was supposed to be their last confrontation. Wasn't it about time he tried to kill this boy, even though it was pretty dangerous to pull the trigger? But for the life of him, he couldn't force himself to squeeze the trigger. He knew he couldn't do it. Maybe Tosan was right. The moment had passed.

After a minute of silence, Tos said, "Before we get into any discussion, there are a few things I think you guys should know about me and the very nasty situation we find ourselves in. I admit freely I have participated in my fair share of the violence in Warri. I even think I'm justified to say I've killed in the crisis. My mother was killed in the crisis. My family house in Koko was burned down. But Conboye, or whatever his name was—I did not kill him. I don't even know him. He died in the war like so many other people. Nobody can be held responsible for his death. In a war situation, people die. And people will always die." Tos knew the last two sentences were the echo of Mike's words during the peace meeting in the Jucee Motel.

Wuru stared at Tos in silence, and then he looked beyond him at Yellow, who was still standing in the doorway, staring pointedly at the gun that was firmly held in Ganiyu's hand.

"Lakemfa, what do you think we do now?" he asked roughly.

Yellow replied in a weary voice, "You know what I think? I think the Itsekiris and Ijaws have lost their priorities. They know what they want, but they don't know how to go about getting it. It's not really complex, if you ask me. We both want local governments, but instead of asking for more local government areas to be created, we're fighting over one single local government. I think it looks more like two mangy dogs fighting over a piece of bone that fell down from the master's table. But they do not know that the master is feasting on the meat of their dead parents."

"You've not answered my question." Wuru's expression had turned a shade darker.

"Wuru, the Itsekiris want more local government areas, just like the Ijaws want more local government areas. There's nothing wrong with that. But because we're intolerant, we went to war. And today we've lost a reasonable number of lives. Maybe the Itsekiris have lost more. The next time we clash, more of such people will die. The question, then, is, What are we killing and fighting ourselves for? Is it written anywhere that at some other time local governments will no longer be created?" The question was directed at Wuru.

But before he could respond, Manager said, "You've still not answered the question, Lakemfa. This man killed Conboye. The commander is asking what we are going to do to this man now."

Yellow knew they had placed him in the middle. He thought ruefully how embarrassing the question was. He said, "I don't know what to say or do right now. All I can say is that when war breaks out, it's not the rich or their offspring who fight. They escape to their safe havens in Abuja, Lagos, and London with their ill-gotten wealth and leave the ordinary people like us to face the mess and kill ourselves. That's the way I see it."

"You've still not—" Manager was saying, but Timi came to Yellow's rescue.

"If Tosan Mayuku's responsible for Conboye's death, then you can kill him. But what about those other people, Itsekiri and Ijaw people, killed? Who's going to avenge their deaths?"

A great silence greeted the question. Tension had gripped the room now.

Never before had Wuru felt so disorganized. Even Yellow had turned yellow. *Is it because of fear?* he wondered. The events of the past few months, beginning with Conboye's death, the military raiding of the creeks, and then the meeting with the university lecturer, the invitation to Lagos by Chief 'Tade Dabiri, and the assignment to eliminate Tos. Now this. "Peace" was the word on everybody's lips. That word alone had muddled his brain as a warrior. A warrior is a man of war. He was supposed to be an assassin, a killer. He was not supposed to spare his enemies and let them live.

Ever since the war, he hadn't felt guilt for the Itsekiri lives he had taken, but now his activities for the past several years were giving him cause for worry.

He was disturbed now by Timi's rhetorical question. That last question was a word of caution to spare Tosan. It was like the rhetorical question Christ had asked the ancient Jews who had been about to stone the prostitute to death. *Was it right?*

The war in the riverside areas was an event in which there were no rules. Now Timi was trying to apply some rules, some logic. He, Wuru, as commander of the EBA, had nursed his mind for this encounter; for the past five months, he had planned how to eliminate Tosan and had traveled hundreds of miles, only to be asked a Christian question: "Is it right?"

"I think you've finally made your point, Timi," he said. He lowered his gun and tucked it into the rear of his waistband.

It didn't surprise him that Timi liked Tos the moment he met him. But the consolation to the whole thing was that sometimes hotheaded militant youth leaders had their moments of rationality. This could be it. After all, it wouldn't do them any good to lose their heads and become trigger-happy.

Tos smiled tiredly and also lowered his gun. The other boys carefully, guardedly, lowered their guns.

Aunt Yemi and Ebi sighed simultaneously, and the former dashed to where her grandchild was lying. The little boy was already sleeping peacefully. She picked him up and walked hurriedly to the bedroom. Ebi walked to Tos's side and held him by the hand.

Wuru, with Yellow and Manager standing beside him, now was staring at Tos, Ebi, and the two boys who were on either side of him, their guns still in sight. Wuru's eyes were really fastened on Ebi, not Tos and his gun-toting companions. *I've seen this girl before,* he thought. *But where?*

Tos also was thinking. Standing and looking at Wuru, he likened him to a great fish stranded in the desert, a warrior without his sword, a commander without his troops, a horseman on foot, and a great leader with only two men to answer to his beck and call.

"What's the saying?" Timi said, and he assumed a thoughtful pose.

"The peaceful are the strongest," Ebi replied, and she smiled for the first time since she had been in the room.

Timi smiled too. Her smile really ignited his, and his unexpectedly illuminated the atmosphere of the room.

"You're not far from the truth," he said, and he winked at Ebi.

"Gentlemen, I think we're all tired of this bloodletting," Tos said quietly. "We're all tired of these mindless killings. Nobody wants it anymore. As youths, our generation has been decimated well enough by these senseless killings. Our generation has traveled far, seen more, and suffered much. We know there's a monster somewhere that's always interested in drinking the blood of innocent people. For once, let's starve that beast of this nourishment. The only way to do that is through peace. Our people want to live in peace. They want an end to the hostility. Or what do you think, Wuru?"

Wuru didn't speak. He was still staring at Ebi.

"Let's forget the past," Timi chipped in. "The crisis is a sad chapter in the history of our lives, and I think there's only one place for it—the garbage can. And that's where we're going to throw it."

Wuru had still not spoken. He was staring at Ebi, and he then asked a question that took them all by surprise.

"Young lady, I want to ask you a question: Are you Chief Ezontade Dabiri's daughter?"

Ebi blinked as if she couldn't comprehend the question. When her reply was not forthcoming, Wuru turned to Timi and spoke in Ijaw: "The girl's Chief 'Tade's daughter."

Timi looked at Ebi and shifted his gaze to Tos and then back to Wuru.

"Are you sure?" he asked.

"Chief 'Tade Dabiri is the girl's father," Wuru said in English this time.

Timi turned toward Manager and said, "I knew there was more to this thing than met the eye."

"But the girl has not answered him," Manager complained.

Tos placed a possessive hand across Ebi's shoulder. "You're right. She's Chief Dabiri's daughter, and she's my fiancée, my princess. But I'll let you guys in on a secret. I'm booked for a flight to the United States. I'll be traveling out of this country with this wonderful lady in some few hours' time."

Tos could see the disbelief spread across Wuru's face.

"America? You? You're going to America? My God—Timi—Manager—I came here to kill this guy, and you, Timi, you gave me a reason why I shouldn't kill him. Now the guy's given me another reason why I *should* just kill him."

Tos, Ebi, and the two Owlsmen were bewildered; Ganiyu and Gafaru were subconsciously fingering their guns.

"What reason is that?" Ebi asked, apprehension quietly settling into her voice.

"Jealousy," Wuru said in mock misery. "He's going to America. That's the richest country in the world. That's a land of unlimited opportunity. Boy! Are you not too lucky? You're going to a country where there's no internal war. The freest country, where you won't be shot at or killed because you're from an oil-producing community, where your home and village won't be bombed or your house burned down because there's oil under your soil. When are we going to be free and happy like the Americans?"

Tos smiled. "Soon, my friend. Soon."

Wuru considered the reply and shook his head sadly. "I'll believe you when all the bad and evil people in our government are dead. But for now that's impossible in a difficult country like Nigeria. Well, I wish you good luck."

"Thanks," Tos replied, touched. "That's exactly what I really need right now."

Wuru held out his hand to Tos, who grasped it in return after a few seconds.

"Good luck," Timi said, and he smacked Tos's shoulders affectionately like an old friend. Then he pointed to the picture. "I like your painting, Tosan. You paint very well."

Tos was flattered. "Thank you."

After they had all exchanged goodbyes, Tos escorted them to the door. He was smiling as he locked the door.

"Jesus…that's something in the Ijaw and Itsekiri relationship."

"Yeah," Ebi agreed. "It's something that even those politicians can't achieve within the close walls of their government-sponsored peace meetings."

Tos smothered a yawn and said tiredly, "I think it's time to hit the sack. We have a lot to do later in the day."

Ebi nodded and went to the bedroom to wake Aunt Yemi.

* * *

The four young men in the Audi were as silent as strangers. Wuru was driving, and he was trying to concentrate. He knew it was a long drive to their hotel, but that was not what was bothering him. Many questions came to him in a mesmerizing stream—many questions, but very few answers. What was Chief Dabiri's daughter doing in Tosan's apartment? Why had the chief given them the job to come to Lagos to kill Tosan? Was it in connection with the attack on his convoy in Warri? Or was the chief trying to use that attack as a smokescreen to convince them? What about the lecturer? Where did he come into this whole sequence of events? The whole thing was confusing. As these questions were running through his mind, he was asking himself how he had allowed himself to be persuaded by Timi. How had he surrendered so easily to reason? So quickly and so cheaply?

Abruptly, he pulled the car off of the highway.

"What's the matter?" Timi asked.

"I have to make a call," Wuru replied, and he pulled out his cell phone and began to search for a particular number.

CHAPTER TWENTY-THREE

Chief Dabiri couldn't sleep. He sat in the big, comfy plush chair in his luxurious bedroom, a glass of whiskey on the headboard near him. But he was far from comfortable. He was very tense. He had every reason to be. The boys had been gone for the past thirty-six hours. They had phoned him regularly to inform him of their progress. A few hours ago, Wuru had phoned him that they were about to strike that night, and by now they had to have finished the job, finished the boy. His eyes strayed to the ornate gold-faced clock hanging like a pendant on the wall. It was five minutes past one o'clock. What could have happened to delay them? he wondered.

As he reached for his glass of whiskey at exactly ten minutes past one, the phone rang shrilly. He paused, his eyes suddenly alive and luminous.

"Who's on the line?"

Wuru's heavy voice floated over the line. "We got him. It's over."

Chief Dabiri smiled. It was a cold, humorless smile.

"Was there any hitch?"

"There was a little problem. We thought he was living alone, but when we got into the apartment, we discovered that three other people were living with him—two boys and a girl. The girl, we discovered, was his girlfriend. But they're all dead."

There was a sudden short silence. "A girl? Was she his girlfriend? Is she dead?"

"Yes sir. They're all dead. Tosan, the girl, and his two other friends."

See! The bastard even was cheating on Ebi.

"So what's next?"

"We're leaving town immediately."

"Why the hurry?"

"Manager was shot. We're taking him someplace for treatment."

* * *

In the Audi, Manager looked at Wuru strangely. Like Timi and Yellow, he suspected that Wuru was phoning the chief, but he couldn't make sense of what they were discussing.

"Is it serious?" the chief asked.

"It's critical. But who knows, he might sail through."

"Will you boys be all right? Is there anything I can do?"

"Don't worry about us, sir. We can manage," Wuru said, and he ended the call, a macabre expression of satisfaction displayed at the corners of his mouth.

"What was that all about?" Timi asked Wuru, who had swerved the car back onto the road.

Wuru gave him a lopsided grin and said smoothly, "Maybe Chief Dabiri wanted his daughter dead. I just told him that she was killed alongside Tosan."

"You lied to him?" Manager protested.

"He lied to us," Wuru replied to him heatedly.

Manager tilted his head to one side questioningly. "Are you sure you're doing the right thing, Commander?"

"I sure hope so. After all, Tosan's traveling to America with the girl. The Chief, I guess, won't know the truth for a long time."

"So where do we go from here?" Yellow asked.

"I don't know," he said. He shrugged his shoulders and stepped on the accelerator. "We'll go back to the hotel."

They had not gone far when he exclaimed, "Ore! We're going to Ore!"

"What's in Ore?" Timi asked.

Eloho! Yes! He had always thought of paying her a visit. This would be the right time to do so. They were looking for an area to get lost in. Ore would be an ideal place.

"What's happening in Ore?" Timi repeated.

Wuru replied, "I've an old friend there. Her name is Eloho. I guess I've mentioned her a couple of times. If she still lives there, I guess we can hide there for some time. At least till the heat cools off."

They continued the rest of the journey in brooding silence.

* * *

Chief Dabiri stared at himself in the mirror over the mantelpiece for a long time and smiled thinly.

It's over. The little bastard's gone from this family. Ebi will cry a little, but she will never know the people who were responsible. She will assume that they were cultists and everything was done for her own good.

He stood up and strolled to the window. He pulled the heavy curtains apart and looked down at the deserted compound. It was as still and as quiet as a graveyard. He saw only two of the security men.

Above the rooftops was a band of light stretching like a plastic ribbon behind the distant clouds. The sky far beyond was dark, but it was laid with a tinge of gray. Even the twinkling stars were losing their brightness. In a few hours' time, it would be daylight.

He replaced the curtains, picked up his whiskey, and downed it in a gulp. He thought of Ebi and decided to check on her before he finally retired to take a three-hour sleep.

He walked out of his bedroom unhurriedly. Ebi's bedroom was in another part of the house. His legs carried him there, though he was feeling a little absentminded, his thoughts on Tosan, the boy he had sent to an early grave.

Turning the knob, he pushed the door open. He entered the beautifully laid out bedroom. The nightstand lamp was off, but a soft shade of blue moonlight filtered into the room. By the wall, but a little bit away from the door, was an ornate bed, and the bed was empty. From the look of it, the bed hadn't been slept in.

Chief Dabiri closed the door softly behind him and walked slowly across the room to where the bed was. It was empty, save for an outsized teddy bear. He snapped on the bedside lamp. His eyes took in the empty bedroom. For over five minutes, he was rooted to one spot, staring at the empty bed. He found it hard to think, hard formulate in his own mind where his daughter could have gone.

What kind of game does she think she is playing? he wondered. It was inconceivable that at this ungodly hour she was not in her room, in her bed.

The room was very quiet, and there was a faint feminine fragrance in the air that he had always associated with her.

He looked around the room again and wondered whether she had taken some clothes with her. He went to the closet and opened it. It was partially filled with her clothes—some designer outfits she had ordered from the United States, and others she had bought right here in Lagos.

Staring at the closet, he noticed two things. Some of the hangers were empty, and the attire she had been wearing that evening was not there among the hangers. One of her traveling bags he so much admired was not in the closet. He closed the closet door angrily, and as he turned to leave, he saw a white note on the dressing table. He stopped and snatched it up. He sat on the bed and held it near the bedside lamp. It was in Ebi's neat handwriting. He read the note.

Papa,

By the time you see this note, I'll already be at Tosan's place. He's traveling out of the country tomorrow, and I'm going with him. Mom has told me everything that happened between Eyitemi and Etan, Tosan's parents. I understand what you went through, but I think you should find a place in your heart to forgive them and free yourself of this hatred you are still carrying in your heart. As for Tosan and me, I think it is our destiny to be thrown together. Tosan is my love and the only man I intend to spend the rest of my life with. In him lies my peace. He's my peace and refuge—my purple prince. Remember Mom's favorite words: peace is a refuge. Don't think too badly of me. I'm following the direction my heart is leading me.

Love,
Akpos

Chief Dabiri's face changed. "It's not possible!" he said fiercely. His jaw sagged, and the note dropped from his fingers. His eyes became dark, and a prickle of alarm ran through him. Wuru's words connected to his brain. *The girl we discovered was his girlfriend. They are all dead.*

That could mean only one thing. *That means she's dead!*

"No!" he screamed, and he grasped his chest. His breathing was coming in painful gasps, and his mind was thinking of his medication. In his eyes, there was sudden fear, and just then the ground seemed to give way under his feet, and he felt himself falling.

For hours he lay where he fell. When the maid found him in the morning, he was dead. He had been dead for hours. The doctor would later tell his wife that he had suffered from an acute heart attack.

When the news of his death was announced a couple of days later, it appeared like this:

EX-MINISTER DIES OF HEART ATTACK

> Chief Ezontade Dabiri, strong man of Ijaw politics, died of a heart attack on the morning of May 31 while taking a walk around his palatial compound in Victoria Island. He was 60.
>
> His personal doctor disclosed that Chief Dabiri had suffered a heart attack several months ago and that it was a miracle the chief had not passed away much earlier because of his nature as an active man with a tendency of high blood pressure.
>
> With Chief Dabiri's demise, it is obvious that somebody very powerful in the Niger Delta has indeed been lost.

* * *

That same night, Wuru and his gang drove to the hotel. It was close to 2:00 a.m. by the time they finished packing their bags and settling their bills. It was odd checking out at that hour, but it did not bother them. They were well armed and could take care of themselves. Even if they attracted armed robbers on the highway, they knew it would be the worst day in those robbers' lives. And if it was the police? Well, the police should know what happens to overzealous cops on Nigerian federal highways at two o'clock in the morning.

Even with all the weapons in the car, none of them felt comfortable traveling in a posh vehicle at that hour. But their luck held. The journey was hitch-free.

It was about 5:00 a.m. when they reached Ore. There was a great early-morning mist in the air, and the weather was chilly. It was still pitch black. "There's the compound," Wuru said, and he pulled the car into the front of the property. He peered through the windshield at the doorway of the house. It was locked.

Wuru sighed. *Is she still single?* he wondered. He had been away for a long time. Once he had told her that he prayed to marry a woman like her in the future. That had been some two years ago. *Will she still be available?*

"You think she'll still recognize you?" Timi asked.

Wuru considered the question briefly. "Maybe. I can't say for sure."

There was some silence. For some strange reason, the fact that Tos was still alive and the lie he had told the chief preyed on his mind. He felt a vague uneasiness coming over him. *Why have I lied to Chief 'Tade?* he asked himself thoughtfully. *Is there a reason why?* There was nothing he hated more than lying.

"Timi, why do you think I let him live?"

"You're still thinking about it?"

"Yeah. It's unlike me. I'm not sure I've done the right thing."

"Wuru, I think you did the right thing."

"If I did the right thing, why am I still thinking about it in this disturbing manner?" Wuru asked him.

"You want an honest answer?"

Wuru nodded.

"I think you followed your instincts. Our instincts hardly disappoint us. Look at it from this angle. Because you allowed him to live, the Chief's daughter is still alive. That's the greatest gift you could have given him. Think about it."

Wuru considered the various theories and reasons advanced a few hours ago by Tos and Timi. He let all that they had said in the heat of the night drop in lazy, slow motion through his mind as he analyzed it. Itsekiris. Ijaws. Neighbors for hundreds of years before the white people had come; people who had lived together before there had been this nation called "Nigeria" and oil and politics.

"Nigeria. Oil. Politics." He muttered the words under his breath. There were no more bases for quarrel between these two neighboring tribes.

"How did you guys meet?" Timi asked.

"Meet who?" Wuru replied.

"The girl we're meeting.'

"Eloho?"

"Yeah."

Wuru said nothing. He just stared at the front door of the house. "It was a long time ago," he said.

It was very quiet all of a sudden.

The thought of how he had met Eloho flashed through his mind. Really it had been a long time ago.

Eloho was made for laughter. His first encounter with her had given him that impression. She was a natural woman, pretty and wellbehaved. She was the kind of a lady who would make a man happy.

When he first met her, it was at a small trado-medical healing home in Ore. The home was a crude hospital of some sort where the owner, Mama Abeni, a Yoruba naturopath, handled cases of chronic poisoning, asthma, tuberculosis, broken bones, and other ailments that had mystified modern science.

From the youngest patient who was suffering from high fever to those who had been given up for death, Eloho made everybody feel at home with jokes. She was so good at cracking jokes that

Wuru, who was in a sour mood from the bullet lodged in his upper thigh, found himself laughing.

Eloho was a figure of fun. He could understand her intentions. Because lots of the patients were suffering and some were dying, she still tried to lift their spirits by putting smiles on everyone's face.

When Mama Abeni introduced Eloho as her niece, and the "Mother-in-Israel" in the home, Eloho quickly cut in, saying, "Don't mind Mama. I'm just a simple Isoko woman." This unexpected response drew laughter. And on and on the joke went.

Later in the evening, after supper, she brought him a glass of water and a pitcher of pure honey. She told him it would reduce excessive fatigue if taken.

In the home, at breakfast, lunch, or supper, Eloho put smiles on the faces of everybody.

Mama Abeni was right. She ran the home as if it were a comedy house and not a place for healing the terribly sick.

One evening, she came to his bed and brought him a specially prepared meal. She said the naturally prepared food would rejuvenate body cells and tissues and provide energy. They ate it together.

The next morning, she led him outside, and they ate breakfast on the balcony. It was the first time he saw the beauty of the place. It was a very picturesque countryside. It was a panorama of rolling hills, gentle valleys, and singing streams. The stream was clean and sun-speckled, and hundreds of colorful birds were singing a million songs. In the distance, little houses dotted the landscape. Winding leave-strewn roads meandered through pleasant meadows.

As they breakfasted, Eloho talked of the community. She had been reared there as a little girl. She pointed to places and things—things he could not see yet could feel through her intensity.

"It's wonderful to be able to talk about your growing up in such a beautiful way," he had told her.

"I didn't make it beautiful; God made it so," she replied.

"Where did you learn to make people happy?"

"I grew up in the West. I was taught humanitarian services by the Yorubas."

After a brief interval, Wuru asked, "Are you married?"

"Yes."

Wuru paused. He knew then that he had fallen for her. Any man would fall for her. The way she looked at him and talked to him had convinced him that she could be interested in him.

"I was married once, but now I'm a widow," she said after a long silence.

Somewhat surprised, Wuru asked, "What happened?"

She closed her eyes for some time, and then said slowly, "He was killed. He was consumed by the waters of the Niger Delta."

"Tell me everything."

She told him everything about herself and how she had met Babatunde Adefusi, her late husband. They had met in early 1996 in Warri. At the time, he had just been transferred to the Public Affairs Division of Chevron Nigeria and posted to the Warri main office. They had dated for eight months, and eventually she had been introduced to Tunde's family. Tunde's father had told her that she was every inch wife material and that she was all that Tunde had said she was. The marriage was conducted shortly after, and they lived as one very happy couple. A few months after the marriage ceremony, she became pregnant, and she bore a son whom Tunde's father named Oluwaseun.

They were enjoying matrimonial life until that black Tuesday—December 23, 1997—when she heard through some of Tunde's close friends and coworkers that one of the company's public affairs' officials was missing in the inhospitable creeks of the Western Niger Delta. When she heard the news, she couldn't eat or sleep. She prayed as she had never prayed before for God to protect her husband, wherever he was. On Christmas Day, people put a name to the missing person. It was her husband. She was devastated. On Sunday, December 28, somewhere in the Benin River swamps, Tunde's bullet-ridden body was discovered. People suspected that Ijaw militant youths had killed him. Her beloved husband had been killed just like that—such a beautiful life taken violently by people who didn't even know him.

Wuru shook his head. Her story touched him deeply. He couldn't understand it. Even in her own grief, she was giving out love. It amazed him. The death of one's husband and the father of one's child has to produce an emotional response. From the way she described her husband, he seemed like a nice man.

"Were you close friends?'

"He was the nicest man I've ever met."

Wuru nodded as if he understood. He saw the pain in her eyes.

"Are you married?" she asked him at last.

"No."

"Why not?"

"I'm not the marriage type. I know this may sound funny to you, but it's the truth. Women need stability in marriage, and it's something I can't provide right now. The major reason why I haven't settled down is that in the last several years, I've been living at a frantic pace. It's not easy. It's very difficult when your job is on the road, offshore."

"Any serious relationships?"

"Yeah. I've had a couple of relationships, and you could say I'm still friends with some of my exes, but there was nothing concrete—nobody concrete enough to commit me to matrimony."

"Don't you think it's—?"

"Yeah. I know it's time. I'll settle down one day. I'll definitely settle down one day, but not today. But when I'm ready, I pray I get a woman like you."

She laughed and told him he was not serious.

Wuru told her he was feeling sleepy and needed to rest. She helped him inside and tucked him into bed. When she was gone, it took him several hours to reflect on what she had said. The revelation had disturbed him. On the date she had mentioned her husband being killed on, Conboye had been on a mission in that area of the Delta. He even had heard the news then that a Chevron worker had been killed. Now he knew his boys could have been responsible.

* * *

When Eloho came the next day, she met Wuru as he was sitting close to the window. He had not touched his food or taken his medicine. The other nurses had already disclosed this to Eloho because they felt she was the closest person to him. Some suspected there was a deep intimacy between them.

"Good morning, Isaac," she said warmly.

Wuru looked at her watch. The time was half past twelve.

"It's midday already."

"Oh, I forgot it's past midday. Good afternoon."

"Good afternoon."

"Mind if I sit down?"

Wuru looked at her and shrugged.

She sat close to him. They did not say anything for a long time.

"They told me you haven't taken your medication. You didn't even touch your food. Is anything the problem?"

Wuru said he didn't feel like talking.

"Are you suggesting that I leave?" she asked him quietly.

"No," he replied, though that was exactly what he wanted.

Eloho talked for fifteen minutes. Wuru didn't utter a word.

At last she got the message. She stood up and left him, promising that she would come again when he was in a good mood. When she was gone, Wuru got up and went to the back of the building. For the first time in a long time, he smoked a packet of cigarettes.

Later that evening, she came in with her little boy, Seun. Wuru was lying on his bed when they came.

"Seun wanted to go for a walk, so I brought him with me."

Wuru looked at the little boy for a moment and then looked at the mother.

"How are you, Seun?"

"Fine," the little boy replied shyly.

"They said you still haven't touched your meal or taken your medicine."

As she spoke, Wuru reached across the bed to the side table, took a roll of peppermints from the table, and slowly unwrapped the foil from it. He popped some mints into his mouth, sucked on them, and offered Seun the remainder.

"Is anything the problem, Isaac?"

He shook his head, and after a short interval he said, "Can I ask you a question?"

"Feel free to ask me anything."

"Have you forgiven those who killed him?"

She was puzzled. "Forgiven who?"

"Those who killed your late husband."

She was silent for some time and then said, "At first I thought it was almost an impossible thing to forgive. But actually there was no way to avoid it. My father told me to forgive and forget. If I didn't forgive them, I would be hurting the more, and the people I would hold grudges against in most cases lose no sleep, because most of them are completely unaware of how deeply rooted the pain they've caused me is. Some don't even care. By forgiving them, I've forgiven myself."

But Wuru couldn't forgive himself, and he knew it was a big problem. He couldn't bear to be in the same building with her. His mind was too worked up. The next day, his colleagues came to see him, and he talked them into moving him somewhere else for treatment. They obliged him, paid the outstanding bills, and moved him to Irrua, a small town in Edo state.

His hasty departure, he knew, had caused quite a stir in her heart. She was a wonderful companion and a pleasure to be with. *Has she remarried?* He shook the thought from his mind.

"Timi?"

"Yeah?"

"What do I tell her if I meet her?"

"How the hell do you want me to tell you what to tell her? I've never even seen or talked to her once."

"Just tell me anything. It's been a long time since I last saw her. Think of something creative. You're the book guy here. What did you go to school for if you can't be creative?"

The two other young men in the car said nothing. They just stared at the commander with what looked like pity.

"Somebody is opening the door!" Yellow said excitedly.

They all turned to look at the house. The door swung wide open, and in the doorway of the house was a boy of about seven years, staring at the car.

"That must be Seun!" Wuru said under his breath. "Man, tell me what the hell to tell her!"

Timi shook his head meaningfully. "You really fancy her, man—"

"Tell me what to say—"

"Okay. When she comes out, tell her hello—"

"Hello! You think I can't say hello!"

"No. I know you can say hello. But if she asks you what kept you so long, tell her there's nothing enduring in life for a woman except what she builds in a man's heart. Tell her that. It's a fine line. I read it somewhere; I just can't remember where."

"You think it's cool?"

"Trust me."

A woman came out of the house. She, too, stared at the car.

Eloho!

"That's her!" Wuru exclaimed. He opened the car door and stepped out.

"Hello," he said casually. "Good morning."

The woman did not reply. The others came out and stared at Wuru. "Why isn't she responding?" Manager asked.

Wuru took a long, deep, breath. "Maybe she has forgotten me."

"Eloho." Wuru called her name again lightly.

The young woman still did not reply. There was a total lack of expression on her face. She just stared at the four young men with vacant, innocent eyes.

"Eloho, it is me." This time Wuru's voice was calm and clear.

Recognition brought a huge smile to her face.

"Isaac!"

Wuru sighed. *She recognizes me! Nobody has called me Isaac in a long time.*

"Oh my God!" she came running over. "Isaac, you bad boy!" she yelled as she threw her arms around him.

Wuru put his arms around her tenderly and grinned self-consciously. After a while, she released him, stepped back, and looked at him as if she couldn't believe her eyes.

"Where did you vanish from?"

"Nowhere."

"What took you so long?"

"So many things."

Eloho closed her eyes. "When I open my eyes, will you still be here?"

"Yeah. I'll still be here. Of course I'll be here, for a long, long time."

"So tell me, why are you here?"

"I came because I wanted to see you."

"Is that all? Just to see me?"

"There's nothing enduring in life for a woman except what she builds in a man's heart. I'm here because of what you've built in my heart."

"And what's that?"

"Love."

"You're not serious," Eloho said, and she led him toward the house. When they came to the veranda, Wuru looked at the little boy.

"Seun, do you remember me?"

The boy shook his head.

"Don't worry. I'm a friend of Mom. This time I'm not going to run away without knowing you really well. Now give me five!"

The others were still resting on the car.

Timi shook his head and said, "Vaswani was right. Truly, a single touch of love can convert a savage into a civilized man."

"What the hell's the meaning of that?" Manager asked.

"Nothing, brother," Timi replied. "Let's go inside."

Leisurely, they walked up into the house.

* * *

Twelve hours after Wuru and his gang had left Tos's apartment, Tos found himself in a Bellview airplane bound for Ghana. As there was no direct flight from Lagos to New York at that time, it was a trip he had to take. It made no difference to him, though.

Before the boarding announcement was made at the Kotoka International Airport departure lounge, Tos exchanged pleasantries with a pretty lady whom he deduced to be Nigerian from her accent. He suspected they would be on the same flight. He had no idea they would be sitting side by side until he took his seat and she was right there beside him.

Around him on the airplane were well-dressed businessmen and businesswomen and politicians. It was obvious that this was not their first time traveling across the Atlantic by air. But this was *his* first time. It frightened him.

He looked through the tiny window and stared down at what view he could get of Africa's huge landmass. *Will I ever be coming back to Africa again?* he wondered.

Tos, deep in thought, didn't pay attention to the fair-complexioned lady sitting next to him. She was dressed in an Yves Saint-Laurent silk umbra leopard blouse with a tie hanging loose on her neck, a blue skirt, and a jacket. She smelled of Chanel No. 5, one of Ebi's favorite perfumes.

"Is this your first time?"

Tos turned to look at her. "First time what?"

"I mean is this your first time in the air?"

Tos nodded. "Yeah. How do you know?" *I've tried not to show it.*

She smiled, her lipsticked lips revealing very white, perfect teeth.

"I didn't mean to invade your privacy, but I just wanted to tell you that first time air travelers are prone to experience some queasiness, dizziness, nausea, et cetera. Believe me. It has happened to me."

Tos glanced around him. Nobody was watching him. "Do you travel often?"

"I've traveled quite a lot. London. Paris. Amsterdam. Athens."

Tos was impressed. "I guess you're in that private club called highfliers."

She laughed heartily. It was a sincere laugh. "I'm not in any such club. I'm just a simple Nigerian."

Tos gave her his most straightforward smile. "I think we should introduce ourselves. I'm Tosan Mayuku."

"Dora Tinubu. I'm pleased to meet you," she replied, and they shook hands.

"Are you in anyway related to the governor of Lagos State?" Tos asked.

She shook her head. "No such luck." After a while she asked, "Where are you heading?"

"New York."

"I know. I mean which city in New York?"

"New York City. What about you?"

"I'm going to Queens to see my mother. So what are you going to do in New York?"

"My mission in New York is twofold. I'm a painter, and the primary mission is that I'm billed to attend an art exhibition featuring my paintings."

"The second one?" she queried.

"The second one, however, is to continue my studies at Pratt Institute."

She was really impressed. "So I'm sitting next to a painter."

"Just an amateur," Tos replied.

"Where's this exhibition taking place?"

"Frank Reese Gallery."

Dora's penciled lashes fluttered upward. She couldn't contain herself. "Are you in the Reese exhibition?"

"You know of it?" Tos was surprised.

The girl nodded. She was stunned. She didn't tell him Frank Reese was *prestige* in the art community in New York. She didn't mention that exhibiting in the Frank Reese Gallery meant more than just getting there, in art parlance. It meant that you were already there. His gallery was one of the major art galleries in New York, and he had an exotic collection of artworks from all over the world.

"That means we'll be seeing much of each other then," Dora said with a friendly smile.

Tos nodded, but he actually prayed that the girl would just shut up and let him rest his mind. He was thinking of Ebi. He was missing her already.

His mind replayed the wild lovemaking they had engaged in several hours prior, the memory of her soft, succulent body that wickedly conquered his strength and drained away all his energy until he was weak both in the legs and at the groin.

She couldn't make the trip with him. Early that morning, about 6:30 a.m., she had received a phone call that her father was in the hospital and that it was terribly important that she come to the hospital straight away. He had told her not to go, that it was a ploy to stop her from traveling with him. But she had said it could be that her father was really sick, and she had to go and see things for herself. Tos had insisted that she should travel with him, but she had insisted on going straight home. She had kissed him and promised to be in New York by the next week. She had promised him that.

Will she keep her promise? he wondered.

EPILOGUE

All the funeral rites for the late Chief Ezontade Dabiri were held two weeks later. His remains were committed to Mother Earth after a long funeral service at St. Philip Anglican Church, Lagos Island. The church was filled to capacity. Sympathizers, friends, and relatives; political associates; and his "militant boys," people from all walks of life, paid their last respects to Chief Ezontade Dabiri, whom the NTA anchorman described as "…a man of forbidding power who was fiercely fearless and uncompromisingly focused on the agenda of the Ijaw people…a man who worked terribly hard to position the Ijaws as the face of the Niger Delta."

From all indications, the "strong man of Ijaw politics" was given a large ceremonial burial befitting his expansive reputation and wealth.

A month after her father's funeral, Ebi kept her promise and joined Tos in New York, creating art.

Nine Months Later

Dr. Vincent Ubangha was taking a light breakfast on a large, cluttered table. It was Monday morning, and the February sun filtered softly through a large curtained window, the warmth of the sunlight caressing his shoulders. He didn't mind the warm heat on his off-white cotton shirt. As he ate, from a habit that was too strong to break, he reviewed some papers that he had prepared for his morning class. After breakfast, he cleared the dishes, picked up his suit, locked the front door of his two-bedroom apartment, slipped the key into his pocket, and strolled to where his car was parked.

Five minutes later, he brought the car out of the parking lot and swerved carefully onto the main road. But as he did so, he glared furtively around to see whether anybody was paying him more attention than usual. He didn't see anything that raised his danger signal, so he concentrated on his driving. Being a careful and methodical man these days, he remembered to keep the speedometer well on the safe side. To him, the safe side was forty.

After fifteen minutes of sedate driving, he entered the school compound and maneuvered the car expertly into the parking lot clearly marked "ACADEMIC STAFF ONLY," which was situated a few yards away from the Department of Fine Arts. He got out of the car and followed the river of neatly dressed students along the clean sidewalk and up the steps leading to the lecture auditorium.

Dr. Ubangha now worked at New Herald University. The university was one of those pristine new private varsities recently given operational license by the National University Commission. It was situated on one of those stretches of land between the Gateway State and Lagos. It was a brilliant strip of land near Shagamu, a dense jungle that good money had transformed into a completely developed intellectual, arty dreamland just a few kilometers away from the chaotic city of Lagos.

Since its inception as one of the first private universities in the country, the school had distinguished itself by the presence of modern, towering buildings, a well-appointed library, and the technological facilities that it had placed at the fingertips of its students.

Dr. Ubangha loved this new school—*his* new school. He loved the lecture halls and the staff quarters. He loved the huge library with its thousands of new and up-to-date books. He loved the immaculate cleanliness of the place and the obvious fact that all the things inside the school campus were kept well and in good repair. Like in virtually all of the few private universities that had been given license by the NUC, it was clear that refurbishing and maintenance work never ceased throughout the campus and the residential villages.

There was no comparison between Aliu Zamani University and New Herald University. While the former could be described as a place of dust and decay, the latter was an impressive institution situated on ninety-eight hectares of a garden of Eden—a place that was clean, cared for, and orderly, and where any student, if he was prepared to learn, could accomplish anything.

The lecture hall was almost filled by the time Dr. Vincent Ubangha entered. As was his tradition, he walked to the middle of the stage and placed his lecture notes on the lectern. Not that he needed them, but they served their purpose just by being visible and within reach.

He studied the class quietly.

The lecture theater was large and neat, the semicircular auditorium seating no more than three hundred. The wooden seats were elegant, the lighting was perfect, and all the conditioning systems were in perfect working condition.

For six to seven hours every day, he lived and breathed in this universe of fresh young people—a universe of rich students, children of top politicians, army generals, naval admirals, captains of industries, royalty, aristocrats, and technocrats. In the first semester alone, he had personally met fifteen very famous people—people who were ruling and ruining the country. Some of their offspring were in his class.

The hundreds of students in the auditorium waited patiently for him to make his opening statement. His opening line was always a maxim by a famous person. He didn't disappoint them this morning.

"'Art is not a handicraft, it is a transmission of feelings the artist has experienced.' Can anybody in this class tell me the name of the person I have just quoted?" His voice was uncommonly loud, and he was one of the few lecturers in the department who could talk in the auditorium without the benefit of a microphone.

The class was quiet. For a whole minute, nobody shifted in his or her seat. Some of the students had already started sweating. It was a trick of his. If nobody answered the question, he would convert it immediately to an assignment and charge the entire class to do research on it. And it was beginning to look as if that would be the case already.

"So there's nobody in this class who can impress me." It was a statement.

The class was quiet still.

"Shall we make it an assignment then?" he asked, his sharp eyes traveling around the large auditorium. He saw a timid hand reluctantly raised. "Yes. Can you help us?"

A little girl, no more than sixteen, rose to her feet. She was at the back of the theater, an attractive little thing wearing a beautiful red dress.

"It's Leo Tolstoy." Her voice, though surprisingly loud for one so small, was uncertain. Dr. Ubangha had seen that posture many times before in various lecture halls and lecture theaters. It was the posture of a student who was not sure whether she was 100 percent correct.

"Are you sure?"

The little girl hesitated briefly but nodded vigorously.

"You must be an A student," the lecturer said, and the class broke into cheering. It was obvious that the students liked his way of testing them.

In just three months, he had created an image for himself. It was unlike when he had been in Jankara. Here he was liked, and that was an unusual thing for him. When he had been in Jankara, he had made lots of people unhappy and angry. And he knew that lots of the students there had been glad to be rid of him. But right here in this quiet university, he was gaining an unusually good reputation, winning the trust of people. In the first semester he had had a powerful understanding with a great percentage of his students, and for the first time in his life he had discovered intense happiness in his vocation as a teacher. He was appreciated without fighting or asking for it.

Now he really wanted to spend the rest of his life in front of these young minds, in these immaculate classrooms, in the garden, in the serene forests, teaching them how to paint and how to appreciate the true value of art. He wanted to turn them into good artists—people who could learn art, breathe art, and live art. He wanted to spend the remaining part of his working life doing that. And that was doing good. Maybe he was trying to change partly because of the psychological fallout of the violence he had orchestrated in Jankara.

Now he had discovered that he could be a good teacher. He *wanted* to be a good teacher. Was this because a great percentage of his students were the offspring of rich and powerful families?

"Now ladies and gentlemen, what is art?"

The lecture hall had grown so silent that the question was rhetorical.

"I would like to define art with five quotes by five famous people," Dr. Vincent Ubangha said quietly.

Over two hundred faces stared down at the tall, neatly dressed man. He was wearing an immaculate, conservatively cut black suit, a dark narrow tie, a white shirt, and expensive-looking Italian shoes.

"But before I state these famous quotations by these famous men, I must register this: Art is not for every Tom, Dick, and Harry. Art is for worthy minds, for *fine* souls. And there are many reasons why you should not practice it here in this country. Nigerians are not interested in art. It baffles our society that some people are interested in pursuing it. It baffles me why your parents, your guardians, would want beautiful people like you to study art. The sons and daughters of rich and wealthy people are not supposed to study art. The reason is that art not only stinks regarding the sensibilities of the rich; art stings their consciences. Art is for ordinary people. Art is for irrational people. It's not for respectable people like you, whose fathers are governors or senators or generals—except maybe, after your graduation, you'll be drafted to the NFA to manage our soccer team or be sent to head NEPA."

There was some general laughter. They appreciated the joke, though they knew it was a jab at their social status. Sometimes his tongue could be acerbic.

"But there's only one reason why you should practice art. I think it's simply to express your own personality. If this is so, then I think the sons, daughters, grandsons, granddaughters, or even dogs of generals can study art." Another burst of laughter broke out.

All eyes were focused on him. He walked away from the lectern and began to stroll slowly up the aisle.

"To those of you who still wish to pursue studying art for art's sake or simply to express your own personality, knowing fully well that art is not respected in this part of the world, I would say, welcome to my lectures and the world of parochial dreams. I must confess that I have nothing to teach you. The truth is that art is in you. You can attend my lectures, but you'll learn nothing from me. *Art is in you.* You're just a step away from discovering it. I'll only guide your steps. I'll only guide your steps in the search for it, just as Jason went in search of the golden fleece. And to those of you who have credits in the sciences, I must advise you to switch courses. Go and study engineering if you can or geology if you must. You can benefit society more by helping the white people to siphon our oil wealth or helping make NEPA inefficient."

There was another major round of laughter at this juncture.

"Or"—he continued as if he had not been interrupted by their laughter—"you may study law and not use it to help society. In the light of recent events, I know, and you all will agree with me, that we don't need lawyers. This is more so because a minister of justice was killed in coldblood in this country, and justice was sacrificed for injustice." Dr. Ubangha had begun to retrace his steps. As he moved back toward the lectern, he exuded the faint mixture of an actor and a scholar. "New Herald University remains a popular place for fine minds seeking a place in the silken canvas of the avatars. We have a thespian environment for those who want to be like Professor Wole Soyinka. Art has much to offer fine minds in terms of painting, sculpture, literature, music, architecture, philosophy—name it. This school is built for it. But the kind of art we are interested in right now is the fine arts: painting and sculpture. And this branch of art is best appreciated if you are fully prepared to immerse yourself in the same creative pond that Ben Enwonwu bathed in, and the one Bruce Nobrekpeya once bathed in and is still bathing in. So, ladies and gentlemen, art is not just about aesthetics. Art is ugliness. Art is life. So let me start with my first famous quotation: 'The true artist will let his wife starve, his children go barefoot, his mother drudge for her living at seventy, sooner than work at anything but his art.'" The class broke up into laughter, but the majority of the students had already started scribbling away on their notepads.

"Those were the words of George Bernard Shaw," the lecturer said quietly, but loudly enough for even those at the back of the hall to hear without straining their ears. "He was a very brilliant man, this guy called George Bernard Shaw." His eyes traveled once again around the lecture theater. He knew they were warming up to what he was saying.

"Artists are magicians. They make things happen on canvas. But they don't *just* make things happen on canvas. They make *impossible* things happen on canvas. Like engineers and scientists, they invent and create, but unlike them, they don't destroy nature. Artists are people who share a common paranoia, a common passion and moving force, people with great influence who have defined the beauty of the human spirit. And that brings us to the second quotation. Oscar Wilde told us that 'The secret of life is in the art.'" The lecturer paused and gave one of his famous grins to the captive audience. The students were hanging on every word that was issuing from his mouth. The majority of them had come to the quick conclusion that he was a nice kind of guy—intellectual, scholarly, sardonic, and cool.

"Oscar Wilde was a genius, and I believe wholeheartedly in his submission. But I also believe that in life, there is good art and there is bad art. It's not my place to teach you good art or bad art. The element of good or bad in art is in each individual. It's also relative. And what I know is this: for you to become a great artist, you must first sell your soul to the devil. However, some really good artists prefer to sell their souls to God." He looked terribly serious as he said these words. "It's a combination of good and bad in you that brings out the force of your creativity—but most especially the bad aspect.

"As artists, you imitate nature. You create something as beautiful as or more beautiful than what you've imitated. As artists, you make something good happen. You create eternity with your work. You create immortality. Art is beautiful. And I suspect that was what George Nathan was trying to tell us when he said that 'art is reaching out into the ugliness of the world for vagrant beauty, and the imprisonment of it in a tangible dream.'" He paused for a moment. It was as if he were in a trance. He continued abruptly. "But to me the greatest definition of art is the one that Edgar Allan Poe gave us. The highly esteemed Poe defined art this way: 'Were I called upon to define very briefly the term "art," I should call it the reproduction of what the senses perceive in nature through the veil of the soul.'" The lecturer nodded as if he alone understood what he had just said. "But let me conclude the quotations with the words of James Whistler: 'Art happens—no hovel is safe from it, no prince may depend on it, the vastest intelligence cannot bring it about.' That concludes the quotations of today's class. The lecture now begins. Why do we study art when we know that the true artist, according to Shaw, will starve his wife, let his children go …"

Forty-five minutes later, Dr. Vincent Ubangha came to the end of his lecture, and he was surprised by the way the students applauded him, deafening the hall with their shouts for an encore as if they had been listening to him sing rather than teach an "irrational" subject. He knew he had delivered a powerful lecture. That was how his lectures always ended. It was now the tradition that he must leave them with a famous quote. And every time, he was always surprised by the students' response to his lecture. To a great many of them, he was fantastic, phenomenal, incredible, astonishing, and utterly wonderful. Those who had missed today's class would definitely hear of the lecture from their classmates. It was unfortunate that many of them would not become real artists.

There would not be three Ben Enwonwus or Bruce Nobrakpeyas. Or Kraks Idonijes. Or even Tosan Mayukus. Sometimes he would think of them, his former students in Jankara. Not many of this overfed bunch would make it to their third year, but he would try to encourage the really serious ones among them to excel.

By the time the applause ended, Dr. Vincent Ubangha had left the lecture theater and was hurrying toward his car.

It was five minutes later that he arrived at his office. He walked across the marble-floored hall, pushed the key into the lock, and twisted it. His office was an extravagant affair with high-quality furniture. As he walked in, his foot kicked something. He turned his attention to the floor and saw that it was a plain khaki envelope with his name written boldly and clearly on the front. He looked at it, but he ignored it at first. He suspected it had been pushed under the door by one of those timid students who wanted his favors. Dr. Ubangha always admired the way students here in private universities got their problems sorted out. It was either by a quiet phone call accompanied by a large envelope pushed under the door, or simply by a thick envelope pushed under the door. In Jankara, the students had been more direct and informal. Here it was practically refined.

He went to the small, newly installed WestPoint fridge, took out a can of mineral water, poured it into a glass, and drank to his satisfaction. As he reached to close the fridge, he saw a book on top of it. He picked it up. It was a book he had bought a few days ago, but he had been too busy to read it. It was *A Small Place*, written by the West Indian writer Jamaica Kincaid. He was contemplating the book when his eyes fell on the envelope. He studied it thoughtfully, and then, after a brief moment, he dropped the book and picked up the envelope. He tore it open and took out a single sheet of paper. The sheet of paper had something attached to it. He studied it curiously and discovered that it was a black feather—the feather of an owl.

He read the words written on the note: "There is a popular saying in Jankara: 'The owl cried last night, and the child died this morning.'" He paused and frowned as if he could not make a thing out of the note. Then it dawned on him. *Owlsmen.* "Oh my God!" he whispered. *"They are here!"* With this exclamation, his breath failed him, and he wobbled and went down with a thud.

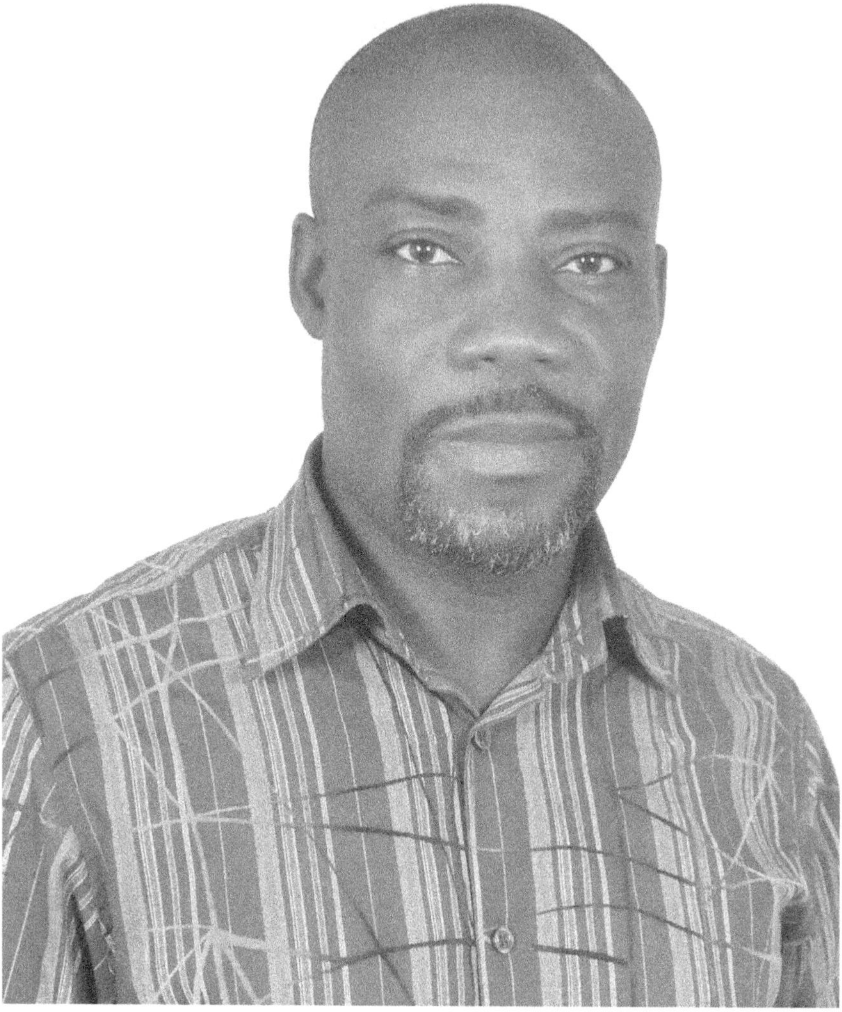

CPSIA information can be obtained
at www.ICGtesting.com
Printed in the USA
BVHW092044220722
642786BV00006B/640